Karen Rose was born in Maryland an horror at the tender age of eight when ... *and the Pendulum*.

After marrying her childhood sweet........ .... engineer (she holds two patents) and a te..... before taking up a full-time writing career when the characters in her head refused to be silenced. Now Karen is more than happy to share space in her head with her characters and her writing has been rewarded with a series of bestsellers in the UK, the US and beyond.

Karen now lives in sunny Florida with her family.

By Karen Rose and available from Headline

Have You Seen Her?

Don't Tell
I'm Watching You
Nothing to Fear
You Can't Hide
Count to Ten

Die For Me
Scream For Me
Kill For Me

I Can See You
Silent Scream

You Belong to Me
No One Left to Tell
Did You Miss Me?
Watch Your Back

Closer Than You Think
Alone in the Dark

Novellas available in ebook only
Broken Silence
Dirty Secrets

Karen ROSE

no one
left to tell

headline

First published in 2012 by
HEADLINE PUBLISHING GROUP

First published in paperback in 2012 by
HEADLINE PUBLISHING GROUP

This edition first published in paperback in 2015 by
HEADLINE PUBLISHING GROUP

1

Cataloguing in Publication Data is available from the British Library

ISBN 978 0 7553 7396 3

Typeset in Palatino by Avon DataSet Ltd, Bidford-on-Avon, Warwickshire

Printed and bound in Great Britain by Clays Ltd, St Ives plc

Headline's policy is to use papers that are natural, renewable and recyclable
products and made from wood grown in well-managed forests and other
controlled sources. The logging and manufacturing processes are expected to
conform to the environmental regulations of the country of origin.

HEADLINE PUBLISHING GROUP
An Hachette UK Company
Carmelite House
50 Victoria Embankment
London EC4Y 0DZ

www.headline.co.uk
www.hachette.co.uk

*To my sweet mom, who has demonstrated strength, grace,
and faith throughout a very difficult year.*

*To my sensei, Sonie Lasker. I miss you, girl,
but am so very proud of you!*

And to Martin. I love you always.

Acknowledgments

Thank you to my friends for your consistently generous flow of information!

Danny Agan, for answering all my police 'how-to' and 'what-if' questions.

Shannon Aviles, for the Spanish phrases.

Marc Conterato for helping my characters' wounds to be more realistic.

Kay Conterato for her constant stream of interesting articles, facts, and links to people she meets. I get all manner of ideas this way!

Sonie Lasker for fight scene choreography and introducing me to karate.

To Claire Zion, Vicki Mellor, and Robin Rue – your support has meant more than you'll ever know.

Finally, to my dear friends for all your love and unflagging encouragement. I love y'all right back.

Prologue

Six years earlier

He was near. Crystal could hear his heavy breathing, feel him watching her. If she looked to the right, past the perfectly manicured hedge, she'd see him. His eyes would be hungry, his body aroused. But she didn't look at him. Wouldn't give him the satisfaction.

Instead she glanced over her shoulder. The door to the gardener's shed was ajar, just as he had said it would be.

The gardener's shed. She lifted her chin. He could have had her meet him anywhere on the grand estate, but he'd chosen the gardener's shed. She'd make him pay for that. She'd make him pay for everything he'd done.

She quietly pushed at the door to the shed, taking a last look behind her. The party by the pool was in full swing, the music loud enough to be heard in the next county. Luckily the estate was as big as the next county or the cops would have already been here, handing out citations. She smiled bitterly, the very idea ridiculous.

The cops would never hand out citations here.

Which was a good thing for the dancers, she supposed. *And for me*. Everyone was so busy having fun that no one had seen her slip away. The partiers in the pool were having the most fun – coke and sex the party favors of choice. But not everyone was in the pool. The dance floor under the bobbing Chinese lanterns boasted its share of gyrating bodies. Every woman still clothed was dressed to the hilt, making Crystal grateful she'd had the good sense to go for the tiny, expensive dress and the even more expensive shoes. Her credit card was maxed out.

But I fit in. Well enough to get her entrée to the party of the season – and that was the important thing. She wanted – no, she *needed* – to be here. To see his face when she told him who she really was. That she had evidence that would ruin him.

That she now owned him.

He'd be shocked. Stunned. He might even beg.

Crystal smiled. She really hoped he begged.

She flicked a final glance at the big house, looming large and powerful on the hill above the partying crowd. *He could have had me there, in one of the bedrooms.* There were, after all, ten of them, each one decorated like something out of a magazine.

But here she was, stepping into the gardener's shed. No matter. *Someday all of this will belong to me.*

She closed the door behind her and frowned. This really was a gardener's shed. It was filled with tools and smelled of gasoline. Meticulously organized, the walls were covered with anything and everything a gardener would need to keep up an estate this size. Two riding mowers took up most of the concrete floor. There was no convenient cot in the corner as she'd expected. Not really any room to do anything.

Crystal rolled her eyes. *Except maybe kneel.* It figured.

The door behind her opened, closed again. 'Amber,' he said.

Crystal took a moment to still her racing heart. *Amber.* That's how she'd introduced herself. If he'd known her real name, he never would have met her here. He would have ignored her, just as he'd ignored the phone messages she'd left with the damn butler in the big house. That was the tricky part about blackmail. You actually had to get the target's attention to lay out the terms. She had his attention now.

Showtime, girl. Make this count. Your future rides on the next five minutes.

'You came,' she murmured seductively. 'I wasn't sure you would.'

He chuckled, the sound far from friendly. 'You knew I was there,' he said, 'watching you.'

She kept her voice smooth. 'Yes. I was hoping for somewhere a little more . . . comfortable. Somewhere we can . . . talk.'

He made a humming sound, considering. 'Talk? I don't think so. *Crystal*,' he added and her heart leapt to close her throat.

'You knew,' she whispered.

'Of course I knew. I had you followed. Pretty thing like you, coming on to me. I have to be careful. There are all kinds of bad people out there, Crystal. You never know who might try something stupid. Like blackmail. Are you going to blackmail me, Crystal?'

Fighting panic, she slowly lifted her arm to retrieve the lipstick-tube of pepper spray she'd slipped into her tiny handbag, glad she'd come prepared. Mentally she counted the steps to the door. Six steps. She could do six steps. She'd get by him.

She had to.

Go for the spray slowly. No sudden moves. Don't let him see your fear. He likes your fear.

He came closer and she could feel the heat of his body. 'You never should have come.' There was a mocking lilt to his voice that chilled her to the bone.

'I have pr—' Something silky brushed against her jaws a split second before it slid down to her throat and tightened. *Proof. I have proof.* But the words wouldn't come.

Can't breathe. She flailed instinctively, her nails clawing at her throat. She kicked backward, trying to hit his knees, his groin, anything she could reach, but he yanked her up until her feet no longer touched the ground.

No. Please. No. Her lungs were burning. She pawed at her purse, grabbing the pepper spray, fumbling as she pulled at the cap. *Just get away. Have to get away.*

She wrenched the cap from the tube. *I don't want to die. Please don't let me die.*

'Bitch,' he muttered. 'You come here, threatening me. My family. Did you think that would work? Did you think any of this would work?'

She aimed the spray, but his hand clamped over her wrist, twisting, forcing the tube lower. Forcing her finger to press. New pain shot through her eyes, burning, blinding her. She screamed, but her voice was trapped. She was trapped. She dropped the tube, her hands desperately rubbing her eyes.

Make it stop. Please, make it—

He stepped back, breathing hard. Her hands swung limply at her sides. He dropped her to the floor. She was dead. He'd killed her.

I did it. For a long time he'd wondered how it would feel to drain the life of another. Now he knew. He'd finally done it.

The bitch. *She thought she could come here. Control me.* She'd learned. The hard way. *Nobody controls me.* He wadded the silk scarf with which he'd choked her, shoved it in his pocket. Leaned over to scoop her purse from the floor and hid it under his coat. He opened the door a fraction.

Nobody was coming. Nobody was watching. Everyone was partying. Having a great time. The music of the band would have covered any sounds they'd made. He slipped from the shed and disappeared behind the hedge. It was done.

One

Baltimore, Maryland
Tuesday, April 5, 6.00 A.M.

Paige Holden pulled her pick-up into the last parking place in the lot, a scowl on her face. Of course it was the one farthest from her apartment. Of course it was raining.

If you were back home, you'd be pulling into your own garage right now and you'd stay warm and dry. You never should have left Minneapolis. What were you thinking?

It was the mocking voice. She hated the mocking voice. It seemed to slither into her mind when she was least prepared, usually when she was most exhausted. Like now.

'Fuck off,' she muttered, and the Rottweiler in her passenger seat gave a low growl that Paige took to be agreement. 'If we were back home, that little kid would still be with that bitch of a so-called mommy.' Her teeth clenched at the memory, only hours old. She wasn't sure she'd ever erase the sight of that child's terrified face from her mind. She didn't want to.

She'd accomplished something tonight. Someone was safe who otherwise wouldn't be. That was what she needed to hold on to when the mocking voice intruded. The faces of the victims she had kept safe were what she needed to remember when she woke from the nightmare. When the guilt rose in her throat, choking her.

Zachary Davis would be okay. Eventually. *Because I was there tonight.*

'We did good, Peabody,' she announced firmly. 'You and me.'

The dog pawed at the truck's door. He'd been cooped up with

5

her in the cab for hours, patiently waiting out the night. Doing his duty. *Guarding me.*

That he did so made her feel safe. That she still needed a protection dog to feel safe in the dead of night annoyed her. That she still jumped when anyone made a sudden move pissed her off. But for now, that's how it was and she was learning to live with it. Her friends back home told her to give herself more time, that it had only been nine months, that recovery from an assault could take years.

Years. Paige didn't intend to wait that long. Briskly, she pulled her hood over her head, clipped Peabody's leash to his collar. She'd walk him, then grab a coffee and a shower before her next appointment.

And then she'd catch a few hours' sleep. When she got tired enough, she didn't dream. A few hours of dream-free sleep sounded like heaven.

Peabody made a beeline for his favorite spot, the lamppost where the neighborhood dogs stopped to pee. He was sniffing when her cell jangled. Juggling the umbrella, she glanced at the display before wedging the phone between her ear and shoulder. It was her partner of three months, who until she was a licensed PI was really her boss.

'Where are you?' Clay Maynard demanded, bypassing any greeting as usual. He was brusque, maybe even a little rude, but he was very smart. And still grieving a devastating loss. Because Paige keenly understood his grief, she cut him some slack.

Under the gruffness resided a good man who, in the three months since she'd moved to Baltimore, had become more like a big brother than a boss. She'd trained with dozens of over-protective 'big brothers' just like him during the fifteen years in her old karate *dojo*, and she knew how to deal with his irritation. Keep it cool, make him laugh.

'Standing under a lamppost watching Peabody pee. If you want,' she added wryly, 'I can send a photo. Peabody won't mind an invasion of his privacy to ease your mind.'

There was a beat of silence, then a grudging chuckle. 'I'm sorry. I called your landline and you didn't answer. I figured you'd be home by now.'

6

Paige wanted to remind him she was thirty-four, not four, and that he was her partner and not her keeper, but she did not. He'd found his last partner brutally murdered. He didn't want to feel responsible for anyone else's death, and this Paige completely understood, maybe even better than Clay himself.

Thea's face, always hovering somewhere on the edge of her mind, now barreled front and center. Terrified, with that gun to her head. Then dead.

And no matter how many Zachary Davises you save, she'll still be dead.

'I had to give my statement to the cops.' Thea's face faded to the edge of her mind, replaced with what she'd witnessed through a window just hours before.

'Had you seen anything like that before?' he asked.

'The mom snorting coke, sure.' It was one of her earliest memories, one she rarely shared. 'The mom letting her son be groped by her strung-out boyfriend, no.'

Six-year-old Zachary Davis was the subject of a brutal custody battle. Mom had developed a cocaine addiction. Dad filed for divorce and sole custody. Mom was fighting for joint custody, claiming she'd gone clean. Worrying the court would side with Mom, John Davis hired Clay to provide proof that his wife was actively using drugs.

Which was why Paige, as the junior member of Clay's PI agency, had been sitting outside Sylvia's apartment all night, taking pictures. They'd expected Sylvia to do coke. That she'd let her boyfriend put his hands on Zachary . . . Paige hadn't expected that.

'He would have raped a little boy,' Clay said evenly. 'You stopped that from happening. Now Sylvia will have a record – for possession and for prostituting her son.'

'I was lucky. A cruiser was a minute away when I called 911. If it had been any longer, I would have gone in myself, kicked in the door if I'd needed to. I couldn't have stood there watching that child be assaulted.'

'I couldn't have either, but the boyfriend had a gun. Your black belt wouldn't have protected you from a bullet.'

Paige found herself rubbing her shoulder where an ugly puckered scar marred her skin. Clay had been kind. He easily could have added, *like it didn't last summer.*

Her palms suddenly clammy, she wiped them on her jeans, straightening her spine. 'I had my gun.' Which she hadn't that night. *I'll never make that mistake again.*

'He would have shot you first.'

'Then show me your commando tricks so I can enter a room without getting my head blown off,' she said, her voice gone hard and brittle.

Before becoming a PI, Clay had been a DC cop. Before that, he'd been a Marine who'd trained new recruits, which was essentially what she was – a PI white belt. Her years of martial arts had ingrained within her a deep respect for her teachers, so she softened her tone. 'Please,' she added quietly.

'I will. Tomorrow. You had a hard night and I need you sharp. Take the rest of today off.'

'Maybe I will. Or maybe I'll work from home. I've got work to do on Maria's case.'

'The case you took pro bono,' he said, slightly disapproving.

'You would have done the same, Clay.'

He sighed. 'Paige, every con in jail has a mama that thinks her boy's innocent.'

'I know you think I'm naïve,' she replied. 'All the evidence said Ramon Muñoz was guilty, but a few things don't add up. Worst case is I dig through trial transcripts, learning to structure a case of my own.' She thought of the tears in Maria's eyes as she'd begged for help. 'Best case, I give a mama some peace.'

'Just don't spend too much time on it, okay? We have to pay the electric bill.'

'Maria's stopping by this morning to give me some new information. If it's worthless, I'll quit. If it's got merit, I'll bring it to you. Gotta go. I need coffee.'

The squeal of tires had her spinning to face the road. The sight of the minivan racing toward her had her leaping out of the way, dragging Peabody with her. She landed hard on her knees in the mud as metal crunched behind her and for a moment she hung there, breathing hard.

Peabody's barking filled her ears and she looked up, still dazed. 'Sit,' she snapped and he dropped into a sit, but quivered, awaiting her next command.

'Paige? Paige!' Clay's shout was tinny coming from her cell phone a few feet away. She scrambled for the phone, twisting to stare at the van, her heart beating wildly.

'I'm okay. I'm okay.' She made herself calm. *Breathe*.

'What the hell happened?'

'A minivan.' That was now wrapped around the lamppost she'd been standing under only a minute before. Bullet holes were sprayed across the hatchback and the windshield and windows had been blown to oblivion. 'It's been shot up.'

'I'm calling 911,' Clay said brusquely. 'Get somewhere safe.'

She jumped to her feet, then came to an abrupt stop as her eyes shifted from the bullet holes to the driver-side sliding door. It was rust colored while the rest of the van was blue. 'It's Maria's van.' Paige ran to the van and her heart stuttered. A woman was slumped over the steering wheel. Blood covered her upper body and the deployed airbag. 'Clay, tell 911 that a woman is bleeding to death. *Hurry*.'

'Stay with me on this line, Paige,' he commanded. 'I'll call 911 from another phone.'

Paige shoved her phone in her pocket without hanging up. *Déjà vu*, her mind hissed and she pushed the insidious memory away. 'Maria? Please.' She wrested the driver's door open and had to still her panic.

There were holes in Maria's threadbare coat. Bullet holes. She pressed her fingers to Maria's throat. A pulse. Faint, but there. *She's alive. Oh, thank God.*

Paige eased Maria back, then sucked in a breath. This was not Maria, but Elena, her daughter-in-law – Ramon's wife. Who would want to shoot—?

'Oh, God.' Dread settled like a dark cloud. They'd had information. Her fear heightening, Paige looked over her shoulder for another car. Elena couldn't have driven far in this condition. Whoever did this must still be close by.

She unbuttoned Elena's coat, trying to find a wound to attend, but there was too much blood. *I don't even know where to start.* 'Tell me what happened. Who did this?'

'No cops.' Elena's whisper was too soft, her breathing too shallow. 'Please.'

'Don't you dare die on me,' Paige said harshly. Hands trembling, she undid Elena's blouse. 'Dammit. I can't see where you were hit.'

Then she jumped as Elena's bloody hand grabbed her wrist. Elena's eyes blinked furiously, trying to open. 'No cops,' she whispered hoarsely. 'Just you. *Promise me.*'

'Fine,' Paige said desperately. 'I promise. Who did this to you?'

'Cops. Chasing me,' Elena mumbled. 'Bra.'

Paige heard the sirens approaching. *Thank you, Clay.* If nothing else, it would scare away the shooter, if he was still nearby. She pulled her scarf from around her neck, pressed it to what looked like the worst of Elena's wounds. 'Help is coming.'

'Flash. Drive.' Struggling to breathe, Elena clawed at her own chest, fumbling with the edge of the bra that was now dark, soaked with blood. She reached for Paige's hand, holding tight. 'Tell Ramon. I love him.'

'You can tell him yourself. You're going to make it.'

But Paige didn't believe that, nor, from the agony in her eyes, did Elena. 'Tell him I never stopped believing him,' Elena begged, her voice almost inaudible. '*Tell him.*'

'I will. I promise. But you have to promise to hold on.' Behind her the ambulance screeched to a halt and she heard the slamming of doors and pounding of feet.

'Miss, you have to move,' someone from behind her ordered. 'Control your dog.'

She glanced over her shoulder to see Peabody standing between her and a gathering crowd of onlookers, his teeth bared. But before she could move, she heard a whine like a mosquito and Elena's hand went limp. Horrified, Paige stumbled back.

There was a hole in Elena's forehead that hadn't been there before.

Numb, she could only stare, her hands clenched into bloody, impotent fists. And as her heart started to beat again, she realized one fist clutched something hard. And small. A flash drive. Elena had hidden it in her bra. Had pressed it into her hand.

Cops. Chasing me.

Maria had been convinced the police had set up her son. It had sounded far-fetched at best. Now her daughter-in-law was dead, saying police had done it.

Whatever Paige held in her hand had gotten Elena killed.

Tuesday, April 5, 6.04 A.M.

Silas lowered his rifle. His hands were steady, but his heart pounded in his throat. *Goddammit.* He hadn't wanted to kill her.

The woman with the long black hair backed away from the wrecked van, her footsteps far less steady than they'd been minutes before. He'd thought the woman a goner when she stood in the minivan's path, and then she'd leapt like some kind of fucking ninja, dragging her monster dog with her.

Who the hell was she? Had Elena said anything to her? He hoped not. He'd hate to have to kill the woman too. He almost had.

Luckily she'd turned around when the medics arrived or he would have been forced to shoot her too, just to get her out of his line of fire. He wouldn't have liked that. He hated to kill unnecessarily. Unfortunately, Elena had signed her own death warrant.

He closed the lid on his rifle case, picked up the spent casing, dropped it in his pocket. People were screaming, just now realizing what he'd done. That Elena was dead. The paramedics were ducking behind their rig, per their procedure.

And . . . there was the cruiser, screeching to a stop. Two uniforms sprang from the vehicle, weapons in hand. Those in the crowd who hadn't fled were pointing vaguely, but close enough to his general direction.

Move your ass, boy. It wouldn't take the cops long to drop a

11

surveillance net over this whole area. Crouching low, he made his way to the edge of the rooftop, dropped to the fire escape and took the steps two at a time.

He'd had only seconds to choose a spot from which to stop Elena. Luckily the small business park he'd chosen had offered a good view and access to an escape route where he'd left his car.

He eased into traffic. Then on his cell, he dialed a number from memory. 'It's done.'

'She's dead?'

'Yeah,' he muttered. 'No thanks to that idiot Sandoval. He couldn't wait for me to finish it. He shot up her van before I could run her off the highway. I would have shot her more discreetly.'

There was a moment of very displeased silence. 'Why?'

'I don't know,' he said. 'Maybe you should ask him. Maybe you should ask him why he let her get that close to him to begin with.' *Then I wouldn't have had to kill her.*

'Maybe I won't bother to ask.'

Silas shrugged, knowing what would transpire. Denny Sandoval deserved it. Keeping records for Elena to find. Idiot. 'Make it look like a suicide.' He kept it a suggestion, knowing a command would not be tolerated. 'What she found out would have buried him anyway.'

There was another beat of silence. 'What did she find out?'

'That he'd been paid off to lie in court, that Muñoz's alibi was real, after all.'

'It would have been her word against his.'

'Unless she took proof with her. He was scared shitless enough to call me for help.'

'And obviously enough to follow her and fire at her vehicle.'

'He was sloppy. He went for the windows, not for the tires.'

'Why?'

'Probably because he wasn't a good enough shot to hit the tires while he was driving.' Probably because the moron was drunk. Again. 'She made it another five hundred feet, then turned into an apartment complex and hit a lamppost. I was just within range. If he'd shot her up a minute earlier, I wouldn't have been able to hit her.'

'But she *is* dead.'

'Yes.' He'd fired on enough people to know a kill shot when he saw one.

'Then thank you. You'll be compensated the usual way.'

Which meant a great deal of money deposited to his offshore account with speed and efficiency. It had taken time to grow accustomed to such polite discussion of such a dirty deed. After all this time, it still made him cringe inside. 'Thank you.'

'One more question. Who else is implicated in whatever it was he kept?'

'I don't know. *I* didn't pay him off. That would have been you. Did you go as yourself or did you play dress up?' He wished the words back as soon as they exited his mouth. *Keep the sarcasm leashed or you'll be a 'suicide' yourself.*

Another beat of silence. 'I was disguised.'

'Then you have no worries,' he said, his voice mild.

'Again, thank you. I'll be in touch.'

Yeah, you do that. He wasn't sorry for the idiot Denny who'd signed his own death warrant by keeping incriminating evidence. And for what? Blackmail would have been suicide and insurance would have been unnecessary, had he kept his big mouth shut.

He did feel sorry for Elena Muñoz. She should have forgotten about her husband, gone on with her life. She'd still be alive. *And I'd have one less mark on my soul.*

Tuesday, April 5, 6.20 A.M.

Three and two and one. With a grunt, Grayson Smith pushed the weight bar back to the rack. *Two-ninety-five used to be a hell of a lot easier.* Then again, he used to be a lot younger. He was officially on the downslide to forty. Which bothered him a lot more than he'd expected it would.

He relaxed his shoulders onto the bench, gave his spotter a nod. Without missing a beat, Ben resumed the story he'd been telling before Grayson had started the set.

'So the punk sets off running and tosses the fucking gun down the goddamned storm sewer.' Ben made a disgusted face. 'It's gonna take me forever to get the smell out of my shoes. Asshole.'

'Did you find it?' Grayson asked.

'Hell, yeah. Guy's a three-timer. You'll be able to put him away.'

Which Grayson had heard from detectives more times than he could count. Unfortunately, 'putting them away' wasn't always as easy as it appeared. Still, he had one of the better conviction rates in the state's attorney's office. Knowing he'd put assholes like the one Ben had just cuffed behind bars let him sleep at night. Most of the time.

'It'll be my pleasure.' Grayson gripped the bar and prepared for his final set. He'd pressed three reps when phones started ringing all over the gym and all chatter ceased.

In a gym full of cops, this was a damn bad thing.

Grayson racked the bar and sat up, his eyes on the men and women around him. It looked like the officers called were out of the eastern precinct. 'What's going on?'

'I don't know,' Ben murmured. He waited until the guy closest to them had put away his cell phone. 'Well? What's gone down, Profacci?'

Profacci started for the showers. 'Sniper. Woman in a minivan hit. Sergeant's just called all hands to search for the gunman. Hell of a way to start the day.'

For a moment Grayson said nothing. His mind was racing back ten years to when a sniper had terrorized the DC Metro area. The closest victim to Baltimore had been a few counties over, but the entire area had lived in fear for three weeks. By the time the snipers were caught, ten people had died and three others were critically wounded.

He looked at Ben. 'I hope this isn't what we're all thinking it is,' he said, then turned to the woman at the front desk. 'Sandi, can you switch the channel to the news?'

Sandi complied and the sixty-three-inch plasma screen mounted on the wall above them switched from replays of last night's hockey game to the local station, where a reporter stood in front of a large sign that said *Brae Brooke Village Apartments*.

Seeing who the reporter was, Grayson had to swallow his annoyance. Phin Radcliffe shoved a mike in his face every time he left the courtroom. A lot of reporters shoved a mike in his face, but Radcliffe always took it a step further. And stopped at nothing to get a story.

'. . . killed by a sniper's bullet,' Radcliffe was saying. 'The police have not yet given the all-clear, and residents are being told to stay indoors. We know that the victim is dead. We don't know the status of the shooter at this time, but we do have this exclusive footage of the events as they unfolded. Be warned. The following images are graphic and may upset some viewers.'

The image switched to a woman in the path of an oncoming minivan and Grayson found himself staring in disbelief. The woman went into a crouch and sprang, flying at least eight feet before she landed on her knees, dragging a big Rottweiler on a leash.

Milliseconds later, the minivan crashed into a pole. There was no sound on the video, but the dog was clearly barking like a lunatic. *And who could blame him?*

'Did you see that?' Ben demanded. 'Fucking gazelle.'

Grayson had seen it and he still wasn't sure he believed it. The camera ignored the minivan, zooming in on the woman's face, and Grayson slowly released the breath he'd been holding. Her eyes were black as night, large and stark against the paleness of her face. Her hair was black as well, pulled into a ponytail that hung halfway down her back.

Grayson couldn't tear his gaze from her face, and neither could whoever was doing the filming. Curiously, the lens stayed focused on the woman and not the wrecked van.

Instead of running away, the woman got up and ran toward the van, followed by the Rottweiler. The camera moved, focusing through the van's front passenger window where a female victim lay trapped in the driver's seat. The camera's angle remained constant, pointing down.

'The camera's on one of the apartment balconies,' Grayson said, his chest going tight with dread. A woman in a minivan was dead, Profacci had said. But not *her*, Grayson hoped, and felt instantly

15

guilty. But he couldn't change the outcome, and one of them was dead. Nor could he stop himself from thinking, *Just not her. Don't let it be her.*

'And the cameraman's got a thing for the gazelle,' Sandi added.

'Can you blame him?' Ben asked. 'She's . . .'

The picture skipped, a clumsy edit. In the next frame the dark-eyed woman was frantically putting pressure against the victim's wounds. From the angle of the lens, the victim's face could not be seen. *A blessing for the family*, Grayson thought.

He knew what was coming, but found himself unable to turn away. One of the women would be dead in moments. The dark-eyed woman worked feverishly, her lips moving as she talked to the victim.

In the background the enormous dog could be seen planting himself between the minivan and the growing crowd. Nobody dared approach, although several in the crowd held out phones. More pictures. More video. *Vipers*, Grayson thought viciously.

But you're watching. What does that say about you?

An ambulance pulled up, EMTs spilling out. The woman turned to look over her shoulder at her dog and then . . . Grayson flinched as a portion of the screen became intentionally blurred, hiding the minivan, the victim and the dark-eyed woman.

The camera wobbled wildly, then stabilized, the angle now changed. 'Whoever is filming this just dropped to his stomach,' Ben murmured.

'Still filming,' Sandi said incredulously. 'Tough guy. Or totally stupid.'

The dark-eyed woman stumbled out of the blurred area, away from the minivan, her face frozen in shock. Grayson's shoulders abruptly relaxed. *Not her.* For a moment the woman stared, horrified, as shouts rang out around her. A uniformed police officer ran toward her, drawing his weapon when the dog lunged, teeth bared.

Bystanders were screaming and running and still the woman stood there, staring, motionless in a sea of chaos. Abruptly she blinked, looked at the cop whose gun was pointed at her dog. She grabbed the leash, bent at the waist and ran to the passenger side of the van for cover where she dropped to sit, the dog at her side. She draped her arm around the dog and closed her eyes, and again the camera zoomed in on her face.

Grayson couldn't tell if the moisture on her face was rain or tears. Probably both. But there was no more time to stare as the screen changed, splitting to show both Radcliffe and the morning anchor who was still flinching, her reaction sincere.

'Amazing footage,' the anchor said soberly. 'That poor woman. Do we have any more information, Phin? How is the Good Samaritan who stopped to help?'

'She appears unhurt,' Radcliffe said. 'The police haven't given the all-clear yet and to our knowledge, no further shots have been fired. When we're able, we'll move closer to interview the witnesses and the Good Samaritan who risked her own life.'

'And we'll have that for you live,' the anchor said to the viewers. 'While we wait, we have another video to show you, one uploaded to YouTube just minutes ago by one of the bystanders in which the events unfold from a different angle. Again, this clip is graphic and might upset some viewers.'

This video was significantly grainier, taken by a cell phone. The holder of the phone focused in on the snarling Rottweiler, grumbling that the dog was keeping him from getting a better view. The picture shifted to the victim. Once again the station had blurred her face and torso, but the abundance of blood was more than apparent as the Good Sam with the dark eyes struggled to stop the bleeding.

'Sonofabitch,' Ben said, shocked. 'Look at the minivan. It's shot full of holes. She was shot before she crashed. Somebody wanted that woman dead.'

But Grayson barely heard him. *No.* His brain tried to reject what his eyes were seeing as his heart began to beat hard and fast. *It can't be.* But it was. The victim had grabbed the black-eyed woman's arm, her hand just visible below the blurred portion of the video. Even covered in blood, the ring on the victim's middle finger was discernible. Unique. It was a cross, flared at the four ends, a large stone in its center.

It's not the same ring. It can't be the same ring.

'I've gotta go,' Grayson said. Leaving Ben and Sandi staring at the screen, he went to the locker room and brought up YouTube on his phone.

Sniper in Baltimore, he typed in the search field. The video already had thousands of hits. As he'd expected, the videographer with the cell phone hadn't blurred anything. The victim's face was there, for her family and all the world to see.

'Oh, God,' he whispered, staring at the victim's face as she writhed in pain.

He knew this woman. He'd seen her not even a week before – when she'd come to his office to beg for a new trial for her convicted husband.

As he watched the video, Grayson flinched again when the sniper's shot came.

Elena Muñoz was dead.

Tuesday, April 5, 6.20 A.M.

'Miss? Miss! Are you hit? Do you need medical attention?'

Paige could hear the man, but kept her eyes closed tight. Her shoulder burned as memories churned, the images all jumbled in time. Yet each picture was crystal clear.

Her teeth were clenched to keep from replying. *Yes, I was hit. Just not today.* Nobody needed to know what happened nine months ago, that there were days she worried over her own sanity. *Because this isn't about me.* It was about Elena.

Paige held her body motionless against the minivan's tire, gripping Peabody for dear life. Her gun was pressing painfully into her back, but she didn't touch it. The cops hadn't called the all-clear and she and Peabody weren't moving a muscle until they did.

That cop had threatened to shoot Peabody. *Because you were in danger.* Paige heard the logical words in her mind and forced herself to grab on to them as a shudder shook her. She'd stood there, deer in the headlights, while a sniper had her in his crosshairs. *But he wasn't after me.* Still, his bullet had come so close.

On its way to Elena's temple. The bullet left a small hole. The exit wound wasn't so small. The back of Elena's head had simply disappeared, brain matter splattering.

'Is she hit?' a woman demanded.

'I don't think so,' the male voice said. 'Burke. Burke! Goddammit, stay here.'

'If she's hit, she's not gonna bleed out,' the woman said. 'Not while I'm here.'

'Dammit, Burke.' The man's shout was furious. 'You're gonna get suspended.'

Paige flinched, hearing a sound next to her ear. Whoever Burke was, she was here. She felt a vibration. Peabody, growling. *Guarding me*. Wearily, she leaned against him.

'Are you hurt?' Burke asked softly.

'No,' Paige murmured. 'I'm not hurt.' *Not today*.

'Easy.' Burke spoke soothingly. 'I'm not going to hurt her, boy. What's your name?'

'Peabody,' Paige said dully. 'He's Peabody.'

'What's *your* name?' Burke asked.

Paige had to think a moment. 'Paige. Paige Holden.'

'Okay, that's good. I'm Dr Burke. I need to know if you're okay.'

'Why?'

'Because you look like you're hurt.'

Paige's brows knit as she tried to think. 'No. Why are you here if you're a doctor?'

'Oh.' The woman sounded a bit surprised by the question. 'Because I'm a resident, getting my field hours. Are you hurt, Paige?'

Paige drew a shuddering breath. 'No. I'm okay.'

'Then why are you holding your shoulder?' Burke asked kindly.

Because it burns, Paige wanted to snarl. Except . . . it didn't. She opened her eyes carefully to see her right hand clutching her left shoulder. Her shoulder didn't burn. Not any more. Not like it did when she woke from the nightmare in a cold sweat, the pain ebbing as soon as she realized where she was. *Not Minneapolis*. Not on the floor bleeding out, staring into Thea's dead eyes.

This is Baltimore. And today the dead eyes belonged to Elena

Muñoz. *Déjà vu, baby*, the voice mocked. *When you fuck up, you do it right.*

Paige forced herself to relax. She dropped her hand from her shoulder, brushing it against her coat before resting it on her knee. The flash drive was still in her pocket, hidden. It would stay that way. No cops. Elena had made her promise.

Until I know what really happened. Paige drew a breath, steeling herself for what she already knew to be true. 'Is she dead?' she asked.

'Yes,' Burke said quietly. 'I'm sorry.' She was young, maybe a few years younger than Paige. Her eyes were calm. She wore a bulletproof vest over her windbreaker.

Hell of a lot of good that would do against a bullet in the head.

'You shouldn't have come to me. The man said you'd be suspended.'

'I can't do anything for that poor woman, but I wasn't going to lose anyone else.'

'What do we do now?'

Burke shrugged. 'We wait for the all-clear.'

TWO

Tuesday, April 5, 6.40 A.M.

Paige let out an even breath when she heard the shout of 'All clear!'

'Thank God,' Burke murmured. 'Let's go get you checked out.'

'No.' Paige felt a wave of panic grab her throat. 'No hospitals.'

'Just your vitals,' Burke said. 'Let's clean you up, make sure you're okay.'

'I'm fine. I just need to go home.' Grabbing Peabody's leash, Paige tried to stand but her knees turned to rubber. 'I'm okay. Really, just fine.'

'You keep saying that,' Burke said. 'In a few hours it might even be true.' She helped Paige to the rescue squad, Peabody padding along next to them.

At least the rain had stopped. As they passed the minivan, Burke turned so that Paige couldn't see, but it didn't matter. The image was seared in her mind.

'You're limping,' Burke said, diverting her attention from the van. 'What hurts?'

'I fell on my knees when I jumped out of the way.'

Burke gestured for her to sit in the rescue squad's bay. 'You need an X-ray.'

'No hospitals.' Paige heard her own desperation. *Breathe*. 'Please,' she added.

Burke checked her pupils, then probed her shoulder. 'What happened here?' She looked up sharply. 'Don't tell me "nothing".'

'I was shot. Last summer.' She scanned the crowd that had gathered. One out of three held out cell phones. Filming Elena, the bastards.

21

'They piss me off,' Burke said, shielding Paige with her body. She pulled Paige's arm from her jacket to take her blood pressure. 'At least they won't see you.'

'Thanks,' Paige murmured. 'When will the ME take her? I don't want those assholes taking pictures of her. This is going to be hell on her family.'

'CSU will be putting up a tarp to keep the cameras away. The ME probably won't take her for a while. I'm sorry. All that breathing you were doing while we waited worked. Your BP is almost normal. But you should get your knees checked.'

'I know my body. I don't need an X-ray. If there's a form I have to sign to cover you, give it to me.' She pushed to her feet and beside her, Peabody stood. She scratched behind his ears, waiting out the wave of nausea. 'I'm going home.'

'Not just yet, miss.' A man walked up, his face sober. He wore a suit and tie and had a badge clipped to his breast pocket. 'I'm Detective Perkins. I need to talk to you.'

Paige lowered herself to the ambulance. She'd known this was inevitable, but she'd hoped for a few minutes to herself. 'I'm not feeling very well at the moment.'

'I'll make it brief. First, name and address.'

'Paige Holden and that building, right there.' She pointed over her shoulder. 'Three-A.'

'Did you know the victim?' he asked.

'Just to see her around. I—' She broke off, looking past Perkins to where a tall man was elbowing his way through the crowd. Clay was here. A piece of her settled.

The cop saw him too. 'Wait over there,' Perkins said sharply, pointing, and Clay's eyes flashed fury.

'Please, let him stay.' She held out her hand and winced when Clay grasped hard.

'Are you all right?' Clay asked quietly and she managed to curve her lips upward.

'Shaken *and* stirred, but okay.' She turned to Perkins. 'I'm ready.'

'Did you know the victim?' Perkins asked again.

'Elena Muñoz. She and her family do the maintenance here at the complex. Empty trash, mop the floors, clear sidewalks when it snows, cut the grass when it grows. Maria is their mother. She manages the business.' She'd been forced to work after Ramon's arrest. *This will break her heart.* 'The building super will have a number.'

'I'll be sure to ask him,' Perkins said. 'So what happened?'

'I was walking my dog when the van came at me. I jumped out of the way, the van crashed, and I tried to help. The EMTs had just arrived when the last shot was fired.'

Perkins gave her a long look that made her want to squirm. The steady pressure of Clay's hand holding hers kept her focused. 'Did she say anything?' Perkins asked.

Paige had thought this through while waiting for the all-clear. There had been a small crowd behind her toward the end, but thanks to Peabody, probably not close enough to have overheard. 'She begged me to help her, but that was about all.'

Perkins nodded, his expression unreadable. 'Most people would have run.'

Paige shrugged. 'It didn't occur to me.' And that was the truth.

'What do you do for a living, Paige?' Perkins asked.

'Lots of things. I work part time in a gym. I'm a personal trainer. I also work for a PI.'

Perkins's brows rose. 'What do you do for the PI, exactly?'

'Mostly take pictures of cheating spouses.'

'Could *you* have been the sniper's target this morning? Maybe somebody who didn't like you taking their picture?'

Paige blinked, startled. 'No. Somebody shot her before she got here. I assumed whoever fired the last shot was . . . finishing what they'd started.'

Clay cleared his throat. 'Can she go now, Detective? She's pale as a ghost.'

Perkins took a notepad from his pocket. 'And you are, sir?'

'Clay Maynard,' Clay said.

'Your relationship to Miss Holden?' he asked.

'We're friends,' Clay said and squeezed Paige's hand again. 'If that's all . . . ?'

23

'For now. Please stay available. We'll have more questions as we investigate.'

'Thank you,' Paige said to Burke. 'I hope you don't get suspended on my account.'

'Just promise you'll come to the hospital if you have any issues later on.'

'I will.' *When hell freezes over.* 'Thanks again.'

'I'll get an officer to escort you to your apartment,' Perkins said. 'There are a lot of reporters who will want your story. I hope you won't talk to them.'

'I won't. That you can count on.' Keeping a tight hold on Peabody, Paige started for her apartment. The reporters began shouting for her attention and she ignored them.

Until one called, 'Hey Paige, where'd you learn to jump like that?'

'What does that mean?' she asked Clay. 'What are they talking about?'

Clay urged her forward. 'Keep walking, Paige.'

She held her tongue until they reached the door of her apartment. 'What did they mean about my jump? The crash had just happened. Nobody was out there but me.'

'Somebody was taking a video of you when the crash happened,' the officer said, looking pained on her behalf. 'It was on the news minutes later. You're an Internet star.'

Paige closed her eyes, wondering what else the video had shown. 'Shit.'

Tuesday, April 5, 7.30 A.M.

'Honey, what's wrong?'

Adele Shaffer looked over to see her husband lifting their daughter from her highchair for a hearty hug that had Allie squealing happily. Adele's lips curved despite the knot in her gut. 'I never get tired of hearing her laugh,' she said.

Baby on his hip, Darren planted a warm kiss on Adele's mouth. 'Me either. And you didn't answer my question. What's wrong?'

Adele pointed at the television on the kitchen counter and gave an answer that would satisfy him. 'There was a shooting this morning. They said it was a sniper.'

Darren frowned. 'No way. Not again?'

'That's what they said. You have to drive near there on your way to work.'

He kissed her again, then passed Allie into her arms. 'Don't worry. I'll be fine.'

'You always say that,' Adele murmured.

'And I'm always fine,' Darren said with a smile. 'What are you going to do today?'

'I'm meeting a client this afternoon. I finally got her to narrow her choices from about a thousand carpet samples to five.' It was a lunch meeting, actually. After which she had an appointment with someone she hadn't seen in years. Hadn't needed to see.

Didn't want Darren to know she'd ever seen in the past, much less now.

She'd put this off for as long as she was able. Hopefully one time would be enough.

Darren tipped up her face. 'Don't worry about me, okay? I'll call you when I get to the office. You shouldn't need to stop anywhere. I filled your gas tank last night.'

Guilt swamped her. He was always doing nice things like that for her. He didn't deserve to be lied to. But she didn't think she could stand the look in his eyes if he knew the truth. 'Thanks. I'll be careful if you will.'

'It's a deal.' He kissed the tip of her nose. 'What's for supper?'

'Chicken and couscous, just how you like it.'

He waggled his brows. 'I can think of things I like a whole lot more.'

She drew a breath, forced a smile. 'Go to work, you letch. I'll see you later.'

She waited until she heard the front door close before letting the tears fall. Cuddling her baby close, she rocked them both. *Please*, she prayed, *make it stop. Please. I'll do anything, I promise. Just don't let it be like it was before.*

Getting hold of herself, Adele turned the volume up on the TV. She heard the words 'wife of convicted murderer Ramon Muñoz', 'execution', and 'probably not a random sniper' and let out a relieved breath. At least the city was safe.

Herself, not so much.

Tuesday, April 5, 7.30 A.M.

Silas was right, the man thought as he picked the lock to Denny Sandoval's back door. Sandoval had long outlived his usefulness. Denny had to go. Especially if he'd had evidence that Elena had considered worth dying for.

He entered the bar through the back door and thought back to the night he'd last been here. Six years had wrought changes, both in the bar and in his own life. Sandoval had spruced up his bar. *And I am now very rich.*

He intended to stay that way. Whatever evidence Sandoval had kept here, he needed to get it back. He paused, listening. Sandoval was upstairs in his apartment over the bar. He crept up the stairs and stood outside Sandoval's open bedroom door.

The television was on. It was the news. The shooting, of course. A video was playing. His eyes narrowed as he watched the footage. *What the hell?*

Elena had talked to the woman who'd tried to save her. God only knows what she told her Good Samaritan. *Silas must have seen this. He should have taken out both women.* But most disturbing was that Silas had lied about what truly transpired. Maybe Silas was outliving his usefulness, too.

Sandoval appeared in his bedroom, backing out of his closet, a suitcase in his hand.

Not so, little man. I want information. He wanted to know what Elena had seen. He wanted to know if he was in any way implicated. *And I always get what I want.*

Tuesday, April 5, 7.30 A.M.

'Here. Drink this.'

Paige glanced away from her living-room window to take the cup of hot tea from Clay's hands. It was the third cup he'd forced on her as she'd watched the police processing the crime scene through the blinds, thinking about the flash drive in her pocket, and wondering what the hell to do.

She'd watched the videos. She knew exactly who'd taken the one of her jumping. The kid upstairs had a crush and always carried a camcorder. Once she'd caught him taping her walking Peabody late at night. She'd thought she'd scared Logan Booker from future videotaping by threatening to tell his mother. *I guess not.*

She hadn't seen Elena's flash-drive hand-off in Logan's video or any of the others shot with the cell phones behind her. *Thank God for Peabody.* He'd kept the vultures far enough away that none of Elena's words had been caught on tape.

Still, they'd captured Elena's murder, her brains splattering against the windows of her van. The videos were online, viewable by anyone. Including the Muñoz family. It made Paige's heart ache to think about them seeing Elena die.

Clay nudged her shoulder. 'Drink it,' he repeated.

She sipped the tea obediently. 'I'm going to float away,' she murmured.

'You should have let that doctor check you out.'

'I wasn't hurt. Just rattled. Anyone would have been.'

'You could have been killed.' His voice was raw and she knew he was reliving finding his old partner's body.

'But I wasn't. And I don't think I would have been. I'd just turned to look at Peabody when the killer pulled the trigger. A second earlier I'd been leaning over Elena.'

His eyes widened. 'Like he was waiting for you to get out of the way?'

'Exactly.' She let the warmth from the cup seep into her cold fingers as she looked back to the crime scene. 'The MEs are finally taking her. It's about time.'

'It was a messy crime scene,' Clay said. 'They needed to be careful.'

'"Messy" would be the word.'

'If you're worried about the videos, don't be. You'll be an Internet sensation for a day, maybe two. Then some starlet will go into rehab and it'll be over.'

'That's not what I'm worried about,' she said quietly.

'Somehow I didn't really think so.' He was studying her intently. 'So let's get to it. You told that detective that she hadn't said anything to you,' he said. 'You lied. Why?'

Paige pulled her phone from her pocket and laid it on the windowsill. At some point her call to Clay had been terminated. She had no idea when. 'How much did you hear?'

'Only you. Her voice was too faint. You asked who'd done it. What did she say?'

Paige ran her fingers over her pocket, feeling the outline of the flash drive. Abruptly she stepped back from the blinds and met his eyes. '"Cops. Chasing me."'

His frown was immediate and severe. 'A cop shot her?'

'No. She said that a cop *chased* her. I assumed the chaser and the shooter were the same. Then the medics arrived and that other shot came out of fucking nowhere.'

'Same shooter?' Clay asked and she shrugged.

'I don't know. One of my first thoughts was that the shooter had to be close, that Elena couldn't have driven far with injuries like those.' She paused, thinking. 'It might have been the same shooter, but not the same gun. The entry wounds in her torso were bigger than the final hit to her temple. The exit wounds in her body were . . . smaller.'

'I'd guess the final shot was made by a high-speed rifle. The cops were all over the rooftops, looking for signs of the shooter. They're scared right now, the cops. I heard a couple of them wondering if they had another serial sniper.'

Paige frowned, not understanding, then she remembered the DC sniper. 'It's been years.'

'Ten years,' Clay said harshly, 'but for any of us who lived through it, it seems like yesterday. You can be sure this will stir up a lot of fear in the community.'

'Elena wasn't a random target like the sniper's from before,' Paige said. Sitting at her desk, she took a latex glove from her drawer of supplies and pulled it on. She brought the flash drive from her pocket, holding it flat on her palm. Elena's blood had dried on the gadget.

'Holy hell, Paige,' Clay whispered, his eyes wide. 'What is that?'

'Elena's flash drive,' she whispered back. 'She put it in my hand seconds before she died. She made me promise not to tell any cops.'

'So what? This is evidence. You can't just sit on it.'

She gave him a disbelieving look. 'Like you always rush to hand over everything to the cops? You don't trust the cops any more than Elena did.'

His face flushed uncomfortably and Paige knew she'd scored a direct hit. Clay had known who'd killed his partner, and for a lot of reasons – not the least of which was the need for his own revenge – had held back information while he investigated on his own.

'Shit,' he mumbled. 'Doesn't mean that's the right thing to do this time.'

'What part of cops chasing her did we miss here? I mean, who do I hand it over *to*? The detective who questioned me? What if *he* was the cop chasing her?'

'Shit,' he said again, then sighed. 'What's on the damn thing?'

'I don't know. She died before she could tell me. Whatever it is, somebody killed her over it.' Paige held it under the desk lamp. 'I hope whatever's on here is readable.'

'You're going to plug that thing into your computer?' he asked, eyes even wider.

'What, worried about viruses?'

'Along with about a million other things. Look, I did keep information from the cops after I found Nicki's body, and I was wrong. People died, Paige.'

Paige leveled him a hard stare. 'Elena thought the cops planted evidence against Ramon. What if this is proof? The man is in prison

29

for murder, Clay. Now his wife is dead. You can stay or go, but I'm going to see what's on this damn drive.'

'And if the cops somehow find out?'

'I'll say I was stunned. In shock. That I couldn't remember getting it and didn't check my pocket until later to find it. So stay or go. Choose and make it quick.'

He rolled his eyes. 'You know I won't go. Hell.'

'Okay.' She opened a box next to her desk and Clay whistled.

'How many laptops do you have in there?'

'Six.' She pulled one out. 'Rich kids at the university in Minneapolis throw them out when they get a new one. These old machines are useful if you're checking out any file that might be a risk. If there's a virus, you can wipe the drive and not risk your own PC.'

'How did you get them?' he asked suspiciously.

'Friends who are students. They dumpster-dive occasionally. They're geeks.'

'And hackers?' he asked dryly.

'Of course.' She plugged the drive in the USB port and it opened quickly. '*Yes*,' she whispered.

'That's a lot of files,' Clay said, looking over her shoulder.

'Most of them are old, except for these three picture files – saved three hours ago.' She opened one and stared at the photo of two men drinking beer at a bar. 'Bingo.'

'It's a bar,' Clay said.

'It's *the* bar,' Paige corrected, 'where Ramon Muñoz claimed he'd been the night of the murder. Ramon's on the left and the time stamped in the corner is the same time he was supposed to be murdering a college girl on the other side of town.'

'Time codes can be faked.'

'Yes, they can. But this picture never made it into the trial exhibits.'

'Are you sure?'

'I've studied every page of the transcripts. Ramon said he was there with a friend.'

'The guy next to him?'

'Yes. The friend denied seeing him there that night, as did the bar owner. Under oath.' Paige opened the other two picture files. The first showed two men exchanging a piece of paper. 'The guy taking the paper is the bar owner, Denny Sandoval. He's looking up at the camera, like he's posing almost.'

'His insurance policy,' Clay said quietly. 'Who's the guy with the fake mustache giving the paper to the bar owner?'

'I don't know. The mustache is cheesy, but it does the job of disguising his face.'

'Nice hands,' Clay noted. 'The guy gets regular manicures.'

Paige zoomed in on the man's hands. 'And wears a pinky ring. Maybe a diamond, but it's too grainy to be sure.' The third file was a receipt. 'Wire transfer. Lots of zeroes.'

'Fifty Gs would be enough to get a lot of guys to lie under oath.'

'And enough to kill a woman who found out about it?' she asked.

'I've known murderers to kill for a lot less. Look, I know you told me about this case when you first took it a month ago, but all I really remember is that Ramon's in jail for murder and his mama thinks he's innocent. Tell me the details again. Who do they say Ramon murdered?'

'A college girl named Crystal Jones. She'd gone to a party at a big estate where Ramon worked as head gardener. She was found dead the next morning in the gardener's shed, strangled, then stabbed to death. One of the pruning shears was missing. Cops found the shears in the closet in Ramon and Elena's bedroom. They said most of the blood had been wiped off, but there was enough to do a DNA check and link the shears to the dead woman. They also found one of Ramon's hairs on her dress.'

'Pretty damning stuff.'

'I know. Plus there was a note found on the body. "*Gardener's shed, midnight.*" Signed "*RM*". Ramon said it wasn't his. Hand-writing analysis was inconclusive. Ramon claimed he was innocent, that he had an alibi, but nobody would confirm it.'

'The DNA on the weapon gave the prosecution a slam dunk.'

'Exactly. Ramon was the gardener, he had access to the shed and the shears.'

'Did he live on the estate?'

'No, the job didn't include living quarters. He and Elena had an apartment about a mile from Maria's house. But he had a key for the back gate, so he had access. The prosecutor presented Ramon as a player, that he killed this woman when she teased him, then wouldn't give him sex. The jury came back in a few hours. Guilty on all counts. Maria met me after I moved into this apartment. She was cleaning one morning and we got to talking. When she found out I was a PI—'

'In training,' Clay interrupted.

'In training,' Paige acknowledged. 'She and Elena begged me to help them. They were so sure someone was dirty. That the cops were involved. Elena said she'd get proof. She did.'

'What made them believe cops were involved? What did the cops do?'

'Maria said people in the neighborhood avoided them after Ramon was arrested. There were whispers that they'd been intimidated by the cops on the case to keep quiet, but nobody would tell her the truth. Elena believed that the bloody shears and the note that was found on the body were planted.'

'Who were the investigating detectives?'

'Gillespie and Morton. This was all six years ago. Morton is still Homicide, but Gillespie retired a few years ago.'

His eyes flickered for the barest instant. 'Who was the prosecutor?'

'Assistant State's Attorney Grayson Smith.'

'I've heard of him. Never met him.'

'Me either. I did check out his record, though. Smith has the best conviction rate in his office. But he didn't have to work hard in this case. The evidence all pointed to Ramon being guilty.'

'So what's next?'

Paige transferred all three picture files from Elena's flash drive to her old computer's hard drive. She then removed Elena's drive and dropped it back in her pocket. 'I'm going to put this computer in my safe, then I'm going to put this coat in a plastic bag. If I decide to hand over the drive later, I can say I put the coat in a bag until I could launder it, then found the drive when I was cleaning out my pockets.'

She bit her lip as she bagged the coat. 'I want to do the right thing. I just don't know who I can trust. I tell the wrong person and I could end up like Elena.'

'Was Detective Perkins involved in Ramon's investigation?'

'His name wasn't in the court records, but that doesn't mean anything. Who knows who he knows? Has loyalties to? You've lived here for years. Do you have any cops you can trust? I mean, really, with-your-life trust? Because we're talking my life now.'

He was quiet for a long moment, which said a great deal. 'I haven't lived in Baltimore all that long. I know cops I'd trust with my life, but they're elsewhere. Here in Baltimore I may know one. But I'm not sure.'

'Then we say nothing.' Paige disconnected the old laptop, put it in the safe bolted into her china cabinet. She heard Elena's voice again. *Cops. Chasing me.* With a sigh she shoved the bag in, too.

She'd no sooner locked the safe and closed the cabinet doors when there was a sharp knock on her front door. Peabody came to his feet, a low growl in his throat, and Paige and Clay exchanged a quick look. 'Who is it?' she called out.

'Baltimore PD.' It was a woman's voice. 'We'd like to speak with you. Please.'

Peabody at her side, Paige cracked the door open, leaving the chain in place. On her doorstep stood a man and a woman, both wearing suits.

'Yes?'

'I'm Detective Morton and this is my partner, Detective Bashears. We'd like to talk to you about what happened this morning.'

Morton? The same cop who'd arrested Ramon. *Shit.*

It took an effort to keep her face blank and she could only hope she pulled it off. There were only so many detectives in Baltimore's homicide department, but this was still too much coincidence. 'I told the other detective everything that I know.'

Morton attempted a smile. 'This case has been reassigned to my partner and me.'

Paige leaned against the doorframe, genuinely weary. 'Fine.' She closed the door and turned to Clay, who looked as unhappy as she felt. 'What next?' she mouthed.

He pointed to himself, then to her bedroom. 'Tell them nothing,' he mouthed back. With that, he disappeared into her bedroom, his step soundless.

Tuesday, April 5, 7.45 A.M.

'Grayson, Anderson's looking for you.' Assistant State's Attorney Daphne Montgomery held up a note scrawled in their boss's hand as Grayson rushed past her cubicle. 'He's growly. You should call him before he has a stroke.'

His boss was always growly, Grayson thought. Besides, he knew exactly what Anderson wanted and would be damned before he gave it to him. Anderson could wait.

He stuffed the note into his pocket, eyeing the plate of muffins on Daphne's desk. 'How did you get here so early? Took me forever to get through security.'

The line had reached around the corner and people were understandably scared, despite another report from Phin Radcliffe, who, Grayson hated to admit, had gotten a decent handle on the situation as a whole. Radcliffe had revealed the woman's association to a convicted murderer without giving her name and had posited that, given she'd been shot before arriving at the scene, she was not a victim of a random sniper attack.

Still, people were on edge. *So am I.* He couldn't get the picture of Elena Muñoz's face out of his mind. He needed information, and he needed it now.

'I got here at six,' Daphne said. 'I was expecting a call from Ford.'

Grayson had turned toward his office, but stopped at the worry in her voice. Daphne's son Ford was on a college spring break trip to Europe. 'Is he okay?'

She nodded and Grayson relaxed. 'He's enjoying the hell out of Italy,' she said.

'Good. I thought something was wrong. You don't sound like yourself.'

She hesitated. 'When Ford called, he was scared. He'd already heard about the sniper attack. He was worried because he knew I sometimes take that route to work.'

Grayson blinked. 'He'd already heard about it? In Europe?'

'One of his friends posted it on Twitter. There were already videos online. One of them shows the victim's face as she's being shot.' Her voice trembled. 'The bastard who took the video gave her name, too. Before her family was notified. It was Elena Muñoz.' She met his eyes and sighed. 'You already know all this?'

'Yeah. I don't know much more than that, but I'm going to find out.'

'She was here. Last week. I saw her go into your office. Why was she here?'

'She wanted a new trial for her husband. He was convicted of murder.'

'I remember reading the case when I was still in law school. What did you tell her?'

'I said there was nothing to warrant a new trial. No new evidence.' He blew out a breath. 'And now she's dead. I need to get some answers. If Anderson comes by again, can you hold him off for a while? He just wants me to cut a deal with Willis.'

Daphne's brows shot up. 'Franklin Willis shot two women to death over a hundred bucks in their cash register. We have him on tape. Why the hell would you cut a deal?'

'Because the defense is saying the police recovered the gun in a bad search and the tape is grainy. I've been trying to find a way around a deal. Buy me a little time if you would. I need answers on Elena Muñoz first. I'll have to prepare a statement.'

'Wait. Ford wasn't the only one calling me, all worried.'

Something in the way she said it told him who it had been. 'My mom? Why?'

'She wanted to be sure you were okay as you weren't answering your cell phone. She asked me to remind you that you're having dinner with her tomorrow night. I told her I'd fuss at you to call her. So call your mother, Grayson.' She smiled kindly, taking the edge off her admonition. 'And have a muffin.'

'Poppy seed?' he asked and she nodded.

He used to be annoyed when Daphne brought baked goods into the office, but that was because she'd baked with peaches, which gave him hives. As soon as he'd come clean about his allergies, she'd made it a point to bake his favorite treats.

Somewhere in her forties, she was brazen and bold, wore her hair too big and her suits too neon. She mothered the entire office, himself included. But she was smart and resourceful and a fierce combatant in the courtroom. She'd gone to law school when her son was in high school, which couldn't have been easy. In the year they'd worked together Grayson had come to respect her highly. He had also grown to like her far more than he'd ever admit.

'I'll hold off Anderson as long as I can, but please call him soon so he stops yelling.'

Grayson snagged a muffin. 'Soon,' he promised. He closed his office door and called the person he could trust to give him the truth. While the phone rang, he found the video on the news station's website. By the time he heard 'Hello?' he was staring once again at the woman with the dark eyes.

'Stevie, it's Grayson.'

'Grayson?' Homicide Detective Stevie Mazzetti's voice was immediately concerned. 'What's wrong?'

He frowned. 'Why do you always ask me that when I call?'

'Because you only call when something's wrong.'

He considered it. 'So maybe I do. But you only call when you want a warrant.'

She chuckled. 'Fair enough. What's up?'

'The sniper shooting. I need everything you know.'

'Hell.' All the humor fled from her voice. 'Not much. The vic was shot at two different locations. Ballistics is still out, but it's two different weapons. A woman walking her dog stopped to help the victim and narrowly avoided being shot herself.'

On his screen the woman had jumped out of the minivan's path and was now rushing to aid the victim. 'I know. I'm watching the video.'

'You and everyone else on the planet,' Stevie grumbled. 'It looks like he shot her from a business park, one driveway up. But we're still not sure.'

'All those video cameras and nobody got the shooter?'

'All the cameras were pointed at the victim in the minivan.'

'Where were the first shots fired? Before she crashed?'

'We don't know yet. Right now, just about everyone's searching for the sniper. I don't have to tell you that tensions are high around here. Ten-year anniversary and all.'

'Here, too.' He hesitated. 'Has the victim been ID'd yet?'

'Elena Muñoz. Grayson, what's going on? What's with all the questions?'

Eyes on his screen, Grayson flinched once more when the shot was fired, waiting until the dark-eyed woman staggered out of the blurred zone. 'I prosecuted Elena's husband. Who's primary?'

'Perkins was the first on the scene, but as soon as Hyatt heard "sniper", he pulled him. Perkins's partner hadn't even made it to the scene yet. Hyatt made Bashears and Morton primary. It was simply a question of experience. Perkins has never dealt with a high-profile case and Bashears and Morton have.'

Grayson searched his mental archive. 'Morton was on the husband's case.'

'Really? When was that?' Stevie asked. 'I don't remember the Muñoz case.'

'Six years ago.'

Stevie's breath came out in a little rush. 'Oh. Well, that explains it.'

Stevie's husband and son had been killed six years ago, leaving Stevie seven months pregnant and grieving. She'd taken a leave of absence until after Cordelia had been born. There was a period of several months Stevie didn't remember and nobody blamed her for it, Grayson least of all. Stevie's husband had been his friend.

'Why aren't you and Fitzpatrick lead on this?'

'Probably because we weren't in the office yet when all this went down. We'll get pulled in before it's all over, but right now we're on a case of our own. Gang shooting a few hours ago. We're off to inform the parents of a seventeen-year-old boy. Which', she added flatly, 'is my very favorite thing to do in all the world.'

'Sorry. Be safe.'

'We will.' She hesitated. 'Call me if you need me, Gray. I mean that.'

'Thanks.' Grayson hung up and watched the video once again. Ramon Muñoz had been denied bail, so he'd been locked up ever since his arrest six years ago. *Why did Elena come to see me last week? Why now?*

He wondered who she'd gone to see after she'd left his office, fighting back tears of despair. He wondered who else she'd sought out for help. He wondered whose apple cart she'd upset badly enough to end up riddled with bullets.

He picked up his phone. 'Daphne, can you get a number for Detectives Bashears or Morton? They're primary on the Muñoz murder.'

'You want me to call them, tell them she was here last week?'

'No, just have them call me. I'll tell them. Thanks.'

'Anything else? Another muffin?'

'No, but thanks. Do we have word on the Samson jury?' They'd been deliberating another one of his murder cases for four days. He wished they'd hurry the hell up.

'Just entering the jury room to resume deliberations. Sounds like they may be close though. Hopefully this morning. Hey, Anderson called again. He knows you're in the building. Said if you didn't call him, he'd plead down Willis himself.'

'Man has goddamn spies,' Grayson muttered. He hung up, closed the video of Elena and the dark-eyed woman, and dialed his boss, ready for a good fight.

Detective Stevie Mazzetti slid her phone into her pocket with a frown.

JD Fitzpatrick glanced away from the road to study her face. 'So? Spill.'

'It's nothing,' she said. 'Just Grayson being odd.'

'Grayson isn't odd. He's always too mad.'

'He's not always mad. Just when he's working.'

JD gave her a pointed look. 'He works always. Therefore he is mad always.'

'Almost always. So you're almost right. So what?'

'I'm always right,' JD said smugly, and Stevie grinned in spite of herself.

'You're full of yourself today. Why?'

He grinned back, the look of a well-satisfied man. *Which is how it should be.* Her partner of one year was getting married in a month and she'd never seen him so happy. Still, 'she put on her grump', as her six year old called it. 'I hope you two are using birth control. Otherwise, you're gonna be procreating like bunnies.'

He said nothing and Stevie's grump faded like mist. 'Lucy's pregnant!' She clapped her hands. 'How long have you known?'

'Since this morning,' he confessed. 'Don't tell Lucy I told you. And don't tell anyone else yet. We want to keep it a secret for a few months.'

'Good luck with that,' she said, and laughed out loud.

'I know. Tell me what's making Smith odd today so I can practice my serious face.'

'He asked about the sniper's victim. Said he thought he recognized her. That he prosecuted her husband.'

Abruptly he sobered. 'Makes you wonder who Mr Muñoz pissed off in jail. Still, it is odd that Grayson remembered the wife after all this time.'

'Do you remember the faces of the spouses when you inform them of a murder?'

'Every single one,' JD replied.

'Grayson once told me that every conviction is a bit like a death to the family. When the jury says "guilty", it's like a piece of them dies, too.'

'Except their loved one took away someone else's loved one forever.'

'He knows that, and he's more committed to getting justice for those victims than any prosecutor I know. But he remembers the mothers who cry when their children are hauled off to jail. It's

39

the price the bad guys pay. Unfortunately their families pay too.'

'Like Elena Muñoz.'

'Maybe,' Stevie said. 'I guess we'll see what Bashears and Morton dig up. Oh, heck. That's our exit, right there. Whose turn is it to inform the parents?'

'Yours,' JD said grimly.

Stevie sighed. 'That's what I thought. Let's get this over with.'

Three

With Clay safely out of sight, Paige opened her door and let Detective Morton and her partner in. With a hand signal, she sent Peabody to lie down at her side.

Bashears looked impressed. 'That's some dog.' He started toward Peabody, but Paige held out her hand in warning.

'He's a protection dog. He knows I'm tense right now, so he's tense too.'

Bashears studied her front door with its three brand-new deadbolts, then nodded. 'Fair enough. I don't suppose it's every day you witness a murder.'

If you only knew, she thought. And then she realized he probably did. It wouldn't be hard to find out about her 'incident'. Google was only a cell phone away.

'Not every day,' she agreed evenly. 'Look, I want to help you, but I'm really tired and I was about to take a shower. Can you ask me what you need to ask me?'

'Of course,' Morton said. 'Can we sit?'

'I'd like to get this done fast. I prefer to stand,' she said and Morton frowned.

'Of course.' Morton proceeded to ask the same questions that Perkins had asked.

Paige sighed. 'With all due respect, Detective Morton, I have already answered all of these questions. I'm so tired I can't think. Can we please be finished soon?'

'If you'd sit down, you wouldn't be so tired,' Morton said snidely.

41

Paige had to bite back a snarl. 'If I sit down, I won't get back up again.' She moved to her door to show them out and Morton made a huffing noise, clearly annoyed.

'Miss Holden, what do you do for a living?' she asked.

'I work at a gym. I also work for a private investigator.'

'Are you licensed?' Bashears asked. By the look in his eyes she knew he'd known exactly what she did for a living, just as he'd known about her 'incident'.

'Not yet.'

Morton took a half-step forward, stopping when Peabody growled. 'Why do you think Elena Muñoz was shot in her vehicle, then shot again by a sniper?'

'I don't know,' Paige said, and even she would have believed herself.

'You're a PI,' Bashears said. 'Were you working for her?'

'No,' Paige said, and that was actually the truth. Technically. Maria had approached her, begging her for help. Not Elena. A cold shiver raced down her spine as she realized that Maria might be in danger, too. 'Are we done?'

'Almost,' Morton said. 'Who do you work for, Miss Holden?'

'The Silver Gym. I'm a trainer there.'

Morton leveled a stare that had become hostile in a single blink. 'I'm talking about your PI job. Who do you work for?'

Bashears cut in smoothly. 'We'd like to know in what capacity are you acquainted with Clay Maynard? He stood with you while you spoke with Detective Perkins.'

'We're associates. And friends.'

Morton lifted a brow. 'And he had nothing to do with the fact that Elena Muñoz happened to crash into the lamppost next to your apartment?'

Paige didn't back down. 'No. Look, I'm tired and I've cooperated. Please leave.'

'You haven't told us the truth,' Morton bit out. 'But I'll go, for now. By the way, when you see Mr Maynard next, tell him that Detective Skinner finally returned to work after months on disability. But he'll never work Homicide again. He'll sit at a damn desk until he's old enough for his retirement Timex.' She leaned closer, this time ignoring Peabody's warning growl. 'And you tell your associate and your *friend* that I'll be watching you both. Because something stinks here and it reeks of *him*.'

Morton yanked Paige's front door open, then turned for a parting jab. 'If you know something you aren't telling me, I'll nail your ass to the wall. I don't care how many YouTube hits you get or how many reporters are calling you a Good Samaritan.'

Wide-eyed, Paige stared at the two detectives as they walked down the stairs. Bashears looked annoyed, but with his partner, not with Paige. *At least there's that*, she thought, closing her door and locking all three deadbolts. She turned, unsurprised to see Clay standing behind her even though he hadn't made a sound. His jaw was hard, but his eyes were turbulent. And filled with guilt.

Wearily, Paige sank into the chair at her desk. 'So who is Detective Skinner?'

Clay sat on her sofa, staring at her carpet. 'Morton's old partner. Skinner was shot by Nicki's killer after I discovered her body. Because I didn't tell the cops what I knew right away, Skinner almost died. When I heard Morton ID herself at the door I thought that there might be trouble. She doesn't like me much.'

'Yeah,' Paige said dryly. 'I got that. I have to tell someone. I don't want a Skinner on my conscience. But I'm not gonna tell Morton. She scares the hell out of me.'

He glanced up to meet her eyes. 'Me, too.'

Paige sighed. 'So Ramon's alibi was true. There was no way he could have killed Crystal Jones in a gardener's shed six years ago. Yet the murder weapon was found in his bedroom closet, wrapped in a canvas apron, stuck down in one of Elena's boots. It was planted. Maybe by cops. God, we sound so OJ.'

'It's been known to happen,' Clay said. 'Cops planting evidence.'

She studied him shrewdly. 'And someday you'll tell me about it?'

'Probably not,' he murmured. 'Not one of my better memories.'

'You didn't . . .' Paige let the thought trail and watched him shake his head.

43

'Never. And I tried to stop it, but it was too huge.'

'So you left the force.'

'Yeah. If cops were involved, this is already bigger than you and me, Paige.'

'Well, cops *are* involved on some level – assuming they were chasing Elena this morning. Then Morton, who worked on the Crystal Jones murder, comes in as a pinch hitter. This does not bode well. I have no idea where to turn.'

'I can call the cop I mentioned before. I think we can trust her.'

'How do you know her?'

'She worked Nicki's homicide.'

'So she works with Morton. Look, even if Morton hadn't been the one to investigate Ramon's murder, she has a vendetta for you, Clay. And I promised Elena I wouldn't take this to the cops. Call me superstitious, but I don't like to renege on a deathbed promise.' Paige rubbed her aching forehead. 'So where do I go to do the right thing?'

Clay shrugged. 'What about a defense attorney?'

'Elena contacted one of those innocence organizations that help wrongly convicted prisoners. They said she was so far back in line that it could be ten years before they even got to Ramon's case. They told her that she needed new evidence. And so did I.'

'You can't blame yourself, Paige. Besides, you have that evidence. A defense attorney will listen to you now. Maybe the innocence organization would move Ramon up in line so he wouldn't have to wait ten years.'

'Ten minutes is too long for Ramon to stay in jail.' Peabody laid his head on Paige's knee and she scratched behind his ears. 'I could talk to the defense attorneys, but if dirty cops are involved . . . Someone in law enforcement needs to know.'

'We could try the state's attorney's office.'

'ASA Grayson Smith.' Paige considered the trial transcript she'd spent the last few weeks poring over. 'He ran a clean trial. Cut and dried.'

'Any indication he could have been corrupt?'

'Not to my knowledge. He only used the evidence that Morton

44

and her old partner collected. Maria said that he tried to get Ramon to take a deal but Ramon refused. When the case came to court Smith was harsh with Ramon, but kind and respectful to Maria. Compassionate, even. She and Elena wanted to hate him, but couldn't. Elena was even considering visiting him, asking for his help.' She bit her lip. 'I'm going to have to trust someone. I've got enough ghosts haunting my mind. I don't need someone dying because I held back.' She swiveled in the chair and opened her everyday laptop.

'What are you doing?'

'Pulling up my file on Grayson Smith.' The most recent photo she'd found had been taken on the courthouse steps the previous winter. He was a very handsome man, tall and linebacker-big. His double-breasted wool coat hung from his broad shoulders like it was custom-made for him. His hair was dark, his skin golden. 'He doesn't look like a Grayson. Or a Smith.'

Clay looked over her shoulder. 'What does it matter?'

She lifted a shoulder. 'It doesn't. It's a game I play. Just trying to figure out where people come from. Probably due to the fact that I was the only one with black hair and black eyes in a family of blond, blue-eyed Norwegians.'

'Are you adopted?' Clay asked, interest in his tone.

'No.' Although there had been a hell of a lot of days growing up that she wished she had been. 'But I never knew my father, who I have to assume was not a blond, blue-eyed Norwegian. I think I'll take a shower, then go meet Mr Smith.'

'What, you're going to look into his eyes and see if he's trustworthy?'

'Something like that.'

'Has it ever worked before?'

Paige thought of the failed relationships that littered her life. 'I wish. I would have run from about ninety per cent of my old boyfriends.'

'Then why even bother?'

She considered her answer. 'Because I don't know what else to do.'

'You want me to come with you?'

'It would be better if you went to check on Maria. I'm worried about her. If anyone thinks she knows what Elena was carrying, her life could be in danger.'

'If they find out you've got what she was carrying, your life could be in danger, too.'

An icy finger ran down her spine. 'Yeah. I know.'

Tuesday, April 5, 8.55 A.M.

Silas swallowed hard when he saw the caller ID on his cell phone. 'Yeah?' he answered before the last ring, his voice flat. He'd learned to be a hell of an actor.

'You lied to me.'

Silas's jaw tightened. 'No, I did not.'

'You never said that Elena spoke to anyone. But there's video all over the Internet that shows that she did.'

His blood went cold. *Video?* 'From my vantage point I saw no words exchanged.'

'You also didn't mention the Good Samaritan who stopped to help her.'

'Had I known they exchanged words, I would have killed her too.'

'I need to know what they said. I need to know what Elena knew.'

'Did you speak with Denny? Ask what the woman had seen?'

'Of course, but I haven't gotten a straight answer yet.' There was a touch of amusement in his tone, punctuated by a guttural moan in the background. 'But Mr Sandoval did, after a little convincing, tell me that Elena saw you. That you arrived at the bar as she was escaping. That's not what you told me either. So, you did lie to me.'

'I didn't tell you she didn't see me. By the time I got there she was already driving away. I had her in a place where I could run her off the road when Denny started shooting. I saw her heading into the apartment complex and I chose the building at the next driveway. That's the truth. I got to the roof seconds before she crashed.'

Just as the woman leapt out of the way.

There was no answer, only heavy, angry silence. Silas closed his eyes. He couldn't win this. He just had to survive. 'What do you want me to do?'

'That's much better. Listen and obey, or you will not be a happy man.'

He listened, his palms clammy. He'd do as he was told. The risk of disobedience was too high. When the instructions were complete, he disconnected. Just in time.

He made his lips smile as he opened his arms to the little whirlwind who'd brought him back to life from the ashes. 'Hey, baby.'

'Papa.' She hugged him hard, then flattened her little seven-year-old hands on either side of his face, her eyes very serious. 'You looked sad on the phone. Why?'

He kissed her forehead. 'Because your Fluffy ate the pie that Mama made me for dessert tonight.' He didn't lie unless he absolutely had to, but he'd say anything, do anything to keep her from knowing the real world. *From knowing the truth about me.*

She laughed, a twinkling sound that soothed him. 'Mama will make you more.'

He brought her close, wished he could hug her with all the emotion in his heart. But he could break her if he wasn't careful. He was always careful. 'You be good today.'

'I'll try.'

'There is no try,' he said with mock severity.

'There is only do,' she responded, as she always did.

'I love you, baby.'

She burrowed into his neck. 'I love you too. I hafta go. The bell's gonna ring.'

He put her down, the smile still on his face as she darted away, waving over her shoulder. He turned for his van, waiting until he was inside before letting out the breath he'd held. But there was no relief. He'd been holding his breath for seven and a half years.

Seven and a half years since he'd made a horrible choice. He watched her rejoin the other children, happy, safe. Loved. And he knew if he had to do it all over, he'd make the same horrible choice again.

Tuesday, April 5, 11.15 A.M.

'Did you call Anderson?' Daphne whispered as they sat at the prosecution table waiting for the Samson jury to come in. 'Please say you did.'

'Yeah, I did,' Grayson whispered back. 'I had to deal that bastard Willis down.' And he was very unhappy about it. With good behavior, a man who'd murdered two convenience-store workers in cold blood would be out in three years. It sucked. He glanced up at the jury door as it opened and the first juror entered the courtroom.

Anderson had wanted him to deal this case down too. The Samson jury had been out too long and the boss didn't believe they'd be delivering a guilty verdict.

Grayson was betting on the jury. *I guess in a few minutes we'll know who was right.*

'Dammit. I'm sorry.' Daphne pursed her lips. 'Did you tell Bashears about Elena?'

He nodded. 'They're trying to find out who else she talked to about her husband.'

'Did you call your mother?'

He grimaced. 'Crap.'

'Grayson,' she scolded.

'I've been busy.' He'd been going over his files on the Muñoz case, when he really should have been doing other things. Like calling his mother. 'I'll call her when we're done. Ah, finally,' he added as the last of the jurors filed in. 'Cross your fingers.'

'And toes,' Daphne muttered. 'Defense is looking damn smug.'

The judge entered, the tension in the courtroom palpable. 'Does the jury have a verdict?' the judge asked.

Grayson held his breath. Having to deal a murderer down still stung. Grayson didn't want another loss on his conscience. *Elena's murder is a tragedy, but not your fault.* Except he'd been telling himself that all morning and it wasn't helping. Rereading the file had left him with the uncomfortable feeling that he'd missed something.

'On the charge of murder in the first degree, we the jury find the defendant guilty.'

'*Yes*,' Grayson breathed, indulging in a single hammer of his fist against the table.

Chatter broke out through the courtroom, celebration from the victim's family and devastation from the defendant's. An anguished scream had Grayson twisting left to where Donald Samson's mother had thrown her arms around her son.

Ramon Muñoz's mother had done the same. As had his wife.

But of course, every con in the joint had a mother or wife who swore six ways to Tuesday that they were innocent. Muñoz had been guilty. There was DNA on the weapon found in his closet. And there was no alibi. *So put it out of your head.*

Grayson gave a nod to Daphne. She'd worked hard on this case. They both had. He turned to shake the hands of the victim's family seated behind him.

Then froze. It was her. *Her.* The woman from the video. She stood on the back row, watching. *Me. She's watching me. Why? What's she doing here?*

His heart began to race as he stared back. She was even more stunning in person than she'd been on the television screen, taller than he'd expected, her black hair longer. Her face was no longer stark white with shock, but a beautiful bronze, whether left over from a summer tan or a result of her parents' genetics he couldn't tell.

She was dressed in a way that was both professional and sensual all at once. The tailored black trousers couldn't hide the fact that her legs were long, her hips curvy. The black sweater was one of those that draped at the neck, clinging to well-endowed breasts without actually showing a damn thing.

Her eyes were just as black as he'd remembered. And piercing in their careful scrutiny. She was watching him, all right. Why, he had no clue.

'Thank you, Mr Smith.' The quavering voice jerked Grayson's focus away from the woman and into the face of the elderly woman who'd taken his hand. She was the grandmother of the newly convicted murderer's victim. Tears shimmered in her eyes as she shook his hand. 'Thank you,' she said again.

'You're welcome,' he said quietly. He covered her hand with his. 'Are you all right?'

Her chin lifted. 'Yes. My granddaughter can rest now. So can I.'

The other family members gathered. This was closure. While he could never bring their lost one back, he could give them this. When the last hand was shaken, he looked up. The woman was still there, still watching him, a red coat neatly draped over her arm.

He didn't need a law degree to know this was all about Elena Muñoz. When he started toward her, she slipped out the doors at the back of the courtroom. By the time he made it into the hall, she was nowhere to be seen.

'That woman from the video,' Daphne said. 'Do you know her?'

'No,' Grayson answered, troubled. 'Do you?'

'Nope. But I'd lay you dollars to donuts that you will. Are you gonna tell Bashears and Morton that she was here?'

'No,' he murmured and was happy she didn't ask why not, because he didn't know himself. 'It's showtime.' Together they headed out to the sea of reporters.

'Mr Smith! Mr Smith!'

Pushing the woman to the edge of his mind, Grayson gave his attention to the reporters. 'This was a victory for the victim,' he said. 'And closure for her family. We're satisfied with the jury's decision. Justice was done here today.'

A flash of red caught his eye and he glanced left. She was standing alone, despite the people milling around her. She gave him the briefest of nods before she lifted the blood-red hood of her coat, hiding her face as she walked away.

He stepped around the cameras. 'Any more has to come from the Public Affairs Office.' He took the courthouse stairs two at a time, heading in the direction she'd gone.

'You're going to talk to her?' Daphne asked, her heels clicking on the pavement as she barely kept up with him.

'If I can catch her,' Grayson said grimly. *She must have already turned a corner.*

'And if you can't?'

Grayson thought of the sign behind Phin Radcliffe when he'd

reported the story that morning. *Brae Brooke Village Apartments.*
'Then I know where she lives.'

'As does everyone in the free world with an Internet connection.'

He thought of Elena, of the bullet hole in her head. 'I know. Do me a favor. Go back to the office and find out everything you can about her.'

'Starting with her name?' Daphne asked.

'Yeah. Start with that. Thanks, Daphne.'

The woman lived on the outskirts of the city. If she'd driven in, she had to park somewhere. There was a parking garage a block ahead. *Be there. Let me catch you.*

Tuesday, April 5, 11.50 A.M.

Well, that was useless. Paige walked back to her truck, her step as brisk as her stiff knees would allow. *I'll know if I can trust him,* she thought sardonically. *I'm an idiot.*

She came, she saw, she left more conflicted than before. All she could honestly say was that Grayson Smith's photographs didn't do him justice. He was broodingly handsome in the newspaper photos, but in person he ... dominated. It was his physical size, true. The man could have been a linebacker, but it was more than that. He had a presence. Like ... *Don't worry. I'm here. I'll fix everything.*

The people who'd gathered to shake his hand had felt it too. It was written all over their grateful faces as they thanked him for getting justice for their murdered loved one.

She could say he was a successful prosecutor with a passion for his work, but she'd known that already. What she suspected by watching him was that he had a passion for a great many other things, most of which she hadn't done in way too many months.

She might admit, in a weak moment, that he'd fascinated her. And that she had been entirely too attracted for her own good.

What she still didn't know was if she could trust him. Damned if she didn't want to, though. But she'd been taken in by a pretty face too many times in the past to succumb.

She'd wanted to trust every man she'd let into her life.

Too many times. Too many men. But 'in the past' was key. There'd been a time when she hadn't let a week go by between breaking up with one disappointment, only to fly to the next one.

Looking for love in all the wrong places, hating myself for being so pathetic.

No more. It had been eighteen months since she'd allowed herself to succumb. Eighteen months since she'd watched her best friend find the real thing. What Olivia had with David made every one of Paige's relationships pale in comparison.

She wanted what Olivia and David had. She wanted to find the one who'd be her happy ever after. And so she'd gone cold turkey on her man habit, waiting until she found the right one.

Which meant she'd gone cold turkey on sex, too. Eighteen fucking months.

Or . . . non-fucking months, as Olivia would always say.

Olivia. Hell. I should have called her. She'll be so worried. All of her friends would be worried. The light turned red and Paige halted at the corner. Checking her phone, she was chagrined to find her voicemail full, mostly numbers she didn't recognize. Apparently the press had obtained her number. Not too hard if they were any good at their job.

The Minneapolis numbers she did recognize. Olivia had called six times. Paige hit speed dial one and prepared for a tirade. She wasn't disappointed.

'Oh. My. God. David and I were so worried.'

'I'm okay, Olivia,' Paige said calmly. 'I wasn't hurt and I'm fine.'

'You were almost *shot*. What the hell were you *thinking*?'

'That somebody needed help? Hello? Pot calling the kettle much? Like you guys wouldn't have done the same?'

Olivia was a homicide detective, her husband a firefighter. They made their living putting themselves in danger for people who needed help.

'Well, yeah,' Olivia admitted grumpily. 'But you should have called us. I had to get the news from David, who had to get it from one of the guys at the firehouse who saw you on YouTube.'

'It's been an . . . eventful morning.'

'I guess so. Are you really all right? You looked like you took a hard fall.'

'I'm okay,' she said again. 'Shaken, but okay.'

There was a moment of silence, then Olivia sighed. 'That's not what I'm really worried about,' she confessed. 'Paige, you've seen two women gunned down in front of you, in less than a year. You can't be okay. I was just thinking that maybe you'd want to see someone.'

'Like a shrink?'

'Yes.'

'I don't need a shrink,' Paige said decisively.

'I never thought I would either. Seeing all the death creeps up on you, though. I found talking to someone really helped. At least I can sleep at night. Can you?'

'No,' Paige murmured.

'The same dream?'

Paige swallowed hard. 'Yes.'

'What happened today can't make that any better. Promise me you'll consider finding a counselor. Do it for me. Please.'

'I promise.'

'Which? That you'll consider it or that you'll do it?'

'At least the first one,' Paige hedged.

Olivia sighed. 'I didn't expect any more than that.' There was muted conversation in the background. 'David says to tell you he posted pictures of his belt ceremony on Facebook. He missed having you there last night. We all missed you.'

Paige stared up at the light, willing it to turn green. 'I wanted to be there for him. Second dan black belt.' It was an honor. An achievement. She should have been there. But she'd been doing something important – saving Zachary Davis. 'Tell him I'm proud of him.'

'Have you found a *dojo*?' Olivia asked, in a way that said she knew the answer.

'No, not yet. I've been working out at the gym. Practicing on my own.'

'You said that the last time I asked you.'

And I'll say it the next time too. Her karate *dojo* had once been like

53

her second home, her family. But after what happened last summer, Paige hadn't been able to walk through a *dojo* door.

There were bloodstains on her *gi* that she'd never get out. A few months after the attack she'd bought a new *gi*, brightly white, but she'd never put it on. She simply couldn't. She'd tried. Many times. Finally she'd packed the *gi*s away.

Someday she'd be ready to go back. She'd kept her body toned, her skills sharp. But the *dojo* with its sense of family . . . Yes, someday she'd go back. *Soon*.

The light finally turned green and Paige took off like a rocket. Her other coat pocket started to buzz, startling her until she realized it was her disposable phone. Clay was the only one who called her on the disposable. 'I have to go, Liv. Give everyone my love. I'll call you later.' She hung up before Olivia could protest and flipped the disposable open. 'What's up?'

'Where are you?' Clay asked tersely.

'Still downtown. Why? What's happened?'

'Maria Muñoz is in the ER,' Clay told her.

'*What?* Why?'

'Heart attack. Her younger son said it wasn't the first one she'd had. She collapsed when the cops came to tell them about Elena. She's conscious now and her son told me she'd said nothing about the case or you to the cops. None of them have.'

'Dear God. Did you tell them about the flash drive?'

'No. I figured the fewer people who knew, the better. From what I can tell, Elena didn't tell anyone in her family that she had it. They knew she was going to the bar and all of them had begged her not to go, but she was determined to get proof.'

'We need to find out how she got the drive to start with. She just didn't walk into the bar and find it in a bowl of nuts.'

'I think I can guess.' Clay sighed. 'Elena looked different six years ago.'

'I know. She said she lost almost a hundred pounds after Ramon was jailed.' The family business was a physically taxing one. 'Why is that important?'

'Because Ramon's little brother said Elena told everyone in their circle that she was tired of cleaning toilets and sweeping floors because Ramon couldn't keep it in his pants six years ago. She wanted out of the family business. The brother said the family knew it was a ruse, but they all played along. Elena got hired at the bar.'

'Ramon's alibi bar? I told her to stay away from that place. That I'd check it out.'

'Yeah, well, she didn't listen.'

'How long was she working there?'

'For the last two weeks. She wanted to get close to the owner. Find out why he lied on the stand. Apparently she laid it on thick and followed through with . . . action.'

Paige grimaced. 'Oh, God. Tell me she didn't have sex with that sleazy slime.'

'Apparently she did. At least that's the story Ramon got inside. Denny Sandoval was pretty satisfied with himself, bedding Ramon's wife – and he made sure Ramon heard about it. News like that travels damn fast. Ramon blew a gasket. His brother said he lit into some big guys in the yard during recess. They were riding him about it.'

Paige felt sick. 'Is Ramon alive?'

'He's in the clinic. He'll live, but one of the guys he pummeled might not make it.'

'And then he'll be a killer for real. That's not fair,' she hissed fiercely.

'None of this is fair. Ramon told Elena he wanted a divorce when she went to see him in the clinic on Saturday.'

'You can't blame him, I suppose, based on what he'd heard. I guess Elena's taking such a huge risk to get those pictures makes sense. I guess she didn't feel like she had anything to lose.' Paige headed into the parking garage where she'd left her truck.

'That's my take, too. What did you decide to do about the prosecutor?'

'I don't know yet. I didn't actually talk to him.'

'Why not?'

'He was surrounded by reporters, for one, and I don't want to be in anyone else's video. He was in court by the time I got down here.'

She frowned. 'I'm still not sure enough about him to risk it. He was in court for a jury verdict – they found the guy guilty of murder. He looked really happy about it.'

'They usually do when they get a conviction. Most of the guys he tries are probably guilty as hell, Paige.'

'I know, I know. I'm just worried that the pictures Elena died to get will get "lost" or worse. Going the defense attorney route might be safer, after all. I tried to talk to Ramon's old attorney, but he passed away a few years ago. Do you know any others?'

'A few. Where are you now?'

She pulled her keys from her pocket. 'In a parking garage. About to come home.'

'*No.*' He barked it with such intensity that she flinched. 'Not yet,' he added.

'What the hell's wrong with you?' she snapped. 'You gave *me* a heart attack.'

'Check your truck for a tracking device. Look up under the bumper.'

'Damn reporters.' Paige crouched, doing as he'd instructed. 'Why here?'

'A, it's the easiest place to hide a tracking device, and b, it's where I found mine.'

She paused, her hand up under the grille. 'Before or after you visited Maria's family?'

'Before. I drove to the office and switched vehicles with Alyssa. I told her to take the day off and just drive wherever she wanted to go.'

Paige chuckled. 'They'll be spending a lot of time waiting outside the nail salon if they're tracking Alyssa.'

'Exactly.'

Paige's fingers closed over a small device and she pulled it free. 'Found it. Asshole reporters.' Her knees, still sore from her hard landing, started to protest the crouch and she rose stiffly. 'I need to stretch my—'

The next word was forgotten, the step behind her the only notice she had before an arm like iron wrapped around her neck. From the corner of her eye she saw the glitter of a blade and she twisted, jabbing her elbow into a rock-hard gut and throwing her body to the right with all her strength.

Get away. She twisted again, slipping free. Momentum sent her to the concrete floor and out of sheer instinct she rolled to her back, striking a vicious kick to the man's knees.

He was a mountain, a goddamned mountain, and her kick might have been that of a child. As fast as she had been, he leaned forward to grab her hair, the knife in his hand, coming at her. *I'm going to die. I'm going to die. Fight. Fight.*

Watch the knife. She struggled to kick out at him again, her eyes on the knife.

And then the mountain crumpled, the man staggering to his knees in a thump that made the floor shake. Paige kicked, sending the knife flying to land harmlessly under her truck. The sound of the knife skittering along the concrete echoed in her ears.

The man fell forward, as if in slow motion, and Paige rolled out of his path.

Lying on her side, she looked up, her racing heart beating a hole in her chest.

Him.

It was him. Grayson Smith. He stood over the knife man, face dark with fury, his arm still outstretched, a briefcase clenched in his fist.

A warrior in a three-piece suit.

Time began to move again as Smith reached to grab the man, who leapt to his feet and ran. Smith started to chase him, then cursed and dropped to his knees beside her, his briefcase hitting the floor with another loud thud that made her flinch. 'He got you.'

Paige's hand flew to her throat. Warm and sticky. She stared at her hand, covered with blood for the second time that day. 'Shit.'

Smith yanked a handkerchief from his breast pocket, pressed it to her throat, then lifted her chin, forcing her to meet his eyes. 'Who the hell are you?' he snarled.

Four

*G*oddammit. She was white as a sheet. Blood steadily flowed from the slice on her throat, turning her red coat black. Grayson gently tilted her face up to the light, willing his hands not to shake as he continued to press his handkerchief against her wound. An inch lower and she'd have been dead. Her pulse was like a goddamn rocket.

He spared a glance in the direction the man had run. The bastard was gone. He fumbled for his cell phone, managed to call 911 while keeping pressure on her throat.

'This is 911. What is your emergency?' the operator asked.

'A woman's been stabbed in the throat. I need an ambulance at the parking garage four blocks west of the courthouse. Second floor, close to the stairwell.'

'I've dispatched emergency services. Is she conscious?'

'Yes.' *Thank God*.

She'd closed her eyes. Her hands clenched, relaxed, then clenched again. He freed the top buttons of her coat, checked her pulse. It had already slowed substantially.

'Are you in a safe place?' the operator asked.

'I think so.' Grayson's breath still came in hard pants while the woman had hers evening out. 'The man with the knife ran away.'

'Can you describe him?'

'He was six-four, two hundred thirty or forty pounds. He had on a black baseball cap, so I couldn't see his hair color. He was wearing a black nylon jacket and black cargo pants. I only saw his back.'

'Okay, stay on the line. Help is coming.'

'I'm going to put the phone down to keep pressure on her neck,' Grayson said. 'I'll put it on speaker.' He set his phone aside and cradled the woman's head, lifting her gently until her head rested on his thigh. His handkerchief was soaked through so he tugged his tie from his collar and pressed it to her neck instead.

'I'm all right,' she murmured and he let out a harsh breath. She opened her eyes, looking straight up at him, compelling him to answer her.

Except he didn't know what she wanted. 'What's your name?' he asked.

'Paige. Paige Holden. Thank you. You probably saved my life.'

His lips twitched, relief rushing through him at her slightly arch tone. 'Probably?'

One side of her mouth lifted. 'Gotta leave me a little dignity.'

'I'd say you did more than okay, Miss Holden.' Now that it was over he was amazed that she'd fought against a man nearly twice her weight. 'That was one hell of a kick.'

'That's one hell of a briefcase.' She struggled to sit, but he restrained her gently.

'Don't move. If you sit up you could start gushing again. Which would be bad since I don't have any more ties or hankies. The ambulance is coming.'

Her eyes flickered. 'I lost my phone. I was talking to someone. He'll be worried.'

He? Emotion rose quickly, stunning him. Annoyance, anger. Jealousy? *Yeah, all of the above.* Which was crazy. 'Who were you talking to?' he asked, trying not to growl.

'My business partner. He's going to be out of his mind. Can you find my phone?'

Her phone lay against the tire of the car in the next parking place. He stretched as far as he could, just able to scoop the phone up with his fingertips. Studying it, he frowned.

It was the brand sold in convenience stores. 'Exactly what business are you in?'

She studied him for a long moment. 'Private investigation. I'm still a newbie.'

Oh. Elena Muñoz had hired a PI to help clear her husband. That made sense. *Finally something does.* He redialed the last call received, then handed her the phone.

Her eyes never left his as she waited for the call to go through. Wary, she was.

'I'm okay,' she said into the phone without preamble, then winced. 'Don't shout at me. I said I'm okay.' She winced again. 'A guy attacked me with a knife, but I'm fine. Grayson Smith is here.' She glanced up at Grayson uneasily. 'Of course he wasn't. He chased the guy with the knife away.'

Grayson took the phone from her hand. 'This is Smith. Who is this?'

'Her partner, Clay Maynard.' The man sounded frantic. 'Is she really okay?'

'No. The guy sliced her throat with his knife. An ambulance is on its way. She shouldn't need more than stitches. I'll let you know which ER.'

'Thanks,' Clay said gruffly. 'She'll fight you over going in the ambulance. Make her go. Please. And Smith? Don't leave her till I get there, okay?'

Grayson frowned. He recognized Maynard's name but couldn't remember from where. 'Sure.' He picked up his own cell. 'I'm disconnecting,' he said to the operator. 'The medics are almost here. Thanks.' He dropped both phones in his pocket.

Paige struggled once more to sit up, reaching for her phone. 'Please give it back.'

'After you're in the ER,' he said and she glared.

'Extortion.'

'Whatever works.' He leaned closer, so close that he felt her breath on his cheek. She was connected to Elena, and he needed to know how. Once they got to the ER, he might not have the privacy to ask. 'You were working for Elena Muñoz?'

She hesitated. Then gave him the same brief nod she had on the courthouse steps.

'In what capacity?' he asked.

'Proving her husband is innocent. She found new evidence. It's compelling. It also got her killed.'

If he had a nickel for every claim of new evidence . . . Still, considering the events of the morning, he'd give her the benefit of the doubt. For now. 'Why come to me? The police will investigate . . .' His words trailed away when her eyes flashed, violently. 'You didn't tell the police about this evidence?'

'No. And I don't plan to.'

Anger bubbled up. 'Why the hell not?' She hesitated again, longer this time. 'Hurry,' he hissed. 'The ambulance is coming.'

'Elena told me cops did this to her, right before she was shot the last time.'

For a moment he was speechless. It was quite an accusation, one he didn't believe. But she obviously did, and she had been attacked. 'Why come to me?'

'I want to do the right thing. I have information and I need to trust someone. I needed to know if you were an honest man. Are you?'

Her question left him uncomfortable. 'I saved your life.'

'I know. Now I need your help to save someone else's. Are you an honest man?'

Most of the time, he thought. 'Yes.'

'Good. Now help me sit up. I'll let them check me out here, but I'm not getting in that damn ambulance.' She struggled to sit and he held her down. Not, he discovered, an easy feat. She obviously hadn't really been trying before. 'Let me up,' she hissed, her struggles becoming desperate. '*Please.*'

Panic flared in her eyes and he realized that this woman, who seemed so fearless, was scared of ambulances. He'd found there was usually a reason for such fear. He wanted to know what that reason was.

She was valiant, but for the moment vulnerable. 'You want my help?' he asked coolly. 'You go in the nice ambulance.'

'That's extortion,' she said again, this time through clenched teeth. She was trembling and he was tempted to let her run. But

61

he held her firmly. For her own good.

'Like I said,' he said, still holding her shoulders in place, 'whatever works.'

'Don't hold me down.' She was breathing hard, fighting him, her panic rapidly escalating as the ambulance drew closer. Her feet were planted firmly on the concrete and she was trying to rise. 'Let me go. Please.'

A different kind of dread filled him. He'd known enough victims of assault to see the signs. The wound on her throat could be stitched. Whatever was behind this fear went far deeper. He lightened his grip. 'I'm sorry. I didn't know.'

She fell back against him, her forehead beaded with sweat. 'I'll go. I promise. I'll go in the ambulance. Just . . . don't . . . don't hold me down.'

'I'm sorry,' he said again as gently as he could. 'I didn't mean to scare you.'

She met his eyes, hers haunted. 'Don't go. Please.'

Grayson brushed his hand over her hair as the ambulance came to a halt. 'I won't leave you. Close your eyes and breathe.' She obeyed, visibly attempting to regain control of herself. He found himself doing the same, because his heart was pounding like hell, his gut churning with adrenaline and dread and . . . admiration.

She'd been afraid this morning, still she'd done the right thing. *She came to me.*

She'd fought an attacker, but now lay against him. Still frightened. *But trusting me.*

He hesitated, then brushed the backs of his fingers across her cheek. Her skin was flushed. But soft. 'You'll be okay,' Grayson murmured. 'I won't leave you.'

Tuesday, April 5, 12.30 P.M.

He looked up at his handiwork. The body swung nicely, the knots in the bedsheets holding firm. To even the best-trained eye, this was a suicide. He should know. He'd had a great deal of practice at making murder look like it wasn't.

Cleanup had become his specialty and Denny Sandoval had been a worrisome loose end for a long time. But that time was over.

Denny had finally spilled his secrets. *All the ones I care about anyway.*

He inspected the bedroom, making sure everything was in place. The note Denny had been gracious enough to write was on his dresser. His suitcase was put away, his clothes back in his drawers. There would be no indication that he planned to run away.

He'd already checked Denny's cell phone. There were no calls in or out that were troublesome. Except the call to Silas. Fortunately Denny had called Silas's 'business' phone. The police might look at the number because he'd called it shortly before Elena was shot, but it would take them nowhere.

Now, Elena Muñoz was an entirely different matter. Her ruse had gotten her killed. *And caused me a hell of a lot of trouble.* She'd turned out to be far more resourceful than he'd given her credit for. Not that it would have taken much to outsmart Denny.

I should have killed him six years ago. But it would have raised too many of the wrong eyebrows, so he'd let the bar owner live. He looked up at Denny's swinging body with contempt. The prick just had to go and bang Muñoz's woman.

Of course that stupidity was completely topped by his keeping photographs of the payoff. Photographs, for God's sake.

Denny had denied it. Vociferously at first. Not so vociferously after a few rounds of 'encouragement'. Then he'd spilled it. He'd hidden a security camera behind the bar that night. *The night I paid him to keep his damn mouth shut.*

Denny had actually thought he could use them. *Against me.* As insurance. *Idiot.*

And had Elena seen these photographs? Oh no, Denny had whined. But of course she had. That she'd seen something important didn't take a genius to ascertain. Denny had shot her, but not well enough. He'd had to call Silas for backup.

He still wasn't sure what to do about Silas. Silas had lied to him. That couldn't be condoned. But . . . Silas had his skills. *I'll have to think on that for a while.*

63

Now, he had bigger issues to consider. Not only had Elena Muñoz seen Denny's pics, she'd downloaded them. Apparently Denny didn't realize his computer recorded every access and every save of every file. Because Denny was a goddamn idiot.

Elena had walked away with damaging pictures. *Of me. Giving money to him.* He looked up at Denny's swinging body, fury bubbling within him. *Luckily I was smart enough to disguise myself that night or Denny would have met with a much crueler fate.*

He went downstairs to the bar and pried open the cash register. The cash held within wasn't enough to gas his car for a week, but it would look like a robbery. He surveyed the mess behind the bar, broken glass and rivers of booze. He'd been looking for more cameras and had found them. The camera feeds all went to Denny's laptop, which he'd also taken. *Asshole. Keeping insurance on me.*

As a final note, he opened the front door a crack, then left through the back. Teens would be all over this place like jackals on a carcass. They'd further wreck the joint and steal everything that wasn't tied down. Eventually somebody would find Denny swinging. Any cops suspecting foul play would have to sort through a lot of debris.

Good riddance, Denny. He slid Denny's laptop into his backpack. No police would find the pictures in a search. But the pictures were out there, somewhere. He needed to assume they would be found. People would know Sandoval and Muñoz's friend had lied under oath. Muñoz would probably be freed, eventually.

Luckily he'd always had a backup plan. Convicting Ramon Muñoz had never been a done deal.

His cell phone rang as he started his car, the one number he always answered on the first ring. 'Good afternoon,' he said.

'I saw the news. What did the Muñoz woman know?'

He wanted to snarl at the note of rebuke but did not. 'I fixed it. Don't worry.'

'That's what you always say. What did you do to fix this?'

'The bar owner is dead.'

'What about Ramon's friend?'

'He'll be taken care of too.'

'No loose ends?'

'Of course not.'

'Good. And speaking of loose ends, I found the last one.'

The hairs rose on the back of his neck. 'What do you mean? Where?'

'She was gone for years. Moved out of the country. Now she's back.'

He swallowed hard. Nothing good would come of this. 'What do you plan?'

'To kill her, like all the others. Then there will be no loose ends. No one left to tell.'

'Look,' he hedged. 'Maybe it would be better to leave that alone for a little while. At least until all this Elena Muñoz hoopla dies down.'

'But I've already started. I can't back away now.'

'Of course you can,' he snapped and instantly regretted it.

The voice on the other end grew cold. 'You snip your loose ends and I'll snip mine. Call me when you've taken care of everything.'

The phone clicked. 'Dammit,' he muttered. But there was nothing to do about that now. For now he'd follow instructions and make sure his loose ends were snipped.

Tuesday, April 5, 1.20 P.M.

Grayson Smith hadn't left her. He'd held her hand the whole way to the hospital. Had stood next to her when a police officer took her statement, and again when Detective Perkins showed up to take her statement a second time.

Now he stood in the doorway of the little ER room in which they'd placed her, his arms crossed over his chest, filling the space. *Guarding me.*

'Just like Peabody,' Paige murmured.

She'd been instructed to stay still until her throat could be stitched. But even lying flat on her back she could easily see him. He was a big guy, tall and broad.

The man who'd attacked her had been even bigger. *What would I have done had Grayson Smith not come along when he did? I'd be dead.* Except that he hadn't just 'come along'. He'd followed her and she wasn't sure how to process that. Yet.

'Who is Peabody?' Grayson asked.

'My dog.'

His brows lifted. 'Why am I like your dog?'

'He stands between me and the world.'

His face settled, satisfied at her answer. *He stroked my hair. My face. Cradled my head. Held my hand. Calmed me.* She wanted to trust him.

Well, he did save your life. That racked up major brownie points right there.

'Why does your dog guard you?' he asked.

'Long story.' One she did not want to retell.

His eyes narrowed in speculation. 'All right. Then why do you hate hospitals?'

'Same reason,' she said quietly but firmly.

'Excuse me.' It was a woman's voice, unflurried and familiar. Grayson stepped aside to let Dr Burke through. Burke gave Paige a wry look. 'You're a busy girl today.'

Paige grimaced. 'I just wanted to walk my damn dog this morning and take a nap.'

Burke sat on a low stool and rolled it to the edge of the bed before looking over her shoulder. 'That's not the same guy you were with this morning. Who is this one?'

'Grayson Smith,' Paige said, noting Grayson's jaw go tight. 'He's a prosecutor.'

'He's cute,' Burke said with a wink. 'You planning to keep them both?'

Paige laughed, then sucked in a pained breath when Burke removed the temporary dressing. 'Ow. You did that on purpose.'

'You can't laugh and cry at once,' she said. 'I'll do a local, but it's still gonna hurt.'

Paige controlled her anxiety. Until Burke produced a syringe with a needle that looked about fourteen inches long. 'I don't want . . . I . . . I need to go.' She tried to sit up.

Burke gently pushed her down to the bed. 'Stay put, Ninja Girl. It's going to pinch.'

'Look at me,' Grayson said. He crouched by her side, his hand out. His eyes were steady, his face calm. 'Squeeze as hard as you need to.'

Paige focused on his eyes, greener under the fluorescent light of the ER than they'd been in the garage when he'd leaned close to ask her about Elena Muñoz. A thought nagged at her mind, but scattered when Burke's syringe pierced her skin. She took Grayson's hand and tried not to cry. It wasn't the pain. It wasn't.

It was fear. And she hated to be afraid. She bit back a whimper. *Don't cry.*

'I know,' he murmured. 'It'll be over soon. Just hold on to me. And breathe.'

Paige obeyed, closing her eyes and squeezing Grayson's hand as hard as she could. 'Did you get suspended?' she asked Burke, her teeth clenched.

'Yep,' Burke said. 'After this shift I am in the proverbial doghouse until Thursday morning.' Her voice was conversationally chipper, but Paige felt horrible.

'I'm sorry. I should have answered when the other EMT called to me this morning.'

'You were in shock, so cut yourself some slack, Ninja Girl.'

'Stop *calling* me that,' Paige gritted. '*Ow.* Are you almost finished?'

'Nope,' Burke said cheerfully. 'Only halfway done.'

'Paige,' Grayson said soothingly. 'Look at me. Where do you come from?'

'Minnesota.' Paige ground out the word, knowing he was trying to get her mind off the pain and snooping at the same time. She had to hand it to him. The man was good. Really good. She had to be killing his hand right now, but he hadn't complained.

'Peabody, too?' he asked.

'Yes. He was a gift from my friend. She trains dogs. Names them all after—' She grunted when Burke pulled too hard. 'Dammit, that *hurt.*'

'Sorry,' Burke said mildly. 'I did tell you that it would.'

'So,' Grayson said smoothly, 'your friend names the dogs after . . . ?'

'After cartoon characters. Peabody's from *Mr Peabody and Sherman*.'

'I loved that cartoon,' Burke said. 'Bullwinkle and Rocky and Boris and Natasha.'

'Why did your friend give you a dog?' Grayson persisted.

Paige took a moment to choose an answer that would satisfy him. 'She thought I needed some company.'

'Because of last summer?' Burke asked, and from the corner of her eye Paige saw the doctor bite her lip, wincing her regret at having asked. 'Sorry.'

'How did you know?' Paige asked.

'I looked you up after this morning,' Burke said. 'It wasn't hard to find. That you'd want a protection dog is perfectly understandable under the circumstances.'

'So tell me the story,' Grayson said. 'Since it was so easy to find.'

Paige muttered a curse. 'I was shot last summer, okay?'

There was a long moment of silence as Burke continued to stitch.

'And?' Grayson finally asked, very quietly.

'Her friend was killed,' Burke said, just as quietly, and Paige closed her eyes again, the pain from the needle completely over-shadowed by the tightness in her chest.

Grayson smoothed a lock of hair from her forehead and Paige felt her throat closing again. She could deal with fear, she could deal with physical pain. But she didn't do well with tenderness.

'I'm sorry,' he murmured. 'What was her name?'

'Thea,' Paige said roughly. 'I can't do this now. I can't breathe.'

'What's safe?' he asked. 'Baseball? Hockey? Championship poker?'

'It's okay,' Burke said. 'I'm done. I read about your work in Minnesota and about your friend. I admire what you did, last summer and this morning.'

Paige pushed the image of Thea to the corner of her mind. She'd think about her friend later. *Not now, not here.* She was feeling dangerously close to tears. *I can't break down.* 'I didn't do anything this morning.' *Or last summer. That was the problem.*

'Sure you did,' Grayson said gruffly. 'Most people would have run away from a bullet-riddled vehicle. You ran toward it, to help another person. That's a lot.'

'It is.' Burke taped a bandage over the stitches. 'Try not to get yourself attacked again.'

'I'll do my very best,' Paige said dryly. 'Can I sit up now?'

'Sure. I'll leave care instructions with the nurse.' Burke turned to go, then paused. 'If you want to teach again, call me. I have some contacts here who'd be interested in working with you.' With a wave she was gone, leaving Paige and Grayson alone.

'What did she mean?' he asked.

He still held her hand and Paige still grasped his too hard. She loosened her grip, but he didn't let go. 'Burke must work with abused women,' she said.

'Which means you did, too,' he said, and she lifted a shoulder.

'Among others.' She sat up, swallowed against a sudden rush of lightheadedness, then dropped her voice so that only he could hear. 'You followed me. Why?'

His eyes shuttered and carefully he released her hand. 'You wanted me to see you, both inside and outside the courtroom. You might as well have dropped breadcrumbs.'

'Do you follow every woman who watches you in the courtroom?'

'Only the ones who witnessed a murder hours before.' His already-stubbled jaw scratched her face as he leaned close to whisper in her ear. 'What did Elena claim to have found?'

'She didn't *claim* it,' she whispered back fiercely. 'She *had* it. I've seen it. Ramon couldn't have killed Crystal Jones. His friend lied. The bar owner lied. Somebody didn't want Elena to tell. But she told me.' She touched her throat. 'And here we are.'

He looked away, his expression grim. 'I'll take you home. Then we can talk.'

Tuesday, April 5, 2.05 P.M.

Grayson and Paige had just entered the hospital lobby when they saw two men and a woman standing outside, the woman giving one of the men a piece of her mind.

Paige came to an abrupt halt. 'Ah, hell. This day just keeps sucking even louder.'

'That's Morton and Bashears. You know the other guy?'

'My partner, Clay Maynard.'

'Morton seems to be very unhappy with your partner.'

'They have history. Morton's partner was shot last year. A guy named Skinner.'

A puzzle piece fell into place. 'I thought I'd heard Maynard's name before. He was involved in a case last year – a killer who left corpses for the ME. Maynard's partner was a victim. What was her name?'

'Nicki Fields. Clay helped the detectives ID the killer, but not before Detective Morton's partner was shot and almost killed. I guess Morton is unloading baggage.'

'The detective that led that case is a friend of mine.' He remembered Stevie's terror when Cordelia was targeted. 'When her child was threatened, Maynard told her what he knew.'

Paige gave him a quick, odd glance. 'Morton and Bashears came to see me this morning. Because I'm Clay's partner, she distrusts me. Because she was primary on Ramon Muñoz's case, I distrust her.'

The words she'd whispered in the parking garage had been circling in his mind. *Elena told me cops did this to her.* Grayson shook his head hard. 'No way. I've known Liz Morton for years. She's a good cop. And Bashears has got every decoration there is.'

'But I don't know them. And I'm not talking to them.'

'That's obstruction of justice,' Grayson said severely, but she looked unimpressed.

'This morning I was interviewed by Detective Perkins. A few hours later, Morton, who discovered the murder weapon conveniently hidden in Elena's winter boot while her partner was questioning Ramon, shows up saying Perkins has been "reassigned" and threatening to "nail me to the wall" if she finds out I'm with-holding information. Why would she even think I was withholding information if she didn't know it existed?'

'She found out you were a PI. You had last contact with a woman before her murder. Those dots aren't hard to connect, Paige.'

'Fine. Let's say she made the leap because I work with Clay. A few hours later, somebody tries to kill me. You might connect the dots differently, but I'm taking no chances. I want to do the right thing, but I'd like to live to see my next birthday.'

'All you know is that a sniper wanted Elena Muñoz dead. Maybe he knew about this alleged evidence. Maybe he came back to make sure you didn't tell anyone.'

Her eyes narrowed. 'If that sniper wanted me dead, he'd have killed me back at my apartment. I was standing there like a statue for several seconds after he shot Elena. He could have shot me walking out of the courthouse or from anywhere in that garage. A knife to my throat is up close and totally personal. He didn't have to risk it.'

That point was more valid. 'You've obviously thought this through. I still don't buy that Liz Morton is involved in any way. Goes double for Bashears.'

'Bully for you. Either way, I'm not telling her what I told you. I told you because I had to tell someone. Because I had to trust someone. I assume she's here because I got attacked and I'm happy to answer her questions about that. Only that.'

'And if I tell her?'

Her eyes flashed. 'Then we part ways. I'll thank you for saving my life, you'll go back to your office. And I'll get hauled downtown in cuffs for obstruction, but I won't tell them anything.' She started to walk toward the doors, toward Morton and Bashears.

'Wait,' Grayson said, and she stopped, hands clenched at her sides. 'You said you came to the courthouse to see if you could trust me. What had you decided?'

'I still didn't know. Your saving my life tipped the scales in your favor.'

'And if you hadn't been attacked? Where were you going?'

'Back to my place to find a defense attorney who'd handle this information properly and represent Ramon,' she admitted. 'I guess I'll still be contacting one. For me.'

Paige was right, this did suck. He thought about Elena's insistence that her husband had been framed. Her fierce determination to get evidence to prove him wrong.

And then he thought about her brains, blown all over the interior of her minivan.

Someone had wanted the woman silenced. Someone had wanted Paige silenced.

Paige had come to him to do the right thing, but suddenly Grayson wasn't sure what the right thing was. 'I want to see this evidence you say got Elena killed,' he said.

She didn't blink. 'I'm more than happy to turn it over to you.'

'I'll probably end up taking it to the cops.'

'I know. And I hope the ones you take it to are trustworthy. Look, I want Elena to be wrong, but I have to proceed believing she was right.'

He looked over his shoulder. Morton was no longer in Clay Maynard's face, but the tension outside the double doors was still obvious. 'Even if I say nothing, Morton and Bashears aren't stupid. They'll suspect something when they see us together.'

'Let them speculate. Or tell them. It's up to you,' she said and walked away.

Morton's eyes narrowed when she saw Paige. She entered the lobby through the double doors, followed by Bashears and Maynard. 'Miss Holden.' Her gaze flicked to the bandage at Paige's throat. 'I trust you're okay.'

'I gave my statement to Detective Perkins.'

'I know,' Morton said. 'I have follow-up questions. Let's find a private place to talk.'

'Detective,' Paige said with an overly patient smile, 'I'm tired and now my throat hurts like a bitch. Please just ask your questions and let's be done.'

Morton's jaw grew tight. 'I could take you downtown. We could talk there.'

'Let's take this outside,' Grayson said calmly. He rested his hand against Paige's lower back, surreptitiously urging her forward. 'Not so many cellphone cameras.'

Once outside, Paige angled her body so that she could see both Bashears and Morton without turning her head. This put her closer to Grayson who couldn't stop himself from drawing a deep breath. Despite everything she'd been through that day, her hair still smelled really good. And despite being tall and lean, she was soft against him. His brain churned through the complications, but his body cut right to the chase.

He wanted her. He'd wanted her from the moment he'd seen her on the TV screen. He wanted her more now. This was dangerous. *She* was dangerous. *I need to keep my head clear. Be able to make the right call, even if it means she walks away.*

And if it put her life at risk? He couldn't let that happen. There had to be a way. He lifted his eyes to find Liz Morton giving him a distrustful glare.

'I didn't know you two knew each other, Mr Smith,' Morton said. 'I was very surprised to read your name in the first responder's report.'

'Detective,' Grayson said, 'Miss Holden narrowly escaped with her life. She'd like to get home and I'd like to get back to work. Can we move this along?'

Morton gave a stiff nod. 'Certainly. Tell me what happened, Miss Holden.'

Paige sighed, then repeated the story she'd told Detective Perkins.

'And you can't describe his face?' Morton asked, her skepticism clear. 'Really?'

Paige didn't try to hide her irritation. 'Really, Detective. I'm a black belt, third dan. I've been competing in tournaments for years. I've fought dozens of opponents in the ring and most of the time I can't describe their faces either. I can tell you if they're male or female, short or tall. Brown hair or blond. But eye color? No. Features? No.'

'So, what *can* you describe, Miss Holden?' Morton asked.

'Their hands. Their feet. Whatever is coming at my face at striking speed. I can tell you what kind of knife the man used today, down to the pattern on the hilt. But I cannot describe his face and I resent your implication that I'm lying.'

She's good, Grayson thought. *Really good.* Morton's cheeks had gone a dull red.

'Why do you think he attacked you?' Bashears asked kindly. Grayson hoped that he and Morton had planned the good cop/bad cop routine. If they hadn't, Morton was a real bitch. Of course she'd nearly lost her old partner, for which she blamed Maynard. And by association, Paige. Grayson decided to cut Morton some slack.

'I don't know why,' Paige said, and he watched her visibly relax. She seemed to be good at calming herself. Being shot last summer had apparently given her lots of practice.

'Did he say anything when he grabbed you?' Bashears asked.

'No, not a word. He wore gloves so I doubt you'll get prints off the knife.' Paige bit at her lip, considering. 'He was a trained fighter, though.'

'How do you know that?' Bashears said, surprised.

'He didn't anticipate my first move. I surprised him enough to avoid getting my throat slit in the first five seconds. But after that, it was like kicking an iron post. I wasn't going to get away.' She swallowed. 'His knife was inches from my gut and he had a good hold on it.'

'But you kicked it away,' Bashears said. 'It landed under your truck.'

'Only because Mr Smith stunned him. If he hadn't . . .' A genuine shudder shook her and Grayson ran his hand halfway up her back and down, to soothe.

Maynard noted the touch and frowned. Grayson ignored him, keeping his eyes on Morton who watched him like a hawk. He wasn't buying that Morton was a dirty cop. But she was a pain in the ass. She'd taken bad cop too far.

'Which brings us to you, Mr Smith,' Morton said, her temper restrained, but still evident. 'What were you doing there, in the garage with Miss Holden?'

'Right place, right time.' Which was not untrue, he told himself. 'Maybe it was karma. Miss Holden provided assistance to the gunshot victim this morning and I was able to provide assistance this afternoon.'

'Had you met each other before the incident in the garage?' Morton asked.

'No. I saw her on TV, so I knew who she was as soon as I saw her in person.'

Morton appeared unconvinced. 'You'd have us believe that you were attacked at random, Miss Holden? That it had nothing to do with your Good Samaritan actions this morning or your relationship to Elena Muñoz?'

'I never said they were unconnected, Detective,' Paige said, her patience strained. 'My face is all over the goddamn Internet. People know exactly where I live, thanks to reporters and people making videos. Crazies are bound to come out of the woodwork.'

Morton smiled. 'You said he was a trained fighter. Not a crazy.'

'I did, because he knew how to fight. Doesn't mean he was sane. Or rational. People find out you're a black belt and they want to prove themselves against you.'

'That's happened before?' Bashears asked, not unkindly.

Paige clenched her jaw. 'Yes. You know it has. I know you've looked me up. And if you haven't, you're not doing your damn job.'

Seems like everyone knows her story except me. Grayson opened his mouth to speak when his cell phone began to buzz in his pocket. 'I'll be right back,' he murmured, then stepped aside to take the call just as Bashears did the same.

Maynard took Paige's arm and led her to a bench, positioning himself between her and Morton, silently daring the detective to say another word.

'This is Smith,' Grayson said, not looking away from Paige to check the caller ID. Only family and a few friends and co-workers had this number.

'It's Stevie.' And she sounded worried. 'JD and I were the only ones not on the sniper so we got sent out on a fresh one. Vic's name is Denny Sandoval. He owns a bar in a Latino neighborhood. He was found hanging in his bedroom.'

Grayson felt a shiver slide down his spine. He'd seen that name this morning while combing through the Muñoz file. Sandoval owned the bar that Ramon had given as his alibi, but had sworn under oath that Ramon had not been there.

The bar owner lied, Paige had said.

Grayson cleared his throat. 'Why are you telling me about a suicide?'

'Because he left a confession note,' Stevie said. 'He says he killed Elena Muñoz because she'd cheated on him and he'd attacked her in a rage. He says he shot her when she slowed down for a traffic light. He says he got scared and finished her off with his rifle. He couldn't live with what he'd done so he hanged himself.'

Elena had alleged new evidence and one of the most damning witnesses for the prosecution had confessed to her murder.

And now that witness was dead. 'Did you find the weapons?' he asked.

'Not all. We found a .22 under the seat of his car, same caliber as the torso shots on Elena. The pistol's on its way to Ballistics. No sign of the rifle. You asked me about Elena this morning. You never ask unless it's important. I thought you needed to know.'

You have no idea. 'Are you working this case?'

'We're handing it off to Bashears and Morton. It closes their case. The brass are so damn relieved it's a murder-suicide and not a serial sniper that they're all rushing to do a news conference.'

Grayson looked over at Bashears, who was intent in his own phone conversation. Presumably being told the same news. 'When did the victim die?'

Stevie hesitated. 'Why, Grayson?'

'I need to know.'

'ME estimates time of death at between eleven-thirty and one. The guy's still warm.'

Not a lot of time to attack Paige and get back to his bar, but just possible on the tail end of the time frame. 'How tall was he?'

'Five-ten. Grayson?'

Definitely not Paige's attacker. 'Is CSU there?'

'Should they be?' she countered.

Hell, yeah. 'Yes. I have to go.'

'Don't you dare hang up on me,' she snapped. 'What the hell is this?'

'I'll tell you when I can,' he said. 'I'm not where I can right now. I'll call you soon.' He hung up in time to hear Bashears tell Morton that they had to leave.

Morton gave them all a severe look. 'You know there are no coincidences. Miss Holden knows something. I just hope it doesn't get her killed next time.'

'Thank you for your concern,' Paige said politely.

Bashears gave her his card. 'If you have any questions or remember anything that might be useful.' And with that, Bashears and Morton were gone.

'What was your phone call?' Maynard asked. He'd been watching, his eyes sharp.

Grayson debated, then shrugged. 'Denny Sandoval is dead.'

Paige sucked in a stunned breath. 'Oh, my God. How?'

'Suicide. He hung himself.'

She turned her body so that she was looking at Maynard. 'He's the bar owner.'

Maynard appeared to be considering. 'Interesting.'

No, Grayson thought. *Not interesting. Bad, very bad.*

Could it be true? Could Muñoz have been innocent? If he was, that weapon had to have been planted. Who could have done it? The cops, as Paige thought?

Ramon Muñoz might have been innocent. What have I done?

Nothing. You didn't convict him, he told himself. *A jury of his peers did.* Based on the evidence available. Which might be false. *Oh, God. What have I done?*

Don't assume. See the new evidence. Then figure out what to do.

'Ramon's alibi-buster is dead,' Grayson said quietly. 'Ramon's wife is dead, Paige gets attacked, all in the same day. We really need to talk.'

Tuesday, April 5, 2.25 P.M.

Stevie hung up and walked back to JD, who stood next to the CSU van they'd requested as soon as they'd walked onto the scene.

'We were right, weren't we?' JD murmured.

'I think so,' Stevie said. The brass was racing to calm the public, but something hadn't felt right. Years of experience in Homicide had Stevie trusting her gut.

'It's too perfect,' JD went on.

He was right. The bar had been trashed, bottles strewn, the register emptied while the victim's body swung from the rafters in an upstairs apartment. But the most expensive liquor had been smashed and wasted, not stolen.

'The liquor alone was worth thousands of bucks,' Stevie agreed. 'Any self-respecting punk would have taken it, not trashed it.'

'Still, it's not a random sniper,' JD said. 'We can all breathe a little easier over that.'

'Everybody but Elena Muñoz and Denny Sandoval.'

Five

'You have got to be kidding me,' Grayson said, staring at the VW Beetle while Clay unlocked the doors. 'We'll be in traction if all three of us squeeze into that thing.'

'It's my assistant's car,' Clay said. 'Mine was compromised.'

'Tracking devices,' Paige said. The overabundance of testosterone raging between the two men was getting on her nerves. 'We think reporters hid them under our cars.'

'So that's what you were looking for,' Grayson said. 'When you were up under your truck in the parking garage. Tracking devices.'

'Yeah. I'd just found one when the guy attacked.'

Clay's mouth tightened as he studied the bandage on her throat. 'You were lucky.'

'I know,' Paige said.

'Not entirely luck,' Grayson said. 'You fought back. Pretty amazingly, too.'

'I'll say.' A voice from behind had the three of them whipping around to stare. Then glare. It was Phin Radcliffe and he had a microphone in his hand. There was a cameraman with him and the little light on the camera was blinking red.

So was Paige's anger. 'You put me on TV, without my permission.'

'I didn't need permission. The sidewalk and street are public property. As was the parking garage where you narrowly escaped death today at the hand of an attacker with a knife. Can you tell us what happened?'

His tone had changed as he'd uttered 'parking garage', going from coolly rational to booming catch-this-at-eleven.

He's going to put me on TV again, the bastard. No way.

Paige took a step forward, but Grayson held her back. 'Careful,' he murmured.

She drew a breath, knowing that Grayson was right. 'No comment,' she said.

'We're running this story, Miss Holden. We'd like to have your side of it.'

'My side?' She pursed her lips when Grayson squeezed her arm. 'No comment.'

Grayson helped her into the front seat. 'I hope your day improves, Miss Holden.' His back to Radcliffe's camera, he gave her a hard look when she opened her mouth in surprise. 'Later,' he mouthed and she understood what he wanted her to do.

'Thank you. I don't know what I would have done if you hadn't come along.'

He shook her hand professionally. 'I was happy I could help.' He wrote something on the back of one of his business cards and handed it to Clay. 'My direct line. Don't hesitate to call if the police need any additional information from me for their report.'

'Thanks,' Clay said. 'We appreciate it. Can we give you a lift?'

'No. Like I said, I'd be in traction. But thanks for the offer. I'll get a cab.'

'Mr Smith,' Radcliffe pressed, still smiling, 'you became the Good Samaritan for our Good Samaritan when you saved Paige's life. How does that make you feel?'

'I was just in the right place at the right time,' Grayson said. 'Anyone would have done the same.' He turned then and hailed a cab.

Clay drove away. When they'd turned the corner he handed the card to Paige. On the back was an address. 'Smith wants us to meet him at this address.'

'Upscale,' she murmured. 'Is this his home?'

'No. He has a townhouse in Fells' Point.'

'Also upscale. Difficult on a prosecutor's salary. What else did you find out?'

'Not a lot,' he admitted. 'He was engaged once. The announcement was in the paper, but there was never a wedding announcement and no license on file.'

'Society girl? The engagement, I mean.'

'Yes. Why?'

Because he held my hand and stroked my hair. 'I'm thinking about his finances, which I should have done before jumping into my look-into-his-eyes plan. If he's living this far above his means, he could be on the take.'

But even as she said the words, she knew, *knew* they weren't true.

'You don't think so, though,' Clay said.

'No. I have no reason to believe this and I've been wrong about men before.' More times than she wanted to think about.

'But you trust him. Sometimes following your gut isn't bad,' Clay said. 'Besides, to get into his finances deep enough to really know how he gets and spends his money would have taken a long time. Longer than we have. What I want to know is why he was there in the garage, in the nick of time? I'm glad he was, but what was he doing there?'

'He was following me.'

Clay rolled his eyes. 'I never would have guessed. *Why* was he following you?'

'He saw me in the courtroom and recognized me from the video, but he didn't know who I was.' And now she remembered what had nagged her in the ER. 'He whispered.'

'What? What does that mean?'

'When we were in the garage, he saw that my cell was a disposable. He asked me what I did for a living. I told him, and then he whispered in my ear. Asked me if I was working for Elena. How would he know Elena wanted a PI?'

'Good question. And why did he whisper?'

'Maybe because he was expecting me to answer exactly as I did.'

'Which was how?'

'I told him yes, I was working for Elena. Then he asked me in what capacity.' She sighed. 'And I told him.'

Clay frowned. 'Told him what, exactly?'

'That Elena had uncovered evidence. That it was credible. That I didn't tell the cops and didn't plan to because Elena said they did it.'

'Did he believe you?'

She bit her lip. 'I think he believed I wasn't lying. He didn't believe the cops were involved and still doesn't. But he said he understood how I could believe it. I don't think he really accepted that there was credible new evidence until he got that call.'

'About Denny Sandoval. I was watching his face. Smith looked stunned.'

'I know. That's just too much coincidence, even for him.'

'Did you tell him what Elena found?'

'Yes.'

'Will you give him the file?'

'I have to,' she said slowly. 'Because Denny Sandoval's dead too.'

'Smith said that he hung himself.'

'If he thought Elena had evidence that could send him to jail, he *might* have killed himself. Although he didn't strike me as the type. Besides, Elena said the cops were chasing her. Denny Sandoval was no cop. That still leaves cops in the mix. And the guy that attacked me. Can't forget about him.'

'Trust me, I haven't. What do you mean, he didn't strike you as the type? You've met Sandoval?'

'Weeks ago, when I agreed to take the case, I went to his bar. Really sleazy guy. Elena had to have been desperate to let him touch her.' She thought about Ramon in the prison infirmary. *Probably the safest place for him right now.* 'I need to talk to Ramon. I'll see Maria first, though. Even Morton couldn't fault me for paying my respects. Where did they take her?'

'Saint Agnes, but . . .' Clay's mouth tightened and Paige's heart lurched.

'No,' she whispered, fearing the worst.

Clay blew out a harsh sigh. 'I'm sorry. I really am. That's why it took me so long to get to you. I was leaving when I saw a doctor pull Maria's son aside. The poor kid nearly fainted. I stayed. I called the ER you were in to check on you. They said you had arrived and were stable. So I stayed with Rafe until the rest of his family got there.'

'She's gone? Maria's gone?'

'Yes. She'd already had two heart attacks. One when Ramon had the fight in jail and the second when the cops delivered the news about Elena. The third killed her.'

'Oh, God.' Hot tears burned her eyes. 'This just keeps getting worse.'

'I know. I didn't know how to tell you. What can I do for you?'

Paige wiped her eyes with her fingertips, then dragged her hands down her face. *Be angry. Be furious.* She thought better when she was angry than when she was crying. 'Drive me to the parking garage. If CSU is done with my truck, I'm taking it.'

'Should you even be driving?'

'I haven't taken any painkillers.' And it hurt. A lot. But getting shot last summer had forced her to learn to deal with pain. 'If that guy with the knife comes at me again, I don't want to be too groggy to fight back. Which is why I want my truck. My guns are locked in a safe under the rear seat of my cab. I couldn't go armed into the courthouse.' She touched her throat gingerly. 'If he comes back, I don't want to be unarmed.'

Clay grimaced. 'Do you have your concealed carry permit on you? Morton'll have a field day with you if she catches you without it.'

'Never leave home without it.' It'd been damn hard to get a concealed weapon permit in Maryland. No way was she chancing getting caught with a gun without it.

'Good. Where are Elena's files?'

'I got nervous after you left and took the original flash drive and put it in my bank safe-deposit box on my way into town. I made a copy on another flash drive that's still locked in my safe at home. And I printed copies and mailed them to my old attorney in Minneapolis just in case something happens to me.'

'Let's not even go there,' he said. 'Still, it was good thinking.'

'I try.'

Tuesday, April 5, 3.00 P.M.

'Come in, Adele, come in.'

Adele Shaffer walked into the office, its scent familiar and surprisingly welcome. She'd hoped to never come back here. She hoped never to tell Darren she'd been here today.

Dr Theopolis waited until she'd chosen a chair before sitting down. A gentleman. He'd always been that way. Maybe the first true gentleman she'd ever known.

He smiled, trying to put her at ease. 'It's been a long time.'

'I wish it could have been longer. No offense.'

'None taken. So . . . you've changed your name.'

'I got married.' Her chin came up, along with the old defenses.

'Relax. I'm not here to turn you in. I never was.'

Turn you in. Abruptly she stood. 'I shouldn't have come.'

'Adele. Sit down.' He waited until she did. 'So, you're married. Tell me about him.'

'His name is Darren. He's a good man.'

Theopolis smiled warmly. 'Then I'm happy for you.'

She drew a breath. 'He . . . doesn't know.'

'Hm.' He didn't look shocked. 'Why not?'

'I . . . don't know how to tell him.' Tears filled her eyes. 'I can't tell him.'

'Is that why you're here?'

'Not exactly.'

'Okay. You've finished school?'

'Yes. I'm an interior designer. I have my own business. Mainly old ladies.'

He chuckled. 'Lots of paisley and chintz.'

'Exactly.' She swallowed hard. 'I have a child,' she blurted. 'A daughter.'

'Oh, that's wonderful.'

Tears hit again and this time she had no choice but to let them fall. There were too many to hold back. 'She is wonderful. She's everything.' Adele covered her face with her hands, unable to control her sobs. 'I can't lose her. I just can't.'

'Why would you lose her, Adele? Are you afraid you'll harm her in some way?'

'No.' Adele tore her hands from her face, glaring. 'I would never harm my child.'

'I didn't think so. So why are you afraid you'll lose her?'

Adele lurched to her feet and walked to the window. She'd spent hours standing at this window. There was a garden below. Daffodils. She focused on the bright yellow flowers blowing in the wind. The pain in her chest eased.

'It's happening again,' she whispered. 'The panic. Paranoia. I can't make it stop.'

'What's panicking you?'

She felt the panic rise, a gorge in her throat. 'They'll put me away. Take my baby.'

'Let's cross that bridge when we get there. Talk to me. Like you used to.'

She fixed her gaze on the brave yellow flowers. 'Somebody's trying to kill me.'

Tuesday, April 5, 3.00 P.M.

'Where have you been?' Daphne demanded when Grayson stopped at her desk. 'I've been calling your cell for two hours. Why do you have a hospital bag?'

He put the bag on her desk. 'Files from today's trial. Can you re-file them?'

'Why aren't they in your briefcase?'

'Because the cops have my briefcase.' He held up his hand when she would have stormed him with questions. 'I followed the woman.'

'Her name is Paige Holden,' Daphne said and tapped a thick folder. 'This is all her.'

'I know her name. Tell me what you think of her.'

Daphne lifted her shoulders and let them fall. 'She had an amazing life.'

'Had?'

'She was an advocate for victims' rights, taught self-defense classes, competed internationally for martial-arts titles. Until last summer.'

'When she was shot.'

Daphne's eyes widened. 'How did you know?'

'I met her, in the parking garage. She was being attacked at that moment.'

'Oh, my God.'

'Yeah. Big guy, really big knife. She fought like a tiger.'

Daphne cringed, bracing for the bad. 'But?'

'She's alive and mostly unhurt. I hit the guy with my briefcase.'

Daphne straightened, a smile dawning. 'Grayson Smith, you're a he-ro. Bona fide.' She drew it out with more of a twang than normal and his lips curved in spite of himself.

'Yeah. Anyway, the guy got away and the cops took my briefcase as evidence, in case I got his blood or hair caught in the corners. I went to the ER with Miss Holden.'

Daphne's smile dimmed. 'Did you find out why she was watching you?'

'Yes and no. And I can't tell you much more than that because I don't know.'

'But it's all about that woman who got killed this morning. Elena Muñoz.'

'That much seems certain. Can you clear my calendar for the rest of the day? I have some things I need to do.'

Grayson closed his office door and opened his desk drawer. The Muñoz file was on top of the pile. For a long moment he simply stared at the folder and counted the beats of his own heart. What if Paige was right? What if the 'alleged' new evidence Elena had possessed wasn't so alleged? What if it *was* real?

What if the murder weapon *had* been planted?

Who could have done it and why? And the million-dollar question: had an innocent man spent six long years behind bars? *And what part did I play in putting him there?*

He remembered the case so very clearly. He remembered Ramon Muñoz specifically. Remembered how earnestly the man had maintained his innocence.

But they all did. All the murderers claimed they were innocent. Grayson felt contempt for them all. And here, in the quiet of his office, he knew exactly why he felt that way. At the time it hadn't really mattered. Now, it did. It mattered a lot.

He turned away from the file without touching it. Found himself staring at his reflection in the small mirror some former occupant of the office had left hanging on the wall. Green eyes stared back. His mother's eyes.

His green eyes narrowed. He'd inherited his father's shoulders, his dark hair, olive skin. But nothing else. *Thank God*.

His other features had come from his mother's side of the family, luckily. It had made it so much easier for her to pass him off as 'Grayson Smith' when they'd escaped their old life with little more than the clothes on their backs. They'd even left their names behind, telling no one who they really were. No one, not even the Carter family who'd taken them in, given them a home. Grayson loved the Carters like they were blood, but he couldn't tell them the truth. He didn't want them to know. He didn't want anyone to know.

It was their deepest secret, his and his mother's. Their greatest shame. That someone would learn the truth was his worst fear.

He'd been only seven years old the last time he'd seen his father, but he needed no photograph to remember his face. Or the face of his father's final victim.

He had to make himself breathe. Even now, almost thirty years later, the memory of that young woman still had the power to turn his gut to water.

She'd been a blond co-ed. Just like Crystal Jones. She'd been pretty. *Until my father murdered her*. Just like Ramon Muñoz murdered Crystal.

Or so he'd believed. The evidence had been strong, Ramon's alibi unverifiable.

But had his own father not been a murderer, would he have prosecuted with less zeal? He'd never know. Because his father *was* a convicted murderer and Grayson had spent the last twenty-eight years of his life proving that he wasn't his father's son in any way that mattered.

Are you an honest man? He heard Paige's voice asking the question. He wanted to be an honest man. He'd spent his life trying to be. *And if Ramon is innocent? What will you do?*

He'd make it right somehow. No matter what it took. *I want to do the right thing.*

Paige had said the same thing as he'd fought to keep her blood from spilling. *She held on to me. Trusted me when she was at her most vulnerable.* She'd done nothing to get sucked into all this. She'd only done her job.

Just like you did. Prosecuting Muñoz had been his job. His duty.

But if the man was not guilty, it was also his duty to set him free.

Resolutely he looked away from the mirror, down at his suit. Paige's blood had stained his clothes. He reached for the clean suit on the hook behind his door. He always kept a spare in the office for the times he worked through the night and had to be in court first thing. He changed, then opened the Muñoz file. It didn't take him long to find the witness profile page he was looking for.

During the trial Grayson had been convinced Muñoz was guilty. Every witness was sure, unshakable. Except for one. That one had been nervous. Ramon's best friend.

Jorge Delgado had been pale, repeatedly wiping his perspiring brow with a neatly folded handkerchief as he denied Ramon's alibi. But he'd stuck to his story, even under a rigorous cross by the defense. At the time Grayson had chalked Delgado's nervousness up to the fact that he fully understood that his testimony would be a nail in his best friend's coffin.

Both Ramon's best friend and the bar owner had lied, Paige had claimed. The bar owner was dead. *I need to have a chat with Jorge Delgado.*

Blocking his own phone number, he dialed the number on file for the Delgado home. Then frowned. The recorded message said the number had been changed. No new number was available.

That wasn't uncommon. Many times witnesses in high-profile cases changed their phone numbers to avoid the press. His own mother had, before they ran away.

Grayson jotted Delgado's last known contact information on a piece of paper, then stuffed the folder into his gym bag.

'I rescheduled everything,' Daphne said when he emerged. 'You want me to drop your suit off at the dry cleaners?'

'You don't have to do that. You know that.'

'I know, but I'm going anyway.' She held up the thick file she'd compiled on Paige. 'You'll find her fascinating.'

I do already. He shoved the file into his bag. 'Thanks, Daphne. There's something else you can do for me, if you don't mind.' He gave her Delgado's contact information. 'I need to talk to this man. This was his address five years ago. Can you verify that he still lives there and get a current phone number, then text it to me?'

Daphne skimmed the page, then looked up, puzzled. 'Okay. Sure. Be careful.'

'Always.'

Tuesday, April 5, 4.15 P.M.

Grayson let himself into the building in which he'd told Paige and Clay to meet him, glad he'd arrived before they did. The place belonged to his sister Lisa and he needed to prepare her for visitors. The reception area was deserted, but someone was back in the kitchen.

He drew an appreciative breath. Something smelled absolutely delicious. His stomach growled, forcefully reminding him he'd had nothing to eat since Daphne's muffin that morning. There would be plenty to eat here.

Lisa Carter-Winston owned the Party Palace, a catering business and party venue. Lisa was the party planner, her husband Brian, the chef. They did a brisk business, hosting everything from weddings to Bar Mitzvahs to birthdays. The oldest of the Carter siblings, Lisa had a knack for setting a table and making people feel welcome. She'd had excellent role models in her parents, Jack and Katherine.

He'd met Lisa, her parents, and the three other Carter kids when he was seven, scared and scarred by the arrest and conviction of his father and all that had come after. He'd retreated into his shell, terrified he'd say the wrong thing or forget his new name, putting him and his mother in danger yet again.

Mrs Carter had hired Grayson's mother to be the children's nanny, a position that came with a small apartment over the garage, a boon since they'd been living in a shabby hotel, his mother's money mostly gone. The first person he'd met on the estate was Lisa. She'd been fourteen and self-assured. And bossy as hell. But her heart was compassionate and she'd seen how frightened he'd been. She'd taken him under her wing, just another sibling to herd.

The four Carter children became five and Mrs Carter treated Grayson's mother more like a sister than an employee. The Carters had absorbed them into their family.

And slowly, after months had passed, he'd begun to feel safe again. The Carters had saved their lives and Grayson never stopped being grateful.

'Lisa,' he called. 'Are you here?'

A door from the back opened, and Lisa appeared, wiping her hands on an apron that had started out blue, but was now mostly white. Flour smudged her nose and one cheek. But when she saw him, she smiled. 'Grayson. What are you doing here?'

'I tried to call. Nobody answered.'

'We had the music up. We're catering a big corporate party downtown. Busy, busy.'

Grayson leaned down to kiss her cheek. 'You always are. Where are the kids? I thought they were on spring break this week.'

Lisa and Brian had produced the only Carter grandchildren so far – four of them, all under ten. Katherine and Jack Carter and Grayson's own mother never let the rest of them forget that they needed to catch up.

'Our mothers took them to the museum because they were driving me crazy.'

'I'm sorry,' he said ruefully. 'I picked a bad day to drop by.'

'There's never a bad day for you to drop by. But why did you?' Lisa lifted a hand to his face, smoothing his forehead with her thumb. 'You get this crease in your forehead when you're worried. It's starting to be permanent. Why are you here, honey?'

He let out a breath. 'I need some space,' he said, and Lisa pulled back, instantly.

'I'm sorry,' she said, looking more worried. 'I'll leave you alone.'

'No,' he said, 'not personal space. Meeting space.'

Her eyes narrowed. 'Why? What's wrong with your office downtown?'

'I need a place where I know nobody will eavesdrop. No reporters.'

'Are you in trouble, Grayson?' she asked quietly.

Maybe. 'I've got a situation I have to fix. I'm expecting two people to join me. They should be here soon. Can we use one of the party rooms?'

'Of course. Do you need me to call Joseph?'

Their brother – Lisa's brother – was FBI. 'Not yet. If I need him, I'll call him. I promise.' He hoped he wouldn't need to. He'd made a stop by his own house on the way and now felt a good bit more confident with the pistol holstered in his right boot. 'For now, I'm so hungry I could eat the whole kitchen.'

'I'll bring you some . . .' Her voice trailed away as the front door opened and two people entered, along with a very large dog.

'You made it,' Grayson said, relieved. He hadn't been entirely sure Paige would show. That she'd brought the dog was a surprise, but probably shouldn't have been, based on what he'd gleaned from the ER doctor. He hadn't read any of the file Daphne had compiled. He would, later, but he rather hoped Paige would tell him herself.

'I'm sorry we're a little late,' Paige said. 'I had to change my clothes.'

And had she ever. Once again she wore black, but that's where any similarity to her earlier outfit ended. No longer did she wear tailored slacks and a sweater that somehow simultaneously draped and hugged every curve. He had to draw a steadying breath and try very hard not to stare, because now her pants clung to every curve too.

She had amazing legs. The sweater had been replaced by a tight turtleneck that almost hid the wound on her throat. Only about a

91

quarter-inch of white bandage showed. But nobody would be looking at the bandage, he thought darkly. Their eyes would never make it up that high. The jacket she wore over the sweater closely molded breasts that would be more than a handful for any man.

Or a mouthful, if that man was really, really lucky.

Her boots changed her look from bombshell to lethal. They were combat boots, made for running. And for kicking the shit out of anyone who came too close. His eyes traveled up, pausing at her jacket. There was a slight bulge under her left arm.

Hell. She was packing. He wasn't sure if he was appalled, relieved, or intrigued. Maybe all three. Plus a healthy dose of totally turned on.

Grayson cleared his throat, conscious of Clay watching him with a mixture of suspicion and wry understanding. 'I hope this place wasn't hard for you two to find.'

'Not at all,' Paige said. 'But I wasn't expecting . . . well, all this. Can Peabody stay?'

Lisa was staring. 'Grayson? Perhaps introductions are in order?'

'Sorry. Lisa Carter-Winston, Paige Holden and her associate, Clay Maynard.'

Clay inclined his head. 'Ma'am.'

'And that's Peabody,' Grayson said, pointing at the dog.

'I'm so sorry.' Paige's cheeks flushed. 'I shouldn't have brought my dog.'

Lisa regained her composure and offered Paige her hand. 'I'm Grayson's sister. You're the woman from TV, aren't you? The one they're calling the Good Sam.'

Paige's flush deepened. 'Yeah, that'd be me.'

Lisa studied the bandage on her throat. 'They didn't say you were hurt.'

Paige touched her throat self-consciously. 'This happened . . . later.'

Lisa's eyes flew to Grayson's. 'Are you sure you don't want me to call Joseph?'

Grayson looked at Maynard. 'Were you followed?'

'Not that I could see.'

'I think we're okay,' Grayson told Lisa. 'Can we lock this main door?'

'Yes,' Lisa said. 'Go on into the Gingerbread House. I'll bring you some food.'

'What about my dog?' Paige asked and Lisa smiled at her kindly.

'The Gingerbread House is used for kids' parties and sometimes we have service animals in there. For today's purposes, he can be a service dog, okay?'

Relief flashed in Paige's eyes. 'Thank you. I'll make sure he behaves.'

'Not a problem,' Lisa said. 'He can't be any worse than a party of spoiled four year olds. Go, get comfortable. No one will bother you here.'

Paige followed Grayson and Clay into the room and then stood in the middle of the Gingerbread House, turning in a slow circle.

'Wow.' It was like being in a real gingerbread house. The walls looked like cookies and had giant lollipops sticking out at random angles. '*Kids* have parties here?'

'In this room,' Grayson said. 'There are eight party rooms, plus a banquet hall for wedding receptions. Lisa's husband started the catering business and Lisa turned it into a one-stop party shop.' He pointed to an adult-sized table. 'We can talk here.'

'This place is damn creepy,' Clay muttered, sitting in a gingerbread-man chair.

Paige couldn't stop the chuckle that escaped. 'If your friends could see you now.'

'That's the point,' Grayson said soberly. 'Nobody knows you're here. Nobody can listen in. We can discuss our situation and figure out what the hell we need to do.'

Paige took a seat, Peabody obediently at her feet. She met Grayson's eyes, and cut to the chase. 'Why did you follow me before you knew I was a PI, working for Elena?'

He lightly drummed the table, considering. 'She visited me last week. She wanted a new trial for her husband.'

'She said she might try. What did you tell her?' she asked.

'I said there was no evidentiary reason for a new trial. If she had this evidence, why didn't she tell me about it then?'

'She didn't have it then,' Paige said. 'She just got it last night, from Denny Sandoval.'

Grayson leaned back, his doubt clear. 'Elena told you the cops did it.'

'I asked her who'd done this to her. Her exact answer was "Cops. Chasing me". If it had been a legitimate pursuit with shots fired, there would be a record of it, right?'

'Yes,' Grayson allowed.

'Did the cops find both weapons used to shoot Elena?' Clay asked.

Grayson hesitated a long time. 'No,' he finally said. 'Only one. Not the rifle. Look, we won't begin to get to the bottom of all this until I know what the evidence was.'

'It's files on a flash drive. Three photographs.' From her backpack Paige took out the pages she'd printed when she'd changed her clothes. She slid the first picture across the table to Grayson and watched his eyes flicker. 'You remember this man?'

'It's Ramon Muñoz's best friend. Jorge Delgado.'

'Some best friend,' she said. 'Ramon swore that they watched a ball game on the bar's TV. Time and date stamp on this photo are six years ago, the same time and date that the murder of the college girl was happening. Trial transcripts show that both Sandoval and the "best friend" swore that Ramon wasn't there. Sandoval swore there weren't any cameras focused on the bar patrons, only at the cash register. He lied.'

'A photograph can be Photoshopped. Date and time stamps can be easily faked,' Grayson said evenly. 'That's all you have?'

'There were three files,' Paige repeated. She gave him the second photo. 'This is Denny Sandoval and another man I don't know. The really bad fake mustache and eyebrows are an obvious disguise. The only thing identifiable on the man is that he has nice hands and a sparkly pinky ring that might be a diamond. The man is giving Sandoval a paper.'

Grayson studied it. 'You can't tell what's written on the paper.'

'The third is a receipt for wire transfer,' Clay said. 'Fifty grand to Larabella, Inc.'

'I ran a background check before we came here,' Paige said. 'Sandoval's mother's name was Lara. I know that Sandoval did a major bar renovation a few years ago. Installed big-screen TVs, replaced pool tables. New wooden booths, tables, and chairs.'

'Pricey stuff,' Grayson said. 'How do you know this?'

'Maria . . .' She swallowed hard. *Poor Maria. Poor Ramon.* 'Maria and Elena both knew Sandoval was lying in the trial. For a long time they watched for any indication that he was spending money. But he didn't, and the women ended up working so hard to make ends meet that they didn't have time to keep checking on Denny. Then Elena went by the bar a month ago and noticed its new front door. She went in and noticed all the upgrades. She noticed Denny had himself a new car.'

'Did she confront Sandoval?' Grayson asked.

'No.' She glanced at Clay. 'That must have been when she put her plan into play.'

'When she came on to Sandoval,' Clay murmured.

'Yes. When Maria came to me, weeks ago, she said she was afraid Elena would do "something desperate". I thought at the time she meant that Elena was going to shoot Sandoval. But Elena got real cozy with him. I didn't know that when I visited the bar.'

'You visited?' Grayson asked.

'Sure. I wanted to meet Sandoval, see what I could find out about him.' She met his gaze pointedly. 'To see if he was an honest man.'

'And was he?' Grayson asked.

'No. I told him I was new in town, looking for a place to hang. Sandoval gave me the tour, ending with his apartment upstairs. And his bed. He's one smooth operator.'

Grayson's eyes flashed angrily. 'Did he try anything?'

'Yes. I told him no. He tried . . . harder. I put him in a choke-hold.' She watched most of the fire in Grayson's eyes bank. His fury at Sandoval's advances made her feel good. His acceptance that she'd taken care of herself made her feel oddly better. 'He left me alone and I didn't go back. Fast forward to today, when Elena discovers these files. She's shot, she says cops are chasing her, and she's murdered. I, the last person to see her alive, am attacked, and the man she stole the files from "kills himself".'

She leaned forward. 'Assuming these pictures are authentic, the murder weapon found in Ramon's house had to have been placed there.'

Grayson pressed his fingers to his temples. 'Dammit.'

Seconds of tense silence ticked by. Then, at Paige's feet, Peabody began to growl. The door opened a crack and Lisa stuck her head in. 'Food?'

Grayson rose abruptly. 'Yes,' he said, clearly relieved. He took the tray from Lisa's arms, put it on the table. Then he looked into the hall, his smile suddenly so warm that Paige couldn't tear her eyes from his face. 'Holly,' he said. 'You're here, too.'

A young woman followed Lisa, pushing a cart laden with food. Smaller even than the petite Lisa, her hair was the same shade of rich mahogany. Sisters, Paige thought.

When the young woman looked up at Grayson her face broke into a smile even more dazzling than his. She was somewhere in her twenties and she had Down Syndrome.

'Of course, silly,' she said as he wrapped his arms around her. 'I work here.' She hugged him back. 'You haven't been to visit in a long time. Why not?'

'Been workin', babe,' he said, then tilted up her chin. 'Just like you.'

'And I got a raise.' Then her eyes grew wide. 'Oh, my God. That's the lady from TV.' She pulled away from Grayson to peek under the table. 'And her dog.'

Grayson caught her arm before she could run over to Peabody. 'Just a minute, honey. Paige and Clay, this is my sister, Holly. This is Paige and her friend Clay. And that's Peabody under the table.' He looked at Paige. 'Is Peabody dangerous?'

Paige smiled at Holly. 'No. You know how to let the dog smell your hand, right?'

Holly nodded, approaching with her hand out. 'He's pretty.'

'Thank you.' Paige murmured a command that had Peabody all

but melting at Holly's feet. 'He likes to be scratched behind his ears.'

'Did you train him yourself?' Holly asked, laughing when Peabody rolled over to have his belly rubbed.

'Not exactly. One of my friends trains dogs. I helped her out by feeding the dogs when she was out of town or busy working. She gave Peabody to me.'

'For your birthday?'

'No. Because . . . because another friend of mine died and I was sad and lonely. And scared. Peabody makes me feel safe.'

'I'm sorry,' Holly said, her lips drooping sadly. 'I lost my friend too.'

'When?' Paige asked.

'Last month. He had a bad heart and he died.'

Grayson and Lisa looked at each other, stricken.

'I'm so sorry, Holly,' Paige said. 'What was his name?'

'Johnny. He was my age. What was your friend's name?'

'Thea. I miss her.'

'I know. I miss my friend too.' She paused, lips pursed. 'I saw you on TV today.'

Paige winced. 'I'm sorry you had to see that woman killed.'

'I didn't watch the part where the lady died. I turned it off.'

'You're very wise.'

'I'm very smart,' Holly said. 'I have a job.'

'Where you got a raise,' Paige said, smiling at her. 'Congratulations.'

'Thank you.' Holly nodded firmly. 'I saw you jump. That was . . . amazing.'

'I was really scared,' Paige admitted. 'I've never jumped that far before.'

'The lady on the news said you do karate.'

'That's true.' Paige could see the question in Holly's eyes. She'd seen that question so many times before. 'You're wondering if you could do karate.'

Holly lifted a careless shoulder. 'Oh, I couldn't. I'm not very co . . . coordinated.'

'Do *you* have a heart problem?' Paige asked. Grayson and Lisa watched, their expressions filled with warning. Paige had seen this too, in families that watched out for their own.

'No,' Holly said. 'I did, but I got surgery. I have a big scar. But I'm fine now.'

'If your doctor says you're fine, then I can teach you,' Paige said.

Holly's eyes lit up. 'Really?'

Grayson shook his head, hard. 'No,' he mouthed.

'Really,' Paige said to Holly. 'I'll give you my phone number before I leave. You can call if you're interested.'

'I'm interested,' Holly said, giving Grayson a quelling look. 'Will I be able to jump?'

'No,' Lisa said firmly. 'You won't.'

Paige smiled at Holly, deliberately misunderstanding the older sister's concern. 'Not like I did this morning. I'm not sure I'll ever jump like that again. I hope I never have to. You might not jump far, but you'll have better balance. And more confidence.' She glanced at Lisa. 'That's never a bad thing.'

'I'm glad you came.' Holly cast a wary eye at Clay, who'd remained silent. 'You too,' she added politely, then turned to Grayson, her chin lifting defiantly. 'Don't tell me no, Grayson. I can do it. I can do all kinds of things.'

Grayson chuckled, but the sound was strained. 'I know you can.' He kissed her forehead. 'We have to work now. I'll come see you before I leave.'

'You'd better,' Holly said, then waved to Paige. 'Bye, Paige. Bye, Peabody.'

Lisa put her arm around Holly's shoulders, throwing a worried glance at Grayson before leaving. Grayson closed the door then turned, furious. 'What the hell, Paige?'

Paige regarded him levelly. 'Does she have any medical conditions that keep her from moderate physical exertion, like walking up stairs?'

'No.' Grayson's jaw was taut. 'She's healthy now. We will keep her that way.'

'You love her, I can see that.' And it tugged at her heart. 'But she's a grown woman. If a doctor says she's physically healthy and she wants to learn, let her learn.'

'She is not to be hurt.' It was almost a growl. 'You know she can't do karate.'

She smiled at him gently. 'I know no such thing. And neither do you.'

He faltered. 'Look, we just . . . She's been hurt before. She took a dance class and people . . . they laughed at her. It devastated her. We won't let that happen again.'

Paige's heart cracked. 'I've had several students with Down Syndrome. No one laughed at them, I can promise you that. I can teach her if she wants to learn.'

She stood up. 'Let's eat, then you tell me what our options are. I'd like to teach Holly and I want to get justice for Elena and Ramon, but I can't do any of that if I can't stay alive.'

Six

'Let's hear it,' Clay said harshly, pushing his empty plate to the center of the table. 'Paige has told you everything and we need answers. What are our legal options?'

'The first step is easy,' Paige said. 'We get Ramon out of jail as soon as possible.'

'I don't think so. Hear me out,' Grayson said quickly when Paige opened her mouth to protest. 'Let's say all this is true, that the pictures are authentic and that Muñoz is innocent. As you've pointed out, multiple times, it means someone framed him.'

'Duh,' Paige muttered. 'And I don't even have a law degree.'

'But I do. Now that I know this, I'm responsible for what happens next.'

She met his eyes, unwavering challenge in hers. 'You'd prefer not to know?'

'No,' he said. 'I believe in the system, but the system is run by humans and humans make mistakes. They even lie. Everything seemed . . . believable. The evidence, the witnesses. I don't regret the way I prosecuted him.'

Except, he thought, *I do. Now, I do.* All the witnesses had been credible, except one. *You felt it then, but ignored your gut because he said what you wanted to hear.*

He rubbed his forehead. 'If Ramon was framed, who did it? You think it was the police and obviously Elena believed that too. Maybe it was and maybe it was someone else. Until we know, I think it's a bad idea to change Ramon's status.'

'We tip our hand,' Clay said.

Grayson nodded. 'Exactly. I—'

'*No.*' Paige stood up and, fists on the table, leaned close, her dark eyes flashing. 'You're not seriously saying we leave him in prison while we sort this out all polite-like, are you? Because that is *so* not going to happen.'

'Sit down,' he said calmly, though the sight of her avenging and angry was enough to make his mouth water. 'Please.' He waited until she'd sat, arms crossed over her breasts. 'Nothing will get Muñoz out of prison today or even tomorrow. These things—'

'Take time,' she finished coldly. 'That's bullshit. Bureaucratic bullshit.'

His jaw tightened. 'You're right, but that's also reality.'

'*Your* reality,' she snapped. 'You sit there in your expensive suit and play games with other people's lives. Motions, objections, paperwork.' She lurched to her feet again, her fists clenched at her sides. 'Ramon has lost six years of his life. He's lost his wife, and his mother worked herself to death to feed the family because he wasn't there to do it. And you want me to sit idly by while you drag this out for maybe years with *bullshit*?' Her voice had risen and she checked herself. 'Your reality sucks, Counselor.'

He looked up at her, his eyes gone flat. 'What alternate reality do you suggest, Miss Holden?'

'I don't know, but I'll be damned before I sit and watch an innocent man continue to pay.' She snatched up her backpack and Peabody's leash. 'Come.' The dog followed.

Grayson pushed back from the table, catching her before she made it to the door. He grabbed her arm. 'Where the hell do you think you're going?'

Peabody went still, a growl rising from his throat. Grayson froze, his gaze dropping to his hand still wrapped around her upper arm. He released her and stepped back.

'I'm sorry,' he said, stricken. 'I didn't mean to hurt you.'

'You didn't,' she murmured. 'Peabody, down.'

Grayson watched Peabody drop to his belly, then looked back at her. 'Where were you going?'

'I'm going to visit Ramon at the prison clinic. He needs to know that Elena loved him until the very end, that she died for him. You do your paperwork, push your pencils. I'll do what I need to do to get him out of there.'

'You planning to take him a cake with a file in it?' Grayson asked acidly.

'No,' she said, equally coldly, 'I plan to find out who killed his wife. Who stole his life. And if the cops are dirty and you lawyers are caught up in your own red tape, I'll take it to the media. I imagine I can muster enough people who are fed up with your reality. I imagine your boss won't like that, especially in an election year.'

A muscle twitched in his cheek. 'My boss is layers below anyone who's elected. We just play games and push papers and set rapists and murderers free to run amok.'

For a moment their gazes locked. Then Paige drew an uneven breath. 'I'm sorry. I've read your record. I know you've put away a lot of bad guys. It's just . . .' Her mouth bent plaintively. 'Ramon's lost six years of his life and he did nothing wrong.'

'I know,' Grayson said quietly. 'If he's innocent, he shouldn't have to wait six more minutes. But, whether you and I like it or not, these things do take time.'

'I *don't* like it,' she said. 'Can't you have him moved somewhere? Out of the general prison population?'

'Eventually, but to do that now, as Clay said, would tip our hand. The cops have a confession from Sandoval. The brass want this to go away because it calms the public from serial-sniper fears. Whoever killed Elena will want this to go away, too. They must know she had something valuable – they killed her for it.' He gave Paige a pointed look. 'They must think she told you something because they tried to kill you, too. If we make any sudden moves, whoever killed Elena will go under.'

'And any remaining evidence will be destroyed,' Clay said from the table where he sat, watching them with interest.

'Almost certainly,' Grayson agreed.

Paige sighed, the fire in her eyes banked. 'Ramon's in the

infirmary. Prison-yard fight over Elena sleeping with Denny,' she added when Grayson's brows rose in question. 'As long as he stays there, he'll at least be out of the population.'

'I'll see if I can keep him there,' Grayson said. 'It's an acceptable compromise.'

She nodded, holding his gaze. 'Thank you.'

'I want to do the right thing here, too, Paige.'

Color rose in her cheeks and she looked away briefly before lifting her eyes again. 'I'm sorry. You're right. I'm letting my emotions have too much control. So what next?'

He touched her arm briefly as they walked back to the table. 'Somebody killed Elena today,' he said. 'But another woman was killed six years ago.'

'Crystal Jones,' Paige said. 'Ramon didn't do it, so the real killer is still out there.' She rolled her eyes. 'Damn, we are sounding more OJ by the minute.'

'It's a cold case,' Clay said doubtfully. 'Odds aren't good.'

'We have to try,' Paige insisted. 'Ramon's lost his wife and six years of his life.'

Grayson thought of the knife at her throat. 'They won't stop coming after you either.'

'And you won't always be around with your trusty briefcase to save me.'

Yes, I will. The promise was irrational in too many ways. But he silently made it anyway. 'Then we'd better get to work.'

She pulled a folder from her backpack. 'This is the trial transcript. We can start piecing together Crystal's life and her movements before the night she was murdered. We'll have to start at ground zero. If some of the testimony was tainted, more could be.'

'Assuming these pictures are valid, that's true.' Grayson aligned the three photos, tapping the man sitting next to Ramon at the bar. 'Based on that same assumption, we also need to find this guy. Jorge Delgado. Ramon's best friend.'

'Delgado lied under oath,' Clay said. 'Somebody put him up to it.' He pointed to the face of the man wearing the disguise. 'My money's on this guy.'

'Mine too. Somebody ordered that hit on Paige. Sandoval was dying at the time.'

Paige studied him. 'You don't believe it was suicide?'

'We can't afford the luxury of believing it. I think someone's tying up loose ends.'

'Like Paige,' Clay said grimly and Grayson nodded.

'I just hope Sandoval wasn't Delgado's handler. If so, we're screwed.'

'How do we know Delgado's still alive?' Clay asked.

Grayson checked his email on his phone, relieved to see a message from Daphne. 'Delgado's alive all right. At least he was as of an hour ago.'

Paige frowned. 'How do you know?'

'I asked my assistant to check Delgado's last known before I came here.'

Paige blinked. 'You believed me, even before I showed you the pictures.'

'I watched somebody try to kill you,' Grayson said, knowing the memory of those moments would stay with him for a long time. 'Whatever you knew, somebody didn't want you to tell.' *Plus, I didn't believe Delgado five years ago. I just didn't want to admit it then. But I can't hide from it any longer*.

'So where is Delgado?' Clay asked. 'And how do we know he's alive?'

Grayson clicked the link Daphne had included. 'A reporter did a follow-up to Elena's murder. Delgado was quoted along with other people in the neighborhood. He says, "This is a sad day. To lose Elena was a senseless tragedy, but to lose Maria in the same day . . . Our prayers go out to the entire Muñoz family." ' He lifted his eyes sharply to find Paige looking stricken. 'What does he mean, "to lose Maria"?'

'Ramon's mother had a heart attack this morning when she heard about Elena's murder. She died.' Paige balled her fists. 'For that *liar* to even say their *names* . . .'

Grayson closed his eyes for a moment, remembering the mother's wild sorrow when Ramon's jury had announced their verdict. 'When you said his mother worked herself to death, I didn't . . . I thought it was just an expression. I'm sorry.'

'Me, too,' she whispered, jumping when one of the phones on the table vibrated.

Clay grabbed it. 'Yeah?' he answered, then his expression changed. 'When? . . . Keep him calm and keep him there.' He shoved away from the table. 'Did BPD file an Amber? . . . Good. Print copies of the photos we have on file. I'll be there in fifteen.'

'What?' Paige asked. 'What's wrong?'

'That was Alyssa. Sylvia Davis made bail.'

'You've got to be kidding,' Paige said. 'She took Zach? How?'

Clay was yanking on his coat. 'John left Zach with Sylvia's mother while he went into the office to pick up some files. Grandma put up a fight, and now she's in ICU.'

Paige pushed to her feet, her face gone pale. 'Oh, my God.'

Grayson rose, uncertainly. 'Who is Sylvia Davis?'

'Clay's client,' Paige said. 'Custody battle. Dad wants custody because Mom's an addict. Mom got arrested last night for trying to pimp out her kid. I'm going with you.'

Clay glared. 'You will not. One, you are injured and two, you have a goddamn target on your head.' He glanced at Grayson. 'She can stay here till I get back?'

'Of course.' He followed Clay to the front door, Paige behind him, suddenly so close he could feel her warmth against his back. So close that the breath he drew filled his head with her scent, lush and heady. 'If you need to stay, I'll see her home safely.'

'Take her home soon.' Clay looked over his shoulder, meeting Paige's eyes. 'She hasn't slept in more than a day.'

'For God's sake,' Paige muttered as Clay disappeared down the street at a fast jog.

Grayson locked the door and faced Paige, who looked annoyed. This close, he could see the purple smudges of exhaustion under her makeup. He barely resisted the urge to run his fingertips under her eyes. 'Why haven't you slept since yesterday?'

'I worked all night, watching that mom pimp out her kid.'

'What did you do about it?' That she'd done something was a given in his mind.

'Grabbed a cop. They stopped her.' Her mouth tightened. 'Part of me wishes the cops hadn't been so fast. I'd have broken her damn door down and made sure she wasn't ambulatory enough to steal her kid back. He's only six years old.' Her voice grew harsh. Brittle. 'He'll be terrified.'

There was something there, the shadow of fear, a deep rage that had both everything and nothing to do with what had occurred the night before. Grayson recognized it all too well. He kept his own voice mild, but gave in to the need to touch her, sweeping his thumb over her cheek. 'Is your partner good at his job?'

She swallowed hard, her eyes on his. She was holding herself rigid, as if she were afraid she'd shatter. Grayson recognized that feeling, too. 'Yes,' she whispered.

'Then let him do his job. You saved the little boy last night. He'll save him tonight. Right now, you staying alive is just as important.'

Something that looked like guilt flittered through her eyes. 'I don't know about that.'

Irritation flared within him. 'If you're dead, how many little boys will you save?'

'Not enough,' she said softly. 'Never enough,' she added, as if to herself. She took a step back and he let his hand fall to his side, the moment over. 'What about Delgado? We need to talk to him, if he's still around. Knowing him, he's probably run away.'

'You've met him, too?'

'No. I've gone by his place a few times, but he was never home.' She frowned. 'Wait. He doesn't live in the Muñozes' neighborhood. What was he doing there?'

'What do you mean, he doesn't live there? His address is a block from Elena's.'

'His wife and kid still live there, but Jorge moved out four years ago. Ramon's brothers were trying to convince him to admit he'd lied. They were running out of time to file an appeal and tempers boiled over. Delgado got roughed up by one of the older Muñoz brothers. Maria said his wife also thought he was lying and made him move out. He rents a room in DC and sees his daughter on the weekends, supervised by the wife.'

'If the wife thought he was lying, why didn't she go to the police?'

'I asked Maria that and she said Tina Delgado was scared that "something bad" would happen to her and her daughter.'

'What, like Jorge would hurt them?'

'Don't know. Maria forgave her because she was protecting her child. I'm thinking Jorge came back after he heard about Elena to see his kid before running away.'

'Before running? Or to see her one last time because he thought he was next?'

'Don't know. Not sure I care. All I know is that I need to talk to him.'

'If he fears for his daughter's safety, he's not going to talk to you, Paige.'

Her eyes narrowed dangerously. 'He might. If the incentive were right.'

Grayson shook his head. 'No. Not gonna happen. Having to prosecute you for assault would suck.' He leaned forward, closing the space she'd put between them. 'Burying you would be far worse. I didn't save your life this morning to watch you throw it away on some ill-conceived excuse for a plan. You run out of here half-cocked and whoever started the job in the garage this morning might just finish it.'

She crossed her arms over her breasts, a stubborn look on her face, but he could see his words had hit their mark. Her dark eyes churned and her chest rose and fell with the measured breaths she took. 'Then what's your plan, Counselor?'

An image flickered in front of his eyes, and the breaths he took were far from measured. Black hair stark against his pillow. Black eyes churning with need. All that lovely golden skin. He pushed the image aside by deliberately remembering his hands applying pressure to her sliced throat. Her blood soaking her red coat.

'To send someone whose face isn't all over the TV. You're too recognizable. You show up asking questions and we show our hand. You might as well go to the cops right now, because you'd be doing the same thing.'

She shook her head. 'If I was going to any other neighborhood, that would be true, but I can visit the Muñoz house while I'm there. Pay my respects. I was with Elena when she died. Nobody will think a thing about my going there tonight.'

'And the target on your head?' he demanded. 'Did you forget about that?'

She rocked up on her toes, bringing her close enough that he could count each eyelash. 'Of course not,' she hissed. 'I'm not stupid. The sooner I find out who put Delgado up to lying, the sooner the target comes off my head and I can go back to my regularly scheduled life, already in progress. Otherwise I might as well change my name, don a hooded robe, and move to a convent in Tibet, because my own life won't be worth a damn. It's not the greatest life going, but it's mine and I aim to keep it.'

He slowly straightened. Of all people, he understood what it was like to have to hide from someone bound and determined to kill him. It was why he and his mother had run away. Why they'd taken new names. He'd spent a lifetime looking over his shoulder. They hadn't deserved it nearly thirty years ago. Paige didn't deserve it now.

'You're right,' he murmured.

She eased back as well, suspicious. 'I am?'

'Yes. You can't hide forever. We need to know. Sooner versus later and before Delgado goes under. Get your things. We'll take my car.'

She hesitated. 'Wait. What? You're coming with me?'

'You're not going alone. Call me old-fashioned, but that's how I roll.'

She regarded him warily. 'Okay. But you'll have to stay in the car with Peabody.'

He narrowed his eyes at her. '*Now* you're bordering on stupid, Paige.'

'I'm serious. If someone sees you, they'll remember the trial. If they see us together, they'll know something is afoot.'

'Afoot? Really?' Despite everything, his lips twitched and a moment later hers were twitching too.

'I read too many detective stories,' she confessed and he was charmed.

'Well, be that as it may, I'm not staying in the car. We'll have to find another explanation for our mutual presence.'

'Oh, I can think of one,' a woman drawled behind them. He and Paige turned to find Lisa watching them, the expression on her face putting him on instant alert. 'Before you two go playing Holmes and Watson, you need to take a look at this. Follow me.'

Tuesday, April 5, 5.25 P.M.

'I won't leave you. Don't make me leave you.'

Jorge Delgado gathered his sobbing wife in his arms. 'Only for a little while,' he said softly, holding back his own anguish. 'Only until it's safe.'

'I have waited, for *six years*. I thought that soon . . . that you could come home. That we could stop living this lie. Then Elena had to go and do what she did. Damn her soul.'

Jorge wiped the tears from her face. 'Don't ever say that. You can't say that. If it had been me that was accused and rotting in prison, would you ever have given up?'

'No. But she's dead for nothing. And now he's going to finally kill you too.'

'No, because I'm going to hide. And you and CeCe are going away, where it's safe.' He took off the chain he wore around his neck and fastened it around hers. At the end of the chain was a key. 'I've already mailed the account number for the safe-deposit box to where you're going. If anything happens to me, you open this box.'

Tina began to cry again. 'Jorge, please, don't make me go.'

He grasped her shoulders. 'For CeCe, you'll go. I'll find a way to contact you. Make sure she knows I love her. Tell her every day. Tell her I did the best that I knew how.'

'I will. I promise.'

'Good. Now dry your eyes, my love. You've got one more performance and it's got to be good enough to fool CeCe and the neighborhood.'

She straightened her back, pasted a disapproving frown on her face. 'CeCe,' she called impatiently. 'We have to go. It's getting late.'

CeCe came down the stairs, a sullen frown on her face. 'I don't wanna go to Grandma's for dinner. There's nothing to do there and she always makes me eat eggs.'

'Listen to your mother,' Jorge said, more sharply than he'd planned to. His heart was breaking and it was all he could do to hide his misery. His baby wasn't going to Grandma's. She wasn't going for dinner. She was going far away, maybe forever, with only the clothes on her back. To keep her safe. Everything was to keep her safe.

Nobody could suspect that his wife and child were running for their lives.

Chastised, CeCe's gaze lowered. 'I wish you could come with us.'

Jorge dropped to his knee and wrapped his arms around her, holding her tightly. 'Cecilia, my baby. Remember that I love you always. Now you be good for your mama.' He let her go and buckled her into her booster seat, then watched the only woman he'd ever loved get behind the wheel and drive away.

Tuesday, April 5, 5.30 P.M.

Grayson at her side, Paige followed Lisa into the kitchen where delightful aromas filled the air. A lean man wearing a Ravens cap backward was icing a tall, three-tiered cake while Holly kneaded a large lump of what looked like white paste.

'This is my husband, Brian,' Lisa said.

Brian gave Paige a measuring glance. 'Pleased to meet you, Paige.'

'Likewise,' Paige said slowly. 'Thank you for the food. It was delicious.'

'Hi, Paige,' Holly sang. Then she grinned cagily. 'Hi, Grayson,' she added slyly.

'Hi, Holly,' Paige said, then turned to Grayson. 'What is this?' she whispered.

'I don't know,' he whispered back. 'But I don't think it's good.'

110

'That would depend entirely on your point of view,' Lisa said. 'You're not going to be happy, I imagine. Your mother, on the other hand, will be ecstatic.' She turned on the TV. 'I started recording as soon as they mentioned your names.'

'Oh, no.' Paige's heart started to pound. There she was on the TV screen again, but this time in the parking garage. The shot was from far away and very off-center, but there was no mistaking that it was her. 'No, no, no.'

'Oh, God,' Grayson murmured.

Brian came to stand behind Lisa, resting his hands on her shoulders. 'This isn't the part that Grayson's mother will like,' he said to Paige, then bent to his wife's ear, his tone chiding. 'You make Judy sound like a sadist.'

Lisa's reply was lost as Paige recoiled at the sight of a knife at her own throat, at her desperate struggle to get away. Her hand lifted to her bandage of its own accord.

'Why? How can they do this?' She looked up at Grayson, whose face was dark with fury, both on the TV and in real life. On screen, he'd just knocked the guy down. In real life he looked like he wanted to do the same to Radcliffe.

'That's why Radcliffe wanted a comment, outside the hospital,' he said.

'They were there in the garage the whole time.'

'And they never called for help,' Grayson said coldly. 'And they don't even get the bastard's face.' He shook his head in disgust as the attacker ran away.

'At least they don't show me bleeding.' That had been edited, cutting to Grayson pressing his tie to her throat to stem the bloodflow. 'That tie looks expensive.'

'It was,' he muttered. 'Lisa, exactly which part of this will have my mother ecstatic?'

'Wait for it . . .' On screen Grayson lifted Paige's head to his thigh. 'Right about now.'

Paige heard him utter an oath, but she didn't look away from the TV. His expression was ferocious as he tended her wound, but at the same time tender. She watched, knowing what was coming but still feeling a thrill when he bent to whisper in her ear. Then stroked her hair. Then her face.

There was something in his expression. Something sweet. Unexpected.

'*That's* what your mother will like,' Lisa said, satisfied. 'It's about time.'

The clip ended and Phin Radcliffe was back on screen. 'State's Attorney Grayson Smith declined to comment other than to say he was in the right place at the right time. I'm sure Paige Holden agrees, and so do I. Miss Holden had no comment, but we here at the station wish her a speedy recovery. This is Phin Radcliffe reporting.'

Lisa turned off the TV and the only sound in the kitchen was Holly's rhythmic kneading of the doughy paste on the table. The silence was charged. Awkward.

Paige chanced a glance up at Grayson. He stared straight ahead, not looking back at her. So she kept her tone light. 'At least now you don't have to stay in the car.'

'That's not funny,' he ground out and she fought the urge to flinch. He was angry. Very angry. And horrified. The anger she could understand. The horror hurt.

Grayson pointed at Lisa. 'And you stay the hell out of this.'

Lisa didn't back down. 'Pull that stick out of your ass. What is wrong with you?'

'What is *wrong* is that now half the city has seen *that*.' He gestured at the screen.

The little thrill Paige had felt at being touched so tenderly was long gone. His cheeks were red, his eyes blazing. He was furious. *And who can blame him?* He'd saved her life and what did he get? A demanding female wanting to play Sherlock and an asshole reporter who'd just splashed his face all over the TV.

He'd been dignified this morning. Now he was tabloid fodder. *Just like me.*

She couldn't blame him for being angry. *If I were him, I'd wish I'd never met me.*

'*I* thought it was sweet,' Holly declared, but her lip quivered. 'You're a hero.'

Grayson went to the table and hugged Holly to him, not caring that she was covered in flour. 'That you think so means a lot to me. What are you making?'

Holly settled against his side. 'Fondant. For the cake Brian's making.'

'It'll be delicious.' Laying his head against Holly's, he closed his eyes and Paige watched him grow calmer. Eyes still closed, he stretched out his other arm for Lisa and she joined the hug without hesitation, the three of them standing together. A unit. 'I'm sorry,' he murmured. 'I shouldn't have yelled at you.'

'I'm sorry too,' Lisa murmured back. 'But I'm not sure for what.'

A wave of longing smacked Paige as she watched, a lump rising in her throat that she had to swallow hard to dislodge. Because she understood that the way he'd touched her face was not special or unique. It was just his way. His family's way.

Quietly she backed out of the kitchen, her eyes stinging. *I need to get out of here*. But she didn't have her car. Had she been in Minneapolis, she could have had any one of ten friends pick her up in as many minutes. But here, life was a little different. She'd made a few friends, like Clay and Alyssa, but they weren't the friends she suddenly missed so much her chest ached. They certainly weren't family.

She all but ran back to the Gingerbread House, shoved the trial transcript into her backpack. Peabody sat up, ready for her command.

I will not cry. Not here. 'How am I going to get you home?'

No cab in town would transport a ninety-pound dog and it was miles to the office where she'd left her truck. Too far to walk, especially as fatigue was beginning to pull at her mind. She'd have to ask Grayson to give her a lift. *Then I'll drive to Delgado's*.

Peabody came to attention, staring at the doorway. She didn't have to look up to know Grayson was standing there. She could feel him watching her.

'Are you ready to go?' he asked.

Paige kept her eyes down. 'I've had a long day. I was hoping you could drive me to my office so I can get my truck. I want to go home, take a hot bath, and call it a night.'

113

Hearing his footsteps cross the floor, she braced herself. Still she shivered when he cupped her cheek in his palm and tugged until she looked up. His eyes were very green in this light. And still angry. But his hand was as gentle as his tone when he spoke.

'I'm sorry, Paige. You've had a hell of a day.'

Hot tears filled her eyes and she blinked, sending them down her cheeks as she turned her face away. After a moment's hesitation he threaded his fingers through her hair, making her shiver again.

His palm was warm against her skull and it was then she realized just how long it had been since she'd been touched. The tears started anew. 'I don't cry, it's—'

He'd pulled her against him, muffling her words. The hand in her hair urged her head to rest against him while his other hand stroked the hair down her back. 'It's okay.'

Just for a minute. He felt so good. For a minute she let herself breathe him in. And cry. And pretend that this day had never happened, that she hadn't seen a woman murdered before her eyes. That she hadn't nearly been killed herself. That she'd never seen Elena's pictures. That her throat didn't hurt like a bitch.

That this man stroking her hair so gently was hers to keep. That he wasn't just being kind to her out of duty or, even worse, pity. And that she couldn't still feel the anger roiling beneath his outward calm.

The crying jag passed. 'You have every right to be angry,' she whispered, 'and I don't have any right to ask for more help. I'll go home.'

He kept stroking her hair. 'After you go see Jorge Delgado.'

She sighed. 'Yes.'

'I told you that I'd take you. Get your things. We'll leave right now.'

'No.'

'Why the hell not?' he asked, exasperated.

Her throat was closing again. 'Because you're mad at me and I don't like that.'

He leaned back so that she could see his face. 'I'm mad, but not at you, Paige. You didn't ask for any of this. I'm mad at that

114

sonofabitch Radcliffe because he's getting ratings at your expense. I'm mad that anyone involved in this has already figured out that you came to me for help. If they weren't sure if you knew anything, they sure as hell will be now.' He swiped at her cheek with his thumb. 'But I'm not mad at you. Okay?'

That he'd avoided the topic of his mother's glee and his own horror hadn't escaped her notice, and it hurt. Still she nodded. 'Okay.'

'I need to bring in the police. Now that I've seen the pictures, I have a responsibility to do the right thing.'

She closed her eyes. Her heart was pounding again. 'I know. But it doesn't make me any less terrified.'

'I told Morton and Bashears that Elena came to see me last week asking for a new trial. I told them this morning, as soon as I confirmed she was the victim.'

She wasn't sure if she was comforted by that or not. 'So they really did know. Will you give them the copies of the pictures I made for you?'

'No.'

She blinked up at him in surprise. 'No?'

'I've got a friend, another homicide detective. I'm going to give them to her. Her name is Stevie Mazzetti and I trust her with my life.'

'That's very good,' Paige said slowly. 'But I need to trust her with mine.'

'I know. She wasn't involved in the Muñoz investigation. She hadn't even heard about it until today. She was on bereavement leave when Crystal was killed, followed by maternity leave. She was out for several months and not watching the news.'

That Paige hadn't expected. 'How can you know she wasn't watching the news?'

'Her husband and five-year-old son were murdered in a robbery when Stevie was pregnant. She focused on keeping her baby and her sanity. She refused to watch the news out of self-protection. Her husband and I worked together. He was a damn good prosecutor. He was also my friend. I've known Stevie for years. She'll do the right thing.'

115

Paige remembered what Clay had said that morning and some of her panic quieted. Mazzetti had investigated the murder of Clay's former partner and was the cop he thought they might trust. 'I always knew you'd have to tell someone. Okay. Do it.'

Something moved in his eyes. 'I'll call her on the way. Summon your hound.'

She hiccuped a surprised laugh. 'Summon my hound?'

He shrugged. 'I read too many detective stories, too.'

Tuesday, April 5, 6.15 P.M.

Silas stepped back from the mirror, barely able to see his own reflection through the blood. His stomach was churning and it took every last ounce of control not to heave its contents all over the small bathroom with its Dora the Explorer wallpaper.

He hadn't wanted to do this murder either. Jorge Delgado had heeded every last warning. Until today. He'd come back to the neighborhood.

Silas wasn't sure why Delgado had come back. Maybe to make sure Sandoval was really dead. But Silas didn't think so. *Were it me, I would have run when I heard Sandoval was dead*. And, were it him, Silas wouldn't have been able to leave without holding his daughter one last time. He hoped Delgado had gotten that last hug.

Tina Delgado and the child hadn't been home when he'd killed Jorge. He'd waited until they'd left the house before slipping in the back. He was so glad they'd gone. If they hadn't . . . he didn't want to think of it. Didn't want to consider the choice he would have had to make. He couldn't have killed Jorge and left his family alive to tell.

Because if they hadn't left he would have made the choice. His child came first.

Silas looked down at his double gloved hands, latex covering the leather. The tip of his forefinger was red. The message in the mirror would be clear enough.

He slipped out the kitchen door to the alley. No one was out, no one was watching. It was raining again and everyone was inside. He pulled his hood up, covering his head and shrouding his face. No one would be able to identify him even if they did see him.

Pausing at the dumpster two blocks down, he tossed the gun he'd just used. The dumpster was the closest to the Muñoz family home. The gun was untraceable to him. He threw the latex gloves down the sewer. They'd wash out to the river by morning.

Silas drove away as if he hadn't just ended the life of a man who had done nothing more than be in the wrong place sitting next to the wrong guy. At the worst of wrong times. Grimly he made a call on his work cell.

'It's done,' Silas said.

'Good to hear. And the wife and kid?'

'They were gone by the time I got there.'

'Hmm.'

Silas held his breath, hoping there would be no kill order on Tina Delgado and the child. *Please, no. I can't.* But he knew that he could. If he had to.

'I suppose that's just as well. That would have been too messy.'

Silas let out a careful breath, lightheaded from relief. 'Exactly.'

'Did you search his room at the boarding house?'

'Yes. I was there all day, waiting for him. He wasn't supposed to be here.'

'Then it's a good thing he got interviewed. We might have missed him.' The meaning of the silky words was clear – *you nearly failed again*. 'I have another job.'

'No,' Silas gritted, then bit his tongue, regretting the outburst. 'Who?'

'An MMA fighter. Roscoe "Jesse" James. He's got a fight tonight. You may want to follow him to the bar afterward. It's where he goes to chill.'

'What should I do with him?'

'Kill him. And make sure he's never found. You know, the usual.'

Silas knew. The shootings of Elena and Jorge were unique. Normally his jobs were much less public. And less frequent.

Silas didn't ask why James had to die. He'd seen the video of the botched attack on Paige Holden while he'd waited in Delgado's rented room. Her attacker had been big, muscled, and fought like a pro. A secret part of him was thrilled she'd gotten away.

That Silas had been tasked with the job of killing the man who'd botched her hit was also a message. He hadn't been trusted with the parking garage assignment. Because he'd failed to kill her this morning when he'd had her in his sights.

When a kid with a camcorder also had her in his sights. Silas had watched that video while waiting for Delgado as well, troubled to see that the tape had been spliced. He needed to know what was contained in those missing minutes. He needed to know if the kid who'd taken the video had captured his face in any capacity. With all the facial recognition software, even the slightest glimpse might be enough to ID him.

His source in BPD said that everyone knew who'd taken the video – a kid named Logan Booker who lived in the unit above the Holden woman. But both Logan and Phin Radcliffe were refusing to give the cops the uncut version without a warrant.

Silas needed to see that uncut tape. *Just for my own peace of mind*. But first he had another job to do. Roscoe 'Jesse' James would learn the penalty of failure tonight. *And in teaching it, so will I.*

Seven

Grayson checked his rearview mirror yet again. There appeared to be no one following them, but it was hard to tell in the dark and in the rain that had started up again while they'd been at Lisa's. The interior of his car was silent except for the swishing of his wiper blades and the panting of the dog taking up most of his backseat.

Paige had fallen asleep minutes into the drive, head tucked against her shoulder. But even in sleep her brows were knit. Grayson wanted to smooth the worry away.

He figured they'd achieve little from their trip. Delgado wouldn't talk. Not unless he had one hell of a heavy conscience. In Grayson's experience, people rarely confessed secrets they'd kept for years. Especially when protecting someone else.

They were a few miles away from Delgado's house when Grayson's cell buzzed in his pocket. He'd put in a call to Stevie half an hour ago, but got her voicemail. He tapped his hands-free earpiece. 'This is Smith,' he said softly, so he didn't wake Paige.

'I know.'

Grayson swallowed the sigh. *Here we go*. 'Hi, Mom.'

'Why are we whispering?' his mother whispered loudly.

'Because I'm in the car and my passenger is asleep.'

'Your passenger is photogenic. That you are also goes without saying. Of course.'

'Of course. So . . .' He sighed. 'What do you want to know?'

'Just remember that you asked,' she said tartly. 'When will I meet

119

your passenger? She has good taste in clothes. I loved her red coat. Very chic.'

'Until it got soaked with her blood,' he said grimly.

'There was that,' his mother acknowledged. 'Are you in danger, Grayson?'

'No. But she is.'

'Then you'll keep her safe.' It was a statement of fact. Of faith.

His mother had kept *him* safe, guarding their secrets, standing between him and those who would have literally torn him apart. A lioness protecting her cub, she fiercely defied anyone who had threatened him. 'I learned from the best.'

'You always know what to say,' she murmured. 'Your passenger is very lucky.'

He glanced back at the dog whose gaze never left Paige's face. *He stands between me and the world.* That her guardian was a dog and not a person who loved her made him sad. Somehow he knew she'd never had a mother like his. 'I think you'd like her.'

'I plan on finding out. You promised me dinner tomorrow. I have reservations at Giuseppe's. For three. Because I had intended to invite Carly.'

Grayson winced. He and Carly hadn't been together in months. 'About her . . .'

'Except you hadn't called me back as of lunch,' his mother interrupted. 'So I called her.'

His heart sank. 'You called Carly?'

'And wasn't I surprised to learn that you and she had broken up? Months ago.'

'I'm sorry, Mom.'

'Were you ever going to tell me, son?' He heard the hurt in her voice.

'Of course I was. I just couldn't find the right time.' It sounded lame, even to him.

'Why did you break up?' she asked. 'I thought things were getting serious.'

He was certain Carly had thought so. He shifted, uncomfortable. 'Mom.'

'Don't "Mom" me,' she said sharply. 'I asked Carly myself.'

He sat up straighter, his neck growing warm. 'You had no right.'

'She said she left you because you were always working. That she didn't want to play second fiddle to your job.'

'It was true.' It was his MO. Make them hate him for neglect before they discovered the truth. They always left, taking their dignity with them. It was the least he could do.

'It's been true for every woman you've ever known,' she pushed.

'Mom,' he warned her. 'This isn't your business.'

'You didn't tell her, did you? Carly. You didn't tell her.'

'Of course I didn't tell her,' he said wearily.

'She was a nice woman and you pushed her away, just like all the others.'

'It was for the best.'

'Bullshit,' she snapped, startling him. 'You've more than proven yourself not to be *him*. He can't hurt you. Any woman who can't accept who you are doesn't deserve you, but you do them a disservice by not giving them a chance to make the right choice.'

'I can't tell them because I can't risk them telling,' he said quietly.

'So what if they do? Nobody's coming after you. Not any more.'

'It has nothing to do with that.' Even though it did.

'You think people will think less of you. That they'll think you're like *him*, but nobody will. Nobody except yourself. How long will you go on paying for someone else's sins?'

He didn't know what to say, so he said nothing at all.

Finally she sighed. 'I'm sorry. I shouldn't yell at you.'

'It's okay.'

'No, it's not. You needed to hear the words, but not the tone. I look back and wonder what might have happened if I'd never made us run. Never made you afraid.'

We'd be dead, he thought. 'I know you want what you think is best for me.'

'What I want is for you to have a family. Which you'll never allow yourself to have.'

'I'm sorry, Mom,' was all he could say.

'Don't be sorry. Just bring your Good Samaritan to meet me.'

The hairs on the back of his neck lifted in alarm. 'Promise me you won't tell her.'

'I promise. Eight o'clock tomorrow night. Wear a tie.'

'All right,' he said, relaxing a little. But only a little. His mother was a woman on a thinly veiled mission – to have him settled sometime this decade. He'd spent a lifetime making her proud, proving he was a good man and not . . . his father. Not disappointing her. But in this, she would be disappointed.

He looked at Paige, guilt already eating at him. He wanted her. He'd wanted her from the minute he'd seen her jump from the path of a bullet-riddled minivan, then run back to check on the driver.

He should walk away, or better yet, send her running before she got any ideas of permanence. Of anything more than a few days or weeks. Months at the outside. Because if she wanted more, she'd end up hurt. Just like the others.

He'd never raised a hand to a woman. Ever. But he'd broken a few hearts, despite his best intentions. The thought of breaking Paige's left him feeling physically ill.

At least his timing was good. He was in Elena's neighborhood. 'I have to go, Mom.'

'I love you.'

'I love you too. I'll see you tomorrow.' He tapped his earpiece to disconnect and slowed his car, focusing on reading the house numbers.

The Muñoz place was dark. Grayson assumed the Muñoz brothers were all together, grieving. He didn't want to imagine losing his mother or any of the Carters. Much less to have lost a mother and sister in the same day. His heart ached for them.

His heart always ached for the families.

Unfortunately, by the time he entered the picture, there was nothing to be done but get justice for the victims. And protect future victims by putting murderers behind bars.

He thought he'd done the right thing by Crystal Jones. He thought he'd put a murdering bastard behind bars. He thought he was one step closer to balancing the scales. But it was never enough.

Never enough. He glanced over at Paige, still asleep. She'd said that, too. *How many little boys will you save?* he'd asked. *Never enough.* He wondered what she'd meant. He intended to find out, but it would need to be later.

He stopped his car in front of Delgado's row house. It, too, was dark. No one was home. He was tempted to leave, but Paige needed to make the attempt for her own peace of mind. He shook her shoulder lightly and she opened her eyes.

'We're there?' she asked.

He'd brushed his thumb across her cheek before he could stop himself. 'Yes.'

'Then let's do this.' She was out of the car before he could assist her, telling Peabody to stay before closing the door. 'Doesn't look like anyone's home,' she said.

He followed her to the Delgados' front door, glancing from side to side, wondering who was watching. Paranoia wasn't fun. He glanced at the bandage peeping up from Paige's collar. Except it wasn't paranoia when someone was really trying to kill you.

She knocked on the door lightly. 'Mrs Delgado? Are you home?' she called.

When no one answered, Grayson knocked harder. Then both of them sucked in a startled breath when the door creaked open. It hadn't been closed.

'This feels bad,' Paige whispered, then raised her voice to call again. 'Mrs Delgado? Are you all right?' She sniffed deeply. 'Oh, God. Do you smell that?'

'Someone's fired a gun. Recently.' He took his cell from his pocket then cursed as Paige walked straight on inside, her hand on her holstered gun. '*Paige. Stop.*'

She looked back, her dark eyes snapping. 'A little girl lives here.'

Muttering, he followed her into the narrow house and down the hall. 'This is insa—' He stopped abruptly in front of the bathroom, as had she.

'Oh, no,' she whispered. 'No.'

Grayson couldn't speak. Could only stare. The wallpaper was from a child's cartoon. Now it was splattered with blood and brain.

123

He made himself look at the tub. Delgado knelt, hands and feet bound. His body listed to the right, propped up by the side of the tub. He'd been shot in the back of the head.

'Executed,' Grayson whispered hoarsely.

Paige turned to the mirror, where a message had been scrawled across the glass. ' "*Pago del saldo*," ' she read, her voice barely audible. 'It means "Paid in full".'

'I know.' Grayson had understood the meaning of the words as soon as he'd seen them. Both literally and symbolically. The message had been written in Jorge Delgado's blood. 'What does it say at the bottom?'

Without stepping over the threshold, Paige leaned in and squinted. ' "RIP Elena." '

'Shit. Let's go.' He headed back for the front door, cell phone in hand, but she'd already started up the stairs, her gun drawn. 'Paige,' he hissed. 'Dammit.'

She looked back, eyes shattered. 'His little girl is only eight years old,' she said fiercely, her voice thick with unshed tears. 'If she's alive, she needs help.'

He clenched his jaw, torn between knowing she was right and the need to get her the hell out of here and to safety. He quickly dropped to one knee and drew the Glock from his boot while her eyes widened. 'Fine,' he said. 'Just stay close.'

He slipped past her on the stairs and carefully ascended, listening for any noise. Any moans. Any whimpers. But the house was silent except for their breathing.

There were two bedrooms upstairs, one belonging to a little girl, the other to an adult woman. Both were painfully neat. And appeared empty.

The little girl's closet was slightly ajar and Grayson nudged the door with the toe of his boot. School uniforms hung on the rack, shoes in a pile on the floor. No child.

His shoulders sagged in relief. He'd braced himself for the worst.

The mom's closet also held only clothes. There was no sign that a man lived there, in the closet or the upstairs bathroom, which was thankfully empty.

Grayson pointed to the stairs. 'Now we get the hell out of here.'

Outside, they took great gulps of the rainy air as Grayson slid his pistol into his coat pocket then hit the redial on his cell phone.

Stevie answered on the first ring. 'I just got your voicemail. What's wrong?'

Where to start? 'I need your help. *Now*. I'm at the home of Jorge Delgado. He testified in the trial of Ramon Muñoz. Delgado's dead, bullet to the back of his head. His wife and child are not in the house. Nothing else appears to have been touched. There's a message on the mirror, in Delgado's blood. "Paid in full. RIP Elena." '

'I'll be there as fast as I can. Are you safe?'

He looked up and down the street. 'I don't know. Paige Holden is with me.'

A half-beat of silence. 'You're going to tell me what this is about, right?'

Grayson nodded, numb. 'Yeah. But only you. I mean that, Stevie. You do your investigation, get CSU and the ME out here, do whatever you need to do. But what I tell you stays with you until we know what the hell is going on here.'

He hung up, then reached for Paige. She turned into him as his arms came around her. For a long moment they held on to each other, shaking as they stood in the rain.

He'd seen countless crime scenes, but most were photographs. It had been a long time since he'd seen one in person. He was stunned. Sick to his stomach. Paige had also been stunned, he thought, but her first instinct had been to protect Delgado's child.

My mother's going to love her.

His arms tightened around her, one hand running down her spine. And coming to a halt when he touched a second holster in her waistband. It was a smaller gun than the one she held by her side, pointing at the ground. Another tentative touch revealed the hilt of a knife. It was reassuring and terrifying all at once. And left him wondering how many more weapons she'd concealed. And where.

'You need to put your gun away,' Grayson murmured against her hair. 'If they get here and your gun's out, it'll make for questions you don't want to answer.'

She slid the gun in her hand into the shoulder holster, then looked up, devastated. 'I got that man killed. I should have told Morton and Bashears. I should—'

He shook his head, pressing his fingers to her lips. 'No. I still don't believe Morton and Bashears have anything to do with this, but we'll continue according to plan. We tell Stevie and no one else. Someone executed Jorge Delgado. Now three of the four people who knew the truth about Ramon's alibi are dead. You're the fourth.' He lightly gripped her chin. 'We keep you alive, understand?'

'I understand. Grayson, you're the fifth. You know that, too.'

'Yeah, I know.' And standing here, they were sitting ducks. He led her to his car and opened the back door. 'Get in the backseat and keep your head down.'

She frowned as she obeyed, giving Peabody a reassuring pat. 'What about you?'

'I'm going to drive.'

'We're leaving the scene?' she asked, shocked.

'No, but I want to be able to see all the exits.' He drove down the block, picking a point that was close enough to see the front of the house and the alley.

'There are binoculars in the front pouch of my pack,' she said. 'On the floor.'

'Thanks,' he said as they settled in to wait for Stevie.

Tuesday, April 5, 6.55 P.M.

'What have we got?'

Stevie turned when JD entered the Delgado home. 'Jorge Delgado, twenty-eight-year-old Hispanic male.' She stepped back to let him look. So far, they were the only ones there. CSU hadn't arrived. Stevie hadn't called her boss yet either.

When she'd arrived at the scene she'd found Grayson grim and shaken. Except when he looked at the black-haired woman sitting in his backseat, her arm hugging a very large Rottweiler. When Grayson looked at Paige his whole face softened in a way she'd never seen before. Except on the TV news. If he hadn't called her, she'd been ready to call him about the parking-garage incident.

But it wasn't only infatuation Stevie saw in his eyes. He was afraid, for Paige. The mystery woman was equally shaken, her face so pale that her dark eyes appeared bottomless.

He'd been adamant that no police except Stevie should know Paige had been there. He'd been equally adamant that Stevie keep the Delgado case.

Because it was Grayson, Stevie would do everything in her power to do what he'd asked. She'd sent the two to get coffee, hoping to pull a little color back in Paige's face.

JD stepped back from the bathroom. 'Who is this guy?'

'Jorge Delgado was the best friend of Ramon Muñoz.'

JD threw her a startled glance. 'So in less than twenty-four, we have Ramon's wife dead, her alleged lover dead, and now the best friend. Why this guy?'

'Ramon gave him as his alibi. But Delgado testified that Ramon was nowhere near the bar where he'd claimed to be the night he was accused of murdering that co-ed.'

'Crystal Jones.'

'Yeah. I downloaded the report. Meant to read it after I put Cordy to bed, but I haven't had time to do more than skim the top few pages. I'll make you a copy.'

'Execution, vengeance message on the mirror, a two-liter cola bottle on the floor.'

'Amateur silencer.'

'Or somebody wanted it to look that way,' JD said. 'The ties on his hands and feet were done by someone who knew their knots.'

'That's what I thought.'

'And that entry wound placement? Instant death. Other than the terror of knowing he was going to die, this guy didn't suffer.'

And as a former Army sniper, JD would know. 'No evidence of forced entry,' she said. 'Front door askew, back closed but no deadbolt. Empties into an alley.'

'Who found him?' Stevie didn't answer and JD turned to meet her eyes. 'What's going on here, Stevie?'

'I don't know. Yet. I'll tell you as soon as I can.'

'Stevie,' he said, warning and annoyance clear.

'You know I trust you. I will tell you, I promise. First I have to get the facts myself. Can you handle this scene? I have to take off for a few minutes. I've checked the house. Nobody else is here. Doesn't look like any bags were packed and the car is gone, so the wife and daughter may be coming back. I've called CSU and the ME.'

JD looked at her shrewdly. 'And Hyatt?'

'No. Not yet.' Their lieutenant could be tyrannical and theatrical, but ultimately he was a good cop who operated best on facts. 'When I know more, I'll tell him.'

'Will we have to give this one to Morton and Bashears, too?' JD asked.

'I hope not. Check things out quickly, in case we don't have a choice.'

'You got it. Who should I say found the body?'

'Right now, an anonymous informant. I need to go talk to said informant.'

'Tell him I said that was a good save with the briefcase in the parking garage,' JD said dryly, and one side of her mouth lifted.

'I'll call you when I'm on my way back. Thanks, JD. I owe you one.'

'A helluva lot more than one.'

Tuesday, April 5, 7.20 P.M.

'I got you guys some coffee.' Sitting next to Grayson up front, Stevie Mazzetti handed a cup to Paige, who still slumped in the backseat. 'Easy, boy,' Stevie murmured to Peabody, who'd sat up to check her out.

'Thank you.' Paige shivered as the warmth hit her throat. She was numb, the image of Delgado's body filling her mind until it was all she could see.

After filling Stevie in at Delgado's house, Paige and Grayson had driven a few miles away to a burger place where they'd parked in a corner of the lot and waited.

'Thanks,' Grayson echoed, his jaw set grimly. 'Thanks for coming.'

'You're welcome,' Stevie said. 'So. Tell me a story, kids.'

Paige and Grayson did. Stevie showed no reaction until they'd finished.

'That's one hell of a story,' she murmured, shaking her head.

'It's true,' Paige said defensively.

'I don't doubt you,' Stevie said, then pointed to Grayson. 'Because I don't doubt *him*. It's just . . . a hell of a story. So what do you want to happen next, Miss Holden?'

'You need to—' Grayson began, but Stevie cut him off with a look.

'You'll get your turn,' she said, then patted his arm. 'I want to hear from Paige.'

Paige laid her head on Peabody's neck. 'I want to go to sleep and wake up and find this was all a bad TV show. But it's not.'

'No,' Stevie agreed. 'So what next, Paige? What are you prepared to do?'

Paige's eyes flew to Stevie's, alarmed. 'What does that mean?'

'It means that if you pursue this, you'll inevitably be questioned by guys in suits. Some will be kind, some will rip out every secret you own. It means that you'll likely make enemies of a few cops who don't like squealers. It also means that if you're right, and there *was* police misconduct on Ramon's investigation, most of the cops will thank you in the end. The bad apples make us all look bad.'

'I can handle being interrogated,' Paige said, quelling the urge to rub her shoulder. She'd been interviewed by the police after the shooting last summer, again and again. At times it had grown downright ugly. *But last time you had Olivia by your side, supporting you. This time you're on your own.*

'Then again,' Stevie said levelly, 'they might find that Elena was wrong, that cops weren't chasing her. That no cops were involved today or back then.'

'You mean someone might say Ramon is still guilty. That he stays in prison and all of this was for nothing.'

'Pretty much. So what happens next, Paige? What do you want?'

'I want the truth. I want everyone to know what Elena gave her life for. I want not to be hated by cops, because I'm going to need them in the future. I'm still in the honeymoon phase with my new partner and if I don't work out, we call it quits. I'd have to relocate again and I finally unpacked my pots and pans.'

'Which is a total pain in the ass,' Stevie murmured. 'Anything else?'

'Yeah. I want whoever attacked me this afternoon to be caught. I came here to stop looking over my shoulder, yet I find myself there again.'

Stevie's brows lifted. Grayson's lowered. Neither spoke.

Paige sighed. 'And I don't want to have blood on my hands. Ever again.'

'All fine wants. So what are you prepared to do?' Stevie persisted.

She met Stevie's eyes. 'Whatever it takes. What did I just sign up for?'

'I don't know yet,' Stevie said. 'Grayson, what's on your agenda?'

'A meeting first thing tomorrow morning with you, your commander, and me.' He'd arranged for it already, making the call to the commander as they'd waited.

'What will you tell him?' Stevie asked.

'The truth, just like we told you.'

'He's not going to like that Paige is accusing a cop of involvement.'

'I don't like it either. And it may not be true. Elena could have been mistaken. Assuming evidence was planted, anyone could have done it. But a victim – who somebody took a big risk to silence – accused the police in her dying declaration. The individual who heard that declaration was nearly killed this afternoon. We have to consider Elena's accusation credible until we've disproven it.'

'The commander's going to bring IA in,' Stevie said, 'before you've even left his office.'

'He can bring them in,' Grayson said, 'but not to take over.'

'Ah,' Stevie said softly. 'The list of demands. Let's hear them.'

'First, I don't want Paige hurt. If this escalates, my office will hide her in a safe house and IA won't have access to her.'

'Hey,' Paige protested. 'I should get some say in—'

Stevie held up her hand. 'Not your turn. I figured as much,' she said to Grayson.

130

'I will keep this investigation under the control of the state's attorney's office. I will lead it. I want police backup – you. No other unless all hell breaks loose. IA is to be involved on an inform basis only. And I want access to any ongoing investigations into the deaths of Elena Muñoz, Denny Sandoval, and Jorge Delgado as well as the personnel files of anyone involved in the investigation of Crystal Jones's murder.'

Stevie gave him a long look before replying. 'You ask for a lot.'

Grayson pulled folded papers from his shirt pocket. 'These are copies.'

'Of course they are.' Stevie studied each one. 'Where are the originals?'

Paige looked at Grayson and he nodded. 'In my safe-deposit box,' she said.

'On the flash drive Elena gave you before she died,' Stevie said. 'Okay. We'll want one of the techies to verify the files haven't been compromised. But given the events of the day, I'd say that's pretty damn unlikely. I'll also want the drive.'

'First, I get the commander's agreement to my terms,' Grayson said.

'Then why did you even call me?' Stevie asked.

'Because I trust you,' he said simply. 'I need someone I can trust.'

Stevie sighed. 'You know I'll stand with you, but first I have some questions of a more personal nature. How long have you known each other?'

'We met today,' Paige said.

Stevie looked incredulous. 'If you're not going to take this seriously . . .'

'She's not lying,' Grayson said firmly. 'She came to court today to meet me.'

'I'd seen his picture,' Paige admitted. 'I had to know who I was looking for.'

'I'd seen her on the video,' Grayson added. 'Along with everyone else in creation.'

Stevie pursed her lips. 'That's gonna be a hard sell, guys. I know the brass has seen that video of the parking garage by now. Along with everyone else in creation.'

Grayson's jaw clenched. 'Damn that Radcliffe.'

'Pictures don't lie.' Stevie waved the copies. 'You two can't have it both ways.'

'We. Met. Today,' Grayson said, gritting his teeth.

'O. Kay,' Stevie replied tartly. 'Are you two "in a relationship"?'

'No,' they both said at the same time.

'Okay,' Stevie went on, 'do you plan to *be* in a relationship?'

Paige opened her mouth to say no, but the word wouldn't come. She chanced a glance at Grayson and found him glaring at Stevie, who clucked her tongue thoughtfully.

'At least that's honest. If this goes south, you could face sanctions, Grayson.'

'Wait,' Paige blurted. 'Then no. I answer no. He's done nothing wrong.'

'Too late,' Stevie said. 'Grayson? Do you understand?'

He looked away from both of them. 'Yes. I understand.'

'I don't,' Paige said. 'I don't want anyone else to die. *I* don't want to die. But I won't let you sacrifice your career. This isn't your fight.'

He turned to look at her then, his eyes so intense that for a moment she didn't breathe. 'I watched you nearly killed today, so yes, it's my fight. And even if you weren't involved at all, I knew something was off with Delgado when I put him on the stand.'

Yes, you must have, Paige thought. Otherwise he never would have asked his assistant to track Delgado down. 'How so?' she asked quietly.

'I thought he was afraid of the community backlash, of not giving Ramon an alibi. He had a wife and a daughter. Maybe he was protecting them, maybe not. Whoever did this didn't want Delgado to talk. That person manipulated my trial. Manipulated justice for Crystal Jones. Manipulated *me*. So, hell yes, this is my fight.'

Paige nodded, moved. 'Then we should make sure that nothing goes south.'

'Coming back to the body in the tub,' Stevie said. 'If the person who killed Elena also did Sandoval and Delgado to shut them up, what's with the mirror? "*Paid in full. RIP Elena.*" Makes it look like someone on Elena's team did it out of revenge.'

Paige shrugged. 'It's no secret in the neighborhood that Ramon's family hated Jorge Delgado. They've already had one fight that ended in Delgado's being forced out of town. Why not frame one of the Muñoz brothers for this? It worked the first time.'

'It's a theory,' Stevie allowed. 'The hit itself looked professional.'

'It was too formal,' Grayson said thoughtfully.

'The hit?' Stevie asked and he shook his head.

'That, too. But I meant the message on the mirror.'

Paige remembered his words. *Paid in full*, she'd said. *I know*, he'd replied.

'It said "*Pago del saldo*",' he said. 'That's a more formal way to say "paid". If one of the Muñoz brothers had done this in a fit of anger, I'd think they'd say something more direct, like simply "*Pago*", or an insult. "*Pago del saldo*" is . . . almost respectful.'

Stevie blinked at him. 'After all these years . . . I didn't know you spoke Spanish.'

He looked uncomfortable. 'I don't advertise it. Sometimes it's nice to have people think no one can understand what they say. They say a whole lot more.'

'Huh. Just when you think you know somebody . . . Look, I have to get back, so let's take care of the incidentals.' Stevie held out her hand. 'Gun.'

Grayson took his from his pocket and handed it to her, grip first. Stevie sniffed it and handed it back. 'Last time you shot it?' she asked.

'A month ago, at the range with my brother Joseph. Permit to carry up to date.'

'Okay.' She looked at Paige pointedly. 'You're carrying?' Paige nodded and Stevie extended her hand over the seat, making Peabody growl.

'Easy,' Paige told him. She took the Glock from her shoulder holster. 'Glock. Hasn't been fired in two weeks. Firing range near Hopkins.' She reached behind her and pulled out her .357 with the two-inch barrel. 'Smith and Wesson AirLite.'

133

'Nice.' Stevie tested it in her palm. 'I've been eyeing one of these.'

'Fits anywhere.' Paige drew her knee to her chest and released the side snap on her right boot, withdrawing another AirLite. 'They were having a sale,' she said dryly when Grayson's brows lifted.

Stevie sniffed them, checked cylinders and clips, then handed them back. 'Permit?'

'Of course. There's a copy in my backpack as well as the one on file with Maryland State Police. You want to see the knives too? I've got five.'

'Not necessary,' Stevie said. 'You're remarkably well armed, Paige. Why?'

'I was attacked last summer. Shot, along with my friend.' Paige waited for the tightness in her chest to ease. But it didn't. 'Thea died. I almost did.'

Stevie looked sympathetic. 'I'm sorry about your friend. But this is the kind of thing I want you to prepare yourself for. The suits will grill you about that night. They'll have you relive every moment and they probably won't be gentle about it. You're producing evidence that possibly implicates cops. That's a big hairy deal.'

Paige systematically checked the safeties on each of her guns before reholstering, preparing herself to recount her assault yet again. It never got easier. 'You need to understand one more thing then. Especially you, Grayson, considering your career may be on the line.' She met his eyes. 'Last summer, back in Minneapolis . . . Thea and I were attacked by a group of four men. Two of them were cops.'

A muscle twitched in his cheek. She could see the furious questions in his eyes, but all he asked was, 'Did you get them?'

'Not really. Three got away. One of them attacked me a second time. He broke into my house the night I got out of the hospital. Tried to finish the job.' Peabody made a rough noise and Paige realized she was clutching his neck too tightly. She released him immediately, stroking him instead. 'I had a knife under my pillow.'

'Did you kill him?' Grayson asked, his voice steady.

'No. I wanted to. I got him in the side, but not deep enough to stop him. I was too weak. He didn't know my friend was staying with me. She's a cop. Real light sleeper. She woke up when he cursed me for stabbing him, found his hands around my throat.'

'She killed him?' Stevie asked, and Paige's mouth curved bitterly.

'No, but she wanted to, too. Liv followed procedure. Yelled "Police" and everything. Got him off me and kept him on the floor until backup came. The next day, our other friend Brie gave me Peabody. Brie used to be a cop too. Now she trains police dogs. The two of them took me to the shooting range and I killed a lot of paper targets. Then we had major mojitos and they let me cry. After I'd sobered up, I bought the guns.'

'And the knives?' Stevie asked.

'I had those before. I'm trained in weaponry. I can knock you on your ass with a staff, break your neck with nunchucks, carve you into pieces with a knife. But a gun trumps all of the above.' She rubbed her shoulder. 'I know from experience.'

'I guess so,' Stevie murmured. 'Your hesitancy to trust a cop enough to reveal Elena's evidence made sense before. It makes more sense now. It's a wonder you're even talking to me.'

'My best friends back home are cops. I know there are good ones. I hope to heaven you're one of them.'

'I hope for your sake that I'm better than good.' She glanced at Grayson who was way too quiet. His face was dark, his fury a tangible thing. 'The suits will ask you why the cops did it,' she told Paige. 'They may insinuate you were to blame.'

'I know. I'll tell them the same thing I told the cops back home. The truth. It's all documented. They won't even need to ask me. But they will. They always do.'

'And for that I'm sorry. It's hell to relive the moment again and again. What's the name of your cop friend? The one who was with you the night of the second attack?'

'Detective Olivia Hunter. She's Homicide.'

'Okay. I've got to get back. I'll be in touch.' With a backward wave Stevie was out of the car, leaving Paige and Grayson alone.

The car was silent again, the only sound the rain steadily drumming on the roof. Paige rubbed Peabody's head, dreading the question even as she knew that he needed to ask and she needed to answer. 'Ask,' she said. 'Get it over with.'

'Who did it?' He hesitated, then released a weary breath. 'And why?'

Tuesday, April 5, 7.30 P.M.

'Adele? I'm home!' Darren called. 'Are you here?'

Standing in the kitchen, Adele Shaffer braced herself as the dog barked a frantic welcome. *Tell him.* It had been Dr Theopolis's advice. *It's the stress of living as a person separate from yourself that's causing your paranoia. Just like before.*

Just like before, when she'd spent six weeks in a psychiatric hospital because she'd tried to kill herself. Before somebody else could. That 'somebody' had been nobody back then. Just her soul crying out for retribution. For acknowledgement.

For justice. But there was no justice then and she'd come to terms with that.

At least she'd thought she had. Theopolis didn't seem to agree. Adele knew he was right. Why else would she be so paranoid? So delusional? Why else would she be thinking someone was trying to *kill* her, for God's sake?

'In the kitchen,' she called. 'Rusty, stop that barking.'

Darren came in the kitchen, Allie squealing happily on his hip and Rusty following at his heels, happily wagging his whole wiener-dog body. 'I was worried about you two,' he said. 'I called all afternoon and you never answered your cell or the home phone.'

Tell him. But where did she start? *Hey, Darren, my life's been a lie and now I've got paranoid delusions. You want Stove Top or potatoes with dinner?* Hardly.

'I turned off the ringer,' Adele lied. 'I had a terrible headache when I came home.'

'Must be this rain. Lots of people at work had headaches. How was your meeting?'

'It went well.' *Tell him, Adele. For all that's holy, tell him.* She opened the oven to check on the chicken, pushing Rusty out of the way. Stupid dog would eat anything not tied down. 'She ordered three rooms, just like I'd designed them.'

'Fantastic. We should celebrate. Why don't I get a sitter for Allie and I'll take you to that Indian place you've been asking about.'

'No,' she said, so quickly that he blinked. 'It's just . . .' *That I'm afraid to leave my house.* 'I still have a headache. I took some aspirin, so can we do it a different night?'

'Sure. Go put your feet up and watch TV. I can feed Allie and finish dinner.'

She hugged him hard. 'I don't deserve you.' Adele went to the living room, stopping by the little table near the door where she'd put the day's mail. And she frowned. There was a box there that wasn't there before. 'Darren? Where did this box come from?'

'It was on the porch when I came in. Looked like it came from one of your clients.'

Adele stared at the box while her heart beat wildly. Tentatively she picked it up. It wasn't that heavy. She held it to her ear. Not ticking.

'Silly,' Darren said behind her. He produced a kitchen knife. 'Open it.'

Her hands trembled as she cut the shipping box open, revealing a smaller, foil-wrapped box inside. She lifted the lid, terrified of what she'd see.

Then she let out her breath. 'Chocolates,' she murmured.

'Mmm. Truffles.' He reached for one and she smacked his hand lightly.

'You'll spoil your dinner.'

He laughed. 'You're such a mom since Allie was born. I remember a time that box would have been inhaled, no matter what time of day. Who are they from?'

'No card.' Adele checked the outer box. 'Trammell and Trammell. I did their lobby six months ago. Why send chocolates now? It's not a holiday.'

'Maybe you got them by mistake.' He frowned, tipping up her chin. 'Go sit. You're looking even paler. I'll bring dinner to you.'

'Okay.' Adele sat on the sofa and put the box of truffles on the end table. She turned on the TV, mainly to make Darren happy. She was changing channels when her finger paused. There was the woman from this morning. The one who'd jumped like Wonder Woman. Adele's eyes widened.

Holy shit. She was being attacked. Unable to look away, Adele watched to the end, breathing a sigh of relief when they said the woman was okay. *Glad I'm not her.*

Eight

Grayson had asked her to move to the front seat, but Paige had declined, saying she needed the physical space. Based on the way she clung to the dog, he suspected it was more the emotional space she needed.

'I taught self-defense,' she began. 'In Minneapolis. Most of my students were women, most had abusive spouses. A few were victims of random violence.'

He'd put that much together on his own. 'Who was Thea?'

'One of my students. She was afraid to leave her husband, but she had a sister who convinced her to learn to defend herself.'

'Did she ever leave him?'

'Eventually. She got a job at the women's center. Her husband gave her an ultimatum – quit or get out. She shocked him by moving in with her sister. Time passed, then one night he tried to grab her when she was walking from the women's center to her car. He'd been leaving notes in her mailbox, ordering her home.'

'Why didn't she report him?' Grayson asked quietly, although he already knew.

'He was a cop. She was afraid no one would believe her, or worse, that there would be retaliation. In the end, she was right. The first time I saw him grab her we'd just finished class. I restrained him, threatened to report him if he didn't leave. He did.'

'Did you report him anyway?' he asked.

'No. I was going to, but she begged me not to. Promised she would do it herself. I believed her. And I have to live with that, because she didn't report him and he tried again a week later. She was outside her sister's house, but her sister screamed and scared him off, then filed for a restraining order.'

'What happened?'

'We heard that her husband was facing disciplinary action by the department because of the TRO. She was scared, but what can you do? We went on as usual. I'd taught class that last night. Everyone was gone except Thea and me. I heard them break in, dialed 911 on my cell, dropped it in my pocket. The operator heard it all.'

Her hands clenched and unclenched as she maintained an outward calm. But the look of raw panic in her eyes when she'd begged him not to hold her down in the garage flashed in his mind and he dreaded what he was about to hear.

'There were four of them?' He'd wanted to ask gently, but his tone came out harsh.

'Yes. But it's not what you're thinking. They didn't rape me.' She blew out a breath as his shoulders sagged in relief. 'The four guys wore masks. One of them had Thea, had a gun to her head. I knew it was her husband.'

'He planned to kill his wife?'

'I don't know. To this day, I don't know. He definitely wanted to scare her. And discredit me. He told his friends to "show the black belt a thing or two".'

Grayson swallowed back the anger. 'Like you said to Bashears outside the ER.'

'Yes. The men had drawn straws on who got to attack first. It was a big joke to them. Thea was so scared.' Her voice cracked then, broke. 'I can still see her, staring at me. Begging me to do something. To help her. But I didn't help her.'

She was trembling, one hand pressed to her shoulder. 'I couldn't help her.' Her voice had become ragged. 'I couldn't even help myself. And I have to live with that, too.'

To hell with space. He got out of the car and opened her door, pulling her out and into his arms. He guided her hands to his back, under his coat. 'Hold on to me and breathe.'

He wrapped his coat around her, laying his cheek on her head to shelter her from the rain. And camera lenses or, God help them, snipers' scopes. She held on tight. He held on tighter.

And admitted that he needed to hold her as much as she needed to be held. There was a loneliness in this woman that called to him. Because he was lonely too.

'I'm sorry,' she mumbled against him.

'Hush,' he murmured, stroking his hand down her hair. 'You're fine.' He looked around, conscious of the danger of standing out in the open, wishing he were just being paranoid and knowing he wasn't. 'We can't stand here. Get back in the car.'

She got in the backseat and kept her head down until he'd pulled away from the parking lot. 'What next?' she asked.

'Same song, second verse. We find out who killed Crystal Jones.'

Tuesday, April 5, 8.10 P.M.

Silas lowered his rifle as Grayson Smith drove away. He looked down at his shaking hands. He'd had Paige in his sights for a brief moment.

But he hadn't been able to pull the trigger. He'd seen them drive up to Delgado's house as he was driving away. He'd followed them here, to this burger joint, waiting for his clear shot. He'd failed this morning. He needed to make that right. Regain trust.

But Paige had stayed down. *Smart girl*. That they'd brought in the cop dismayed him on too many levels. When his employer found out, it would be far worse. Hopefully the man had a Plan B, or they were all going down.

Silas calmed himself. His employer always had a Plan B, as did Silas.

That's how Silas himself had become entangled with the man, after all. His employer had been Silas's Plan B. *Now, I'm his. For the rest of my life*.

He'd had a clear shot for a single moment, when Smith had pulled her from the car and into his arms. But the look on her face had shaken him. She'd been so valiant, all day, through everything. But in that moment she'd been devastated. Afraid.

141

Silas's hand had trembled. Then he couldn't take the shot without hitting the prosecutor, too. His employer would have been fine with the collateral damage. But Silas couldn't bring himself to do that, either.

He'd never killed a friend. Not yet. But that might have to change.

He brought out the picture he always carried next to his heart. His little girl smiled out at him, one tooth missing, a smudge of chocolate ice cream on her chin. He rubbed the heel of his hand over his aching heart. Cherri had been five and it had been the Fourth of July, twenty long years ago. The picture was faded now, its edges worn from constant handling.

I miss you, baby. Every damn day of my life.

He slid the photo back in his pocket and flipped open his phone. His baby's baby smiled at him now. Violet had Cherri's smile. He'd keep his granddaughter safe. He'd make sure she never found out the truth.

Even if that meant killing a valiant woman who'd done nothing more than be in the wrong place at the wrong time. Even if that meant killing a friend.

I failed again. At least his employer didn't have to know about this one.

Silas put his rifle back in its case and, shifting his focus to his next assignment, picked up the picture he'd printed from the Internet. Roscoe 'Jesse' James was an ugly sonofabitch who'd taken way too many punches to the head over his fighting career.

James had been arrested many times, but always managed to skate. He was just one lucky sonofabitch. Silas chuckled bitterly. James's luck was about to run out.

Tuesday, April 5, 8.15 P.M.

He lowered his binoculars as Silas drove away. *Busy parking lot tonight*, he thought wryly. He shook a cigarette from the pack and lit it, inhaling deeply.

He'd learned more than he'd planned. He'd learned that Paige

Holden really did know something. He'd learned that they'd called in a cop on the QT. Not good.

It meant they knew cops were involved, otherwise Miss Holden would have handed over whatever she'd found to the police that morning. Mazzetti had been a good choice on their parts. She was . . . untouchable. He should know. He'd tried, long ago. She hadn't taken the bait. She was one of those foul creatures – an honest cop.

He'd also learned that there was definitely something going on between Holden and Smith. He'd figured it after seeing the news, but now he knew for sure. That was especially useful. Smith had a family. Men with families were so . . . easily persuaded.

And finally, he'd learned what he'd actually come for. *Silas is getting soft.* He'd suspected it for some time. He'd followed Silas, to find out for sure. That he'd balked over killing Roscoe James was bad enough. That Silas looked ill after leaving Delgado's house was worse. But then he'd had Holden and Smith in his sights and he'd choked.

The boy needs a refresher course. That would be easy enough to provide. And if the refresher didn't work, he had no compunction in following through with his threat.

Now he needed to decide what to do about Holden and Smith. He considered briefly, then made his decision and took out his phone.

The call was immediately picked up. 'Well?'

'The cops are involved now,' he said.

'You *said* you'd fixed it so they'd never find out.'

'Well, unfortunately they did. We always knew positioning Ramon Muñoz to take the blame wasn't guaranteed. We need to move to our alternate plan.'

There was a long, tense silence. 'Damn that bitch. She should have left it alone.'

He wasn't sure if the reference was to Elena or Crystal Jones. 'Are you agreed?'

'Yes.' The word was bitten out. 'Do what you have to do. Just fix it.'

The connection was abruptly broken, leaving him staring at his phone. 'I always do.'

Tuesday, April 5, 9.00 P.M.

Paige was quiet as she walked Peabody up to her apartment. Grayson stayed a step behind to cover her. He'd walk her dog once she was safely inside.

He was on alert, listening for the smallest noise. But the stairwell was empty and by the second flight he found his eyes straying to the view provided by the skintight pants she wore. From this angle he could see the shadow of her glutes flexing with every step she took. That she wore three guns and five knives under all those clothes made the overall picture even more appealing.

When they got to her front door, his focus was shifted jarringly back to her safety. She'd taken every precaution, he thought grimly. Third-floor unit, steel door, three new deadbolts. Not to mention a large dog and a veritable arsenal on her person. That she felt she needed all those precautions made him angry all over again.

'The deadbolts are probably overkill,' she said quietly, 'but it makes me feel better.'

'Then it's not overkill,' he said, and a smile tipped her lips.

Once they were inside, she locked the three deadbolts, then dropped her backpack on an old-fashioned secretary desk. 'Make yourself comfortable,' she said and went to the kitchen, leaving him to study her apartment, surprised.

He'd expected a sleekly modern look. Instead, she'd surrounded herself with brightly painted antiques that made him think of lederhosen and cuckoo clocks.

A large antique-looking pie safe dominated one wall in her living room, again surprising him. Her place had an old-time, prairie feel that he wouldn't have paired with the woman he knew. But oddly, it suited her. It was comfortable. Homey. He sat on her sofa, relieved to find it comfortable as well. He'd be able to sleep here. His eye drifted down the hall to what was most certainly her bedroom. Her bed would be a hell of a lot more comfortable than the sofa. But once he got there, he wouldn't sleep.

And neither would she.

The buzzing in his pants pocket startled him until he remembered he'd never given her back the disposable cell she'd dropped in the garage. 'Your disposable is ringing.'

'It's Clay.' She rushed from the kitchen, her hand outstretched. He tossed her the phone and she flipped it open. 'It's me,' she answered. 'Where are you?'

Her face grew dark and angry. 'What a bitch.' She closed her eyes. 'Yeah, we saw him. He was dead.' She met Grayson's eyes. 'He brought in a cop that he trusts. You recall a Detective Mazzetti? . . . I promise I'll be careful. Call me when you've got Zach.'

'Zach's the one whose mother took him,' Grayson said. 'What's the mother done?'

'She wants ten thousand from Zach's dad for returning their six year old, safe.'

'After all these years, I'm still occasionally stunned at what parents do to their kids.'

Paige shrugged. 'It's the drugs. They'll do anything, say anything for the drugs. Because the reality is that they love themselves and the drugs more than their kids.'

There was a hard yet wistful note to her voice. Grayson had talked to enough kids of addict parents to know he was listening to one right now. He followed her into the kitchen where she was putting a kettle on the stove.

'I'm making tea. Would you like some?'

'Sure.' He leaned against the doorframe, watched her spoon tea into a pot. 'Your décor surprises me. I wouldn't have pictured you as the Little House type.'

Her lips curved fondly. 'My grandfather made the cupboard and my desk. His grandfather made the table. I'm the end of a very long line of Minnesotan Norwegians.'

He laughed. 'You're kidding. Norwegian would have been my last guess.'

Her chin lifted, ever so slightly. 'Because of my hair?'

He moved closer, stroked her hair down her back. 'And your eyes,' he said softly.

Her cheeks heated. 'Blond Norwegians are something of a

stereotype,' she said lightly. 'There are dark ones, too. Just not in my family,' she added ruefully.

'Your mother was blond?'

Her hands stilled on the teacups she'd just taken from the cupboard. 'Yeah.'

'And your father?' He was snooping now, but he wanted to know.

'Don't know,' she said tightly. 'Never met him. Would you like some pie?'

Not the most elegant of subject changes, but he went with it. 'Did you make it?'

She glanced up at him. 'I did. I'm not the chef Brian is, but I make a very good pie.'

'Then, yes, please.' She put two slices in the oven, then returned the rest to the refrigerator. 'Wait. If you keep pie in the fridge, what's in the pie safe in the living room?'

'Come see.' She brushed by him, unzipping her jacket as she went, and he let out a breath. The tight black sweater left very little to the imagination. Mutely he followed, his hands itching to touch.

She opened the pie-safe doors, revealing a tall gun safe inside. 'My friend made it for me for Christmas.' She punched in the combination so quickly he missed it.

Well, that wasn't exactly true. He missed it because he'd been staring at her breasts and he thought she was very aware of that fact. 'Your friend is a carpenter?'

'No, he's a firefighter. But David does a little bit of everything on the side.' Paige pointed to a framed photo on a shelf. 'That's him.'

He studied the photo, hating the jealousy that instantly rose within him. The man standing next to Paige could have been a model. Together they made a beautiful couple. Both wore *gis* and black belts.

'He's a black belt, too.'

Of course he was.

'David's married to my best friend Olivia,' she said, and he felt better as the jealousy melted away.

'The friend who stopped the guy who came back,' he said, and her eyes shuttered.

'Yes.' She checked her watch with a grimace. 'I was supposed to call her two hours ago to let her know I'm okay. She worries. I hate that she feels she has to.'

'Did you introduce them?'

'No, she met David through her family. I met him through my old *dojo*.' She removed the shoulder holster. 'He was my *uke* when I taught my self-defense classes.'

'What's an *uke*?' he asked.

She unloaded her Glock and placed it in the safe. 'An *uke* is the receiver in martial arts. He let my students practice on him. He had a way of making them feel at ease.'

'You miss him.'

She dropped to one knee and loosened her boots enough to remove the small pistol she'd concealed. 'Every day. He and Olivia and Brie are my best friends.'

'Where was he the night of your attack?'

She put the small gun in the safe. 'On his honeymoon. He and Olivia cut their trip short the moment they heard.'

'Why did you leave Minneapolis? If your friends are there, why come here?'

Her jaw tightened, her hand stilling on the safe's door. 'I was suffocating.'

The teakettle whistled and she closed the gun safe before hurrying to the kitchen. He noticed she'd kept the small pistol holstered at her back. He wondered if she always felt the need to be armed in her own home or if today was especially terrifying.

He had a feeling it was the first one. Which made him wonder what, or who, it would take to make her feel safe again.

Tuesday, April 5, 9.20 P.M.

Paige dialed Olivia on her cell phone as she turned off the burner under the kettle. She braced herself for another tirade and once again, was not disappointed.

147

'You never call, never write,' Olivia said sarcastically.

'I'm fine,' she said, forcing her voice to at least sound calm. Being around Grayson Smith was making her edgy.

'How many stitches?' Olivia asked and Paige knew she'd seen the garage video.

'Fifteen.'

Olivia sighed. 'Did they catch the bastard?'

'Not yet. And frankly I've been a little too busy to even worry about it.'

There was a long, long pause. 'What the hell is going on there, Paige?'

Paige rubbed her forehead and told it all again, from Maria hiring her, to Delgado.

'I can be there tomorrow,' Olivia said. 'Noah's already said he can cover our caseload and David's all but bought plane tickets for me and Brie.'

Just hearing their names made Paige so homesick her stomach hurt. Noah was Olivia's partner and his wife Eve had been one of Paige's best students. And having Olivia and Brie here . . . it would have been like old times.

Except not. If she could go back to the time before last summer, she would have in a heartbeat. But all Paige could see was the worry in her friends' eyes. It was one of the many things that had been suffocating her. 'Not yet. I'll let you know if I need you.'

'No, you won't,' Olivia said harshly. 'Because you turtle. You've been turtling for nine goddamn months. You pull your head back under your shell and shut us all out. Why won't you let me help you?'

Olivia was right. Didn't mean Paige knew how to fix it. 'I'm okay. I've got help.'

'The prosecutor. I could *see* that he was helping.'

Paige's cheeks burned. 'If he hadn't been there, I wouldn't have gotten away.'

'Fifteen stitches. I saw the tape. Why didn't you tell me about him?'

There was hurt in her friend's voice that Paige wouldn't have put there for the world. 'I just met him today and that's the truth.'

'Oh. That's . . . I'm not sure what that is.'

'Me either,' she said, turning to find Grayson at the window, looking at the parking lot through the blinds. He still wore a suit, although he'd tugged the tie loose. His coat had to have been custom-made, his shoulders too broad for off the rack. He stood still, a fine tension around him. He was ready. For what she wasn't certain.

Unfortunately she was ready too. And she knew exactly for what.

'Just don't rush into anything,' Olivia said, as if reading her thoughts.

'I'm not stupid, Liv,' she whispered. 'I've stayed on the Waiting for Mr Right Express for eighteen fucking months. I'm not going to jump ship today.' *Maybe tomorrow, but not today.*

'Or eighteen no-fucking months, as it were,' Olivia said dryly, then sighed. 'I just want you to be okay. We all do. We're scared and we feel helpless.'

'And I love you all for it. Truly. I'll call you tomorrow. I promise.'

'If you don't, I'm buying those plane tickets. Is the prosecutor with you now?'

'Yes.' He'd left the window and was back in the kitchen where he watched her, a frown line bisecting his forehead. She wanted to smooth it away but didn't trust herself to touch. He was too much, too soon. And when he held her it felt too damn good. 'I'm safe,' she told Olivia. 'I have to go, but I will call if I need you. You have my word.' She hung up and met Grayson's avidly curious stare. 'My friends worry. It makes me crazy.'

'Doesn't your family worry?'

She took their pie from the oven and slipped by him to put it on the table. 'My grandparents raised me and they're both gone. So it's just friends left to worry. Come and eat some of this pie so I don't feel so guilty for eating dessert instead of dinner.'

He looked like he had more questions, but asked no more. 'It smells good.'

'Tastes better. Can you get my backpack? I'd like to work on that trial transcript.'

'I can start on the files, Paige. You need to sleep.'

She shook her head. 'I can't sleep. I close my eyes and see Delgado. And Elena. The hours are slipping away. I need to do something.'

'Then let's start looking at Crystal Jones. But first let's eat. I didn't know I was hungry until I smelled the pie.'

And I didn't know how much I'd missed a man's touch until you held me. Now she wanted more. A lot more. And that could be worse for her than eating dessert for dinner.

Tuesday, April 5, 9.35 P.M.

Grayson took the Muñoz file from his gym bag, leaving the file Daphne had compiled on Paige. He'd look at it later, when Paige was asleep.

The trial transcript sat on the table in front of her, a spiral notebook next to it. She'd already filled several pages of the notebook with shorthand, surprising him.

'Why do you know shorthand?' he asked.

'I was a paralegal for several years. I transcribed depositions and did some low-key investigation.' She waited a beat. 'I even worked for the defense for a while.'

He wasn't as surprised as she apparently thought he'd be. 'Were they *all* innocent?'

'Hell, no. They were all guilty as sin. I didn't work for that law office for long.'

'Did you ever work for the prosecution?'

'No. I worked for a family law firm, doing a lot of the same things for them that I do for Clay. Taking pictures of cheating spouses, et cetera.'

'Did you ever think about going to law school?'

'Only every day at the beginning. But that required money for university and I could only afford community college.' She tapped the transcript. 'Just like Crystal Jones.'

'Your avoidance of my questions is improving,' he said.

Her glance was rueful, then she sobered as she began to read from her notes. '"Crystal Jones, age twenty, went to a party on the night of September 18. She was discovered the next morning in the garden shed by one of the gardeners – not Ramon, who had not yet arrived to work. Crystal had been stabbed three times and there were ligature marks around her throat. Her dress was pulled up to her waist, her upper body exposed."'

'They did a rape kit,' Grayson said. 'No sign of sexual assault.'

'At least there's that,' she said, then continued reading. '"Crystal attended community college where she majored in Business, but was also auditing a political science class at Georgetown University where she met her date for that night, Rex McCloud, a senior at Georgetown."'

'Ah, Rex McCloud,' Grayson murmured. 'Grandson of retired State Senator James McCloud. As soon as the word "Senator" popped up, the powers-that-be ducked for cover. It was like walking through a damn minefield, every day.'

'The transcript doesn't say much about Rex,' she observed carefully.

'The cops cleared him early, so we were asked to tread lightly for the family's sake.'

'Special treatment?' she asked.

'Yes and no. There are a few powers-that-be that count on the McClouds for political support, and naturally they wanted to shield them from any "unpleasantness". If Rex had been a person of interest I would have grilled him. But he wasn't.'

'Then,' she said.

'Then,' he agreed. He consulted his own notes. 'Crystal told Rex that her name was Amber and that she was a full-time Georgetown student, too. He realized she'd been lying to him after she was killed, that she had just wanted an entrée to his party. Apparently Rex's parties were legendary among his crowd.'

'Sex, drugs, and rock 'n' roll?'

'Mostly sex and drugs,' Grayson replied dryly. 'Any rock 'n' roll was just for show. Rex insisted that if the partygoers were doing drugs, he didn't see it.'

'Did you believe him?'

'No, but I wasn't prosecuting him on drug charges. I was prosecuting Ramon Muñoz for murder. Rex was drinking that night, said he'd lost track of Crystal. He assumed she'd left because he'd been fooling around with some of the other guests.'

'Where were the adults during all this partying?' Paige asked with a frown.

'Technically Rex was an adult. He was twenty-one at the time. Rex's mother was out of town on business. His stepfather said he'd taken a sleeping pill. His grandparents said they "retired early". Didn't hear a thing.'

She looked skeptical. 'How could they not know that sex, drugs and rock 'n' roll was happening in their own backyard?'

'It's a big estate. The pool's a fair distance from the house, so it's possible they didn't hear. It's more likely that they chose not to know. Rex was wild and his mother seemed absentee. Stepdad seemed like a nonentity in the family. The grandparents may have felt unable – or unwilling – to control him.'

She frowned, considering. 'I read up on the McClouds.'

The way she said it gave him pause. 'Why?'

She looked him in the eye. 'Because Rex was barely mentioned in the transcript even though he was Crystal's date for the night, and because I find it difficult to believe that somebody on the estate didn't know what was going on at that party.'

'Rex had an alibi,' he said mildly.

She shrugged. 'Alibis can be bought if you're rich enough. The McClouds are.'

He leaned back in his chair, studying her. He'd verified Rex's alibi himself, because he'd thought the same thing. But he was interested in the conclusions she'd obviously drawn and how she'd arrived at them. 'So you read up. What did you find?'

The look she gave him said she knew he was indulging her. 'The McClouds have a buttload of money, originally made in coal. They still own mines in western Maryland and are stockholders in several public utilities, here and in Europe. They give a lot of money to charity and started the McCloud Foundation in the early eighties. They do fundraising, matching donors to causes, that kind of thing.

The senator retired from his senate seat after thirty years in 2000, planning to play golf every day, but a mild stroke a year later left one hand too weak to hold the club.'

Grayson blinked. 'How do you know the part about golf?'

'James McCloud gave a commencement speech the year after the stroke and mentioned it as a means of preparing the graduates for life's little disappointments.' She checked her notes. 'He has two daughters, Claire by his first wife, who is deceased, and Reba by his current wife, Dianna. His daughters run the businesses and non-profits now. Claire makes the money and Reba gives it away.'

'Claire is Rex's mother,' Grayson said. 'I met her briefly when we were interviewing Rex about the party and his whereabouts. She was . . . intense. A real control freak. Rex was terrified of her. So was her husband – what was his name?'

'Louis Delacorte. Claire's grown the business every year since the nineties. Unfortunately Louis doesn't have her Midas touch. He used to be a bigwig in the McClouds' European business division, but was dismissed when their profits took a dive. He was given a position in the non-profit foundation, reporting to Reba.'

'They put him where he couldn't hurt anything,' Grayson said.

'Essentially. A few colleagues were anonymously quoted as saying that Louis was caught having an affair with a young blonde in Europe and that's why he was reassigned. They also said that he drinks and he's surly. He has a record for misdemeanor assault. Bar brawl here in Baltimore.'

'True,' he said, impressed with her thoroughness. 'He has a history of violence.'

'So had Ramon not been accused, both Rex and Louis might have been suspects.'

'Perhaps Louis. He did have an alibi, but it was the word of one of the servants. Rex's alibi was strong. I verified it myself. Assuming Ramon's innocence, Crystal's killer could have been a party guest.'

She'd frowned at his insistence of Rex's alibi, but didn't push it further. 'No guest list for the party was entered as evidence according to the transcript.'

'There wasn't a guest list *per se*. It was one of those parties that if you knew about it, you were invited. Rex gave the police enough names to establish his alibi.'

'Who were the names? Other partiers doing drugs?'

'Some, yes. Ultimately, though, it was the security video that confirmed his alibi and cleared him. He never left the pool. Not once during the entire evening.'

'I thought he was fooling around with some of the other guests,' she said, and when Grayson lifted his brows, she made a face. 'Oh, yuck. In front of everybody? On camera?'

'Verification of which was *not* one of the highlights of my career. At any rate, the cops didn't dig that deeply into the other party attendees. Everything pointed to Ramon.'

'The defense never said that no other leads were followed. This was a wild party where anything could and did happen. They should have tried for reasonable doubt.'

'They did, via Ramon's alibi. They tried to break Sandoval and Delgado, but they stuck with their story. We had DNA from Ramon's hair found on the body, the weapon with his prints and her blood, found in his closet. It was a slam dunk. Or so we thought.'

'Elena said she and Ramon wanted his attorney to introduce the theory of evidence tampering. They wanted to accuse the cops, but the attorney wouldn't allow it.'

'I would have said the same thing had I been his attorney,' Grayson said. 'Saying the cops planted evidence is sure to turn the jury against your client. It's so . . .'

'So OJ,' Paige muttered. 'I know. That's what I told Maria and Elena. But "Cops. Chasing me" kind of changed my mind.'

'You need to open your mind to the fact that, assuming Ramon was innocent, the evidence could have been manipulated by anyone. It didn't have to be the cops.'

She frowned. 'The cops had Ramon's keys while he was being questioned. They had access to his home. And his closet.'

'Anyone could have broken in.'

'There was no sign of forced entry.'

'Paige,' he said. 'If Clay wanted to get into a place and didn't want to leave a trail, could he?' He'd scored a point, he could see.

'Elena may have been mistaken about who was chasing her. Or maybe she thought saying that would keep you on the case.'

She shrugged. 'Either way, someone killed Crystal and it wasn't Ramon.'

'All right. There was no sign she was dragged into the shed. She entered under her own power, either by choice or by force.'

'What was her blood alcohol level? Had she been drinking?'

He looked through his own file and found the autopsy report. 'Zero point two, so she wasn't anywhere close to drunk. Her tox reports were clear. No drugs in her system.'

'Let me see that report.' She dragged her chair around the table so that she sat closer. Much closer. So close that her scent filled his head, chasing everything else away. So close that when he slid the autopsy report in front of her, his hand brushed her breast. And if he'd said it had been unintentional, he'd have been lying.

For a moment he let himself breathe her in. Let himself look. His hands itched to run themselves over every curve but he flattened his palms on the table, fully intending to keep them there.

Her face was hidden by hair that he knew was as soft as it looked. Indulging himself a little more, he lifted one hand and slid it under her hair. And felt her shudder.

'Did you leave anyone behind in Minnesota?' he asked, very quietly.

She didn't pretend to misunderstand. 'No. No one.'

He massaged the base of her skull, gratified at her soft hum. He wondered what sounds she'd make if he massaged somewhere else. 'You need to sleep,' he said.

'In a little while.' She rolled her head, meeting his gaze, and again he let himself stare. And want. Her cheeks grew flushed, her eyelids heavy, and he knew she wanted too. But before he could say anything more, she looked away, straightening in her chair, the moment gone. 'The autopsy says cause of death was the stabbing.'

'Three times,' he said. 'She was strangled beforehand.'

'This also cites inflammation in the bronchial pathways and in the eyes and mouth.'

'Because she was pepper-sprayed. The ME testified to that. It just made Ramon look worse then, that she'd tried to fight back and he'd used pepper spray on her.'

'I read that in the transcript. But no pepper spray was found at the scene.'

'No. Either her assailant brought it and took it with him, or she brought it and it was taken from her. Why?'

'I don't know. Do you have crime-scene photos?'

Intrigued, he handed her the police report. 'Where are you going with this?'

'I don't know. I'm just thinking about her, that night. She goes to a lot of trouble to meet Rex McCloud and get invited to a party where everyone's drinking and doing God knows what, but she doesn't get drunk. Instead she goes to the shed.'

'CSU said her attacker came at her from behind, that he was taller by at least six inches based on the angle of the ligature marks around her throat. That fit Ramon.'

'Along with half the men in town. Okay, so she walks into the shed, he comes from behind and strangles her. She fights, maybe takes out her pepper spray . . .' She frowned and leafed through the police report until she came to the crime-scene photos. 'Her dress is pulled up to her waist. What was she wearing that night?'

It was Grayson's turn to frown. 'What does it matter what she was wearing?'

She glanced up at him. 'Not because her dress sent out "rape me" vibes. I'm wondering where she hid the pepper spray. Her dress doesn't look like it has pockets.'

'You're assuming it was *her* pepper spray.'

'It's not usually something a man carries, but it *is* something a woman carries.'

'Do you carry it?'

'Always. I didn't have it on me today because I was in the courthouse. I carry it in my backpack unless I feel unsafe. Then I stick it in my bra so it's on my person. This dress looks tiny and the way it bunched, was probably very tight. I don't think she could have fit even a lipstick-tube pepper spray on her. She had to have had a purse.'

He frowned again, mostly because his mind instantly conjured the picture of Paige wearing nothing but a bra. 'Did Crystal have a purse? I can't remember.'

'The report doesn't list one among the items found at the scene. She would have had a phone and credit cards. She'd need a purse for all that.'

'We ran her financials. Her credit cards were maxed out and she had no cash in the bank before the party, so maybe she didn't have credit cards. She didn't have a cell phone, not one that was traceable anyway.'

'She'd have car keys or cash or a bus ticket. Some way to get home. And a girl doesn't go to a party without at least lipstick. She had to have a purse. Whether the pepper spray was in it is a different question.'

'Why is that important?'

'Because if she went to the party to play, she'd have played. She didn't play. She stayed pretty sober and had pepper spray with her. She was prepared for something.'

'Like?'

'Hell, I don't know. She was financially strapped, right? Maybe she was planning to steal something from the rich people at the party. Maybe she knew about the drugs and sex and planned to blackmail them, or maybe even sell to them.' She paused. 'Wait. She had no cash in the bank?'

'Less than fifty dollars. Why?'

'Because she paid to audit that class at Georgetown and that's not cheap. Why would she have paid? Why not just meet Rex in the cafeteria and lie about being a student? She was living paycheck to paycheck. Why spend her money to audit?'

He blinked. 'I don't know. Maybe she was afraid he'd check up on her.'

'Maybe. This makes her reason for going to the party even more important. She didn't just lie to Rex, she spent a few hundred bucks to be near him. Then she didn't stay near him, but went to the shed. Why?'

'The note found near her body said, "*Gardener's shed, midnight.*" Signed "*RM*".'

'Ramon Muñoz,' she murmured. 'Or Rex McCloud.'

'Which was why I watched all that video of drunk, naked people having sex in the swimming pool. I needed to be sure Rex hadn't left the party at the time of the murder. I didn't want to rock the political boat if I didn't have to. It would have been a hassle for nothing and would have made it harder the next time I really needed to rock the boat.'

Plus, he'd known Ramon was guilty. *And I didn't look as deep as I should have.* The admission shook him. Shamed him. Paige watched him steadily and he got the uncomfortable feeling she knew that.

'Did you see Crystal on the video?' she asked.

'No. She never got in the pool and the camera was focused on the pool area. Rex McCloud never left.'

'Do you still have the video?'

'Not me personally. It may be saved on the server downtown. I can get it for you if you want to check for yourself.' He heard the defensiveness in his own voice.

She met his eyes, having heard it too. 'I believe you about Rex. And Crystal. I want to see who else was at the party. There's no ID listed among the items found with her body. She told Rex her name was Amber. How did they ID her as Crystal Jones?'

'They ran her prints. She had a record. Mostly little stuff like shoplifting, but there was one prostitution charge, when she was barely eighteen.'

Paige had started to yawn, but blinked instead. 'The defense didn't mention that.'

'They tried, but I had it suppressed during pre-trial. Crystal was the victim. Even if she'd lured Ramon to the shed to sell a trick, she didn't deserve to be murdered.' His voice had gone hard. 'Her previous bad acts had no bearing on this case.'

'Good for you.' She nodded sleepily. 'I hate it when they blame the victim.'

'Tomorrow I'll get the party video. I have to locate the guests, question them to find out if anyone knew why Crystal came to the party. You're right. If she'd come to have fun, she would have. She was there for another reason. For now, go to sleep.'

'I think I will. Would you mind walking Peabody before you leave?'

'I'll walk Peabody, but I'm not going anywhere. I'll sleep on the sofa.'

For a long moment he thought she'd argue. Instead she sighed. 'I don't want to need you to guard me. But I'm not going to be too stubborn to accept help. I need to sleep and I won't if I'm alone. Thank you. For everything today. For staying.'

'Lock up behind me. I'll knock when Peabody's ready to come back inside.'

Nine

'Another, please.' Silas pointed to his empty glass and the bartender nodded.

Next to him sat Roscoe 'Jesse' James who stared balefully into his drink, the picture of a man who wanted to get drunk and be left alone.

Sorry, pal. Tonight you die.

There was a goose egg on James's skull, most likely courtesy of Grayson Smith's briefcase. Smith was built like a damn tank. James had to have one hell of a headache.

The bartender slid another drink his way. Silas did a quick swish with the hollow stirrer that held about a quarter ounce of Rohypnol. Now he just had to wait for the right time to switch the glasses. The way Roscoe was gulping them down, it wouldn't take long for him to be out like a light.

Silas's family phone buzzed in his pocket. He'd call his wife back later. He had to stay focused. He had to stay alert.

He got his chance a moment later when the bartender had to break up a fight at the other end of the bar. Roscoe and everyone else looked. In seconds, the glasses were switched. Roscoe blindly grabbed for his glass, not taking his eyes off the fight.

It was the fighting that the man was addicted to, Silas understood. Not the booze. The booze just deadened the disappointment. He glanced at the puddle near his foot, the remnants of his own first glass, dumped so that no one would realize he wasn't drinking too.

He needed to stay sharp until Roscoe was dead. He'd deaden his own disappointment later.

Tuesday, April 5, 11.00 P.M.

Adele stood over Allie's crib, watching her baby breathe. *I'd cut off my arm before I'd hurt you. But what if I am losing it again? What if I did something to you?*

'Adele?' Darren whispered from behind her and she stiffened.

'You were snoring,' she lied, injecting a smile into her voice.

He wrapped his arms around her waist. 'You haven't been yourself. What's wrong, honey?' He hesitated. 'Are you sick?'

Yes. Yes. Yes. 'No,' she soothed. 'Nothing like that.'

'Then what?' he persisted. 'Is there . . . Is there someone else?'

Stunned, Adele turned to stare up at him. 'No. Oh, my God, no. Darren . . . *no*.'

He shuddered out a relieved breath. 'I was so scared. Please tell me what's wrong.'

Adele opened her mouth, trying to find the words, when a light caught her eye. On the street. A car. Black. It slowed to a crawl as it passed her house . . .

And she was *there*. Back *there*. She was twelve years old and it hurt. *God, it hurt.*

Tell a soul and you'll die. No one will believe you anyway. The car slowed to a crawl and the door opened and she was pushed out. Into the dirt. She curled up in a ball and cried. She cried. But nobody came. Nobody helped. Nobody believed.

'Adele?' Darren's hands were on her upper arms, squeezing hard. 'What is it?'

Adele looked out the window. The street was dark. Deserted. Had the car even been there? She burrowed her head into his chest. 'Don't leave me.'

'I won't.' Darren rocked her where they stood. 'I'll never leave you.'

Tuesday, April 5, 11.30 P.M.

Silas rolled his shoulders as he straightened, watching the dark, fast-moving river. Listening for the splash, he nodded when the sound was small. Good. That was done.

With all the rain, the Patuxent River was swollen, the current even faster than normal. With any luck, Roscoe James would be in the Chesapeake by morning. In any event, he wouldn't be washing up on shore. Silas had weighted the body down well.

Exhausted, he got in his van. He'd need to detail it completely. Roscoe had thrown up in the back. Silas had cleaned up most of it, but forensic science was just too good. One speck of puke and they'd be able to connect him to a dead guy.

Silas pulled off the eyebrows and mustache he'd applied before entering the bar. The cheek implants came out next. Even if he'd been caught on the bar's camera, nobody would recognize him. He reached for his business cell to call his employer, relieved when he got voicemail. He didn't want to deal with the bastard. 'It's done,' he said and hung up.

His family cell was next. The list of missed calls in the log made his pulse race. His wife had called five times. She picked up immediately when he dialed.

'Why didn't you call me back?' she cried. 'I've been calling for two hours.'

'I'm sorry,' he said. 'What's wrong? *Tell me*. Is it Violet?'

'Yes. I went in to check on her tonight and her window was open. I'd shut it, I know I did. I set the alarm, too, but the phone's out. I think the wire's been cut.'

Silas's blood turned to ice. 'Is Violet all right?'

'Yes, she's asleep. But Silas, on her nightstand, there was a folded-up hamburger wrapper. From Bertie's Burgers.'

Silas opened his mouth to breathe, but no air would come. *He'd been there.* At the drive-through hamburger place tonight. *He'd seen. He knew I failed again. Oh, God.*

'I'm here,' he managed. 'Did you call the police?'

'Not yet. I wanted to talk to you first.'

'Get a gun from the safe. I'll be home soon.' Silas hung up, but didn't move.

That sonofabitch. The threat had always been dangled. *But to touch my child.* He'd gone too far. Because Violet was his child. She had been from the moment the nurse had laid her in his arms, all wrinkled and pink and yelling at the top of her lungs.

He'd held her, tears streaming down his face as he stared at his own baby girl lying on a hospital bed, covered with blood, eyes wide open. Seeing nothing.

'I'm sorry,' the doctor had said, so sadly. 'We did everything we could.' Then the doctor closed Silas's daughter's eyes and called her time of death.

It had been one minute after his granddaughter's first breath of life.

I'll send you to hell before you touch a hair on her head.

And he knew just how to do it. But it wasn't as simple as a bullet to the head. It never had been, or he would have done it years ago. His employer kept careful records and made it well known that, were he ever to meet with an unfortunate accident, his 'operatives' would be revealed.

And most of us wouldn't last a week in prison.

But the man had crossed the line. *He was in her bedroom. My child's bedroom.* What he might have done . . . The man had to die.

Silas needed those records or his own life was forfeit. There were two ways this could go. Best plan was to force the SOB to give up his records before killing him. Silas and his wife stayed in their home, their child growing up with her friends, none the wiser.

Worst plan was to hide his family, then kill the SOB and let the chips fall where they may. It might mean that he'd be a wanted man for the rest of his life. But his child would be safe. And that was the most important thing.

But today's video, the one that kid took of Holden when the van crashed, had the potential to make him a wanted man regardless of anything else he did. Hiding his family and killing the SOB would then become the only plan. He needed to know if his face had been caught on that video. Tonight.

Wednesday, April 6, 2.30 A.M.

Paige came instantly awake and went completely still. The noise came from the window. Somebody was coming in her window.

Hell no. Not again. Not ever again. She shoved her hand under her pillow, then froze. *It was gone.* The knife was gone. She whipped to her back to try to leap from the bed, but he was there. Holding her down. *Let go. Let me go. I'll kill you.*

'Paige. Wake up.'

She opened her eyes with a jerk. She was sitting up, fists lifted and ready to fight – and a half-naked Grayson Smith had his hands on her shoulders. Peabody snarled and lunged, his teeth bared, but Grayson didn't back away.

'Dammit, Paige, *wake up.*'

There was no one at the window. She'd dreamed it. Again. She relaxed her fists. 'Peabody, down,' she croaked. The dog dropped to his belly, but watched, untrusting.

Wearing only a pair of sweats hung low on his hips, Grayson stood over her, breathing hard. He slowly released her and, hitching his sweatpants a little higher, lowered himself to sit on the edge of her bed. 'You scared the fucking shit out of me. You screamed. It was bloodcurdling. Are you all right?'

No. Her heart raced like a bird's. 'Yes. Of course,' she said and he shook his head.

'Of course you're not. I'm not all right and I only heard you. What did you dream?'

She looked away. 'Same thing I dream every night.'

He shifted his body so that he was looking at her squarely. 'What do you dream?'

'He's always coming through the window and I never have my knife.'

'And he holds you down?'

'Yeah.' She clutched the blanket in her hands so he wouldn't see her tremble.

'Did he break into your women's center through a window?'

'No. Into my house. My bedroom.'

'The second attack,' he said grimly.

'Yeah. The first attack in the women's center . . . they talked about what they'd do once they beat me up. How they'd hold me down and rape me. But they never got a chance. The man in my bedroom . . . he . . . he'd already unzipped his pants.' She glanced up to find his eyes flashing fire. 'But Olivia stopped him and he's in jail now.'

His shoulders visibly relaxed. 'Where every con knows he was a cop?'

'Oh yeah,' Paige said with grim satisfaction. 'I think it's safe to say that he knows how it feels to be held down now.'

He nodded once, hard. 'Good. Can you go back to sleep now?'

No way in hell. 'Yes. Of course.'

One side of his mouth lifted wryly. 'Would you like some tea?'

'I usually have some when I can't sleep.'

'I figured that. I saw you'd already set up the teapot. No, don't get up.' He stopped her when she tried to climb out of bed. 'I'll bring it to you.'

'You don't have to do that, Grayson. I've already put you to enough trouble.'

'Hush,' he said gently. Tipping her chin, he skimmed his thumb over her lower lip, across then back, ending with just enough pressure so that there was no confusing his intent. It was a kiss, or would be when she was ready. 'Let me take care of you.'

She watched him go, then, mind racing, she got out of bed, testing her shaky knees. She went to the window. The parking lot was quiet, the crime-scene tape gone. No one would ever know a woman had died there not even twenty-four hours before.

Paige closed her eyes and let herself grieve Elena. There'd been no time before. She'd been in shock or fighting for her own life. Or discovering the body of Delgado, executed. She wondered why Jorge had lied. Why he'd betrayed Ramon.

She heard Grayson's footsteps long before she heard his voice. He was walking more heavily than normal. Probably to let her know he was there. *So I won't be afraid.* It was sweet and thoughtful and another mark in his favor. If she'd special-ordered a knight in shining armor, she couldn't have chosen much better.

'I thought I said to stay in bed,' Grayson said.

'I was thinking,' she said, letting out the breath she held when he slid his arms around her waist. Without hesitation she leaned into him, having no idea how this would turn out, but grateful he was here now. Her bare ankle brushed against a wool trouser cuff and she had only a moment to wonder why he'd changed out of his sweats before it became apparent.

He wanted her. A great deal. The soft fabric of his sweats would have done nothing to disguise the arousal that pressed against her. Her body wanted to turn, wanted to slide her arms around him. Wanted to say to hell with her eighteen-month drought. Bring on the damn rain already.

In her mind she could hear Olivia scold her for moving too fast. Then again, Liv wasn't alone. Olivia had David. *I don't have anyone.* And she didn't think she ever had.

Grayson pressed his lips to her jaw, making her shiver. 'You're cold,' he murmured. 'Go back to bed. You can think there.'

She wanted to go back to bed. But she wanted him there with her. She just *wanted. Needed.* All the months of being alone swelled, filling her mind, sweeping away all the reasons she shouldn't do what she was about to do.

She turned quickly, before the reasons rushed back. Slid her hands over those muscled shoulders, lifted on her toes and kissed him. He stiffened in surprise for a split second before his arms tightened around her and he was kissing her back, hard and deep. *Good.* The word pounded in her mind. *So good.*

'More.' The command rumbled from his chest. Vibrated against her lips. 'Open.'

She opened her mouth and his tongue swept in, probing. Promising. His body was hard, throbbing against her. *So good.* Her arms wound around his neck and she lifted higher on her toes. *Closer.* She needed to get closer. *Now.* 'Please.'

The warmth of his hand burned through the thin fabric of her underwear as he pushed her nightshirt aside, covering one cheek. She shivered again, far from cold. His fingers teased at the elastic and she bent her knee, bracketing his hip. *Closer*.

A growl had them freezing in place. They turned as one to see Peabody poised, ready to spring. 'Easy,' Paige murmured, as much to herself as to the dog. She'd let things get out of hand. 'Peabody, go to your crate.'

Peabody obeyed and Grayson let out an uneven breath. 'That was . . . different.'

Paige lowered her heels to the floor. His green eyes were still hot, his mouth damp. She wanted to kiss him again. But there were reasons to take it slow. Good reasons.

She just had to remember what those reasons were. Which she would, once the blood returned to her brain. 'Different, how?'

'Mostly you.' He pressed a fast, hard kiss to her mouth. 'Nearly being bitten in the ass by Peabody ranks up there, though.'

She had to restrain herself from touching the ass Peabody had nearly bitten. It was probably as hard and amazing as the rest of him.

She slid her hands down his chest, enjoying the flex of his muscles under her palms. The man worked out. Seriously. And what she'd felt throbbing against her? If and when the time came, it would be worth the eighteen-month drought.

'I'm sorry,' she said. 'He's not used to seeing people with their hands on me.'

He lifted his brows. 'People?'

'Men . . . type . . . people.'

'Good.' He pressed a kiss to her forehead. 'Come on. Your tea's getting cold.'

She let him lead her back to bed and climbed in when he held the blanket back. He tucked her in like she was a child, then gave her the cup of tea. 'Drink.'

She took a sip and blinked up at him. 'It's perfect.'

'You don't have to look so surprised. I know my way around a kitchen. I used up all your eggs, by the way. I got hungry and you were asleep.'

'I think a few eggs are a small price to pay for my own guardian.' She patted the edge of the bed and he sat down. 'How much do you bench?'

'Two-ninety-five,' he said.

'Not many of my clients can do that,' she said, impressed, as he looked puzzled.

'You make your clients lift weights? What kind of PI are you?'

She chuckled. 'I work at the Silver Gym part time as a trainer.'

Puzzlement turned to surprise. 'You said you'd been a paralegal.'

'I was, until a few years ago. The lawyers I worked for retired and by then I was working at a gym, just to make ends meet. I got a nice severance package when the firm shut down, so I used it to buy a share in the gym.'

'What happened when you moved here?'

'I still own the share.' She studied him over her teacup. 'You don't know that much about me, do you?'

'No.' He looked away for a moment, then back, his eyes intense. 'I saw you this morning and it was like . . . I don't know. Something clicked. It was like I'd always known you. Or maybe I just wanted to. My assistant made a file on you. It's very thick.'

'Really? Where is it?'

'In my gym bag. She had it for me when I went back to the office after the ER.'

'Oh.' That stung. 'So you knew everything about last summer before I told Stevie.'

'I haven't read the file. I wanted to learn about you on my own. And I did. I looked for Peabody's food when you were asleep. I thought maybe it was in your spare room.'

She wanted to frown, but didn't. 'It's not.'

'I got that. There have to be a hundred trophies in there.'

'A hundred thirty-five. I used to compete on the US and world circuits. Weapons and *kata*. Did a little fighting, too.'

'And now all those trophies are sitting there collecting dust.'

'Past life,' she muttered. 'On to something new.'

He looked at her for a moment. 'Why?'

'Because,' she said impatiently, 'I'm done being Super Karate Woman.'

'Because of what happened last summer.'

'Yes,' she said evenly. 'Which, I imagine, is in the file your assistant created. If not, you should hire a new assistant.'

'I didn't hire her, which is a good thing.'

She blinked. 'What? Why?'

'Because if it'd been my call, I wouldn't have given her a chance. She's brash and bold and . . .' He shrugged. 'Damn good. If I'd listened to myself, I would have lost out.'

She narrowed her eyes. 'And aren't you the clever armchair shrink?'

He grinned, so artlessly that she couldn't stay mad. 'My sister Zoe is a shrink, so I learned it honestly.'

'How many sisters do you have?'

'Three. Lisa, Zoe, and Holly. Then there's Joseph, our brother.'

'They're all Carters? No other Smiths?'

His grin all but disappeared. 'They're all Carters. My mother and I are Smiths.'

'Then how did they come to be family?'

'My mom and I came to live with the Carters when I was a kid,' he said carefully. 'We were just about homeless when Mrs C gave my mom a job. We became close. The Carters are wonderful people.'

'They sound like it. Why were you homeless?'

'Because my dad left us.'

She knew there was a lot more story there. She wanted to know it all, but his expression had tensed and she decided to ask more about his father at another time. 'What did Mrs Carter hire your mom to do?'

'To be a nanny. Holly was a newborn with health problems. Mrs C needed help with the other kids. She offered us the apartment over the garage and, seeing as we had no home, Mom jumped at the opportunity.' He hesitated. 'By the way, she wants to meet you. My mother, I mean. She's invited you to dinner tonight.'

Paige bit her lip, guilt pricking her conscience. *Yes, I know.* 'Grayson, about that . . . I need to tell you something.' A loud thud from the apartment above shook the walls. Her teacup clattered on the nightstand and a photograph fell off the wall.

Peabody sprang from his crate, once more crouched and growling. 'What was that?' Grayson said, looking up.

'Peabody, easy.' Paige glared at the ceiling. 'It's those idiots that live upstairs.' Another thud had her whipping back the blanket and throwing open the closet door.

'Holy shit, Paige,' Grayson hissed. 'What the hell *is* that?'

He pointed to the shotgun propped against the closet wall. She rolled her eyes. 'I'm not going to shoot them, for God's sake.' She grabbed the next tool in the closet.

'Okay,' he said more calmly. 'I repeat. What the hell is *that*?'

She brandished her weapon of choice, a mop to which she'd bungied a heavy book. She jumped on the bed, grasped the handle in both hands and banged the book against the ceiling. 'Shut up!' she yelled. 'Just shut the hell up!'

Grayson watched, astonished. 'I take it they make noise often.'

'Five times a week. The mom has this boyfriend who only comes over at night. They're either having really rough sex or doing the polka. Unfortunately she also has a kid, who's only fourteen. I'd feel sorry for him if he weren't such a damn creep.' She gave the ceiling another pounding for good measure. 'That's for taking video of me and sending it to that rat bastard Radcliffe.'

'The kid upstairs took the video? You knew all along?'

'Sure. Logan's taken video of me before. Kid's a stalker. I told him if he didn't stop, I'd sic Peabody on his ass. I didn't see him taping me again, but obviously he did.'

'Why don't you complain to the building manager?'

'I have. Many times. He just says boys will be boys. One of these days . . .'

Another crash from above shook the walls. 'What are they doing up—'

A gunshot cracked the air, followed by a terrified scream.

Paige stared at Grayson for a split second before jumping off the bed and grabbing the shotgun. She ran to the front door, Grayson right behind her.

She flipped the three deadbolts, freezing when Grayson's hand came down hard on the door. 'Wait,' he said. 'Let's see what's out there before we go off all half-cocked.'

He bent to look through the peephole. Then took her shotgun

from her, saying, 'Call 911. The kid upstairs is being dragged down the stairs by a guy in a ski mask.'

He opened the door and slid through before she could utter another word. She ran back to her bedroom to get her cell phone and the .357 from her nightstand drawer.

She described the situation to the 911 operator as she ran to the front door. 'Tell the cops it's the same building where the woman was shot by a sniper this morning.'

She headed down the stairs to Grayson but stopped at the sound of a tormented cry. Logan's mother was on the landing above, covered in blood, clawing her way across the floor.

Paige pressed the phone to her ear. 'Are you still there?' she asked the operator.

'Yes. Emergency responders are about two minutes from your location.'

'My neighbor's been shot. She needs an ambulance. Fast.'

'*Stop*,' Grayson shouted. 'Let the boy go or I'll shoot your damn head off.'

The man abruptly halted on the sidewalk, holding Logan in front of him, a gun pointed at the boy's head. Logan was bleeding from his leg.

'Drop the shotgun,' the man snarled. 'Put it on the ground and step away.'

Grayson weighed the options, wondering where Paige was, hoping she'd stayed inside where it was safe. 'If I drop the gun, you'll kill us both. I like a little leverage.'

The boy started to whimper. Grayson tried to ignore him. *Focus or he'll die.*

The man in the mask jerked the boy to his toes, jamming the gun hard against his skull. 'I don't have anything to lose here. I didn't want to hurt him.'

'Then why did you?' Grayson demanded. 'You shot him.'

'No, I didn't. His mother did by accident when she shot at *me*. Look, I just want to get outa here. Unload the shotgun, then drop it and I'll let him go.'

171

'Please,' Logan whimpered. Tears ran down his face. 'Please don't kill me.'

'I don't want to kill him,' the man said fiercely. 'I don't want to hurt you.'

Grayson drew a breath. Desperate men did unpredictable things. Carefully he unloaded the shotgun, hoping to defuse the situation until the cops arrived.

'Throw me the cartridges and drop the shotgun,' the man said. 'Now.'

Keeping eye contact with the man, Grayson complied. He bent his knees and laid the shotgun on the ground. 'I put it down. Now let him go.'

'Go over to that lamppost. The broken one.'

Grayson didn't move. 'Let him go.' Sirens were faint in the distance.

'I will shoot him in the head. Do you want that on your conscience, Counselor?'

Grayson started. *He knows who I am.* 'No. I don't.' Slowly he backed away and the man drew an unsteady breath.

'Fine, take him.' The man shoved the boy forward and on a howl of pain, Logan's leg collapsed beneath him.

Grayson caught the boy and eased him to the ground then took off after the man, crouching behind a car, flinching when the man fired a shot that deliberately went wide.

'Damn it, Grayson, stay back,' the man shouted. Then he ran, disappearing into the darkness of the business complex in the next block.

Gone. He was gone. 'Dammit.'

Logan was groaning pitifully. Grayson knelt, inspecting the wound. It was bleeding sullenly, and he could see leg bone protruding from the skin. Afraid of making it worse, he didn't touch the boy's leg. Instead he took his hand, wincing when Logan squeezed.

'Logan, my name is Grayson. We called for help. Why did that man grab you?'

Logan's face was deathly pale. 'He wanted my computer. But I didn't have it.'

'Why? Why did he want your computer?'

'For the video.' Logan was rocking in agony, tears rolling down his cheeks. 'It's worth money. TV stations wanted to buy it off me. But I sold it already. I sold the exclusive and I gave the guy my computer.'

'Who? Radcliffe?'

'Yes, that sonofabitch. He promised to give it back in a day, when he'd gotten a twenty-four-hour scoop. He didn't want me sending the video to anyone else.' He gritted his teeth and moaned. 'My mom. He shot her. Where is she? Is she okay?'

'I don't know.' For the third time in twenty-four hours Grayson watched the flashing lights of emergency vehicles approach. He looked over his shoulder, expecting to see Paige, but she wasn't there. 'We'll find out. For now, stay still. Help is coming.'

As Logan crushed his hand, Grayson stared in the direction the man had gone. That someone would break into the kid's apartment in the middle of the night to steal the video at gunpoint for money wasn't completely impossible, but he didn't believe it. Logan believed it, clearly, and that was probably best for now.

Because Grayson had the very bad feeling that he'd just looked into the eyes of the sniper who'd killed Elena. Who might have attacked Paige and even killed Delgado.

Worse yet, the man's voice was familiar. *He knew me. He called me by name.*

And I let him go.

Wednesday, April 6, 4.15 A.M.

Stevie sat on the sofa as Paige wearily twisted three deadbolts. Grayson was pacing the floor, uncharacteristically disheveled. His feet were bare and dirty and the shirt he wore was untucked and buttoned only halfway.

Paige didn't look much better. Her nightshirt was smeared with blood and she looked even paler than she had after finding Delgado's body.

Stevie knew the two of them had already given statements to

Morton and Bashears who'd been called to the scene, but she couldn't ask the other detectives for details. Not without generating questions she didn't want to answer. 'Take it from the top.'

Paige looked at her bloody nightshirt. 'I'm going to change. You can tell her, Grayson. I'll be back.' She disappeared into the bedroom, leaving Grayson staring after her.

'Anytime would be good,' Stevie said.

The look Grayson shot her was miserable. 'The kid's in surgery. He might lose his leg. His mother died on the way to the hospital.'

'Shit.'

'The kid said he and his mother were asleep when they heard Paige scream. He said they ignored it, because she screams most nights.'

'She has nightmares,' Stevie said. 'Understandable.'

'And terrifying. I had to wake her up out of one. Logan said he couldn't go back to sleep, so he got up to get a snack and found the guy with the mask looking through his things. The intruder tried to run, knocked over a table. Paige and I heard the crash.'

'Okay.'

'Logan said his mother came out of her room, half-drunk and waving a gun. The intruder grabbed Logan and the mother fired. She hit Logan's leg. The intruder shot the mom in the chest. We heard Logan's scream, but only one shot.'

'So one of them had a silencer.'

'The intruder did. We gave Morton and Bashears a statement. Except . . .' He met her eyes, his haunted. 'He knew me, Stevie. And I knew him.'

'The shooter?' Stevie sat up straighter. 'Why didn't you tell them that?'

'Because I don't remember where I knew him from. I recognized his voice. I know lawyers and cops. I don't have many friends outside.'

'So do you think this guy was a lawyer or a cop?' Stevie asked carefully.

'I don't know. He called me "Counselor". Cops call me that.'

Cops. Stevie needed a moment to consider how she wanted to probe this. That he hadn't told Morton and Bashears was significant. 'Paige had blood on her nightshirt,' she said, changing the subject.

'Logan's mother's. I stopped her from running after the intruder. Paige stayed with the mother, tried to stop her bleeding before the EMTs came, but it was too late.'

'Plucky thing, isn't she?' Stevie asked and he closed his eyes.

'She's going to get herself killed,' he said hoarsely.

And that would kill Grayson, Stevie thought. She'd met a few of the women with whom he'd had relationships over the years. Knew he'd held back a part of himself with each one and had no idea why. But he wasn't holding back with this one and Stevie wondered if he knew it.

'Does she know you think you know the shooter?' she asked.

'Yes. I told her after Morton and Bashears left.'

'Do you think you'd recognize the guy if you heard him again?'

'Maybe. I don't know. His voice was pretty thin and desperate.'

'Then how did you recognize him?'

'I don't know,' he said, frustration in his voice. 'I've been wracking my brain, trying to remember. It wasn't "Hey that's Joe Blow". It was more like a feeling.'

'Then we'll leave it for now.' This was a Grayson she didn't know. Rarely did he show so much emotion. He felt it, she knew. He just didn't show it very often. Only with his family. And now with Paige Holden.

'Did the shooter say anything to Logan? Before the shooting started?'

'He wanted Logan's computer. He wanted the video, the one of the minivan crash.'

'And of Paige,' Stevie said. 'Hell. So what do you want from me?'

'I want to ID the shooter.'

'Duh.' Stevie rolled her eyes again. 'Specifics, Grayson.'

'He wants video and audio clips,' Paige said from behind him. Grayson stepped back, his eyes searching Paige's face. 'I'm okay,' she said. 'I'm more worried about you.' She ran a hand down his arm. 'Sit down. Please.'

He dragged a chair from the dining room as Paige settled in the easy chair, her dog at her side. She was scared but she was otherwise sharp, her eyes alert.

'Grayson gave the other detectives a physical description of the shooter,' Paige said. 'Is it possible to get video or audio on file for the officers that match the height and weight? He can see if any of the voices match the one he heard tonight.'

Stevie grimaced. 'I honestly don't know. IA has their ways, but . . .'

'But it violates a whole hell of a lot of civil rights,' Grayson finished.

'So? He's shooting people for fun and profit. He should have no civil rights.'

'I agree with you,' Stevie said. 'Unfortunately, cop or not, he does have rights. I don't want some judge throwing out evidence because we overstepped the line. When I catch this guy, cop or no cop, I want it to stick.'

'We have more than one man to catch,' Grayson said. 'Tonight's shooter probably killed Elena, but he wasn't the man paying off Sandoval in the photo. If Sandoval was five-ten, the man in the photo was six feet, but slim. This intruder was my height.'

'You're six-two?' Stevie asked.

'Yes. But the guy who attacked Paige was taller than me. Six-four at least.'

'So we have three, maybe four men,' Stevie said. 'This intruder, Paige's garage attacker, and the guy who made the payoff to Sandoval. If tonight's intruder didn't kill Elena, her killer would be the fourth.'

'This intruder took a big risk, breaking into a fourth-floor apartment,' Grayson said. 'Why would he want the video that much? It was all over Radcliffe's station website.'

'Not all of it,' Paige said. 'I watched it several times this morning. There's a portion cut out. I tried to stop Elena's bleeding for two minutes, but that wasn't in the video. It was cut and spliced. There were missing minutes of tape on the version on the news.'

'Oh, great,' Stevie muttered. 'Shades of Watergate.'

'Logan said Radcliffe took his computer for a day so that he couldn't send the file anywhere else,' Grayson said. 'Radcliffe wanted to keep it exclusive for twenty-four hours. Radcliffe would know what was on the tape. We need to talk to him.'

Stevie pointed to the window. 'You don't have to go far to find him. He's outside.'

Grayson jumped up and peered through the blinds. 'When did he get here?'

'He was setting up when I got here,' Stevie said.

Paige didn't move from her chair, but the hand that rested on the dog began stroking his neck. She'd done the same thing in the car.

'Radcliffe seems to have an uncanny ability to show up at opportune moments,' she said mildly, but there was strain beneath her words.

'This one is a little different than his filming your attack this afternoon,' Stevie said. 'It went out over the police radio. If he has a scanner, he'd know.'

Grayson turned from the window. 'I want to know why he was in that garage. And why he thought it was okay to not call 911. I'd like to charge his ass.'

'He was at the courthouse, filming you after the verdict today,' Stevie said. 'It was on the news at five. I assumed he followed you both to the garage and just got lucky, but I'll double-check. I'd like to know what the connection is between Radcliffe and Logan. How did the kid know to call him in the first place?'

'Logan's done some citizen journalism,' Paige said. 'He started working for his school newspaper and one day filmed a fight at school. It went viral. Radcliffe contacted him, said if he got more stories like that he'd get him legit time on the news.'

'How do you know this?' Stevie asked.

'Logan told me so when I first moved in. He wanted to do a story on me. He'd Googled me and knew what happened last summer. I told him no, but he filmed me anyway, without my permission. I caught him doing it and I lost it.'

'How was he filming you?' Stevie frowned. 'Through your window?'

'No. I was walking Peabody, who caught him hiding in the

177

bushes.' She patted the dog's neck. 'Logan nearly wet himself.'

'Good dog,' Stevie murmured.

'He was waiting for me on the front stoop a few days later. He said that if he had a story like mine, he'd be able to impress this reporter, Radcliffe. That Radcliffe was always looking for stories. I told him I didn't care, that he should find another story or I'd tell his mom. I thought it worked. I didn't catch him filming again, until yesterday morning.'

Paige closed her eyes. 'I was banging on the ceiling when he was being attacked. I probably woke them with my screaming every night and he never said a word. He's hurt and his mom's dead because he had a fixation on me.'

Grayson brushed the hair from Paige's face in a gesture so tender it had Stevie feeling like a voyeur. 'He was filming you yesterday without your permission,' he murmured. 'That was stalking, honey. None of it was your fault.'

'I know,' she said miserably. 'So why do I feel so damn bad?'

'Because you're human,' Stevie said. 'Look, the kid didn't deserve what happened to him, but he's not an innocent bystander in all this.'

'Thanks,' Paige said, her smile strained. 'We need the uncut version of that video.'

'That's not going to be easy,' Grayson said. 'I can't see Radcliffe giving it up without a court order.'

'Morton and Bashears were trying to get a warrant today, but then they found Sandoval's body and the suicide-confession note and let it slide.' Stevie stood up. 'Grayson, I recommend you sleep before the meeting with the commander in a few hours. You might remember more about the shooter once your brain's had a chance to rest. We'll talk with IA and figure out what can be done. If we've got a bad cop, we need all hands on deck to stop him. I'll ask Radcliffe on my way out about the tape. The worst he can do is say no.'

'Thanks, Stevie. I really appreciate this.'

'I guess I owe you for all the warrants over the years,' she said with a tired smile.

Stevie had her hand on the doorknob when Paige spoke again.

'Detective, what about Delgado? Have you found his wife and daughter?'

'No. We've got a BOLO out. If I was her and had a child to protect, I'd be hiding.' Stevie hesitated, then decided Paige needed to know. 'We found the gun that killed Delgado. It was in a dumpster behind the Muñoz house. We rounded up the Muñoz brothers and took them in to interview.'

Paige pursed her lips hard. 'Somebody wanted it to look like the brothers did it.'

'My partner and I knew we were supposed to think it was amateurish the minute we saw the scene, even before I'd heard your story. I had to pull strings to keep the case and I didn't want anyone to accuse me of not following every lead.'

'Morton and Bashears,' Paige said.

'Maybe. That you discovered Jorge's body so soon after he was shot helped. The Muñoz brothers have an alibi. They were at church and their priest confirmed it.'

'Good,' she said fervently. 'That poor family. Poor Ramon. He's got to feel so helpless, stuck in prison while his family suffers. I really need to see him. To tell him not to give up. To tell him that Elena really loved him, up till the end.'

'Not yet,' Grayson said sympathetically. 'We need whoever's behind this to believe we don't know what's going on. We need them to get cocky and make a mistake, not to hide from us. If Ramon knows, he could let on, even if he never says a word.'

'It could put his life in danger,' Stevie added. 'We need to know who's involved in all this before we tell him, okay?'

Paige sighed. 'Okay. I guess.'

'As soon as it's safe I'll take you to him,' Grayson said. 'I promise.'

Grayson's promise seemed to make the difference. Paige nodded. 'Thank you.'

'We'll get to the bottom of all this,' Stevie said. 'You try to get some sleep.'

179

Ten

Wednesday, April 6, 4.15 A.M.

Silas drove away from his house, leaving the Toyota and his van parked in the garage. This vehicle was safe, clean of any tracking devices. Silas had taken it apart himself. Just in case a day like today arrived.

He'd stored the car under an identity he'd been building for years. It was his escape plan, and Silas had attended to every detail. Except how he'd tell his wife the truth. She sat at his side, silent because he'd asked her to be. But soon he'd have to tell.

Violet slept in the backseat, clutching her tattered doll, the only possession he'd allowed them to take and only because his wife had insisted. Violet couldn't sleep without the doll. An hysterical child was the one thing he did not need.

Their house would remain as it had been. Nobody would know they'd gone.

Ironically, Jorge Delgado's wife and child had done the same exact thing. If karma was real, Silas would end up the same way as Jorge.

But my child will live. He wished the same for Jorge's daughter. But that was for Mrs Delgado to deal with. He had his own problems.

All of my own making. Which didn't matter. All that mattered was getting away.

Because he'd lost it tonight. Panicked. He'd shot dozens of people in his life. Why had he so completely lost it?

It had happened so fast. He had a gun to the kid's head to scare him. *Just to scare him.* But the kid kept saying the computer wasn't there. He kept lying. Then the mother staggered out of her room, reeking of whisky and waving a goddamn pistol.

She'd shot her own son by mistake, then raised the gun to fire . . . *at me*.

The shot he'd fired had been simple reflex. *I should have left the kid there. I should have run.* A few seconds faster and he would have avoided Grayson Smith entirely.

And that's where it all fell apart. That's where his problems had started. The counselor had been armed. And Silas knew the man could shoot. They'd been to the range together. *I should have shot him.*

Smith hadn't recognized him, but Silas knew he would figure it out. It was just a matter of time before the cops he'd served with for so long came to his own door. Silas needed to hide his wife and child before that happened. He couldn't protect them once he was locked in a prison cell.

'I gave her Benadryl like you said. She'll sleep for hours,' his wife whispered.

'She needs to sleep for at least eight hours. If she wakes up, give her more.'

'Why eight hours?' she asked fearfully.

'Seven hours to Buffalo. I need her to sleep until we cross the bridge into Canada.'

'*Canada?* Why are we running away like thieves in the night?'

'Because that's what I am. Among other things.' Things he didn't want her to know.

'What happens when we get to Canada?'

'I have money put away there.' A hideout of sorts. 'You'll need to stay there.'

'And you?'

Silas would return to Baltimore. He could hide from the cops, but his employer would track him like the dog he was. Killing the man who owned his soul was the only way to keep his family safe. 'I have some business to finish. Then I'll join you for good.'

'What about our house? Our friends? Violet's school? Silas, what have you done?'

'What I had to do.'

181

She stifled her sobs. 'This is about Cherri, isn't it?'

He'd always known he'd married a smart woman. 'Yes.'

'I'm scared, Silas.'

A very smart woman indeed. 'So am I.'

Wednesday, April 6, 4.45 A.M.

Grayson closed the door when Stevie left, locking the three deadbolts. He wished he could make this whole day go away. But then he never would have met Paige, and he found he wasn't quite selfless enough to wish that.

She sat, hand on the dog's neck, looking spent. Grayson tugged her to her feet and into his arms. She rested her head against his shoulder and some of his tension ebbed.

'When you ran after that man, I was so scared. You could have been killed, too.'

'I chased him after he let Logan go,' Grayson confessed and felt her stiffen. 'He shot wide, warned me to stop. He could have gotten me then.'

'But he didn't.' She said it as if trying to reassure herself.

'No, he didn't. And trying to remember where I know him from is making me crazy.'

'Grayson . . . was he Morton's partner? Her old one, the one before Bashears and Skinner? The one that retired. Detective Gillespie.'

'Gilly?' He tried to think back. 'No, it didn't sound like Gilly.'

'You're sure? He had access to Ramon's keys. He and Morton were primary.'

'Sure as I can be without talking to him again.'

'I could look up his phone number. You could call his house. This early we'd probably catch them asleep. We'd wake them, but at least they wouldn't have left for work yet. And then you'd know for sure if you can eliminate him or not.'

'Cops and their wives are used to being woken in the night,' he said. 'Do it.' It took her only minutes to find Gilly's phone number. Grayson dialed using her disposable cell, hoping he'd hear the voice over the pulse pounding in his head.

'Hello!' It was an older woman's voice on their answering machine. 'Gilly and I aren't here right now 'cause we're doin' something cooler than you are. If we want your call, you've got our cell. Otherwise, leave a message. We might just answer it.'

Grayson waited till the beep, hoping someone would pick up but no one did. He hung up. 'Gilly's wife on voicemail,' he told Paige. 'I'll have to rely on IA to bring him in so that I can hear him. Come. Let's get you back to bed so I can get some sleep, too.'

His arm around her, he walked her to her bedroom and checked the windows. 'They're locked.' He turned down the blanket. 'Now get in.'

Her smile was wobbly as she got into bed. 'Nobody's tucked me in for a long time.'

He kissed her mouth softly. 'Sleep.' Walking away was hard to do, but he managed it. At the door he turned to find her sitting up, looking troubled. 'What is it, honey?'

'Nobody's called me honey in a long time, either.' She drew a breath. 'I don't have any right to ask you this, but I'm going to. Would you mind sleeping here? Just sleep?'

Meaning he'd have to lie next to her and not touch. The look on his face must have shouted volumes, because she looked away. 'Never mind. I shouldn't have asked.'

'No, it's fine.' It would be fine. *If it kills me. Which it just might*. He climbed under the covers next to her, still wearing his trousers and shirt.

She settled on her side, facing away from him. 'I set the clock for seven.'

'Fine.' This close, he could smell her hair. He fought with himself for a minute, then gave in and put his arm around her waist. She relaxed into him and he relaxed too, despite the hard-on that he couldn't ignore.

She went still and he knew she hadn't been able to ignore it either. 'Wow.'

'Sorry. I can't help that.'

She rolled to her back, staring up at him. 'Don't be sorry. I'm . . . very flattered.'

The awareness flaring in her eyes sent the remaining blood straight out of his head. She'd said 'just sleep' but his body didn't care. He dipped his head, as her hand curved around the back of his neck. She pulled him closer, making it clear it was a yes.

He'd meant to keep it sweet, but as soon as she opened her mouth under his, his control snapped. He ate at her mouth, making her moan. Making her writhe. Making his blood pound in his ears when she thrust her hips against his hand.

He stopped, panting. His hand was between her legs and her eyes were closed. She looked like a woman on the verge and he cursed himself even as he drank her in.

She was hot and he could feel her getting damp through the layers of fabric that kept her from him. He wanted to rip the pants down her legs. He wanted to taste. Needed to thrust long and hard and as deep as he could. He wanted her. All of her.

He brushed her lips with his. 'I want to eat you alive,' he whispered and she shivered convulsively. She opened her eyes and for a moment they simply stared.

Then she spoke, her voice husky and pained. 'I can't have sex with you.'

Stunned, he blinked. 'Not this minute, or not ever?'

Her eyes stayed steadfastly on his. 'This minute.'

'But not, not ever?'

'No. Definitely *not*, not ever.'

'Okay.' He tried to think. 'But since you opened the door to this specific line of questioning . . . When?'

'I don't know. Just not tonight.'

'But you want to?'

'God, yes,' she breathed. She moved his hand. 'We need to talk first.'

He frowned, his mind immediately going in all kinds of bad directions. 'About what?'

'Nothing like that. I'm . . . okay.'

'How long has it been?'

'Eighteen months,' she said and his frown deepened.

'Why?'

'Because that's when I saw my best friends find the real thing and finally realized what I was missing.' She bit her lip. 'I've made a lot of mistakes in my life. Lots of men.'

Lots of men. The shame in her eyes told him it had been hard for her to admit. 'Did you love any of them?' he asked roughly.

'No,' she said with brutal honesty. 'I wanted to, but I knew they were temporary.'

He wasn't sure what to say. What she needed him to say. So he asked what he needed to know. 'Why?'

Her smile was filled with a self-loathing he understood more than she could ever know. 'I could claim my childhood sucked and I never knew my father, but the truth is that I didn't want to be alone and accepted what I could get. Then Olivia found David and my life was glaringly . . . empty.' She shrugged. 'I got fed up with hating myself. I decided I'd rather be alone than waste my time and dignity with Mr Wrong.'

Shit. Just . . . shit. 'So this time you're holding out for the real thing?'

She winced at the caustic tone he hadn't meant to use. 'Yes,' she said. 'I thought you should know before we go any further.'

'It's way too soon . . .' He let the words drift off as her mouth curved wryly.

'I don't believe in love at first sight. But there's something between us. You're here, in my bed, for God's sake.'

'You asked me to sleep here,' he said defensively.

'I know.' Again the shame flickered in her dark eyes.

Guilt stabbed him deep. She'd been through hell and simply asked not to be alone. To just sleep. And he hadn't been able to keep his hands off her. 'I'm the one who pushed it,' he said and she shrugged again.

'If I said I hadn't anticipated this, I'd be lying. But I was hoping to put it off a little longer. We can call this attraction, fascination, pure lust. Whatever. If you're open to the real thing, I'm interested in seeing where this goes. Very interested. But if you're not . . . I can't. I can't go back to the person I was. It's important to me.'

'I don't do relationships.' The words were lame, especially after what she'd shared.

'Why not?' she asked and he had no answer. Seconds ticked by and her eyes changed, going carefully expressionless, driving the spear of his guilt even deeper.

She cleared her throat. 'I guess that tells me everything I needed to know.'

His throat closed, panic and despair overwhelming him. 'I won't leave you alone tonight. I'll sleep on the sofa.' But he didn't want to leave her bed. 'If you want me to.'

Indecision filled her eyes, but the shame was still there. 'I'd sleep better if you stay.'

'Then I'll stay.' And he wouldn't touch her again.

She nodded stiffly. 'I appreciate it. Let's . . . just go to sleep.' She rolled back to her side. The next breath she drew was ragged and he knew she was holding back tears.

His hand reached to stroke her arm before he knew it. He snatched it back. *Leave her alone. You're just going to hurt her, like all the others.*

He never meant it to end this way, and it always did. This was ending a hell of a lot faster than it had with all the others, but it had been that kind of a day. The others had always declared him insufficient and gone on with their lives. Now, lying in Paige's bed, he realized he'd picked them for their ability to do just that.

But he hadn't picked Paige. She'd slammed into his life like a freight train. And he knew that when he hurt her, she'd stay hurt for a long time. That he couldn't stand. He would stay with her until she was safe. Until this was over. Then he'd leave her alone.

He knew that this time, he'd hurt for a long time, too.

He lay on his back, wondering how he'd managed to so royally fuck everything up. He didn't know how much time had passed when she spoke, still turned away from him.

'I have a confession. When I'm not caught in a bad dream, I'm a very light sleeper. Things wake me up. Conversations. On cell phones. In cars. About Carly.'

Carly? *Carly.* Understanding came, followed closely by dread as he tried to remember what he'd said in the car. 'You heard me talking to my mother.'

'Yes. You told her she'd like me. Then you said you couldn't tell "them" because you couldn't risk them telling. You told her not to tell me. Tell me what?'

Anger bubbled up. 'You should have told me you were awake.'

'I know. I almost did, but you got upset with her and I didn't know what to say. I'm sorry. I shouldn't have listened, but I did.'

'And you're hoping I'll tell you now?' he asked harshly. 'Just like that?'

'I don't know.' Her voice grew small. 'Maybe. I've told you everything about me.'

'This is different.' Seething, he rolled out of her bed, sitting on the side, his back to her. 'Dammit, Paige. You had no *right*.'

'I know. I said I was sorry. What else can I say?'

He didn't answer, the anger continuing to burn in his gut. She'd spied. Listened. *I trusted her.*

Well, no, you really didn't. If you had, you would have told her.

I have no reason to trust her. I just met her.

She trusted you. With her life. That was a harder one to negate. Because she had.

He heard the sheets rustle, felt the mattress dip. He looked over his shoulder to find her sitting up, watching him, her expression a mixture of apprehension and hurt.

'What?' he snapped defensively and she flinched.

Then her chin came up. 'I won't tell.'

He narrowed his eyes. 'Tell what, exactly?'

Her brows knit, nonplussed. 'That you've got a secret. Which is all I really know.'

'And?'

'No "and". That's all.'

'No, it's not. You'll need to know. Wheedle. Nag. Pry.' Anger became bitterness. 'Cry, even. And then I'll feel guilted into spilling my guts when all I wanted was privacy.'

'You're wrong about that,' she murmured.

He frowned. 'What does that mean?'

'It means that I won't have the opportunity to wheedle, nag, or pry because this will be the only night I'll see you here, this way, in my room.' She said the words evenly, without heat, but this time he flinched, his chest tightening painfully. She shrugged. 'You're the one who doesn't do relationships.'

'So now you're punishing me.'

She closed her eyes. 'No. I'm being honest. And, in my opinion, a good bit more rational than you. You say you don't want forever. You just want now. I say that I deserve better than that. I deserve forever with someone who wants . . . *me*. And I won't settle for less.'

Her words took his anger and squeezed it dry, leaving shame in its place. She was right. 'I'm sorry,' he murmured.

'You should be. You don't know me well enough to know that I never wheedle, nag, or pry, so I'll cut you some slack on that one.' She was utterly serious. And, it would appear, a bit angry as well. 'But that you thought I'd *cry* to manipulate you into "spilling your guts" is downright insulting.'

'You're right,' he said simply. 'I'm sorry.'

'I know.' Her temper faded quickly, leaving an expression of sadness that hurt his heart to see. 'Let's just get some sleep. It'll be daylight soon.' She scooted back under the blanket, pulling it up to her chin. 'Stay or go, but do something quickly.'

He hesitated, then gave in to the yearning she'd brought forth from him. He lay down beside her and let out a quiet breath. 'I can tell you that I haven't done anything illegal or that should make you be afraid of me.'

She rolled over to look at him, warily curious. 'Why would you think I'd be afraid of you?'

He shrugged. Improvised. Lied. 'I'm a big guy. You've been hurt before.'

She held his gaze for so long that he wanted to run away. She saw too much. But 'Okay' was all she said before closing her eyes and within minutes she was breathing steadily. He'd thought her asleep until she put her hand in his, threading their fingers. 'Rest,

Grayson. I won't ask you any more questions that you don't want to answer.'

He should have been relieved. And he very well might be, once he could breathe again. But that wasn't going to be tonight.

Wednesday, April 6, 6.30 A.M.

Adele woke to Darren shouting, 'Goddammit, Rusty! What did you do?'

She hurried down the stairs. 'Darren, what's wrong with—' She stopped abruptly at the bottom of the stairs, the stench turning her stomach inside out.

Darren stood in the kitchen doorway. Garbage lay strewn around the trash can. Vomit and diarrhea covered the floor.

'Oh, God.' Adele had to fight to keep from retching. *I don't need this. Not today.*

'Where is that dog?' Darren demanded. 'God only knows what he ate.'

Rusty had the most sensitive stomach of any dog she'd ever heard of. The least bit of human food had him runny for a week.

'You go find him and put him in his crate,' Adele said. 'I'll start cleaning up.'

'I'll put him in his crate,' Darren muttered. 'Then I'll send it to Abu Dhabi, one way.'

It was his usual threat, but Rusty was safe. Darren would never give the dog up. He'd fought his ex-wife for custody of Rusty in what had been a toxic divorce after his ex had cheated. Rusty was a permanent fixture. Luckily Adele liked him.

But not today. She began sweeping the trash when she noticed the box. *Oh, no.*

It was the box the chocolates had come in, the chocolates that had come from a client she hadn't dealt with in six months. She'd thrown the box away, too paranoid to even risk keeping them around. But the box was empty. Rusty had eaten the chocolates.

Relax. This is normal. Chocolate made Rusty spew, but he was always fine after.

189

'Adele!' Darren's panicked shout came from the den. He ran into the kitchen, Rusty's limp little body in his arms. 'I can't wake him up. He's unconscious.'

'Take him to the emergency vet. I'll take Allie next door and meet you there.'

Wednesday, April 6, 9.30 A.M.

Paige looked up from her notebook, reaching for the china coffee cup on the very expensive table in Grayson's dining room. She'd checked in with Olivia and Clay and was now trying to plan her day, but the man sitting across from her was openly staring, unnerving her.

Grayson had brought her here to change his suit, then wait while he met with the cops. She had deadbolts and a dog, he said, but his place had a security system.

Apparently a critical component of the system was its installer, Grayson's 'brother' Joseph Carter who had been tagged for baby-sitting duty until it was Paige's turn to face IA as a confidential informant. Thinking about the questions they'd ask made her feel sick, so she looked at Joseph instead.

Grayson's brother wore a gun holstered at his side and gave off a darkly menacing vibe. She didn't feel threatened – she had Peabody at her feet as well as all of her weapons – but she didn't know what to make of the man. He had one of those faces that wasn't exactly handsome, but still . . . compelling. About Grayson's age, Joseph was tall, dark and broody.

Just like Grayson. Who was in one hell of a surly mood. He still couldn't remember where he'd met the shooter and hadn't even managed an hour of sleep.

Paige hadn't slept much longer, waking to find him holding her hand, watching her with a desolation that made her eyes sting. They'd exchanged only the most necessary words. He'd walked Peabody while she'd showered. His surly mood appeared when she'd emerged from the bathroom, clean and clothed. He'd been snapping and issuing orders ever since.

But the desolation in his eyes had remained so she forgave him the rest.

She closed her eyes, waiting for the tightness in her chest to recede. She'd known him one day. Technically less. But walking away was going to hurt. It already did.

So don't think about him now. She needed to think about Elena and Ramon. She needed to think about Logan's mother. And Crystal Jones. She needed to figure out who on her long list of names she'd talk to when she was done with the cops.

Who were going to make her tell . . . *everything*. Panic began to rise and she forced it back down. She'd be professional. Concise. She'd tell the story like it happened to someone else. She'd answer their questions and get their help.

She jumped when her pencil lead snapped. She looked at her notebook, at the dark scribble she'd made while thinking about all the things she wasn't going to think about.

She looked up, found brother Joseph still staring at her, his dark brows lowered.

'I'd appreciate if you'd stop watching me like I was about to steal the family silver,' she said.

'I never thought that at all,' he said quietly, his voice a deep rumble. 'I was actually thinking that you're holding up pretty well, considering.'

She touched the bandage at her throat. It hurt, still. 'I'll live. Unlike the others.'

'Damn straight, you'll live. Grayson made it pretty clear that if anything happened to you, my ass would be toast. So thus, the watching.'

She narrowed her eyes at him. 'I'm not a child.'

He lifted his forefinger. 'Don't ruin my opinion of you by saying "I can take care of myself".' He said it in a slightly mocking, singsong way.

'I wasn't going to say that,' she said flatly. 'Because it's no longer true. But, way to rub my face in it. Thanks so much.' She looked back to her notes as her eyes welled up, embarrassingly.

'Hey,' he said. He leaned forward, tapped the table next to her book. 'Aren't we feeling sorry for ourselves?' he asked, the mocking tone back.

She looked up, furious. 'You're . . .' Then she shrugged, depleted. 'You're right.'

'You used to take care of yourself very well,' he said, 'but lately not so much.'

'Right,' she said glumly. 'And now I have to be babysat. By you. No offense.'

'None taken.' He dug into his pocket and pulled out a roll of Lifesavers. 'Butter Rum. Haven't been opened, so no pocket lint. Want one?'

It was so unexpected, she had to laugh. 'Why not?' She popped the candy in her mouth and took a minute to study him as he'd studied her. There was something stiff and unyielding about the man, but his eyes were kind. 'Who the hell are you, anyway?'

'Just Grayson's brother,' he said mildly.

'He said you're government,' she said. 'But the question is, whose? Ours?'

His lips twitched. 'Yes, ours.'

'FBI? CIA? NSA? I think we can safely cross off the Library of Congress.'

He chuckled. 'I read. It's FBI.' He shot her a warning look. 'Please don't ask.'

'Damn. I got me a high-priced babysitter.'

Joseph shrugged. 'Grayson called me last night after you went to sleep. He was worried. I'd say he had a right to be. And that was before the kid incident.'

'He told you about what's going on?'

'The series of events, yes. You, specifically? Not a word. So when he asked me to stay with you, I was curious. Naturally.'

'Naturally,' Paige murmured. Unwilling to satisfy his curiosity, she met his eyes squarely. 'So what do you think about the Muñoz case?'

'I think you two have one hell of a mess. Where were you going with the scribbles?'

She glanced at her notes with a frown. 'I was thinking about the scope of all this. All of these names on my list. Somebody had to have a lot of money to pay off all the people involved. We know Sandoval at the very least was paid off. A person would have to have significant money to be able to write that kind of a check and not miss it.'

'Most of the guests at that party would have considered fifty Gs pocket change.'

'I can't imagine considering fifty grand to be pocket change.' She looked around her. Grayson's townhouse was prime real estate, filled with expensive antiques. The thought was disturbing. 'Do you?'

'Do I what?' Joseph asked blandly, but his eyes had grown cool once again.

'Consider fifty thousand dollars to be pocket change?'

'No.' He paused, watching her. 'Neither does Grayson.'

His meaning was clear and it made her angry. 'I'm not after his money. I may have to work two jobs to make ends meet, but financially I can still take care of myself.'

'I know,' he said calmly, watching her over his coffee cup. 'Because I checked you out. I find it exceedingly odd that Grayson didn't.'

I don't like you, she wanted to say, but bit back the words. 'Okay, look. You care about your brother and I can be all jiggy with that. But you can run back to your *family* and assure them that I'm not after his money. In reality, he and I are not even—' She broke it off when his eyes shifted, her temper going stone cold. 'You're a jerk, you know that? You're just baiting me to get information.'

He looked disappointed. 'Now my sisters are going to be mad at me.'

'Like you're afraid of them,' she said with a sneer.

'You obviously have no sisters,' he said.

'Like you don't know that, too?' she demanded, then caught herself. *Whoa*. She hadn't been angry when Grayson's assistant had compiled a whole file on her. Why wouldn't a family check out a woman who'd captured the interest of one of their own? She wondered if they'd be so interested if they knew nothing was going to happen.

Not unless one of us changes. And that can't be me. She remembered the emptiness of all those relationships, how much she'd hated herself when they imploded. The pity she'd seen in the eyes of her friends. *Poor Paige. Can't pick 'em.*

And were they ever right. Still. *Why can't I meet a forever guy, just once?* Although she knew she'd met them, many times, but had passed over them, going for the losers instead. And somehow she'd always known they were losers, right from the get-go. Looking back, she realized she'd picked them for exactly that reason.

But Grayson wasn't a loser. She knew that. He carried something inside him, something large and dark and heavy. But it hadn't stopped him from being kind. It didn't stop him from seeking justice. *It just stops him from being available to me.*

She rubbed her temple, conscious of Joseph's scrutiny. 'Of course you know I have no immediate family. I'd want to know if I were you. I have friends, but no sisters. Or brothers. No parents. Just me.' She straightened her back. 'For the record, I'm not interested in your brother's money. I'd have been far more comfortable if he'd been poor.'

Joseph didn't respond, instead pulling a ringing phone from his shirt pocket. He answered while keeping his eyes on her face. 'Yeah?' he answered. 'Okay. I'll bring her to you. Where?'

'Is that Grayson?' she asked. 'Ask him what I should do with Peabody.'

Joseph did, then said, 'He wants you to leave the dog here. Anything else?'

Yes. What did you make your mother promise not to tell me? But she herself had promised to ask no more personal questions so she shook her head. 'No. Nothing else.'

Wednesday, April 6, 9.30 A.M.

His empty plate was removed and his coffee cup refilled. 'Anything else, sir?'

'No. That's all.' Once his maid had left him, he returned his cold gaze to the TV news. There had been a shooting, just hours ago. He recognized the building right away. Everybody who'd been near a TV yesterday recognized that building.

The boy who'd made the video was in a serious condition. His mother was dead. State's Attorney Grayson Smith had chased after the gunman, saving the boy.

Wasn't that nice. He picked up his cup and sipped, barely noticing the coffee was hot until it burned his tongue. *Silas, you fool. You just had to go back. Don't tell me you were worried they got your face on film. You idiot.* There was no way that the kid could have filmed Silas from where he'd been shooting. The angle was wrong and the distance would have made any facial features indistinguishable.

Silas was clearly rattled. And rattled men did really stupid things.

He dialed Silas's cell, got his voicemail. Silas was gone. He'd cracked. But Silas was predictable. He'd never leave his wife and the girl he'd passed off as his own child.

On his laptop he opened his tracking program. Silas's cell was at his home, just as he'd expected. Silas would know the phone was trackable and would leave it behind.

Silas's van was also at his home. Again, expected.

He pulled up the third item and frowned. Silas's little girl was on the move, headed north. At least her doll was. Predictably, Silas had been so shaken by finding the hamburger wrapper on Violet's nightstand that he'd ignored the possibility anything else was left behind.

Idiot. How many times have I told him that he cannot run from me? He twisted the ring on his pinky, contemplating how to proceed. He'd leave the wife and child alone for a little while, he decided. Not letting Silas know he knew where they were would fill his formerly trusted employee with confidence. With relief.

Because he knew Silas was coming back for him. *I can identify him. And he me.* It was time to terminate their business relationship.

Wednesday, April 6, 9.45 A.M.

Adele found Darren pacing in the waiting area. 'Is he . . . okay?' she asked.

'He's not dead. But he's really sick.' Darren shuddered. 'All the times I said I'd send him away in a box, I never meant it.'

'Of course you didn't.' *When I tell you the truth, don't mean it with me either.*

The vet tech beckoned them back. 'The doctor can talk to you now.'

The vet wore scrubs and a face mask hung around his neck. He looked beat. 'Your dog's alive, but he's very sick. Did you leave him outside for any length of time?'

'It was raining yesterday,' Adele said. 'He was indoors all day.'

'Why?' Darren asked. 'He ate the trash, right? That was in the kitchen.'

'I don't think so,' the vet said. 'Your dog shows signs of being poisoned.'

Poison. Adele grabbed blindly behind her, finding the edge of the examination table. The box of chocolates. Her name had been on the label.

Oh, my God. They were for me.

'Are you all right, Mrs Shaffer?'

Adele nodded numbly. 'Poison? What kind? How could that have happened?'

'I don't know yet, but if he pulls through, it'll be because of his sensitive gut. He threw most of it up.' The vet patted Darren's shoulder. 'Why don't you two go home and rest? We'll call you the moment there's a change. One way or the other.'

'Okay.' Darren slid his arm around her waist. 'Let's go home, honey.'

Adele let him lead her out. Her legs were like rubber.

It was clear. She'd made no mistake. *Somebody really is trying to kill me.*

Wednesday, April 6, 10.05 A.M.

'Thank you,' Grayson said to Joseph, who'd delivered Paige safely to the hotel where she was about to meet with the police department brass. 'Where will you be?'

'Standing here in the hall,' Joseph said. 'Call if you need me.'

Grayson turned to Paige who stared at the door in front of her as if gathering her strength. He drew in her scent. He now knew it was the lavender soap in her shower.

He'd tormented himself, imagining her in the shower. All that golden skin. Bare. Knowing he'd never have her had put him in a foul mood. Which was squarely his own fault. She had a right to far more than he could offer. Than he was willing to offer, he thought.

'Are you okay?' he murmured and she shrugged the question away.

'Why are we here? I appreciate the name of the place, but why a hotel?'

He'd gotten two suites at the Peabody Hotel. The suite next door would be hers. The meeting-room suite would later be used by whoever he hired as her bodyguard. Even with three deadbolts, he didn't want her staying in her apartment alone.

And after last night, there was no way he could stay with her.

He wanted her with a desperation he'd never felt before and it scared the hell out of him. He could actually see himself telling her everything and that scared him even more.

'The Peabody has an elevator from the parking garage to the rooms,' he said. 'It gets people up here without being seen.' He'd wait until after the meeting to tell her she'd be staying here. No use in stirring the pot unnecessarily.

She looked at the door. 'How'd they take the news?'

'Like you'd expect. Not happy to be accused by Elena, who can't be questioned.'

'Because she's dead,' Paige muttered. 'Did you tell them you knew him?'

'I did. They weren't happy about that either. Are you ready?'

'Sure,' she said grimly. 'Let's roll.'

The men in the room stood when they came in. Stevie remained where she was, perched on one of the stools at the counter between the kitchen and the living room.

Paige studied the face of each man, then nodded once. 'I'm Paige Holden.'

Stevie's boss inclined his bald head. 'We know.'

'That's Lieutenant Hyatt,' Grayson said. 'He heads the homicide division. To his left is Commander Williams. To his right, Lieutenant Gutierrez of Internal Affairs.' He motioned to the man standing in the bathroom doorway. 'Sergeant Doyle, also IA.' He pointed to the man standing off to one side. 'That's my boss, Charlie Anderson.'

Who insisted on coming, but had said uncharacteristically little during the initial hour. The uncertainty as to Anderson's intent left Grayson feeling even edgier.

Paige slid her backpack off her shoulder. 'I'm sure you've all got places to be, things to do. Bad guys to catch. So if we could begin?'

Hyatt placed a wooden dinette chair facing the sofa. 'Miss Holden, if you please.'

Grayson's eyes narrowed. Despite the 'please', it was an obvious attempt to put Paige in a position of being the interrogated, answering to a tribunal of stern-faced law enforcement. Paige's smile was pleasant. 'With all due respect, I'll stand. You're welcome to sit here if you'd like. Although it doesn't look as comfy as the chair you were sitting in.'

The men stared at her, then IA's Gutierrez snorted. 'I've got bunions. I'm sitting.'

The others followed, sitting on the more welcoming chairs. From the corner of his eye Grayson saw Stevie hide a smile. Hyatt wasn't her favorite person, but Stevie was a good cop and respected the chain of command. Hyatt crossed his arms, not bothering to hide his scowl. Paige hadn't made a friend, but she'd asserted her place in the pack.

Good for you, Grayson thought, leaning against the counter, prepared to step in if needed. Paige seemed relaxed, but he knew better. The clenching and relaxing of her hands gave her away. He'd seen her do it before, trying to keep herself calm.

Paige told the whole story, finishing with the attack on Logan and his mother. The only parts she'd left out were the personal moments between the two of them, although she needn't have bothered. Grayson had already been taken to task by Commander Williams for becoming too personally involved. It had been an exchange throughout which Anderson had been conspicuously silent.

She took a few seconds to look each man in the eye. 'That's all.'

'That's hardly all, Miss Holden,' Hyatt said aggressively. 'You've made a serious allegation of police involvement, both in the murder of Elena Muñoz and the framing of her husband. But you have a habit of accusing cops of things, don't you?'

Grayson's hackles rose. *Hell no.* He almost stepped in, but Paige beat him to it.

'My accusation against two officers was proven,' she said calmly, 'in a court of law.'

'This is a different court,' Gutierrez said. 'We need to find you credible.'

She lifted her chin. 'What would make me more *credible* in your eyes? Sir?'

'What do you believe motivated the attack on you and your friend last summer?' Commander Williams asked kindly, but Grayson wasn't fooled. Hyatt was always the bad cop. Williams was being good cop. Paige's glare said she'd figured this out.

'If you are asking if I did anything to provoke the attack, then no,' she said coldly. 'I absolutely did not. If you are asking if I am placing sole blame on the heads of the four attackers, two of which also happened to be police officers, then yes, I absolutely am.'

'Why don't you tell us what happened, Miss Holden?' Williams asked, still kindly.

Her jaw was taut. 'It's all in the police reports.'

'I'd like to hear it from you,' Williams said. 'If you wouldn't mind.'

'Yes, of course you would,' she said. 'There were four men. One was married to my friend. She'd accused him, a cop, of domestic abuse. He was angry with me for interfering in his efforts to "bring his wife back into line" and because I once made him look bad after he'd attacked her.'

'So you made him angry,' Williams said evenly. 'Then?'

'He complained to some friends. And they came to teach me a lesson.'

'Had you ever met or had contact with the other assailants?' Williams asked.

'Not that I know of. One was never caught, so I don't know for certain who he was.'

Grayson stiffened. She hadn't told him that one of them got away.

'The men forced their way into our women's center. They were masked. And armed. Thea's husband put a gun to her head. The others attacked. Two weren't trained to spar. The third was. He was also a cop, as we later found out. I called 911 as they came in. My cell was in my pocket. Everything was recorded.' She lifted a sardonic brow. 'In the event you don't find me *credible* enough.'

'How did you stop them?' Gutierrez asked.

'I threw one of the men into the wall. He was stunned. The second I kicked in the ribs but the third grabbed me from behind. He was the cop who would later break into my home. He had me in a choke-hold and I was . . . struggling.' She swallowed, her calm evaporating. 'The intruder with the broken ribs got up and started punching.'

'He wasn't a police officer,' Hyatt said, and Paige's eyes narrowed bitterly.

'No, but his punches still hurt. The *cop* behind me tightened his hold and gave his club to the non-*cop* who struck me with the club, in the head, ribs, and legs. They were all laughing. "Not so tough now, are you, bitch?" ' She cleared her throat. 'They, um, talked about what they'd do to me when they'd knocked me down to size.'

Grayson realized he'd been holding his breath, trembling with rage. That she'd let him touch her at all was a fucking miracle.

'I'd started to see stars when my friend Thea made her move. She tried an evasive technique I'd taught her. She succeeded in twisting out of her husband's hold.'

'But he still held the gun to her head,' Williams said.

'Yes.' Paige swallowed, tears welling in her eyes. She didn't blink, but she didn't look away from the men watching her either. 'She startled him and he fired. The bullet went through her neck and struck him under his arm. Pierced his artery. She was dead in seconds. He lasted a few minutes more. That she died trying something I taught her . . .' Her voice broke. 'That's hard to live with.'

The room had gone utterly silent. Paige cleared her throat again. 'The cop choking me let me go so that he could help Thea's husband. I had a knife in my bag and was trying to get it when I . . . dropped like a rock. The first man I'd stunned came to and he had a gun. He'd shot me, here.' She rubbed her shoulder.

'The men ran, except for Thea's husband who was dead. The medics were almost too late. I nearly bled out, but the docs sewed me up. The three men were still at large. I couldn't identify them, except to say that one of them would have broken ribs and they'd called the guy who choked me "Mike". The hospital sent me home a few days later.'

'When one of them came back,' Commander Williams said.

'Yes. The cop who'd choked me. He was afraid I could ID him, once the trauma wore off. My best friend, also a cop, saved me and cuffed him.'

'The friend who arrested him is a decorated homicide detective in Minneapolis,' Stevie said. 'Thea's husband and Mike Stent, the officer who choked her, were cousins. The man who hit her with the club was Stent's brother. He was picked up the day after.'

Paige gave her a surprised look and Stevie smiled encouragingly. 'I could see that telling your story wasn't going to be easy for you,' Stevie said, 'so I went to another source. Detective Hunter says hi, by the way. It's all documented, Commander.'

'I know,' Williams said. 'I made some calls of my own last night, after Mr Smith requested this meeting. What about the man who shot you, Miss Holden?'

Paige's eyes narrowed at the commander. 'You made calls. You already know.'

'I don't,' Gutierrez said, sounding a little annoyed, and she shrugged.

'Best guess is that he was Thea's husband's brother. His mother was his alibi and there was no evidence putting him at the scene. He's . . . disturbed. Still blames me. For months after, he followed me, watching me. Never said anything, never approached. The kid knew how far he could go before he was charged with stalking or harassment.'

'How did you make him stop?' Gutierrez asked.

'I moved here,' she said flatly.

'Have you seen him here?' Grayson asked, hearing in his voice the menace he felt.

'No. My friends keep an eye on him. He's going to university like a good boy.' She met each of their eyes, clearly exhausted. 'Look, I'm here because I heard the dying declaration of a murdered woman. She blamed a cop. If you don't find me credible, then don't. If you believe me, fine. Either way, I've done my duty and no more blood is on my hands.' She grabbed her backpack. 'Now if you'll excuse me.'

'I believe you about Muñoz,' Hyatt said. 'At least I believe *you* believe this.'

'Gee,' Paige said, her mouth smiling, but her eyes angry. 'Thanks.'

'We'd like the victim's flash drive before you leave,' Gutierrez said.

Paige took a plastic baggie from the pouch of her backpack. Grayson had asked Joseph to take her by her bank on the way. 'This is Elena's.' She gave it to Gutierrez.

'You touched the drive?' Hyatt asked and she nodded, warily.

'Yes. I needed to see what it was so I could know what to do with it.'

'I assume you kept a copy?' Williams asked.

She looked Williams squarely in the eye. 'Yes, sir. I absolutely did.'

'I would have done the same,' Williams admitted. 'Thank you, Miss Holden.'

Hyatt stood. 'I hope it goes without saying that you are now out of this investigation. The state's attorney's office and the police department will take it from here.'

She nodded again, dutifully. 'Yes. Of course. Sir.'

Which was her way of telling them to fuck themselves, Grayson thought. 'If we're done dredging up Miss Holden's past, I'd like to get to work.'

'As would I,' Gutierrez said. 'We'll begin our internal investigation. You, Mr Smith, will begin re-interviewing the witnesses from the original trial.'

The men nodded to Paige as they filed out, until only Grayson, Stevie, and Charlie Anderson remained. Anderson had said not one single word during the entire exchange but Grayson had never forgotten he was in the room.

Anderson stayed where he'd stood for the entire meeting, leaning against the door to the bedroom. From there he spoke. 'Detective Mazzetti, could you see Miss Holden is taken home? I need to speak with Mr Smith. Alone, please.'

Grayson said nothing. Something was up. Something was wrong. 'What's this about, Charlie?' he asked when Paige and Stevie were gone.

'I was going to ask you the same thing. Yesterday you were a logical prosecutor.'

Hot anger mixed with cold dread. 'And today?'

'You're throwing your career away on that woman,' Anderson said.

'My relationship with Miss Holden, whatever it is or is not, is none of your business.'

'It is when you disrupt my office. I came to tell you that you're reassigned.'

Grayson could only stare. 'What?'

'You'll transfer your caseload to Joan Danforth. You'll take her cases.'

He shook his head, hoping he wasn't hearing right. 'But she's in Fraud Division.'

'Yes, she is. You've been working Homicide too long. You've let it become personal.'

'What about this investigation?'

'Joan will take the lead. I will assist her in any way I can, but she's a very competent attorney. Well respected on both sides of the aisle.'

Grayson's mind was reeling. 'This is insane. You can't just move me.'

'Oh, yes. I can. I absolutely can,' Anderson said acidly, mocking Paige's words. 'You should be grateful. I'm saving your career.'

Grayson's eyes widened as the words sank in. 'My career does not need saving.'

'When this investigation opens up, you might see yourself in a different place.'

'What the fucking hell does that even mean?'

'You tried the man. You're the one who got the conviction.'

'Because there was *evidence*,' Grayson said through gritted teeth.

Anderson's almost amused look had Grayson staring, stunned. 'Oh, my God,' he whispered. 'You knew. You *knew Muñoz didn't do it.*'

'Don't be a fool,' Anderson said quietly. 'Five years ago you had promise, but you were no superstar. Now you get the good cases. The winnable ones that give you that conviction record you're so proud of. The high-profile ones that get your face on the news. The Muñoz case got you noticed by all the right people, who will now wonder if you possibly could have been *that* naïve. If yes, then how savvy are you really?' He lifted a brow. 'How long do you think it will take them to figure out where all your zeal in that courtroom *really* came from?'

Grayson's blood went ice-cold. 'What are you talking about?'

'Muñoz was a big, bad Hispanic who murdered a blond co-ed. Sound familiar? You were the perfect choice to prosecute.'

No. Grayson opened his mouth to speak, but no words came. *This isn't possible.*

'Take a few days off, Mr –' Anderson paused – '*Smith*. Think about it. I have every confidence that you'll agree that abandoning this case is in your best interest. And that of your mother as well.' With that, Anderson left the room

Knees weak, Grayson sank into a chair. *Oh, God. Oh, my God. He knows. How does he know? How did he find out? We were so damn careful.*

Dully he stared at the table-top until the panicked noise in his mind began to quiet and Anderson's words sank in. *You were the perfect choice . . .*

Anderson had known the truth about Muñoz five years ago. *He picked me.* Grayson closed his eyes. Last night he'd said that his courtroom had been manipulated. Last night he hadn't included himself as a victim of that manipulation.

As of this moment, that changed. As of this moment, everything changed.

He knew what he had to do. He pulled out his cell phone, dialed his mother.

She answered immediately. 'Don't even think about ditching me for dinner.'

'No, I'm not,' he said grimly. 'I just need to change the venue.'

'Grayson, honey,' she said, alarmed by his tone of voice. 'What's wrong?'

'Pretty much everything.'

Eleven

Wednesday, April 6, 11.00 A.M.

Paige looked around the hotel room suspiciously. It adjoined the one she'd just been in with the suits – a mirror-image layout. Joseph and Stevie had whisked her inside as soon as she'd been dismissed by Charlie Anderson.

'Why am I here?' she asked.

Stevie shrugged. 'You need to talk to Grayson. I'm just following orders. Why don't you sit down before you fall down, Paige?'

Paige eyed the soft sofa. 'If I sit down there, I'll go to sleep.'

'Not a bad idea actually,' Joseph said. 'You got circles under your circles.'

Paige dropped her backpack on the small dinette table and dropped her ass onto one of its chairs. 'I'll stay awake, thanks. Dark circles notwithstanding.'

Stevie sat next to her. 'You did good in there, kid.'

'Thanks.' Parts had felt simply awful, other parts almost cathartic. 'But they could have read the report and know everything they needed to know.'

'They're trying to catch you in a lie,' Joseph said. 'I take it that they did not.'

'No. Because it's all the truth. I wish it were someone else's truth, but it's all mine.'

'I'm sorry it happened to you,' Stevie said kindly. 'I'm sorry they were cops.'

'There are bad apples in every barrel,' Paige murmured, ready to think about something else. 'I called the hospital but they wouldn't tell me anything about Logan.'

'He's stable,' Stevie said. 'Out of surgery. In shock. They saved his leg, though.'

Paige closed her eyes. 'Thank goodness.' She still felt guilty as hell, even though she knew she hadn't directly caused any of this. 'Did you get his video and computer from Radcliffe?'

'No,' Stevie said. 'He told me to get a warrant. Although I think I played it wrong. I asked him in front of the other reporters. I got the impression that if we'd been alone, he would have given it to me. He had to save face.'

'How long will the warrant take?' Paige asked.

'My partner's working with Grayson's assistant to get it signed. If they get the right judge, by lunchtime. If not . . . we'd need to wait until Radcliffe gives it back to Logan.'

Paige gritted her teeth against the sudden roil of rage. 'Did he show any remorse?'

'He looked like he cared. But it's hard to say for sure.'

'He makes his money looking like he cares,' Paige said, then paused. 'What the hell?' A suitcase sat next to the TV. 'That's my bag. And . . . what the fuck?' Beside it was a bag of dog food. She twisted in her seat. Met Joseph's inscrutable stare. 'This is my room? Are you trying to tell me that this is *my* room?'

'Yes. And yes,' Joseph said.

Stevie winced. 'Ooh. Grayson didn't ask you first?'

'No, he did not.' Paige lurched to her feet, pacing. 'How long am I supposed to stay here? Who packed my things?' She stopped, pointed at Joseph. 'Well?'

'I don't know. Grayson. While you were sleeping,' he added before she could demand to know when he'd done so.

'Oh, this is great. Just rich. I guess he is, at that. Booking a goddamn suite.'

'You don't like it?' Joseph asked blandly.

'That's not the point. The point is, he didn't *ask*.' Another thought struck her and she recoiled. 'Is this a safe house? Am I some kind of prisoner here?'

Joseph didn't blink. 'Kind of. And sort of.'

'Are you my babysitter?' she demanded, her breath hitching in her throat.

'No,' Joseph said.

Paige looked up at the ceiling, fighting tears of fury. 'Then who is my babysitter?'

'That I don't know. I'm only the temp.'

Paige looked at Stevie, who said, 'Sorry, Paige. I didn't know about any of this. Although I have to say it makes a lot of sense. I'm surprised last night's shooter didn't come after you instead of Logan.'

'He didn't need me,' Paige ground out. 'He needed the tape.'

'Still.' Stevie tapped her throat. 'You're a target. Somebody wants you dead, girl.'

This yanked some of the starch from Paige's ire. Stevie was right. But . . . 'I can't be locked up like some prisoner. This could take a long time to resolve. I've got a job to do, rent to pay. Responsibilities. I can't just sit around and—'

The door opened and Grayson walked in. Paige opened her mouth to rail at him, but her anger fizzled. He looked terrible. Pale. Like he was in shock. Instead of yelling, she ran to him, bracketing his face between her palms.

'What happened to you?' she asked.

His eyes were stark, filled with devastation. And fear. 'My boss knew too. He knew Ramon was innocent.'

Paige stared. 'Oh, my God.'

'What the hell?' Stevie said, stunned. 'How do you know?'

'He told me.' He slumped on the sofa.

'Just like that?' Stevie demanded. 'He just came out and told you?'

'Pretty much. This is much, much worse than I'd ever thought possible. And on top of that, I've been reassigned. To the fraud division.'

'As of when?' Joseph asked.

'As of three hours ago.' Grayson scrubbed his face with his palms. 'I just tried to access my files on the server but was denied.

Tech Support said they'd received a request to transfer my access and that it would take a few days.'

Stevie sat on the arm of the sofa. 'Damn. You've been locked out.'

'Yes. They don't want me getting to the bottom of this.'

Paige sat on the coffee table, facing him. 'Who exactly is "they"? How high does this go? How many people knew Ramon was innocent? And how many other trials might they have manipulated?'

Grayson shook his head. 'Good questions. At least Anderson. Could be others are involved. As for other trials, I can't even contemplate. This is . . . mind-boggling.'

'And potentially life-threatening.' Joseph stood, arms locked over his chest. 'They've already killed three people to cover their tracks.'

'Four,' Grayson murmured. 'Logan's mother made four.'

Joseph scowled. 'I won't let you become number five. What will you do next?'

'I'm going to find out who gave the order to frame Ramon and who carried it out. And who knew it was happening. Which will hopefully answer the big question – who should have been prosecuted instead?' Grayson looked at Stevie. 'You can go, if you want. This won't be pretty for either of our careers if it goes wrong, which it probably will.'

She gave him a quelling look. 'Shut up. You know I'm not walking away from you.'

He nodded, his eyes flickering relief. 'Thanks.'

'I should hit you for even suggesting it. I've got work to do. I got Hyatt to give me and JD last night's shootings. Since they've declared Elena's case closed because of Sandoval's suicide note, they can't say Elena and Sandoval are connected to Delgado and Logan's mother. Not unless they agree that the sniper is still on the loose, and they aren't ready to backtrack on that yet.'

'Smart,' Paige murmured.

'I have my moments,' Stevie said. 'I'll check with Ballistics on yesterday's shootings when I get to my desk. JD will call as soon as he and Daphne get the court order for Radcliffe's tape. Be careful, both of you.' She left, closing the door behind her.

Paige frowned. 'Why did Anderson tell you? How does it benefit you to know?'

'He threatened me with it. Said that if the truth came out, "the right people" would wonder if I wasn't in on it too. And if they did believe I prosecuted honestly, that they'd find me too naïve to be effective. He said he was "saving my career".'

'Sonofabitch,' Joseph gritted. 'Who does he report to? The state's attorney?'

'No. There are three layers of management between Anderson and the state's attorney. Enough room to do real damage if any of the people in between are dirty.'

'Then take this straight to the top,' Joseph said.

'And prove it how?' Grayson said wearily. 'Once I can prove it, I can have him disbarred, but right now, it's my word against his.'

'You're right,' Joseph said, his jaw tight. 'But dammit.'

Paige had a disturbing thought. 'Grayson, if you can't access your server, does that mean we can't get to the video taken of the pool party where Crystal Jones was killed?'

He looked grimly satisfied. 'It might have meant that, if I'd waited until this morning to go looking for it. I downloaded it last night while you were sleeping.'

She lifted her brows. 'You were a busy bee while I was sleeping last night.'

Grayson glanced at Joseph, who shrugged. 'She guessed. I didn't lie.'

Grayson's mouth hardened. 'I'm not going to apologize. I need you safe.'

'I appreciate that.' She could fight him, but he looked beaten already. She looked around her. 'I appreciate all this. But you should have asked me first.'

'I figured you'd say no.'

She controlled what would have been an irate huff. 'Because I'm apparently stupid.' She flicked her hand when he tried to backpedal. 'Don't even try. What about Peabody?'

'He can stay here with you. The manager approved it.'

Paige weighed her words. 'I'm not going to be a prisoner,

Grayson. I'm *not* stupid, and I don't take foolish risks, but I can't stay here indefinitely. The sooner we get this cleared up, the sooner we can all go back to our lives.'

'Already in progress,' he murmured.

Her heart squeezed without warning, startling her. They'd go back to the lives they'd been living before yesterday morning. Before they'd met. Because he didn't do relationships. Even though every instinct she possessed told her that he yearned to.

But look how well her instincts had served her in the past. Not.

'Already in progress,' she repeated. 'I'll be careful. You have my word. But I won't be idle. If you don't want to work with me, I'll work on my own. I won't go anywhere alone. I'll wait for Clay or I'll call my friend to come from Minnesota. She's offered to come if I need her. I won't risk my life, but I will not be a prisoner. So what will it be?'

A muscle twitched in his cheek. 'What about at night?'

'If you want me to stay here instead of my apartment, I'll do that as long as they let me have Peabody. It's your dime. If you want me to have babysitters, I'll agree. I assume that's who the adjoining room is for.'

Again the muscle twitched. 'It is.'

'Fine. Just don't try to lock me up and we'll have no disagreement.'

He looked away. 'Okay.'

She was surprised. 'Okay? That's it?'

'You promised to take precautions. That's all I can ask. For now, I'd like you to review the video of the pool party and match as many of the guests as you can to the partial guest list that Rex McCloud gave us five years ago. Most of them have an online presence. You should be able to locate a current photograph to compare to the video. I want to know who left the pool area at any time during that party.'

'What will you be doing?' Paige asked.

'Reconstructing my witness list. I need to track them down and talk to them again.'

'While they're still alive,' Joseph muttered. 'Your witnesses are dropping like flies.'

211

'True enough,' Grayson said evenly. 'I want Anderson and everyone who manipulated this case to pay.'

Wednesday, April 6, 11.35 A.M.

Adele held her breath while Darren opened their front door. 'Oh, God,' she said, grimacing. The smell was still strong. 'I set up fans and sprayed and everything.'

'It didn't help.' They hadn't said much on their way home. He was waiting for her to talk to him, but she still didn't know where to start. It sounded crazy. *Maybe I am crazy.*

She followed him to their bedroom where he began taking off his clothes.

'Where are you going?' she asked, her voice small.

'Work. I barely have time for a shower and a shave before my afternoon meeting.'

'Can I fix you some food?'

'I can't eat.' He went into the bathroom and she heard the shower. She stared out the window, down to the street where the black car had been last night. Or had it?

She pressed her fingers to her temples, not sure of anything anymore. Except someone had poisoned Darren's dog. And the box of chocolates was empty.

Poor little Rusty. She swallowed back the bile that rose in her throat. *It could have been me that ate the chocolate.* Worse, it could have been Darren. Or even Allie.

The water shut off. Darren stood in the bathroom doorway, a towel draped over his hips, watching her. 'Adele?' he said quietly. 'You need to tell me the truth because the possibilities I'm making up in my mind are driving me crazy.'

Interesting choice of words. 'I think the poison came from the chocolates,' she said.

He stared, stunned. 'The ones that you got in the mail yesterday?'

'They weren't mailed. They were just dropped off.'

'Whatever. Why would you think that?'

'Lately some things have been happening. Strange things.'

212

'Such as?' he asked, guarded.

He already thinks I'm crazy. 'I was run off the road two weeks ago.'

'When you popped the tire. You said you swerved to avoid a cat.'

'No. It was a car. A black one. It ran me off the road and I almost hit a tree.'

'Why did you lie?'

'Because a few days earlier someone pushed me down an escalator.'

'You said you fell.'

'I told myself that I had, because nothing else made sense. I was meeting a client in DC, near the zoo. There's that long escalator in the subway.'

'I know it,' he said, no emotion in his voice.

'My hands were full of shopping bags and all of a sudden I felt someone push me. I fell down a bunch of stairs before I caught the railing. When I looked back up, there wasn't anyone there. Then that car ran me off the road.' She glanced over at him. His face was like stone, unreadable. 'Then it happened again.'

'When?'

'Wednesday. Allie was in the car that time.' So she'd gone to see Dr Theopolis. 'Then last night the chocolates came. I haven't worked with the client whose name was on the label in six months. There wasn't any reason for them to send me a gift. So I threw them away.'

'You think your old client did this?'

'No. But anyone could get my client list. It's on my website.'

His jaw squared. 'Why didn't you tell me?'

'Because I sound crazy. I didn't think you'd believe me.'

'I believe you, Adele.'

There was something in his voice that filled her with new fear. 'You do?'

'Rusty was poisoned. I'd like to know why someone would want to harm you. You of all people.'

She thought of the black car cruising by the night before. Had she really seen that last night? Or was it just another hideous memory

213

snaking its way out of the box in which she'd locked it? 'I don't know,' she whispered. Darren stood, waiting for her to say more. Finally she shrugged. 'I don't know,' she repeated.

Darren nodded once. 'I see,' was all he said. He went about choosing his clothes, his movements robotic. 'I'll get Allie from the neighbor and take her to the babysitter. My mother will pick her up this afternoon. You and I can discuss this more later.'

Adele nodded, bewildered. She'd known he'd be upset. She'd known he'd protect Allie. *I thought he'd be more concerned for me.* Instead he seemed hurt. Withdrawn. Even wary. 'Sure,' she murmured. 'I'll be waiting for you.'

Toronto
Wednesday, April 6, 12.45 P.M.

'Papa, I don't like this place.' Violet stood in the hotel room, her lips in a pout. She hugged her ratty old doll. 'I want to go home.'

Silas shared a glance with his wife. Rose knew enough to be afraid, but not enough to hate him. Not yet anyway. She sat on the bed. 'Come sit. We'll watch some TV.'

'I'll be back as soon as I can,' Silas said. He hoped. He gave Rose an ATM card. 'I have an account at the bank next door.' He told her the pin code. 'Buy what you need.'

His wife studied the name on the card, the same name he'd given at the border stop. She looked back up at him. 'You've been planning this.'

'Yes. But I hoped I'd never need it.' He held open his arms for Violet, but she turned her head. 'Honey, I'm sorry,' he murmured. 'I know you're confused. I'll be back soon and we can do some real fun things together, okay? Like . . . horseback riding. You'd like that, wouldn't you?'

She looked back at him warily. 'Really?'

'Sure. Where we're going on vacation has horses all around.' The vacation part was false, but the horse part was true. His cabin was near a working ranch. At least he didn't have to lie about everything. 'You'll love it.'

214

'If we're going on vacation, why are you leaving? We just got here.'

'Papa's got a few things to do first. I'll be back soon.' He tickled her, making her giggle. She wrapped her arms around him and hugged hard. 'Be good.'

'I'll try.'

He swallowed hard. 'There is no try.'

'There is only do,' she said dutifully, then kissed his cheek. 'Love you, Papa.'

He held on tight, wondering if Jorge Delgado had gotten that last hug before his wife had driven away with their child. 'I love you, too. Always.' He stood, kissed his wife good-bye. 'Remember what I said.' He'd told her where to find his stash of cash. Where to hide in the event he did not come back.

Her eyes were terrified. 'I'll remember. Be careful. Come back to me.'

'I will.' He would be careful. Whether or not he'd come back to her . . .

He returned to his car, allowing himself one last look back at the hotel. They were safe. It gave him the strength to get back in his car and start the long drive home.

Baltimore, Maryland
Wednesday, April 6, 2.30 P.M.

'This is weird,' Paige said, blinking to bring the computer screen back into focus. She and Grayson had set up their situation room on the dining-room table of his townhouse. They needed space to work and secure Internet. And snacks.

They'd arrived back at his home to find his refrigerator filled with food from Lisa and Brian's kitchen, 'leftovers' from the party they'd catered the night before. Paige had been so nervous this morning that she hadn't been able to stomach the thought of food, but her appetite had returned with a vengeance and her workspace at Grayson's table was cluttered with empty bowls. The computer monitor she stared at was huge, taken from the desk in his home office. Which smelled like him.

215

She'd ignored that fact as she'd gathered the equipment she needed. She'd ignored that fact as she'd sat across from him while studying naked, privileged college brats cavorting in Rex McCloud's swimming pool.

Grayson had files spread in a semi-circle around him and had been making phone calls to the names on his old witness list while she reviewed video and tried to identify the faces in the pool from their society photos, Facebook pics. And mugshots.

They were a rowdy group, Rex McCloud and his friends. They'd gotten into more trouble in the intervening six years than she could fathom. Interestingly enough, not one had served any real time. *Money talks.*

Right now, money was screaming all around her. The dishes from which she'd eaten Brian's Mac-a-Chee were antique Wedgwood. The furniture exuded the same kind of quiet wealth and breeding, leaving Paige more curious about Grayson than the naked people in the pool.

Unfortunately, the naked people could be key to keeping her alive. And one of the naked people had her frowning. 'This video's not right,' she said.

He looked up from his notes. 'Besides being bad porn, what's wrong with it?'

'This woman, Betsy Malone. Come see what I mean.'

He got up, wincing as he stretched, then came around the table, his expression grim. He'd been watching her, stealing peeks as they worked. She knew because she'd caught him several times. The rest of the time she could feel his gaze.

Combined with watching naked people for two hours, Paige found herself a little warm. Gripping the back of her chair by her left shoulder, he rested his hand on the table at her right, caging her in. He leaned closer to see the screen and for a second she had to close her eyes. *Okay, a lot warm.*

Definitely not one-sided. His head dipped lower until his jaw rubbed against her temple and he inhaled. For a moment they hung there, the air growing charged between them. She wanted him. For a moment she let herself wish.

216

I don't do relationships.

Abruptly she broke away. 'Focus, okay?' she snapped.

'Okay,' he said, his voice husky. His swallow was audible. 'What's not right?'

'This woman. Betsy. She's one of the names on Rex McCloud's guest list.'

'Right. I interviewed her before the trial. She verified Rex's alibi.'

'Of course she did. She was probably scoring crack from him. They got arrested together for possession at a party a year later.'

'That doesn't prove she was lying about that night.'

'No. That's not what wasn't right. I've been watching the video on your laptop.' Which she'd connected to the large monitor. 'I've been going through the guest list pulling Internet social networking pages and mugshots and running other searches on my own laptop. Look at Betsy the night of the party. It was mid-September.' She expanded the frozen frame until Betsy filled the large monitor, *all* of her. The young woman was naked in the shallow end, being pummeled from behind by Rex himself.

Grayson cleared his throat. 'Okay. Interesting choice of frames. What's not right?'

'Her breasts. They're small. Maybe A cup, if she's lucky.'

'Are you fishing for compliments here? Because you've got her beat. In every way.' His voice grew gruff. 'I really hope you're about to show me what's not right soon, otherwise I have to leave.'

Paige brought up a screen on her laptop. 'Look at Betsy on her MySpace page.'

She could feel him tense in surprise. 'Whoa. Somebody had some work done.'

Betsy was wearing a tiny bikini in the second photo, her hand on her hip. Her smile for the camera was huge. As were her new breasts.

'This MySpace photo is dated August 15 of the same year.' Paige glanced over her shoulder to see if he was following. From the frown on his face, he was not. 'She was a D cup in August, and an A cup a month later, in September. Either the date on the MySpace photo is wrong, which I don't think it is because she's at her birthday party, or the date on the video is wrong.'

'This video isn't from the night Crystal Jones was murdered,' he murmured.

'Exactly.'

'That changes everything.'

'It would mean the McClouds' security men gave you the wrong tape. One could only assume they did so on purpose. To alibi Rex.'

He straightened, leaving her cold. 'One could assume. One couldn't say with certainty though.' He looked at her shrewdly. 'Was Betsy's MySpace locked down?'

'You mean did I hack into it? I'm flattered that you think I could, but the answer is no. I'm no hacker. I got into Betsy's account the old-fashioned way. Search and click. Betsy never locked her privacy settings. And this is an old account. There's been no activity for about three years. She started her Facebook account about a year ago and the pictures there are a lot tamer. Apparently she was in rehab and has been clean for a year. But she never took down the MySpace.'

'So anyone with her password could have posted to it.'

'That's true with any social media. Which is what I thought you'd say.' Turning back to the large monitor, she moved the video to another point and froze the frame. 'The night is clear, the moon is three-quarters full.' She twisted in her chair to look up at him. 'According to the charts, the moon was only a quarter full the night Crystal died.'

Grayson was clearly unhappy. 'Goddamn. Why didn't we see that?'

'You weren't looking to disprove the video. You were looking for confirmation of Rex McCloud's alibi.'

'You could have just told me the moon part,' he said grumpily. 'You didn't have to flash Betsy's boobs in my face.'

'Possibly true. But I had to watch all this video of naked people behaving badly and it seemed a shame not to present my theory with a little pizzazz. So now what?'

'Like I said, this changes everything. But I'm not optimistic about getting our hands on the real video, all these years later.'

'But this, along with the photos Elena found, provide enough reasonable doubt to get Ramon a new trial, right?'

'We might be able to get his conviction overturned without a new trial. That would be better. And faster.'

'Faster is better. This Betsy woman looks like she's turned over a new leaf. She's volunteering at one of her old rehab centers. She might be more willing to tell you the truth about what happened that night now than she was five years ago.'

'I'll call her next.'

'You don't sound like you've been having a lot of success finding the old witnesses,' she said carefully.

'Not a lot, no. Some have moved. Some have died, including the security guard who provided the alibi video. But I did find Rex McCloud.'

'Maybe we should see him first, in case he runs.'

Grayson shook his head. 'No "we". I'll talk to him. You won't go near him.'

She sat back in her chair. 'And why the hell not?'

'Because you're not . . . officially on this case,' he said, ending lamely.

'And you are, Mr Fraud Division?'

He rolled his eyes. 'Rex McCloud is not going to run. He was released to house arrest after his last conviction. Now that he has no alibi for that night, he's first on the list of suspects. But I need to think of all the possibilities, not just Rex.'

'Because he has a powerful family?'

'That's part of it,' he admitted. 'His family makes it very difficult to investigate, even with the mantle of the office.'

'Maybe it'll be easier without it,' she said. 'You don't have to worry about stepping on the toes of wealthy campaign contributors. You can ask what you want.'

'That's true. But when I do start stepping on toes, I want them to be the right ones. Most of the people in that pool were kids of very rich parents. If one of them did it and the real tape shows that person interacting with Crystal Jones, the parents could have bribed the McCloud security.'

It was possible. 'Then why not start with Crystal?' she asked. 'She went to that party for a reason. She used an assumed name and lied her way in. Once there, she didn't party. Maybe somebody knew her intent. She lived with her sister at the time of her murder. Maybe she told her something.'

'I talked to her sister five years ago. She didn't know anything.'

'Grayson, who's to say that whoever convinced Jorge Delgado to keep quiet didn't intimidate Crystal's sister or any of the other witnesses, on both sides? Who's to say that five years might not make a difference? We need to know why Crystal went to that party and right now the closest link you have to Crystal Jones is her sister.'

'I called her house but she didn't live there anymore,' he told her.

'When you called,' Paige said gently, 'you said you were from the state's attorney's office. I might not have been honest with you either, especially if I'd lied before.' He was still hesitating and she thought she knew why. 'If you'd had the right evidence, you would have gotten justice for her sister. You have nothing to be ashamed of.'

His eyes flashed, but he said nothing, so she stood up. 'Come on,' she said. 'Let's find Crystal's sister. If she's moved, we'll track her down.'

He nodded stiffly. 'Does the dog need to be walked first?'

'It's been a while since he's been out. I'll do it.'

'*No.*' He bit out the word. 'I don't want you out in the open yet.'

'Grayson, you looked the shooter in the eye last night. He's gonna be after you too.'

'I don't think so. He had the opportunity and he didn't take it, unlike the guy who attacked you yesterday. He's still out there and he might try again.'

A shiver scraped her skin. 'I talked to Detective Perkins this morning. They don't have any leads. His knife was clean. No prints.'

'I know. Stevie told me.'

'He might not even be connected to any of this. We could find out who killed all the others and never know who did this.' She touched her throat. 'I hope that's not true, but I know how to live with it, if it is.'

'You didn't tell me that they never caught one of the men who attacked you last summer.' His hand lifted to her face and she couldn't bring herself to push him away.

'I hate to say it out loud. I don't know why.'

'Maybe it makes it more real.'

'It never stops being real. That's why I have so many locks. And guns. And Peabody.' She leaned into his palm, savoring the contact. He caressed her cheek, tracing her lower lip with his thumb. She wanted so much more. Sending up a silent prayer for strength, she stepped back. 'We need to get busy. Working.'

His hand dropped to his side. 'Is there any chance that the guy in the garage yesterday was the one who got away last summer?'

She shook her head. 'No. That guy was barely five-eight, if that. Weighed about one-fifty, soaking wet. Nothing like the guy yesterday. He was a damn cage fighter.'

'If we don't find him through all this, we'll rattle all the cages until we do,' Grayson promised grimly. 'I want you to sleep without nightmares after I'm gone.'

Her mouth opened to speak, but her throat had closed. He met her eyes, his so damn sad, and her heart cracked a little more.

'Just . . . don't,' he said. 'Don't say anything. I'll be back in a little while.' He called Peabody and together they went outside. Paige watched from the front window until she could no longer see Grayson's dark head. She was jumpy, edgy inside.

Damn needy. If the man walked back in right now, she'd throw herself at him.

She needed to be busy. She went to the table and gathered their dirty dishes, loaded the dishwasher. But he still wasn't back so she disconnected the large monitor from his laptop and carried it back to his desk where she reconnected it to his desktop computer. She was reaching behind his desk for an adaptor cord when her cell phone buzzed in her pocket and she jumped, smacking her head on the shelf over his desk.

Muttering, she rubbed her head with one hand while answering the phone with the other. It was Clay. 'About time you called me,' she said. 'Where are you?'

'Back at my place, finally. Zach is safe with his dad.'

She sank into Grayson's desk chair. 'I'm glad. What happened to ho-mommy?'

'She's in jail. Hopefully they'll set an astronomical bail. Zach was okay, physically anyway. His father promised to get him counseling. Hopefully the kid will heal.'

No, he won't, she thought. 'Hopefully,' she said aloud. 'I'll be needing a babysitter tonight. You up for a stay in a suite at the Peabody?'

'Excuse me?'

'Grayson got me a suite at the Peabody Hotel since my apartment seems to be the hotbed of violent activity. He got two adjoining rooms. One's for my babysitter.'

'It won't be him?' Clay asked carefully.

Paige bit her lip. 'No.'

'Okay,' Clay said. 'Text me the room number and make sure they have me listed to get a key. I've got to catch some sleep, and then I have a meeting at six with a client in Towson. When I'm done there, I'll come straight over. Shouldn't be later than ten.'

'Thanks.' She hung up, then looked up. 'Dammit.' She'd knocked all of Grayson's picture frames on their face when she'd hit the shelf with her head.

She studied each one as she picked them up. There were at least a dozen, most of them of Grayson with the Carters over the years. She recognized Lisa and Joseph. Holly would be the littlest, but there was a third girl Paige hadn't yet met. Grayson had mentioned a Zoe, so she assumed that's who the third sister was. Several included a smiling couple with the Carter kids. *Must be their parents*. The Carters looked like a happy family. Paige wondered if they knew how lucky they were.

The next photo was Grayson in a cap and gown, arm in arm with a tall, statuesque red-head. Paige held the picture up to the lamp, studying the woman's face. She was fair where Grayson was dark, but their smiles were the same. As were their eyes, sober and green.

This was his mother, then, who clearly loved him. Paige didn't have to wonder if Grayson knew how lucky he was. She'd heard the gratitude and respect in his voice when he'd spoken of her. And the regret in his voice when he'd been talking to her the night before, during the cell-phone conversation Paige never should have heard.

She reached for the last of Grayson's photos, and her hand stilled. There was a picture that hadn't fallen, but had been wedged into the back corner of the shelf, behind all the others. It was small, about the size of her palm, in a cheap silver frame that was tarnished around the edges.

It was Grayson and the same red-head, but taken much longer ago. Grayson looked about six or seven. *So cute.* He smiled boldly for the camera, the kind of smile kids did when they were told to say 'Cheese'. The photo's colors were faded, but she could still tell that the blazer and short pants he wore were navy. He carried a satchel over one shoulder. *He went to private school.*

His mother knelt beside him, her plain gray skirt draped modestly over her knees. She wore the same navy blazer, which had stitching on the breast pocket, an insignia of some kind. Her arm was around him and she smiled.

Differently, she thought. His mother smiled differently than in the later picture. She was happier here. Grayson had said his father left them and Paige wondered if the abandonment had happened yet. She didn't think so. His mother looked too happy.

Behind them was what looked like a school with wooden crosses on the front doors. The sky was blue, unbroken by clouds. And there were palm trees in the background. Tall ones. With coconuts. *Florida maybe? Or California?*

The photo was bent to fit into the frame, the right side hidden. On the fold was half a schoolbus, and on its side were the letters *St Ign. St Ignatius?* she thought.

He'd said they'd been homeless, that his mother had gotten a job as a nanny. But her blazer matched his, down to the stitching on the pocket. She worked at that school. Had his mother been a secretary? A teacher? Why had his father abandoned them?

Promise me you won't tell her. Whatever had happened, it had been bad.

Paige put the picture back, straightening it. She realized that she hoped down deep that Grayson would tell her himself. Knew it was likely he would not.

Pushing her emotions aside, she surveyed the shelf to be sure she'd put everything back as she'd found it. And just in time. The front door opened and she heard the patter of Peabody's feet against the hardwood in the foyer.

'Paige,' Grayson called. 'You ready to go?'

She took a last look at the bent photo. 'Yes. Of course.'

Twelve

'This is it,' Paige said, pointing at a run-down row house. 'The address listed for Brittany Jones. Crystal was twenty at the time of her death. Brittany would have been barely eighteen. No parents.'

Grayson brought the car to a stop. It wasn't a bad neighborhood, but it sure as hell wasn't a good one. 'At the time of Crystal's death they lived in a better part of town.'

'Crystal was a community college student. Where were they getting their money?'

'I don't know.' He stared at the house, dreading meeting the woman who lived inside. 'I should have known. I should have asked.'

'You were lied to. Manipulated by your own boss. Did you have reason not to trust him?'

'Not at the time, no.'

'Lately?'

'He's a prick. He's a micro-manager. He wants us to plead everything down. But I've never believed him to be dishonest. Not until today.'

'So, he's on the take or maybe being manipulated too. There was lots of money in that pool the night Crystal was murdered. She must have known that, too.'

'It got her killed.'

'Yep. But not by you. *You* didn't kill her. You just tried the man the cops said did it. You looked at their evidence and, right or wrong, you felt it was strong enough. You were lied to, Grayson. You were

225

manipulated. Should you have guessed? I don't know. Hell, I wasn't there.'

'I *was* there,' Grayson murmured, 'and I still don't know.'

'And you might never know. It doesn't alter the fact that Ramon's life is forever changed and *that's* what you have to find a way to live with. You can't bring Crystal back. You never could. You can only give her sister the opportunity, if she does know anything, to set the record straight, punish who did this, and set Ramon free.'

She had a way of distilling things down to bare truths. 'And then?'

'And then you go after everyone who looked the other way. You lock their asses away forever, but first you give Ramon five minutes in a room with them.' Her eyes shadowed. 'He's lost so much . . . he's the real victim here. Him and his family.'

'You should have been an advocate,' he told her, and she smiled sadly.

'Thank you. Are you ready to talk to Brittany Jones now?'

He shook his head. 'Yes,' he said, borrowing her phrase. 'Of course.'

Her dark eyes flickered with humor. 'You learn fast.' She looked over her shoulder, serious again. 'You want me to talk to her? If she lied before, you might scare her.'

He considered it. Considered his own frame of mind. And put away his pride. 'Let's try that. See what happens. But I still go with you. That's not negotiable.'

'Hell, I didn't expect as much as I got. Just try to act like my bodyguard and not a lawyer who could charge her for perjury. Let's roll, Counselor.'

He let her take the lead, watching for anything that might harm her, realizing with a quirk of amusement that he really was acting like her bodyguard. The amusement faded when the door opened and a young woman's face appeared. Brittany looked like she'd aged fifteen years.

'Yes?'

Paige smiled. 'Hi, I'm sorry to bother you. I'm looking for Brittany Jones.'

The woman's eyes flicked up to Grayson, then back at Paige. 'Why?'

'Well, that's between me and Miss Jones,' Paige said. 'Who I think is you. Yes?'

'Why?' Brittany repeated more forcefully.

'It's about your sister.' Paige put her hand on the door when Brittany would have slammed it. 'I'm not a cop,' she said softly. 'Or a lawyer. My name is Paige Holden. I'm a private investigator and I need your help. Please talk to me.'

Brittany's gaze flicked to him again. 'He's a lawyer. I remember him.'

'Not today he isn't. Today he's more like . . . my partner.'

'I don't understand.'

'Then let us come in and we'll explain.'

Brittany was clearly conflicted. Her lips quivered, her eyes closed. 'I can't.'

Paige sighed. 'Brittany, three people who testified in Ramon Muñoz's trial died yesterday. At least two of them were murdered. Maybe all three.'

Brittany's eyes widened in genuine terror. 'Oh, my God.'

'Whatever you know, you need to tell. It's all starting to unravel.'

Brittany's hand covered her mouth. Tears filled her eyes. 'I can't.'

Paige abruptly crouched and slipped her hand inside the door, by Brittany's foot. When she rose, she held a red Matchbox car in her hand. 'You have to. Please.'

Pale and trembling, Brittany opened the door and let them in. She ran a self-conscious hand over her hair. 'I'm sorry. I was asleep. I work nights.'

'You're fine,' Paige murmured. 'Where do you work?'

'I'm a nurse's aide. I work in a nursing home.'

'Hard work,' Paige commented as Brittany led them to an old table covered in crayons. When Brittany began scooping the crayons into a plastic bin, Paige helped her. 'It's got to be even harder raising a son and going to school.'

Brittany looked up, startled. 'How did you know I was going to school?'

Paige pointed to the coffee table. 'Your physiology textbook. Nursing degree?'

'Yes. Aides don't get paid squat.'

'I know. I was a paralegal working for lawyers. Big pay difference. Shall we sit?' She didn't wait for an answer, sitting at the kitchen table. 'Brittany?'

Brittany sat on Paige's left. Grayson sat at the end of the table and waited.

'Where is your son?' Paige asked.

'Kindergarten. I have to go get him soon.'

'Then he's five years old?' Paige asked, looking unsurprised.

Grayson did the math and his heart sank. 'You were pregnant when Crystal died.'

'Yes.' Brittany looked away, her whole body shaking. 'I'm going to be sick.'

'Try to relax,' Paige said soothingly. 'Take a deep breath. Tell me about Crystal.'

'She was a good sister.' Brittany squeezed her eyes shut. 'She was all I had.'

'And she was taken from you.'

She clenched her fists on the table. 'By Ramon Muñoz.'

'No,' Paige said and Brittany's eyes flew open, uncertainty flickering there. 'That's the problem, isn't it? You knew it wasn't Ramon.'

'*No*. I didn't know. They said it was Muñoz, the cops that came. They said they found the weapon in his house.' Brittany's eyes filled anew. 'But it didn't matter who did it. It was all my fault. She did it for me.' The tears spilled, ran down her cheeks.

'What did she do for you?' Grayson asked.

'She went to that party for me. Because of me.'

'She planned to make money at the party,' Paige said. 'Because of the baby.'

Brittany shrugged wearily. 'Yes. She took care of me. Tried to keep me out of trouble. I got a scholarship to Maryland and I'd just started my first semester. And I screwed it all up.'

'You got pregnant,' Paige said. 'How?'

Brittany's lips twisted. 'The usual way. Bottle of wine, nice words. I was so stupid and Crystal was so angry. She ranted that she hadn't sacrificed everything to see me ruin my life. Then she saw me crying and said she'd fix it. That she knew where to get some really big money. That we wouldn't have to scratch for food anymore.'

'You two lived alone, right? How did you pay the bills?'

Brittany's eyes became suspicious, her tears slackening. 'We worked. We weren't hookers.'

'I didn't say you were,' Paige soothed.

'Tiger doesn't change its stripes,' Brittany said bitterly. 'It's what everyone said. It's what that cop said, the detective who investigated Crystal's case. God, I hated her.'

'Detective Morton?' Paige asked.

'Yeah, that bitch,' Brittany said angrily. 'She acted like my sister deserved what happened to her, that she lured the gardener to the shed. For sex. That simply wasn't true. It couldn't have been.'

There was something in the woman's voice, an acidic note that stood apart. 'Why not?' Grayson asked. 'Why couldn't it have been true?'

'She hated sex,' Brittany said. 'Because of what happened to her.'

'She'd been abused?' Paige asked, and Brittany looked away.

'She was a good person. We ended up in two different foster homes, but she promised she'd come for me when she turned eighteen. She kept that promise.'

'She was arrested for hooking right after that,' Paige said.

'Yeah. She turned tricks to buy food, but she got caught. They were going to send me back to foster care, so we ran away. We came here and started over. She got a job waiting tables. I worked at a drive-through before and after school. Things were going so well until I got pregnant.' Brittany sighed. 'And then she went to that party.'

'To make big money,' Paige said. 'She couldn't have made that much by turning tricks, not in one night anyway.'

'Exactly,' Brittany said.

'Did you tell this to Detective Morton?' Grayson asked.

'No.'

'Why not?' Paige asked.

Brittany closed her eyes and shook her head. 'I can't tell you.'

'Brittany,' Paige urged. 'Whoever paid you for your silence may be involved in the killings yesterday. One of the men murdered was also persuaded to stay silent. His daughter isn't much older than your son and will grow up without him. You don't want your son to grow up without you.'

Brittany's face hardened. 'How did you know I was paid?'

'I didn't,' Paige admitted. 'I guessed.'

Grayson had guessed the same thing. Still, Paige had played it well.

'You tricked me,' Brittany snarled, furious. 'You're as much a bitch as that Morton.'

'Yeah, I did trick you,' Paige said, letting some of her own anger show. 'Because I'm trying to save your damn life. I saw two of yesterday's victims. Both had bullet holes in their heads, brains sprayed everywhere. You don't want to be like them. Trust me.'

Brittany paled. 'That's where I saw you. You're the woman from the videos.'

'Yeah.' Paige touched her throat. 'I almost got killed yesterday, too. These people mean business. If you want to protect your son, talk to us. *Now*.'

Brittany looked anguished. 'Don't you understand? If *they* kill me or *he* puts me in jail for perjury, it's the same. Nobody's here to care for my son. He's got only me.'

A blast from his own past hit Grayson like a brick. He could hear his own mother saying the same words. *He's got only me.* But his mother had been made of stronger stuff than Brittany Jones. His mother had made a different choice.

And they were still living with the results.

'I can't make promises,' Grayson said. 'Until I know what you did. I won't be able to. But I'll do my best to see that no charges are filed against you for lying on the stand.'

Brittany met his eyes for the first time. 'I loved my sister. But I had this life . . . this baby growing in me. I didn't know how I was going to survive. I got a phone call telling me that if I kept my mouth shut until the trial was over, I'd get ten thousand at the beginning and fifteen more when the trial was over. I didn't want to take it, but I was desperate.'

'Twenty-five thousand dollars is a lot of money,' Grayson said carefully. There was something in the woman's eyes that he didn't trust. Calculation. And still a lot of fear. They were probably hearing some of the truth, he thought. But nowhere close to the whole truth and nothing but the truth.

'Would have been if I'd gotten it all. I got the first ten, but two months before the trial I had my son. I got a letter saying if I wanted to stay healthy for my baby, I'd keep my mouth shut for free. By then I was in too deep to tell anyone and really scared. I would have lied to anyone, good or bad, to keep him safe.'

That last phrase, Grayson thought, was probably true. 'Did you keep the letter?'

'No. It wasn't mailed and it wasn't handwritten. And it wasn't like I was going to tell Detective Morton. She'd already done enough, accusing Crystal of being a whore at that party. "Tiger doesn't change its stripes", my ass,' she muttered.

'Do you have anything that belonged to Crystal?' Paige asked. 'Any old diaries or notebooks or anywhere she might have written something about that night?'

'I kept some of her things. I'll get them for you.' A few minutes later Brittany reappeared, a medium-sized manila envelope in her hand. 'There's not much here.'

'You'll get it back,' Paige said. 'Do you have a place to go for a few days?'

'No. If I don't show up at work, I'll lose my job and we're barely hanging on.'

'Then be extra careful. Invite a friend to stay over if you can. Borrow a big dog,' Paige said. 'Keep your doors locked. We'll be in touch.'

Wednesday, April 6, 4.00 P.M.

He checked his laptop screen. The doll hadn't moved in almost two hours. It was in Toronto. Specifically, in a hotel on Yonge Street. Therefore he could only assume Violet was there, too. He would be foolish to assume Silas would stay with her.

If I were Silas, I'd be trying to kill me. So he'd just have to deal with Silas first.

He dialed Silas's business phone and got his voicemail once again. 'It's me,' he said, leaving a message. 'I have a job for you. Call me when you get this.'

He had no intention of tasking Silas with anything important. And this job was. He'd found that Paige Holden had met with IA, that she was their 'confidential informant'. The woman had caused enough headache. It was time for her to meet with an unfortunate accident, which he'd already put into play. It would be a two-fer, getting rid of an irritant and creating a beautiful new path for IA's investigation.

Yeah, the job was legit, so he had already assigned it to another. If Silas was back in time, he'd invite him to the party too. *That way, I'll know exactly where he'll be, and when.*

Wednesday, April 6, 4.05 P.M.

'She's playing us,' Paige said when Grayson had driven away from Brittany's house.

'I know. We got a slice of the truth, I think.'

'You're being generous. She got to you,' she murmured.

'What do you mean?'

'When she said "He's got only me" you looked like you'd seen a ghost.' Actually he'd looked more like he'd been poleaxed. 'She totally picked up on that.'

'What can I say?' he said blandly. 'I'm a marshmallow.'

Paige thought about the picture, the one with the palm trees. He'd said his father had left them. She wanted to ask questions, lots of questions, but she held back. Her questions would keep and she didn't think he'd answer them right now anyway.

'One giant rock of a marshmallow,' she said. 'Brittany knew Ramon was innocent. If the part about the phone call offering her hush money was true, she had to know.'

'It wouldn't make sense to be paid for silence if Ramon was guilty,' he agreed. 'I'll pull over into that parking lot and we can look in the envelope.'

She reached for her backpack and the gloves she kept in one of the pouches. Snapping them on, she held out her hands like a surgeon. 'I'm ready.'

'I'm impressed. What else is in that backpack?'

'Magnifying glass, safety flares, dog treats. My laptop and my WiFi modem. Extra ammo. Makeup. Rope. Flashlight. Trail mix and a bottle of water. Nunchucks. A Swiss army knife. And an Ellery Queen novel. You know, tools of the trade.'

His lips curved as he parked. 'Just don't mix up the trail mix with the dog treats.'

'I did once. Dark alley surveillance, couldn't risk a light. Dog treat wasn't as bad as I thought it would be.'

He winced. 'That's just gross, Paige. Do you have any more gloves?'

She gave him a pair, then opened the envelope. He leaned over to look into it with her. 'A checkbook register,' she said, and handed it to him. 'A high-school class ring. A man's.' She held it up. 'Class of 1973. That's an odd thing for her to have.'

'What school?'

'Winston Heights.'

'Never heard of it,' he said. 'It's not local. We'll look it up. This checkbook register is all deposits. The same amount every month. A thousand bucks.'

Paige met his eyes. 'Sounds like Miss Crystal had some hush money of her own coming in. You'd think Brittany would have looked at this at some point.'

'I'm sure she did. She was eighteen, working her own part-time job. She had an idea of what waitresses made and had to know it wasn't enough. The last deposit was a week before Crystal's death. There's a motive for you.'

'Especially if she'd upped the price tag to pay for baby-on-board. How long did this go on, the deposits?'

He flipped pages. 'For two years. Starting right after her prostitution arrest. We need to trace where this money came from.' Then he frowned. 'Wait. I ran Crystal's financial records. This account didn't show up. I would have noticed a grand a month coming in. Her credit cards were maxed and her checking account was empty.'

'Is it an offshore account?'

'The register book says it's a local bank. I can get the account holder's name without a warrant. I know someone who works at the bank and can ask her to run it for me. We'll need that information anyway, for when we request a warrant to trace the funds.' His expression grew dark. 'But I won't be requesting a warrant anytime soon. Anderson will block it.'

'Sonofabitch,' Paige muttered, then pushed her own spurt of fury aside. Their energy would be better spent proving Anderson was dirty slime. 'What if we tackled this from the other end?'

'What do you mean?' he asked, still scowling.

'You said the deposits started after her prostitution arrest. Did they arrest her john with her? Would that have been in the report?'

He shook his head. 'If they'd arrested him, it would be public record. There'd be no need to blackmail him.'

She winced. 'True. Dammit. We have the class ring. We might be able to find out who she was servicing.'

He looked doubtful. 'Maybe. A call to the arresting officer wouldn't hurt, but I'm not holding my breath that he'd remember, not after this much time. Let's find out who owns the account first. Then we'll reevaluate. What else is in there?'

'This.' She drew out a ribbon, red, white and blue striped, from which a gold-colored plastic medallion dangled, the inscription on which made her whistle. 'It says "*I'm a MAC, Loud and Proud*". MAC, Loud. It looks like one of those freebies you see at rallies. Maybe from Senator McCloud's campaign?'

'I've never heard the slogan, but that doesn't mean anything. McCloud last ran for office in the nineties and this isn't his district. I wonder how Crystal came to have this.'

'From Rex, maybe?'

'That was my first thought, but we can't assume that.' Gingerly he took it from her and held the ribbon pooled in his palm. 'Look at the ribbon.'

'It's . . . kinked. Like it was wrapped around something small,' Paige noted. 'The class ring?'

'No. It had small sharp points.' He looked up, a gleam in his eye. 'A key. The kinks look fresh. It was wrapped in the ribbon recently. I'm thinking Brittany took whatever that was out of the envelope.'

'And left us exactly what she wanted us to find.'

Grayson put the car into gear. 'Let's pay her another visit.'

Paige put everything back in the envelope. 'I think so.'

Wednesday, April 6, 4.20 P.M.

'She's gone.'

Grayson's fist paused mid-knock and he and Paige turned to the right where a woman stood on her front stoop, watching them. 'When did she leave?'

'About ten minutes after you left she did too, and with a suitcase.' The woman's eyes widened. 'You two were on the news. That was so romantic, how you took care of her. I hope you're okay.'

'Yes, ma'am,' Paige said, 'but we need to talk to Brittany. Do you know where she went?'

'Has she done something wrong?' the woman asked.

'Not that we know of,' Grayson said.

'Good. I'd hate to think of that sweet little boy being in any danger.'

'She said she was about to pick him up from school,' Paige said urgently. 'Do you know where he attends?'

'Private school. Brit was determined he'd have the best. He goes to St Leo Academy. It's downtown. Very exclusive.'

And very expensive, Grayson thought, hiding his surprise. 'Do you know why she chose that school in particular?'

'I asked her once. She got sad and said it was something her sister had wanted. I don't get it myself. The local public school was good enough for my kids. Brittany works her fingers to the bone paying his tuition. Lots of overtime. Sometimes I watch little Caleb when she works an extra shift.' She looked distressed. 'I hope they're okay.'

'If she comes back, can you call me?' Paige gave the neighbor a card. 'My cell's on there. We're not trying to get her in trouble. We're trying to keep her safe.'

'I know,' the woman admitted. 'I heard you through the wall. Most of it was muffled, but at one point you raised your voice and that's what you said.'

'You never told me if you knew where she might have gone,' Paige said.

'She has family north of here, but I don't think they're close.'

'What, like, New York?' Paige asked.

'No, like Hagerstown.'

'Up near Pennsylvania,' Grayson clarified when Paige shot him a puzzled look.

'She's also seeing a guy,' the neighbor volunteered. 'His name is Mal.'

'Last name?' Grayson asked.

The neighbor grew uncomfortable. 'I only heard her call his first name . . . you know, in the throes, but only when her son was at school. Mal works for the cable company. The van was parked out front during his lunch hour.'

'When was the last time Mal was here?' Paige asked.

'Yesterday.'

'Can I have your name and number in case we need to reach you?' she asked.

'Miriam Blonsky.' She gave her phone number. 'Should *I* be afraid?'

'No, just careful,' Paige said. 'Thank you.'

They hurried to the car and Grayson started driving. Paige took out her phone. 'I'll get the address for the St Leo Academy.'

'No need. I know exactly where it is. We all went there, the Carter kids and me. It's very exclusive and very expensive.'

'How did Brittany afford it?'

'Good question. The Carters got me admitted and I had a scholarship.' Which Mrs Carter had probably arranged, bless her forever. 'Maybe Caleb does, too. Do me a favor.' He gave her his phone. 'Look them up and call the main office. Ask to speak to Miss Keever and say it's me. Then activate the bluetooth. I'll use my hands-free.'

He drove aggressively while she did as he asked. When the call connected, he felt a spear of pleasure at the sound of Miss Keever's voice. 'How are you?'

'Still here. Are you in some kind of trouble, young man?'

He had to chuckle. It was what she'd always said when he got called to the office. 'No, ma'am,' he answered. He'd been the model student. The model everything. Just to make his mom proud. To make her smile again. 'I've had a long stretch of good.'

'Happy to hear it,' she said tartly. 'How's your mother?'

'Doing well. Miss Keever, I need your help. Do you have a student named Caleb Jones? He's in kindergarten.'

'You know I can't give you that information, Grayson.'

'I wouldn't ask if it weren't important. I'm trying to reach his mother. She could be in danger, Miss Keever.'

He heard her dusty sigh. 'Yes,' she said. 'We do.'

'I think his mother is on her way to pick him up. Can you delay her until I get there?'

'Grayson, what's going on here?'

'It's too long to tell. Please, just keep her there. I'm less than fifteen minutes out.'

'All right. But I expect some answers.' She hung up on him.

'She's going to hold Brittany there,' Grayson said to Paige.

'Good. Brittany told the neighbor that the private school had been important to her sister. I wonder if she meant private school in general or St Leo's specifically?'

'If she meant private school in general, there are a lot less expensive schools.'

'But it's kindergarten,' Paige said. 'Why spend the money at all?'

The light changed and he sped up as quickly as traffic would allow, grinding his teeth over the slow drivers. 'Some people think it's entrée for their kids,' he said.

'I was happy to go to school period. Well, no I wasn't, really. I hated school.'

'That's sad. I loved it.'

'You would. I bet you never got into trouble.'

'No. Never.' His phone rang and he tapped his earpiece. 'This is Smith.'

'It's Miss Keever. Caleb's mother is already gone.'

'What? How could she be gone?'

Next to him Paige sighed heavily. 'Shit,' she muttered.

'I just missed her,' Miss Keever said. 'The desk said she signed Caleb out early. Said she had an appointment. She looked . . . frazzled. More so than usual.'

'She usually looks frazzled?'

'She's a working single mother. She drops him off after her shift at work and picks him up looking like she hasn't slept enough before going to work again.'

'How is Caleb's tuition paid?'

'Grayson,' Miss Keever snapped. 'Financial information is confidential.'

'She's in danger, Miss Keever. She's involved in an old case, one on which a lot of associated people are being killed.'

'Oh, my. Oh, dear.' She paused a moment. 'This has to do with the woman you were with in the garage yesterday, doesn't it?'

'Yes, ma'am. Can you please tell me about the tuition?'

She blew out another dusty sigh. 'He's not on scholarship. She pays it all herself.'

'Wow. What is tuition running these days?'

'Thirty-five thousand per year, including books and fees.'

Grayson swallowed hard. 'That's a lot for a single mom. How does she pay for it?'

'She writes a check every month. She'd applied for a scholarship and it looked like Caleb might have been eligible, but it fell through at the last minute. I don't know why, but if the committee discovered she was sitting on cash, that would have been cause. She reapplied for financial aid for next term. The application is here in her file.'

'Did she get it?'

'Only twenty thousand of it. They noted she had the ability to pay fifteen thousand. None of which I was supposed to tell you. So don't get me in trouble, Grayson Smith.'

'Thanks, Miss Keever. If anyone comes looking for her, you call me. On second thought, call the police first. Ask for Detective Mazzetti in Homicide. Then call me.'

'Who should I be looking for?' Miss Keever asked. Her voice was brisk, but he heard the slightest tremble of fear.

'I don't know. If I knew, I'd tell you.'

Paige tugged at his sleeve. 'Ask her if Rex McCloud went to the school.'

I should have thought of that. 'Miss Keever, did Rex McCloud ever go to St Leo's?'

'Yes, he did.'

Her quick answer surprised him. 'That was more than ten years ago. You don't need to check?'

'No, I remember him well. He attended here from kindergarten until high school. Then he was . . . withdrawn and sent elsewhere.'

The little pause told him a great deal. 'He was asked to leave?'

'I didn't say that and I can't say more. Only that I'm not exactly stunned to hear his name come up in a conversation like this.'

'Got it. Thanks, Miss Keever. I really appreciate it.'

'Give my regards to your mother.'

He hung up and looked at Paige. 'Good thinking on Rex. He was expelled.'

'Interesting, but not a big shock. So where are we going?'

'We need to find Mal, the cable guy. I want to know why the hell Brittany chose those things to give us.' He did a U-turn at the next intersection. 'Call my assistant, Daphne Montgomery, on her cell. I'll talk to her on the hands-free again.'

'Grayson!' Daphne exclaimed as soon as she picked up. 'Where are you?'

'Driving around town, thinking.'

'I'm not in the office. You can speak freely.'

'Good. Did you hear what happened?'

'I heard you asked to be reassigned. I knew it was a crock,

239

but I just smiled and said hey to the new gal. She likes my cobbler, by the way.'

'I'll never diss your cobbler again,' he promised. 'Are you comfortable finding information for me?'

'Depends,' Daphne said warily. 'What do you want to know?'

'I need to find a guy who works for the cable company. His name is Mal and he's seeing Brittany Jones. She's the sister of Crystal Jones, the victim in the Muñoz trial. That's all I know.'

'Okay,' she said slowly. 'Can I assume that Muñoz was really innocent?'

'Why would you?' he asked carefully.

'Maybe because I'm not stupid? Elena Muñoz is murdered after asking for a new trial for her husband. The woman who tries to save her – a PI, according to the media – is nearly killed hours later. Last night, there's another shooting and you're there. Now you're asking for information relating to the victim's sister. You've reopened the case.' She drew a breath. 'And Anderson doesn't want you to. That's why he moved you. What did that little SOB do?'

Grayson sighed. 'I don't know yet . . . exactly. If you don't want to get involved, I'll understand. I promise.'

She was quiet for a moment. 'Which cable company does Mal work for?'

Gratitude and respect mixed with a bit of frustration. 'I forgot to ask.'

'Don't worry. I'll find out for you and text you with his information.'

'I miss you already, Daphne.'

'You should. I'll take care of that as soon as I get a signature on JD's court order for Radcliffe's video. I want to get that done before the new boss comes in.'

'Good plan. I don't intend to stay reassigned, by the way.'

'Glad to hear it. I gathered all your stuff for you and put it in my trunk. Anderson was insistent that your office be cleared as soon as possible.'

Fury at Anderson made his blood boil anew. 'Thanks, Daphne.'

'You're welcome. Be careful, Grayson.'

'I will. Call when you have a name for Mal, okay?' He hung up and drove, focusing on the road instead of the rage that bubbled in his gut. *When this is over, I'm gonna nail Anderson's ass to the wall.*

'Where are we going?' Paige asked.

He glanced over at her. 'Pardon?'

'Where. Are. We. Going? I asked you three times already, but you zoned out.'

'Sorry. Office shit.'

'Your boss who knew Ramon was innocent?'

'Yes. He's already cleared my office.'

She frowned. 'The man really wants you out of the way. You know, I was so mad that he knew Ramon was innocent, I didn't think about the implications. How did he know Ramon was framed? Why did he go along with it? What was in it for him?'

'I've been asking myself the same questions,' Grayson replied. And so far he'd come up with nothing but new rage. 'I'm guessing money. Maybe influence.'

'Money is easier to trace,' Paige said. 'I could run some checks. See how he's situated financially, if he paid off any big loans five years ago.'

'Not without a warrant. I mean it,' he snapped when she tried to protest. 'If we do an illegal search we can't use anything that comes from it. And I want him to pay. He might have known that Elena Muñoz came to visit me last week. Hell, he could be involved in her murder. If he is, I want him charged. I won't risk it. We do this right.'

She blew out a breath. 'I figured you'd say that. At least we know that he wasn't the guy who talked to you last night. Anderson's too old and too thin. But he could have paid off Sandoval. He's got the right build. I didn't notice his hands, because he didn't offer to shake mine. Does your boss have a manicure like the guy in the picture? Wear a ring?' she asked hopefully.

'I never noticed his hands, honestly. I don't remember him wearing a pinky ring.'

'That photo was taken six years ago. Maybe he doesn't wear the ring anymore.'

'Maybe,' he allowed. 'It is possible that he's the man in the

241

photo. It would be damn hard to prove. If it is him, I doubt that the money he paid Sandoval came from his own pocket. It came from whoever really killed Crystal that night, or someone trying to protect him. Maybe Rex McCloud's family, maybe the parents of one of the other rich kids in the pool. So once again we're back to finding Crystal's killer.'

She bit her lip. 'Does he really think that moving your office will make you back off?'

No, he thought. *He thinks threatening me and my mother with exposure will make me back off.* 'Obviously he does.'

'So what if he was involved in Elena's murder?' Paige asked. 'What will he do if he knows you're still investigating?'

The hairs on the back of his neck raised. 'If he is, we still have to prove it. We have to prove all of it. And that still means finding who killed Crystal, so for now we do nothing differently.'

She gave him a long look. She hadn't missed that he hadn't answered her other question, about what Anderson would do. If Anderson was involved in murder, he could be dangerous. Again, they'd do nothing differently. They were already being careful, watching for snipers and cage fighters.

'And once we prove it?' she asked.

'He'll be disbarred at a minimum. Hopefully he'll do time. If he's actually killed someone, he'll do a lot of time.'

She nodded, satisfied. 'So where are we going?'

He realized he didn't know. 'Daphne's going to find Mal the cable guy. Next on the list was Betsy, right? A-cup playgirl turned D-cup clean-and-sober rehab volunteer?'

'Men always remember the cup sizes. Betsy's working in the burbs. Get on I-95 and I'll tell you where to go from there. So, how much is tuition at that fancy school?'

He hesitated, then told her and watched her mouth drop open.

'You've *got* to be *kidding*. Thirty-five *grand*? For fucking *kindergarten*? Why was that so important to Brittany? And to Crystal? Why would they care?'

'The "why" is a damn good question. The Carters sent their kids because Mrs C went to St Leo's. My mom just wanted me to get a good education.' And she wanted him to be shielded from cameras. 'Some people send their kids there for the security.'

From the corner of his eye he watched her study him. 'What kind of security?'

'Tall walls around the place,' he said. 'Heavy gate, discreet armed security force. The wealthy are afraid their kids will be snatched. Celebrities are wary of the paparazzi.'

'You think Brittany was afraid for Caleb?'

'Maybe. Between tuition for this year and the next term, she'll have shelled out fifty Gs in cash for it.' As soon as he said the words, the picture of the check to Sandoval flashed in his mind.

'The amount Sandoval was paid by Mystery Man,' Paige said. 'Coincidence?'

'Hardly. I'm thinking Brittany wasn't honest with us on the amount she was paid. She was a little too . . .'

'Angsty,' Paige said. 'I wondered why they didn't just threaten her to start with. Giving her money then pulling back didn't make sense. She threw in the stuff about protecting her baby to sway you.'

'I know she did. I saw that calculating gleam in her eye. It's pretty common when people fabricate some or all of a story. So let's play this out. She's contacted after Crystal's death, bribed to keep quiet. She took the money. She couldn't have spent any, because she's been paying St Leo's all year and will pay fifteen thousand next year.'

'I still can't believe that,' Paige murmured. 'It's just kindergarten. What's she planning to do in the future?'

'Apply for scholarships, I guess. Once her money runs out, Caleb would be eligible.'

'But it doesn't make *sense*.' Her brows knit. 'Why *that* school? My gut says that the fact that Rex McCloud went there somehow connects. I just don't know how. Yet.' She rubbed her forehead. 'Okay, so continuing to play it out . . . She deposits the dough and lives on what? Her part-time job at McDonald's? Don't think so. She managed to get her nursing assistant certificate and she pays rent on that place we just left.'

'How do you know?'

'I checked her out last week. I was going to talk to her when it was still a pro-bono case for Maria.'

'You mean Maria and Elena didn't even pay you?'

'With what? They were barely making ends meet. That's why all this took me so long. I could only work when I had downtime from all of Clay's other cases. Oh, he said he could babysit me tonight. He'll be at the Peabody by ten.'

Grayson frowned. 'Great.'

'I'm just following orders, Counselor,' she said quietly.

'I know,' he said, hating the jealousy that gnawed at him. 'I don't have to like it.'

Paige looked out the window. 'What was Brittany living on after Crystal died?'

He forced his mind back on topic. 'Not on part-time Mickey D's and it would be hard to work with a baby. Why would she give us that check register?'

'I guess we'll find out when we find her. Maybe she'll go to work tonight.'

He felt like smacking the steering wheel again but he didn't. 'We didn't ask which nursing home she worked in, assuming she was telling the truth about that.'

'She'd have listed her employer on the forms she filled out for Caleb's school, especially if she was applying for financial aid. We could call your Miss Keever again.'

'I will.' He scowled when he got voicemail. 'She may be gone for the day.'

Paige took her laptop from her backpack. 'Then I'll call nursing homes till I find her.'

Thirteen

Wednesday, April 6, 5.00 P.M.

Betsy Malone looked a lot older than she really was, Paige thought. The woman who'd partied her twenties away now faced thirty looking more like she was forty. She led them to a small room at the rehab facility where she volunteered.

'We can talk here,' she said, closing the door.

'We're here to ask you about Rex McCloud,' Grayson said when they'd sat down.

Betsy's eyes widened. 'As it pertains specifically to?' she asked guardedly.

'Not your drug arrests,' he said, and she looked relieved. 'I wanted to talk about the night of a pool party at which a young woman was murdered. Crystal Jones.'

Betsy's shoulders seemed to sag. 'Okay.'

'What happened the night she was killed?' Paige asked.

'I don't remember much. Rex and I were high. I remember Crystal, a little. I more remember that Rex was pissed because he'd hoped she'd put out, but she left. He had a lot of guys there that night and she was part of his entertainment plan. I didn't pay a lot of attention to her. I'd just gotten . . . well, I was new and improved.'

'You'd just gotten your implants,' Paige said evenly. 'For your twenty-first birthday. I saw your MySpace page.'

She laughed incredulously. 'That's still up? I'll have to go look for old times' sake. Yes, I'd just gotten the okay from my doctor to go into the pool.'

'Did Rex leave the pool that night?' Grayson asked.

'A couple of times. I couldn't believe you guys bought his alibi.'

'We had a video of the party,' Grayson said. 'He didn't leave the pool all night.'

Betsy shook her head. 'That's not possible.'

'We've just discovered that the video wasn't made the night of the murder. It was a different night,' Paige said. 'Before your surgery.'

'I'm in it?' Betsy looked away, horrified. 'What was I doing?'

'Rex,' Paige said dryly and Betsy's cheeks flamed red.

'Let's focus on that night in general,' Grayson interrupted, 'and not you specifically.'

'That sounds fine,' Betsy said, relieved. 'Please.'

'Did you see Ramon Muñoz there that night?' Paige asked.

'If I did, I didn't know him. I remember thinking afterward that Rex was lucky they'd found the person who did it, that he'd have had a hard time proving his innocence otherwise.' Betsy paused, frowned. 'But you didn't find the right guy, did you?'

'You don't seem terribly surprised,' Grayson commented.

She sighed. 'I guess because I always wondered if Rex had done it.'

'You said he left the pool,' Grayson said. 'When and why and for how long?'

'A couple times he went to snort more coke. Once he said he was going to find that "Amber bitch". That's how she introduced herself that night. She didn't go by Crystal.'

'Was he angry enough to strangle and stab Crystal?' Grayson asked.

'I don't know. He was mad, but Rex had never been violent. More self-destructive. He hated himself, hated his family. They looked all perfect on the outside, but they were one fucked-up tribe. I mean, look at the parties they allowed.'

'The senator and his wife said they didn't know about the parties,' Grayson told her. 'They said they were asleep that night. Stepdad was, too. Mom was out of town.'

'Rex said they knew exactly what went on. Of course when he got high he said all kinds of things.' She shrugged. 'My folks were absentee, but not like Rex's parents. When my parents found out about the drugs, they shoved my ass into rehab. Four times. It finally took. Rex wasn't so lucky. His mom traveled all the time and his stepdad wasn't involved in his life, really. Rex grew up with his grandparents, mostly.'

Paige found no sympathy for Rex McCloud. 'How long had you known each other?'

'Since we were little. Rex was always trying to impress his grandparents, but they just weren't that into him. Freshman year of high school he started acting out, got expelled. Finally he got shipped away to military school. When he came home and started college, he wanted a good time. He partied hard, looking for it.'

'You said he had a lot of guys there that night,' Grayson said. 'How many?'

'More than usual. Maybe twice as many.'

Paige took out her notebook. 'Do you remember any of their names?'

'I'd never met most of them. There was a guy named Grant. One they called Bear.' She grimaced. 'Hairy.'

Paige looked up from her book. 'A boy named Harry?'

'No. Bear was hairy. Very. That's why I remember him.'

'Grant, Bear, anyone else?'

'The normal crowd. There was TJ and Brendon and Skippy. And a couple guys from Georgetown that I can't remember. It was six years ago and I was high. Am I going to be in trouble for lying about Rex's alibi?'

'I don't know,' Grayson said. 'Maybe. It would have been so much better if you'd told the truth. A man may have spent six years in prison for a murder he didn't do.'

Betsy flinched. 'I'm sorry. I made a lot of mistakes when I was high. I don't know how to make amends for that.'

'You can't,' Paige said sharply, then felt Grayson's shoe brush her ankle and she bit her lip to keep from saying more.

'Is there any more you can tell us?' Grayson asked.

Betsy wagged her head sadly. 'No. Nothing about that night.'

Paige thought about Brittany's envelope. 'Do you know what a "MAC" is?'

Betsy looked up, confused. 'Like a computer?'

'No. Like, "I'm a MAC, Loud and Proud".'

'No. I've never heard that before. I'm sorry.'

Grayson stood. 'Thank you for your time, Miss Malone. We appreciate it.'

Paige seethed silently as they walked back to Grayson's car and she buckled up.

He started the car. 'Go ahead. Get it out.'

'It was all "poor, poor Rex" and "poor, poor me". Born with all the opportunities and she pisses it away. Ramon worked hard, built a life for himself and his family and he's accused, while they . . . party naked with preppy boys named TJ and Brendon and Bear. And Skippy,' she spat. 'What kind of mother names her son Skippy?'

'Usually a Skippy's given name is really stuffy and ends with "the fourth".' Grayson glanced at her. 'You didn't have anything growing up, did you? Materially, I mean.'

'No, because I had a mother who'd rather shoot herself up than feed me.' She told herself to *shut up*, but the words kept coming. 'By the time I was Caleb Jones's age I was running cons, the cute kid they'd send in first to cry for my mommy. I'd distract the mark while my mother and her bed-buddy *du jour* would steal them blind. If I'd had one millionth of what those assholes shoved up their rich noses, I wouldn't have gone to bed hungry every night.' She drew a breath and let it out. 'I'm sorry. That was total TMI.'

'I figured as much,' he said evenly. 'Not the con part, although I've heard it before. So what happened?'

'What do you mean?'

He met her eyes for a moment. 'How did you become wonderful?'

His question slapped her hard and her eyes filled, humiliating her. She turned to the window, focusing on the pretty trees lining the streets. 'My grandfather.'

'He saved you?'

'Yes. I was eight years old and hadn't been to school in months. He'd been looking for me, ever since the last time my mother came and took me away.'

'You stayed with them sometimes?'

'Yeah. When my mother couldn't stand the sight of me anymore.' Her words were bitter, but Grayson didn't seem to mind. 'She'd come for me when she "missed me".'

'When she needed you to run cons.'

'Yes. She left me at my grandparents' one summer and never showed up when school started. My grandmother enrolled me in school. I was . . . happy. Then my mom came one day and got me out of school early. She took me away and months passed. I thought nobody was coming for me, but my grandfather had hired a PI to find her. The PI did and together he and my grandfather came for me. I didn't see him coming.'

'You didn't expect him to come?'

'No, I physically didn't see him coming. I was hungry and was rummaging in a garbage can. The neighbors threw away some damn good stuff.'

A muscle twitched in Grayson's cheek. 'And then?'

'He grabbed me in his arms and said, "*Skatten min*." It means "my treasure" and he used to say that to me when he'd tuck me in. I knew I'd be okay.'

Grayson's throat worked for a minute before he spoke. 'He took you home with him?'

'Yes. He and my grandmother filed for adoption and my mother agreed.'

'Did you take their name? Holden doesn't sound very Norwegian.'

'It's not. We were Westgaards. My mother married when I was a baby and changed my name too. I always thought I'd change it back when I turned eighteen, but by then I was into martial arts and my name had started to mean something.'

'You loved your grandparents,' he murmured, as if to reassure himself.

'Oh, yes. Lord knows I didn't deserve them half the time. I was a hard-to-handle kid.'

'Like how?'

'I got in trouble because I didn't know how to interact with the normals. Broke my grandparents' hearts more than once. It was Granddad that got me into karate. He'd heard about this guy on TV who was working wonders with the bad kids. Granddad signed me up. Sold some furniture to pay for my lessons. I guess he saved me again.'

'I'm sure he thought you were a worthwhile investment.'

She swallowed hard. 'He lived long enough to see me pull it together. Never saw me win a tournament though. But Gran was there, every time she could be. I know rich kids have their problems too, but to throw so much away for so little . . .'

'Money can make things too accessible.'

She shook her head. 'I don't accept that. You had money and you didn't party naked in a pool, snorting coke like air. Did you?'

'Hell no,' he said, sounding shocked at the thought. 'My mother would have grounded me for life.' He paused thoughtfully. 'Actually, no. It would have broken her heart if I'd gone wild, and I respected her too much to even consider it.'

She felt a pang of longing. He was a good man. *Who you will have to walk away from when this is over.*

'And *we* didn't have money,' he added. 'We lived with the Carters and *they* had money. They were, and still are, incredibly generous. I was lucky. But you're right. Rich or poor, people make choices. Bad choices have consequences. At least that's the way it's supposed to be. It's why I do what I do.'

The pang in her heart became a physical pain. Here was the kind of man she'd been waiting for . . . forever. 'You *were* lucky,' she said. 'You had a mother who loved you. Taught you to be a decent man. That's everything.'

He kept his eyes straight ahead, his body seeming to still. 'That's true.' He was quiet for a long moment. 'I think it's time we had a chat with Rex McCloud.'

She blinked, surprised at the abrupt subject change but more by the solemnity with which he said it. 'You said he's on house arrest. Where, at the estate?'

'No. The family owns a building downtown. Mostly offices, a few penthouse condos. Rex is there. No need for the GPS. I know where it is.'

Wednesday, April 6, 6.15 P.M.

A martini was placed at his elbow. 'I hope you had a productive day, sir.'

'I did, actually.' A few well-placed sets of eyes and ears had informed him that Mr Grayson Smith had taken two rooms at the Peabody Hotel. He'd later been seen leaving with Paige Holden who had left her suitcase behind. Now he knew where she'd be tonight. So far she hadn't stumbled on anything he couldn't fix. He needed to make sure that did not change.

'Can I get you anything else, sir?'

'No. Thank you.'

The woman nodded and backed out of the room in the old school way. She'd come recommended for her skills and her discretion. He was never sure what a servant might see, so he paid for their silence. It had been an important lesson, taught him by someone who'd learned through experience.

He'd taken a few sips of the martini when his business cell rang. It was a call forwarded from one of his older numbers. A six-year-old number, to be exact. 'Hello?'

'Hi. This is Brittany Jones.'

His brows lifted. 'It's been a while,' he said. To his knowledge, she'd been a good girl, following the dictates of their arrangement to the letter. 'What can I do for you?'

'I have some information that you'll find valuable.'

He had to smile. The girl possessed guts. And avarice. She'd been an easy target six years ago. She realized she was being paid more than a fair price for her silence and didn't balk. Unlike Sandoval, who'd never been satisfied.

251

'Tell me what you have and I'll tell you what it's worth.'

'I got a visit this afternoon from Grayson Smith and the woman from those TV videos, Paige Holden. They're convinced that Ramon Muñoz didn't kill my sister.'

'And this surprised you?'

'Being contacted? Yes. That Ramon Muñoz wasn't guilty? No. You wouldn't have paid me so well to keep quiet if he'd been the one.'

'So what do you have for me that I really need to know?'

'You knew they'd come to see me, didn't you?'

'I'm not surprised. They now have a cold case. Re-interviewing the victim's closest relative makes perfect sense. What else do you have?'

'I know where they'll be tonight at eleven o'clock.'

It was such a specific time, his curiosity was piqued. 'Where?'

'I'd like to be paid.'

'Where are you calling from, Miss Jones?'

'From a pay phone, which was damn hard to find.'

'But smart.' She'd called the number he'd given her five years ago in the event of an emergency. That she'd kept it all this time spoke volumes. 'I could see my way clear to pay you. Tell me what you know and we can set a price.'

'At eleven tonight they'll be at the Carrollwood Nursing Home. They called earlier and asked the front desk about me. They pretended to be a doctor and wouldn't tell the desk what it was about, but it was them. I'm sure. I gave them some things of Crystal's that will make them ask a lot of questions.'

He frowned. 'What did you give them?'

'Evidence of one of Crystal's old marks. She was blackmailing him at the time of her death. He didn't kill her, but it'll give them a rabbit to chase for a while.'

He was reluctantly impressed. She'd become very smart. 'Who was this mark?'

'His name is Aristotle Finch. He lives in Hagerstown, where Crystal was arrested for prostitution when she was eighteen. He was one of her regular customers.'

'How long did he pay?'

'Up until she died. So how much is this worth?'

'Ten thousand.'

'Twenty.'

He laughed. 'You've already told me everything. You have no chips.'

'I've got a son to raise,' she said, her voice going from amiable to thin and bitter. 'Ten thousand more means nothing to you. It means everything to me right now.'

'I'll go twenty, but I want you to do something else.'

'What?' she asked warily.

'I want you to call your friend at the nursing home and tell her that when Smith and Holden get there, she needs to keep them inside as long as she can. Got it?'

'What are you going to do?' she asked, alarmed.

'Exactly what you thought I'd do when you called me.'

'If I tell my friend to keep them longer and then they die, she'll know I was involved.'

'You didn't expect ten grand more for nothing, did you?'

'Make it an even twenty-five to make up for the extra trouble and I'll do it.'

Greedy bitch. 'Do you have the same account information?'

'Yes.'

He heard the relief in her voice. 'I'll make the arrangements. And Miss Jones?' he added mildly. 'Greediness was very bad for your sister's health. It would be a shame for that son you're raising to become an orphan.' He hung up, shaking his head.

Without the kid, she might have been a potential hire. But kids made people do stupid things. Silas was the perfect case in point. And without the kid, he doubted Brittany Jones would have pushed for the money. She worked at a nursing home. That wasn't the behavior of someone who had grand schemes.

He ran a search on the Carrollwood Nursing Home. It was located in a fairly rural area, with undeveloped acreage around it. Lots of hills. Hills were good for what he had in mind. And a rural location was more appetizing than the bustle of the Peabody Hotel. The Peabody had too many cameras. Too many staff and too many witnesses.

He sipped on his martini as he placed the next call. 'It's me.'

'We still on?' Kapansky asked gruffly. It was his natural voice after his larynx had been damaged in a prison fight. Kapansky claimed women found it a turn-on.

He thought Kapansky was a few bulbs short of a chandelier. But the man did have his skills. 'Yes, but we're changing the venue and adding a guest.'

'Who?'

'You remember a guy named Silas?'

Kapansky growled. 'Yeah. Every goddamn day. He's the one who put me in the joint. Stole fifteen goddamn years of my life.'

Which, of course, he'd known. Having cops on the payroll meant knowing how to deal with them if the need arose. He knew many of the cons Silas had put away. Kapansky was particularly bitter. Combined with his other skills, he was very well suited for this job. 'How would you like to take him out?'

Kapansky laughed, a scraping sound. '*I'd* pay *you*.'

He chuckled. He'd known that, too. 'I hoped you'd be interested.'

'Where?' Kapansky demanded. 'When?'

'Hopefully tonight. I'll call you when I know for sure.'

'I can't wait. Can I hurt him first?'

He chuckled again. 'As long as you make it quick and get out. Plus you still have to do the first job. Silas is just gravy.'

'You'll get your first job. As for Silas, it'll be quick and extremely painful.'

He drained his martini. 'Excellent.'

Wednesday, April 6, 6.25 P.M.

Grayson slid the car to a stop on the curb outside the McClouds' building, ready to go to work. Damn ready to get the truth from Rex McCloud. He'd lost his mojo there for a while. Been a little rudderless. Having the rug ripped out from under him by Charlie Anderson had shaken him even more than he'd thought.

But I'm back, he thought. Paige's outburst had somehow knocked him back on course. Probably because she was damn right. She'd never lost her focus. This was all about Crystal Jones and Ramon Muñoz. They were the real victims here.

Everyone else . . . 'They're all going down,' he murmured.

Paige looked up from her laptop. 'Who? Who's going down?'

The drive through rush-hour traffic had been quiet. She'd withdrawn after sharing yet another heartbreaking chapter in her life, taking her laptop from her backpack and muttering that she was going to look for MAC. He'd let her have her space.

He'd had plenty to think about. 'Everyone who lied about, covered up, and in any way benefited from the murder of Crystal Jones and the framing of Ramon Muñoz.'

'Even if they have family connections?'

He frowned. 'Fuck their family connections.'

She nodded once. 'That's more like it.'

Her approval warmed him. 'Any luck with the search?'

She blinked at him. 'What do you mean?'

'The search for "I'm a MAC, Loud and Proud".'

'No,' she said. 'There isn't much here on Senator McCloud's campaign. I searched eBay too. Sometimes they have political memorabilia for sale.'

'Made of plastic?'

'A local person might have had it in a box with a bunch of other stuff they cleaned out of their garage. It was worth a try. The slogan itself may not be important. What is important is how Crystal came to have it. Especially if she got it from Rex.'

'We'll just have to ask him, won't we?'

'I guess we will.' She closed her laptop and slid it in her backpack. 'I did locate Winston Heights High, the school that the class ring came from. It's outside Hagerstown, where Crystal was arrested on the prostitution charge.'

'The neighbor said she thought Brittany had family there.'

'She also said the family wasn't close. Given that it came with the checkbook, my gut says it's connected to the prostitution. Have you heard from Barb at the bank about who owns the account on Crystal's check register?'

Grayson looked at his phone. 'No messages from her, but it's only been two hours since I called.' He'd asked Paige to find Barb's phone number in his contact list on the way to Betsy's rehab center. That Paige's eyes had narrowed when she'd heard him decline Barb's offer of a late-night drink hadn't hurt his ego, he was forced to admit.

'Think she'll still help after you blew her off for drinks?'

'I think so. She's one of Joseph's old girlfriends, actually. If she invited me out, it's because she's angling to get Joseph back.'

'Ah, my babysitter. Brother Joseph. I don't see him as the type to bend to angling.'

He lifted his brows. 'What *do* you see him as the type to do?'

'I don't know exactly and I think he likes it that way. He's got that broody, this-tape-will-self-destruct-Jim thing going on. A little dangerous.'

His lips twitched. 'He'd like hearing that.'

'I kind of thought so. I also don't think he's as mean and bad as he wants everyone to think he is. If this Barb chick doesn't want to help us, maybe he'll sweet-talk her.'

'Oh, he can be every bit as mean and bad as he looks. But I think she'll come through. She's not as astute as you. She thinks she can still get him back.'

'What did she do to lose him?'

'She was uncomfortable around Holly. Ignored her and made her cry. Nobody disses Holly and gets welcomed to the family.'

'I would hope not,' she said quietly.

'You passed with flying colors. Lisa and Holly are singing your praises.'

'I didn't do anything special.'

'You treated Holly like she was . . . not different.'

'Like I said, nothing special.' She shouldered her backpack. 'Ready, Counselor?'

'Absolutely.' Grayson felt a hum of anticipation as he walked into the building's lobby, Paige at his side. After five years, Grayson was going to get some answers out of the spoiled rich boy.

He gave their names to the security guard manning the front

desk who copied their IDs and waved them through to a bank of elevators. Rex McCloud's condo was on the twenty-fifth floor. Grayson pressed the up button while Paige scanned the directory of businesses with offices on the lower floors.

'Ninety per cent of these aren't McCloud family businesses,' she noted.

'The McClouds own a lot of real estate here in the city,' he said. 'Most of it they lease. The top three floors are condos. My interview with Rex regarding the party was here, in his condo. Six years ago they were only using the estate on weekends. The family lived here during the week. I don't know if they still do that or not.'

'I knew about the condos,' Paige said. 'The senator and his wife and youngest daughter Reba live here full time now. I found an article about Reba in the society page archives. She was throwing an intimate soirée for one of her charities. They still use the estate for the really big functions. Seems wasteful though, maintaining that big house when no one lives there.'

The elevator took them to Rex's floor and they stepped into a lushly decorated hall.

'House arrest,' Paige muttered. 'Such hardship. Money certainly talks.'

'I know.' The earlier hum of anticipation he'd felt had leveled out, becoming grim determination. This was it. His chance to set things right, to bring the real killer to justice. He lifted his fist to knock on Rex's door, but was surprised when Paige stayed his hand. 'What?' he asked.

'You can say "fuck family connections", and I can cheer you on, but you realize that this will get out. If we start asking questions about that night, Rex will almost certainly contact his attorney.'

'Who will contact my boss,' he said evenly. *Who might follow through on his threat to expose . . . everything.* He'd let every possible scenario play out as he'd driven. With the exception of Anderson keeping his mouth shut, none of the scenarios were good.

But he knew that he stood at one of those crossroads that defined a life. *I will not look back with regret.* And he would *not* be blackmailed. 'Yes,' he said. 'I know.'

Worry flickered in her eyes. 'Be sure. This could mean your career.'

He wasn't sure whether to be touched by her concern or angry that she thought he'd put his career ahead of justice. 'My career would mean nothing if I let this slide.'

She frowned. 'I never thought you'd let it slide. But there may be ways to manage this through more . . . diplomatic channels.'

'Which could take months if not years, if they work at all. While Ramon sits rotting in jail and a killer walks free, smug in the knowledge that he got away with it.' He saw the worry disappear, the approval return. 'I know what I'm doing, Paige.' *At least, I hope to God I do.* 'But thank you.'

She smiled and gestured to the door. 'Then have at it. I've got your back.'

His knock was answered by Rex himself, wearing nothing but a skimpy pair of gym shorts, his ankle bracelet, and a cocky smile. 'Well, well. I thought the doorman had made a mistake. I don't often get visitors.' He raked Paige with an openly suggestive leer. 'Especially ones that look like you.'

Years of drug use had not been kind to Rex's face. Despite the smile, he looked hollowed out. Gaunt. He'd been a handsome young man. Now, he looked pathetic.

Grayson could find no pity. 'I'm Grayson Smith with the state's attorney's office.'

Rex's lip curled. 'I know. I remember. I did a stint in rehab because of you.'

Paige looked up at Grayson in question.

'It was a deal in exchange for the security video of the pool party,' Grayson said. 'His family said they would give it to us if we didn't press charges for the drugs.'

'I wasn't using that night,' Rex insisted. 'Booze, yes. Coke, no.'

'We're not here about that,' Grayson said. 'Exactly.'

'Then what are you here about? Exactly?'

'Let us in and I'll tell you.'

Rex waved them inside. 'By all means. Come in. Not that I could stop you.'

'No, you can't,' Grayson agreed. As a condition of house arrest Rex had to submit to unannounced searches and visits from cops and the court. Rex turned on his heel and left them to follow him into a very expensive room complete with an impressive home theater and a pool table. To be incarcerated in a place like this . . . *Why even bother?*

Rex gestured to a long leather sofa. 'Make yourself at home. I'm going to get a shirt. If that's okay.'

'Just make it fast,' Grayson said. 'We don't have all day.'

Paige said nothing as she sat on one end of the sofa. Grayson stood beside her, close enough to touch. Except he didn't, only because he'd shoved his hands in his pockets. Together they waited until Rex McCloud sauntered in, fifteen minutes later. He'd shaved and changed into a silk shirt and pants, looking every bit the rich heir to a large fortune. He flopped in a chair and propped his feet on the coffee table.

'Sorry it took so long,' he said mockingly, flicking his wrists where diamonds winked. 'Had to find my cuff links. So to what do I owe the honor of this visit?'

'Crystal Jones,' Grayson said.

Rex put on a frown of confusion. 'Who?'

'The woman who died while attending your pool party six years ago,' Paige said.

'Oh, you mean *Amber*. I keep forgetting her name was Crystal. You know, since she *lied* to get into my party and all. So what about her?'

'I'm looking into what really happened that night,' Grayson said.

Rex's jaw cocked, his eyes dark with anger. 'What happened is the bitch, who lied to get into my party, went trolling where she shouldn't have been and did it with the gardener. Who fucking killed her, probably in that order.'

Paige stiffened, but said nothing.

'If I thought that was true I wouldn't be here,' Grayson said evenly. Rex's eyes flickered. Panic? Fear? 'I have reason to question your alibi for that night, Rex.'

'It's Mr McCloud,' Rex snarled, then visibly calmed himself. 'I wasn't anywhere near the garden shed that night. The tape showed I stayed in the pool all night long.'

'It might have,' Grayson said, 'had it been the right tape.'

Rex's brows crunched. 'What the hell are you talking about?'

'The tape wasn't made the night of Crystal's murder,' Paige said. 'It's indisputable.'

Rex gave her a condescending sneer. 'And who the hell are you, Pocahontas?'

Grayson wanted to knock the sneer off Rex's face, but Paige only smiled at him placidly. 'The tape was switched, Mr McCloud,' she said. 'It's not up for debate. Do you want to know how I know? Or do you want to waste your words on lame taunts?'

'You're bluffing,' Rex said flatly.

'Oh, no, I'm quite serious. "Pocahontas" is a lame taunt.'

Rex gritted his teeth. 'About the tape, bitch.'

'Betsy had a boob job,' Paige commented as nonchalantly as if she spoke of the weather. 'Six weeks before that night. It's documented in her medical record.'

Rex stared at her in confused anger. 'What?'

'She had her breasts augmented,' Paige said. 'But on the tape – which exhibits very impressive acrobatics on your part, I must add – she's really small. Plus the moon is the wrong size.'

'What moon?' he demanded.

'The one in the sky,' she explained, pointing upward as if Rex was a child. 'Wrong phase for the night Crystal was killed.' She shrugged. 'But, you know, that's only, like, science and shit.'

Rex was visibly seething. 'You're lying.'

'Somebody switched the tape,' Grayson said harshly and Rex's eyes whipped up to meet his. 'My only assumption at this time is that it was you. Your alibi is worthless. So maybe you'd like to tell me what happened that night.'

'Maybe you'd like to get the hell out of here.'

'I'm an officer of the court. You are under house arrest. There are consequences here if you choose not to talk to me.'

Rex's temper was ready to explode. 'Fuck you, Smith. I was in that pool the whole fucking night. I. Never. Left.'

'We have witnesses that say otherwise,' Paige said.

Rex's feet came off the table. 'Who?' he demanded.

Paige's body went still. She watched Rex like she'd watch a cobra, ready to strike. 'That's privileged information,' she said. 'But our witnesses say you were mad that night. And that you went off to search for Crystal. Because you were so *mad*.'

'Who?' Rex said furiously. 'Who said that?'

'What did you do when you found her, Rex? Tell me. Did you try to make her put out? Did you try to make her *pay* for her party invitation? Because you were so *mad*?'

'Dammit, I *did not*. It wasn't like that. Who told you that? Was it that bitch Betsy?'

Paige ignored him, keeping her tone smooth in stark contrast to her words. 'Did Crystal tell you no? Did you strangle her then? Did it feel good, Rex?'

It happened so fast that Grayson would have missed it if he'd blinked. Rex charged Paige, his hands outstretched and his mouth forming the word, '*Who*?'

But what came out was a muffled shriek because Paige had risen in a move so fluid it was fucking ballet. She bent Rex over the sofa, his arm pulled behind his back, her fingers squeezing the pressure points on his hand while she stood relaxed, not even breathing hard.

It was the hottest thing Grayson had ever seen in his life and for a moment he could only stare. And be very glad he wore the jacket to his suit because he was suddenly and almost painfully erect. *God*.

'Get off me!' Rex was screaming. 'I'm calling my lawyer. This is police brutality.'

Paige leaned close enough to snarl in Rex's ear. 'I'm not a cop, asshole, and you can't sue me for squat. You came at me and I defended myself. So you'd better hope that *I* don't press charges against *you*.' She tightened her grip on Rex's thumb when he continued to fight. His body jerked, going rigid in pain. 'This is what's going to happen, *Rex*. You're going to quiet the fuck down and listen to me.' His struggles ceased. 'Okay. I'm going to let you go and you're going to behave yourself, as novel a concept as that might be. You understand, *Rex*?'

He nodded, still furious. 'Let me go.'

She kept the pressure on his hand. 'One move toward me or Mr Smith and you are done. And next time, you might want to reconsider that temper. It's going to get you into trouble. Oh wait, it already did. You *are* in trouble. That's why we're here.'

'I didn't kill her,' he gritted. 'Let me go.' He gasped. 'Please.'

She released him and Rex shuddered, breathing hard. She offered him a hand, but he shot her a look of hateful contempt and pushed himself to his feet. 'Fucking cunt.'

'Sticks and stones,' she murmured. 'What a fine, fine opinion of women you have.'

He rubbed his hand, glaring. 'I didn't kill the bitch. Somebody else did.'

'That's real original,' she said sarcastically. 'Sit down, Rex.'

He looked like he'd argue, but he sat. 'I did not kill her. You have no evidence that I did.' He looked up at Grayson, belligerence burning in his eyes. 'Your career is over, Smith. When my lawyers get through with you, you'll be lucky to keep your license.'

'I'd be more worried about a murder charge, were I you,' Grayson said. 'I know the tape was falsified. I know you have a temper. You have a history of drug use and now a documented display of violence against women. You came at Miss Holden with your hands reaching for her throat. A jury will eat that up. And then you'd go to real jail. No cuff links required.'

'Anything you have on me is only circumstantial,' Rex blustered.

'Maybe. There were prints in that shed that we never matched because you didn't have a record at the time. We didn't fingerprint you because you had an alibi, which you no longer have. So maybe they're yours. Plus, we can't forget the note that was found on Crystal's body. "*The gardener's shed, midnight.*" It was signed "*RM*".'

Rex rolled his eyes. 'Ramon Muñoz, you retard.'

Grayson heard the offensive word used often, but it still steamed him. 'I don't think so, *Rex McCloud*.'

Rex's eyes flickered as if realizing the gravity of his situation for the first time. 'I didn't do it.'

'Famous last words,' Paige murmured.

Rex opened his mouth to say what would be undoubtedly unprintable, then reconsidered. 'If you're going to charge me, then charge me. Otherwise I want my lawyer present. See yourselves out.' He rose and walked from the room.

'You should ice your hand,' Paige called after him.

Rex flipped her the bird without turning around.

Grayson pulled the door closed behind him, his heart pounding in his chest. Paige had been magnificent. And Rex was guilty as hell.

'Grayson,' she whispered. 'Grandparents, dead ahead.'

Indeed they were. Both the former senator and his wife stood in front of the elevator. Mrs McCloud looked coolly reserved. The senator looked tired. And sad.

Only one elevator served the penthouse suites, so Grayson and Paige would not be able to avoid a confrontation with them if they wanted to exit the building.

'Security guard must have told them,' Grayson whispered back. Preparing himself for trouble, he walked toward them, his expression blank. 'Senator. Mrs McCloud. I'm Grayson Smith with the state's attorney's office.'

'We know,' the senator said. 'We remember you from the trial.' He leaned on a cane that he grasped in his right hand. His left hand was tucked in the pocket of a gray cardigan. Grayson remembered Paige telling him that the senator had had a stroke years before, which had weakened his grip.

'Can we ask why you're here?' Mrs McCloud asked. Her hair was blond, pulled back elegantly from a face that was nearly wrinkle-free. She was in her early sixties, but she didn't look it. Her dress was tasteful and timeless, as Grayson's mother would say. A string of pearls completed her look. She was ever a politician's wife, even though her husband was long retired.

'I came to speak with Rex.'

The senator lifted bushy white brows. 'About?'

'That's between my office and Rex. Of course, should he choose to share it with you, that's his business.'

'Is our grandson in any trouble?' Mrs McCloud asked. Her voice was composed, but her eyes held an underlying despair she didn't quite hide.

The senator's shoulders sagged. 'What has he done *this* time? What possible trouble can he get into on house arrest? I swear, he's going to be the death of us.'

'My business was with Rex, sir,' Grayson repeated, keeping his tone respectful.

The door to Rex's condo opened behind them. 'He thinks I killed Crystal Jones,' Rex said in a loud, scornful voice. 'Can you believe it?'

The senator's brows snapped together, shock in his eyes. 'Crystal Jones? That's simply not possible. This is a mistake. She was killed by our gardener. Roberto.'

'Ramon, dear,' Mrs McCloud murmured. 'It was Ramon Muñoz.'

'Of course,' the senator said. 'Ramon. He was convicted of her murder. You were there. You convicted him. Why would you tell Rex you suspect him?'

'He was cleared, Mr Smith,' Mrs McCloud said, but her chin wobbled. 'Our grandson is many things, but he is not a murderer.'

'Senator, Mrs McCloud,' Grayson said as calmly as possible, 'I realize this is upsetting you. I can assure you that was not my in—'

'He says my alibi is a fake,' Rex called. 'He says somebody switched the security video for the night of the party. I told him he was full of shit.'

'Rex!' Mrs McCloud scolded. 'Please.'

The senator was looking hard at Grayson. 'What do you mean, the videos were switched?'

'The video that your security chief provided for Rex's alibi was not made the night Crystal Jones was murdered.'

The senator shook his head. 'How is that possible? That's not possible.'

'I can prove it to you, sir,' Grayson said. 'I'd have to show you the video.'

'No,' the senator said forcefully. 'I saw it the first time.' His throat worked as he tried to swallow. 'That that kind of party was going on in my house . . . On my land. Disgraceful. We didn't allow it. We don't condone it.'

'We put a stop to those parties,' Mrs McCloud said, but she was also shaken. 'Rex was left to run wild, I'm afraid. His mother . . . She was often busy. Too busy.'

'Claire was taking care of the business, dear,' the senator asserted, his voice low.

Mrs McCloud pursed her lips and said no more. Clearly it was a point of contention.

The senator looked at his grandson with a mix of anger, sorrow, and frustration. 'What did you do, Rex?'

'Nothing,' Rex snapped from his doorway. 'I did nothing wrong.'

'You never do,' Mrs McCloud murmured. 'It's always someone else's fault.' She straightened her shoulders. 'Rex's alibi is a moot point, Mr Smith. As much as we hated to see it happen, Ramon was convicted. The evidence presented at the trial was damning. Even if Rex did switch the videos, he did not kill that girl.'

'I didn't switch the videos,' Rex said angrily. 'Smith's lying.'

'Rex, that's enough!' the senator said. 'Mr Smith, you remember this case. The girl was at my grandson's party under false pretenses. She'd lied about her name and other facets of her life, namely her occupation. She seduced my gardener and was unfortunately murdered. Her unwise behavior almost guaranteed she'd meet with a bad end somewhere. It was merely a matter of time. We had nothing to do with it, yet our family name was dragged through the dirt because she happened to meet her bad end on my property.'

In other words, Crystal had it coming. Grayson's temper bubbled, but he held it back. 'I apologize for any negative publicity you had to endure,' he said politely, 'but I'm taking another look at this case. I have reason to believe that Ramon Muñoz was innocent.'

Mrs McCloud's gasp was audible. 'How can that be? Jim, it's going to start all over again. The reporters and the photographers . . . We have to stop this before . . . It's going to become another scandal.'

'We won't let it become a scandal,' the senator said, glaring at Grayson, his warning clear. 'I'm sure someone in the state's attorney's office will be able to convince Mr Smith that he's mistaken.'

Grayson had known the McClouds would complain about his visit to Rex. He was prepared to accept the consequences of pushing forward, whatever they were. But . . .

Mrs McCloud's words had triggered memories of his own. The reporters and the photographers had swarmed him and his mother back then. Harassed them. *Terrified me*. They would again, if Anderson revealed the secret they'd guarded for so long.

And? So? The truth of it hit him hard, quashing his dread. *It doesn't matter*. Whatever scandal would be unleashed . . . *doesn't change who I am*. Staying silent, however, would. And that Grayson would not allow.

He looked the senator in the eye. 'Sir, did you hear what I said? An innocent man – one of your employees – may have spent years of his life in prison for a crime he didn't do. Surely that means something to you.'

The senator's face turned red, whether with embarrassment or anger Grayson was unsure. 'Yes, of course it does, and if Roberto is truly innocent, the guilty party should be punished.'

'Ramon,' Paige murmured. 'His name is Ramon.'

'Ramon,' he repeated impatiently, then turned back to Grayson. 'If Ramon is innocent, by all means exonerate him. But be very sure before you drag my family through it again. These things are difficult on Mrs McCloud. Her heart is as big as all outdoors, but it's not as strong as it used to be.'

'Jim,' Mrs McCloud said softly. 'Please don't. I don't want my problems aired.'

'He needs to know, Dianna. If he pursues this and something happens to you . . .' The senator drew a breath. 'I couldn't bear it. I just couldn't bear it. You're *my* heart.'

Mrs McCloud smiled weakly. 'Jim.'

Grayson wasn't sure if he was being threatened, begged, or snowed. 'We'll endeavor to keep the negative publicity to a minimum,' he said. 'But the tapes were switched and I will be asking who did it and what they hoped to gain.'

Mrs McCloud seemed suddenly frail. 'Jim? Is he accusing us?' she whispered.

'No,' the senator said. 'He would never be so foolish.' He jabbed the elevator button and the doors opened. 'Don't be foolish, Smith. Be very certain. Come along, dear.' He walked into the elevator, holding the door for his wife.

The doors closed, leaving Paige and Grayson staring at each other.

'Well,' Paige said as Grayson hit the elevator's down button. 'I wonder what they'll do now.'

'What they'll do,' Rex called from his doorway, 'is have their lawyers on your ass before you're in your car. Avoiding scandal is the most important thing, doncha know. Which is why I'm such a disappointment. Have a nice night.' He slammed the door.

'Hell of it is, he's probably right,' Grayson said. A few moments later, the elevator doors opened for them and he followed Paige in. The doors had started to close when his eye caught a movement. It was a man in another condo, watching them from his doorway. He said nothing to them, just watched as the doors slid closed.

'That was Louis Delacorte, Rex's stepfather,' Paige said.

'I know. I met him briefly during the trial. I wonder how long he'd been listening.'

'From the moment we approached the McClouds. I saw him.' She said no more until they'd left the building, although he could tell she had something on her mind. When his car was in sight, her words rushed out.

'I didn't like that old man,' she declared. 'Insinuating Crystal deserved to die and that Ramon's freedom was less important than his family's good name. Selfish.'

'They *are* politicians,' Grayson said.

'And threatening you like that, while pretending to be doing it for his wife. "You're my heart", my ass. I wanted to smack him.' Then she sighed. 'I know you took a risk, going up there.'

You have no idea. He wasn't afraid of Anderson or scandal, but it was going to be a hell of a mess. Still, the bigger truth remained. 'It was the right thing to do. For Crystal and Ramon.'

She glanced at him. 'I wanted you to know ... For what it's worth, I'm proud of you.'

His chest felt full so suddenly that he had to wait to breathe. 'It's worth a lot.'

The need to touch her swelled, overwhelming him. He gave in, running his hand up the length of her spine and down again, sliding his arm around her waist. And breathing a sigh of relief when she laid her head against his shoulder. They walked the rest of the way in a silence that grew more intimate and warm with every step.

He put her in the car, then sat behind the wheel, wincing. He'd been hard as a rock when she'd dealt with Rex with such fluid finesse, but her words had the same effect. Even more so. He wanted, more than he ever had before.

But it wasn't as simple as want. He yearned. Needed. Surreptitiously he adjusted himself, then looked over to find her watching him, eyes heavy-lidded. Aroused.

'If we weren't on a busy street, I would have you up against the car,' he said, his voice low and rough, and he watched her swallow.

'I know,' she whispered and his hands gripped the steering wheel so he didn't grab her where she sat. She looked away. Cleared her throat. 'We, um, didn't ask Rex about the medallion.'

Grayson started the car, forcing himself to think about Rex McCloud and not about driving himself into her until they both were sweaty and satisfied. 'It's okay. I'm going to give it to Stevie, see if there are any prints on it. We could luck out and find his.'

She took her laptop from her backpack. 'I'm going to see if I can find any more information on the Winston Heights Class of 1973. We have a few hours until Brittany shows up for her shift at the nursing home, if she shows at all. I'd like to know why she put that ring in the envelope before we see her again. We need a way to sort her truth from her lies, and every little bit of background information will help.'

'That's fine, but you don't have hours. You have less than thirty minutes.' He glanced over, saw her confusion. 'Dinner with my mother. Remember?'

Her eyes widened. 'I thought that was canceled. Because . . . we're . . . not going to . . . you know. Have a relationship.'

He clenched his jaw, unwilling to accept that possibility anymore.

If he ever really had been willing, which he hadn't. 'My mother doesn't take no for an answer.' Plus, he had plans, things he needed to do. Things that, now that the time had finally come, were twisting his gut into new knots. 'It's only a few hours. It would make her happy.'

Her eyes dropped to her laptop screen. 'And get her off your back?'

'No,' he said dryly. 'Even meeting you couldn't accomplish that.'

Fourteen

Wednesday, April 6, 7.05 P.M.

The front door slammed and Adele flinched. Darren was home. She didn't call out to him. Didn't say a word. Just waited at the kitchen table, staring at the glass of wine that she'd poured two hours ago and hadn't touched.

Darren set his briefcase on the table. Tugged at his tie, then sat down. She'd hoped he'd be back to normal when he came home, but he was still aloof. And angry.

'The vet called,' she said quietly. 'Rusty's improving. I called your cell but you didn't pick up.'

'I know.'

'That Rusty's doing better?'

'That too,' he said flatly.

She swallowed hard, looked down at the table. 'So you ignored my calls.'

'I called the vet on my own. I also made a few other calls today.'

He said nothing more and finally she looked up again. 'To who?'

His expression was cold. Hardened. 'To the client you had an afternoon meeting with yesterday. Except she told me it was lunch and you were gone by one. You didn't pick up Allie until five. Where were you all afternoon?'

Stunned, her mouth dropped open. 'You were checking up on me? Why?'

Darren's mouth twisted bitterly. 'Not a good answer, Adele.'

'I . . .' *Was at my psychiatrist because I think I'm losing my mind.* But

270

she couldn't bring the words out of her mouth. 'I went shopping.' Which she had, after leaving Theopolis's office. She'd wandered the mall aimlessly, seeing nothing.

'Which store?' Darren asked acidly.

'I . . . I don't remember.' And that was the honest truth.

'Hm. So, what's his name, Adele?'

Again her mouth dropped open, this time in anger of her own. 'You think that I'm having an affair?'

'Just be honest with me.'

'I am. I am not having an affair. That you could even think that . . .'

'You usually do wounded so much better than this,' he said. 'It's like this. You say someone's been following you, trying to harm you. On a different day I might have made you an appointment with a psychiatrist. But my dog is in the clinic, because he's been poisoned. You didn't want the chocolates. You knew something was wrong with them.'

'No, I thought so. But I thought a lot of things.' *Like you loved me.*

'Whatever. I asked you why someone would try to harm you, but you said you didn't know. Adele, we are a normal couple from Baltimore. We are not celebrities. We have no enemies. At least I thought so until today. I wondered why someone would target you. You specifically.'

'It could be random.'

He laughed, the sound harsh and painful. 'Stalkers don't just open the phone book and pick a name. That happens in movies, baby. Not real life. Not our life.'

He'd always called her 'baby' with tenderness. Now, it sliced. 'So you assumed.'

'I did. I do. Seems that if someone's stalking you, you caught their eye somehow. I asked you if there was someone else.'

'I said no.'

'So convincingly, too. Were you laughing at me, Adele?'

She stared at this man she didn't know. 'No. I told you the truth.'

'Whatever. I can't believe anything you'd even say now.'

'So you think I had an affair,' she said, fighting back the tears. 'And then what?'

'I don't know. Maybe his wife finds out. Maybe he's the possessive type and you wouldn't leave me. Because of Allie. So somebody goes all Glenn Close on your ass.' His fists tightened. 'Except they fuck up and send poison into *my* house. Allie could have gotten it, for God's sake. What were you thinking?'

'You're wrong. About all of it.'

'My mother was right about you. I'm going to her house tonight. When I come back from work tomorrow, I want you gone.'

She gaped at him in shock. 'What?'

'You heard me. You cheat, you leave. This is my house. I'm not leaving this time.'

She opened her mouth, unable to speak. His ex-wife had cheated. Adele had always known that. His ex-wife had gotten nearly everything but the dog, including the house. But . . . she never dreamed he could believe this. *Not of me.*

He waited. 'No more lies, Adele?'

She found her voice. 'I didn't cheat on you.'

'Then tell me where you were,' he said, leaning forward. 'Please.'

'I told you,' she said weakly. 'I went shopping.'

He straightened. 'Fine. If that's how you want to play this.'

'I'm not playing,' she said desperately, a new fear gripping her. 'You can't have Allie.'

'Watch me. I've already got a lawyer. The one my ex used last time when she drained me dry. I'll fight for custody.'

Panic gripped her. 'I've done nothing wrong. You can't prove any of this.'

Pain flashed across his face. 'Then prove me wrong. I want to be wrong. Tell me where you were yesterday.'

Her mind raced. If she told him about Theopolis, he'd dig deeper. He'd find out everything. Then he really would take Allie. 'I went shopping.'

He let out a breath. 'That's your final word?'

Her own breath stuck in her chest, she nodded.

'Then go. I don't want you here.' Taking his briefcase, he

walked to the kitchen door, then turned and she saw the hurt raging in his eyes. 'I treated you like a queen,' he said brokenly. 'How could you do this to me? To our family?'

Adele stiffened her spine. She had some pride. 'How could you believe I could?'

He shook his head. Said no more. Then he left the house, closing the door very quietly behind him. It was silent. He was gone.

He'd ripped her heart out. *If you tell him, you can stop this.* Or maybe hasten it. She needed to figure out what to do. She needed to figure out how to keep Allie.

She forced herself to stand and, leaving the wine glass untouched, stumbled up the stairs into her bedroom. From her closet she pulled her suitcase and began to haphazardly pack, not knowing where she would go. She moved a few boxes, looking for the photo albums she'd packed away when they'd moved from their last home.

Her hands stilled when she spied the box in the back corner of the closet. Almost on autopilot she dumped the contents, finding a smaller box at the bottom. It was about the size of her hand. She stared at it for a long time, not wanting to remove the lid.

There were secrets in the box. Things she never wanted to remember. Yet she'd kept it. *How crazy was that*, she thought bitterly. She recalled the black car last night and shook her head hard. 'Don't be crazy.'

She'd recited those words to herself many times. *Don't be crazy.* Some of those times she'd been struggling in a bed, her arms restrained. Guys with white coats giving her meds out of really long needles. *Don't be crazy.*

Eventually they'd stopped the meds. She hadn't been mentally ill. But her mind had been fractured, Theopolis had said, through trauma. She needed to be glued back together. The glue had failed. *I'm falling apart.*

Carefully Adele opened the box that had remained closed since the day it was given to her. She stared at the contents for long, long minutes as she remembered that day. She'd gotten good at locking the memory away, but every now and then it escaped, roaring to life with a vengeance that left her shaken.

Someone is trying to kill you. The words whispered through her mind, sifting through the panic that clawed at the thought of Darren taking Allie away.

She lifted the little medallion from the box. 'I'm a MAC,' she whispered. 'Loud and Proud.' It had started as the best day in her life. It had ended as the worst. Until today.

Someone is trying to kill you. Darren had believed her. Maybe someone else would too. Maybe it was finally time to tell.

Wednesday, April 6, 7.35 P.M.

Paige glanced at Grayson as he drove. He was talking to Stevie Mazzetti who'd gotten the court order for Radcliffe's video. Mazzetti and her partner were trying to track Radcliffe down to execute the order.

'Somebody should attack me,' Paige muttered. 'Radcliffe would be right there.'

Grayson shot her a that's-not-funny look before going back to his conversation with the detective, leaving Paige to her laptop screen.

Which did have a browser window in which she'd typed *Winston Heights 1973*. Which she'd get back to in a minute. She'd been running another search earlier, as they'd driven from Betsy's to talk to Rex. The results had just popped up as Grayson stopped in front of the McClouds' building so she hadn't reviewed the information.

She did so now, toggling to the background search on *Judy Smith*. She'd heard Lisa's husband call Grayson's mother by name the day before. Handy, as a search on *Grayson's mother* would probably not have yielded much. Unfortunately, neither did the search on Judy Smith. Grayson's mother was very low profile. She'd lived at the same address for twenty-eight years. Grayson was thirty-five. She knew that from one of the articles she'd pulled before Elena was killed.

That meant Judy had lived over the Carters' garage since the time the picture under the palm trees was taken. A search on palm trees revealed Florida to be the only mainland state where coconut-bearing palms grew. Specifically, the southernmost tip. *Miami*.

Here goes nothing, she thought and typed *St Ignatius-Teacher-Miami* along with the year Judy Smith had moved above the Carters' garage and the two years preceding. It was all she had.

But her finger hesitated, hovering over the *submit search* button. It was an invasion of privacy. Grayson hadn't wanted her to see that photo. It had been hidden.

Yet she had seen it, through no nefarious intent of her own. She'd made the decision to start the search based on a simple question.

When did you become wonderful?

She wanted this man. Not only for sex, although her body was primed and ready because he was totally magnificent and it had been so long. But she also liked him. Admired him. Respected him. That wasn't a combination she'd found in a long time.

She sensed that he wanted more, too. But it wouldn't happen if she walked away, which she'd have to do soon or risk falling into bed with him.

So just do it. She held her breath and hit *submit search. Let's see what pops up.*

What popped up was . . . more than she'd hoped to find. Paige glanced over at Grayson, who was on the phone with Stevie, his eyes firmly on the road. He was deep in conversation, telling Stevie about what had just happened with Rex and his grandparents. For the moment he wasn't paying any attention to Paige.

Later. Do this later. But she could not bring herself to turn away. The picture that filled her screen compelled her to look. To read on. To understand.

Her search had returned a grainy newspaper photo of Judy Smith, the same age as she'd been in the school picture. But her eyes were haunted, her face drawn. There was no sign of the happiness she'd shown the day under the palm trees. Whatever had happened, had happened.

Paige scrolled down to the headline – ST IGNATIUS TEACHER AND SON DISAPPEARED, PRESUMED DEAD. Her heart began to beat, hard and fast as she read. And read.

And then she understood. *Oh, God.* She understood.

Oh, Grayson. He'd lived with this . . . *this*, all these years. *He was just a little boy.* She continued to stare at the screen, her heart breaking.

The car stopped. 'Paige?'

Oh, God. She understood why he couldn't risk telling anyone. *Anyone.*

'Paige?' He grasped her shoulder, massaging gently. 'We're at the restaurant.'

She closed the laptop, making her expression as blank as possible, steeling herself not to give anything away. 'I'm ready.'

He tilted her chin, swept his thumb over her lip. 'You look like you've seen a ghost.'

She searched frantically for something to say. 'An article on Elena's death. I . . . It all came back.' She wanted to wince at the lie, but she was numb. 'Let me put on my lipstick.' She actually managed to get the lipstick on her lips, even though her hands wanted to shake.

'You don't need lipstick.' He touched her face with a gentleness that broke her heart even more. 'You're beautiful the way you are.'

She closed her eyes. Tried to calm herself, but she trembled. 'Thank you.'

His hand slipped beneath her hair, gently massaging her neck. 'My mother won't bite you,' he said. 'You don't have to be afraid of her.'

She let him touch her, let the comfort he didn't know he was giving seep in. 'We should go. I don't want to keep her waiting.'

Wednesday, April 6, 7.55 P.M.

Grayson hadn't expected Paige to be so nervous. Then again, meeting a man's mother did seem like a big deal. He got out of the car, told the waiting valet to leave his car as he wouldn't be staying long, then helped Paige to her feet.

She looked up at him, her eyes wide. She was still pale. 'You're not staying?'

'I'm going home to walk Peabody, remember? I'll be back soon.'

'Peabody can wait a little while. Just stay here. Please.'

Her plea squeezed at his heart, but he had things he needed to do. He and his mother had arranged this when he'd called her from the hotel, right after Anderson had dropped his bomb. 'We may not have time to walk him after dinner. We have to get to the nursing home in time for Brittany's shift.'

'Oh. Right.' She nodded unsteadily as he walked her under the awning. She seemed dazed and he frowned, a little worried.

'Are you okay?'

She looked up, uncertain. 'Yes. Of course.'

He threaded his fingers through her hair, cradling her head in his palm. 'Relax. She's going to like you. And I won't be long. I promise.'

He brushed his lips gently over hers, calming her. She shuddered and lifted on her toes, following him, continuing the kiss when he would have pulled away. Forgetting where he stood, he threaded his other hand through her hair and took control, tilting her face so that their mouths fit. Perfectly. She fit him perfectly.

'Grayson?'

The familiar voice cut through the fog and he broke the kiss, lifting his head only enough to see Paige's face. Her eyes were closed. Her lips beautifully plumped. Her cheek a little red from the burn of his five o'clock shadow. He kissed that too, running his lips over her skin. She was warm and smelled so good. *Mine. All mine.*

'*Grayson!*'

He jerked away. His mother stood behind Paige, looking both amused and exasperated. 'Mom?'

'Mom?' It came out of Paige's mouth in a squeak and she whirled, hitting him with her backpack. 'Oh sh—' She cut herself off, pursing her lips, her cheeks blushing a deeper red.

Grayson's mother extended her hand, lips curving. 'You're Paige. I'm Judy.'

'I'm sorry,' Paige blurted, shaking his mother's hand. 'I . . . We just . . . Never mind.'

'Don't think a thing of it. I'm freshening my lipstick and what should I see?' Her eyes twinkled. Oh, his mother was enjoying this *way* too much. 'I've got a table, dear. Why don't you sit and wait for me? I need to talk to Grayson for a moment, if you don't mind.'

Paige shot him a nervous look over her shoulder. 'I'll just . . . go in. There.'

'There's someone waiting for you,' his mother said to her. 'Holly begged to come. I hope that's okay.'

His mother was a goddess, he decided, because she'd not only solved a sticky situation for him, she'd also managed to put Paige at ease.

'It's totally okay,' Paige said, visibly relieved. 'I'll go find her.'

He waited until she was gone. 'Thank you,' he said.

'Uh-huh,' his mother replied blandly. 'She's very pretty.'

He let out a breath. 'Yes, she is.'

Her expression grew sober. 'I figured I'd keep Holly with me while you talk to the family.'

'It's a good idea. They'll want to decide how much to tell her. And how. And when.'

'I should be there with you. This is my doing. My fault.'

He grasped her shoulders and squeezed lightly. 'It's your doing that we're alive and well. You did what you needed to do to protect us. To protect me. And don't think a day goes by that I don't thank you for it, even if I don't say the words.'

She drew an unsteady breath, her eyes glittering. 'I can't cry. I just put on mascara.'

He gave her his handkerchief, watched as she dabbed her eyes. 'What I'm about to do, to say . . . This will change everything.'

'I know,' she said. 'I told you not to be afraid to tell, just yesterday, but now that the moment's come . . . I'm scared to death. Tell Katherine that if she wants me to move out of the apartment, I will. I've hated every day that I've lied to her.'

He knew the feeling. Still he shook his head. 'She loves you like a sister. She's not going to make you move. That apartment's been your home for almost thirty years. Katherine would smack you for even suggesting it.'

'I know. I just had to say it aloud. Though I have to tell you, if I ever get my hands on that boss of yours, I'll be doing the smacking.' Her eyes now snapped with rage. 'He'd better never show his face.

Blackmailing my son. Of all the outrageous things.'

'Well, it's a whole lot more than just us,' he said. 'He knew about other things. Things that could get him disbarred if I'm able to prove them.' *Hopefully more than disbarred. Hopefully* behind bars *for a long time.*

'Then prove them. Son of a *bitch*,' she muttered.

'Mom. Language.' He kissed her on the cheek. 'Go on now. I'll call you when I'm done to tell you how it went. Have a nice dinner. And sit away from the window.'

'I already asked for a table where your Paige will be safe. You stay safe too.'

Wednesday, April 6, 8.01 P.M.

Paige was escorted to a table where Holly sat, looking preoccupied. And worried.

'Hi, Holly.' Paige joined her, then covered the young woman's hand with her own. 'What's wrong?'

'I'm so glad to see you,' Holly said urgently. She looked around. 'Where is Judy?'

'Outside, talking to Grayson. What's up?'

'Well, you know how yesterday you said you could teach me? You know, karate?'

'Yes.' Paige leaned closer. 'What's happened, Holly?'

'I just need to learn. Fast. Now.'

'Somebody bothering you, honey?' Paige asked soberly.

Holly nodded. 'There are these guys.'

A cold shiver snaked down Paige's back. Women like Holly were even more vulnerable. 'Where?' she asked, keeping her voice calm. 'And who?'

'At my center. I go there after work, to see my friends. I went last night.'

'Do these guys go to the center?'

'Yes. They're jerks,' she said angrily.

'Did they hurt you?' Paige asked, heart sinking at the shadows that filled Holly's eyes.

'They push me. They . . . poke me. They grab, sometimes. You know.'

'You know about sex, right?' Paige asked, and Holly's cheeks went pink.

'Yes. But they didn't do that. They talk about it though.' Her mouth firmed. 'A lot. They laugh and say what they'll do if they get me alone. I used to have Johnny. He was my friend. He would make them stop.'

'Oh,' Paige murmured. 'But he died, didn't he?'

Holly nodded miserably. 'He was my friend. He kept the bad ones away from me.'

'Now you're afraid.'

'Yes. I want to be able to kick them and make them *stop*. Teach me. I can pay you. I have my own money.' She frowned, worried again. 'How much do you cost?'

Paige hated the thought of taking Holly's money. Still, she understood about pride and Holly was entitled to hers. 'You'll be able to afford me, I promise you that. I need you to do something for me first, though. I need you to talk to your doctor and have him sign a paper that says you're healthy enough to train.'

'That'll take days. I need to learn now, Paige.'

Paige smiled at her gently. 'It'll take years to learn.'

'Years?' Holly paled. 'I don't have years. I'm afraid *now*.'

'We need to address that. Have you told the manager at the center?'

'Yes,' Holly said, tears forming in her eyes. 'He talked to them. They said they were just playing around. But they're not. He believed them. Not me.'

Paige made a mental note to have a chat with that manager. 'Well, *I* believe you. And it's always better to be safe than sorry. How about if Joseph takes you to the center next time you go? He could tell those guys to back off.'

Holly shook her head. 'No, you can't tell Joseph. He'd . . . he'd be mad.'

'At you?'

'No.' She said it like Paige was silly. 'At the boys. Joseph would hit them and he'd get into trouble. He could go to jail. That's why I couldn't tell anyone. They always tell Joseph. He can't go to jail. He'd lose his job.'

Bless Holly's heart. 'That would suck,' Paige agreed. 'How about if I go with you?'

Holly's eyes widened. 'You'd do that?'

'I absolutely would. I hate a bully.'

Holly considered. 'Would you teach the other girls too?'

Something fell into place. A sense of completion, the knowledge of what she'd been missing. She'd been focused on herself for months. Had felt sorry for herself. Poor karate master, foiled. Beaten. Humiliated. Now it was time to look outward again.

'I absolutely would. We'll figure it out. We need to tell your folks, though. And until we get this sorted out, I don't want you going there alone, okay?'

'Going where alone?'

Paige looked up. Judy Smith had just stepped up to the table and she'd been listening. Judy didn't look much older than the pictures Paige had seen, and for a moment all Paige could think about was the articles she'd read. The sheer hell Grayson's mother had been through. Then her mind cleared and Paige could see the woman Judy had become. She'd survived. Warmth bloomed, pride for another woman who'd suffered and come out stronger on the other side.

Paige leaned close to Holly and whispered in her ear, 'It's up to you. Tell or don't.'

Judy sat down and gave Holly a motherly, chiding look. 'I will find out. You know that. You also know you can trust me. I hope I've earned that.'

Holly blinked, surprised. 'I trust you, Judy. I just don't want to make Joseph mad.'

Judy patted Holly's hand. 'That boy was born mad. You leave Joseph to me.'

'Okay.' Holly told her while Paige watched Judy's face. The older woman was furious that someone would threaten her child, as she obviously considered Holly. Paige imagined she'd reacted the same way twenty-eight years ago when her little son was in danger. This was a mother bear who protected her cubs, no matter what.

Paige liked her already.

'We need to stop those boys from coming to the center,' Judy declared.

'That's a place to start,' Paige said. 'But there will always be bullies, no matter where Holly goes. Don't you think it's better to prepare ourselves – and our families – to face dangers every day?'

Judy nodded, her gaze going faraway for a moment. Then she focused sharply. 'So what's our plan, girls?'

Holly's chin lifted, ready for an argument. 'Paige is going to teach me karate. Me and all my friends. It was my idea. We'll be able to beat up the guys that bother us.'

'Self-defense within karate,' Paige said. 'You probably won't ever be able to beat up a guy. They're just stronger. But you will learn balance and awareness and ways to get away if you're attacked. Which is the best defense.'

Holly frowned. 'Can I still wear an outfit?'

Paige smiled. 'A *gi*? Of course. You'll earn belts, too. But you should never forget that karate is a defensive art. Not for beating people up. Even when they deserve it.'

Judy put her napkin on her lap with a snap of linen. 'I think a self-defense class is a very good plan, Holly. You're wise to think of it.'

Holly beamed. 'Thank you.'

'I might even come,' Judy said. 'If Paige can teach this old girl a few new tricks.'

Paige regarded her for a moment. 'I'd be more than happy to try, but I think you've done pretty well on your own. All of these years.'

Judy's eyes registered shock and Paige could see that Judy knew she knew. Judy recovered, admirably. 'I still want a *gi* of my own.' She opened her menu and frowned. 'I've left my reading glasses in my car. Holly, can you be a dear and go get them for me?' She dug her keys from her purse. 'You remember where we parked, right?'

'Sure. I'll be right back.'

Judy waited until Holly was out of earshot before turning to

Paige. In a heartbeat she went from affable to terrifying. 'Paige, you've got about three minutes. Talk.'

'I know what happened to you and Grayson in Miami. It wasn't hard to find.'

'*How?*' It was an agonized question, incredulously asked. 'I left no trace.'

'People always leave *some* trace, Mrs Smith. Yours was a photograph Grayson keeps on a shelf over his computer monitor. He was seven, you two stood in front of St Ignatius Catholic School. It was a simple search. Took me less than an hour.'

'I didn't know he kept it,' she murmured. 'Foolish of him.'

'I'd say it's a moment in time he never wants to forget. His mom, when she was happy. And not afraid.'

Pain tightened Judy's face. 'What do you plan to do?'

'This was what Grayson asked you not to tell me, wasn't it?'

Anger mixed with the pain. 'What do you plan to do?' Judy asked again.

'I'll never tell. You have my word. But I got the impression that this was keeping him from forming attachments. Of a romantic nature.'

Her eyes narrowed. 'And you want such an attachment? Of a romantic nature?'

'Yes, ma'am,' Paige said, with all the longing in her heart. 'But I want it to be with the right one. That may not be your son, but I want a life with someone. This secret of his is going to keep me from finding out if he's the one.'

'You could have waited,' Judy said, but some of the anger had faded from her eyes.

Not really, Paige thought uncomfortably. 'I've made mistakes, ma'am. Lots of mistakes. I'm . . .' She looked down, embarrassed. 'Um, I'm attracted to your son.'

'Of course you are,' Judy said, as if it were expected. 'Any woman with sense is.'

Okay. 'He's attracted to me. Which I guess you figured out. Things have moved very quickly between us. I needed to know if we even had the promise of something, before things got out of hand. Because I've made mistakes before. Which I think you understand, too.'

Judy looked grimly accepting. 'Yes, I do.'

'If he's the one and I had let him get away because of a secret, one it sounded like you were urging him to tell . . . well, I hope you'll forgive me for finding out for myself. But I'd still do it all again.'

Judy settled back in her chair, her jaw cocked. 'You won't tell anyone?'

'No one. I gave you my word.'

Judy tapped the table with a manicured nail. 'His boss knows. That Anderson.'

Paige's mouth fell open. 'What?' She remembered Anderson's silence as she'd told her story. The way he'd dismissed them to have a word with Grayson. And the look on Grayson's face when he came back to her. *Oh.* 'And still he knocked,' she murmured.

Judy frowned. 'What are you talking about? Knocked on what?'

'We confronted Rex McCloud tonight. He's the grandson of Jim McCloud. He was a state senator in the nineties,' Paige added when Judy's brow remained furrowed.

'Okay. What about the grandson?'

'A girl was murdered six years ago. It looks like Rex did it, but someone covered it up and framed an innocent man. I told Grayson that knocking on Rex's door would get back to his boss and ruin his career.'

'And change his life,' Judy said harshly. 'Because his boss threatened to tell about us if Grayson didn't back off the case.'

'And still he knocked on that door.' A new wave of emotion crashed into her. 'You should be so proud. You've raised an amazing man.'

Judy regarded her levelly. 'Thank you. Will you tell Grayson you know?'

'I want him to tell me himself. If he never does, I don't know what I'll do. But even if it doesn't work out for the two of us, I still won't tell. I'm not wired that way.'

Judy nodded her approval. 'It might be easier for him to tell after tonight.'

'Why?' Paige asked, and Judy's eyes grew shadowed.

'He's telling the family. He wanted them to know before his boss leaked it publicly.'

Paige looked at the front door. Holly was back, looking satisfied with herself. 'The family didn't know? After all this time?' That stunned her.

Judy grimaced. 'There never seemed to be the right time to tell them.'

'You're not telling Holly?'

'Of course we will. But she'll need to be spared certain . . . details.'

Paige thought of what she'd read. 'I understand.'

Judy looked over her shoulder to make sure Holly was still far enough away. 'I think you're probably all right.' She met Paige's eyes. 'But if you *ever* hurt my son, you will regret it. I don't care how many black belts you have.'

Paige had no doubt Judy Smith could make her suffer. 'Yes, ma'am.'

'But if you make him happy, I will love you forever.'

Paige swallowed. 'I'd like the second one better myself.'

'I thought you might.' Judy looked up and smiled at Holly, who held out a pair of glasses with a taped bridge. 'Oh, good. You found them.'

'These are your old ones. I couldn't find the pretty new ones.'

Judy took the glasses from Holly with one hand, brushing the pocket of her jacket with the other, and Paige figured the new glasses had been there all along. 'Thanks, honey. I am starving and Giuseppe has the best carbonara in town.'

Wednesday, April 6, 8.15 P.M.

The incoming call came from the only number he always picked up on the first ring. 'What do you need?'

'They visited Rex tonight. Smith and the woman.'

Damn. He'd rather hoped they'd be chasing Brittany's blackmail victim to Hagerstown. But a visit to Rex was not unexpected. 'What did they say to him?'

'They told him the security tape of the party had been switched. They picked up on the Betsy Malone discrepancy. They visited her before they saw Rex.'

'How do you know that?'

'I have my sources. Betsy told them everything. A soul-cleansing, as it were.' The words dripped in contempt. 'The girl is weak. Always has been.'

That was definitely true. When Betsy was an addict she'd been far easier to control. He blew out an impatient breath. 'What did Rex tell them?'

'What you'd expect. That he was innocent. That he wanted his lawyer present the next time they visited.'

That made him smile. 'Let Rex call his lawyer.'

'You find this funny? I can assure you that it's not. You said the prosecutor had been dealt with. You *said* he wouldn't cause trouble.'

'He hasn't done anything major yet.' And as of around eleven-thirty tonight Smith would cease to be a problem. He'd cease to be much of anything. He'd cease to be.

'Stop him before he does.'

'You can count on it. I need to go.'

'Wait. I have another matter.'

Dread pooled in his gut. 'What have you done?'

'Nothing. That's the problem. This last one is incredibly lucky. She keeps surviving.'

'I asked you to back away from that.'

'I can't now. She knows.'

The dread grew. 'What does she know?'

'That I'm trying to kill her.'

Shit. 'Wait. Does she know *you're* trying to kill her or just that someone is?'

'The second one, I believe.'

He sighed silently. 'I'll take care of her.' He usually did. 'Where is she?'

'She left her house with a suitcase about an hour ago. Her husband left with a foul expression earlier this evening. I think they've fought. She's staying at the home of a friend who lives at

3468 Bonnie Bird Way. What a ridiculous name for a street.'

'Where are you now?'

'On Bonnie Bird Way, sitting a few houses down from the friend.'

For the love of God . . . 'Go home. Now.'

There was an ominous pause. 'Don't command me. Ever.'

'I'm sorry,' he said contritely. *'Please* go home. I can't have Adele Shaffer putting too many loose ends together. Not right now.'

'Very well. Take care of her. Fix this.'

'I will. Wait for my call.'

Wednesday, April 6, 8.25 P.M.

By the time Grayson walked Peabody and made it to Lisa and Brian's Party Palace, the family was gathered in Brian's kitchen and chowing down on pot roast.

The chair at the head of the table was empty and Grayson looked at Jack Carter in surprise. The head of the family always sat at the head of the table.

'Your meeting,' Jack said, pointing to the empty chair with his fork. 'Your seat.'

Jack and Katherine Carter sat together. Katherine had taken them in, all those years ago, but Jack had never said no. Instead the man had taken him under his wing. When Jack took Joseph to play ball in the park, Grayson was automatically included. When there was a game or any school award function, Jack and Katherine had been there, sitting next to his mother, beaming with pride.

When time came for college, Grayson watched Joseph fill out applications to all the best schools. Grayson had enough saved for a local school, grateful for the opportunity to even go to college. But they'd turned his world on end yet again by revealing that they'd been putting money aside in a college fund for Grayson along with their 'other kids'.

Jack and Katherine had made it possible for him to become the man he was today. Now, Grayson found himself staring at his family, his heart in his throat and his stomach turning inside out as he faced telling them who he really was.

What if they were angry? Or worse, ashamed or repulsed? He wasn't sure he could handle that. But he knew they needed to hear the truth from him. He knew the news of his visit to Rex McCloud would be reaching Anderson soon if it hadn't already.

'What's wrong, Grayson?' Lisa asked. She slid a plate onto his place at the table. 'You look sick. Sit, honey. Eat.'

'I don't think I can yet,' Grayson said, still standing.

Lisa took her place next to Brian. 'Don't let it sit too long. It'll get cold. Plus I only have the sitter until ten.'

'Then I'll make it quick.' Like ripping off a Band-Aid. 'Thanks for coming out.'

Six sets of eyes met his. Jack and Katherine. Brian. Lisa and Joseph and Zoe.

'I have something to tell you that Mom and I should have told you years ago, but we could never find the right time. At the beginning, we were scared. We'd been homeless and Mom would have done almost anything to keep me safe. Later . . . I wouldn't let her tell. I didn't want anyone to know. And for that, I'm sorry.' He closed his eyes. 'I don't even know where to start.'

There was a long, long silence. Then Jack cleared his throat. 'How about "Once upon a time I was a kid in Miami"?' he said.

Grayson's eyes flew open. Six pairs of eyes watched him, kindly. Unsurprised. For what seemed like an eternity, he couldn't speak. Then he said hoarsely, '*You knew?*'

Katherine smiled. 'Before I offered your mother the job as nanny. Do you think I'd trust my own children to just anyone? What kind of mother do you think I am?'

'You *knew*?' he repeated. 'And you didn't *care*?'

'Of course we cared,' Jack said. 'We cared about you and Judy. Whatever happened was not your fault. Ever. You didn't want to tell us and we understood. That was then. You're part of our family now and we take care of our own.'

Slowly Grayson sank into the chair, his heart hammering in his chest. 'How?'

'You made the national news when you disappeared,' Jack said. 'Your mother cut her hair, but she couldn't change your appearance

288

that much. When she showed up for her interview, she had you with her. Katherine recognized you right away.'

Grayson looked at Katherine who shook her head, remembering. 'You were this terrified child with big green eyes that had seen things no human should ever see. Your mother was desperate. We had the means to keep you safe. So we did.'

Grayson's heart filled his throat. Tears stung his eyes. 'I don't know what to say.'

'Mom and Dad told us the basics soon after you arrived,' Joseph said. 'We watched over you at school. Made sure nobody ever took your picture. By the time you were on the news saying "no comment" every other week, we figured you were ready to take care of yourself.'

Lisa rolled her eyes. 'And then you get yourself on YouTube yesterday. Freaking worldwide celebrity overnight. We all thought that was extremely ironic.'

They laughed and Grayson felt a load lift from his shoulders. 'I never even considered that. I haven't worried about being photographed since I graduated from high school. I don't look like him, thank God.'

'You're nothing like him,' Lisa said fiercely. 'I'll fight anyone who says otherwise.'

Although she was a whopping five-foot-nothing, Grayson would put his money on Lisa any day of the week. 'Thank you.'

'We learned the rest when we were old enough to do the research ourselves,' Zoe said, her eyes growing haunted. 'I remember the day I found the articles. I . . . was never the same. It changed my life. That's why I became a criminal psychologist.'

'And why I joined the Bureau,' Joseph added quietly. 'It changed us all.'

Grayson blew out a breath. 'I thought you'd be mad.'

Katherine rose, came to his chair and put her arms around him. 'We love you, Gray. We hoped you'd tell us yourself someday. But we would have been fine if you never had.'

'Mom said to say that she'll leave if you want her to.' He winced when Katherine smacked his arm, even though it didn't really hurt. 'Ow,' he said without feeling.

'That was for your mother,' she said. 'The very thought.'

'What we want to know is, why today, Grayson?' Jack asked. 'Why tell us today, and like this?'

Grayson looked at Joseph and saw his brother had figured it out. Joseph shrugged. 'This is your party.'

'You know?' Jack asked his son. 'And you've said nothing?'

'I don't know for sure,' Joseph claimed and Jack scoffed.

'Hah. So will *you* satisfy this old man's curiosity, Grayson? Since my other son has a terminal case of poker face.'

Grayson found himself smiling. 'You'll never be old, Jack. You're too damn wily.' He picked up his fork, suddenly starving. 'Let me eat a few bites. Then I'll fill you in.'

Fifteen

Wednesday, April 6, 9.30 P.M.

Silas dragged himself into his house, dropped onto the sofa. No cops were waiting outside, so he knew he was safe for now. Grayson Smith hadn't recognized him.

I should be hurt, he thought dryly. *All those years and he didn't know me.*

To be fair it had been dark. *And I was wearing a mask. And my voice may have been a little higher than normal.* Adrenaline did it every time. Still . . .

I shouldn't even be here. I should be driving across Canada like there's no tomorrow. But as long as his boss breathed, his wife and child would not be safe.

He reached for the business cell he'd left out in plain view. He figured if the cops were on to him, he might as well incriminate everyone he could. His boss's number was in his phone log. A smart cop could put it together. He knew smart cops.

His old partner was one of the smartest. That he'd had to lie to her hurt. Every time he'd taken a life to protect his child he told himself she'd understand. But he knew it wasn't true. Now he could only hope he didn't put her in the position of having to take him down. Because she would, he had not a single doubt.

He opened the business cell and frowned. His employer had called eight times. There was a message. *Another job. I have to say no.* But that would alert the man and that was the last thing Silas wanted. He hit speed dial. 'It's me,' Silas said.

'Where have you been?' The question was not kindly asked.

'I had a migraine. Leveled me all day long. I never left my bed. Dry heaves.'

'I'll send you a fucking potted plant,' he said sarcastically. 'I need you at the Carrollwood Nursing Home at half past eleven.'

Silas frowned. 'Why?'

'Because I want you to read bedtime stories to the Q-tips,' he snapped. 'Fuck it, man. I want you to shoot someone, for God's sake. Remember? That's your *job*?'

Silas drew a steadying breath to keep from snapping back. 'Who?' he asked.

'I'll tell you when you get there. I've sent you an email with a map showing where you need to wait. Be prepared to take a shot from about a hundred yards. Questions?'

About a million, first of which is how do I fry your ass. 'No.'

'Good. This is your last chance, Silas. You fuck up again and somebody's going to need a priest. You'll only wish it was you.'

Silas flinched when the phone clicked in his ear. Sonofabitch.

So don't go.

No, he'd go. He needed to know what the bastard was up to. He found the nursing home on the map. He had an hour before he needed to leave. Time for a shower and shave. And a meal. But first, a phone call to Violet to say good-night. Priorities.

Wednesday, April 6, 11.00 P.M.

'Are we there?'

Grayson looked over to the passenger seat as Paige opened one eye, then the other, still half-asleep. But totally beautiful. She'd fallen asleep minutes after he'd picked her up from Giuseppe's, where his mother had nodded her approval.

'We've been here for ten minutes,' he said. 'I've been reading emails.'

She covered a yawn with one hand. 'I guess I fell asleep.'

'You needed it.' He smiled at her. 'All that girl talk must be exhausting.'

'We had fun, your mother, Holly and me. We missed you, though.'

He'd arrived as they were finishing their meal. 'Next time.'

'Where did you go?'

'I went home to walk Peabody and got sidetracked.' He didn't want to lie, but he didn't want to tell her the whole truth either. 'What did you girls talk about?'

'Oh, all kinds of things. Karate and fashion. Your mother and I are going sale-ing.'

He frowned. 'My mother hates boats.'

She laughed softly. 'Sale-ing as in finding sales. Shopping. Your mother likes that.'

'Don't I know it.' He traced her mouth with his fingertip. 'She liked you.'

'It was mutual. Of course we talked about you. A lot. She's a proud mama.'

He played with her lower lip, his breath catching when her tongue licked his finger, barely enough to feel. He swallowed hard, his body responding.

Really responding. He wished he knew what he was going to do about Paige. Joseph and Lisa had separately urged him not to blow it with her. His mother had done the same thing. In two days Paige had managed to impress all the family that she'd met.

He wasn't surprised. She'd impressed him within two seconds of seeing her on TV.

He had about two hours to figure out his own mind, because that's how long it would take to find and talk to Brittany Jones, then get back to his townhouse to pick up Paige's dog. He'd take them to the Peabody Hotel where he *should* leave her under the guard of her partner. Possessive fury bubbled up at the thought and he knew he would not be leaving her under the care of another tonight. *I will guard her myself.*

She was watching him, dark eyes aroused and potent. Maybe they'd never leave his townhouse. He had a big bed. A really big bed. His mind tortured him with what he could do to her there. He'd make sure her eighteen-month fast was worth the breaking.

No, you can't. Not unless you plan to keep her. He went still. To keep her meant he'd have to tell her. She needed to know. Then she could leave if she wanted.

'What am I going to do with you?' he whispered.

Her eyes changed. The arousal remained, but it was tempered with a tenderness that made his heart hurt. 'What do you *want* to do with me?' she whispered back.

His body clenched, the breath leaving his lungs in a rush. He touched her cheek, caressing her smooth skin in the way he already knew she liked. 'Everything,' he said gruffly, and he knew it was true.

She continued to study him. 'Everything is a lot,' she said quietly.

He leaned toward her, smelling her hair, finding it soothed the rush of emotions churning inside him. 'I know.'

She closed the distance between them, brushing his lips with hers. 'I wish it didn't make you so sad,' she said. 'I don't want you to be sad.'

Startled, he stared as she pulled away and resettled herself in her seat. 'What's in your email?' she asked before he could think of a thing to say.

'What?'

'Your email. You said you were reading your email.'

His heart still hurt. His body still wanted her. With difficulty he forced himself to focus. 'Stevie and Fitzpatrick found Radcliffe. He voluntarily surrendered Logan's computer once they showed him the court order. They've got the video at the lab, but they're not hopeful that Logan caught the sniper's face.'

'That would be too easy.'

'That it would. Ballistics tested the gun the detectives found in Sandoval's car and the gun used to kill Delgado. No obvious connections.'

'Again, too easy. What about Barb the banker?'

'Barb came through. She said the account on Crystal's check register belongs to Brittany Jones.'

'What? *Brittany* was blackmailing someone? That doesn't make sense.'

'Apparently Brittany's middle name is Amber.'

'Which is the name Crystal used to get into Rex's party. She also used Brittany's name to open the account. Smart, actually.'

'Barb said the account had been active until six months ago. That's all she could say without a warrant.'

'So either their mark didn't find out that Crystal was dead or Brittany renewed the threat,' Paige said thoughtfully. 'The girl's bold.'

'She continued getting money every month. She just didn't record it in the register.'

'That's also how she could afford to pay fifty grand to St Leo's, assuming she got paid what Sandoval did. She used Crystal's blackmail money for food and rent. I wonder why the payments stopped?'

'Maybe the mark finally found out Crystal was dead.' Grayson checked his watch. 'It's almost eleven. Let's visit Brittany.'

'If the front desk tells her it's us, she might run. We need a ruse.'

His lips twitched unexpectedly. 'A ruse?'

One dark brow arched. 'Are you making fun of me?'

'Only a little. So, Watson, what shall our *ruse* be?'

'Why do you assume you're Sherlock?' Paige asked.

'Good point. You can be Sherlock if you want.'

'If anyone inside recognizes us from that damn news video we're stuck being ourselves. If not, I'm her friend from nursing school and you're my date.'

My date. It gave him a kind of sophomoric pleasure. 'Why do you assume I can't go to nursing school too? Now you're being sexist.'

'No, now I'm being realistic. Few nursing students could afford a suit like yours.'

'Plus you just want to be my date,' he said lightly.

Now it was her eyes that grew sad. 'Yes. I would.' Abruptly, she opened her car door. 'Let's go. I want to know how Crystal got that McCloud medallion.'

The reception area of the nursing home was an institutional white. The front desk was occupied by a woman whose nametag read *Sue*.

Paige stopped at the desk. 'Hi. Has Brittany Jones come in yet?'

Sue's eyes narrowed suspiciously. 'What do you want with her?'

'I go to school with her,' Paige said. 'I missed a class and she was going to give me some notes.'

'What's your name?'

'Olivia Hunter.'

Sue lifted an inquiring brow towards Grayson. 'And him?'

Paige slid her arm around Grayson's waist proprietarily. 'My boyfriend, David.'

'Ma'am,' Grayson said, wondering at Paige's choice of names. She might have picked the first ones that came to her mind, but that they were her friends who'd found forever happiness was not lost on him. He put his arm around Paige's shoulders.

'Let me see if Brit's available.' She paged Brittany to come to the front desk, then pointed to a row of vinyl chairs. 'You two can wait over there.'

Wednesday, April 6, 11.20 P.M.

Silas frowned. He'd known deep down who his target would be, but his anger boiled when he drove past the silver Infiniti parked in the nursing home's lot. It was Grayson Smith's car. Silas had no doubt that Paige Holden would be with him.

It was a goddamn test.

Which meant his boss was probably nearby, watching him. *Asshole.*

But if his boss was nearby . . . Silas's rifle had a night scope. If he could figure out where the bastard was hiding, he could put an end to all of this tonight.

And then he'd take his family far away. They wouldn't like it at first. His wife would miss city life and her friends. Violet would miss her school and the toys she'd left behind. But they'd be alive, and together. The rest they'd get used to.

He cruised to the end of the parking lot, searching the hills beyond. There were a lot of places to hide. If the bastard was up there, he'd be difficult to find. *I'll have to make him come to me.* How he'd accomplish that, he wasn't quite sure. Yet.

And if he's got a scope trained on you? That idea was laughable. The bastard couldn't shoot his way out of a paper bag. *That's why he 'hired' me.* If the bastard planned to take Silas out, he'd do it up close and personal. *Except I'd be ready for him.*

Silas drove his van around the parking lot. No security cameras, which was good. He left the lot. He would not stay here. He didn't intend to kill Grayson and Paige, but he'd at least make it look like he'd made a well-planned attempt. Once shots were fired, people would come running. There was no way he'd park here.

He'd seen an access road on his way in. He'd park there and find a place within the trees to set up his shoot.

He wondered why Grayson Smith was in the nursing home. The man's mother wasn't ill. Judy Smith was, in fact, in fine, fine shape. Silas had admired her more than once. Of course he wasn't that kind of man, even if she'd been that kind of woman.

She had sacrificed much for her son. From the few times he'd observed them together, Silas got the impression that Grayson fully understood the value of that sacrifice. He also wondered how long it would be before the bastard who believed he owned Silas's life would spill the Smiths' secret.

He wondered if Grayson was aware of just how many people knew who he really was.

It had never mattered to Silas, but he knew it mattered to Grayson. That's the kind of man the prosecutor was. When his boss had told Silas the truth about Grayson Smith, the reason for the prosecutor's zeal had become painfully apparent.

It had also made Grayson the perfect, unwitting patsy. *Join the club, Counselor.*

Wednesday, April 6, 11.35 P.M.

Paige and Grayson had been waiting a half-hour and there was no Brittany Jones to be seen. After calling her cell, Sue said Brittany was on her way in but she'd been delayed. Apparently, she'd had to scramble to find childcare for her son. Based on the fact that Brittany had run from her neighborhood, that had made sense. Now, Paige wasn't so sure.

Sue had begun casting them nervous looks. The last time she'd called Brittany's cell, she'd turned her back to speak into her phone, hiding her face from them.

Paige leaned close to Grayson, pressing her lips to his jaw just below his ear. It was part of the ruse, but she took a moment to draw in the scent of him, to savor the tingle of his stubble on her lips. Now that she knew what he'd held so secret all of these years, she understood how hard it would be for him to reveal it to anyone.

She could be patient. Grayson Smith was a man worth the time it would take to find out if the undeniable spark between them could become more.

He'd knocked anyway. The thought kept playing through her mind. Knowing he'd be revealed, that his life would be forever changed, he'd still knocked on Rex's door. Because it was the right thing to do.

She wanted this man. He was handsome. Sexy. Intelligent. Kind when he didn't have to be. Protective. He had a body that she wanted to explore for hours, then start all over again. But it was his integrity that called to her. This was real. *I want him for my own. I want him to want me for the same reason.* She wanted him to want her the way David wanted Olivia. *I want my turn at happy ever after. I want it with this man.*

She had to swallow her thrumming heart back down to her chest. 'Do you think she's coming?' she whispered in his ear.

He turned to look at her, his green eyes aroused, full of want. And a yearning she understood because she felt it too. 'I don't know,' he whispered back, his breath hot against her neck. He brushed his lips over her ear, making her shiver. 'See if you can get Sue to give you Brittany's cell number. We'll call her ourselves.'

Paige rose, only to find Sue watching them, clearly interpreting all the physical signals correctly. The receptionist looked at Grayson in a way that made Paige want to claw the woman's eyes right out of her head.

Paige glared and Sue blinked innocently. 'I'm so sorry,' Sue said, her voice husky. 'He's . . . You can't really blame me, you know. It's pheromones.' She held up her left hand where a ring glinted in the overhead light. 'I'm married. Happily. I promise.'

Paige chuckled and the tension was broken. 'Is Brit really coming in?' she asked, letting herself whine, just a little. 'I need those notes, but I'd really rather be doing other things right now than waiting for her. You, um, understand.'

'Oh, yes,' Sue breathed. 'Perfectly. I told her that you were waiting. She said she's coming. That she's late to begin with is really unusual. She's so dependable.'

'I know. That's why I asked her for the notes. She's always in class. Look –' Paige lowered her voice conspiratorially – 'I have to get up early tomorrow and I really want to get back home and . . . well, you know. Can I get Brittany's cell-phone number? I can arrange to get the notes tomorrow or maybe she can scan them and email them to me.'

Sue hesitated. 'I really shouldn't give out her number.'

'Please?' Paige wheedled. 'You have no idea what I'm missing right now.'

Sue sighed. 'I bet he's every bit as incredible as he looks.'

He'd knocked anyway. 'Better,' Paige told her.

With another sigh, Sue wrote a phone number on a notepad and handed the sheet to Paige. 'Have fun. Maybe *you* could take some notes and send them to me?'

Paige chuckled again. 'Your heart couldn't take it.' She turned and gave Grayson a nod. 'We're good. Let's go home.'

Grayson stood and the room felt smaller. His eyes rested on her and she felt . . . hot. Flushed. *Claimed.* 'Anything you say,' he said.

Wednesday, April 6, 11.45 P.M.

From his vantage point on the tree-lined hill, Silas watched Grayson and Paige exit the nursing home. They were alone, Grayson's hand on the small of Paige's back. That the prosecutor's hold was proprietary could be seen, even from here. Silas wondered again what they'd been doing there, how it connected to the case. He hoped Grayson would uncover every facet of this crime, down to the involvement of both their bosses.

Except that Silas needed to be sure his own boss wouldn't talk. *Because prison would be a really unhealthy place for me.*

He put his eye to his rifle sight, brought Grayson into focus as he put Paige into the car. The prosecutor kissed her on her mouth, then lifted his head, like a predator sniffing his prey. Silas guessed he'd become accustomed to looking over his shoulder, at least at one time in his life. *Stay vigilant, Grayson. Or you'll be dead, too.*

Silas shifted the gun a few inches from Grayson's head and fired, the bullet harmlessly pinging off a lightpost. Grayson moved fast, barking an order to Paige before disappearing in front of the car. Paige ducked down and the driver's side door opened from the inside. Grayson got in and drove like a bat out of hell.

Good. They'd be on their guard from here on out. *And if the boss is here, he saw me try.* Silas slowly rotated his body so that he was looking through the sight at the hills, searching for a shadow, falling stones, anything to tell him the bastard's position.

One more squeeze of the trigger and his problem would be sol—

'Don't move, cop.' Cold steel pushed against the back of his skull.

Silas froze, his finger still on the trigger. It wasn't his employer. He didn't know the voice. It was male. Gravelly and rough. Full of venom. His heart began to beat a little faster. 'Who are you?'

He didn't wince when the gun barrel shoved harder into his skull. 'You have the right to remain silent,' the man said. 'Do I sound familiar, *cop*?'

'No, you don't.'

'That's because some crackhead busted my larynx when I was in Holding,' he rasped. 'Where *you* put me. Before that, I had the voice of a motherfucking choir boy. I said, put the goddamn rifle down.'

There was no way Silas was dropping his weapon. He lowered the rifle a few inches, still keeping his finger on the trigger. 'Who sent you?' As if he had to ask.

Before the man could answer, Silas ducked and spun, knocking the guy's feet out from under him. The man crashed to the ground and Silas shot both wrists before he could blink. His scream was nearly silent, the gun falling out of his hand to bounce harmlessly in the grass, his face twisted in pain and hate. He tried to rise to his knees.

Silas shot out one knee and the man's mouth yawned open on another rasping scream that could barely be heard. Silas leaned close. 'Who the hell are you?'

'Go to hell.'

It was dark, but there was just enough moon to make out his face. It was familiar. Silas aimed at the man's other knee. 'Give me your name or I shoot again.'

'No.' It was a pathetic gurgling noise. 'Don't shoot.'

'I know you. I obviously arrested you.' Silas had a damn good memory and the puzzle pieces in his mind interlocked. 'Harlan Kapansky. You killed a family because the father owed money to his bookie. You got twenty-five years.'

Kapansky glared up at him. 'Got out on good behavior.' That must have struck him as funny because he began to laugh hysterically, great gasping guffaws that left him even more wild-eyed and breathless.

'How much did he pay you to kill me?'

An unholy glee joined the wildness in Kapansky's gaze. '*You* were free.'

'I was – *what*? Oh, God. Oh, my God.' Silas's heart stopped as another puzzle piece fit. Kapansky wasn't an ordinary killer. He was a demolition expert. He planted bombs. He'd killed that family with a car bomb.

Grayson and Paige. Silas shoved the barrel of his rifle against Kapansky's unwounded knee. 'Did you plant a bomb under that car that just drove away?'

Kapansky laughed.

You have to warn them. Silas hadn't heard the bomb blow. Timer. The little shit writhing on the ground must have used a timer. *Warn them.*

Silas slung the rifle over his shoulder and dug for his cell phones.

He still had Grayson's cell number on his personal cell. On his business cell he dialed.

Wednesday, April 6, 11.48 P.M.

Grayson had his hand on Paige's back, keeping her bent forward in her seat. He drove like a man possessed while she dialed 911 and reported their situation.

Faster. Faster. It was all he could think. *Get her away. Keep her safe.*

Paige asked the operator to contact Stevie Mazzetti, then looked up sideways. 'They shot at *you*, Grayson,' she said urgently. 'Not me.'

'I guess our visit to Rex McCloud rattled a few chains.'

'The operator says they dispatched squad cars, that we should find a well-lit area and wait.'

'Like hell,' he muttered. A well-lit area would just give the sniper a better view. He kept driving. And then the cell in his pocket vibrated. *Stevie.*

He released Paige to reach for his phone. 'Stevie—'

'Get out of the car.'

Grayson's foot froze on the pedal. It was the voice. From last night. The shooter who'd called him by name. 'No,' he said.

'Dammit, Grayson, if you value your life you will get out of the car.'

'You just tried to shoot me,' Grayson said, incredulous.

'Goddammit, if I'd wanted to hit you, you'd be dead. I was trying to miss. Get out of the car, or you and your woman will die. There's a bomb under your car. Trust me.'

'Why should I trust you? Who the hell are you?'

'A friend who doesn't want to see either of you dead. *Get out of the damn car.*'

Grayson calmed abruptly. His brain began to work. They'd been lured. Brittany had never planned to come to work. She'd kept them there, stringing them on. He slammed on the brakes, making Paige curse as her head slammed into the dash.

'*Get out*,' he barked. 'Get out of the car.'

He bolted, running around the car to grab her as she stumbled. He picked her up and ran, diving over the shoulder and down an embankment.

Just as his car exploded. Grayson clutched her to him and they rolled down the hill. He covered her with his body, hunched over, grimacing when pieces of twisted, burning metal rained down around them.

And then it was quiet, the only sound the crackle of flames.

Grayson lifted his head, stared into her dark eyes, wide with terror. Glazed with shock. Together they labored for air.

'Are you hurt?' he asked when he could speak.

She shook her head. 'Your back.'

'I'm all right.'

She closed her eyes and tears seeped from the corners. She was trembling, her hands convulsively gripping his shirt. He pushed himself to his knees beside her. Saw with new horror that the grass around them was on fire.

'Get up. We have to move.' Wincing, he forced his body to rise. She came to her feet with the same fluidity he'd seen when she'd taken Rex McCloud down a few pegs.

Had Rex arranged this? Or his grandparents? Or even Anderson?

Grayson grabbed her hand and together they began to move, not stopping until they were standing in a small copse of trees, away from the blaze. Luckily the ground was wet from all the rain. The fire wasn't spreading their way.

Paige slid to the ground, her back against one of the trees. 'He warned you?'

'Yes. It was the intruder. From last night. And I still can't see his face in my mind.'

She'd closed her eyes, her hands flexing and clenching. Calming herself. 'Call him back. Check your log.'

Shit. I should have thought of that. But his thoughts were coming in uncoordinated fits and spurts, his heart still pounding like a wild thing in his chest. He followed her lead, controlling his breathing until his hands had stopped shaking enough to pat his pockets for his phone.

It wasn't there. Balefully he glared up at the burning car. 'I must have dropped it when we ran. I'll have to wait till the fire cools and hope it's not melted.'

'If it is, the phone company will have the record. It's okay, Grayson. We're okay.'

They were alive, he thought grimly, watching the car burn. They were far from okay.

'He had your cell-phone number,' she murmured. '*I* don't even have your cell-phone number.'

He frowned. 'That I can fix.'

'That's not what I meant. Who do you give your cell out to?'

Oh. 'Not many people. Family. A few friends. Colleagues. Cops. Lawyers.'

'Any of them could have given it to someone else,' she said thinly.

'But he called me by name.'

'True. But anyone would know your name if they read the paper.'

'Brittany knew this would happen. She set us up,' he said and Paige nodded.

'She kept us there while whoever did that –' she pointed at the car up on the road, still burning – 'planted the bomb.'

Fury boiled in his gut. 'Crystal's little sister just crossed a big line. Blackmail was bad enough, but attempted murder . . .'

She brought his clenched fist to her lips. 'It seems you've saved my life again.' She looked up at him. 'What do you have planned for tomorrow? Today will be a hard act to top.'

He stared at her for a moment, then threw back his head and laughed. And if he sounded a little hysterical, then so be it.

Wednesday, April 6, 11.50 P.M.

Silas looked down at Kapansky's body. A well-placed bullet in his temple had ended the man's thrashing. He couldn't leave the body here. His employer had sent Kapansky to finish him off. If he believed he'd succeeded, even for a little while, Silas would be able to move about more freely.

I'll be able to hunt him down. Take him by surprise.

Quickly he gathered his tools and Kapansky's guns and stowed them in the back of his van. Then he dragged Kapansky's body through the woods. He'd left a trail in the dirt, but he couldn't help that now.

Kapansky had a vehicle, but he didn't have time to look for it. This place would be swarming with law enforcement in minutes. He put Kapansky's body in the back of his van, covered him with a paint-stained tarp, slammed the doors, and drove away.

When he'd gone far enough, he pulled over. His heart still pounded.

Had he called Grayson in time? He'd heard the blast, seen the fireball. Had they gotten out? He'd done the best he could. They were on their own for now.

Would he have warned them had he not gotten Rose and Violet to safety?

He wasn't proud of his answer. Because he knew it would have been no.

Pushing the well-deserved self-loathing aside, he opened the flip phone he'd found in Kapansky's pocket. In the call log was a familiar number. Zero surprise there.

Silas had been sent to kill Grayson and Paige, but it was a double trap. Even if he'd failed, Kapansky had already planted his bomb, so Grayson and Paige would have been dead anyway. *And then Kapansky got to kill me.*

You were free. Silas imagined Kapansky had dreamed of the day he could take him out. Too bad the ex-con had savored the moment a little too long. He'd dropped his guard, just enough. He got cocky. *And I got lucky.*

Silas couldn't expect his luck to hold out for too much longer. On Kapansky's phone, he texted a short message to the familiar number. *Both jobs done.* Unless Kapansky had been expected to call in personally, that should buy some time. He needed his employer to think he was dead. Hopefully the arrogant SOB would drop his guard, too.

Silas removed the batteries on both Kapansky's phone and his own business cell, then removed the chips, just to be certain. No one would be able to track him now. He needed to get rid of the body.

Then he needed to go to sleep, for just a little while. When he made his move, he needed his mind clear, his hand steady, and his trigger finger ready.

Wednesday, April 6, 11.58 P.M.

His cell buzzed in his pants pocket. That should be Kapansky, reporting in. He folded his napkin, smiling at the other faces around his table. 'I'm going to have a smoke. No, no, don't get up. I'll be right back.'

He strolled out to his terrace, closing the French doors behind him. He lit a cigarette and took a single drag. Surreptitiously he checked his phone. *Both jobs done.* Excellent. Grayson Smith and Paige Holden could no longer dig into things that were better left untouched.

Silas was no longer a threat.

Brittany Jones had done her job, keeping Smith and Holden in the nursing home long enough for Kapansky to plant his device.

Now he could kill her. He took another long drag on the cigarette, then set it on the balcony railing. He searched his other messages, pleased when a new text came in, exactly as anticipated. *Calls to the Carrollwood Nursing Home were made from the Donnybrook Hotel, Dunkirk, NY.*

It had taken his resource at the phone company less than ten minutes to pinpoint Brittany's location from the cell towers, even simpler as she'd stopped for the evening. Lugging a kid around made everything harder. Luckily Brittany wouldn't have that worry for much longer. Brittany wouldn't be worrying about anything for much longer.

He texted Kapansky. *Proceed. Donnybrook Hotel, Dunkirk, NY.*

Thursday, April 7, 12.30 A.M.

Stevie slammed her car door, her fury still fresh. Seeing the charred remains of Grayson's car sent her temper boiling even higher. They'd have been dead.

Her heart was still stuck in her throat. She had a handful of friends who had been part of her and Paul's circle. JD was one. Grayson another. They'd held her hand in the days after Paul's murder. Kept her sane.

Not having Grayson in her life . . . Stevie couldn't, wouldn't even think of it.

She stopped at the still-smoking car, flashing her badge when one of the local cops approached. 'Detective Mazzetti,' she said. 'Baltimore PD.'

'Smith and Holden are in the back of my squad car. CSU has something for you.' The cop pointed to the CSU van parked over the hill. 'They're over there.'

'We appreciate you allowing us in,' Stevie said to him. This area was way out of their jurisdiction. 'Smith said he was okay when I talked to him.' On a phone he'd had to borrow from one of the first responders as his own was somewhere in the twisted wreckage. He'd made it out, but it had been too close. 'Is he really all right?'

'A few cuts and scratches, bumps and bruises. His suit's seen better days.'

'He has a million others just like it,' Stevie said, relieved. 'Thanks.' She found CSU's Drew Peterson with a guy wearing a white cover-up. 'What do you have?'

Drew pointed to the man beside him. 'Detective Mazzetti, Art Donovan, Bombs.'

'This one was planted under the car,' Donovan said. 'Held in place magnetically. It's a pretty common design. Used a tilt fuse. Mercury.'

'So the car drives, jostles,' Stevie said. 'The mercury rolls from one end of the tube to the other where the wires are. Burns the coating off the wires, sends the spark to the explosive device, then . . . *pow*.'

'Exactly.' Donovan held out his gloved hand, a small clock in his palm. 'This one also had a timing device. The bomb was activated, but delayed. Probably so that the bomber could escape undetected. The prosecutor and the PI are damn lucky.'

Her heart fluttered again. 'I know. Any idea who might have done this?'

'Somebody who knew his stuff.' Donovan shrugged. 'These days that could be any teenager with an Internet connection. I've got a list of perps who've used this type of bomb in the past. I'll email it to you.'

'I'd appreciate it.' She turned back to Drew Peterson when Donovan walked away. 'Can we narrow down where the mercury in the tilt fuse came from?'

'We can try, but I wouldn't count on it. It's not something you're gonna find in the store, but if someone wants it bad enough there are plenty of back-alley sources. It's just as likely it came from an old instrument or thermometer someone had lying around.'

'Shit,' Stevie muttered.

'We did find other stuff, though,' Drew went on. 'Back by the nursing home where the shot was fired.'

'The shot that had Grayson and Paige fleeing the scene,' she said. 'Did you find the cartridge?'

'No, but something went on there,' Drew said. 'There was a struggle, one person lost a lot of blood and was dragged away. The trail ends at an access road. There's evidence a large vehicle was parked there, probably a van. No decent tire prints.'

'Two people were there,' Stevie mused. 'Grayson said the sniper told him he'd deliberately missed. He was the one who warned Grayson so I assume the second guy planted the bomb. I wonder which one went down? Bomber or sniper? Did you get blood samples?'

'That wasn't a problem. There was a lot of blood.'

'We've got four dead and someone trying to blow up a state's attorney. When can I have DNA?'

He shrugged. 'Best I can promise is a twenty-four-hour turn-around.'

'Fine,' she said grudgingly. 'We'll compare results to DNA samples in the database and to Donovan's bomb perps. Hope we get a match. What else?'

'A car, stolen plates.' His brows lifted. 'Explosive residue in the trunk.'

'So the sniper won. The bloody bomber got dragged away or he'd have driven his own car instead of leaving it with detectable explosives in the damn trunk.'

'That was my take. We'll take the car in, dust it for prints, vacuum for hair. And hope to hell this guy left something. I'll let you know when I find anything else.'

'Thanks. I'm going to talk to Grayson now. When I'm done with him I'll get down to the nursing home to check out the scene of the shooting. Thanks, Drew.'

She gave him a wave and made her way to the squad car where Grayson sat with Paige in the backseat. He had a gash on his forehead that had been butterfly bandaged. She was wrapped in a blanket, her head on his shoulder. The bandage at her throat was bright white, probably freshly changed by the paramedics.

His arm was around her, holding on tight. Both looked grim. Stevie slid in the cruiser's front seat. 'We have to stop meeting like this,' she said lightly.

Grayson didn't smile. 'I know him, Stevie. I can't figure it out. It's making me crazy.'

'I called IA on my way over. They don't have voice samples yet. Or so they say.'

He met her eyes and in his she saw controlled rage. And a healthy amount of fear that she suspected was mostly for Paige. 'What did CSU find?'

She told him about the bomb and the scene of the struggle she'd assumed was bomber versus sniper. She probably shouldn't have done so in front of Paige, but Stevie figured the woman had earned information. 'I'll let you know when I know more. In the meantime, I'll start a trace on the number that called you. We can pull it from your phone records if you give us permission.' When he only nodded, Stevie studied his haunted eyes. 'You think you might have tugged the tiger's tail by talking to Rex McCloud?'

'Yes,' he said. 'But it was Brittany Jones who made sure we were stalled in the nursing-home lobby while the bomb was set.'

'The sister of Crystal who gave you interesting evidence.' Stevie rolled her eyes, frustrated. 'Which was in an envelope, which was in the car when it blew sky high.'

He shook his head. 'No, it wasn't. I went home to walk Paige's dog and put the envelope in my safe. I'll give it to you tomorrow.'

'Brittany connects to the sniper who doesn't seem to snipe all that well.' Paige forced a small smile. 'Not that I'm complaining, mind you.'

'He said he tried to miss,' Grayson said. 'Said if he'd wanted to hit me, I would have been dead.'

'He snipes really well when it counts,' Stevie said. 'He hit Elena Muñoz and not you, Paige. Why didn't he shoot you?'

'I don't know,' she said. 'I've wondered about that a lot. He could have taken me out and pumped a second bullet into Elena before anyone even knew what happened.'

Grayson made a low sound of rage and Paige patted his knee comfortingly, meeting his eyes. 'But he didn't,' Paige whispered. 'He didn't kill me and he deliberately missed you today. He saved our lives with that call, Grayson. We need to know why.'

The temperature in the car seemed to climb a few degrees. Stevie cleared her throat and the two stopped staring at each other and looked back at her.

'Thank you,' Stevie said dryly. 'Elena connects to Sandoval and to Delgado. Logan and his mother connect to the sniper through the video. How does Brittany connect?'

'She may have taken money from the same person who paid Sandoval,' Paige said. 'He's a connection. We told Brittany that people who'd been involved in the case were being killed. Maybe she offered up Grayson and me to keep the payer of fifty Gs happy and not killing her.'

'Or her child,' Grayson added. 'Her child is important to her.'

'I'll put out a BOLO on Brittany and her kid. Hopefully she'll turn up.'

'Alive,' Paige muttered.

'That would be ideal,' Stevie said. 'You guys look pretty bedraggled. You're staying at the Peabody, Paige?'

'That's where my overnight bag is. Shit. My backpack was in the car.'

'I'm sorry,' Grayson murmured. 'Your laptop, too.'

'I know. At least I back up nightly so I didn't lose much data. But my makeup bag was in there too. I know that sounds dumb to worry over, but damn, I had a lot of time invested in buying all that makeup.'

'We'll get you some more,' Stevie said. 'My sister Izzy collects makeup samples every time they have one of those promotions at the department store.'

For a moment Paige looked like she'd refuse. Then she inclined her head. 'That would be very kind of your sister to do. Thank you.'

'You guys go clean up. I'll have one of these officers drive you back to the city.'

'You'll call when you know anything about the shooter or the bomber?' Grayson asked.

'Absolutely. We'll get to the bottom of this, Grayson.'

His lips thinned. 'I'm going to hold you to that.'

Sixteen

Grayson hadn't let her go, not once since the medics had bandaged them up. One of Paige's stitches had ripped out when they'd rolled over the embankment. *When he covered me with his body. Protecting me once again.*

The medic told her to go to the ER, but this time Grayson hadn't forced her to go, much to her relief. She couldn't take several hours in a small white room.

Now they sat in the back of a cruiser on their way to Grayson's townhouse, his arm locked around her shoulder. She lifted a trembling hand to the bandage on his forehead. She couldn't make herself go to the ER, but he should have gone.

'You should have let them take you,' she murmured.

'I wasn't going without you.' He pressed a hard kiss to her temple with a dark desperation she understood, because she felt it too.

Before . . . it was just me. Now he was in danger too. She turned her face into his chest. Underneath the smell of smoke was his scent and she breathed it in. His arm tightened and they steeped in each other until the cruiser stopped outside his house.

The officer turned to look over the backseat. 'I'll come in, check out the place.'

'That's okay,' Grayson said. 'I have a good security system and she has a big dog.'

'The Rottie,' the officer said. 'I see him through the side window. Nice-looking animal. You two take care.'

The townhouse was quiet. Peabody stood in the foyer, head cocked slightly. Alert.

'Good boy,' Paige said, and the dog relaxed. Grayson disarmed the alarm, flipped on the lights. Everything was how they'd left it. She went to the study door. Everything was in place, including the photos on the shelf over his desk. Including the one that he hadn't wanted her to see. The one of a little boy and his smiling mother.

She turned to find him watching her, eyes stark. 'I thought I could keep you safe,' he whispered fiercely. 'I need you safe.'

'You did.' She went to him. 'You have. Every time someone or something's come at me, you've protected me. It's been a long time since anyone has done that.'

His mood abruptly changed. His gaze heated, moving down her body slowly before taking the return trip to meet her eyes. She felt scorched, her skin too taut for her bones. But she couldn't look away, even if she'd wanted to.

'It's been a long time since anyone's done a lot of things for you. And to you.'

Her breath caught. She wanted to say something. Anything. But her heart was beating like a hummingbird's and her mind had gone blank. As he had done the night before, he ran his thumb over her lips, the promise of a kiss to come. Her lips tingled, remembering the kiss outside the restaurant before his mother had interrupted them.

There was no one to interrupt them now. The thought teased. Enticed. Tempted.

Grayson stepped back, breaking the moment before she could decide what she wanted to do. He snapped his fingers for Peabody, reaching for the dog's leash.

'*No*,' she said, shocked into vehemence. 'You can't walk him outside. Someone could shoot you. Whoever tried to kill you tonight won't just stop.'

'I won't walk him out front,' he said. 'I have a courtyard out back with a privacy fence. It's a small area, but it will do for now.'

He walked around her toward the kitchen and she turned to follow him.

Then stopped dead in her tracks. 'Grayson.' It came out a horrified gasp.

He paused in the doorway, but didn't turn. 'I'm okay,' he said. 'Don't worry.'

She ran to him, reaching for him, then snatched her hands away before she touched him. 'Your back.' She wrung her hands, staring. 'There are holes. In your coat. *Burns*.' Great jagged holes with charred edges. 'You said you weren't hit.' She remembered them rolling, then him shielding her. 'You're burned.'

'I'm okay,' he insisted. 'I was wearing—'

But she'd ceased listening. She grabbed at his coat, pulling it off his shoulders. The holes went all the way through. All the way through his shirt. She yanked the shirt from his pants. Her hands shook and she fumbled the buttons.

Then realized she couldn't see anything through her tears. 'You should have gone to the ER. Why didn't you go to the ER?' she demanded, her voice breaking.

He brought her hands to his lips. 'Paige. I'm okay. I was wearing Kevlar.'

The breath shuddered out of her. 'Kevlar? How?'

'Sometimes I get threats from the accused or their families in court so I got a vest. I put it on when I walked Peabody earlier, when you were with my mom. It seemed . . . prudent at the time. Joseph's getting one for you, too. You'll wear it. Promise me.'

She blinked up at him. 'Kevlar?' she repeated numbly. 'Where is it?'

'I took it off when the medics checked me out. CSU took it. To get burn residue.'

She nodded mechanically. *Burn residue*. Hearing but not yet believing his assurances, she pulled at the buttons on his shirt, popping a few. She pushed the shirt from his shoulders, baring his chest with all that beautiful skin.

She flattened her hands on him, touching him, needing to feel him. His muscles flexed under her palms and his breathing changed. Hitched. Grew more shallow.

Her hands slowed, no longer frantic. She took her time, touching him the way she'd wanted to the night before when he'd lain beside her, not sleeping. She pressed her mouth to his powerful chest, feeling him tense beneath her lips, his breath coming out in a hiss. She reached around him, her hands tentative, searching his back.

No burns. Just smooth skin. 'You're okay.' Rippling muscle. 'You're perfect.'

He said nothing, gripping her hips, pulling her against him. He was aroused. Very, very aroused. *For me. This is all for me.* And she wanted it all. She wanted him.

He kissed her neck, hot wet kisses that made her hotter and wetter . . . everywhere. One big hand rose to cover her breast, gently shaping and reshaping, and she closed her eyes on a throaty moan. It felt so good.

'Good,' he said huskily and she realized she'd said it out loud. He kissed the curve of her shoulder, bit lightly, making her gasp. Then he sucked hard, marking her. 'Stop me,' he whispered harshly against her skin. 'Unless you plan to finish this, stop me.'

She lifted her hands to his face, felt his stubble tickle her palms. Knew she wouldn't be stopping him tonight. She leaned up on her toes and kissed him, a hot, open-mouthed kiss that yanked a guttural groan from his chest. He unbuttoned her jacket, pushed it off her shoulders to the floor.

'Be sure,' he ground out. 'I won't do this if you're not sure.'

She said nothing, but unsnapped her shoulder holster with quick, economical movements and let it land on top of her jacket. He pulled her shirt off, then unhooked her bra with a practiced finesse she wouldn't think about. Ever.

He was staring at her breasts, his eyes dark with greed. 'You're beautiful, Paige.'

She'd heard it before. Too many times to count. But this time . . . *Please let it be him. Let him be for me.* She closed her eyes, waiting for him to grab. To pluck and pinch. But he didn't. Instead she felt hot breath against her skin and opened her eyes to find him bent, his dark head at her breast. It made her knees weak.

She waited for the touch of his mouth. Waited for him to suck. Instead his hands spanned her waist and she found herself lifted off her feet, whisked to the edge of his dining-room table with devastating ease.

'I want you,' he whispered. He planted his hands on either side of her, caging her in. Leaned forward, kissing her with an intensity that left her lungs empty and burning. 'I fantasized about having you here, on this table. All afternoon, when you were watching other people having sex in that pool. Tell me to take you. Tell me I can have you. *Tell me.*'

She opened her mouth, but no words would come. His head was close to her breast, his breath hot against her nipple. But he didn't touch her. Anywhere.

'Tell me, Paige. Say the words.'

She swallowed hard. 'Do it. Please.'

He laughed, low and wicked. 'Please is nice, but you need to say what I tell you to say.' He brushed lightly between her legs, making her jump. 'Tell me to take you.'

'Please. Please.' She whimpered it and he looked up, his gaze razor-sharp.

'Say it.' He increased the pressure between her legs, his thumb finding the place that made her gasp. She lifted her hips, trying to get more. More pressure. More of him.

He took his hand away and she protested. 'Grayson.'

'Say it.' He delved under her waistband, finding the holster, setting the gun and knife aside. He peeled her pants to her knees, leaving only her lacy black panties. 'Pretty.' He bent, kissing the inside of her thigh, inches from where she needed him.

'Grayson.'

He looked up, his gaze intense, demanding. '*Say it.*'

She closed her eyes, her heart pounding like a wild thing. 'Take me. Please.'

He moved fast then, yanking at the laces on her boot, pulling one off and letting it fly. It landed somewhere in the foyer. She didn't care where. 'Hurry,' she whispered.

He stripped her pants off one leg, leaving her with one boot on, throwing her bare leg over his shoulder, opening her wide. Then she cried out when his mouth closed over the black lace, sucking hard.

She came in a blinding rush, her head falling back, gasping for air. *Too soon*. It was over too soon. It had been so long. *Too long*. She wanted to scream. She wanted to curse. But she didn't have any breath.

'Again,' he muttered, pulling her panties down, freeing her bare leg. Finally his mouth closed over her breast and he plunged two fingers deep into her. Her body went rigid as he sucked, long draws that had her writhing and bucking on the edge of his dining-room table. 'Come, Paige,' he demanded. 'Again.'

He moved to the other breast, sucking, while his thumb found her most sensitive flesh. He pressed and rubbed and sucked and she came apart again, her cry strangled in her throat. 'Grayson.' It was hoarse. Barely discernible as her own voice.

She could only watch as he straightened, his lips wet from sucking her breasts, his fingers glistening from her arousal. He fumbled with his belt, let his pants fall to the floor.

He cursed, bent over and pulled a condom from his back pants pocket. By the time he'd straightened, he was covered. He caged her in again, moving between her legs, leaning over her until all she could see was green, green eyes.

'Tell me again,' he whispered. 'Tell me you want this.'

He'd leave her no way to blame him, she understood. 'I want this,' she whispered back. 'I want you. Do this. Take what you—' She cried out again, this time in surprised pleasure. He was big. All over. She was filled and she could feel him, deep.

'I want you,' he said gutturally, beginning to move. 'You're mine. You understand?'

'Yes.' She met his thrusts, watching him. Watching them. 'I understand.'

He slid his arms under her back, hooking his hands on her shoulders, and he thrust even deeper. 'Do you like this?'

He hit the spot that sent a jolt of current singing across her skin. 'God yes. Don't stop.'

'I couldn't.' He closed his eyes, sweat beading on his brow. 'You feel too damn good. I want you. I want you.' He set a rhythm and she let herself be swept away. And when she came, her scream made no sound at all.

317

He found her mouth, covered it with his. Kissed her until she couldn't breathe. And then he went rigid, throwing his head back with a grimace that was beautiful to behold.

He laid his cheek against her shoulder, panting. Weakly she ran her fingers through his hair, then stroked his back. Once. Twice. Her hand fell to her side, useless. Limp.

'Are you all right?' he murmured, still out of breath. Still buried inside her.

'I don't know. Am I?'

He lifted his head. Looked into her eyes and her pounding heart fluttered. 'You're more all right than I deserve,' he said. 'I've just had you and I want you again.'

She brushed a lock of hair from his forehead. 'Do I have to beg each time?'

One side of his mouth lifted. 'Depends. If you jump me, then no.'

She laughed softly, keenly aware that for a few precious minutes she'd thought only of him and the magic he'd worked on her body. Even if things didn't work out between them, those moments were worth the risk. 'Jumping you requires a softer surface.'

'I have a bed,' he said silkily. 'It's very soft.'

She sucked in a breath, her core muscles clenching around him, and he groaned quietly. *Again*. She wanted him again. 'Can we have a shower first?' she asked.

'I have one of those, too.' He kissed her jaw tenderly. 'You go upstairs. I'll lock up down here and meet you in a few minutes.'

Thursday, April 7, 2.15 A.M.

Silas had dumped Kapansky's body into the Patuxent, switched his van for the untrackable car and now pulled into the storage unit he'd rented under one of his aliases. *I was a damn good cop. Now I have untrackable cars and aliases*.

He locked up, found his sleeping bag, shook it out, settled onto the floor. Sighed as his bones creaked and his muscles ached. He needed a hot shower, not cold concrete.

It was dark. And quiet. Too quiet. He could hear himself think.

He hated to think. When he let himself think, he was deluged with regret over what he'd become. The people he'd hurt. It had all started with a choice that hadn't seemed so terrible then.

He'd needed to save his daughter from ruining her life.

She'd been such a precious child, his Cherri. And then adolescence arrived and the fights began. Sneaking out, smoking. Boys. He hadn't had the time to guide her, to keep her straight. He'd been busy catching bad guys. Being a goddamn hero.

The day the nightmare started . . . he'd thought it would be the most terrible day of his life. He'd find he was wrong about that. He'd been watching a re-run on TV when two cops had knocked on his door, a man and a woman. They had a search warrant.

He'd looked up the stairs. Seventeen-year-old Cherri stood on the top step and one look at her face told him she knew why those cops were there. There had been a robbery and the stolen goods were found hidden under his daughter's bed.

Cherri was guilty. Of that he'd had no doubt. But taking the rap . . . She would have gone to prison. The daughter of a cop. Her life inside would have been hell. He couldn't let that happen.

All of those thoughts passed through his mind as he watched his only daughter taken away in handcuffs, sobbing, begging him to help her.

Mere minutes after the police car had driven away, the phone rang. And then came the offer. Like the serpent in the Garden of Eden, tempting him.

I can make that evidence go away. As if it never was. I can make it so that your precious daughter never sees the walls of a prison. But you have to act fast. The cruiser is taking her in. When they arrive at central booking, the offer disappears, as if it never was. Think fast, Silas. The clock is ticking.

What do I have to do? he'd asked.

Whatever I say. Whenever I say.

And if I don't?

Those two cops that got your daughter asked the same question. The woman cop's son spent a week in the hospital. Hit and run. She doesn't ask that question anymore.

What will you do?

Someone else will take the blame.

Who?

Do you care? As long as your daughter is safe, do you care?

He hadn't. God help him, he had not cared.

The voice on the phone had chuckled. *If it makes you feel better, the one who'll take the blame has already served time. She can take care of herself inside. Can your daughter take care of herself?*

Silas had said nothing, frantically trying to choose, and then the voice on the phone hit it home. *A cop's daughter, in prison. They'll eat her for breakfast, lunch, and dinner. The clock is ticking, Silas. I need your decision.*

And so he'd decided. *Yes.* He'd blurted it out before he could change his mind.

Excellent. I'll be in touch.

And so it was done. Another girl had been framed. And Cherri had been released. Spared. It hadn't had the effect he'd hoped for, though. Free from jail, she'd run off again. There would be more trouble. More heartache for him and for Rose. He'd always thought it couldn't get worse.

And then, not even a year later, Cherri was gone forever. He'd held her newborn child in his arms and vowed Cherri's baby would always be safe.

The voice on the phone had contacted him again two weeks later. It was time to pay his debt. The first job was one like Cherri's, framing a young man for a crime he did not commit. But Silas had been able to justify it. The boy had already been convicted. He'd reoffended. He hadn't done the crime for which he'd been accused, but he sure as hell had done others.

Years passed. The jobs got harder. His first kill . . . He'd balked and his employer had reminded him of the cop whose child had been hit by a car. The boy still walked with crutches. So he'd killed his mark, then thrown up afterward. But over time, the kills got easier too.

He thought of Cherri. Of Violet. Even now, knowing what he knew, he was sure he'd make the same choice.

Habit had him reaching for the photo in his shirt pocket, even though it was too dark to see the little girl with chocolate on her chin. He slid two fingers in his pocket.

Then sat up straight, panicked. *It was gone*. Cherri's picture was gone.

I've lost it. Where? He made himself breathe. Mentally retrace his steps. He'd come home from Toronto. Showered and changed. Had he put the photo in his pocket?

What if I dropped it? What if someone finds it? If he dropped it at the river, no one would find it. No one ever went there. *What if I dropped it in the woods at the nursing home?* The area was crawling with cops. CSU would be sure to find it.

What if the cop who finds it is the one cop who'd know who it is? That Silas himself had been there would be their eventual conclusion. He'd be found out.

Then so be it. Grayson would realize who he was sooner or later, so it really didn't matter in the end. If that one cop did find the photo, it would be cared for. She would give it back to him. She would know how much the picture meant.

He lay back down, forced his eyes to close. And made himself sleep. He needed to be sharp tomorrow morning when he pulled the trigger for what would hopefully be the last time. And if his employer had arranged for incriminating records to be made public in the event of his death, so be it.

Of course, the other 'operatives' might be pissed, because their records would be made public, too, but that was their problem. Silas just had to survive a little longer.

Thursday, April 7, 2.25 A.M.

'Hmm.' Paige snuggled against him, her head on his shoulder as they lay in Grayson's bed, her hand resting lightly on his abdomen. He didn't seem to be able to let her go. They were clean, and he'd had her again, in the shower. Up against the smooth tile wall.

He hadn't planned it. He'd joined her in the shower after letting her dog sniff around his courtyard and locking up his house. Never had setting his alarm seemed so important. Now, it was keeping her

321

safe. *For me*. He'd planned to get clean, then tell her. Tell her everything.

But he'd been unprepared for her reaction when she saw his back. He was black and blue from whatever had fallen from the sky after his car had blown.

She'd cried, great gulping sobs. He'd kissed her mouth, trying to comfort her. But he couldn't kiss her and not have her. Then she'd begged. Again. He'd lost control. He'd made her come twice, changing her sobs to sensual pleas.

And then he'd come so hard. Inside her. Without a condom.

He'd never done that before. He'd always been careful. Never lost control. Never made that kind of commitment. Because he knew none of the others were ones he'd keep.

But this one . . . the woman cuddled up against him, trusting him. *I want to keep her. I need to tell her. Now. Before this goes any farther*. Before he took her again, lost control again. Made her pregnant.

His heart clenched in his chest so hard it hurt. She lifted her head and looked into his eyes, hers filled with worry. 'What is it?'

'I . . .' *Need to tell you*. But fear bubbled up and he blurted the first thing that came into his mind. 'We were careless.'

She bit her lip. 'I know. But it's the wrong time of the month for any . . . pregnancy.'

He blinked, stunned to find himself disappointed. The wrong time. Suddenly, desperately, he wanted it to be the right time.

'I'm . . . It's just that . . .' He closed his eyes, unable to find the words. He made his living with compelling arguments, but right now he was as scared as a small boy.

As the small boy he'd been.

She kissed his forehead, next to the bandage. 'What's wrong, Grayson?'

'I need to tell you.' He forced the words out. 'I need you to know.'

She stilled. Then let out a slow breath. 'What can I do to make it easier for you?'

His chest swelled, emotion swamping him. *I could love you, Paige Holden*. Now he was even more scared. He opened his eyes. She was watching him with a mix of compassion and tenderness.

322

'Let me finish. And if it makes a difference . . .' He filled his lungs with air. 'If it matters, if you need to go, then go. But please, promise me you'll keep it to yourself.'

'I promise,' she said solemnly, and he believed her.

He nodded, wondering where to start. Then he shrugged. 'Once upon a time there was a boy in Miami. His name wasn't Grayson Smith.'

Her eyes shifted, something indefinable moving in their black depths. She said nothing, so he continued.

'The boy had a mom,' he said. 'A great mom.'

'Judy.'

'Yes. But that wasn't her name then, either. I had a dad. I thought he was great, too. Until one day we found out that he wasn't.' He drew another breath and took the plunge. 'My name is Antonio Sabatero. I was named after my father who tortured, raped, and killed fourteen young women. Most of them were college age. A few younger. By the time we found out, he'd been killing for years.'

For an interminably long moment she said nothing, then finally spoke. 'I didn't think you looked like a Smith,' she murmured. But there was no disgust in her eyes.

And no surprise. Realization was like a fist in his gut. 'You already knew.'

She nodded. 'I was putting your monitor away this afternoon. I bumped my head on your shelf and knocked your pictures down. I was fixing them, when I found the one with you and your mom. Standing in front of the school. I really wasn't intending to snoop.'

His mind was reeling. 'How did you find out?'

'You were standing in front of a bus that said "St Ign". There were palm trees. I did the math, then did a search. I needed to know, because I was about to break my own rule and sleep with you. I needed to know if you might be . . . mine. Someday. Maybe.'

Mine. That he understood.

Her brows furrowed. 'Are you angry that I knew?'

'No.' He swallowed hard. 'Relieved. Incredibly relieved.'

'Good. I was worried. I only know what I read in an old newspaper article. That you found one of the bodies. That more bodies were found later and your father was arrested. And that you and your mother disappeared. You were only seven years old. I . . . I can't imagine that.'

He didn't have to imagine. He remembered every detail with brutal clarity. 'The paper didn't print everything,' he said quietly.

Her eyes shifted again, steeling herself for something bad. 'Tell me. If you want to.'

He tugged her head back to his shoulder and she cuddled against him, her hand splayed on his chest. Over his heart. Which clenched again. She'd known. *And yet here she is. In my bed. She knew and still she trusted me. She wanted me.*

'I'd seen a pirate movie,' he began. 'They'd found a treasure map between some stones in a wall. I knew about a stone wall, in a barn on a neighbor's property. The neighbor was old, mostly deaf and didn't see well. My mother visited her every week, brought her food. I didn't think the lady would mind if I played pirate in her barn.'

'But your dad had "played" there first.'

'Yes. I found a loose stone. I worked it free, thinking I'd find something wonderful behind it.' He stopped, the memory as fresh, as frightening as if it had been yesterday.

'You found the body then?' she prompted gently.

He stared at the ceiling, the self-hatred clawing inside him. 'She wasn't dead yet.'

He heard her sharp intake of breath. Felt her tense. 'Oh, God. Grayson.'

'He'd beaten her. Cut her. He had her shackled to a wall. She turned her head to look at me and started to . . . gurgle. It was . . .' He swallowed the bile that rose to burn his throat. 'It was the most terrifying sound I'd ever heard. I've seen more murder victims than I want to remember, but that sound . . . to this day it makes my blood run cold.'

'You were only seven,' Paige breathed, shaken. 'What did you do?'

He hesitated, not wanting to speak of it. *Tell her.* 'I ran,' he admitted. 'I ran away and hid in my closet. The girl was trying to ask for help. I found out later that my father had cut out her tongue so she couldn't scream. I was terrified. So I ran.'

'Of course you did. You were *seven*,' Paige repeated protectively. 'Most adults would have run and hid.'

He'd always known that, but it never helped. 'My mother came looking for me, found me in my closet. I kept stammering about the hole in the stone wall. I couldn't say more, couldn't find the words, but she knew something was terribly wrong. She found the girl, but she was dead by then.' He swallowed hard, remembering the guilt. The nightmares. 'I hid too long. If I'd found my mother, told her . . . the girl might have lived.'

'That she didn't live isn't on your head,' she said. 'But knowing that doesn't help, does it? I feel responsible for Thea's death, even though her husband was to blame.' She sighed. 'What did your mother do?'

'She called the police. They found knives with fingerprints.' He swallowed again. 'Semen on the body. In the body. He'd assaulted her. Repeatedly. It was the eighties – before DNA profiling. But the prints matched my father's. The semen matched his blood type. And, he kept souvenirs. Jewelry. He gave some of it to my mother.'

'Monster,' she whispered, and his mouth twisted bitterly.

'I remember her wearing it. He'd make a big production about getting a bonus at work and spending it on his "beloved". My mother couldn't get past having worn the girls' jewelry for a long time. Some people thought she knew, that she'd helped him.'

'Some people are stupid,' Paige declared fiercely.

'The woman I'd found was identified as a college girl missing from University of Florida. The police found evidence there'd been others in the room where he'd tortured her. They arrested him and started digging around the barn. They found his burial ground not far away. Thirteen more bodies.'

'Why did you and your mother disappear?'

'Because we feared for our lives. My father was furious that my mother had discovered his secret, that she'd called the police. So he made her pay. His defense was that he was a loving family man. He could never have done such a thing, he said. He had a son of his own, after all. Later, when the evidence began to mount and he knew he was truly caught, he claimed that my mother knew. That she'd helped.'

'Surely the police didn't believe him, did they?'

'The police didn't, but enough other people did to make our lives hell. One of the fathers of the victims went off the deep end. He was one of the ones convinced that my mother had known. He came after us, me and my mother. He was going to kill Mom for her involvement. He was going to kill me as an "eye for an eye", because my father still insisted he loved me. He came damn close to succeeding.'

'The police didn't help you?'

'At first, yes. We'd had to move. Our house and the old neighbor's property were crime scenes for months while they searched for bodies. The police put a protective detail on the house my mother rented and she got a restraining order on the victim's father. But a few weeks passed and they decided we were safe and left us on our own.

'There were constant picketers protesting that my mother hadn't been arrested. She got death threats from multiple sources. This went on for weeks. The reporters had swarmed too, microphones and cameras every time we left the house. It was a circus, but ironically they'd protected us. One night some other news happened and the reporters left us alone for a few hours. The victim's father broke into the house and grabbed me out of my bed, stuck a gun to my head, and started to drag me away.'

She tensed. 'What happened?'

'My mother grabbed a baseball bat and slammed him with it. Knocked the guy out.'

'Good for her. I like her even more now.'

'He was going to kill us. She knew he would never stop until we were dead. Or he was. I remember her standing over his body, his gun in her hands, pointing at his head. She stood that way for a long, long time. Her hands shook and she cried.'

'But she couldn't kill him,' she murmured.

'No. That's not who she was. Is. He'd tried to hurt me, but

my father had brutalized the man's child. My mother had . . . compassion. And fear. She could have called the cops, but she'd done that before. They would have arrested the victim's father, but there were so many others who hated us. So she took all the cash she had left, filled the tank with gas and we headed north. We left everything behind.'

'Except for one picture,' she said softly.

'I hid it,' he confessed. 'My mother told me to bring nothing, but I couldn't leave the picture behind. It was my favorite of her.'

'She was happy in the picture. She wasn't scared yet. You could look at it at night and pretend that you were still a little boy in Miami and that none of this had happened.'

That Paige understood didn't surprise him. 'She'll be unhappy that I kept it.'

'She already knows.'

That surprised him. 'You told her?'

'She wanted to know how I'd found out. She told me if I ever used the truth to hurt you that she'd make me pay. I believed her before you told me that she could wield a ball bat.' There was a dry smile in her voice. 'Now I'm doubly afraid.'

'My mother is tough.'

'And so proud of you.' She pressed a kiss to his chest. 'How did you end up here?'

'The car broke down and Mom was running out of money. We lived in a cheap hotel for a few weeks while she tried to find work. We were desperate when she answered an ad for that nanny position with the Carters.' He thought of the story Paige had told, earlier that evening. It seemed like a million years ago. 'But she never left me. Somehow she got us new IDs and kept me fed. I don't know how. I've never asked.'

'Your mom said you were telling them tonight – the Carters. What did they say?'

'They already knew.' It had shocked him then. Now, he was wondering how many people knew the secret he thought he and his mother had kept so well. 'Jack and Katherine Carter had known from the very beginning.'

Paige was quiet a moment. 'Your mother didn't know that. She was worried about what they'd say. Well, not really worried. More . . . sad, I think.'

'She hated lying to them.'

'She did what she had to do to protect you. If the Carters are as wonderful as you've said, they will understand.'

'They did. They protected us.'

'I like them even more now.' Paige hesitated. 'Your mother also said your boss had threatened to expose all of this if you didn't back off the Muñoz case.'

'Yes, he did,' Grayson said.

'Is that why you told me?'

'No. That's why I told the Carters. But not why I told you. I needed you to understand who I really was because I knew that you . . .' He let the thought trail.

She lifted her head, her dark eyes intense. 'When your mother told me about your boss, I wanted to tear his head off. And then I saw you in my mind, standing at Rex's door, knocking. Even though you knew the cost. That's when I knew.'

His heart stumbled. 'Knew what?'

'That the secret you kept didn't matter. What mattered was the man you'd become. That's who I wanted. I don't care who you were. I don't care who your father is. I care about *you*. I want *you*.'

He stared at her, at the face that had entranced him from the moment she'd run toward a bullet-riddled minivan when any sane person would have run away. His heart squeezed in his chest, so hard it hurt. 'Say it again,' he whispered.

She traced his lips with her fingertips. 'I want *you*.' She kissed him sweetly, then nipped at his lower lip. 'I want you,' she murmured, the words turned sultry. Sensual.

His body sprang to life. He cupped the back of her head and brought her close, taking her mouth with all the emotion churning inside him. She lifted her head again, this time her eyes hot. Greedy. She swiveled her hips against him, making him groan.

He rolled, trapping her under him while he searched his nightstand drawer for another condom.

She grabbed it from his hand. 'Does it hurt to lie on your back?'

'Depends. What will I get?'

Her lips curved. 'On your back,' she ordered. 'It's my turn.'

He obeyed, ignoring the bruises as she straddled him. He watched, mesmerized, as she made quick work of the condom wrapper and covered him. Silently he cursed the condom, remembering how it had felt to come inside her. How hot and slick she'd been and how her muscles had squeezed him.

Later. When they'd sorted everything out he'd throw that box away and feel her skin to skin again. For now . . . He gritted his teeth as she teased him, lowering herself onto him, but only an inch. 'Paige.'

She smiled, a cat-in-cream smile that had him lifting his hips, trying to grind himself into her. 'It's my turn,' she repeated. 'I get to do what I want.'

What she wanted was to torture him. She took him in an inch at a time, wriggling her hips, her swaying breasts driving him insane. Finally he broke, pulling her down, filling her. She gasped, then laughed, the sound full of joy. Then she began to move.

She was the most beautiful thing he'd ever seen. She leaned over him, one hand on either side of his head, meeting his eyes in the darkness. 'You made me beg.'

'Twice,' he panted and she licked at his lip.

'Can I make you beg?' she whispered against his mouth.

'You can make me do damn near anything. Just don't ever stop.'

'I can't.' She was moving faster. He could feel his release coming, a dull throb at the base of his spine, but he controlled it. He needed to see her. Needed her to get there first. Abruptly she pushed herself back so that she sat upright, driving him deeper into her. She cried out, her face . . . unforgettable.

His control snapped and he rolled her beneath him, his hips hammering hard as she looked up at him, dazed. He hooked one arm under her knee, sending him even deeper into all that hot, wet heat. His body went rigid. His vision grayed. And he fell.

He wasn't sure how long they lay there, panting. He buried his face in the curve of her shoulder, let out a quiet breath. 'I never told her,' he whispered.

She stroked his hair. 'Told who what, Grayson?'

'My mother. I never told her that the girl was alive when I found her.'

She went still. 'Do you want her to know?'

'No.' He looked up at her, desperate. 'I never want her to know.'

Her mouth bent sadly. 'Do you really think she'd love you any less?'

'No. But it would hurt her. Knowing that it's been eating me up, all these years.'

'Then why tell me?'

'I needed you to know it all. So you could decide.' He hesitated. 'If I'd be yours.'

Her eyes softened. 'You were a child. If I held that against you, I wouldn't be worth your time. Let little Antonio keep his secret. He did nothing wrong. He was a victim, too.'

'Not Antonio.' The words came out harsh and angry. 'My mother called me Tony.'

She caressed his cheek. 'Grayson, you could have taken your past out on anyone weaker than you. But you didn't. You stand for the victims. You are an honorable man, whatever name you choose to call yourself. Your mother is proud of you. And so am I.'

His throat closed. 'Thank you.'

'You're welcome. Now go to sleep. We have a busy day tomorrow. I want this over so we can walk my dog without worrying about you being shot.'

Seventeen

Thursday, April 7, 3.00 A.M.

Stevie exited the Peabody Hotel's elevator, planning to check on Grayson and Paige before heading home to catch a few hours' sleep. Just to make sure they got here okay. It was paranoid, she knew. And a lot overprotective. But Grayson was her friend and seeing his car smoking like that had left her more shaken than she cared to admit.

Stevie put her ear to the door of the suite he'd gotten for Paige. Either they were asleep or not there. She heard a TV in the adjoining room, so somebody was awake.

She knocked lightly. Then had to stop herself from taking a step back when the door opened. It wasn't Grayson Smith. And she wasn't prepared.

Stevie looked up, face to face with the man she hadn't seen in almost a year, but had not forgotten. He'd lied to her, hampered her investigation. He'd falsified federal documents and probably done ten times worse, but they'd caught a killer with his help.

He'd unwittingly put her daughter in danger, but had done the right thing as soon as he'd known. And her daughter was safe today.

Clay Maynard had intrigued her then. And now, here he was. Again.

'Mr Maynard,' she said softly. 'I didn't expect you to be here.'

He frowned, but she barely noticed. His chest was bare and the sweats he wore rode low on his hips. She wasn't in the market, but looking was free. *Oh, my.*

'Detective Mazzetti,' he said. 'I didn't expect you either. Where is Paige?'

Her eyes shot up to his, focused again. 'I thought she was here.'

'She's not. Smith wasn't going to stay with her, so she asked me to. But she hasn't shown up. She hasn't called and she's not answering any of her phones.'

'Well, her phones aren't exactly working at the moment.'

'Why the hell not?' he demanded.

'She and Grayson Smith were involved in an incident tonight. Grayson's car was blown up. Her phone was blown up with it.'

Clay started, his jaw dropping. 'What the hell?'

'I don't want to have this conversation out here. May I?' She gestured to the room.

Immediately he stepped back, opening the door wider. 'Of course. Come in.'

Four handguns lay on the kitchen counter. He'd been cleaning his weapons, an oily rag folded in precise quarters.

Stevie respected a man who took care of his things.

His brows lifted impatiently as she took in the room, his arms folded tightly over his chest. He had a tattoo on his left biceps. *Semper Fi.*

'It was a car bomb,' she said, cutting to the chase. 'We don't know who planted it. Yet. We did recover some pieces of the device and are working to identify the bomber. Grayson's car was destroyed. They got out just in time.'

Clay's mouth tightened. 'Somebody doesn't want them finding out who killed Elena.'

'It's related to that case, yes.'

'And you're not going to tell me any more.'

She regarded him steadily. 'You were a cop once. Did you really expect me to?'

'No.' He all but bit out the word. 'Where is Paige now?'

'A squad car took them to Grayson's house to pick up Paige's dog, then they were supposed to come here. I know they were dropped off safely. I'm thinking they decided to stay there.'

'Paige would have called me.'

'I'm thinking maybe she's been a little busy.'

He rolled his eyes. 'Shit. And she was doing so well, too.'

She frowned up at him. 'What does that mean?'

'She was waiting for Mr Right. Twelve hours ago, that wasn't Smith. Her hormones got the best of her.'

'That's never happened to you?' she asked, feeling the need to defend Paige.

'A time or two,' he said evenly.

'With her?' she pushed. *Shut up*, she told herself. *Let it go.*

His eyes flared. 'No. She's my partner. I don't do partners.'

'Good. Grayson's my friend. I don't want her toying with him.' Not that she thought Paige would. It was merely the best save she could conjure.

'Your friend can take care of himself,' Clay said mildly, as if reading her mind. 'Can you check with your friend to see if he's still got possession of my partner?'

Holding on to a shred of her dignity, Stevie dialed Grayson's home number.

He picked up on the fourth ring, sounding groggy. 'Stevie?'

'Do you have Paige with you?'

'Yeah.' It was said with such satisfaction that she nearly smiled. 'Why?'

'Because I came by the Peabody Hotel to check on you both. Her partner's here and he's been worried sick.'

'Oh.' It was uttered on a blown-out breath. 'I'm sorry. She . . . forgot. *Sshh*,' he said softly and Stevie knew that wasn't meant for her. 'It's Stevie. Go back to sleep.'

'Well, that answers the rest of my questions,' Stevie said wryly.

'I'm sorry, Stevie. It was really nice of you to check on us. Do you have any information?' Grayson asked, more alert now.

'Not at this time.'

'Because Maynard's with you?'

'Yes,' she said, glancing up at the big, dark man who watched her intently.

'Call me in the morning,' Grayson said. 'I have some things to tell you.'

'Case things?'

'Yes and no. I told you that Anderson knew about Muñoz. Well, he also knew things about me. Personal things he threatened to use against me if I pushed this case.'

Her heart began to pound. 'And then, tonight – *kaboom*.'

'Exactly. I'll tell you when you're alone. Get some rest now. I'm more than fine.'

She frowned at the phone as he hung up, then looked at Clay. 'Paige is okay.'

'I got that.' He regarded her carefully. 'How is your little girl?'

She blinked, not expecting the question. 'Safe. Happy.'

'I got the picture you sent of her, in the holiday card. Thank you.'

'I wasn't sure whether to send it. I didn't want you to get the wrong idea.'

His brows lifted. 'What would have been the wrong idea?'

'That it was . . . from me.'

'Hmm. I understand.'

'No,' Stevie said sadly. 'I don't think you do.'

'You're a widow. Your husband was murdered.' He shrugged when she stared. 'I looked you up. Because I was curious, too.'

She could have denied being curious, but he'd know she was lying. 'I'm a single mom with a job that takes too much away from my daughter as it is.'

He continued to study her, not breaking eye contact. 'You said once that you might need my help. On a future case. When you needed information that wasn't available by more conventional means.'

'Or legal,' she said.

'Tomato, *to-mah-to*. But you never asked.'

'I almost did,' she admitted. 'Several times.'

'But?'

She looked away. 'I don't know.'

'The offer still stands,' he said. 'No strings. No expectations.'

She met his eyes. Made a decision she hoped she would not regret. 'Thank you. I think I'll take you up on it.'

'This case? Dirty cops?'

'Maybe prosecutors, too. Grayson's boss for one. He knew Muñoz was set up.'

'You want me to look into this boss? Discreetly?' he asked and she nodded.

'His name is Charlie Anderson. I can't believe he'd look the other way on Muñoz out of the goodness of his heart. There's a money trail somewhere.'

'You want me to dig into his bank records?'

She paused, knowing full well what she was asking him to do. Then in her mind she saw the smoldering wreckage of Grayson's car, and her doubt disappeared. 'Yes, please. But no one can know. Not even Grayson or Paige.'

'Why keep it from them?' Clay asked.

'Because Grayson would stop me. We don't have a search warrant for Anderson's financial statements and Grayson's an idealist. "Fruit of the poisonous tree" as he always says.'

'Almost getting blown up has a way of changing a man's ideals.'

She sighed out a breath. 'True enough. But keep it to yourself for now. Your word?'

He nodded. 'Nobody will know. I'll get back to you when I have something.'

'Thanks.' She moved to the door. 'Do you still have my cell?'

'Yes,' he said without hesitation.

'Good. Then call me when you have something.' She'd opened the door when he stepped behind her and gently pushed it shut, caging her in.

'I never really thanked you,' he said quietly, 'for bringing Nicki's killer down. You gave her family closure and for that we're very grateful.'

She looked up at him. He was too close. Her heart was beating entirely too hard. 'It was my job. Get some rest, Mr Maynard. Your new partner is safe.'

He opened the door without another word. Stevie waited until she was in the hotel lobby to press her hand to her still-racing heart.

Thursday, April 7, 7.15 A.M.

The shrill ringing of the telephone woke Grayson from a sound sleep. It took him a second to remember where he was, but the warm woman in his arms was his first clue. He reached for the phone, a smile on his face despite the sharp twinge in his back.

Taking the brunt of falling burning metal wasn't something he hoped to do again.

'Hello?' he whispered into the phone, stroking Paige's black hair, gently pushing her head back to his chest when she looked up, blinking sleepily.

'You didn't think to call?' It was his mother and she was angry. 'You didn't think it was important to tell me you'd almost been blown to bits? I had to see it on the news.'

He winced. 'It was late last night. There didn't seem to be much use in waking you up to tell you I was okay.' Plus, he'd been a little busy at the time having Paige on the dining-room table. And in the shower. And in his bed. *That was the best time of all.*

'Are you really all right? They said minor injuries.'

'I got hit in the back by a piece of the car, but I'm only bruised. I was wearing Kevlar.'

'Kev—' She stopped short, her exhale audible. 'I want to see you this morning.'

He thought of all he needed to do. 'I'll try.'

'Grayson.' Her voice trembled. 'I need to see you for myself.'

'Then I'll come. I promise.'

'Okay. How is Paige? That rat bastard reporter said she was with you at the time.'

'Rat bastard?' He grinned. 'Mom.'

'That's what Paige called him. Was she hurt?'

He looked down at all that soft, golden skin. Paige propped her chin on his chest, watching him as he talked. 'Just a scratch or two,' he said. 'She's fine.'

'I see.' And he suspected that his mother did. 'Did you tell her?'

'She already knew. But you knew that.'

'I did. She's a smart cookie. I can't believe you kept that photo.'

'I needed to. After . . . you were so sad. You cried all the time. I had the picture to remember you from before. Sometimes I'd hold it and pretend it never happened at all.'

She was quiet a moment. 'I kept a few of your baby pictures. I look at them every time Lisa has another baby and I think about being a grandmother.' Her voice went wry. 'I've been waiting a long time, you know.'

He rolled his eyes. 'Mom.'

'I know, I know. It's too soon. I can dream, though.' She cleared her throat briskly. 'I tried calling your cell phone before the home phone. It went straight to voicemail.'

'I dropped it when I was running from the car. It's pretty well trashed. I'm going to get another phone today. Paige will need another one, too. And a laptop.'

'Sounds like you two have a lot to do today. I'll let you get started.'

'But I will stop by the house this morning so you can count my fingers and toes.'

Her chuckle was watery. 'I'll be waiting. I love you, son.'

'I love you, too, Mom.' He hung up and handed the phone to Paige. 'We made the news again,' he said. 'Your friends in Minnesota will be worried about you.'

She sat up, pulling the sheet to cover her breasts. He tugged at the sheet, but she held it in place, making him scowl. 'We have things to do this morning,' she said primly. 'If I let you start, we'll stay here all day.'

'I could live with that,' he said, but she shook her head.

'You promised your mother. Now hush and let me call Olivia.' She made her call, wincing as he had. She held the phone an inch from her ear as a stream of creative cursing spilled from the receiver. When it quieted a bit, she tentatively put the phone back to her ear. 'No, you don't need to come. I'm fine. Grayson took most of the brunt of it. He's fine, too.'

He tugged at the sheet again and she glared at him. 'Stop it,' she snapped. 'Not you,' she said to her friend, then she sighed. 'Yes, he's here.' She handed him the phone. 'Now you've done it. She wants to talk to you.'

'This is Smith.'

'I would hope you weren't anyone else,' Olivia said dryly, 'since you're in her bed.'

'Technically she's in mine.'

'You don't have to sound so proud of that,' she said, her voice gone hard. 'Look, I checked your record. You're a decent prosecutor. Doesn't mean you're a decent man.'

'I like to think I am.'

'Well, time will tell. Don't hurt her.'

'I'll try.'

'There is no try.'

Grayson froze, the phone pressed to his ear. *There is no try.* He heard another voice say the same words, in the same impatient tone. More than a year ago.

Eight hours ago, that same voice had told him to stop his car and get out. 'Oh, God.'

'What?' Olivia demanded, worry crowding her voice. 'What's wrong?'

Paige took the phone from his hand. 'What did you say to him?' She listened and frowned. 'That's all? "There is no try"?' She met his eyes. 'What is it?' she asked him.

There is no try. 'I know who it is,' he said simply.

'Liv, I have to go. It's okay, but I can't explain now. I'll call you later.' She hung up, tossed the phone to the bed and scrambled to her knees, framing his face between her palms. 'Who?'

'Silas Dandridge. Retired cop.' He closed his eyes. 'I have to be wrong.'

'But you know you're not.'

'No. It's his voice. I just hadn't heard it in a year.'

'You have to call Stevie.'

He stared at Paige numbly. 'This is going to kill her. She won't believe me.'

'Why?'

'He was her partner.'

Thursday, April 7, 7.20 A.M.

Stevie stumbled into the kitchen, yawning. 'Smells good.'

Her sister Izzy stood at the stove, flipping pancakes. 'I know. Coffee's fresh.'

'Morning, Mommy.' Six-year-old Cordelia already sat at the table, her plate nearly empty.

'Morning, baby.' Stevie filled a cup and sat next to the case paperwork Izzy had stacked into a pile. 'I was going to nap for five minutes last night before reading those.'

'You were snoring like a buzzsaw on the sofa when I came down,' Izzy said.

'Like a very loud buzzsaw,' Cordelia agreed soberly. 'You're louder than Grandpa.'

'Am not,' Stevie denied, and watched Izzy and Cordelia share knowing looks.

'Whatever you say, Chief,' Izzy said. 'I got some makeup together for your friend.'

'Thank you. And she's actually Grayson's friend.'

''Bout time he got a friend,' Izzy declared. 'Cordy, time to get dressed for school.' Cordelia grumbled, but obeyed. Izzy put a plate in front of Stevie. The pancakes had chocolate chips in the shape of eyes and a smiling mouth. 'Because you're all scowly.'

'How can you be so damn cheerful?' Stevie muttered.

Izzy leaned close to whisper, 'Because I get some on a semi-routine basis, sweetie-pie. You should try it. Before you're too old to enjoy it anymore.'

Immediately Stevie saw Clay Maynard in her mind and pushed the image away. 'Shut up. Just because your pancakes are good doesn't mean you can butt into my life.'

'My pancakes are great and you have no life.'

The doorbell rang, followed by Cordy's 'I'll get it', and a happy squeal. 'Uncle JD.'

JD had been one of Paul's closest friends and was Cordelia's godfather. That he and Stevie had been paired up the year before had been part luck and part strategic maneuvering on Stevie's part.

JD had needed a change. He'd found it, with a new direction in his career and a new love in his life.

'JD's gettin' some,' Izzy said conspiratorially. 'He's not scowly.'

Stevie rolled her eyes. 'Will you shut up?'

JD came into the kitchen, Cordelia on his hip. 'I smell pancakes,' he said hopefully.

Izzy laughed. 'I have to take Cordy to school. But there's enough batter left for a dozen more cakes if that scowly one over there will pour them on the griddle.'

JD looked at Stevie doubtfully. 'I'd better pour them myself.' He smacked a loud kiss on Cordelia's cheek. 'You be good today.'

'Or don't get caught if you're bad,' Izzy added. 'Come on, kid. Let's go.'

JD watched them go, then poured the pancake batter. 'Why are you scowly?'

Because I haven't gotten any in years. 'Because I haven't slept in two nights.'

'Because?'

'Because I've been working on Grayson's case.'

'Which you're going to tell me about right now, yes?'

'Yes.' She rose. 'Sit down. I'll flip 'em. You always let them burn.'

'I get distracted easily.'

'Yeah, right. You just like other people to cook for you and this is your way of looking helpless.' His grin told her she'd hit the nail on the head. 'It's like this.'

His grin quickly faded as she brought him up to date.

'Oh, my God,' he murmured. 'Smith's boss has dirt on him?'

'I can't imagine Grayson having dirt.' She slid a plate in front of him. 'But there was a threat. I could see it in his eyes after he talked to Anderson yesterday. Then last night his car goes kablooey.'

'Maybe they were after Paige.'

'The guy who shot Logan's mother called *him*. Warned *him*. And shot at *him*. I pulled Grayson's cell records. The number that called him came from a pre-paid phone.'

'I expected as much. I'd like to see the scene,' JD said.

'The bomb took the car out. Not much left.'

'No, the spot in the woods where the blood was found. Where the shot that missed Smith was fired. That's where the sniper set up. I want to see it.'

He'd been an Army sniper once, back in his first career. He might see something the rest of them had missed. Besides, the sun was up. CSU might have missed something in the darkness.

Stevie nodded. 'Finish up and we'll go out there.'

Thursday, April 7, 7.30 A.M.

Paige's mouth fell open in shock, not sure she'd heard what she'd thought she'd heard. 'Stevie's *partner* called you last night?'

'Her old partner. She's only been with JD for a year. Before that she was partnered with Silas Dandridge.'

'For how long?'

'Years. Before Stevie's husband and little boy were murdered.'

She blew out a breath. 'You're sure?'

'No. Now I'm not.' Grayson shoved a hand through his hair. 'What am I going to say to Stevie? The guy who you trusted with your life is a stone-cold killer?'

'Maybe I can find something online with his voice. An old interview or something. Then you can be sure before you tell her. I'll have to use your computer, since mine's in pieces. Where are my clothes?'

'Downstairs where you left them. Use my robe.' He pulled on a pair of sweats. 'I'll log you in to my computer, then I'll walk the dog. It's daylight. It should be fine.'

'I'm not worried about this Dandridge. He spared you, twice. I'm worried about the guy who planted the bomb. And about the guy in the photograph, paying off Sandoval. I'm worried about where Brittany Jones is, and what trouble she's brewing. Just take Peabody out back again. I'll ask Clay to exercise him.' She bit her lip. 'Oh, crap. Clay spent the night at the Peabody Hotel. He's probably worried about me.'

'No, he's not. Stevie found him there last night. He knows you're okay.'

'Good. Then let's confirm Silas Dan—' Fierce barking cut into the quiet and Paige paled. 'Peabody.' She reached for her gun, then realized she wore Grayson's robe. 'Shit.' She threw open the door and ran down the stairs.

He was close on her heels, but not close enough to grab her. 'Paige. Stop.'

She stopped abruptly, halfway down the stairs. He nearly plowed her over, which would have sent them both headfirst into the foyer.

Where Joseph stood very still, his back against the front door. The gun in his hand was pointed at Peabody, who growled low in his throat, teeth bared.

'Peabody, down,' Paige said quickly and the dog instantly obeyed.

Joseph's shoulders sagged. He lowered his gun and raised his brows at the sight of them on the stairs. 'I guess I won't be dropping by unannounced anymore.'

'I thought you put on the alarm,' Paige said to Grayson.

'He knows the master code,' Grayson said, bypassing her on the stairs. He took the leash from the hook beside the door. 'Come on, Peabody.'

'Why doesn't the damn dog growl at *him*?' Joseph demanded.

'Because I told him that Grayson was okay,' Paige said, pulling the sides of Grayson's robe more snugly together.

'Do you plan to tell him that I'm okay?'

'I don't know. I haven't figured out if you are yet.'

'I brought your stuff from the hotel.' He opened the front door and retrieved the suitcase and the bag of kibble from the porch. 'I also brought you both cell phones. They're not your old numbers, but they'll do until you get replacement phones from your providers.' He held up a plastic drugstore bag. 'And a toothbrush for you.'

Paige crept down the remaining stairs, very aware that she was naked under Grayson's robe and that Joseph knew it. His eyes sparkled with laughter even though the rest of his face remained stoically unmoving.

'I could tell Peabody you're temporarily okay,' Paige hedged. 'For the toothbrush.'

'What if I made you coffee?'

'Then I'd worship you forever.' He laughed and Paige blinked. His face was transformed when he laughed. She remembered that Grayson's mother had said he'd been born angry and wondered why. 'Of course there's no deal if the coffee sucks.'

'I wouldn't expect it.' He measured her, up and down. 'Are you both all right?' he asked, suddenly sober again. 'I went out to the scene. There's nothing left of his car.'

'We're okay. We were lucky. If that warning had come thirty seconds later . . .' She followed him through the dining room, where he stopped and she felt her cheeks light on fire. Her clothes were everywhere. Grayson's pants were still in a heap where he'd left them – on the floor next to the table. Next to her pants and a single boot. She had no idea where the other boot had landed.

Joseph coughed, but Paige knew it was a smothered laugh.

'Go ahead and say it,' she sighed. 'Yes, we *were* lucky and we *got* lucky, too.'

'Not touching that with a ten-foot pole,' he said, going into the kitchen, leaving her to pick up their clothes in a rush.

'I'll be back,' she said loudly. 'I need to change.'

'You, um, do that,' Joseph said and she peeked into the kitchen. His shoulders shook as he measured out the coffee. He was laughing so hard he spilled a scoop on the counter and had to start over again.

'How long before your sisters hear about this?' she asked from the doorway.

'Ten minutes, fifteen tops. Less if they're all online.'

'Wonderful.' She took the discarded clothes and her suitcase up the stairs.

Thursday, April 7, 7.45 A.M.

'Thanks for letting me stay last night.' Adele slid onto a stool at Krissy's kitchen counter as her friend made coffee. 'I wasn't sure where else to go.'

She'd met Krissy at the Y shortly after she and Darren had moved back to Baltimore. Krissy's baby was about Allie's age, so they'd attended mommy-baby classes together. But more importantly at the moment, Krissy had just finalized a nasty divorce. When Adele had finished packing her bag the night before, she'd called Krissy, hoping for a place to stay and some advice.

On getting a divorce, if it came to that. Hopefully Darren would calm down and realize he'd overreacted. *And hopefully I'll find a way to tell him the truth.*

Adele had no intention of sharing anything more personal with Krissy, such as the medallion she now carried in her purse. She'd tossed and turned all night, worrying about what to do next. Who to ask for help.

That the medallion and the attempts on her life were connected was a huge stretch. It was more likely a killer had picked her name out of the phone book, despite Darren's belief that that only happened on TV. Except . . . *They threatened to kill you if you told.*

So I never did. She'd told Theopolis only the basics years before when he'd treated her for her suicide attempts. Even he didn't know names, places, dates.

Telling now might do nothing more than help her put her own life back together. But God knew she needed to do that, if only to keep her own child safe. *From me.*

She'd debated all the options in her mind, everything from the police to the media to just telling Darren and getting it over with. She'd decided on the first, but with a step in between. The police would never believe her story without proof. She hadn't even kept the box the chocolates had come in. They'd think she was a crackpot.

So sometime before dawn she'd decided to hire a PI to find out who was trying to kill her. Once she had proof, she'd go to the cops. If the medallion was connected, she'd tell the media, too.

In the meantime, she'd plan for the worst. She had to find a way to fight Darren for Allie. *He will not take her.*

'I can't believe Darren did that.' Krissy poured the coffee with a frown. 'I liked him.'

'I'm hurt that he could believe I'd cheat. That he believed the worst about me.'

Krissy hesitated. 'He doesn't have proof, does he? No pictures or anything.'

'No,' Adele said forcefully. 'Because I didn't do anything wrong.'

'Maybe he's just upset over his dog.'

'That didn't give him the right to treat me that way.'

'No, it didn't. It just doesn't sound like him. He's always treated you like a goddess.' She shrugged and handed Adele a card. 'My lawyer. He was good, but expensive.'

Adele steeled herself. 'How expensive?'

'His retainer was five thousand. But he's good,' she said when Adele flinched. 'If Darren's behaving so irrationally, maybe you can use that against him.'

But I behaved irrationally first. Which Darren would make sure everyone knew.

'Maybe. When you went through your divorce, did you have pictures?'

'Hell, yeah. My alimony doubled when my ex saw the pictures. He didn't want them getting out. They were . . .' Krissy sipped her coffee. 'Damaging.'

'How did you get the pictures?'

'I hired a PI. Best money I ever spent.' Krissy wrote down an address. 'In case you decide you need some ammunition.'

Adele frowned. 'This isn't the best part of town.'

'Just don't go down there at night. He said his cheap rent keeps his rates down.'

'Thanks. I'll give him a call.'

Thursday, April 7, 7.45 A.M.

'Coffee and the morning paper, sir?'

'Yes,' he said. 'Please. You can leave the carafe. I think this is a two-cup day.'

He'd already had his run on the treadmill in his private gym. He'd showered and was ready for a healthy breakfast before work. Back to normal. Normal was good.

It was nice to return to routine. No crashing minivans. No staged suicides. No managing Silas Dandridge. And no PI and state's attorney harassing everyone.

The maid set the newspaper next to his laptop, poured his coffee, opened the drapes across his picture window, and bowed out discreetly, as she did every normal morning.

He settled in his chair and checked his cell phone. Then frowned. He'd expected a text from Kapansky. The man should have been in Dunkirk, New York by now. Brittany Jones should be dead by now. He dialed Kapansky's number.

And his frown deepened when the call went straight to voice-mail. Kapansky had turned off his phone. The man knew better than that.

A bad feeling chipped away at his normal good mood. He unfolded the paper and read the headline with fury, dread, and disbelief. STATE'S ATTORNEY SURVIVES CAR BOMB.

What the hell? He read, fury quickly overwhelming the other emotions. It just got worse. Both Smith and the woman had survived by leaping from the car seconds before the explosion. How could they have known? They couldn't possibly have known.

Unless they'd been warned. He came to his feet, pacing his office floor. Silas. *It had to have been Silas*. But Kapansky had killed him. He stopped abruptly, his blood gone cold.

Unless Kapansky had failed. He'd instructed Kapansky to text him last night. He'd been with credible other people for the express purpose of an alibi. He hadn't wanted to receive a call that people would remember. *I should have had him call me*.

I should have made sure I heard his voice.

Now Silas was on the warpath. His next step was . . . *Me. He thinks his family is safely hidden. So he'll come after me*. He turned, realizing just how Silas would do it.

From far away. With a sniper's rifle. *Fuck*.

He dived and rolled, pressing flat against the wall below the window that ran the length of the room. Just as the plate glass above him exploded. Shards of glass filled the air like snow, catching the morning light like a million prisms.

The moments after were quiet, then he could hear the noise from the street, twenty-five stories below. The door was thrown open, his maid's face ashen.

'Get back!' he barked.

She obeyed, jumping back a foot. 'Should I call 911?'

'No.' He swallowed hard, sitting up gingerly, keeping his head below the window frame. 'Call the glasscutter. Have him replace the window. Then clean up the mess.'

The maid nodded unsteadily. 'Any special kind of glass?'

'Yeah.' The shock was wearing off, rage rapidly taking its place. 'As bulletproof as he can get. And Millie? It was a bird. The biggest goddamn bird you ever saw. Clear?'

She nodded again. 'Yes, sir.'

He waited until she was gone to crawl across the room, avoiding the jagged pebbles littering the carpet. Silas had made a whole lot of critical errors.

Killing Kapansky was one. Not that Kapansky was worth too much mourning, but it meant Brittany Jones was still alive. She was only an irritant, though. As long as he kept paying her, she'd keep her mouth shut.

Warning the prosecutor and the PI was a bigger issue, but still manageable. They were on Rex's trail and that was fine with him. *Lousy, good-for-nothing addict. Let them arrest him.* This time no one would be running to his aid. No attorneys would be defending him. Maybe he'd finally wise up and be the man his family needed him to be.

No. Rex would always be Rex, with that silver spoon stuck up his ass. *Rex McCloud isn't worth my contempt. So let the PI and the prosecutor accuse him.*

And if the prosecutor got testy over the car bomb, there was a money trail for him to follow. It would result in the loss of a key man on the other side of the table, but he had other contacts in the pipeline. Developing a new key man wouldn't be that hard.

And if the prosecutor and the PI continued to press closer? *Then I'll take them out myself.* He certainly couldn't fuck it up any worse than Silas had.

He stood, brushed off his clothes, shook the glass from his hair.

Of all the errors Silas made, pissing me off was the worst. Silas thought his family safe, snug in their little Toronto hotel room. *He'll be rethinking that.*

Stepping from the room, he placed another call on his cell.

'Pearson's Aviation.'

'I'm booking a private flight from BWI to Toronto. Steve Pearson is my usual pilot.'

'I'll put you in touch with him.'

'Thank you.' Steve Pearson had a way of managing to fly without leaving nasty records all over the place. *Because I don't want anyone to know I'm going or that I've been there. Because if you want something done right, you have to do it yourself.*

'This is Steve. I can fly you there this morning. Flight time is forty minutes.'

'Excellent. I'll have at least one passenger on my way back.'

'Not a problem. When should I meet you at the runway?'

He had to get all the glass out of his hair. 'Ninety minutes tops.'

'I'll be waiting.'

Eighteen

Thursday, April 7, 7.45 A.M.

Feeling more confident now that she wore actual clothing, Paige rejoined Grayson and Joseph in the kitchen. Grayson sat staring miserably into his cup of coffee. A shiny new laptop was on the table.

Joseph pointed to it, all smile gone from his face. 'Yours until you get yourself a new one. Grayson said you needed to run a search.'

She sat down and pulled it to her. 'Thank you. You could probably find this faster.'

'I probably could. But I hear you're good at uncovering information. I'm making omelets,' he said before she could respond. 'You want?'

'Please.' She logged into her news article database while Joseph poured her a cup of coffee. *Dandridge, Silas,* she typed and began sorting the results. She glanced at Grayson. ' "There is no try." Why did that particular phrase trigger your memory?'

'He said it when he wanted a warrant and I'd say, "I'll try." He did the whole quote.'

Joseph looked up from whisking the eggs. 'What quote?'

'It's from *The Empire Strikes Back,*' Grayson told him. 'Yoda says it.'

' "Do or do not. There is no try." My karate master said it too.' Paige refocused on the screen. 'Here's a file photo of Dandridge.' She turned the laptop so that he could see.

'It's not the guy who paid Sandoval,' Grayson said, 'but he's the same size as the man who dragged Logan away. Same hands. Silas has hands like frying pans.'

Joseph folded the omelet. 'Would you have believed Silas could kill like this?'

'No,' Grayson said without hesitation. 'I knew him to be honest. Devoted, even.'

'What does that mean, devoted?' Joseph asked.

'He was passionate when he believed in a cause. He was there for Stevie when Paul was killed in ways the rest of us couldn't have been. He was her partner.'

'Then what could have made him turn this way?' Paige asked softly.

'I don't know. It's taking every ounce of my self-control not to call his house, just to hear his voice again. I need to know if I'm crazy or I'm right.'

'Give me a few minutes,' she said. She ate breakfast while she sifted through the videos and articles that were returned on the search of Silas Dandridge's name. Finally she found an old clip in which he spoke. 'He was interviewed by the local news about a homicide.' She hit *play* and Grayson shut his eyes, listening intently.

'No comment. Any questions should be sent to the Office of Public Relations.'

By watching his face she knew.

'It's him,' Grayson said hoarsely. 'I need to tell Stevie. We need to bring him in.'

Paige darted a quick glance at Joseph, saw he shared her misgivings. 'Wait,' she said when Grayson reached for his phone. 'I believe you, but who else will? It's your word – and right now, your boss has painted you as unable to handle Homicide.'

'She's right,' Joseph said. 'If you bring him in now, all he'll do is deny everything. Think about what might motivate a good cop to go so bad. Get some proof first.'

'Maybe his family was being threatened,' Grayson said. 'Or he was blackmailed.'

'Either are options,' Joseph said. 'What do you know about this guy's family?'

'He's married with a daughter.' Grayson tried to recall. 'We never talked much about home or family. We were both all about the job. The only time I ever saw him outside of work was at the gym in the mornings. And twice at the firing range.'

Paige saw the flicker of sad realization in his eyes. 'Good shot, huh?' she asked.

'Really good. He could have made the shot that killed Elena Muñoz. Easily.' Grayson's mouth firmed to a hard line. 'Run a background on him. Please.'

'He's fifty-six years old,' she said when the results came up. 'Wife, Rose, forty-nine, daughter, Cherri, twenty-five, and daughter Violet, seven.'

'Run Cherri,' Grayson said. 'He mentioned Rose and Violet, but never Cherri.'

An entry on the first page of results had Paige sighing. 'Cherri died seven years ago in West Virginia. She was eighteen. I'll pull the official death cert in a minute. She was married in Maryland at age seventeen. Groom was Richard Higgins, nineteen.'

She scrolled further. 'Here's something. Cherri was arrested for armed robbery eight years ago in Maryland. The charges were dropped. Grayson, can you get into your system to get the details on this case?'

'It's unlikely that I can,' he said. 'I'm probably still blocked. But Daphne can.'

Grayson called Daphne while Paige went back to her news database, biting at her lower lip. *Cherri Dandridge Higgins*, she typed. Then added *West Virginia* and *Richard*.

One article popped up. A short article, only four paragraphs. But it was enough.

Disturbed, Paige looked up to find Grayson watching her, the phone to his ear.

'I'm on hold,' he said, 'waiting for Daphne to run the case. What did you find?'

'How Cherri died,' Paige said, and Grayson bent close to read over her shoulder.

'Oh, my God,' he murmured. ' "Police were called to the Vista

351

Motel upon receiving several 911 calls from guests who reported loud screams from a second-story room. Police broke down the door to find Richard Higgins stabbing a woman on the bed."'

'Cherri?' Joseph asked.

'Yes,' Grayson said. ' "On seeing the officers, Higgins attacked them, knife raised. Deputy Derrick Thomas fired three shots, striking Higgins in the chest. Higgins was pronounced dead at the scene. The victim, identified as Higgins's wife Cherri Higgins, was airlifted to University Hospital in Morgantown where she later died. Witnesses at the motel stated that the victim was very pregnant, perhaps as much as nine months."'

Joseph grimaced. 'Shit. Was he on drugs or something?'

'The reporter speculates so,' Paige said. 'It says the cops found bags of oxycodone that appeared to have been for distribution. It also says they found two vials of PCP.'

'Probably for his personal use,' Grayson said. 'We had a problem with PCP labs popping up around Baltimore about ten years ago.'

'I remember,' Joseph said. 'PCP could have caused that level of violence. If she was pregnant, what happened to the baby?'

'It doesn't say,' Paige said.

'Violet,' Grayson said quietly. 'She's seven, same as Cherri's baby would be. Violet must be Cherri's daughter.'

'That makes sense. Silas brought his granddaughter home, raised her as his own child,' Paige murmured, then twisted to look up at Grayson when he abruptly straightened. Apparently Daphne had returned to the line.

'I'm still here,' he said into the phone. His brows lifted high. 'Isn't that interesting?' He listened, then shook his head. 'That should be unbelievable to me, but it's not. Listen, you be careful when you leave the office tonight. Have security walk you to your car. Better yet, take a cab. I don't want anything to happen to you.'

He hung up and sank into the chair next to Paige. 'Cherri's armed robbery charge was dropped when another woman was accused. The stolen money was found in the other woman's bedroom closet, along with the gun used in the robbery.'

'No way,' Paige breathed. 'In her winter boot?'

He laughed, but there was no humor in it. 'No. That would have been a little too much, wouldn't it? But it does get better. Guess who Cherri's defense attorney was?'

Paige narrowed her eyes. 'Bob Bond?'

'One and the same.' Grayson turned to Joseph. 'Bond was defense for Ramon Muñoz, too. And the prosecutor who dropped the charges? None other than my boss.'

Joseph's face darkened. 'Sonofabitch. We'll get him, Grayson. Both of them.'

Paige managed to keep the lid on her own rage, but just barely. 'You won't get Bond. He's dead. Suicide.'

Grayson looked at her with a frown. 'How do you know that?'

'I called his office when I first started investigating for Maria and Elena. I wanted to talk to him, find out if there were any loose ends that he wished he'd followed up on during Ramon's trial, or any leads he could recommend. You know, things he might have done had Ramon been a paying customer,' she added sourly.

'Ramon's attorney was pro bono?' Joseph asked.

'No,' Grayson said. 'The McClouds paid him. Bond was an attorney with the law office the senator had on retainer.'

'Why would the McClouds pay for Ramon's lawyer?' Joseph asked.

'Maria told me that the McClouds liked Ramon,' Paige said. 'That they wanted him to have the best defense possible. Except . . .' she paused. 'Last night the senator couldn't even remember Ramon's name. Called him Roberto. I can't see him footing the bill.'

'Maybe Mrs McCloud paid,' Grayson said. 'I can see her thinking it was just another charity. Or doing it from guilt, especially if she knew the security video had been switched. If she knew Ramon wasn't guilty, maybe she hoped Bond would get him off.'

'I'd buy the second one,' Paige said. 'But once Ramon was found guilty, Maria said the McClouds cut off their support. Maria and Elena hired another attorney for the appeals, but he was unsuccessful. They tried to get one of the attorneys who specialize in retrying wrongful convictions, but he was already booked out for years.'

'And Elena came to me,' Grayson said quietly.

Paige covered his hand with hers. 'What could you have done? Why would you have believed her then? The evidence against Ramon was convincing.'

His jaw tightened. 'It didn't convince *you*.'

'Sure it did. That's why I told Elena we needed more. I'd promised Clay I'd walk away from their case if the new evidence wasn't compelling.' The image of Elena's bloody body suddenly filled her mind, unbidden. She held it there for a moment, let it fuel her rage before shoving it to the side. 'But it turned out to be so compelling that Silas killed her.'

'So how did Silas go from devoted cop to killer?' Joseph asked.

'Let's assume that Cherri was guilty of the armed robbery,' Grayson said. 'Somebody plants evidence and another woman is accused. Maybe Silas is involved in getting his daughter's charges dropped and maybe he's not.'

'But at some point he's either blackmailed into helping frame Ramon or it's his fee,' Paige said. 'Things go well. Ramon is convicted. Nothing happens until Elena walks by Sandoval's bar and sees that he's upgraded the place when he shouldn't have been able to afford to. She and Maria hire me, and Elena manages to copy Sandoval's insurance photos. She has to be eliminated. So do Sandoval and Jorge Delgado.'

'So who attacked you in the garage?' Joseph asked.

Paige shrugged. 'And who is the guy paying off Sandoval? Who paid to have Ramon framed in the first place? Rex? His parents? His grandparents?'

'And did Rex kill Crystal Jones?' Grayson asked quietly. He stood up. 'Give me fifteen minutes to get dressed. We've still got party guests to re-interview. Somebody had to have seen Crystal leave the pool that night. We just have to find that someone.'

She caught his hand, held him in place. 'What about Stevie? We need to tell her.'

'I know,' he said, his expression drawn. 'I'll call her in the car.'

He jogged up the stairs, leaving Paige alone with Joseph. She bit her lip. 'He doesn't have a car,' she said. 'Anymore.'

'I brought him a loaner.' Joseph tossed a set of keys to the table. 'Black Escalade, parked out front. You'll need to drop me off at my house. I left my car there.'

Paige studied him closely. 'I know, you know. About . . . his father.'

He nodded soberly. 'Yeah. I heard. So?'

'So . . . if you're worried that I'll tell anyone, I won't.'

'I believe you. So does he. For him, believing in anyone is huge. Don't hurt him.'

'I'll—' She'd nearly said *I'll try*. But there truly was no *try* in such matters. 'I won't.'

Thursday, April 7, 8.45 A.M.

'I'll be in touch, Mrs Shaffer.' PI Sheldon Dupree shook her hand as they concluded their short meeting. 'Be careful.'

Adele put her checkbook away. The PI's retainer had put a dent in her savings, despite keeping his rates modest through low-rent real estate. 'I'll try. Thank you for seeing me this morning. I know it was short notice.'

'You're quite welcome. Where will you go from here?' he asked.

'I don't know. I guess I'm apartment hunting today.'

'Or you could tell your husband the truth and work it out. Either way, I will proceed with the plan we agreed to.'

Telling Darren wasn't an option even if she'd wanted to. She'd already tried calling him this morning so that she could talk to Allie, to let her baby hear her voice on the phone. He'd declined her calls. She'd drive to his mother's house before beginning a search for an apartment. And if it was possible, she'd take her baby back.

She picked up the bag containing the cameras Dupree wanted her to mount on her car. They'd capture anyone following her. It was the low-cost option on his menu. She simply couldn't afford to have him be her shadow. Hopefully she'd see someone following her in time to call 911 before they ran her off the road again.

'I'll let you know where to reach me when I'm settled.'

He walked her out, leaving with her. 'I have a meeting with

another client this morning. I'll be starting on your case later today. Don't hesitate to call if you're threatened again.' With a businesslike nod, he started off in the opposite direction from where she parked her car.

Adele walked to her car, parked in the alley around the corner.

She had the keys in the lock when she felt someone behind her. Looking up, she saw the face reflected in the window glass. The face from her nightmares. She opened her mouth to scream, but all that emerged was a hoarse cry as excruciating pain overwhelmed her.

A knife. In my back. Her hands scrabbled for the window. *Fight.* She turned, staggering, looking her nightmare in the eye for the first time since that day. Rage exploded and she lunged. Then fell to her knees.

Dully she looked down. The knife was now embedded in her gut. The pain came a millisecond later. 'I'm going to die,' she mumbled.

'Yes, you will.'

Adele looked up, her vision dimming. 'Goddamn you,' she choked. 'I had a life. I made myself a life.'

The knife was pulled free, wiped clean on Adele's jacket. 'That was the problem.'

Adele barely felt the shoe that shoved into her shoulder, pushing her face down into the asphalt.

Allie. She'd never hold her baby again.

She watched as her purse was stripped from her arm, unable to lift her head. Unable to do anything to stop this. *Just like that day*.

Her car started behind her and she could see the taillights from the corner of her eye, blurred through her tears. Adele was alone. *So glad Allie wasn't with me.* She tried to claw her way to the street. But everything went dark.

Thursday, April 7, 8.50 A.M.

'This is the place,' Stevie said, stopping at the crime-scene tape strung around the area on the edge of the woods near the nursing home.

JD walked around the perimeter, then ducked under the tape, staring down at the bloodstained ground. 'The sniper stood here,' he said. 'It's the only place with a clear path to the lightpost he shot instead of Smith.'

'He told Grayson that he missed on purpose.'

'Oh, he totally missed on purpose,' JD said. 'A sniper with cataracts could have made that shot. The shot that killed Elena Muñoz was a halfway decent challenge. This would have been child's play.' He crouched to study the blood left behind. 'There were two guys, the sniper and the bomber. I'm assuming the blood is the bomber's since the sniper was alive enough to call Grayson.'

'I assumed the same. CSU took samples of the blood, but it'll be tomorrow before we have a result. The bomb tech sent me a list of cons who've used the same kind of fuse. I've got DNA lined up for comparison.' She looked toward the road. 'At some point the sniper figures out that the bomb's been set. When? And how?'

'At least after Grayson drove away. If he knew beforehand, he would have stopped the car with a bullet to a tire instead of waiting to call him on the phone.'

'But why shoot at Grayson, meaning to miss?' she asked. 'Why the charade?'

'Somebody was watching him? Maybe he knew the other guy was here.' JD rose. 'Grayson's heard the sniper's voice before?'

'He's sure he has, but can't remember where.' Stevie ducked under the tape and stood beside JD, looking down at the bloodstains. 'It's heavier in patches.'

'Whoever got shot lay here bleeding for a while.' JD pointed. 'Arm, arm, and knee?'

The two of them looked up when CSU's Drew Peterson approached. 'There was a fourth shot to the head. There's brain matter right here.' Drew pointed to a marker. 'We found three bullets in the ground. I sent them to Ballistics.'

'The survivor dragged the injured guy,' Stevie said, walking along the path created in the leaves and dirt, head bent to get a closer look. Something caught her eye. It was almost white. She crouched to see more. 'You guys done here? Can I dig a little?'

'We've taken pictures. We haven't gone over that area with tweezers yet.' Drew crouched beside her, a sifter in his hand. He scooped the dirt surrounding the white paper into the sifter and shook until all that remained was a wallet-size photograph.

'Could it have been dropped here before last night?' JD asked.

Drew shook his head. 'We had so much rain the day before yesterday. Had it been dropped before yesterday morning, it would be falling apart by now, but it's intact. Looks like a little girl. An old picture, from the hair and clothes she's wearing.'

Pulling on gloves, Stevie carefully lifted the photograph and held it to the light.

And frowned. She'd seen this picture before. 'No,' she murmured.

'Who is it?' JD asked.

She said nothing, unable to believe her eyes. A sick feeling grabbed her gut. Disbelief. Pure unadulterated denial. She turned the picture over, devastated when she saw *Cherri* scrawled in the corner in a childish hand. Her throat closed.

'Who?' JD asked again. Kindly.

'Her name is Cherri,' she whispered. 'Cherri Dandridge.'

Drew's indrawn breath was sharp. 'Dandridge? Silas? Not possible.'

JD's brows knit. 'Silas? As in your old partner? This is his daughter?'

'Yeah.' Stevie rose, the photo in her numb hand. 'I can't believe this, JD. Not Silas. It can't be.'

'Could he have made that shot Tuesday? Could he have hit Elena Muñoz?'

Stevie nodded dully. 'With his eyes closed. He carried this picture around with him everywhere. He lost Cherri a year before we got partnered up. Murder. I lost Paul and our son a few months later. Also murder. Silas helped me go on.' Her voice trembled, broke. 'I won't believe he'd kill in cold blood.'

'There's got to be another explanation,' Drew said. 'I knew Silas Dandridge my whole career. He'd never do this.'

'Then let's go talk to him,' JD said. 'Find out how a picture of his daughter ended up in this crime scene.'

'He always carried it,' Stevie murmured. 'In his shirt pocket.' Her cell began to ring. It wasn't a number she recognized so she let it go to voicemail. 'He has another child. Violet's a year older than Cordelia.' Her cell phone began to ring again, the same number. Irritated, she answered. 'Mazzetti.'

'Stevie. It's Grayson.'

Stevie closed her eyes. How could she tell Grayson what she'd found? He'd sworn he'd heard the man's voice before. If it was Silas . . . *God, it can't be Silas.* But if it was, Grayson would know his voice. And Silas wouldn't let Grayson die. That much fit.

'You got a new number,' she said tonelessly.

For a moment all she could hear was road noise, the honking of a horn in the background. Then Grayson's heavy sigh. 'I know who he is, Stevie.'

The tone of his voice had her heart breaking. 'So do I,' she whispered.

'I'm sorry, Stevie,' Grayson said. 'I'm so damn sorry. How do you know?'

'He was here. At the nursing home. He dropped a photo of his daughter.' Her eyes burned. 'How do *you* know? Did you remember?'

'Yes, finally. Paige found a TV news clip where he was talking, so I could be sure before I told you. It . . . it was him, Stevie.'

A sob shook her. 'No. How could he? He killed that poor woman, Grayson.'

'And probably Delgado.'

Stevie thought about the scene, the blood all over the Dora the Explorer wallpaper. The note on the mirror. And the gun dumped near the Muñoz family home. And her devastation trebled. 'He framed the Muñoz brothers.'

'I know. He had a daughter. Cherri.'

She looked at the photo she held. 'She died, years ago.'

'Eight years ago Cherri had armed robbery charges against her dropped. The stolen goods were found in another woman's bedroom closet.'

'Like Ramon,' she murmured.

'Yes. Cherri's attorney also represented Ramon Muñoz. Somehow

Silas got pulled into this. I don't know how or why, but that he framed someone for the Delgado murder isn't contrary to his MO.'

A terrible calm settled on her shoulders. 'We need to find him. I'll put out a BOLO.'

JD tapped her shoulder. 'Can we use his daughter to draw him? Violet, I mean.'

'I think she's his granddaughter,' Grayson said, hearing JD's question. 'Cherri was pregnant when she was murdered.'

'He never told me that. I only knew that he and Rose adopted a baby shortly after Cherri's death. I wonder what else I didn't know.' She thought about what Grayson had said the night before. That he had some things to tell her. Personal things. 'I wonder what else I don't know about *you*.'

'Let's meet, later. For lunch. I'll tell you then. I need you to know. What are you going to do about Silas?'

'Find him,' she said coldly. 'And if he doesn't have one hell of a good alibi, I'll cuff him and bring him in like anyone else. I'll call you when I know something.'

Thursday, April 7, 9.10 A.M.

Grayson tapped his hands-free earpiece, disconnecting with another sigh. Paige had been watching his face, compassion on hers.

'She already knew?' she asked. 'How?'

'Silas dropped a picture of Cherri at the nursing-home crime scene last night.' He drew a breath. 'She cried. I haven't heard her cry since Paul and her son were killed.'

'She's survived worse than this,' Paige said kindly. 'She'll make it.' She patted his arm. 'You said we were going to see party guests. Where do we start?'

'With Brendon DeGrace. He was Rex's best friend then. I found him yesterday afternoon. He works at a brokerage downtown. But first, we're going to see my mother.'

'Oh. Any chance that Joseph was discreet about how he found us this morning?'

He glanced over at her, found her cheeks appealingly rosy. 'Not a prayer,' he said.

'Hell. I was afraid of that.'

'She already likes you. You'll be fine.' He paused, trying to organize the details in his mind. 'How did you find out that Ramon's attorney committed suicide?'

'The receptionist at the law firm told me Bob Bond was deceased when I called to make an appointment with him about Ramon. I pulled his death certificate to be sure she wasn't lying to me. It said "suicide".'

'Do you know how he did it?'

She looked surprised. 'No, why?'

'Because Bond would have been a loose end, like Sandoval. Who committed suicide, too. Supposedly.'

She opened her laptop, did a search. 'Here's an article published the day after Bond's death. He was found hanging from his bedroom ceiling. Bedsheets.'

'Like Sandoval.'

'Exactly like Sandoval. We could ask the ME to review the autopsy reports. See if there were any similarities.'

'I'll ask them if you look up the number. I had the MEs in my contact list, but I've only reset a few contacts in the new phone.'

She looked up the number and dialed. 'Morgue on line one, sir,' she deadpanned.

He was almost smiling when the phone was answered by a receptionist. 'Dr Mulhauser, please,' he said.

'He's not in today. Can I put you through to his voicemail?'

'No, I need to talk to a *live* person.' Paige cleared her throat and he realized what he'd said. 'I mean a doctor, in person. Not voicemail. Is Dr Trask in?'

'She is.' The receptionist sounded as if she were chuckling. 'Let me transfer you.'

A few rings later his call was picked up. 'This is Dr Trask. How can I help you?'

Trask worked more with Daphne, but the times Grayson had dealt with her he'd found her to be smart and efficient. And less of a bureaucrat than her counterparts. That she was engaged to Stevie's partner JD made her trustworthy. 'It's Grayson Smith.'

'Well, hello there. I hear you were nearly our guest last night.'

Thinking about what could have happened still made him flinch. 'Too nearly. But that's not why I'm calling. I was wondering if you knew anything about the recent death of one Denny Sandoval.'

'He was my case. The guy who supposedly hung himself.'

'You don't think he did?'

'No. He had a lot of barbiturates in his system. I don't think he could have stood up, much less put his own head through a noose. I think he was dead before he was hung. But he was strangled first, so it makes it hard to say.'

'Your best guess?'

'He was drugged, repeatedly asphyxiated, strangled, then hung. I'm ruling it homicide based on the barbiturate levels alone. I just have to finish the paperwork.'

'Repeatedly asphyxiated, how?'

'I'd guess it was done with a pillow. Bruising around mouth presented after death. It's in multiple places which leads me to believe the asphyxiation had been repeated.'

'He was tortured.'

'That's my take. I didn't find any feather fluff in his lungs, but it's possible the pillow was synthetic. The detectives assigned to the case should remember what kind of pillows he had. That was Morton and Bashears. Why are you asking about Sandoval?'

'I think this connects to another case. Can you look up a guy named Bob Bond? He also hung himself.'

'Give me a few minutes to pull the file. You wouldn't happen to have a date of death, would you?'

He looked over at Paige. 'Death date for Bob Bond?'

'September 17,' Paige said. 'Four years ago. Ask her to pull Crystal Jones's autopsy report as well. Ask her to see if there's anything . . . odd.'

'I heard that,' Lucy said before he could relay the information. 'Is that the woman I saw on TV? The one who almost blew up with you?'

'Yes,' Grayson said cautiously.

'Good you found her,' Lucy said. 'Daphne worries about you. So does JD.'

He didn't know what to say to that. 'Can you see this cell number?'

'No, you were transferred. Give it to me. I'll look up the reports and get back to you.'

He recited his new number, thanked her, and hung up. 'She's ruling Sandoval a homicide. He was doped up on barbiturates, but first he was repeatedly asphyxiated.'

'Somebody wanted information. Maybe the mystery man making the pay-off?'

'Reasonable assumption,' Grayson said. His phone rang in his hand, startling him. He glanced at the caller ID. Daphne's cell phone. 'Hi, Daphne. What's going on?'

'You've been summoned,' Daphne informed him. 'By Reba McCloud.'

Rex's aunt, who ran the family's charitable foundation. 'Why?' he asked.

'Because Her Highness is not pleased that you're harassing her nephew and dragging the family name through the mud with your "baseless innuendo". She wants to have a face to face with you, to convince you of the error of your ways.'

'My innuendo is far from baseless. And it wasn't innuendo. I called Rex a dirty liar.'

'Hey, I'm only the messenger. You want her number?' she said and he sighed.

'Sure.' He repeated it out loud and Paige wrote it down. 'I'll let her vent her spleen. She might even say something I can use against Rex. When and where?'

'Eleven this morning, at her office downtown. I'll text you the address.'

'It's okay. I know the place. Have you seen Anderson today?'

'Unfortunately,' she grumbled. 'File this, pull that, plead this felon down. Some of these guys are multiple rapists. Makes me sick. I know we're controlling costs, but you'd think he was writing the checks from his own bank account.'

Anderson's bank account. Paige had offered to check the man's finances, find out if he'd been paid to look the other way on Muñoz. Yesterday, Grayson had declined. Fruit of the poisonous tree. This morning, he'd been tempted to let her do it.

Funny how nearly getting killed changed a man's priorities.

But there still might be a legal way. Now he knew that Anderson was involved in at least one other case of tampering – the release of Cherri Dandridge. One could be coincidence. Two was smoke. A few more cases would produce an honest-to-God fire.

Then I'd have cause for a warrant. 'Daphne, I need to run a query.'

'I'll run it for you.'

'No, it could flag you. Too dangerous. I need my access back.'

'Not sure I can do that. But what if I got you somebody else's access?'

He lifted his brows. 'Whose?'

'Anderson's.'

Grayson's grin was sharp. 'I'd buy you a year's supply of hairspray.'

Daphne laughed. 'Look for a text. I'll get you what you need. Just remember the hairspray. Extra volume, extra hold. Extra superglue.'

He hung up, smiling.

'You should do that more often,' Paige said quietly. 'Smile.'

'Maybe I will.' He brought her hand to his lips. 'I never thanked you for last night.'

'Which part?' she asked huskily and most of the blood in his head rushed south.

'All of it,' he said. 'But mostly not being shocked about my father.'

'You can't control who your parents are. I don't even know who my father was.'

'I wish I didn't.'

'What happened to your father, if it's okay to ask?'

Grayson shrugged. 'He was given the death penalty.'

'Oh. Did he . . . did they . . . Is he still alive?'

'No. He got cancer fifteen years ago. Went fast. I have to say it was a relief.'

'I can understand that.'

'Your mother?' he asked. 'Is she still alive?'

'I don't know. I don't care.'

'Yes, you do,' he said gently. 'If only to wish she could have been different.'

'Sometimes,' she allowed. 'But my grandparents loved me. You had your mother and the Carters. The two of us did okay.'

'You must miss them, your grandparents.'

'I do. But my friends got me through. Became my family.'

He glanced at her curiously. 'I asked you why you came here if all of your friends were in Minnesota. You said you were suffocating. I understand that now. But why here? I mean, I'm glad you're here, but why Baltimore?'

'Because of Clay. I was at loose ends around the holidays last year, feeling sorry for myself. You know. Black belt brought to her knees and all that.'

'Normal, I'd think,' he said.

'Perhaps. But unproductive. I was restless and . . . scared. I kept Peabody close by. I woke up one day and looked at myself in the mirror. I didn't like who I saw looking back, so I decided to make a change. I didn't know where I was going. I just started packing when I found the business card Clay had given me at a wedding of some mutual friends, long before last summer. I figured it was fate, knocking me over the head with a two-by-four. I called him to ask for a job and found out his old partner had been killed. He needed a new partner, I needed a new start.' She lifted a shoulder self-consciously. 'So I guess I'm here because I was too much of a coward to stay.'

'You are no coward, Paige Holden.' The words came out far more heated than he'd planned. He calmed his voice. 'You might be the bravest person I know, after my own mother.'

Her dark eyes flashed with emotion. 'That's quite a compliment. Thank you.'

He kissed her hand again. 'You said you knew when I knocked

on Rex's door. I knew when you ran toward Elena. Most people would have run away.' He pulled Joseph's SUV into the Carters' drive, then let go of her hand to hit a button on the dashboard that sent the big iron gates swinging open. 'Home, sweet home.'

Paige's eyes grew huge. 'Wow. *This* is home?'

The Carter home was a mansion, elegant but not ostentatious. 'I remember the first time I saw this place,' Grayson said. 'I thought the big house was an apartment building. When my mother told me only one family lived here, I was stunned.'

'I'm not a small boy and I'm stunned. If I might be so bold, where did the Carters get all this? What does Mr Carter do?'

'When he was growing up, he was one of those geeky guys that built stuff in his dad's garage. He went to MIT, majored in biomedical engineering. His senior project was a new kind of joint for a prosthetic knee. His design won a prize, got bought by an orthopedic company and they hired him when he graduated. Ten years later he owned the company. Biomedical research is still the core business, but they also do robotics, guidance systems, software development.' Grayson smiled fondly. 'And Jack still builds stuff in the garage.'

He pointed to the garage that could easily house ten cars. 'That's his workshop. The apartment on top is where I grew up. Mom still lives there. We won't stay long. Just enough for her to be sure I'm really alive. Then I need you to tell me everything you've read about Reba McCloud. She's summoned us.'

Thursday, April 7, 9.45 A.M.

His phone rang and he let it go to voicemail. He'd been preparing for what he would do once he arrived in Toronto. They'd land in ten minutes. He was ready.

Not ecstatic, but ready. Dealing with children was never simple. He needed the little girl alive. The wife could go either way. If she became too much of a liability to bring home, he'd leave her behind. If so, he'd make sure to take a final picture for Silas's photo album. Because as soon as Silas had taken a shot at him, this had become far more than severing a business association.

He wanted Silas to suffer.

He pictured him now, seething because he'd missed, but secure in the knowledge that he could try again undeterred because his family was safe.

Within an hour, he'd have Silas Dandridge on his knees. *Then he'll come to me.*

His cell had stopped ringing, but started again. He looked at the display and wanted to groan. But of course he did no such thing. 'Good morning,' he said briskly.

'You didn't answer. You always answer on the first ring.' It was, and always had been, an unwritten rule between them.

'I was . . . occupied.'

'Huh. Well, you don't need to be *occupied* on my account. I took care of her.'

He sat up straighter in his seat. 'Who?'

'Adele Shaffer. You said you would, but you didn't. So I did. She was the last. Now there's no one left to tell.'

He closed his eyes, the vein in his temple throbbing. 'What the hell did you do?'

He could feel the frost coming through the line. 'Don't *ever* use that tone with me.'

'I'm sorry,' he said as sincerely as he could muster. 'What did you do?' he repeated, more politely.

'I stabbed her. She's dead.'

His gut began to churn. *I do not need this today.* 'Where? When?'

'In an alley. And about an hour ago.'

'Did anyone see you?'

'Of course not. I moved her car. I took three different taxis back to my own car.'

'You're sure she's dead?'

'I didn't wait for them to put her in a body bag, no. But she'd stopped breathing.'

'Did she see you?'

'Yes.'

His blood ran cold. 'But you're not sure she's dead?'

'She was dead. Trust me. I've done this enough to know.'

And I've cleaned up enough of your messes to know better. Two times out of every three, your victim wasn't dead. He could only pray that Adele Shaffer would be among the one-third that died without his assistance.

'Did you go back and see if she'd been taken anywhere?' he asked.

'Return to the scene of the crime?' The wry amusement in the question had him wincing. 'I'm not stupid.' There was a slight pause. 'Excellent. They're here.'

He leaned forward. He could hear sirens in the background. 'What's happening?'

'Ambulance and two squad cars. She's done, too.'

Too? Holy shit. 'Who? Where are you?'

'Sitting down the street from Betsy Malone's house.'

He kept his tone level. 'What have you done?'

'Made certain she wouldn't air any more secrets. Which you should have done last night. You haven't been very successful lately, have you?'

The churning in his stomach increased but he kept his voice cool. 'On the contrary. Things are going pretty much as I planned.'

'So the prosecutor is dead?' Amusement became contempt. 'Oh, wait. He's not.'

He clenched his teeth. 'He will be. For now, let him gnaw on Rex for a little while. I have some pressing matters to attend to.'

'You go tend to your "pressing matters". I, for one, have checked off the items on my to-do list. I think I'm up for a round of golf. If you want to know where to find the prosecutor and his PI at this very moment, just ask.'

'Where?' he asked, keeping his anger in check. 'Where are they now?'

'On their way to see Reba. She called them in.'

He said nothing for a moment, calculating the outcomes in his mind. 'She'll defend Rex. Uphold the family. Not a game changer.'

'I know. But if you want to finish the job you left undone, they'll be leaving there soon. Have a great day.'

The connection was broken and he sat staring at the phone in his hand. *Reba. I should have expected that.* But there was little to worry about. Reba was like tofu. Soundless, colorless. She was a placeholder. Grayson Smith would learn nothing more than that the McCloud family was above reproach in every way.

Which would further strengthen Smith's resolve to see Rex pay for the murder of Crystal Jones. Then this matter would be put to rest.

Nineteen

'Are you *certain*, Detective Mazzetti?' Lieutenant Hyatt asked.

Stevie stood with Hyatt and IA's Gutierrez in Silas's living room as IA detectives searched the Dandridge house. She could hear the strain in her boss's normally caustic voice. This wasn't easy for him either. Hyatt had trusted Silas. *As did I.*

She still wanted to believe they were wrong. That Silas had been framed. But now that she knew, so many little things made more sense. Silas had been so good at finding evidence that no one else had seen. They'd called him 'The Finder'.

So was she sure? She didn't want to be. But she was.

'Yes. Grayson Smith and I came to identical conclusions via separate paths.'

Grayson had been shaken by the discovery. *As am I.* She was holding it together, but only by picturing Delgado's body in his tub, his blood and brains all over the Dora the Explorer wallpaper. *Silas. How could you?*

His house was empty. No suitcases appeared to have been packed, the family vehicles still in the garage. With the exception of no dead man in the tub, the house felt exactly like the Delgado house. Vacated hastily. Deliberately.

Her cell buzzed. 'It's a text from JD,' she told Hyatt. 'He's with Latent. They got a match on one of the prints from the car CSU found behind the crime scene.'

'The one with the explosive traces in the trunk?' he asked.

'Yeah. Print matches Harlan Kapansky. He's on Donovan's

bomber list.' She winced at the next text. 'Kapansky's arresting officer was Silas Dandridge.'

Hyatt sighed. 'Hell. This just keeps getting worse. Where's Fitzpatrick now?'

'Going to Dispatch to listen to last night's 911 calls. A woman was close enough to see that Paige and Grayson were okay. Maybe she saw somebody else.'

'Lieutenant.' It was Sergeant Doyle, who'd been in the hotel room when Paige had told her story. *Only yesterday.* 'There's a floor safe in his bedroom.'

'I'll call in a tech,' Gutierrez said.

'Wait,' Stevie said, her heart in her throat. She brought up the article Paige had sent to her email. 'Try 1–12–05. Cherri died on January 12, 2005. And Violet was born.'

'Very well.' Hyatt's expression had gone cold. People thought he didn't care. Stevie knew that he did. He'd been her commanding officer for more than six years now. He could be a complete jerk, but the man cared deeply.

When Doyle went upstairs, she, Hyatt, and Gutierrez followed. Doyle knelt on the floor, a throw rug folded and laid to the side. He twisted the dial. The latch sprang open.

'Damn,' Stevie whispered. 'I was hoping it wouldn't work.'

'I know,' Hyatt said quietly. 'Open it, please.'

Doyle shot them a sympathetic glance, then began to pull items from the safe. Ten handguns. *Ten.* He looked up. 'All of these have the serial numbers filed off.'

Stevie nodded, her throat aching. Silas had saved throwaways? 'I didn't know.'

'I know you didn't,' Hyatt said. 'This is going to be a fucking nightmare.'

'Yes, it will,' she said tightly. Every case she and Silas had worked together would be scrutinized. *I'll be scrutinized.* How many of their cases had he tampered with? How many killers went free? *Silas, I could kill you right now and feel totally justified.*

Doyle pulled out a small bound book. 'It's a bank book.' He flipped through the pages. 'Deposit dates begin seven years ago.

The account is with a bank in the Turks and Caicos.' Doyle's eyes twitched slightly. 'There's a quarter mil here. No withdrawals appear to have been made. That's all.'

'Where could he be?' Gutierrez said.

Stevie shook her head. 'I don't know. We had a diner we liked. We'd go to the shooting range together. Other than that, we didn't really socialize. I was busy with Cordelia and he and Rose were raising Violet. I called Violet's school. They said she wasn't there and that they'd heard nothing. He didn't have any other family.'

'Did he have a favorite spot he'd go on vacation? Maybe a getaway cottage somewhere?' Gutierrez persisted.

'He did,' Hyatt said, 'before Cherri died. Up north – Canada. That's all I know.'

'Did you know that Violet was his granddaughter?' Stevie asked Hyatt.

'Yes. Cherri's death hit him and Rose so hard. That baby was his salvation. When Cherri was cleared of that robbery charge, he was so relieved. He thought she'd make something of herself. Have a second chance. If I weren't standing here, looking at this with my own eyes . . . I still wouldn't believe it.'

Doyle stood up. 'What next?'

'We put out a BOLO,' Hyatt said grimly. 'We arrest him. We also trace those funds.'

'And run the guns through Ballistics,' Stevie said. 'He left them for us to find. I imagine they'll tell a story too.' She sighed. 'We also have to locate Rose and Violet. They've run or Silas has them hidden. If we find them, we can lure him.'

'We can get Rose's cell-phone number from Silas's file,' Hyatt said.

'I'll get it,' Doyle said. 'Who should call Rose Dandridge?'

'I will,' Hyatt said.

'No,' Stevie told him. 'Let me. If she thinks we're on to Silas, she'll clam up. I can ask her about the clown she hired for Violet's last birthday party. Cordelia's got a birthday coming up. Rose just might answer a call like that.'

Thursday, April 7, 10.25 A.M.

From the driver's seat of the Escalade, Paige glanced over at Grayson for what seemed like the hundredth time since leaving his mother's apartment. They'd switched places, Paige driving to their appointment with Reba so that Grayson could run his queries on Anderson through the state's attorney's database on Joseph's laptop.

Daphne had come through with Anderson's user name and password and a call to Joseph had reassured them that no searches Grayson did on the wi-fi card he'd provided could be traced back to them. No need to tip their hand until they had to.

Paige had asked Joseph if she could keep it after the case was over and he'd just laughed. She'd taken that as a no.

Grayson hadn't looked up from the laptop screen in thirty minutes, absorbed in whatever he'd found. And whatever he'd found wasn't making him happy, based on the scowl he wore.

A tinny trumpet blast suddenly pierced the silence in the car, startling them both.

Grayson's head jerked up and he glared. 'What the hell was that?'

'It wasn't me.' She hadn't touched the horn. 'I think it came from the laptop. Maybe you have mail.'

He checked, then blew out an irritated breath. 'I do. Joseph set it up to trumpet when I get a new email. It's from JD Fitzpatrick. He says they have a suspect on the bomb. Name's Harlan Kapansky, arrested by Silas years ago, sent up for twenty-five, got out a year ago on good behavior.'

'Then we follow the money,' she said. 'Somebody paid him to kill us. Chances are that the same somebody paid to have Ramon framed so that Rex would go free.'

'And Cherri Dandridge,' Grayson said grimly. 'And the others I've found who went free when someone else took their blame.'

She glanced at the computer in his lap. Apparently his search of the state's attorney's database had been fruitful after all. 'How many have you found?'

'Charlie Anderson and Bob Bond tried cases against each other

ten times in the eight years before Bond's death. In five of the cases
the charges were dismissed because somebody else was discovered
to have done it. Evidence was found leading to the conviction of
other people.'

Paige blinked. 'Half? Wow. That's a lot. Why didn't anyone
catch that?'

'Nobody was looking and they spread it over eight years. Those
are the cases that actually made it to arraignment. I'd need to get to a
different part of the database for the cases that weren't charged at all.'

'Of those five, one was Cherri Dandridge,' Paige said. 'What
about the others?'

'Three are robbery and/or assault. One rape,' he added bitterly.
'Most of the accused are young, from wealthy families who could
afford to buy their freedom.'

'How many times did you meet Bond in court?'

'Just that once, on Ramon's case. He died the year after.'

'Anderson gave Ramon's case to you. Why didn't he keep it for
himself?'

'Partly because it had the potential of being high profile,
especially if we'd discovered that Rex didn't have an alibi. Someone
might see that he'd done it before.' He hesitated. 'But Anderson said
my zeal made me the perfect choice to prosecute.'

'Why?' she asked, although she knew.

'I look at every murderer I prosecute and see my father. I look at
every victim and see that young woman my father shackled to that
wall, trying to beg me to help her. Ramon's case was no different. I
prosecuted like I always did. No mercy. And in so doing, sent an
innocent man to prison and drove his wife to activities that led to
her murder. I have to live with that.'

'But you didn't know Ramon was innocent. If you had, you
wouldn't have charged him to begin with. You're not a machine,
Grayson. Our history, all of our life experiences . . . they stay with
us. Become part of who we are. You prosecute murders with an
almost religious zeal, that's true. But the zeal that worked against
Ramon has worked *for* so many victims and their families. How
many killers have you put away?'

'Dozens. At least I think they were killers.'

'Ah. And there's the rub. Your confidence is bruised. So is mine. I lost more than a friend the night Thea died. I lost part of myself. The part that roared.' She smiled to herself, sadly. 'My old *sensei* used to say I had "the tiger within". Now it's a scared little pussycat that hasn't set foot in a *dojo* in nine months.

'I have to get myself back, Grayson, and so do you. Yes, one of the men you incarcerated was innocent, but dozens more were guilty. By putting them away you made the world a better place. You got justice for the dead. Don't lose confidence in your judgment. I saw you with the victim's family in court on Tuesday morning. You had compassion for them. Maria said you had compassion for her. It's your zeal, tempered with compassion and your personal integrity, that makes you so good at what you do.'

She heard him turn, knew he was studying her profile. She kept her eyes on the road. 'I've seen you fight,' he finally said, his voice husky. 'That was no scared pussycat in the garage on Tuesday or taking Rex McCloud down a notch last night.'

'That was instinct and reflex. Different than the tiger. I really miss the tiger.' She cleared her throat. 'We're almost there. You asked me to tell you what I'd read about Reba McCloud.'

'Then tell me what I need to know,' he said gently, letting her change the subject.

'I told you a lot of it Tuesday night. It's the tale of two daughters. Claire and Reba.'

'You said Claire makes the money, Reba gives it away. But what does Reba have to do with Rex's troubles? She's not his mother, she's his aunt.'

'From what I've read, Reba's always been the family good girl. Claire's life's been a little more checkered. Claire went wild as a teenager, running away from home and marrying a guy from a rock-and-roll hair band. Rex was born five months later. She later divorced the rocker, moved home and married Louis, the son of a Texas oil tycoon. Big wedding splash in the society pages. Lots of gossip about past wildness with the rocker ex and how she was settling down, back in the bosom of her family.'

'The time I met them, Claire seemed to have Louis on a short leash.'

'Claire kept a lot of people on a short leash. She was known to be ruthless in business – Gordon Gekko in Gucci shoes. But she made investors a lot of money. Now she runs the family's domestic and international holdings.'

'I knew she managed the business, but didn't realize she managed so much.'

'She didn't have the international holdings until a few years ago. Her second husband, Rex's stepfather, did. But remember I told you that Louis was dismissed? He lost a lot of money in bad investments, so now he works for Reba and is considered by most to be a figurehead.'

'You got all this online?' Grayson asked and she nodded.

'While I was waiting for Clay's clients' spouses to do whatever nasty behaviors we'd been paid to capture on film. Some of this came from the newspaper. Some from birth, death, marriage, and divorce records. I pieced it together. Not really that difficult. I was trying to find out all I could about Rex and the McClouds because I knew Rex had been Crystal's date, but he was barely mentioned at the trial.'

'You thought I'd given them special treatment,' Grayson said, but without heat.

'I did. At the time. When I started to reconstruct the case, Rex caught my eye. I wanted to know what kind of family he came from that would allow such behavior.'

'So what about Reba?'

'Like I said, Reba was the family good girl. I needed information on Rex and considered talking to her. I thought maybe with all of her charitable activities that she'd be more likely to care about Crystal Jones.'

'Did you ever talk to her?'

'No, I hadn't gotten that far. So, the scoop on Reba. Dianna and Jim McCloud got married when Claire was eight years old, Reba was born a year later. While Claire had her wild phase with the rocker, Reba stuck close to home. She went to college locally, undergrad and graduate school, then went off to the Peace Corps in West Africa. Cameroon, I think.'

'Huh. She really was the family good girl.'

'Exactly. Reba left home around the time Rex was fourteen.'

'Betsy said that's when he started getting wild and got sent to military school.'

'Maybe Reba was a good influence on Rex. When Reba came back from Africa, she and her mother started the non-profit foundation. Dianna retired and now Reba runs it. She's done a lot of good work around the city. According to her website anyway.' Paige slowed the SUV, looking for an empty parking place. 'It won't be easy finding parking for this thing. Why does Joseph have to drive such a big vehicle?'

'This is the one that has the touch-sensor alarm. Once I activate it, the car will screech if anyone touches it. Or any bombs are placed beneath it.'

'Oh. I like that.'

'I thought you might. Look, there's a spot. You don't even have to parallel park.'

She glared at him. 'I can parallel park just fine.' Still, she was happy she didn't have to prove it. She got out of the car, eyes drawn upward by movement on the side of the building. Two men stood on a platform, boarding up a massive window that hadn't been broken when they'd come the night before. 'Look at that.'

He joined her on the sidewalk, looking up. He did a double take. 'Must have been one hell of a foul ball. I pity the kid that has to go asking for that baseball back.'

She looked at him uncertainly. 'You're joking. Right?'

He laughed. 'Yes. If a kid hit a ball up there, the Orioles better be knocking on his door. Must have been a bird.'

She looked up again as he activated the car alarm. 'One hell of a bird.'

'So,' Grayson said, 'to summarize the reason for our summons, we've accused someone in the McCloud clan of aiding and abetting Rex in murder because we pointed out that the video was phoney, and only a family member could have provided it.'

'Which must have irked Reba. Scandal's bad for business. Reba's and Claire's,' she said as he placed his hand on her back, partially moving behind her. He was shielding her again. She frowned up at him. 'You're not wearing Kevlar today.'

'Yes, I am,' he answered. 'I have an old vest. It's a little tight across the shoulders, but I'll live. Joseph's located one for you too, a spare from one of the female agents he works with. He's picking it up from her now. We'll meet him back at my place when we're done here to get it. Until then, I'm your bodyguard.'

The slightly naughty way he said it made her smile. 'You're bad. I like it.'

'Thought you might,' he murmured.

'What's our game plan when we get to Reba's office?'

'Find out why she really called me in. I doubt she'd waste her time bringing me for just a scolding. The McClouds are in scandal-control mode.'

'You think she'll try to bribe you?'

'Or threaten me. Or maybe try to find out how much I know. Mostly I want to get her talking about the family, see what I can glean. Somebody switched those videos. It might have been Rex acting alone, but if he had help from the family I need to know. Someone supplied the fifty thousand dollars that was paid to Sandoval. The more I can narrow it down, the easier it'll be to get a warrant to trace that money.' He followed her into the lobby. 'Daphne says Reba's office is on the tenth floor.'

Thursday, April 7, 10.25 A.M.

Dr Charlotte Burke stepped back from the table wearily. 'Malone, Betsy. Time of death, ten twenty-five.' Gently she closed the woman's eyes. 'Can you clean her up? Her parents are waiting outside.'

'Sure,' the nurse said. 'You okay, Burke?'

'No. Woman makes it through rehab, gets clean, only to OD and choke on her own vomit. What a waste.' *Win some, lose some,* she told herself. It was part of working in the ER. But she hated to lose.

'You saved one earlier, the Jane Doe with the stab wounds.'

'We'll have to see. We got her stable enough for surgery at least.'

'She was dead when she came in, but you brought her back. You did good.'

'She fought hard to stay alive. I hope she makes it through surgery and wakes up enough to tell us who she is. But I have to tell this one's parents now. I hate this part.'

Bracing herself, she pushed through the doors. The Malones immediately wheeled around to stare at her, anguished. *Parents always know*, she thought.

'I'm so sorry,' she said quietly. 'We weren't able to save her.'

Mrs Malone's knees buckled, a sob ripping through her body. Mr Malone caught her, holding her close. 'Thank you,' he managed. 'We saw how you tried. We just . . . we'd hoped this time she'd make it. We had our daughter back for a while.'

'The nurse will take you to see her. Take all the time you need.' Her heart heavy, Burke made her way to her desk to get the next patient's folder. 'You hear anything on Jane Doe up in surgery?' she asked the triage nurse.

'Not yet. But I'll call up again in a while to check.'

'I'd appreciate it. She wanted to live. I hope she does.' Shoving the next folder under her arm, Burke squared her shoulders. Win some, lose some. *I hate to lose.*

Thursday, April 7, 10.45 A.M.

They walked into Reba's office ahead of schedule. Grayson approached the receptionist, hoping Reba had information to impart whether she intended to or not.

'I'm Grayson Smith and this is my associate, Paige Holden. We have an appointment with Ms McCloud. We're early, but we hoped she might see us now.'

'If you'd like to wait, I'll let Ms McCloud know you're here.'

Grayson took a seat on the sofa in the waiting area while Paige wandered, checking out the artwork and photographs on the wall. He took a moment to breathe, to simply watch her. She moved fluidly, no sign that he'd tumbled her down an embankment twelve hours ago. Or tumbled her in his bed after that. When this was over, he intended to tumble her again and again.

He enjoyed watching her, knowing that under her clothes were deadly weapons and wicked curves. She'd stopped at a group of photographs, studying each one as if she was a student in an art museum. And because he was watching, he saw the minute tensing of her body before she relaxed and moved on to the next wall. Eventually she made her way through all the art and sat down beside him.

He bent to her ear, pretending to kiss her neck. 'What did you see?'

She swatted him playfully. 'Not here.' She took her phone from her pocket and typed a text message. He settled back, pretending to rest his eyes, waiting for her to finish.

His phone buzzed in his pocket. She'd hit *send*, but she was still typing. His phone buzzed three more times before she finally stopped texting, opening a game of Scrabble on her phone. 'Is "xylophone" l-o or l-a?' she asked, bored.

'L-o.' Idly he checked his phone. And fought to keep his expression bland.

2 fotos far wall. Group of kids. 12 yr old. Wearing medallions.

I'm a MAC, Loud and Proud. MAC = McCloud Alliance for Children. It's a charity for kids. Run by McCloud family.

1 foto taken 1984. CJ not born then. Other 1999. CJ 13 then.

His heart pounded. Crystal's determination to get close to Rex McCloud had just taken on a substantially different meaning. *Why had she gone to the party that night?*

'Mr Smith,' the receptionist said stiffly. 'Ms McCloud will see you now.'

Thursday, April 7, 10.55 A.M.

The newspaper photographs didn't do justice to Reba McCloud, Paige thought as she took the chair next to Grayson's. Her hair, coiffed in a sleek French twist, shone like gold silk. She had a Grace Kelly look to her, ethereally beautiful. The dress she wore was

Chanel, if Paige wasn't mistaken. And about clothes, Paige rarely was.

Reba smoothed the hair behind her ear, sending the dozens of diamonds circling her watch winking in the sunlight. 'Thank you for coming to see me, Mr Smith.'

Grayson inclined his head, every bit the dignified state's attorney. 'I felt it my duty.'

Reba's lips curved cynically. 'Your duty to whom?'

'To the truth,' he said bluntly. 'A young woman was killed on your family's property six years ago. She was your nephew's guest.'

Her mouth flattened. 'My nephew was allowed entirely too much freedom in those days, Mr Smith. It damaged him. Rex is a drug addict and a thief. But he's no killer. He had an alibi for that night, a security video of the party going on, which he never left. Distasteful as his activities were, he was quite occupied at the time of that girl's death.'

'The video was switched,' Grayson said. 'I'm sure Rex told you we know this.'

Paige caught the merest of flickers in Reba's eyes, acknowledging Grayson's words as fact. 'My parents told me you'd said so,' Reba said. 'I don't believe it.'

'We have a witness,' Grayson continued, 'who says Rex left the pool that night to go looking for the victim, Crystal Jones. The witness says he was angry. Very angry.'

'I'm familiar with the witness that you're speaking of,' Reba said coolly. 'Betsy Malone is an addict as well, and not credible in the least. Let me speak candidly, Mr Smith. You are attacking the wrong family.'

'I'm attacking no one,' Grayson said. 'I'm searching for justice for a dead woman. If the facts point to your nephew, then that's where I go. If someone switched a security video and the security company was paid by your family, then I go there, too.'

'My parents are exemplary citizens,' she said, her voice coldly furious, 'who have done more for this community than ten philanthropists combined. For you to accuse us is outrageous. And wrong.'

Paige had the feeling Reba believed every word she'd said. *I'm a*

MAC. She wanted to ask, but held herself back. 'Can you provide an alternate theory for the switched video? Because it was switched. There is no question about that.'

'Because Betsy Malone said so?' Reba asked, a shrill note in her tone.

'No, ma'am,' Paige said calmly. 'Because the moon in the video was in the wrong phase for the date of Crystal's death. The video provided for Rex's alibi was not made the night of the murder. I'd be happy to show you if you're still unconvinced.'

Reba's cheeks heated. 'That doesn't mean Rex killed her or that my parents are involved in a cover-up.'

'Being very blunt, that's exactly what I do think it means, Ms McCloud,' Grayson said. 'And by bringing these facts to light, I've made someone angry. Very angry.'

Reba's eyes flashed. 'I read about your near miss last night. How terrifying for you.' Any sincerity in her voice was stamped out by her fury. 'But to even intimate that my family was responsible for such a crime . . . Mr Smith, if you don't cease and desist, you'll find yourself at the center of a libel suit.'

'It wouldn't be the first time. But I am willing to entertain, as Ms Holden said, alternate theories. Do you have one? Perhaps another guest was responsible for the death of Crystal Jones and the subsequent switch of the videos?'

'I don't know any of their names other than Betsy, and I only know her because she and Rex got arrested together several times after that night. I wasn't even at the estate during that party. I was in my condo here, in this building.'

'Your sister wasn't there that night either, as I recall,' Grayson said.

'Claire was probably out of the country. She usually was back then. Now her office is in New York. She comes to Baltimore once a month to give my father an update.'

'What about Rex's father?' Paige asked.

'His father OD'd when Rex was ten,' Reba said flatly. 'His stepfather hasn't been very involved in his upbringing. He couldn't help you with details about that night either.'

Paige softened her request with a smile. 'We need someone who was there that night. Anyone who can offer us a lead in another direction. An innocent man has lost six years of freedom. We don't want the same to happen to anyone else, Rex included. So any help you can give us will be appreciated. And followed up.'

'Why should I believe you?'

'Because we want to do the right thing,' Paige said patiently. 'But if that's too hard to swallow, somebody tried to blow us up. The sooner we find out who killed Crystal Jones, the sooner we ID whoever is trying to make us into hamburger.'

Reba's suspicion appeared unappeased, but she answered. 'I remember my father calling the guard at the gate Les. I don't know if it was short for Leslie or Lester. Les doesn't work the gate anymore. He retired the year after the murder. That's all I know.'

That's all she's willing to divulge. And they already knew that Lester Neil had died shortly after retiring. Paige suspected Reba knew it too. It was time to shift gears.

'Thank you,' Paige said. 'I read about your father. He's been responsible for a lot of good work. I don't want to drag him through the mud, not at all.'

'My father is responsible for more good than anyone knows,' Reba said passionately. 'These days, politicians use every small thing they do as a platform to tout themselves. My parents ran many charitable programs no one even knew about. They did it because it was the right thing. They didn't want all the adulation and publicity.'

Yes. The opening she'd been waiting for. 'I hadn't read about the program for the kids, but I saw the pictures outside. MAC, I think it was called?'

Reba's chin lifted. 'My favorite. My parents sponsored a dozen schools every year, from districts all over the state. They provided money for supplies and books and field trips. One child represented each school and my parents gave them an ice-cream social at the estate every year. These were pretty poor kids, from sad circumstances. Most of them never got a square meal. My parents made donations to their families, too.'

'I imagine choosing the schools was hard,' Paige said, 'with so many being needy.'

'It was a lottery system. The school benefited, the kids and the families did too.'

'I wish I'd been in one of those programs,' Paige said ruefully. 'My grandparents raised me and our budget was always tight. How long did the MAC program run?'

'Sixteen years. I have photos of the first and last classes out there. MAC made a difference in the lives of a lot of kids.'

'I like the concept. I admire the work your family's done for children. I'm actually trying to pull together a non-profit of my own. A school.'

Reba's eyes widened, incredulous. 'You have a lot of nerve, accusing us, then asking for my help.'

'If you'd known Rex's alibi video had been switched, what would you have thought?' Paige asked. Reba said nothing, pursing her lips. 'You do good here, Ms McCloud, like your parents did. I'd like to think I've done good too. You can look me up.'

'I did,' Reba said coolly. 'I know what you've done. And what's been done to you.'

Paige fought the urge to flinch. Reba's arrow had squarely hit her mark, but Paige wouldn't let it show. She wanted more information on the McCloud Alliance for Children, but hesitated to ask any more questions lest the suspicious Reba become more so.

Paige had an idea about how she could get to more MAC info. Grayson had become very quiet, letting her take the lead – and for that she would kiss him later.

'I may be nervy, Ms McCloud, but I see an opportunity and I may not have your ear again. I've been planning a martial arts school for kids and adults with disabilities. I have a sponsor who's prepared to provide all the funding I need, but I'll also need publicity and help structuring the project from someone with experience.' Paige noted how Reba's eyes positively gleamed at the mention of funding. 'A joint effort between us could go a long way in signaling your family's cooperation with the investigation and washing away any shadows.'

Reba drummed her fingers on her desk. Paige could see the wheels turning in the woman's eyes. 'Name one charity I've helped fund, Ms Holden.'

'I can name dozens.' She proceeded to rattle off names of Reba's charitable endeavors until the woman lifted her hand.

'All right. You did some research before you came. Submit a proposal.' Reba rose. 'In the meantime, I trust you'll stop these baseless accusations against my family.'

'We'll keep trying to find the truth,' Paige said softly. 'But if we can find any other viable explanation, we'll run with it. You have our word.'

'Thank you,' Reba said frostily. She opened her door. 'Have a good day.'

Paige waited on the sidewalk while Grayson checked the SUV. 'It's clean. Get in.' When he'd slammed his door he turned to her. 'What the hell just happened up there?'

Paige buckled her seat belt. 'We discovered the significance of Crystal's medallion and I laid the foundation to inquire further into the MAC program, separate from the investigation into Rex. We need to know what the program did and when and if Crystal was part of it, but I didn't dare ask all that straight out. Reba would have shut down.'

'How do you plan to inquire further into the MAC program?'

'I plan to return with my sponsor. Did you see how Reba's eyes lit up when I said I had all the money I needed?'

He rubbed his forehead. 'And who might this sponsor with money be?'

'Well, I'm not sure yet. But we'll think of something.' She opened the laptop. 'I'm going to search for the MAC charity, now that we know what it is.' She glanced at him sideways. 'You mad at me?'

'No. I'm just . . . flabbergasted.'

She smiled. 'Wouldn't want you to get bored.'

'No chance of that.' He studied her. 'Are you serious about the school?'

'Oh, yes. That wasn't a lie. Your sister Holly will be my first student. Your mom thought it was a fantastic idea.' She bit at her lip. 'Especially given the circumstances.'

Grayson frowned. 'What circumstances?'

Here we go. 'Holly's been bullied by some men at her social center. The friend she mentioned at Lisa's place on Tuesday, the one that died? He'd been protecting her.'

Grayson gripped the steering wheel, hard. 'Who? Who's been bullying her?'

'Can you calm down? You're about to pop a blood vessel in your neck. She's okay.'

'Nobody touches Holly.'

'Nobody has. She was afraid to say anything, afraid Joseph would blow his cool and get himself arrested. Don't make her worry about you, too.'

He sighed. 'I won't. Holly's a lot more aware than we give her credit for sometimes. Joseph *would* blow his cool if he knew. And that's never, ever good.'

'I told her I'd go to the center with her. Scare the boys into leaving her alone. But she will be alone sometimes and she needs to know how to get away if she's attacked.'

'I know. I don't want to admit she's vulnerable that way.'

'She's a grown woman now. You have to look these things in the eye.'

'I'll keep one eye closed,' he muttered. 'Thank you,' he added quietly. 'For caring.'

She patted his arm. 'Holly asked if I could teach her friends, other women at the center. I said sure. Your mother said she'd join us, but I think she just wants the outfit.'

He chuckled. 'That's my mom.'

'Holly goes to the center on Thursdays. That's tonight. I'm planning to go, as long as we're not busy, you know, fighting crime or anything.'

'I'll go with you. If any guy looks at her any way I don't like, I'll beat the shit out of him.'

Paige sighed. 'I knew you'd say that. So, what next? Meet Joseph for lunch, then back to interviewing the pool-party guest list or run with the MAC charity?'

'The charity. If Crystal was one of those children in the program, she had previous contact with the McClouds. And she'd been at the estate before Rex's party.'

'Grayson, do you still believe Rex killed Crystal Jones?'

He hesitated a fraction. 'Yes.'

'But?' she asked.

'But right now I really want to know why Crystal had that medallion and why she wanted to go to Rex's party.'

'So do I. We could ask Rex. Although he called his lawyers, so he won't talk to us.'

'Maybe, maybe not.' He looked over at her. 'I thought it odd we were summoned to cease and desist by Reba. Normally that would have come through Rex's attorney.'

Her lips bent thoughtfully. 'Is it possible he doesn't have an attorney yet?'

'Very possible. I wonder if this might be the straw that broke the family's back.'

'Good. It's about time they cut him loose.'

'You never said if *you* still thought Rex killed Crystal,' he said.

'The kids in that picture were only twelve,' she said, troubled.

'Yeah, I know.'

'So you're thinking what I'm thinking?' she asked and he shrugged.

'We have Crystal who's already been arrested for hooking. She's blackmailing a man, yet goes to a party to score some really big money. We have Brittany who gave us bank records establishing the blackmail and one plastic medallion.'

'She also helped stall us inside the nursing home,' Paige said.

'I think Brittany's playing both sides of the fence. I believed her only twice. Once when she was sad that her sister was dead.'

'And once when she said she was all her son had.'

He nodded. 'That came off as sincere. She blew fifty Gs on a private school for her kid's kindergarten while working nights in a nursing home. That doesn't add up unless the only person who matters is her son. She'll do anything, say anything to protect him.'

'She's wily. Brittany, I mean. She gives us just enough to send us to the McClouds – the family, not just Rex. Why? She's got an angle. I can feel it.'

'I know. We need to be watching for how that thread weaves into this mess.'

Paige frowned. 'Brittany said that Crystal had been molested. What if something happened to her when she was twelve? When she was a "MAC, Loud and Proud"? What if someone there molested her?'

'Then we have a very big problem.'

'We have Brittany's cell number. We could call her and ask. We both have new phone numbers, not tied to us, so she won't know it's us calling. Maybe she'll pick up.'

'Stevie tried the number several times. Brittany's not answering.'

'She's on the run,' Paige said. 'I would be, too, in her shoes. Especially since she nearly got us killed. I'd sure as hell run from me.'

'Let's find out if Crystal really was one of the MAC kids,' Grayson suggested. 'If she was, it adds all kinds of motives for her going to that party. And motives for whoever killed her.'

'We could start with Crystal's middle school. Ask them if she was a MAC kid.'

'But we don't know where Crystal went to middle school,' he said.

'I can find out. I will need to make a few calls. Three, four tops.'

'Then do it. I want to see how you manage it,' he said, making her grin.

'A challenge. How can I refuse? Call number one, Winston Heights High School, where that class ring came from.' She searched for the school's website and phone number. 'It's in the Hagerstown area and there's a chance it was Crystal's high school.'

'But you want the middle school.'

'Sshh.' She dialed the school with her new cell phone. 'Hello? My name is Mary Johnson. I'm doing a background check on a potential employee. The applicant's name is Jones, Crystal. She should have graduated in 2004 . . . Of course I'll hold. Thank you.'

Grayson didn't look impressed. Yet.

The woman from the school came back to the line. 'She never graduated?' Paige said. 'Did she transfer to another school? . . . I see. She dropped out entirely. That's troubling. I should rip up her application, but I really liked her. I'd like to give her another chance. Can I ask one more question? She's put on her app that she attended Samuel Ogle Middle School. It would be great to confirm that at least . . . She didn't? Where did she attend? . . . Longview Ridge. Thank you for your time.'

Paige hung up. 'Got her middle school,' she said with satisfaction.

'Yes, but you don't know if that school received MAC funds and if she was one of the students.'

'O ye of little faith. Call number two, the middle school's librarian.'

'Why the librarian?'

'Because all the kids go there at some point and librarians don't have to worry about confidentiality policies like the front office. Plus, the librarian would have gotten goodies from the MAC program, but likely wouldn't have had contact with the charity itself, so no worries that she'll report our snooping to the McClouds.'

'What if it's not the same librarian?'

'Then I find the old librarian's name and call her. Hush,' she hissed when he opened his mouth for another *what if*. Paige brought up the middle school's website and dialed the main number. 'Can I have the school library, please?' Her call was transferred and an older lady answered. Excellent.

'This is the library. Mrs White speaking.'

'Hi, Mrs White. My name is Brittany Jones.' Grayson's eyes widened. He opened his mouth but Paige waved him silent. 'My sister went to your school fourteen years ago. Her name was Crystal. Do you remember her?'

'Let me think,' Mrs White said. 'That would have been when . . . 1998? That was the year we got the new computers. Of course I remember Crystal. She had the most beautiful blond ringlets. Like spun gold. Natural, as I recall. How is she?'

'Um, well . . . she's dead, ma'am. She was murdered six years ago.'

'Oh, my,' Mrs White gasped, shocked. 'How terrible. Oh, my dear Lord.'

'It *was* terrible,' Paige said soberly. 'I was moving recently and came across a few of her things. I hadn't been able to look at them before, you know.'

'I know,' Mrs White said sadly. 'Oh, mercy, child. I'm sorry to hear this.'

'Crystal used to read to me all the time. She made me love books. One of the things I found with her belongings was a book from your library. That's why I called you. If it's all right, I'd like to keep it and just send you a replacement copy.'

'Of course, dear, of course. That would be fine. If there's anything else I can do . . .'

'Maybe there is. Mrs White, another of the things I found in her box was a medallion. It's plastic. I remember her getting it when she was at your school, but I can't remember what it was for. It's pretty scratched up, but has M-A-C on it.'

'M-A-C?' The librarian paused. 'Oh. *MAC*. It was a program chaired by one of the state politicians. McNeal. McGee. McSomething. Back in the nineties they chose a few schools and gave endowments for the year. That's where we got the new computers. All of them are completely obsolete now. We've replaced them twice.'

'Do you remember how Crystal got this medallion?'

'I imagine she was awarded it at the party given by the charity. One child was chosen to represent each school. The party happened at the politician's house. They had ice cream, as I recall. The children submitted an essay with their picture and the charity picked one.' Mrs White's swallow was audible. 'Crystal got a new dress. It was blue and she was so proud of it. She wore it to school one day before the party, to show me. I don't guess you girls got new dresses very often. With that hair of hers . . . she looked like a little china doll.'

Paige found her own throat closing. 'Thank you. This has helped me, a lot.'

'Me too. It's nice to know that one of my books was something she kept.' There was a teary laugh. 'Even if the scamp would owe quite an overdue fine after all this time.'

'I'll send the replacement copy,' Paige promised. She hung up and stared at her phone until her eyes stopped stinging. Grayson, too, looked drained.

'She was there.' Paige blinked, clearing the moisture from her eyes. 'She even got a new dress. Something happened that day, Grayson. Something that made her go back the night of the party, eight years later.'

'Something that she was certain would make her a lot of money.' He sighed. 'Things just became a lot more complicated. If something did indeed happen, it could have been anyone on the estate. And it was fourteen years ago.'

'Just to be clear, we're both talking molestation,' Paige said. 'Sexual in nature.'

'That's what my gut's telling me. This is going to be very difficult to even approach, much less prove. Fourteen years and no complainant? Not a good combination.'

'There's no complainant because she's dead,' Paige said, frustrated. 'You're not giving up?'

'Hell, no. I'm just getting started.'

Twenty

Thursday, April 7, 11.30 A.M.

Silas was growing impatient. He'd watched his employer's front door all morning, waiting for him to emerge. All he'd seen were Grayson Smith and his PI going into the building, coming out a half-hour later. *If you only knew how close you really were.*

His trigger finger was itchy. He glanced down at his personal cell. So was his redial finger. He'd been trying to reach his wife for an hour. She was overdue checking in. She might have gotten caught somewhere where she couldn't phone. Inside a store, perhaps. Violet needed new clothes. New everything.

His cell finally rang and he snatched it up. 'Rose.'

'No. Not Rose. Not even close.'

His chest flattened. No breath would fill his lungs. 'No,' he whispered.

'Oh, yes.'

'What have you done with her?'

'What I had to. Say hi, sweetie.'

'Papa?' Violet sobbed. 'Where are you? Mama's—' She was abruptly silenced.

'Violet!' Silas shouted.

'No, we're back to me,' his employer crooned. 'Little Violet has gone to sleep. Not to worry, just a sedative. She'll live – *if* you cooperate. I didn't like that little show of temper this morning, Silas.'

'Don't you *touch* my child.'

'But I've already touched her.'

'*Bastard*.' A sob rose in his throat, furious and desperate. 'You fucking *bastard*.'

'Oh, Silas, surely you don't think . . . I had to grab her, to get her out of that hotel room you had her hiding in. I haven't touched her *that* way. For shame.'

Silas drew a strangled breath. 'What do you want?'

'Much better. I want Smith and the PI dead. Then I want you, unarmed.'

'You'll trade? Me for my family? For Rose and Violet?'

'Sure. Well, for Violet anyway.'

His heart stopped. Just . . . stopped. 'Rose?' he whispered.

'She fought hard. Did you proud. Good cop's wife.'

Silas couldn't breathe. Couldn't breathe. *Rose*. 'You're lying.' He had to be lying.

'Check your other cell. I just sent you a text.'

Silas did and bile rose to choke him. It was a picture. Rose, crumpled on the floor, her head covered in blood. Rage geysered, blinding him. 'I'll kill you, you sonofabitch.'

'Silas,' his boss cautioned in a friendly way. 'Don't throw out the baby with the bathwater. Or so the saying goes. I want Smith and Holden dead. I want it done quickly, before they cause any more difficulty. I want it done today.'

'And if it takes longer?'

'You have until midnight. After that . . . You'll need a small coffin.'

Panic filled him. Seized him by the throat. 'How did you find them?'

'You let Violet take her doll. I'd been in her room. It was a simple matter to place a tracker in the doll's body.'

'I see.' He closed his eyes. 'Just don't hurt her. Please.'

'I like it when you say please. I like it better when you obey me. So, Silas, obey.'

The connection was broken and Silas sat staring at his phone.

I killed her. I killed Rose. He'd never raised his hand to his wife, but he'd killed her just the same. *My baby. That bastard has my baby*.

He covered his face with his hands, his decision made. *I'm sorry*,

Grayson. I don't have any other choices. He'd never killed a friend before. Today would be the first.

Thursday, April 7, 11.45 A.M.

Grayson and Paige found Joseph on the porch of the townhouse, scowling at Peabody through the door's side window. Peabody was staring, his teeth slightly bared.

It made Paige laugh. Joseph was not amused.

'Your dog is a beast,' he said.

'My dog is a sweetie,' she said. 'He just doesn't like you.'

Joseph's eyes narrowed. 'He would if you told him to.'

She shrugged. 'I'll tell him to when I'm sure that *I* like you.'

Grayson was pretty sure she already did, but that she enjoyed needling Joseph. With three sisters, Joseph was more than used to being needled. Down deep, he even liked it. Down deep, Joseph liked Paige, he could tell. With any other man than his brother, Grayson might be jealous.

'One of these days you might wish you'd been nicer to me,' Joseph growled.

Paige rolled her eyes. 'Don't you have, like, a job?'

'I do, *like*, have a job. One I should be doing right now, except Romeo over there wants his Juliet to keep breathing.'

'Play nice, you two,' Grayson said mildly. Joseph had a very important job, but was so rattled by the bomb that he'd taken personal leave, a fact shared privately by his mother that morning. *Paige has her protection dog and I have mine.*

It moved him. *I'm a lucky man.*

Grayson unlocked the door and let them in, scratching Peabody behind the ears. 'Paige, he's brought you a present. The least you can do is tell Peabody to be friends.'

Joseph held out a paper bag. Paige peeked inside, then pulled out the Kevlar vest, hooking it over her pinky. 'What every girl is wearing this year.'

'What every girl who wants to stay alive is wearing this year,' Joseph corrected. 'I borrowed it from a colleague. Try not to get anything on it. You know, like blood.'

Paige sobered. 'Thank you. And I didn't tell Peabody not to trust you. He gets used to most people quickly, but there's something about your scent that scares him.'

Joseph looked taken aback. 'I scare him? Why? I like dogs. Dogs usually like me.'

'More like he's scared for me.' She lifted her brows. 'All that raw danger, y'know.'

'The tape-will-self-destruct-Jim thing,' Joseph said with a smirk. 'I get that a lot.'

Paige glared at Grayson. 'You told him what I said.'

Grayson shrugged. 'He's family. Go,' he said gently. 'Try it on. Please.'

She huffed her displeasure, but went upstairs, the vest in her hand. Grayson watched her, his eyes drawn to her ass. He looked back at Joseph, only to find his brother watching her too. Grayson cleared his throat.

Joseph just grinned. 'Hey, she came downstairs this morning buck naked under your robe and I didn't even sneak a peek. I think I can be trusted.'

'I know you can. It's just all that raw danger.'

Joseph snickered. 'I know, I know. Drives the women crazy.' His head came up, his gaze snapping to the window beside the door. For a long moment he stared, saying nothing. Then he let out a quiet breath. 'Grayson, there is a woman coming up your walk with a lime-green suit, four-inch heels to match, and legs up to her shoulders.'

Grayson knew only one woman who dared to wear lime-green suits.

'Daphne?' Grayson opened the door. She was carrying a dry-cleaning bag with a suit in one hand, and a towel-covered basket in the other. 'What are you doing here?'

'Deliverin' your dry cleanin', darlin',' she said with a drawl. She took one look at Joseph and stopped. 'Well, well, well. I didn't expect you'd have company.'

She was eyeing Joseph with interest, a reaction Grayson had

become accustomed to since he and Joseph were in the fifth grade. It was always Joseph who the ladies preferred. *Except for Paige. Who prefers me.* The thought warmed him.

'I didn't expect you either.' Grayson shut the door. 'Joseph, my assistant, Daphne Montgomery. Daphne, my brother Joseph Carter.'

Daphne studied Joseph through the skinny glasses at the end of her nose. 'I'd *definitely* shake your hand, honey, but mine are a little full.' She held the dry-cleaning bag out to Grayson. 'If you don't mind.'

Grayson took his suit and hung it in the closet and she shook Joseph's hand.

'It's very nice to meet you, Mr Carter.' She pushed the basket into Joseph's hands. 'Poppyseed muffins. Made 'em myself. Grayson's favorite, but there's enough for everyone. Would you mind taking them into the kitchen?'

Joseph did, pausing to glance over his shoulder, his gaze sliding down to check out Daphne's legs once more before heading into the kitchen. It had been Grayson's first reaction as well, the first time Daphne had worn one of her short skirts. It was rumored that she'd been a Vegas showgirl, but if that was true it wasn't in her work history.

She kept a more suitable outfit at her desk for the days she was in court, so Grayson had no cause to complain about her lime-green suits. He'd finally gotten used to her neon wardrobe, but it hadn't been easy.

'Your brother doesn't say much,' Daphne commented when they were alone.

Grayson found himself laughing. 'I have to say I've missed you.'

'Course you have, sugar,' she said wryly. 'I keep you just brimmin' with cheer.'

He grew sober. 'You didn't really come to bring my dry cleaning. What's wrong?'

'Stevie said she was meeting you here, so I hoped I'd catch you. You're such a mobile guy these days.' She pulled a small envelope from her handbag. 'You got a delivery. In person. From one Mal the cable guy.'

Grayson's eyes widened. 'Brittany's boyfriend? What's in it?'

'I do not have X-ray eyes, Grayson,' she snapped. 'Open it yourself.'

Grayson looked up to see Joseph leaning against the kitchen doorframe, half a muffin in his hand, the other half in his mouth. Watching with keen interest.

Grayson tore off the side of the envelope and out slid a small key. 'Safe-deposit-box key,' he said. 'No note. What did Mal the cable guy say, exactly?'

'Not much. Brittany called him, told him where to find the key and asked him to bring it to you. Not to mail it, but to be certain someone in our office signed for it.'

'Did you sign?' Joseph asked and she nodded.

'I did. Mal didn't look terribly happy about the whole thing. He hadn't slept. I asked him where Brittany had gone. He said he'd driven around all night looking for her.'

'She's gone into hiding,' Grayson said. 'What time did Mal say she called?'

'After your car went kablooey. I'd be scared, too. Her with a kid and all.'

'It fits,' Paige announced, her footsteps creaking on the stairs above. 'But severely limits my wardrobe choices.' She appeared, her hand across the V collar of her shirt where the vest showed. Her eyes widened. 'You've *got* to be Daphne,' she said, coming down, her hand extended. 'It's a pleasure to finally meet you. I'm Paige.'

Daphne shook Paige's hand hard. 'It's good to meet the woman who finally got Mr Tight-ass to take a vacation. Can't say I'm partial to the method, but I like the results.'

Paige laughed, then threw a glance over her shoulder at Joseph. 'Her, I like.'

Someone knocked on the front door and Daphne twisted to look through the side window. 'Oh. Stevie's here.'

'She came for Crystal's bank books and the medallion,' Grayson said.

Daphne opened the door. 'Come on in, honey. You look like shit.'

'Thank you,' Stevie said. 'I love you, too.'

Daphne shrugged. 'I call 'em like I see 'em.'

Spying Paige, Stevie held out a zippered bag. 'Makeup from my sister Izzy.'

Paige held the bag as if it were a treasure. 'Thank you. I've felt undressed all day.'

Joseph cleared his throat and Grayson glared at him before turning to Stevie. 'No success finding Silas, I take it,' he said and she shook her head, eyes dull with worry.

'We've put out a BOLO. Armed, approach with caution. Just like any other killer. Rose isn't answering her phone, either. Please give me some good news.'

Grayson and Paige exchanged a look. 'We don't have any either,' Grayson said.

'Just the opposite,' Paige added with a sigh.

'Let's have it,' Stevie said. She sat at the dining-room table wearily. 'I'm ready.'

Grayson, Paige, and Daphne joined her. Joseph stayed in the kitchen doorway, listening while they related the visit to Reba's office, the discovery of the MAC program, and the librarian who'd confirmed that Crystal had indeed been one of the children invited to the estate in 1998.

'Something happened to her there,' Paige said. 'Something that made her come back eight years later planning to make big money. It's hard not to imagine the worst.'

'That's disgusting,' Daphne said. 'And damn tragic.'

'But it happens,' Stevie said heavily. 'All too often.'

'I want to get inside the MAC charity records,' Grayson said. 'Without a live complainant, the only hope is if someone else was also a victim and will come forward.'

'You're making an assumption that Crystal was molested,' Joseph said quietly. 'What if that's not true?'

'We still have to find who murdered her,' Grayson said. 'For now, the best suspect is Rex, but I couldn't even get a grand jury convened on what we have. After this much time, I don't expect any physical evidence to remain. I need a witness who wasn't high or drunk that night, and who saw Rex emerge from the gardener's shed with bloody pruning shears and I don't think that's going to happen.'

Joseph pointed at the key. 'The sister knows something. Brittany.'

'We've got a BOLO on her too, and her kid,' Stevie said. 'If she's using her own car, she's kept to back roads. Hasn't gone through a single toll station.'

'She hasn't used any of her credit cards,' Paige said, and everyone stared at her. 'What? It's not hard to look. My phone alarms if one of her cards gets swiped.'

'She's gone under,' Daphne said. 'Probably terrified she'll get blown up. Too bad we don't know which bank she has her safe-deposit box at.'

'Maybe we do.' Grayson went to his safe and got out the envelope Brittany had given them the day before. 'Crystal had an account in Brittany's name and Brittany kept it active until about six months ago. Maybe her box is there too.'

'We'll need a court order to get into it,' Stevie said. She looked at Daphne.

'Write it up, sugar. I'll get a judge to sign it.'

'We need a court order for Brittany's bank account, too,' Grayson remembered. 'I meant to ask for it last night, but things got a little busy.'

'Can I see that key?' Paige said, then held it up to the light when Grayson handed it to her. 'Remember the little kinks in the medallion's ribbon? I bet they'll match the teeth in this key. Brittany had the key with the medallion. She purposely held it back.'

'What is that girl up to?' Stevie wondered.

'That's why we need to get inside the charity,' Grayson said. 'Brittany was full of shit, but she gave us the medallion for a reason.'

'I can go to Reba's office,' Daphne said quietly. 'I can be Paige's sponsor.'

All eyes turned to her and for a moment there was an uncomfortable silence. Grayson wasn't sure what to say. 'Daphne, I, um, appreciate it, but you're . . . memorable. If anyone's ever seen you in court, your cover will be blown in a heartbeat.'

Daphne's lips curved. 'Memorable. I like that.' She picked up her enormous neon orange handbag from the floor. 'I'll see you later. No, don't get up. I'll see myself out.'

Grayson winced when the door closed. 'I hurt her feelings.'

Paige smacked his arm. 'Y'think? Geeze.'

'But she *is* memorable,' Grayson said, then rubbed his arm. 'Ow.'

'No woman likes to be called "memorable" in that way,' Joseph said, rebuke in his voice. 'Especially a woman like that.'

Stevie gave Grayson a pitying look. 'You're going to have to fix that and don't ask me how. You're on your own.'

'Great.' Morosely he stared at the door. 'I'll think of something. Until then, what do we do about Reba McCloud and the MAC records?'

'We'll need to set up an undercover op,' Stevie said. 'But it'll take a little time.'

'How much time?' Joseph asked.

'Why?' Stevie tilted her head. 'You got another idea?'

'Only a vague one. Probably not actionable,' Joseph said.

Grayson studied him. 'You'd do it? You'd be our sponsor?'

'If we can't get anyone else. I have the bank balance Reba would be looking for and a sister who'd benefit from Paige's school. I could be a credible sponsor.'

'If she doesn't check your employment record,' Paige said. ' "FBI" will kind of stick out.' She patted his arm. 'When I start my real school, I'm hitting you up for funds.'

Joseph frowned. 'I thought it was just a ruse.'

'No, it's not.' She looked at Stevie. 'How much time to get the undercover set up?'

'A day or so.'

Grayson nodded. 'Do it,' he said to Stevie. 'Please.'

'I'll get it started as soon as I get back to the office. Until then, Kapansky's at the top of my list because he's the closest we have to the guy who hired the hit on you two.'

'If he's still alive,' Paige said. 'Silas may have killed him.'

Stevie flinched. 'Based on the blood loss, Kapansky's almost certainly dead. But if he did manage to survive, he would have needed medical help. He's not in any area hospital because I've checked. I searched his apartment. No sign of bank records.'

'Finding his money could take a while,' Grayson said. 'A lot of ex-cons set up accounts in a family member's name so we can't touch them.'

'We're checking his next of kin. He's got a mother, but so far she's not cooperating.'

'Who's working her?' Grayson asked.

'Morton and Bashears.'

Paige rolled her eyes. 'Great. For all we know, they're involved.'

'I don't think so,' Stevie said. 'Bashears wanted to go public that Sandoval didn't commit suicide. He was basically told if he said a word, he'd lose his pension. I don't think they could make that stick, but it's a hell of a threat. Of course I never dreamed Silas could be involved either, so my judgment's not so good right now.'

'Don't beat yourself up, Stevie,' Grayson said.

'Why should I?' she asked bitterly. 'IA'll do that for me. Hyatt believes I didn't know, but with IA, you can never tell. What about your boss, Grayson? He knew about Muñoz. He's definitely involved.'

'He is.' Grayson told them about the search he'd run on the Anderson/Bond cases. 'He's case fixing and I need to tell someone. It just has to be the right someone.'

'You think his superiors know?' Joseph asked, taking the chair Daphne had vacated.

'Don't know. Until I do, I don't want to talk to the wrong person. If I officially report him, it could get back to him and he'll clean up anything that could incriminate him.'

'Including people?' Joseph asked soberly.

'Maybe. That he ordered last night's hit has occurred to me more than once. He may even be the man in the photo, paying off Sandoval.' He grimaced. 'I need to eat. My stomach's been growling since we walked in the door.'

'I brought deli meat if anyone wants a sandwich,' Joseph said.

'Thank you,' Grayson said. 'I appreciate all you've done.'

Joseph shrugged. 'I haven't done anything yet.'

'New phones, computer, loaning us your car,' Paige said. She plucked at the collar of her Kevlar vest. 'My newest foundational garment. You've done a lot, Joseph. I know you have an important job and you've taken time away from it for us. Thank you.'

'You still can't keep the untraceable wi-fi card,' Joseph said, clearly uncomfortable with the praise. 'I'll get the meat and the bread.'

Stevie also rose. 'I can't stay. I have work to do.'

'You gotta eat, Stevie,' Joseph said. 'You really do look like shit. You've been up all night for the past two nights.'

'So have they,' Stevie said, pointing to Grayson and Paige.

'But *they're* having sex,' Joseph said, making Paige sputter. 'It's rejuvenating. You need to eat like the rest of us non-sex-getting people.'

Stevie laughed and Grayson knew that had been Joseph's intent. 'I'll make my sandwich to go,' she said. 'I have to get back and set up our entrée into Reba's inner circle.'

Thursday, April 7, 12.55 P.M.

Silas was set up. And ready to go. But his palms were clammy. *They know it's me.* The cops had a BOLO out. *Like I'm a normal, ordinary criminal.* And wasn't he?

He looked at the street from his position on the roof of the house across from Grayson Smith's home. There was one good thing about old Baltimore row houses – many had façades along the roofline, perfect for hiding behind. The house Silas had chosen was taller than the two on either side. No one could see him, front or side.

Importantly, it had a black roof. Perfect for blending into. Especially if the cops took their search to the air. Which could happen. *I have to be prepared.*

He just needed to be patient, because the other good thing about Smith's house was that it had no garage. Cars were parked on the street. Smith and Holden would have to come out of the house eventually.

They were inside with another man. He was big, although not as big as Smith, whose shoulders were broader than the side of a barn. It would be no issue to shoot Smith through the heart. Except that the second guy kept blocking his view.

Silas could see into the house through the windows on either side of the front door. All he needed was to get a clear shot of either Holden or Smith. Once he shot one, the other would run to their lover's aid. It was human nature.

He'd have to kill the other guy too, because anyone he left behind would call 911. Silas couldn't have that. He needed to be able to get away. He needed to make his employer pay. Because Silas had no intention of trading himself for Violet. He'd kill the sonofabitch and get his child out. Or die trying.

There is no try. He'd get Violet out. And then the two of them would go far away. And heal. *Rose. I'm so sorry.* He needed to get her body. Bury her. Grieve. But grieving was a luxury he could not allow himself. He had to wait, finger poised. As soon as Grayson or Paige walked in front of that window, he needed to shoot.

He needed to kill. It shouldn't be an issue. He'd killed so many already.

But his palms still sweated and his body trembled. He imagined Stevie had found his safe, found the bankbook and the guns. She'd be able to do ballistics on the guns to close all those cases. Give the families peace.

He hoped he hadn't caused her any career damage. Because that wouldn't be fair. She was the best cop he'd ever known. *Certainly better than me.* She didn't deserve this. Neither did Smith. He was a damn good prosecutor. He'd just run afoul of the wrong man. Charlie Anderson had always wanted an opportunity to crush Smith.

It was too bad that Grayson had such an Achilles heel. He couldn't help who his father was. *But we all have our vulnerabilities. Mine was named Cherri. I would have died for her.* And Silas knew, before all this was over, that he just might.

Thursday, April 7, 1.05 P.M.

'Now what?' Paige asked, clearing the remnants of lunch from the table. Stevie had gone back to the office and it was just her and Grayson and Joseph, who made no move to leave. Watching Joseph, Paige had concluded that their near miss had shaken him soundly. The brothers loved each other, even though they shared no blood.

If she hadn't already decided that she liked Joseph, that would have clinched it.

'I'm going to ask Charlie Anderson to meet me,' Grayson said.

'What?' Joseph exploded. 'You said you didn't want to tip him off.'

'I don't plan to. I'm going to try to pay him off. Look, he threatened to tell everyone my secret if I didn't back off the Muñoz case. He doesn't know I've told everyone who matters. I'm going to take advantage of last night's blast and tell him I've reconsidered my position. I'll offer him money for his silence. If he takes it, I'll have my proof.'

Paige's first reaction was the same as Joseph's, but she kept her voice calm. 'What if he uses your bribe to accuse you of corruption? He'd have his proof, too.'

'I thought of that,' Grayson said levelly. 'I'm going to tell Stevie to have Hyatt there, at the meet, and before Anderson gets there, I'm going to tell them both the truth. About my name.' He shrugged. 'It's not that big a secret anyway. Everyone already knows.'

'And if Anderson tries to kill you?' Joseph asked. He'd grown a little pale.

'I need to know, Joseph.'

'Will you at least let me cover you?' Joseph asked.

'Yes, but I want to do it this afternoon. If he finds out I've seen Reba, my decision to fold to his threat won't be credible. I want to mention the bomb. Watch his face.'

'Would you know if he were lying?' Paige asked.

'I think I might. I need to try.'

'You'll wear a wire,' Joseph stated.

'Okay. Fit me up.' They discussed the details, becoming so

engrossed that the knock at the front door had them jumping. Grayson leaned around the table to check the side window. 'Were you expecting a woman, Joseph?'

'Not me. Stay here. I'll see who it is.' He opened the door a few inches. 'Yes?'

'I'm looking for a Miss Paige Holden.' The woman's voice was measured. Cultured.

'May I ask what this is in reference to?' Joseph asked. His own voice had changed, Paige noted. It was normally deep, but it had just gone all smooth. Her curiosity was piqued.

'A business proposition,' the woman said. 'May I come in?'

'Certainly,' Joseph said, and the woman glided across the foyer in very expensive shoes. Her dress was equally expensive. Elegant. Her blond hair was swept into the same French twist Reba had worn.

They could be Stepford Wives, Paige thought. Then sat back as realization hit, unable to believe her own eyes, stifling the urge to laugh aloud. Grayson didn't yet know who stood before him. Joseph closed the door, never taking his eyes from the woman.

'I'm Paige Holden,' Paige said, playing along. 'And you are?'

The woman smiled. 'I understand you need a sponsor for a non-profit enterprise.'

Grayson came slowly to his feet. 'How would you know that?'

'I've talked with Reba. She told me a few of the details. I'd like to hear more.'

Paige chuckled. 'Grayson, look closer. Closer.'

He did and his mouth literally fell open. '*Daphne?*'

Daphne smiled, not the open, delightfully warm smile Paige had seen earlier, but a very subdued, refined smile. The woman was amazingly good.

Paige got up and walked around Daphne. She pointed to the dress. 'McQueen?'

'Yes,' she said demurely. 'You've got a good eye.'

'Champagne taste on a beer budget, I'm afraid.' Paige came closer, studying Daphne's flawless makeup. 'You look ten years younger. What did you do?'

405

'Made herself up to look ten years older before,' Joseph said quietly.

Daphne gave him a considering look. 'You've got a good eye, too.'

'But why?' Paige asked. 'Why would you *want* to look older every day?'

Grayson sat down abruptly. 'It's Ford, isn't it? The makeup. The hair.'

'Who's Ford?' Joseph asked.

'My son,' Daphne said, maintaining her sophistication. Her dignity. 'He's nineteen.'

'Oh,' Paige breathed, doing the math. 'You're, what, thirty-five?'

'Give or take,' she murmured. 'I was two weeks shy of my sixteenth birthday when he was born. If you'd known that, Grayson, what would you have thought of me?'

'Nothing different,' Grayson said. 'Maybe more. Young mother, raised her son to be a nice young man. I'm a little angry you thought I'd think less of you.'

'Maybe you wouldn't, but others have. They question your wisdom and your ability to make decisions for yourself. They think you're flighty. And stupid. And annoying.'

'I wouldn't have,' Grayson said simply.

'You think I'm annoying.'

'That is fair,' he allowed. 'But only because you mother me. And you kept making me peach cobbler. And your hair attracts bees.'

'Was it good?' Joseph asked. 'The cobbler?'

'Best in Riverdale, West Virginia,' Daphne told him. 'I'm sorry, Grayson. I shouldn't have assumed you'd disregard me. But people have.'

'I need to know it all,' Paige said. 'Where did you get the clothes?'

'They're mine. From my life before this one. I was married. Then divorced. Younger secretary, same old story. You think it won't happen to you, until it does.'

'Pig,' Paige muttered.

Daphne's lips twitched. 'Aptly put. The husband wanted a certain kind of wife. I was eager to please. I lost myself during those years. After the divorce, I went back to being me. Big bee-attracting hair and all. What you see now is a façade. What you saw this morning is me.'

'I liked the you I saw this morning,' Paige said. 'But I want to borrow clothes from the façade chick.'

Daphne laughed throatily. 'Anytime. I've got closets of clothes that haven't been worn in years. And that's after I cleaned most of it out for charity.'

'So did you really talk to Reba?' Grayson asked. 'Or was that a façade, too?'

'Oh, I talked to her all right. By now she's checked my credit and my social standing and found me quite desirable as a sponsor.'

'How did you manage that?' Paige asked.

Daphne winked at her. 'Because I'm rich, sugar,' she said in her twang. 'Filthy.'

'You took the secretary-banger to the alimony cleaners,' Paige said. 'Good for you.'

Something flickered in Daphne's eyes. 'Paige, we have an appointment with Reba in ninety minutes. Do you plan to wear that? Because your Kevlar is showing.'

'Don't even think of not wearing the Kevlar,' Grayson said. 'And don't think of going there alone. I'll go with you.'

'Reba didn't like you,' Paige said. 'You dissed her family name.'

'I'll go,' Joseph said.

'No,' Paige said, 'because you'll be covering Grayson when he confronts Anderson.' She lifted her hand to Grayson's face, touched his forehead next to the cut from the night before. 'I won't go anywhere alone. Promise me you won't either.'

He turned his face, pressing his lips to the inside of her arm. 'I promise.'

Daphne frowned. 'What kind of half-assed plan is confronting Anderson?'

'Only a quarter-assed,' Joseph said. 'Tell him to meet you at Giuseppe's.'

'What's Giuseppe's?' Daphne asked Paige in a whisper.

'Italian restaurant,' Paige whispered back. 'Good carbonara.'

'I don't want to endanger Giuseppe or his family,' Grayson said to Joseph.

'Don't worry. I've used his place a few times. He's ... okay with it.'

That's all Joseph said, and although Paige wanted to know more, she didn't ask.

'I'll call Anderson,' Grayson said. 'I'll also tell Stevie that we don't need her to arrange an undercover op. But only if you don't go alone.'

'I'll ask Clay,' Paige said. 'He can play Daphne's bodyguard. He does bodyguard work anyway, so he'll be believable. And capable.' She leaned up and kissed his cheek when he looked unconvinced. 'Don't worry. We'll be fine. Go make your calls.'

She watched him go, then placed her call to Clay. He was terse as usual, especially when he learned of Grayson's meeting with Anderson. But he was ultimately supportive.

'My partner will be here in twenty,' she told Daphne. 'While we wait, we should plan our attack. You'll need to be curious about the MAC program.'

'I can be very curious,' Daphne said. 'What do we want to achieve?'

'I want to get the kids' names, the year they participated, and the school they came from so I can search for wherever they are now. Plus I want the group photos. They ran the program for sixteen years with a dozen kids each year. That's a lot of potential victims. Then we start looking for patterns, similarities. Anything that jumps out at us.'

'You're still assuming Crystal was molested,' Joseph said. 'Maybe she saw something. A murder maybe.'

'Do you really think so?' Paige asked.

'No, but if you're looking for only one thing, you could miss something else.'

'Understood,' Paige said. Her mind raced ahead. 'I'm going to need a micro-camera. I'd be happier snapping photos of her files than outright stealing them.'

'I have a camera you can use,' Joseph said and Paige smiled.

'Somehow I thought you just might.'

Grayson came back in the room, his body tense. 'Anderson agreed to meet. And I told Stevie the truth.'

'What did she say?' Paige asked softly.

'She was a little stunned. Then angry that Anderson would try to use it against me. Then a little mad I hadn't trusted her with it years ago.' He smiled weakly. 'Then I told her about Daphne. I left her sputtering, but not mad.'

Daphne's eyes widened. 'What are you talking about?'

'One more time,' Grayson murmured and met Daphne's eyes. 'I'm trusting you.'

Daphne plucked at her dress self-consciously. 'I trusted you.'

'True. But my secret is a little darker than yours. My father was Antonio Sabatero. He killed fourteen women. My mother and I discovered the body of his last victim and . . . needed to escape the situation. She protected me. She hid me. She changed our names. Anderson found out. Threatened to expose me if I didn't back off this case.'

Daphne lowered herself into a chair. 'Okay. You win. Yours *is* bigger than mine.'

'I'm going to see what it'll take to guarantee his silence,' Grayson added.

'But what if he doesn't bite?' Daphne asked.

Paige met Grayson's eyes, held them. 'Radcliffe hasn't had a story in nearly twelve hours. Poor man might just go into withdrawal. You could give him one to run with.'

Grayson's smile had a razor edge. 'You're sneaky. That's so hot.'

Paige pecked his lips. 'If Anderson doesn't take your bribe, call him out on the case fixing he did with Bond. Let him try to explain. Then let Radcliffe tear him apart on the five o'clock news. You'll need to be prepared to go public with your own story though. You back Anderson into a corner and he's going to make good on his threat.'

'I'm ready. Every time I tell the story it gets easier.'

'Then, let's get busy. We have lots to do, the least of which is me having to change my clothes so my new undies don't show.'

'You want to raid my closet?' Daphne asked.

'Ohhh, so tempting,' Paige muttered. 'But no.' *Time to grow up, girl.* 'I think if I go to pitch a martial arts school I need to look like a martial artist.'

Grayson's smile warmed, pride in his eyes. 'Dusting off the *gi*?'

She nodded, hard. 'Yes.'

'Bloodstains and all?' he asked.

'I have a spare *gi*. It's . . . unstained. I was going to have to put the *gi* back on eventually. I couldn't teach Holly and the others without it. I'm just doing it a little sooner. Besides, if you go public with your story, I'll make my peace with mine.'

Thursday, April 7, 1.15 P.M.

Stevie stared straight ahead for a full minute after hanging up with Grayson. Of all the secrets she'd considered he'd share, being the son of a serial killer was not among them. But it answered so many questions, not least of which was the source of his dedication to the victims and their families.

She picked up the request for an undercover operation she'd just filled out and slowly tore it in half. *Daphne?* Stevie wouldn't believe it until she saw it herself.

And then her humor fled. He was meeting Anderson.

Fury roiled in her gut along with a healthy dose of fear. Stevie knew Grayson could handle himself. She'd seen him box at the gym. Knew he knew how to use a firearm.

And Joseph would be behind the scene, keeping things under control, but still . . .

She thought about Clay Maynard. Wondered if he'd found anything out about Anderson. She stared at her cell phone, working up the courage to call him.

The man did things to her insides. Things she wasn't ready to deal with. Not now and maybe not ever. But this was for Grayson. Any information Grayson had going into this meeting would thicken his armor. *He would do the same for me.*

Her cell buzzed. *It's him.* Of course it was. 'Mazzetti,' she said crisply.

'It's Maynard. Did you know your pal was confronting his boss in two hours?'

'Yes. He just told me. I was about to call you. Did you find anything?'

Across their desks, JD gave her a puzzled look. Stevie just shook her head.

'Yes, I did,' Maynard said. 'How I got it wasn't terribly pretty.'

'I figured on that.'

'Just so you don't come crying about it later.'

'More likely I'd slap the cuffs on you.' Her cheeks heated. 'You know what I mean.'

His chuckle was like dark chocolate. Sinful and smooth. 'You want this info or not, Mazzetti? Last chance to back away from the poisonous tree.'

She hesitated for about a second. 'Tell me.'

'I found three bank accounts in Anderson's name. Two were full. One was a lot emptier. The two full ones together came to half a million bucks.'

'Oh,' she breathed. 'Wait.' She gave JD a 'later' signal, then found an empty meeting room and closed the door. 'Can you trace where the money came from?'

'Not yet. Half of it comes from the same place. All wire transfers from the same account. The last transfer happened four years ago.'

'That's when Bob Bond the defense attorney died. Grayson found evidence that they'd been fixing cases between them.'

'That answers that, then. The other half comes from wire transfers at all different times over the last four years, all different amounts. Tracing that cash flow won't be easy. But I think the third, smaller account will be of more interest to you.'

'Why?'

'It held forty grand yesterday. A wire transfer went out this morning in the amount of thirty grand. It was wired to an account held by Doris Kapansky.'

'Harlan's mother. Anderson arranged the hit. I should be far more shocked.'

'Now you have to find a way to legally acquire that information.'

'I'll figure something out. Thank you, Mr Maynard. Thank you very much.'

'You really need to thank my assistant, who's getting scarily good at the computer stuff. I have to go. I'm playing bodyguard for Paige. We're going to Reba McCloud's.'

' "I'm a MAC, Loud and Proud," ' she murmured. She went back to her desk to find JD. 'I need lunch.'

'You just ate a sandwich,' he objected. 'You gave half of it to me.'

'So I'm still hungry,' she said and saw he understood. 'Come on.'

When they were in JD's car, she told him what she knew. 'We need to be at the restaurant in case Anderson does something we can arrest him for. We can catch Grayson at his house before he leaves and coordinate.'

Twenty-one

Thursday, April 7, 1.45 P.M.

Standing in front of his dresser mirror, Grayson straightened his tie while Joseph tugged at his suit coat, making sure no wires showed.

'You're done.' Joseph backed away. 'How does it feel?'

'I can't even tell the wire's there,' Grayson said. 'How will you record me?'

'The equipment's set up in Giuseppe's office. I use it from time to time.'

'I've been eating at Giuseppe's for years. How did I not know he was an agent?'

'Because he's not. I did him a favor a while back and he's grateful.'

Grayson shifted, trying to get comfortable in the Kevlar. 'I'm ready.'

'Are you sure?' Paige asked from the doorway.

She'd been scared since Stevie called with the revelation that Anderson truly had paid Kapansky to bomb his car. Grayson was more scared he'd climb over the table at Giuseppe's and strangle Anderson with his bare hands.

He would have killed us. Killed Paige. Just thinking about it had his hands clenching into fists. One blow and the bastard would be down for the count. Except Grayson wasn't sure he could stop at one blow. Pummeling the man's skull to a bloody pulp had been running through his mind over and over again.

'I'm sure,' he said. 'I could do nothing and be watching over my shoulder for the next week or month, waiting for someone to kill us. But I'm not willing to live that way.'

'Neither am I. I came to Baltimore to get away from living exactly like that. Joseph, can you give us a minute? And, like, take out the earpiece?'

Joseph put his earpiece on the dresser. 'You've got five minutes. Don't go, *like*, messing with his clothes. He's wired.' He closed the door behind him.

Paige wrapped her arms around Grayson's waist, but loosely. 'Don't want to mess with your clothes,' she muttered.

'Too bad. I wish you did.'

She looked up, her eyes bleak. His teasing hadn't made a dent in her fear. 'This started out being about me, but now it's about you. I can't help but feel responsible.'

'I know. I feel the same. But if none of this had happened, then you wouldn't have come to my courtroom. And I never would have done this.'

He bent his head, kissing her hard and deep until he felt her body surrender and knew that for this moment he'd given her mind some ease.

'Grayson,' she whispered when he lifted his head. 'Just . . . don't get killed, okay?'

He felt the chuckle rise and was powerless to stop it. 'Okay.'

She glared at him. 'This isn't funny.'

'I know. I'm sorry. I'm not laughing at you. I never considered "Don't get killed" to be the words I'd want to hear at a time like this.'

A tiny smile lifted the corner of her mouth. 'What do you want to hear?'

' "Oh, baby, oh, baby, let's go to bed" comes to mind. "Take me" would also work.' He kissed her again, more seriously this time. 'But "don't get killed" is somehow perfect. So, Paige, don't get killed, okay?'

'Okay. When this is over, I promise to say the "oh, baby" line as often as you want.'

A car door slammed outside. 'Somebody's here. Either Clay or Stevie.'

'Let's go then.' She turned for the door, but he grabbed her hand.

'Wait. I, um, need another minute.'

She glanced at the bulge in his pants, her eyes widening. 'Oh. Wow. Seriously.'

'You're not helping.'

She looked up, a wicked sparkle in her eyes, a welcome relief from the fear that had been there before. 'Seems a shame to waste that,' she said and licked her lips.

His brain scrambled. 'The wire's only from the waist up.'

A loud knock had them both jumping like guilty teenagers.

'Clay's here,' Joseph called loudly through the door. 'And don't even *think* about messing with my wire, Paige.'

Paige laughed and Grayson groaned. 'I'll meet you downstairs,' she said, then opened the door, giving Joseph an annoyed pout. 'Spoilsport.'

'Goddamn teenagers have more sense than you two.' Joseph pointed to Grayson. 'You, hurry up and deflate. Stevie's going to be here soon to give us coverage across town.' He replaced his earpiece. 'Just in case something goes wrong.'

'"Just in case" is pretty damn deflating.' His cell rang and Grayson checked the caller ID. 'I'll be downstairs in a minute,' he told Joseph. 'This is Smith,' he answered.

'Grayson, it's Lucy Trask. I'm sorry I took so long to get back to you. I've had a few bodies pop up this morning and we're short-handed. I checked the report on Bob Bond, the suicide victim from four years ago. He also had high levels of barbiturates in his system at the time of death. Same as Denny Sandoval and same approximate level.'

Grayson sighed. 'That's what I was afraid of. Thanks for checking for me.'

'Wait,' Lucy said. 'Don't go yet. I need to tell you about one more.'

She did, Grayson staring at his reflection as her words sank in. 'You're sure?'

'Yes. I'm sorry to be the one to tell you,' Lucy said. 'I thought you should know.'

'Thank you,' Grayson said quietly, then went to join the others.

Paige took one look at him and froze. 'What happened?'

'I got a call from Lucy Trask,' he said. He sat down, heavily. 'Bob Bond had the same barbiturate in him when he died as Sandoval, same levels.'

'We expected that,' Paige said. She knelt next to his chair. 'What's wrong?'

'A victim was brought into the morgue this morning. She'd OD'd. The ME found barbiturate-laced chocolate in her stomach contents. The cops found a box that had held the chocolate on her nightstand.' He swallowed. 'Next to my business card.'

Paige sat back, her dark brows knit. 'Not Brittany?'

'No. Betsy Malone. She's dead. She talked to us and now she's dead.'

'Oh, my God,' Paige whispered. 'She'd just gotten clean. Fucking hell.'

'Okay,' Daphne said. 'Who is Betsy Malone?'

'She was Rex's friend,' Paige said. 'They were in the video the McClouds provided as Rex's alibi. Betsy talked to us last night. Told us she thought Rex might have done it. Reba knew that. She knew that before we came in this morning.'

For a moment they were silent. Then Clay spoke. 'You still want to go through with this, Paige? You don't have to if you don't want to.'

'She doesn't want to,' Grayson said and leveled her a desperate stare. 'You don't.'

'Yes, I do.' Paige lifted her chin. 'Betsy had a privileged life and threw it away. But she did not deserve to die. I have to go.'

Thursday, April 7, 2.00 P.M.

He dropped the duffel bag on the bed and unzipped it enough to see that Violet Dandridge still breathed. She did. 'Leave her in the bag,' he instructed.

'She's pretty.'

He looked up, saw the calculating gaze sizing up his new

leverage. 'She's not yours. She belongs to Silas Dandridge.'

'I thought you were going to kill Silas.'

'I will. But I need to bring him to me before he creates a lot of trouble I'd have to clean up. Speaking of cleaning up, you were lucky. Adele Shaffer is dead.'

'I'm not lucky. I'm thorough.'

'Adele was alive when you left her,' he said as patiently as he was able. 'She died in the ambulance.' His paramedic source had been positive. Unfortunately he no longer had a source in the morgue. He'd have to acquire another one soon.

A shrug. 'Then it's fine.'

'This time. Look, I told you this before. People survive being stabbed in the torso. If you want to kill someone fast, go for the jugular or take a gun and shoot them in the head. Otherwise you leave messes that have to be fixed. By me.'

'You've been paid for all the fixing you've had to do.'

And he'd been paid well, but even more valuable had been the access to power. His acquiescence had bought him influence and control, the likes of which he'd never have found in the hovel from which he'd been plucked. *I'm a MAC*, he thought bitterly, *Loud and Proud*.

'You know I appreciate your generosity,' he murmured.

'Sometimes I wonder.'

He left the bag unzipped enough for the child to breathe. 'Leave her alone. Please.'

'But she's so pretty. What are you going to do with her after her father's dead?'

'I'm not sure. She hasn't seen my face.' He hadn't removed the disguise he'd worn in Toronto until after he'd drugged her. 'I'll kill her if I have to, but I'd rather not.'

'Give her to me.'

He shook his head, knowing what would happen to the child. *I have my faults, but sexual deviancy isn't one of them.* 'She's too young.'

'They all grow. You just have to be patient.'

'I'm patient,' he said, annoyed.

'No, you're not. You never have been. It's one of your more

appealing qualities. You want what you want, when you want it. So you've taken risks. Reaped rewards. But you've also made yourself beholden and dependent. To me, for example.'

He bit back the sharp retort on his tongue. 'She's not your type.'

'I find we get less choosy, the older we get. Don't you agree?'

He saw the glitter of amusement and knew he was being baited. 'I'll be back to check on her in an hour. If she wakes up, give her another pill. No more than one.'

'How about chocolate?' The taunt was mockingly delivered. 'I have some left over.'

He gritted his teeth. 'That's not funny.'

The amusement vanished. 'Why should I help you hide her if I can't have her?'

He took a breath, forced himself to smile. 'Because you love me?' he asked lightly.

After a long pause, a chuckle filled the room. 'You're lucky that that's still true.'

Thursday, April 7, 2.00 P.M.

Dammit. Silas gritted his teeth as another person went into Smith's house. Smith and Holden had still not come out. They hadn't even come close to the window by the door.

And I'm running out of time. A woman had gone in the hour before and just now a third man. There were now five people in the house.

And that bastard still has my baby. His mind was torturing him with all the ways Violet could be hurt. *I will kill him. If he touches a hair on her head I will gut him.*

Violet . . . Oh, God. His heart was pounding, his hands trembling. *Stop it. Stop thinking about him and pay attention to that damn front door.*

Through which no one emerged. He drew a shaky breath, made the decision. *I'll shoot the next person who goes in or comes out.* Then when the others rushed out to help, he'd shoot them all. Then he'd run like hell.

A car drove up, stopped on Smith's side of the street. A big guy got out.

He was a cop, Silas could tell. The man moved like a cop.

Silas leaned forward, keeping the man in his sight, his finger on the trigger. He put pressure on the trigger, aiming at the base of the man's head.

Squeeze, dammit. Squeeze the fucking trigger. For Violet.

His hands were shaking. Shaking. A car door slammed, but he kept his eye on the sight. On the cop walking up to Smith's front door.

He squeezed the trigger just as a petite brunette moved into his sight. His hand jerked and the window shattered. *Stevie. Oh, my God.* It was Stevie.

The man on the front porch dropped to his stomach and rolled, sitting up against a slender tree. That would be JD Fitzpatrick, Stevie's new partner. Fitzpatrick pressed his hand to his shoulder. When he brought his palm away, it was red.

Stevie ran to her vehicle, weapon drawn. Pointed up at the roof. *Toward me. Move.* He left the rifle behind, running in a crouch to the edge of the roof. He jumped, landing on the fire escape. He took the stairs, five at a time.

'Stop! Police!' Stevie was behind him. He drew the revolver from his shoulder holster and turned, firing at the ground between them.

'Silas!' She was crying. Stevie was crying. 'Dammit. Stop!'

He got to the car he'd parked on the next street and hunkered. He trained his revolver on Stevie, who was only steps behind. 'Drop your gun,' he said.

She came to a skidding halt. 'Why, Silas?' She didn't put down her gun.

'Don't make me take *your* child's mother. Drop your gun and back away or I swear to God I'll fire.' His voice was desperate. 'Please don't make me hurt you.'

She stared, shocked. Devastated. Betrayed. Slowly she laid her gun on the ground.

'Hands where I can see them,' he said. 'Kick the gun over here.' She kicked the gun, hands still raised. He picked it up, got in the car. 'I'm sorry,' he said.

He only dared to drive three blocks. She probably had already reported his license-plate number. *Ditch the car. Steal another.* Methodically he worked, finding a car, hotwiring the ignition. Driving away again. He'd failed. Smith and Holden still lived.

And that bastard still has my child.

Clay threw open the door, covering Joseph and Grayson as they dragged JD inside. The window was shattered. Peabody was barking and JD was bleeding.

Paige sent Peabody to a corner, away from the broken glass, then dragged a chair into the dining room, away from the windows. 'Sit him here.'

Daphne had already called 911. 'The ambulance is on its way.'

'I'm all right,' JD said. 'Stevie went after him.' He started for the door, staggered.

Grayson grabbed his arm and forced him into the chair. 'Where are you hit?'

'My partner is out there,' JD said viciously. 'I've had worse. Let. Me. Go.'

'I'll cover her.' With that Clay took off at a run.

'What are we talking about here?' Joseph demanded. 'Is this Silas? The cop?'

'He's a sharpshooter,' Grayson said, taking his gun from the holster at his back. 'But Silas has gone out of his way not to kill me. It doesn't make sense that he'd try to kill me now. I'll take the street to the left. Joseph, you go right.'

Paige bit her tongue as the brothers hit the street. She wanted to beg Grayson to stay put. But she knew he needed to go. She turned her attention to JD. He was bleeding. A hell of a lot. She ran to the kitchen for towels.

When she got back, Daphne had taken JD's jacket off. He was sweating, his face pale. His shirt was already soaked with blood. Daphne had unbuttoned it, exposing the wound, an inch from where his Kevlar ended.

'It's not so bad,' Daphne said, forcing a strong note into her voice. 'Just a graze.'

JD stared at her, his eyes starting to haze. 'It really *is* you. I didn't believe Stevie.'

'Tomorrow I'm back to loud clothes and big hair.'

'Like you better that way,' JD mumbled. 'Hell, I've had worse than this.'

'I'll take care of it,' Paige said to Daphne. 'You're dressed for Reba.'

'This is why I like simpler clothes,' Daphne snapped. 'I'm useless this way.'

'You won't be once we get to Reba's office,' Paige said. She pressed a towel against JD's wound. 'Why do I feel like I've done this before?' she muttered.

'Because he's your third bleeder this week,' Daphne said dryly. But Paige wasn't fooled. The woman's voice trembled.

'Daphne's rattled, so it must be bad. How much blood have I lost?' JD murmured.

'A lot,' Paige said bluntly. 'Looks like the bullet may have nicked an artery. Lie down on the floor.' She eased him to the carpet, kneeling at his side, keeping the pressure steady with one hand while she grabbed a cushion off the chair with the other. She handed the cushion to Daphne. 'Elevate his feet.'

'You do medic work?' he asked. His voice was thickening.

'No. But I had a hole like this one in my shoulder. You'll have a pretty scar.'

'It'll go with all my others,' he said.

'I'll call Lucy,' Daphne said. 'Have her meet you at the ER.'

'Hell no,' he insisted, but his voice was weaker. He was still bleeding. A lot. Paige pressed harder against the wound. 'Not in her condition,' he added, then closed his eyes. 'I didn't say that out loud, did I? I wasn't supposed to tell.'

'I didn't hear anything,' Daphne said, forcing a smile. 'Did you, Paige?'

'Not a word.'

Daphne peeked out the door. 'Stevie's coming back. Clay's with her.'

'Is she okay?' JD asked.

'Not a scratch,' Daphne said. 'You're the one who's bleeding buckets, sugar.'

Stevie and Clay walked into the house, stepping over the glass. Stevie looked devastated, the little color she had left in her face fading when she saw JD. 'Oh, God.'

'I've got him,' Paige said tersely. 'He's not dying. Sit her down before she faints.'

'I don't faint,' Stevie snarled. But she sank to her knees next to JD. 'It was Silas.'

Paige's head jerked up in surprise. 'What? Are you sure?'

'Damn sure. I chased him. He . . . pointed his gun at my head.'

JD patted her leg clumsily. 'I don't like your old partner so much,' he said.

Stevie hiccuped a startled laugh that sounded more like a sob. 'Me either.'

'Where is Silas?' Paige asked, thinking of Grayson still out there, looking for him.

'He got away,' Clay said.

'I radioed his license plate in but he's probably found another car already,' Stevie said. She'd regained a bit of color in her face. 'How much blood loss?'

'It's slowing down,' Paige said. 'A little. He's not dying.'

'I'm not dying,' JD repeated forcefully.

'Grayson and Joseph are back,' Daphne announced.

The brothers were grim-faced. 'No sign of him,' Grayson said.

'He was shaking,' Stevie said. 'Silas, I mean. It's why he missed.'

Grayson frowned. 'It was Silas? What did he say?'

Stevie sat back on her heels. 'He said he didn't want to have to kill "*your* daughter's mother". Rose never answered her phone. This is not good. Silas was desperate. He begged me not to make him hurt me.'

'He said the same thing to me when he had Logan. What if they have his kid?'

'Possible,' Stevie said. 'Violet wasn't at school yesterday. But she was there on Tuesday.'

'Leaving no explanation for the other kills,' Grayson said.

'He could have come to me. Asked for help.' Stevie swallowed. 'But he didn't.'

'The paramedics are here,' Joseph said. 'Give them room.'

'I'm going to the ER with you,' Stevie told JD.

'No, you're not,' JD said wearily, his eyes closed. 'You're going to cover Grayson. I'm not dying. Paige says so. Besides, Lucy will come to the ER and she'll probably cry. She hates for anyone to see her cry. So go, do your job. All of you.'

'All right,' Stevie agreed. 'I'll handle everything here. As soon as I get the scene secured, I'll join you at the restaurant. I've already briefed Hyatt and he'll be waiting for you there. Paige, you and Daphne go to Reba.'

'I'll put Peabody in the bedroom,' Paige said. 'But don't leave him alone, okay?'

'I'll be sure the house is covered.' Stevie stood. 'Go.'

Thursday, April 7, 2.15 P.M.

Silas didn't go far. There were no real places he could hide. It wouldn't take long for news of his botched attempt at Grayson's townhouse to hit the TV waves.

He'd tried to kill a cop. He'd find no one on the force willing to help him now. Especially Stevie. He tried to erase the image of her face from his mind, only to have it filled with the worst possible things that could be happening to Violet.

He pulled a ball cap low on his face and found an alley. He ditched the car, which would be reported missing soon. He slunk into the shadows, leaning against a brick wall and closing his eyes. *What am I going to do?* Grayson was on alert now. He and Paige Holden wouldn't give him another chance to shoot them.

Not that I could get them with my rifle. He'd left it. He had more at his storage unit, but that was miles away. He had two handguns on him. For now they'd have to do.

A low roar had his head jerking up, his eyes scanning the alley as he pressed against the wall. The roar was abruptly cut and a guy pushed a motorcycle into the alley from the street. The guy set the kickstand and straightened, taking off his helmet.

Silas didn't think, he just acted, slipping from the shadows and striking the man with the butt of his handgun, hard, in the base of his skull. The man went limp and Silas guided him to the ground, careful to make no noise. He stripped the man's leather jacket from his body and shrugged into it. Then he put the helmet on, picked up the man's keys where they'd fallen, started the motorcycle and drove away.

The air helped clear his mind. And he knew where he could go to hide, plan, and do what he needed to do to save his child before it was too late.

Thursday, April 7, 3.30 P.M.

'We're turning a few heads,' Daphne murmured as they waited for the elevator to Reba's office. 'Socialite and Ninja Girl accompanied by brooding bodyguard.'

It was true. Daphne wore her McQueen and Paige wore her *gi*. Clay hovered over them all in black, an earpiece in one ear like the Secret Service. The earpiece was really a digital recorder. Everything said would be captured.

'Sounds like a TV show,' Paige murmured back. 'A really bad one.'

'I'm not brooding,' Clay muttered.

Paige tossed him a wry look. 'Sure you are, Mr Don't-say-hi-or-bye.'

'Am not,' Clay said, but there was a smile in his voice. 'I'm taciturn.'

Paige snickered but when the elevator doors closed, she frowned at Daphne. 'She's going to know you're a prosecutor working with Grayson.'

'She would, if I'd told her my correct name. But today I'm Mrs Travis Elkhart, first name Elizabeth. The current Mrs Travis Elkhart is the bimbo using my wedding china, but there were enough photos in the society pages of my ex and me that I'll pass muster with Reba. Daphne is the lawyer. Elizabeth is the woman I left behind.'

The doors opened and Paige walked up to the receptionist whose eyes had widened at the sight of them. 'We're here to see Ms McCloud.'

The receptionist studied Paige's *gi* with confusion. 'I'll tell her that you're here.'

Daphne sat, crossing her legs, her hands folded primly on her lap. Paige spied Clay staring in a way she was certain he thought discreet. She couldn't blame him. Daphne had amazing legs. She was a beautiful woman. Paige had a million questions about the man who'd left her, but held them back, instead standing at attention next to Clay.

She tugged briskly on the lower hem of her *gi* jacket, hearing the familiar snap of fabric. *I've lived in the quiet of my mind for too long*, she thought. It was time to live in the outside again. Her friends had told her to be patient, that this day would come.

Paige hadn't expected it to feel so right.

'Do you like mojitos?' she asked Daphne.

'And martinis. And margaritas. As well as cocktails beginning with many other letters of the alphabet.' Daphne's brows went up. 'Why?'

'I have these two best friends in Minneapolis. We used to go out for major mojito nights, spill our secrets and generally trash the men who'd done us wrong.'

Daphne's lips twitched. 'Sounds like a fun girls' night out.'

'I'm standing here, you know,' Clay muttered.

'If you've never caused a major mojito meltdown, none of this pertains to you,' Paige said, surprised to find him looking almost hurt. 'Have you?'

'Not to my knowledge,' he said seriously. 'But I've been on the receiving end a time or two. Guys don't bitch. They suck it up. And get drunk alone.'

Daphne looked sympathetic. 'You can join us. I'm not discriminatory.'

'Mojitos are not my thing,' he said dryly.

Daphne just smiled. 'I'm sure I can find something that would appeal to your palate. My mother makes a really tasty G and T. Heavy on the G.'

'How heavy?' Clay asked.

'No T,' Daphne said demurely. 'And the G is her own recipe. Sshh.'

The receptionist approached, holding a tray. 'Can I offer you some water?'

Paige instantly sobered on the inside, although she left her polite smile intact. Images of a dead Betsy Malone filled her mind. 'No, thank you. I'm fine.'

'As are we,' Daphne said. 'Thank you, though.'

Clay just gave a taciturn nod.

'If you change your mind, just ask. Ms McCloud is ready for you now.'

Thursday, April 7, 3.35 P.M.

Anderson was late. *I hope he's still coming.* Grayson hated to think he'd gotten all wired up for nothing. He sat down at the table set with fine china and crystal in Giuseppe's private room. The door to the kitchen opened behind him.

'Anderson just walked in the front door,' Joseph said quietly. 'Hyatt's here. He's got a man in the ceiling with a scope trained on Anderson. Stevie will wait in the main dining room, in case he decides to leave prematurely. The back entrance is covered.'

'I have a judge waiting to sign a court order for Anderson's bank records if you can get him to admit anything,' Hyatt said, from behind Joseph. 'We'll be on the other side of this door.'

The kitchen door closed. A few moments later, the door in front of Grayson opened and Charlie Anderson came through it, his step cocky.

He thinks he has me where he wants me. Think again, asshole.

Grayson gestured to the empty place at the table. 'Thanks for coming, Charlie.'

Charlie took his seat. 'I hear you had some excitement at your place.'

'Yeah.' It had been all over the police radio. There was no point in trying to hide it. 'Silas Dandridge just shot Detective Fitzpatrick – trying to get to me.'

'I told you to leave this alone, but you always know better. If you'd listened to me . . .'

Anderson's voice was oily and made Grayson want to strangle him. But he kept his voice humble. Afraid even. 'I fucked up. I should have listened to you. I got influenced by a woman. I should have walked away from Rex McCloud. Now my life is fucked. Somebody's tried to kill me twice in the last day. I'm backing off.'

'Smart. But too late. Even if they leave you alone, which they won't, I'm following through with my promise. You pushed, I tell it all.'

Grayson suppressed his contempt. He leaned forward, let a little desperation show. 'I will do whatever I need to do to make whoever I pissed off happy. I mean *anything*. I can do a lot of good from the prosecutor's table. In many different ways.'

'Aren't you listening? Even if you don't get disbarred, when your family secret comes out, no court will have you. You'll be a media circus. "Son of serial killer wielding the sword of truth,"' Anderson said dramatically. 'Every defense attorney you face will claim conflict of interest and the judge won't have any choice but to agree. You're finished.'

That might actually be true. But Grayson couldn't think about that. He needed to use Anderson's arrogance to line him up where he wanted him. Then he'd use Stevie's evidence to knock him down. He blew out a nervous breath. 'What if you didn't tell?'

Anderson stared at him. 'And why wouldn't I?'

'I'm not without resources.'

Laughter lit Anderson's eyes, filled his voice. 'You're offering to *pay* me? Grayson, I'm appalled. I would never accept money from you. This meeting is over.'

Grayson waited until Anderson had risen from his chair before he spoke. 'Why won't you take money from me? You take it from everyone else.'

Anderson froze. 'I have no idea what you're talking about.'

'Bob Bond's money was good enough when you two fixed cases together.'

'We did not,' Anderson declared. But his eyes had changed. He was scared. *Good*.

'My adopted family is quite well-off. But then you know that, since you know so much about me. Even if I don't borrow from them, I've invested well. I can pay more than Bond did. Much more.' He drew his checkbook from his pocket. 'How much, Charlie?'

Anderson lifted his chin. 'I can't be bought.'

'So you did it for free? Somehow I don't think so. How many wealthy families got their kids off burglary and drug charges with your "help"? How's that going to look when it starts to come out? Bob Bond's death is being reopened as a homicide by the police. We'll get access to all of his bank records. How much will be traced to you?'

Grayson wanted to throw the quarter-million in Anderson's offshore accounts in his boss's face, but technically he didn't know about that. Not all of it anyway. He wasn't sure where Stevie got her information from, but once she'd told the cops to look at Kapansky's mother more closely, they'd uncovered the payment from Anderson.

So the most important information, the thirty grand to Kapansky, he could use. It was back-door discovery, but Grayson found he could live with that.

'Bob Bond committed suicide,' Anderson said, but his eyes said he knew the truth.

'No, he didn't. He died just like Denny Sandoval. Drugged, then hung. Tell me, Charlie, how far are *you* willing to go to keep *your* secrets?'

Anderson was taking deep breaths. 'So *you're* blackmailing *me* now? That's rich.'

Actually, Grayson had been talking about the bomb Anderson had paid for, but he could flow with it. 'Clever choice of words. I might say we're even. I won't expose your dirty secret if you don't expose mine.'

A muscle in Anderson's cheek twitched. 'We might say that.'

'We might, except for the thirty grand.'

The man's eyes flickered. 'What are you talking about?'

'The thirty grand you transferred to Harlan Kapansky's mother. I see that you know who Kapansky is.'

Anderson went pale. 'No. You're lying.'

'You don't know who he is?' Grayson mocked. 'Then it was stupid to pay his mom.'

'I didn't pay him. I don't know anything about that. You're lying.'

'No, I'm not. I have the bank records if you want to see them. Your name is clearly listed as owner of the account the thirty grand was transferred from. Why would I lie?'

'To make me look bad so no one will believe me when I tell them about you.'

'I think all your case fixing will make you look bad enough, Charlie. You don't need my help. And if I was lying about Kapansky, which I'm not, the guy who really paid him will walk free. Maybe he'd even try again. It makes no sense for me to lie.'

Anderson faltered. 'No. It's not possible. I did not pay Harlan Kapansky.'

'Check it for yourself. It's in your bank.'

Anderson took out his phone, wiping a sweaty palm on his trousers. He slowly typed in a lot of numbers and his face went ashen. 'Sonofabitch.'

'Told you,' Grayson said.

'This account isn't mine. I didn't pay Kapansky. I didn't pay to have you killed.'

Yeah, right. But he'd play along. 'Then who did?'

'Let me think.' Anderson shoved his hands in his hair. 'After Bond died there was someone else at his firm. Someone brokering the deals. Not just with me. I can name names of other attorneys fixing deals. But I did *not* pay for your murder.'

Grayson frowned. Anderson sounded almost credible. 'Who's the broker?'

'I don't know. I never talked to him.'

'What about Muñoz? Whose idea was it for me to take lead chair against him?'

Anderson turned for the door.

'We have so much on you,' Grayson said softly. 'It'll be better if you cooperate. Maybe we can even make a deal.'

Anderson's shoulders sagged. 'Mine. It was my idea.'

'Who paid off Sandoval and Brittany Jones?'

Surprise and hate flickered in Anderson's eyes. 'Bond.'

Grayson pictured Bob Bond in his mind. There was no way the man in the photo Elena had obtained was Bond. The man in the photo was too skinny. 'The picture we have can't be Bond. You saw the picture, so you know.'

'That must have been one of Bond's flunkies. Stupid enough to get caught on camera.'

'So are you.'

Anderson looked up in the corners, too calmly. 'They're hidden well.'

'That's kind of the point,' Grayson said mildly.

The next move happened so fast Grayson couldn't stop it. Anderson pulled a gun from his coat pocket, put the barrel in his mouth and pulled the trigger. The shot was deafening, the silence after even more so.

Grayson ran around the table, dropping to one knee beside Anderson. Joseph and Hyatt burst in one door, Stevie in the other, guns drawn. Above their heads a ceiling tile was pushed aside. A guy in tactical gear looked as stunned as everyone else.

Anderson had no pulse. Grayson laid his boss's arm on the floor then stood, staring at the body that seconds before had had a whole head. 'Oh, my God,' he whispered.

For a long moment, everyone stared at Anderson's body, then at each other. Grayson sank into the nearest chair. 'I shouldn't have told him he was on camera.'

'He knew Bond and the others had been murdered. Knew he'd be next.' Joseph grasped Grayson's shoulder, hard. 'My heart stopped when he pulled out that gun.'

'He made a real mess,' Grayson said dully. 'Giuseppe's gonna be pissed.'

'I'll take care of it,' Joseph murmured.

'We need that broker,' Stevie said. 'We need to find out who in that firm is dirty.'

'It's a *law firm*,' Hyatt said. 'They're *lawyers*. They're all dirty. No offense, Smith.'

'None taken. It could be anyone at the firm, so we need a list of personnel. I can subpoena their records, but expect them to fight it, if only on principle. This will take a while. We need somebody inside the firm to get us personnel information, give us the lay of the land. Off the record. Somebody a defense attorney will trust.'

Stevie looked at Hyatt. 'Thomas Thorne might have connections.'

Hyatt grimaced in distaste. 'I do not like that man.'

'He saved Detective Skinner's life,' Stevie reminded him gently.

'I've been in the courtroom with Thorne several times,' Grayson said. 'He's a royal SOB, but I've never caught him in a lie. I'll talk to him.'

'You set it up,' Stevie said, 'and I'll go with you. If he's not in his law office, he should be at the club in a few hours. And if he won't listen to us, I'll sic Lucy on him. Given JD just got shot because of all this, Lucy will be very convincing about now.'

'Who's Lucy?' Joseph asked. 'And why would she be more convincing?'

'Lucy's the ME,' Grayson said. 'She's also engaged to JD.'

'And she owns a nightclub with Thorne and one of their friends,' Stevie explained. 'She can get Thorne to cooperate when nobody else can.'

'I don't care who gets that asshole to cooperate,' Hyatt barked. 'Just do it.'

'I'll call Thorne on my way to meet Paige,' Grayson said. The adrenaline that had him rushing to Anderson's side was ebbing fast. *I need to hold her.* Needed her to erase the image of Anderson blowing his brains out. 'Unless I have to stay here?'

'No,' Hyatt said. 'We'll clean up. You go.' He added in a begrudging voice, 'You did okay, for a lawyer.'

Coming from Hyatt, that was high praise. And yet Grayson wouldn't accept it. 'You'd know none of this if Paige hadn't come forward,' he said. 'She didn't deserve how you treated her yesterday. And now you know she was right about cop involvement.'

Hyatt rolled his eyes. 'I'll send her a handwritten apology.'

'You do that.' Grayson pushed himself to his feet, his body unsteady. 'I'm ready.'

'I'll walk you out,' Stevie said. 'I'm going to the hospital to check on JD.'

'I'll drive you to Reba's building, Grayson,' Joseph said. 'I'll be back to help after.'

Thursday, April 7, 3.40 P.M.

Reba rose when they came in, her eyes showing surprise when Clay followed them.

'My personal security detail,' Daphne said quietly. 'I hope you understand.'

'I do,' Reba said. 'I became accustomed to having my own detail when my father was in politics.' She gestured to two chairs in front of her desk. 'Please.'

It's showtime, Paige thought, steeling herself to speak the words she'd rehearsed in the car, knowing they would leave an acrid taste in her mouth. 'I wanted to apologize. We approached Rex based on information from a source who wasn't reliable.'

Reba's eyes narrowed. 'What do you mean?'

'Betsy Malone told us what happened at your parents' estate the night Crystal Jones was murdered. We believed her. But she also said she'd been clean for a year. We found that was not the case. She OD'd on barbiturates. She's dead.'

Paige watched Reba's face, saw shock spark in her eyes. 'That's terrible. I didn't like her because of what she'd done to Rex, but I wouldn't have wished her ill.'

'I know. But when a witness lies about one fact, the rest of their story comes into doubt.' *I'm so damn sorry, Betsy. You talked to us and now you're dead.* 'We've moved on to other persons of interest. I apologize for any distress we caused your family.'

That Rex had killed Crystal was no longer a certainty in her mind. But that the McClouds as a unit were somehow responsible, was.

Uttering the disgusting apology had the expected effect.

'Everyone makes mistakes,' Reba said regally. 'You've apologized for yours.' Obviously she believed that Paige had offered the apology to clear the slate for her own agenda. Obviously Reba considered this business as usual. 'Now that we've put that unpleasantness aside, how can our foundation help you, Mrs Elkhart?'

'I am prepared to fund Paige's endeavor,' Daphne said, 'but I have questions about how we'd manage to integrate her martial arts program into the community. We want to serve those with disabilities and from lower-income brackets. Those who would benefit from the self-esteem-building aspects of martial arts, but who cannot afford the fees.'

'Interfacing with district schools and adult vocational programs will be a big part of our kickoff,' Paige added. 'I saw that you'd done this successfully at the middle-school level and wanted to reapply any approaches that worked well.'

'Our MAC program,' Reba said. 'The McCloud Alliance for Children donated hundreds of thousands of dollars to two hundred schools over sixteen years. Add to that the assistance to individual classrooms and families and that amount doubled.'

'Did you track the MAC children?' Daphne asked. 'Perhaps discovering how the program changed their lives?'

Reba looked intrigued. 'No, we haven't. Perhaps we should.'

'I'd love to see any material you have on the program,' Daphne said.

'You came to the right place,' Reba said. 'I'm the family historian.' Rising, she pulled a three-ring notebook from a shelf. 'These are the materials used, the letters we sent to the schools and the accounting model for the donated funds.'

'May we take notes?' Paige asked.

'Of course.' Reba pointed to a small table off to the side. 'You might be more comfortable there. Take all the time you need, Miss Holden.'

Keeping the stunned satisfaction from her expression was hard.

433

Paige carried the notebook to the table, positioning herself so that Reba could only see her back. She took out Joseph's camera-pen. Her practice photos had come out crisp and clear.

As Reba detailed many of the other foundation programs for Daphne, Paige looked through the notebook, taking notes for show. Most of the documents were of no importance, mainly invitations and flyers detailing the program itself.

Then she hit the motherlode. Photographs, one group photo for each year of the MAC program's existence. And behind each photo was a typed list of names, middle schools, and home addresses, identifying each child by where they stood in the picture.

She snapped a picture of each photo and each document, pausing when she came to the second to last photo. On the front row stood a little girl with golden ringlets and a new blue dress. She looked sad. Haunted, even.

Paige's throat closed. Twenty-year-old Crystal had gone to that party to commit a crime. She'd had something to blackmail somebody with.

Paige moved on to the final year and left the notebook on the table. 'I've got what we need, Mrs Elkhart,' she said. 'Would you like for me to wait outside?'

'No.' Daphne stood and extended her hand to Reba. 'I'd be happy to sponsor a table at the benefit for breast cancer research. I'll take the other opportunities into consideration and get back to you.'

'That would be fantastic.' Reba walked them back to the receptionist's desk. 'If you'll give Ann your address, we'll get the necessary paperwork out to you.'

'If you'll send the paperwork to Ms Holden, she can be sure it gets to me.'

'I'll write down my business address,' Paige said and, unclipping Joseph's pen from her notebook, wrote the address for Clay's office. She ripped the page out of the notebook to give to the receptionist as the door to the outside hall opened behind her.

Instantly Daphne moved, placing her body between Paige and the door. But Clay had moved faster, now standing between

Paige and Daphne. While not as broad as Grayson's, Clay's back was wide enough to effectively block her view.

Clay was accustomed to protecting people, but that Daphne had put herself between Paige and a potential threat made Paige's heart warm. This was a woman who'd make an excellent friend. And not only because she had a closet of designer clothes. Although that certainly didn't hurt.

'Reba,' a man said.

'Stuart,' Reba said warmly.

Paige heard a kiss-kiss greeting and let herself relax. Clay also relaxed his stiff stance, but only a fraction. The newcomer was just a client.

'Do we have an appointment?' Reba asked. 'You're not on my calendar.'

'Not today,' Stuart said. 'I'm here to see your brother-in-law. Is he here?'

'He's, um, not back from lunch yet. You can wait in his office. But first, I want you to meet one of our new donors. This is Elizabeth Elkhart. Mrs Elkhart, this is Stuart Lippman, one of the Foundation's attorneys.'

'I'm happy to meet you,' Daphne said softly.

'We appreciate the generosity of our donors. I hope you'll keep us smiling,' Stuart added, with a charming smile of his own. The door opened once again.

'Stuart!' The greeting was delivered in a drawl, slightly slurred. 'Good t'see you.'

Paige could smell the alcohol from where she stood. It was like the guy had bathed in it. It was Louis, Claire's husband. Stepfather to Rex McCloud.

Louis had been at the estate the night Crystal was murdered. And he'd been old enough to molest little girls through the MAC years whereas Rex had been a child.

'Let's go to your office, Louis,' Stuart said. 'We can talk there.'

'About what?' There was a tiny pause. 'Rex called you, didn't he? Fucking little asshole. Well, you can just leave. We're not spending any more on that waste of air.'

'Louis,' Reba began, embarrassment clear in her tone. 'Let's go to your office.'

'It won't matter. Claire and I are together on this. Call her if you don't believe me.'

'Let's go call her,' Stuart soothed. 'Sort this out.' The two men moved toward the bank of offices on the other side of the reception desk. Paige leaned right, just able to see them around Clay. The lawyer had his arm around Louis, his hand on the bigger man's shoulder urging him forward, but Louis stopped and turned.

His eyes did a quick trip from her head to her feet and when his eyes met hers she saw surprised recognition. *He saw me last night after we talked to Rex.* Louis looked her up and down, his gaze provocative. An unpleasant shiver went down her back and then he very deliberately winked at her. Startled, she reacted on impulse, her thumb pressing the clip on the pen she held. Snapping a picture of Louis Delacorte.

And then he and Stuart were gone, leaving an awkward silence.

Reba cleared her throat. 'I'm sorry. He's, um . . .'

'Every family has one,' Daphne said kindly. 'Thank you for your time.'

'Thank you,' Reba said, her tone stilted. 'I'll look forward to seeing you at the benefit.' Still flustered, her face still red, Reba opened the door and ushered them out.

Twenty-two

Thursday, April 7, 4.00 P.M.

'You okay?' Joseph asked.

Grayson turned from the stalled traffic to his brother. 'No. I've never actually seen someone blow their brains out. I had no idea the phrase was so accurately descriptive.'

'It's not something that leaves you anytime soon,' Joseph said soberly. 'Look, after you get Paige, I want you two to go to my place and get some sleep. You're running on fumes. I'll sleep on the couch if it'll help.'

'I appreciate it.' And he really did. But right now he needed her. So much it should have scared him. 'But I don't think I could "sleep" knowing you were on the sofa.'

Joseph frowned. 'When I say sleep, I mean *sleep*. You know, REM, out like a light?'

'Oh. I thought you were being discreet.' He turned back to the window. 'When I get Paige alone, I have zero intention of wasting time doing REM.'

Joseph laughed, surprising him. 'You're an asshole to rub it in my face.'

'You'd do the same if our situations were reversed.'

'Damn straight.'

Grayson's phone began buzzing in his pocket. 'Stevie. What's wrong?'

'Nothing at the moment,' she said. 'JD's okay. Lucy's with him and they moved him to a private room for observation overnight. He'll come home tomorrow.'

'Good. I called Thorne's office but he wasn't there. I left my cell and yours.'

'I talked to him already. Thorne was here with Lucy. I told him what we needed. He said to give him a few hours and he'd meet us at my place.'

'Why your place?'

'Because I haven't had a full evening with Cordelia all week and Izzy has a date.'

'Good reasons. I assume it's okay to bring Paige with me.'

'I didn't think you'd be leaving her alone.'

'What about the dog?'

Stevie sighed. 'If he chews up even one sofa leg, you're replacing it.'

'Understood. I'll pick up Paige and meet you at your place in two hours.'

Joseph wore a tiny smirk. 'So much for no REM, out like a light.'

'I can do a lot with two hours.' Grayson looked around impatiently. 'What is with this traffic? They'll have left Reba's before we get there.'

'Look on the bright side,' Joseph said cheerfully. 'There are twelve two-hour blocks in every day. You'll get another crack at it tomorrow.'

'Asshole,' Grayson muttered.

Thursday, April 7, 4.05 P.M.

'Louis versus Reba,' Clay said, driving away from the McCloud building. 'Better than reality TV. Family drama unfolding before our very eyes.'

In Clay's front seat, Daphne shook her head. 'That's an understatement.'

'He saw me,' Paige said, still a little disturbed. 'Louis, I mean.'

'I know,' Clay said. 'I saw that wink. I didn't like him.'

'Neither did I,' Paige said. 'He was at the estate that night Crystal was killed.'

'Isn't that interesting,' Daphne murmured. 'He's cutting Rex off, apparently.'

'With no lawyer to pull his ass out of the fire, Rex might be more forthcoming,' Paige said. 'Might make him willing to dish a little more on that family drama.'

'So exactly what did you get in there?' Daphne asked.

'Everything I wanted. I can't look at the pictures until I get back to Grayson's.' In all the confusion after JD's shooting, she'd left the laptop at the townhouse. 'I should have picked up a spare laptop when I went back to my apartment.'

'You were a little preoccupied,' Daphne said, which was also an understatement.

Paige had found, in the box where she'd stored it, the blood-stained *gi* she'd worn the night Thea died. She'd tried to throw it away last summer, but she hadn't been able to bring herself to do it. She'd put the old garment aside, donning the new *gi* she hadn't been able to bring herself to wear. When she'd tied her belt for the first time in nine months, she'd cried. And then Daphne hugged her and they'd both cried. And then they'd had to fix their makeup.

'It was a very emotional moment,' she agreed quietly. 'Clay, if you'll take me back to Grayson's, I can get to work.'

'And I can get my car,' Daphne said. 'And go home and change back into myself.'

'Getting there could take a little while.' Clay drummed his fingers on the steering wheel. 'We haven't even gone a block.'

'Paige, why don't you try to sl—' Daphne's word was abruptly changed to a tiny shriek by a knock at the back window.

Paige's fists, already clenched and raised, lowered and relaxed when she saw Grayson outside. She unlocked the car. 'You scared us to death.'

Grayson slid in and closed the door, waving to Joseph who sat in his car going the other direction looking very unhappy. 'I didn't mean to scare you. I saw you drive away and didn't want to lose you in traffic. I told Joseph to stop the car and I chased you.'

'Which explains why he looks so angry,' Paige said.

'Joseph was born angry,' Grayson said. 'I'll apologize to him

439

later.' He leaned back, resting his head on the seat, and it was then that Paige saw how pale he was.

And that he had blood on his sleeve. 'Are you hurt?' she asked, trying to stay calm.

'No. Not me. Anderson.'

Daphne turned around in the seat. 'What did he do?'

'He ate his gun.'

'Oh, my God.' Paige and Daphne said it together, horrified.

'Why?' Clay demanded tersely.

'He admitted to everything but paying for the hit last night. Said he worked with a broker on the case fixes, someone with Bond's firm. Didn't give a name, swore he didn't know. I told him he was being filmed, that he was going down for what he'd done. Next thing I knew, he pulled the gun and shot himself. He was dead before he hit the floor.'

'He could have shot you,' Paige said. She held him, pressing her forehead into his shoulder. He was warm and solid and breathing. But he might not have been.

He put his arm around her, pulled her close. 'He could have. But he didn't.' He kissed the top of her head. 'It's all right. I'm all right.'

'Did you believe him?' Clay asked. 'About not arranging the hit?'

'I don't know. He seemed genuinely shocked. But I don't know.'

'Meaning whoever really did it could still be out there,' Daphne said. 'Fucking hell.'

'Out there and working in Bond's old firm,' Grayson said. 'We're looking at everyone who works there. It's a big firm. Six partners and about twenty junior partners.'

'Plus interns, paralegals, office admin.' Paige closed her eyes, overwhelmed.

'You can eat a whole elephant one bite at a time,' Daphne said determinedly. 'We'll keep chewing till we get to the bottom of this.'

Thursday, April 7, 4.30 P.M.

Stevie let herself in her front door, bone-tired. In the grand scheme of bad days, this had been up there among the worst. Her current partner was in the hospital, put there by her old partner. Who'd been killing for more than five years.

And to top off the emotional rollercoaster, Clay Maynard had covered her as she'd chased Silas, waiting silently as she collected herself, wiping her tears away. She'd wanted to walk into his arms. She got the impression he wouldn't have minded.

The afternoon was waning and shadows filled her living room. The house was quiet. Too quiet. 'Izzy!' she called. 'I'm home.'

Stevie tossed her purse on the dining-room table. It skidded to a stop next to the pile of the day's mail. With a finger she spread it out, looking for anything not a bill.

I need to subscribe to a cheerful magazine. With flowers. Or better yet, lingerie. She winced, not needing to be a shrink to know where *that* came from. She opened her gun safe and disarmed, storing both her service weapon and her backup. She didn't leave guns lying around her house. Ever. She closed the safe and spun the combination dial.

'Izzy!' She heard a low murmur upstairs and jogged up. Cordelia's room was empty. The low murmur came from the TV in Izzy's room. No one was here.

Stevie's heart began to pound. She ran down the stairs, barging through the swinging door into the kitchen. Izzy sat at the table, hands flat on the tablecloth.

Her sister turned only her head, her eyes filled with raw panic, tears, and guilt. Then silently directed her gaze to the corner of the room.

Where Silas Dandridge sat in the shadows, a gun in his hand.

And Cordelia on his lap, her sobs muffled by the large male hand over her mouth.

The words came before Stevie could stop them. 'You hurt my child and I swear I will tear your fucking head off,' she said. 'Let her go.'

'I can't,' Silas said. 'You have to help me.'

'I'll help you go straight to hell.'

'Sit down, Stevie.' He pressed the gun to Cordelia's side and her baby's eyes widened in new terror. 'I don't want to hurt anyone. I need your help. He has Violet.'

'And I'm sorry to hear that,' Stevie said, forcing her voice to calm. Silas's eyes were wild. Crazy. Desperate. She thought of her guns, locked up. She thought of Grayson and Paige and Thorne. They'd be here. *But not soon enough.*

'I said, sit down, Stevie,' Silas said. 'Please.'

Needing to buy time, Stevie sat.

'Put your hands on the table where I can see them,' Silas said and Stevie complied.

'Who has Violet, Silas? I'll help you get her back.'

He shook his head. 'That's not what I need from you.'

'What do you need?' she asked, mouth dry. Resolutely she forced her gaze to Silas's face. If she looked at Cordelia, she'd fall apart. And then they'd all die.

'Put your phone on the table and slide it to me. I will text Grayson with an address. When he answers, you will drive me in your sister's car. I will sit behind you, your child on my lap and your sister on the floorboard. You will bind and gag them both. If you don't do it right or if anyone tries to call for help or run away, I'll shoot. Izzy will be first.'

'You're drawing Grayson and Paige out so you can kill them.'

His mouth twisted bitterly. 'Your phone, Stevie.'

'Silas, this is wrong. You know this is wrong.'

'I know,' he said. 'But that doesn't matter anymore.'

'You'd sacrifice my child for your own? Really?'

His jaw squared. 'In a heartbeat. Now slide your phone over here.'

Thursday, April 7, 4.45 P.M.

Paige put Peabody in the back of the black Escalade and waved up at the guy on Grayson's roof who held a high-powered rifle with a scope. 'Be careful up there.'

The police had placed a visible sentry above the roofline. It was more to calm the neighbors, Grayson thought, than to do any real surveillance. Silas wasn't coming back.

The house was cordoned off with yellow tape. A few CSU techs still lingered, along with the SWAT guy above and a uniformed officer below. The front door's side window had not yet been boarded up, but the officer assured him they would take care of it.

Grayson had been asked to leave his own house. There would be no two hours of Paige in his bed. There wouldn't even be a quickie against his bedroom door. *Shit.*

'You don't have to be so cheerful,' he grumbled. 'You'll encourage them to stay.'

Paige gave him a sympathetic peck on the lips. 'That they let us in so that you could change and I could get Peabody was as much as we should have expected.'

He got in the SUV and slammed his door hard. 'I know. I don't have to like it.'

'So where to?'

'Stevie's. We'll be early, but maybe we'll catch Izzy before her date and she can make us some dinner. She's a certified lunatic, but she can cook.'

'I want to thank her for the makeup.' Paige pulled the laptop from a new backpack.

'Where did you get the backpack?'

'From my apartment.'

'When you got your *gi*.' She still wore it over a vivid green T-shirt that came high enough to hide the Kevlar. 'It looks damn good on you.'

'Thanks. It feels good to wear it again. I did pack a few other things to wear later, but I was grabbing kind of haphazardly at my place because we were going to be late for Reba. I doubt anything I got will even match.'

'Then just don't wear anything,' he said and she chuckled, a welcome sound.

She plugged Joseph's camera-pen into her USB port. 'I've got names and addresses on every kid in the MAC program.'

'And the group photos?'

'Yep.' She was quiet as she worked. 'Huh. Each one of these group photos has a blonde girl with curly hair, just like Crystal Jones. How statistically probable is that?'

443

'A blonde every year isn't so strange. That she'd have curly hair is less likely.'

'I'm going to work on locating these people as adults while you drive.'

'Talk me through it,' he said and she looked at him, puzzled.

'Why?'

'I'm dead tired and don't want to fall asleep. And I like the sound of your voice.'

'Okay. I'll check blonde girls, then go back for the other kids. The 1984 blonde was Dawn Porter.' She tapped a few keys. 'There are more than one hundred Dawn Porters nationally. Sorting by birth year . . . yields three. Only one born in Maryland.'

'Where is she now?'

'Checking.' Paige went still. 'She's dead.'

'Of what? She would have been pretty young. Not even forty.'

'I'm pulling the death certs state-wide . . . Dawn Porter's cause of death was listed as suicide.' She looked over at him. 'Less than one month after Crystal Jones's murder.'

A sick shiver raced down his spine. 'Could be coincidence. How did she suicide?'

'Death cert doesn't say. We have to request the autopsy report from the ME.'

'Run a few more MAC kids. Let's see where this goes.'

'Kit Beechum, 1985.' After a few minutes she sighed. 'Suicide, three years ago.'

Grayson's stomach twisted. 'This isn't good.'

'No, it's not. Give me a second. I want to see if I can find any articles on her death. There weren't any on Dawn Porter.' She typed, then was quiet for several minutes.

'What?' he asked impatiently.

'Kit struggled with drugs for years, but she'd gotten clean. One day she OD'd. Her family and friends mourned. They say how hard she worked to get free. And she was a volunteer. Like Betsy Malone. Except Kit worked with victims of sexual assault.'

'Doesn't mean she was a victim herself,' he said.

'No, but it's not good. We're up to 1986. Justine Rains.' She was quiet longer this time. 'Justine was harder to find. She married and moved to Texas. Give me a minute to check the death certificates.' She slowly exhaled. 'Dammit.'

'She's dead too?'

'Yes, but there's no cause listed. Usually that means a natural cause.'

'She was younger than the first two. What's the death date?'

'Six months after Crystal's death,' she said. 'Let me check the newspaper archives for an obit. I feel terrible, but I hope it was cancer. Or she was struck by lightning. Anything that somebody else didn't cause.'

He waited, his heart beating in his throat. 'Well?'

'Justine died in a car accident.'

'That's good, right? She didn't commit suicide.'

'She was charged with DUI.'

'Please say booze,' he murmured.

'Barbiturates. This is a story on the investigation, not an obit. Her husband denied that she abused drugs.' Her voice faltered. 'Especially since their child was in the car.'

'No. Not the kid, too.'

'Yes. He was only six. The investigators discovered that she'd abused narcotics in her late teens. Her friends said she'd been "plagued by personal demons", but never discussed it. Her death was ruled accidental, but the report says the wreck was caused by Justine's drug use.' She made a distressed sound. 'She hit another car, two teens on their way to the mall. They died too. Here's a second article, following up.'

Again she made the distressed sound. 'This gets worse. Justine's husband was being sued by the families of the two dead teenagers. He shot himself. Fatally.'

The image of Charlie Anderson hit him hard. 'Go on to year four. 1987.'

445

Thursday, April 7, 5.30 P.M.

By the time Grayson stopped in front of Stevie's house, Paige was numb. He turned off the ignition and they sat in silence.

'Eight women,' she whispered. 'All dead. Six with the same drug.'

The other two had died of natural causes. One of cancer and one in a fatal car crash when she was fifteen, several years before Crystal's death. The barbiturate deaths started with Crystal Jones's murder.

'And we still have eight years to cover,' he said.

'Seven, actually. We already know Crystal Jones is dead. Why didn't anyone see this?' she demanded, anger bubbling. 'Make the damn connection?'

'They're stretched over the last five years, honey. All over the state.'

'And two in other states. So?'

'They were MAC kids when they were twelve years old. I was a Boy Scout when I was twelve. Nobody would connect me with kids in my troop if something like this were to happen. And it doesn't look like these kids even knew each other back then. That they'd connect with each other as adults . . . It was a perfect setup.'

'We need to finish this,' she said forcefully. 'Find the others.'

'Not here.' He looked around them. 'We can't sit out in the open like this. Let's get inside. You can finish searching and I'll call Lucy Trask and ask for the autopsy reports.'

Paige swung her backpack over one shoulder. 'Grayson, Rex McCloud may have been at the estate the night Crystal was killed, but he wasn't even born when the MAC program started. Whatever happened to these girls, Rex wasn't involved.'

'I know. I don't know what to think about Rex anymore. We'll worry about it inside.'

She got out, snapped Peabody's leash to his collar, then frowned at the darkened house. 'It looks like no one's home. We are early. Maybe Stevie isn't back yet.'

Grayson stopped, suddenly tensing. 'Stevie's car is here and so is the minivan, so Izzy's still here, too. I want to check around the house before we go in.'

'Fine. I'll go around right, you take the left.'

He looked like he wanted to argue, but she didn't give him a chance. She set out with Peabody, leaving Grayson to follow or go the other way. He went the other way.

There was a motorcycle parked at the back of the house. The engine wasn't cold.

Grayson came around the other side and she pointed to the motorcycle. He shook his head. 'Not hers,' he mouthed. He pointed to the back door. A pane of glass was broken. Paige sidled up to the kitchen window.

Shit. Stevie sat at the table, her face deathly pale, her hands flat on the tablecloth. Another pair of female flattened hands could be seen at the end of the table. And barely visible to the left was a man's large shoe on a foot that bobbed nervously.

Paige backed up against the house. 'Silas,' she mouthed.

Grayson peered in the window from his side, then briefly closed his eyes. 'He has Cordelia,' he mouthed back. He pulled out his phone and began to text.

I'll take front and call 911, Paige read. *Only confront if tries to leave. Yes?*

She met his eyes. Nodded. Texted back. *Don't die.*

One side of his mouth lifted grimly as he read it. Then he was gone and she and Peabody stood alone. Paige let the backpack slide silently to the ground, then reached behind her back for her .357, flicked off the safety. And waited.

Thursday, April 7, 5.30 P.M.

Silas glanced at Stevie's phone, willing Smith to answer. He'd texted the prosecutor an hour ago. Why wasn't Smith answering? He'd texted the right number. It had come from Stevie's contact list and was the same number he'd called the night before.

He checked Stevie's call log and frowned. There had been no

calls to Grayson all day. With everything that had happened, that wasn't likely. It hit him and he snarled.

'He got a new phone. A new number.' He lurched to his feet, dragging Cordelia with him. 'Didn't he?' Stevie flinched, giving Silas his answer. 'Goddammit. You lied to me.'

He ran to the front, tightening his grip on Cordelia. He grabbed car keys from the table, opened the door. And stopped in his tracks.

Grayson Smith stood in his path, the barrel of his gun pointed straight at Silas's head. 'Let her go, Silas. Or I'll blow your head off.'

Silas lifted the child, then realized she wasn't big enough to shield him.

A knife cut into his neck. 'Let her go,' Stevie said, her voice cold and deadly.

Silas tossed Cordelia at Smith, then spun, grabbing Stevie's wrist. He'd known her eyes would follow her child and not him, giving him the opportunity he needed. He squeezed hard, bending her wrist back until the knife fell to the floor.

Silas shoved his gun into her temple, clamped his arm across her throat. Cordelia was screaming. Grayson swept her into his arms, turning so that he protected the child with his body. He backed down the steps, his eyes fixed on the gun in Silas's hand.

'Run,' Stevie gritted out. 'Dammit, get her out of here.'

Grayson took off at a sprint, disappearing around the house, and too late Silas realized what he'd done. *It was my chance. I could have shot him. I missed my chance.*

But reflex had taken over and he'd done the unforgivable. *I protected my own skin.*

It wasn't too late. It couldn't be too late. *Go. Move. Find him. Finish this.*

Grayson held Cordelia close to his body as he ran away from the house. She was hysterical, clutching and clawing at him. 'Sshh, it's all right. You're all right.' No, she wasn't. Stevie's child might never be all right again.

Izzy appeared, stumbling around the corner. She'd escaped through the back door.

Paige. Where was she? *In the house*. Without a doubt Paige was in that house.

Izzy was crying. 'He's got her. Stevie's still in there.'

'Go to the neighbor's. I called 911.' Grayson peeled the child's arms from around his neck. 'Go with Aunt Izzy. I'll take care of your mommy. Run, Izzy.'

Izzy took Cordelia and ran next door, banged on the door and was pulled inside.

Grayson drew a breath, getting his bearings. He could hear sirens in the distance. He ran to the front, gun in his hand. Silas was pushing Stevie toward the front door, his arm pressed across Stevie's throat, his gun still to her head.

When Stevie saw Grayson, her body sagged, her eyes filling with tears. 'Cordelia?'

'She's okay, Stevie,' Grayson said, approaching slowly. 'She's not hurt.'

'Drop the gun, Grayson, or I'll kill her,' Silas said quietly. 'I have nothing to lose.'

For a moment Grayson stood there breathing hard, considering what to do.

'You're a good shot,' Silas said. 'I'm faster. You know that. I don't want to hurt her.'

Grayson crouched, placing the gun on Stevie's front step.

'Back away,' Silas said. 'Now.'

Grayson took a step back, saw the change in Silas's eyes a second before the man moved. Silas shoved Stevie away so hard she fell and went still. He raised his gun.

To my head. Grayson raised his hands. 'Don't shoot me, Silas. Let me help you.'

'I'm sorry,' Silas said. 'I'm truly sorry.'

Then Silas pitched forward, his gun dropping harmlessly to the floor. Paige stood behind him, holding his hand firmly in her grip, staring expressionlessly at the agony on his face. She shoved him to the floor face-down, bending his arm behind him, falling so that her knee gouged his kidney.

Silas struggled wildly. 'Let me go.' He bucked viciously, throwing

Paige off him. Paige hit the wall and slid to the floor, dazed.

Grayson leaped, pinning Silas to the floor when he tried to rise, holding him down. 'Silas, stop this. It's over. You can't get your daughter back this way.'

But Silas didn't listen, kept fighting like a wild animal. *Where are the fucking cops?*

Silas twisted, grabbing Grayson's throat, digging his fingers into his windpipe. Gagging, Grayson swung, his fist connecting solidly with Silas's jaw, but the man didn't even flinch. Grayson hit him again and the man's fingers loosened, followed by a cry of pain.

Peabody's teeth were sunk deep in Silas's thigh. Grayson twisted Silas's arms behind him, forcing his knee into the man's back. Glancing from the corner of his eye, Grayson spied his own gun, still on the front porch, out of reach.

'Peabody, hold,' Paige said calmly from behind them. 'I've got a gun pointed at your head, Silas,' she added and Grayson let out a harsh breath. 'I will use it.'

Silas stilled. 'Call off the dog,' he demanded hoarsely.

'Not yet,' Paige said. 'Stevie, you okay over there?'

'Yeah,' Stevie answered, breathless. She approached, pausing to pick up the gun Silas had dropped, unhooking the cuffs from her belt. 'Release the dog, Paige.'

'Peabody, release,' Paige said. Peabody obeyed, sitting at Paige's side, alert. Paige didn't move a muscle, her gun still trained on Silas's head.

Grayson held Silas's wrists with one hand, the back of his neck with the other.

Stevie snapped the cuffs on Silas's left wrist, none too gently. 'Who has Violet?'

Outside, cars screeched to a halt, doors opening. At least three cars. Maybe more.

It was one of those moments that Grayson could see coming and couldn't stop. Stevie's brief glance from the corner of her eye toward the door. His own momentary distraction. And the sudden, subtle tensing of Silas's muscles.

'Stev—' Grayson got out half her name when Silas sprang with the force of a bull, surging to his knees. Grayson threw his body forward, his fist slamming into Silas's jaw a third time. Silas fell to his back, absorbing the blow, then rolled to his feet.

And Grayson froze. Silas leaned, his weight on his uninjured leg. From his left wrist dangled Stevie's cuffs. In his right hand he held a small, snub-nosed revolver.

Once again Grayson found himself staring into the barrel of Silas's gun, watching as Silas pulled the trigger. Then shots cracked the air. Plaster rained down on his head.

And Silas crumpled to the floor. His shirt bloomed red and there was a hole in his forehead. The eerie silence that followed was broken with, 'Police! Drop your weapons.'

Paige lowered her gun, staring in horror at the hole in Silas's head. *I shot his wrist. I swear to God I only shot his wrist.*

Grayson. He was okay. Stark relief bubbled up from her throat in a muted cry that had him turning to her. He met her eyes, his numb with shock.

'Oh, my God,' Stevie whispered. Her gun was still extended, still aimed at where Silas had stood. 'I killed him.'

'I said,' a female voice snarled, 'drop your weapons.'

The words came from the doorway, where Detectives Morton and Bashears stood in full tactical gear, their weapons drawn and pointed at them.

Paige slowly crouched, putting her gun on the floor.

'You too, Stevie,' Morton snapped.

Stevie didn't move. She was frozen in place on her knees. Staring at Silas.

'Stevie,' Grayson said quietly, calmly. He reached for her gun, placing it on the floor. Holding her hands. But she didn't look at him. Didn't look at any of them. She couldn't take her eyes off her dead ex-partner.

'He was going to kill you,' Stevie whispered. 'He wasn't going to give up.'

'I know,' Grayson murmured. 'But he didn't kill me.'

'He was going to kill Cordelia. And Izzy, too.' Her face ashen, Stevie scrambled to her feet. 'I have to find Cordelia.'

'Where's the child?' Bashears asked tensely.

'Next door,' Grayson said, rising also. 'With Stevie's sister. We got them out.'

Stevie rushed to the front door, but Bashears caught her, holding her by the shoulders. 'Stevie, wait,' he said. He and Morton moved into the room followed by four uniformed officers and Peabody came to all four feet, a low growl in his throat.

'Restrain your dog,' Morton snapped. 'Or I'll shoot him.'

And you'd be next, Paige thought viciously but bit her tongue. 'Peabody, down,' she said and Peabody obeyed. 'His leash is in the kitchen.'

'Get it for her,' Bashears said to one of the uniforms. 'Paige, stay where you are.' But his tone was not unkind, so she complied.

Morton knelt by Silas, pressed her fingers to his throat. 'Dead.'

Bashears began checking Stevie for injuries. 'Are you hurt anywhere?'

'Her wrist,' Paige said. 'Silas twisted it hard to disarm her.' She pointed at the butcher knife on the floor. 'He had her daughter.'

'Tried to use both of them as human shields,' Grayson added with contempt.

Bashears cast a dirty look at Silas's body. 'Medics are outside. Anyone else hurt?'

'Just Silas,' Grayson muttered. 'Thank God.'

The officer returned with Peabody's leash and Paige clipped it into place. Having acceptably restrained Peabody, she turned her eyes back to Silas Dandridge. There was blood on his arm, darkest at his wrist. *Where I shot him*. Relief had her shuddering out a harsh breath. *I didn't kill him*. More blood spread on his white shirt.

Silas had been shot in the torso too. *I shot once. Stevie shot once. Silas's shot went wild, hitting the ceiling, and Grayson didn't have time to get his gun. So who shot him in the head?* 'Three shots,' Paige said to Bashears. 'Torso, wrist, head.'

Stevie seemed to refocus. She looked at Silas's body. 'I shot his chest.'

'I shot his wrist. Who shot the third bullet?' Paige asked. 'The head shot?'

'I did,' Morton said. 'We're clearing the room. This is a crime scene.'

Paige's stomach rolled queasily. Morton should have aimed to stop Silas, not kill him. She must have seen Silas waving his gun and made a quick decision.

Quick, but permanent. Silas was dead and only he knew who had Violet.

Silas had framed Ramon. Hadn't he? But Morton had been primary on Ramon's murder investigation. She glanced at Grayson, saw him watching Morton as well.

Why would Morton deliberately kill Silas?

Just because Silas was guilty doesn't mean Morton isn't.

Paige was tempted to take a giant step back, out of the room, away from Morton. But she stood her ground. And hoped she was wrong, that Morton had simply thought to save them from Silas and nothing more.

'I'm going to see my daughter,' Stevie said, pulling away from Bashears. 'Then I'll answer whatever you want.'

'Wait,' Bashears said. 'We received notification from the Toronto PD an hour ago. Rose Dandridge was found in a hotel room. There had been a struggle and she'd been struck repeatedly in the head before being strangled. Violet was gone.'

Stevie swayed on her feet. 'Rose is dead?'

'No,' Bashears said. 'In a coma, though. We need to find Violet.'

Stevie blanched. 'Yes, we do.'

'Then tell us what happened. Then you can go to Cordelia. I promise.'

'He was here when I got home. He had Cordelia on his lap and Izzy was at the table. He texted Grayson from my phone, to have them meet "me". He was going to kill Grayson and Paige so that he could get Violet back. He was working for someone who wanted them dead. I knew Grayson was using a different number, that the text wouldn't reach him. I was buying time.'

'So how did you two come to be here?' Morton asked Grayson.

'We'd arranged to meet for dinner,' Grayson said. 'My house is a crime scene.'

Grayson was lying, Paige thought. He didn't mention Anderson's case fixing or the broker he'd claimed worked in Bond's law firm. Or that Thomas Thorne was supposed to have joined them. *Because Grayson doesn't trust Bashears and Morton either.*

'So,' Bashears prompted, 'Silas had Cordelia and then what?'

'Grayson went around front,' Paige said. 'And I opened the back door and got Izzy out, told her to run for safety and to call for help. Stevie had already grabbed the knife and gone after Silas.' She recited the rest of the events. 'And then you showed up.'

'And now I'm going,' Stevie stated, giving Bashears a warning glare.

Bashears held up a hand. 'Who has Violet?'

'He never said,' Stevie replied over her shoulder as she hurried through the front door.

Bashears pointed to two of the uniforms. 'Walk her to the neighbor's. One stay with her, the other bring back the sister. Her name is Izzy. Thanks.'

Paige thought about her backpack, hoping Izzy had calmed enough to remember that Paige had told her to grab it when Paige pulled Izzy from the kitchen. To keep it safe and not to let the cops have it. *Especially Morton. Just in case.*

'Holy hell.' Hyatt burst into the house. 'What happened here?' He stared hard at everyone in the group, and then started asking all the questions again.

Paige wondered when they'd be allowed to go. *I need to get my backpack back from Izzy. I need to finish looking up all the MAC girls.*

'We'll need to confiscate your weapons,' Bashears said when all of Hyatt's questions were answered. 'For ballistics.'

'I understand,' Paige said. It didn't matter. She had others.

Grayson just nodded. 'You've taken our statements. When can we leave?'

'Any time, Counselor,' Hyatt said. 'You're free to go. You, too, Miss Holden. But as you fired your weapon, we will ask that you be available for follow-up interviews.'

'Of course,' Paige said. 'Don't leave town, right?'

Hyatt inclined his bald head. 'Essentially. Where will you two be tonight?'

'My house,' Grayson said. 'Assuming we're allowed back in.'

'CSU is almost done with your place,' Hyatt told them, then looked at Paige. 'Miss Holden, that was a nice shot, to Dandridge's wrist.'

Her eyes narrowed, unsure if his compliment was sincere. 'Thanks. I didn't want to kill him. I just didn't want him killing us. And I thought you'd want information from him.'

Hyatt scowled at the body then looked over his shoulder. 'Too late for that now.'

Paige thought he'd directed that toward Detective Morton, but she couldn't be sure.

'What are you going to do about finding Violet?' Grayson asked.

'Now that Dandridge is no longer a threat, finding his child is our highest priority.' Hyatt looked at Bashears. 'You go back to Silas's house. There has to be something there, something that connects him to whoever took his kid. Find it. We'll bring in the Feds, coordinate the effort with the Canadians.'

'What about the sister?' Morton said. 'We need to interview her.'

'I'll do it,' Hyatt said. 'Bashears goes to Dandridge's residence. Detective Morton, please wait with the officers outside until a supervisor arrives to escort you to the precinct, where you will complete the necessary reports for discharging your firearm. In adherence to policy,' he added.

Morton's jaw tightened. 'Yes, sir.' She marched out of Stevie's house without a look back.

Paige knew that cops were taken out of rotation for a short period of time when they used deadly force, so Hyatt's command was not unexpected. Paige watched the lieutenant's face for any indication that he thought Morton had acted inappropriately in Silas's death, but saw no sign.

When Morton and Bashears were gone, Hyatt crouched by Silas's body, patted his pockets, and pulled out two cell phones. One was a stripped model, the other a smartphone. Hyatt flipped open the stripped phone. 'The log shows him calling your old cell-phone number, Grayson. Last night.'

'The warning call,' Grayson said. 'Just before the bomb went off.'

'There's a call on the other phone from a blocked number at eleven thirty-two this morning.'

'Two and a half hours before he shot JD Fitzpatrick,' Paige said.

'Also,' Hyatt said, 'within the window the Toronto PD gave for the assault of Rose. This is likely the call from whoever kidnapped Violet, telling Silas to kill you.' He gazed at the phone and let out a quiet breath. 'A picture of Rose. She looks dead.' He studied Silas's body with a mixture of pity and anger. 'A lot of men would have snapped.'

A hoarse cry behind them had everyone turning to the front door. Izzy stood there, her hand over her mouth, her eyes wide with horror. 'Oh, my God.'

Grayson put his arm around Izzy's shoulders, standing so that he blocked her view of Silas's body. 'Didn't Stevie tell you that he was dead?'

'Yes.' Izzy gulped in air. 'But I've never seen a dead body before.'

Hyatt rose. 'Let's go into the kitchen. I need to get your statement.'

'Fine,' Izzy said shakily. She passed by Paige on her way to the kitchen. 'You and Grayson should check on Stevie before you leave.'

'I will,' Paige promised, understanding. Izzy had left her backpack with Stevie.

Izzy hugged Paige hard. 'Thank you,' she whispered. 'You two saved our lives.'

'Thanks for the makeup. We're even now.'

Izzy's chuckle was small and watery. She went to the kitchen, but turned back at the swinging doors, her brows knit. 'He said he had to kill you both by midnight.'

'When did he tell you this?' Hyatt asked.

'While we were waiting for Stevie to come home. He wasn't coherent there for a while. He kept muttering something about cherries. He kept blaming the cherries for everything. Said he'd sold his soul for the "damn cherry".'

'His daughter's name was Cherri,' Grayson told her. 'She died the day Violet was born. She was Violet's mother.'

Izzy blinked. 'I guess that explains it. He cursed a lot. He didn't like Grayson either. He kept muttering, "Damn lawyer. I'll kill him."' She looked at Grayson, troubled. 'He had plans for you. Sick plans.'

Paige, Grayson, and Hyatt exchanged glances.

'What kind of sick plans?' Grayson asked.

Izzy grimaced. 'Gutting, mutilation . . . Slicing off certain body parts and making you eat them. Cordelia was so frightened. I only hope she didn't understand most of what he said. He was sick. And so angry.'

'And he didn't say anything else? Did he call me by name?' Grayson pressed.

'No. He just called you "the damn lawyer".' Her eyes widened. 'Wait. He wasn't talking about you, was he? That makes sense, because later he told Stevie that if she cooperated, he'd make your death painless and fast.'

'What else did he say?' Hyatt asked urgently.

'Just that he was sorry, that he didn't want to hurt us. Then Stevie came and he got all businesslike.' Izzy swallowed hard. 'She asked if he'd really sacrifice her child for his and he said, "In a heartbeat." Stevie knew she couldn't reason with him.'

'So she held on and waited for us,' Grayson said quietly. 'Poor Stevie.'

'Yeah,' Izzy agreed. 'She knew you were coming, but I didn't.' She closed her eyes. 'I honestly thought he'd kill us. I thought we were dead. If you two hadn't come when you did . . . If you don't mind, I think I'll sit now.'

Hyatt held the kitchen door open for her, watching as she sat at the table, new tears streaming down her cheeks.

'We really are looking for a lawyer,' Hyatt said. 'Anderson wasn't lying about that, at least. Somewhere there's a lawyer pulling all the strings and he had Silas under his control. If the bankbook we found in Silas's house is any indication, Silas was his hired gun for years. Are you still meeting Thorne to get information on Bob Bond's old firm?'

'He was supposed to come here,' Grayson answered. 'I'll call him, arrange another meeting place. If you don't need us anymore, we'll check on Stevie and go home.'

Hyatt gave him a scrutinizing look. 'Where will you really be?' he asked.

Grayson didn't seem surprised. 'My brother's house. Joseph Carter.'

'Fine. I'll need your written statements, but I can collect them later. Call me when you get anything on the lawyer. It could be our best lead to finding Silas's daughter.'

'I will call you the moment we know something,' Grayson promised. 'Paige? Let's go.'

Twenty-three

Thursday, April 7, 7.00 P.M.

'That was hard,' Paige said as they drove away, Peabody in the backseat.

'I know,' Grayson said. They'd found Stevie and Cordelia at the neighbor's kitchen table, Stevie rocking as Cordelia clutched her. Stevie's face was blotchy, eyes swollen.

She'd broken down again when they'd entered the neighbor's kitchen and Grayson had led her to another room, so they could grieve together for the Silas they thought they'd known.

Paige and Peabody had stayed with Cordelia, who started to cry again when her mother did. 'She petted Peabody's head like I do when I'm stressed,' Paige murmured.

'It's a wonder your dog has any hair left on his head,' Grayson said sadly. 'I haven't seen Stevie cry like that since Paul died.' The image of her stricken face made him remember a different day, when he was Cordelia's age. 'That's how my mother looked, after she'd hit that victim's father with the baseball bat.' *When he would have killed me.* 'It's been almost thirty years and I can't forget her face.'

Paige looked over her shoulder. 'Speaking of your mother . . . The news crew outside Stevie's house filmed us leaving. We'll be top of the hour again soon and you don't want her to hear about another near miss from Phin Radcliffe. You should call her.'

'You're right.' He handed Paige his cell, gave her his mother's number. 'Can you dial?' His mother answered on the first ring. 'I'm all right,' he said before she could say any more. 'I'm alive, no scratches. My underwear's even still clean.'

459

His mother laughed, but there was a sob mixed in. 'I know,' she said. 'I saw you and Paige leaving Stevie's house. You're on the news again. I'm so glad that man is dead. Both men. I saw that your boss, that horrid little man, shot himself.'

'He did.'

'Then it's over.'

It wasn't over, not by a long shot. But he'd be damned before he told her that. She'd just worry more. 'There are still a few loose ends to be tied.'

'Well, tie them fast. Holly's going to the center and asked if Paige is still coming.'

'Can't she wait till next week to go? We can't get there tonight and I worry about those guys who are bothering her.'

'I'm going with her tonight,' his mother said. 'I'll watch over her.'

Grayson frowned. 'Well, if you're with her, I guess it's okay.'

'I'll carry a trusty briefcase,' she said dryly. 'Love you, son.'

'I love you too.' He hung up, glanced over at Paige, found her smiling. 'What?'

'I like that you tell your mother you love her. In all this mess, it's a nice respite.'

'Thank you. And thank you for saving my life in there, disarming Silas.'

'Then I guess we're even, too.'

'No, because I saved your life twice. In the garage and last night.'

Her smile dimmed. 'Let's just hope we're never able to make it even then. When all those shots were fired, I thought he'd gotten one into you.'

'Me, too,' he said, as she brought his hand to her cheek and held it there. It felt right. 'I'm glad CSU wouldn't let us stay in my house. We would have been too late. Stevie wouldn't have cooperated with him and he'd have killed them all.'

'I don't know,' she said. 'Stevie seems like a rock, but even she can't say what she'd have done if it had gone on further. She didn't cooperate with him at first because she knew we were coming. She was stalling for time.'

'In that case, I'm glad she didn't have to make the choice.'

'Me too.' Paige released his hand. 'Hyatt was angry at Detective Morton.'

'I know,' he said with a frown. 'Morton didn't have to aim for Silas's head.'

'It's possible that she saw Silas pointing a gun at you and made a split-second decision,' she said slowly. 'But . . .'

'But you're wondering about her again,' Grayson said. 'So am I.'

'Yeah. I mean, Silas was working for this lawyer brokering all these deals. It makes sense that he was the one to frame Ramon, right? But there's something about Morton that I don't trust. Maybe it's because I don't like her. I don't know.'

'I think Hyatt was suspicious too. It makes me wonder what IA's dug up that they're not telling us.'

'Exactly. Although we do have our own secrets. I almost told Hyatt about the MAC kids, but I just couldn't.'

'Why not?'

'I don't know. I think part of me wanted to finish the investigation myself, you know, to have my ducks in a row. But the other part of me doesn't trust Hyatt either.' She leaned forward to retrieve the laptop from her backpack, then glanced over at him. 'Are we really staying with Joseph tonight?'

'No. We'll stay at my mother's. She can stay in the main house with Jack and Katherine. Joseph has the property locked down tighter than Fort Knox.'

'Will she mind Peabody coming with us?'

'When she hears the dog bit Silas, she'll probably go out and buy him a bone.'

'He did good today. And I'd have shot that bitch Morton myself if she'd hurt him.'

'I'd have helped you.' His cell began to buzz. 'I don't recognize this number.'

'The last time that happened, it was very bad.'

That was an understatement. 'This is Smith,' he answered cautiously.

'This is Thomas Thorne. I'm a block away from Stevie's house

461

and there are cops all over the damn place. What the hell's going on?'

'Silas Dandridge held Stevie, her daughter and her sister hostage. He's dead.'

Thorne hissed a curse. 'Did Stevie have to do it?'

'No. She shot him, but the kill shot was done by one of the other cops. She's too rattled to meet us. Is there somewhere else we can talk?'

'Come to my club, Sheidalin. My office is soundproofed. Nobody will bother us.'

'Did you get any information on Bob Bond's old law firm?'

'If I did, would you care how I got it?'

'Of course. But I'm getting very good at forgetting things. Who are you, again?'

Thorne laughed, a big booming sound. 'Fine. I got the list of current employees, along with personnel files and photos. Meet me at Sheidalin and we'll sort through it.'

'Thanks.' Grayson hung up and did a U-turn at the next light. 'We're going clubbing.'

Paige looked down at her *gi*. 'I'll look like I'm made up for Halloween.'

'Based on what I've heard about this place, you'll fit right in.' He pointed to the laptop. 'You left off at 1991. Where are the rest of the women who were MAC girls?'

'Susan McFarland, 1991.' A few minutes later she sighed. 'Dead. Suicide.'

'I'll call Lucy Trask,' he said. 'You can give her the names of the autopsy reports we need so far. At least she can get started. Keep going. There are only six left.'

Thursday, April 7, 7.00 P.M.

Silas was dead. Goddammit.

He stood looking down at Violet Dandridge, still breathing evenly, still in a deep sleep. He could kill her now but he had no idea what Silas had told the cops before he was shot. If Silas had named names . . . *they'll come after me. They could be on their way already. I'll need a trade.* A seven-year-old girl would make a good trade.

If it came to that, of course. If Silas had said nothing, there was nothing to fear.

He hit speed-dial nine on his cell. He'd have to change the speed-dial settings. He no longer needed Silas, Roscoe 'Jesse' James, or Harlan Kapansky. Speed-dial nine could move up. Maybe even become speed-dial one.

'What?'

'We need to work on your telephone etiquette skills,' he murmured. 'What did Silas say before he died?'

'Nothing.'

'Good to know.' Very good. Now his main concern was that state's attorney and his PI who continued to dig up what was best left buried.

'Except that someone had taken his kid. Was it you?'

He glanced down at Violet. 'Not your business. I have an assignment for you.'

There was hesitation. 'I did what you wanted.'

'And you'll continue to do so. That's how this works. Silas had his Violet. You have your Christopher. He's what . . . twelve by now? Is he still walking with crutches? Sad, sad thing, that hit-and-run,' he said mockingly. 'Did they ever catch who did it?'

The swallow was audible. The tone impotent fury. 'What do you want me to do?'

'I'm so glad we understand each other. People with families are so predictable, I've found. Grayson has a mother. Call me when you have her in your sights.'

Thursday, April 7, 7.45 P.M.

'One,' Paige said quietly. 'One is still alive. Out of sixteen years. Sixteen girls.'

They'd parked in front of Thorne's club, where they sat, stunned. 'Who's still alive?' Grayson asked.

'Her name is Adele Shaffer, maiden name was Masterson. She

463

married Darren Shaffer six years ago and they have a little girl, Allison. Darren had been working for an overseas company until last year when they moved back. Adele is the only one left.'

'Let's get the law firm's personnel list from Thorne and then we'll find her. Warn her. And find out what the hell happened when she was twelve.'

'What about Peabody?' Paige asked when they got out of the car.

'Do sharp noises bother him? Like cracking whips?'

She swung her backpack to her shoulder, her eyes wide. 'Not that I know of.'

'Then he'll be fine.' He snapped Peabody's leash on his collar. 'Let's go.'

The club was dark, the music loud, and the bouncer was freaking enormous. His nametag said *Ming*. He let them in, not giving her *gi* or Peabody a second glance.

'I was told to expect you,' Ming said. 'Thorne's office is the first door on the right.'

The office door opened and Paige found herself craning her neck to look up. Thomas Thorne was bigger than the bouncer. He had to be six-six and exuded a dangerous sexuality. It was a wonder he didn't have a dozen women pawing him.

There was only one woman with him and she wasn't doing any pawing. She was typing into a computer and scowling at the screen.

'I'm Thomas Thorne,' he said, shaking Paige's hand. 'This is my business partner, Gwyn Weaver. Gwyn, State's Attorney Grayson Smith and his PI, Paige Holden.'

Gwyn was a tiny brunette who would have been beautiful without the angry frown. 'Nice to meet you. Nicer if you could figure out what's wrong with my spreadsheet.'

'Take a walk,' Thorne told her. 'You always find the glitch after you've had a walk.'

Gwyn rolled her eyes. 'Which is Thorne's way of telling me to get lost.' She left the office, her scowl still firmly locked in place. Paige wondered if she scowled all the time.

Thorne closed the door behind her. 'Sorry about that. Gwyn's not been herself for a while.' He pointed to the small table in the corner. 'Let's sit.'

'You have the personnel lists from Bond's law firm?' Grayson asked.

'I said I did.' Thorne regarded Grayson with some suspicion. 'I have to say, though, I was surprised when Stevie approached me.'

'How so?' Grayson asked. The two men, normally on opposite sides of the legal table, assessed one another. Paige wanted to snap at them to hurry up, but realized it wasn't easy for Grayson to trust a defense attorney so she swallowed her impatience.

'I wasn't all that surprised to hear there was case fixing in the prosecutor's office,' Thorne said. 'I've wondered a few times, but never had any proof. And before you ask, I never have, never will fix a case or use illegal means to defend a client.'

'I wouldn't be here if I thought you would. So what did surprise you?'

'Well, that Bond's firm is suspected of involvement, for one. They're an old firm with an excellent reputation. But mostly I was surprised to hear that it was you who wanted the information, Smith. I expected you to insist on a subpoena.'

Grayson flushed, but didn't look away. 'I'm within my rights to request a list of personnel with employment dates, but people are dying,' he said harshly. 'We can't afford to delay and we can't afford for this firm to know we're looking at them. Not yet. Stevie and I needed someone that an employee inside a defense firm would trust enough to give personnel files to. We figured they'd trust another defense attorney. We needed someone we could trust not to share that we'd asked for the information to begin with. Stevie trusts you, so I will too. For now. For this.'

This seemed to satisfy Thorne, who slid a folder across the table. 'These are current employees of Bob Bond's firm who also worked there at the time of Crystal Jones's murder, sorted by gender. Stevie said you were looking for a man.'

The folder was full of employees' personnel records and photos, all male.

'Jackpot,' Paige murmured. 'Do you know any of these guys, Thorne?'

'One of the partners,' he said. 'He's arrogant, but a crook, fixing cases? I wouldn't have thought so. I know several of the junior partners. None of them stand out as criminal.'

Paige began with the photos. Including partners, junior partners, clerks, paralegals, and office administrators, there were dozens. 'We figure the guy who paid Sandoval was about six feet,' she said. 'That narrows the list of employees considerably.'

'The man who paid Sandoval might not be the lawyer we're looking for,' Grayson cautioned. 'Anderson said he was probably one of Bond's flunkies.'

'And maybe he was,' Paige said, not looking up from the photos. 'But he was important enough to get Sandoval killed for keeping his picture and Elena killed for stealing it, which makes me doubt he was a flunky.'

'You could be right,' Grayson said. 'It's certainly a place to start.' They compared the builds of the lawyers to those of the man in the Sandoval photo, whittling the pack down to ten. 'I wish the photo included their hands,' he said. 'The guy who paid off Sandoval got regular manicures.'

'And wore a pinky ring,' Paige added. 'At least back then. We've got ten possibles here. We can run with ten, get backgrounds.'

'I'll go back to my source inside the firm, find out about these ten,' Thorne said. 'But it's possible that whoever brokered the court deals doesn't work there anymore.'

'We know.' Paige thought of Violet. The lawyer who'd brokered all the deals between Anderson and Bob Bond had compelled Silas to kill for him many times. *To kill us because we're too close.* Now the lawyer had Violet. *Violet could already be dead.* 'We'll check out the ten and if we come up with nothing, we'll look at the others who work for the firm.'

The office door opened and a woman came in. Paige found herself openly staring. The woman didn't wear tailored slacks and an elegant silk blouse as Gwyn had. Her dress, what there was of it, was black leather. Her blue eyes were heavily outlined in black and her strawberry-blond hair was streaked with purple.

Grayson blinked. 'Lucy? I'd heard about this place, but didn't expect you to be here. Or to look like that.'

'You're the ME?' Paige asked incredulously. 'Lucy Trask?'

The woman nodded. 'That would be me. You must be Paige. I'm so glad to—'

'Why are you here?' Thorne interrupted. 'Why aren't you with JD at the hospital?'

'Because JD made me leave. Said there were too many germs in the hospital and it's not good for the—' Lucy stopped abruptly and rolled her eyes when Thorne grinned.

'Yes?' the big man asked. 'Anything you'd like to share with the class?'

'It's supposed to be a secret,' Lucy grumbled, her cheeks heating.

Grayson bit back a smile. 'We won't tell anyone.'

'Not a word,' Paige promised for the second time that day.

'I make no such promise,' Thorne declared, then sobered. 'How is JD?'

'Asleep. He was trying to be all macho and wouldn't take the pain pill the nurse kept telling him to take. I promised to leave for a few germ-free hours if he'd take the damn pill, so he finally did. It's farther to go home than come here, so I'll hang here for a few hours, then I'll sneak back in and sit with him.'

She turned to Paige with a grateful smile. 'As I was *saying*, I'm so glad you're here. I wanted to thank you in person. JD told me how you tended him this afternoon. He gave me a message for you. If it's inappropriate, blame him, not me. He told me to tell you, "You show me yours and I'll show you mine."'

Paige smiled. 'He means scars. I've got one on my shoulder. I'm glad he's okay.'

'Me too,' Lucy said fervently. 'He's more worried about Stevie.'

'She'll be okay,' Grayson said. 'Eventually.' He sighed. 'I hope. Did you have a chance to check those autopsy records for us?'

'I did.' Lucy opened her leather handbag and pulled out a CD. 'Here are the reports. The hospital has wi-fi so I was able to download

467

them while I was sitting with JD in his room. All your suicides tested positive for barbiturates. Three were found hanged. The rest were ruled intentional overdoses.'

'Hanged like Sandoval?' Grayson asked.

'No. Sandoval had been repeatedly denied oxygen. These women weren't tortured in any way. Just drugged and hanged.'

Thorne frowned. 'Is it possible that any of them drugged and hung themselves?'

'Possible, but unlikely. They were probably unconscious before they were hung, or at least drugged enough to offer no resistance. I can't see the victims being able to step on a stool and get the noose around their own necks.'

'Why didn't this come up before?' Paige asked. 'Why did no one notice?'

'No one was looking for patterns, but barbiturates at that level should have raised flags.' Lucy sighed. 'The autopsies were done by the same doctor, who died last year.'

'Of course she did,' Paige muttered.

'She quit the ME's office, moved to New Orleans and got a job waiting tables. A month later she didn't show up to work. They found her dead in her car, in her own garage. Carbon-monoxide poisoning. A week later. Nobody had missed her.'

'I remember when that happened,' Thorne said. 'You took off time for her funeral.'

'My boss and I went, out of respect. We were the only people there. It was so incredibly sad. No one knew why she'd killed herself, but we weren't all that surprised. She had always been darker than the rest of us, always preoccupied. We just thought she wasn't suited for ME work. Not everyone is.'

'Did she have barbiturates in her system too?' Grayson asked.

'Yes. At the time that fact didn't seem out of place. Lots of people swallow pills before they get in their cars like that.'

'I'll contact NOPD for the police report and we'll open an investigation,' Grayson said. 'If she received payments for looking the other way while she was here, we'll have another money trail. In the meantime, we have a few more records for you to check.'

Lucy sank onto the edge of the conference table. 'You can't be serious.'

'Unfortunately we are,' Paige said, handing her a list of the names.

'Did any of them die within the last year?' she asked.

'No.' Paige watched Lucy's shoulders slump in relief.

'At least we don't have any other doctors on the take. What the hell is this about?'

'I'd like to know, too,' Thorne rumbled. 'I thought we were looking for deal brokering in the SA's office.'

'We are,' Grayson said. 'The broker connects to a victim named Crystal Jones. The man accused of Crystal's murder was Ramon Muñoz.'

'His wife Elena was murdered two days ago,' Lucy said and Paige nodded.

'Elena and her mother-in-law hired me to prove Ramon wasn't guilty. Ramon was represented by Bob Bond who was brokering deals with Charlie Anderson. It was when we started digging into Bond and Anderson that we found they'd framed a number of people, just like Ramon. Anderson said that there was a mastermind who worked at Bond's firm and that's why we're here – to find out who that is.'

'So what happened to the dead women?' Lucy asked. 'How do they connect?'

Paige exhaled. 'Ramon was accused of killing a woman named Crystal Jones at a party given by Rex McCloud. Ramon was innocent, so we started looking at Rex.'

'Reasonable,' Thorne said. 'The McClouds could well afford to pay Bond to clear Rex's name. But what about the girls?'

'We found out,' Grayson said, 'that Crystal had participated in a charity program run by the McClouds, targeted at low-income twelve year olds from troubled homes all over the state. All the dead girls participated, from '84 until the program ended in '99.'

'Sixteen years of the program,' Paige said. 'And only one of those children is left. Most were killed after Crystal was murdered. All barbiturate-related deaths. We have reason to believe that Crystal went to the party the night of her murder to blackmail someone. We wondered what could have happened to a twelve-year-old girl that she could use as blackmail against a powerful family eight years later. Only one conclusion made sense.'

Thorne's face had darkened. 'Someone molested the girls at the McCloud estate.'

'Oh, no,' Lucy murmured, stunned. Tears filled her eyes. 'Twelve years old?'

'So how does Silas connect?' Thorne asked.

'One of the men who lied under oath in Ramon's trial kept evidence against the deal broker "mastermind". Proof he'd been paid for denying Ramon's alibi. Elena got hold of that evidence and was killed. The same day, the man who'd lied was murdered.'

'Sandoval,' Lucy said.

'Yes,' Grayson said. 'By Silas Dandridge, Stevie's partner before JD. He'd been working for this broker for a number of years. Paige and I started to get close to the truth about the McClouds, and Silas was told to kill us. When he didn't, the broker kidnapped his daughter. Now Silas is dead and nobody knows who has Violet.'

'Which was why we needed the law firm's personnel list tonight,' Paige finished. 'Violet Dandridge is running out of time. We've got ten names to run with. I'll start with background checks.'

Grayson shook his head. 'I promised Hyatt that I'd let him know when we came up with a list. He's bringing in the Feds to help find Violet. She could still be in Canada. The Feds have more manpower to sort these names. If the ten we narrowed it to don't pay out, they can expand their search faster than you can with your laptop.'

'You intend to hand these names over to the Feds?' Thorne said, brows lowered.

'They won't know where we got them,' Grayson promised. 'I've already forgotten.'

Thorne's jaw squared. 'She's how old? The little girl?'

'Seven,' Paige said, and watched a muscle twitch in Thorne's cheek.

'Then do it,' Thorne said.

'Thanks.' Grayson called Hyatt on his cell and gave him the ten names. When he hung up, he sighed. 'Bad news is that there is still no sign of Violet. Good news is that Rose Dandridge just woke up from her coma. They haven't told her about Silas and Violet yet. Plus they found another one of Silas's victims.'

'Who?' Paige asked.

'Remember the motorcycle that was outside of Stevie's back door? It belonged to a man who was found unconscious in the alley outside his house. Silas hit him, then stole his bike. Fortunately the man is stable.' Grayson sighed. 'What a mess.'

'Indeed,' Lucy said. 'Serial child molesters, murderers, case fixers, a cop gone bad, his kidnapped child, and a mastermind eliminating anyone who gets close to the truth. Makes my head spin.'

'Welcome to our world,' Grayson said wryly. 'Did you get a chance to look at the autopsy report of Crystal Jones? I'm hoping you see something the previous ME didn't.'

'I didn't actually, but I have my laptop with me. I'll review the Jones autopsy and pull the reports on the remaining women before I go back to JD at the hospital.'

Thorne was frowning. 'What if the man you're looking for isn't on that list? How will you find the missing child?'

Grayson blew out a breath. 'The broker was paid to frame Ramon for Crystal's murder,' he said. 'That means the broker knows who really killed her. Crystal went there to blackmail her molester.'

'Who killed her,' Lucy finished. 'Who do you think it was?'

Grayson shrugged. 'My first guess? Louis Delacorte, Rex McCloud's stepfather. He's the right age and was at the estate the night Crystal died. He lived at the estate during the years of the charity program and he had a history of violence. He fits the profile in the sense that he's overshadowed by his wife. Passive and needing to control someone. But it could have been any of the long-term employees.'

'We know it wasn't Rex,' Paige said. 'He was just a baby himself. The senator had a stroke a few years before her murder. He wouldn't have had the strength to kill her.'

'So now what?' Thorne asked.

Paige rubbed her temple. 'Adele Shaffer, the only one left. She can tell us what happened at the McCloud estate when she was twelve years old. She's the link to Crystal's killer, who knows the broker.'

'It always comes back to finding Crystal's killer,' Grayson said wearily. 'Do you have a current address for Adele?'

Paige nodded. 'I do.'

'Then let's pay her a visit.'

'Let me change my clothes first. Then we'll go. Thanks, Thorne, Lucy.'

'You two be careful,' Thorne said. 'Let us know if we can do anything else.'

Thursday, April 7, 8.40 P.M.

Grayson stopped the Escalade on the curb in front of the Shaffers' house, a little single family home just outside the city.

'It has a picket fence,' Paige murmured. 'A real picket fence.'

'I like it,' he said and she looked at him, surprised.

'What about your townhouse?'

'I like it, too,' he said. 'But this is homier.'

'Then why did you buy the townhouse and all that fancy furniture?'

'I didn't. Katherine Carter did. It was a gift when I graduated from law school.' He smiled at the memory. 'She cried when I got my diploma.'

'You're a lucky man,' Paige said quietly.

'I know. And grateful every day. But I like your furniture too. I like that your grandfather made it. It's got . . . roots. Roots are good. Let's go find Adele.'

Their knock was answered by a harried man holding a toddler on his hip. He had what looked like strained peas in his hair. 'Mr Shaffer?' Grayson asked.

'Yes. What do you want?'

'We'd like to speak to your wife, Adele.' *Bleach*, Grayson thought. The smell of it tickled his nose and made his eyes water. 'Is she home?'

'No,' Shaffer said with a scowl. 'She's gone.'

'Gone where, sir?' Paige asked.

'I don't know and I don't care. Who the hell are you two, anyway?'

'I'm Grayson Smith, with the state's attorney's office. This is my associate, Paige Holden. We need to find your wife. It's important. She could be in danger.'

'Of her own making. Excuse me, I have to finish feeding my daughter.'

'Wait,' Paige said, urgency in her tone. 'How long has Mrs Shaffer been gone?'

'She was gone when I got home from work today.' Shaffer frowned, as if Grayson's words had just sunk in. 'Why does the state's attorney want her? What has she done?'

'Nothing that we know of,' Grayson said. 'But something may have been done to her. She could be in real danger, Mr Shaffer. This isn't a joke.'

'Yeah, I know. Look, my wife's been having an affair. I threw her out.'

'Oh.' Grayson wasn't sure what to say.

'Mr Shaffer, why does your house smell like bleach?' Paige asked.

Shaffer's eyes narrowed. 'Her lover poisoned my dog, who got sick and now I can't get rid of the smell. Thus, the bleach, if you must know.'

Grayson stiffened. 'Your dog was poisoned?'

'Yeah. Her lover sent her poisoned chocolates.'

Betsy Malone had been sent chocolates. Now she was dead. 'Were they truffles?'

Shaffer looked taken aback. 'Yes. Why?'

'Mr Shaffer,' he asked, 'was your wife afraid of anyone?'

Shaffer stilled. 'Yes. She said someone was trying to kill her.'

'Did she say it was her lover?' Grayson pressed.

'No. She denied having an affair.' He swallowed. 'She wasn't lying, was she?'

'I don't think so, sir,' Grayson said.

'You haven't heard from your wife all day?' Paige asked. 'Is that normal?'

'No. I expected her to come home tonight. To see Allie.' Fear filled his eyes. 'What's going on here?'

'That's what we're trying to find out,' Grayson said grimly.

Thursday, April 7, 9.30 P.M.

Violet Dandridge was still asleep and small enough to be portable. Portable insurance was good to have. He checked his passports. All three of them. Depending on what happened next, he'd decide which nationality he'd be.

He looked again at his cell phone, at the 'breaking news' photograph that had hit him like a rock. *Adele Shaffer.* The police were looking for her as a 'person of interest'. They wouldn't be interested in Adele if Smith and Holden hadn't figured it out. They wouldn't have figured it out if Silas Dandridge had done his damn job.

It was just a matter of time before they found out Adele was dead. It was just a matter of time before someone figured out what the McClouds had done, if they hadn't already. He wanted to be far, far away when that happened.

Steve Pearson had the charter jet fueled up and ready to fly. *I'll go to Toronto, then on to Frankfurt.* He grimaced. He'd have to go coach. He'd be less recognizable. Eight hours in a coach seat would be torture. But necessary.

He planned to leave Violet in Toronto. By the time she was identified, woken up, and questioned, he'd be long gone. She'd never seen his face. Besides, killing a child would heat up the law enforcement and the public. He didn't want to risk that.

But there was still a chance that he could stop the investigation. Stop the trail that would lead to the McClouds. He needed to stop Smith and Holden, once and for damn all. He hit speed-dial nine.

'Do you have her?' he asked, not waiting for a hello.

'I know where she is.'

'When will you have her in your possession?' he asked coldly.

'People are starting to leave this place. She should come out soon. I'll call you.'

'You do that.' *I have a plane to catch.*

Thursday, April 7, 9.50 P.M.

'I hope Rex will talk to us,' Paige said, looking up at the McCloud building from the coffee shop across the street. 'And I really hope the grandparents don't follow him out here to harass us again. I don't have the patience for them tonight.'

Grayson didn't either. He put two cups of coffee on the table and held her chair. 'At least we know Adele's not in the morgue. She doesn't show up in any police reports and we've sent her photo to the local hospitals. Hyatt's got her picture on the TV news. I hope to God somebody's seen her.'

She winced as she sat down. 'Maybe Rex can shed some light on what happened to her when she was a MAC kid.'

Grayson eased onto his chair. 'I hope I can stand back up when we're done.'

'I know,' she murmured. 'I'm really sore. Silas was not gentle.'

The bastard had thrown her into the wall. 'When this is over,' Grayson told her, 'we'll take a hot bath in my tub and I'll rub your back.'

'Mmm. Your fancy furniture made me nervous, but that tub I could live with.'

'And me?' The words were out of his mouth before he knew he'd planned to say them. It was far too late to take them back. Not that he wanted to. He wanted her in his life. But it was too soon to ask. Except now he'd gone and blurted it out.

Her eyes widened. 'What did you say?'

He was saved from an answer by Rex sauntering up to their table. 'Well, well, if it isn't the Lone Ranger and Tonto,' he sneered.

Paige rolled her eyes. 'Sit down, Rex.'

He took a chair and turned it backward, straddling it. He still wore the clothes from the night before. But his attitude was very different. Rex was scared. And angry.

'Thanks for the hall pass, Counselor,' he mocked. 'Always nice to get out among the *good* people of our fair city.'

Grayson had made a call to Rex's correctional supervisor, advising him that he needed to speak with him outside the allowed range of the ankle bracelet. He wanted no family interference this time. Just Rex. *Maybe this time I'll get the truth.*

'Did you know Betsy Malone was dead?' Paige asked, as they'd previously agreed.

Rex's eyes flickered. 'Yeah,' he said quietly. 'She OD'd.'

'That's what someone wanted us to think,' Grayson said. 'She was drugged.'

Rex sat up straighter. 'And you think I did it?'

'No,' Grayson said. 'You're wearing a bracelet. You went nowhere near her home.' He'd asked the correctional officer.

'I didn't kill Crystal either,' Rex asserted. 'You can't prove I did.'

'Then who do you think killed her?' Paige asked. 'We know it wasn't Ramon Muñoz. And I'm not so sure anymore that it was you.'

Rex stared at her for a long moment. 'I thought it was Ramon. I really did. I don't know who did it, and that's the truth.'

'Rex, do you remember a group of kids in the MAC program?' she asked.

Rex's flinch was barely perceptible, but Grayson saw it. From the look on her face, Paige had seen it too. 'Crystal was one of those kids,' she said.

Rex's mouth fell open. 'Oh,' he said so softly it was almost inaudible.

'Explain anything?' Grayson asked.

'No.' But it was obviously a lie.

'Okay, this is the way we see it,' Paige said. 'Someone molested those girls, year after year. Maybe they were threatened, too scared to tell, but for whatever reason, they never told. Or maybe they tried and no one believed them. Until Crystal. She came to your party to blackmail someone. Was it you?'

Rex shot her a cold look. 'You don't know nothin'.'

'I know they're dead, Rex,' she said. 'Most of them murdered.'

He stared at her. 'What?'

'All but one. Sixteen years, fifteen dead women. The killings started after Crystal's death. I know she was found with a note, signed *RM*. I know your alibi was faked. And I know that you are the family fuck-up,' she finished harshly.

He paled. 'You're trying to pin those murders on me?'

'A better question is, is your family trying to pin the murders on you? They've cut you loose, Rex. They're gonna let you take the fall.'

His jaw bulged. 'I didn't do anything. I swear it.'

'I believe you,' she murmured and his eyes narrowed.

'Why?'

'Because you were too young to have done anything to those girls when they were twelve. You were only fourteen when the last MAC group would have visited the estate. That they would blackmail you makes no sense at all.' Paige leaned closer. 'What happened that day, Rex? When you were fourteen?'

His lip curled. 'What makes you think anything happened?'

'Because Betsy said before that you tried to make your grandparents notice you. Be proud of you. After that, you got into fights. You went out of control. What did you see?' When he said nothing, she sighed softly. 'Was it your stepfather?'

'There's no point in my telling you. Nobody would believe it anyway.'

'Try me,' she said. 'I've heard a lot of unbelievable things today. The MAC program went on throughout your entire childhood. If you know anything, please tell us.'

Grayson's mind was uneasy. Something didn't add up. And then it hit him. Rex hadn't even been born in 1984, the first MAC year. His mother was still married to Rex's father at the time. 'When did your mother marry your stepfather, Rex?'

Paige's shoulders stiffened and Grayson knew she was doing the math, too.

Rex looked up, wary. 'When I was three. Why?'

'Because your stepfather wouldn't have been on the estate during the first three MAC years,' Grayson said. *It must have been . . .* He shook his head, disbelieving.

Rex's body tensed as if anticipating a blow. Anger flashed in his eyes, along with shame. And that's when Grayson knew he'd guessed right. 'It was your grandfather, wasn't it, Rex?'

Paige's eyes widened. 'The senator?' She considered it, then nodded, accepting.

Rex swallowed hard. 'He's an icon. A family hero.'

'If he sexually assaulted those girls, he's a criminal,' Grayson said firmly.

'You'll never prove it.' Rex rested his forehead on the back of the chair he straddled. 'No one will believe you. He's Mr Family Values. Loving husband.' His mouth twisted. 'Good father. Hell of a politician.'

'I've been prosecuting a long time, Rex. I know that molesters don't generally wear trench coats and flash people. They're people who look normal. Many have good jobs and serve the community. That's why many of them go undetected – and unpunished – for so long. Am I surprised that your grandfather is a molester? A little. He doesn't fit the profile and he is older. Am I shocked? I wish I were.'

'When I was a kid I thought he was a hero. I thought he could do no wrong.'

'What did you see?' Paige asked. 'We need to know. And you need to tell.'

'Him.' Rex's throat worked. 'She was scared. She fought and he hit her. Hard. She tried to scream and he covered her mouth . . . and did it. She was just a little girl.'

'What did you do?' she asked him, her voice thickening.

'I . . .' Rex's face contorted. 'Nothing. I did nothing. I ran away.'

There was an amazing amount of guilt that came with running away, Grayson thought dully. *I was only seven. Rex was fourteen. Was that old enough to be expected to take action?* He wished he knew the answer. 'And then?' he asked.

'The kids were taken home in our limo. They usually made several trips, a few kids to a carload. They gave them ice cream and cheap plastic medallions,' he said bitterly.

'But the girl was crying,' Paige said. 'Somebody had to have noticed something when they took her home.'

'He told her nobody would believe her,' Rex mumbled. 'He told her that if she told, he'd have her parents killed. He told her if she was a good girl, he'd give her parents money and they'd have food.'

'Your grandfather?' Grayson asked.

'No. The driver. He's dead, so you can't ask him. But I heard him. The old man got done with the girl and left her there, crying. Then the driver came in and got her ready to go home. He . . . cleaned her. Made sure no one would know.'

Paige could barely speak. 'When did the driver die?'

'Right after the parties stopped. Killed himself. OD'd.'

Grayson and Paige shared a glance. 'Where did this assault happen?' Grayson asked.

'In my mother's old bedroom. It was decorated like a little girl's dream.'

Grayson wondered if Rex's mother had been assaulted in that bedroom as well. He filed the distasteful thought away for later. 'Did your mother live at the estate then?'

'No. She was in Europe all the time. When she's in town, she has a condo in the building.' He gestured to the McCloud building across the street with a tilt of his head. 'But she's never here, either.'

'How did you hear the driver?' Paige asked. 'If you ran away, how did you hear?'

'I ran after. I hid during. I was too shocked to come out at first. Then too scared.'

'Did you tell anyone?' Grayson asked quietly.

'My mother. I called her the next day. She said it never happened. She said if I told anyone that she'd call me a liar and say I was delusional. And she'd send me away.'

'She did that anyway, according to Betsy,' Paige said and Rex shrugged.

'She couldn't stand the sight of me from the time I was a kid. It doesn't matter.'

'Yes, it does,' Paige said gently. 'It matters, Rex.'

'Whatever. So now you know. What do you think you're gonna change?'

'We're going to find the only woman left alive,' Grayson said.

'And we're going to ask her to tell. If she does, will you testify?'

Rex shook his head. 'I still have a trust fund. If I tell, they'll cut me off entirely.'

'If they're in jail, they can't control your money,' Paige said, annoyed.

He laughed, a hollow sound. 'You'll never put them in jail. They're the McClouds. They can do whatever the hell they want and get away with it. And if I play by their rules, so can I.' He stood up. 'I'm done.'

'One more question,' Paige said. 'Why were you hiding in your mother's old bedroom? There was an ice-cream party going on downstairs.'

'I wasn't allowed to go to the ice-cream parties, even when I was small. I was told to stay in my room. I was always told to stay in my room, out of sight.'

She just looked at him for a moment. 'You hid something in that bedroom. Weed?'

'You speakin' from experience?' he sneered.

She wasn't baited. 'A teenage boy doesn't just hang in a room decorated like a little girl's dream for no good reason. Either you're gay or you were using. Or both.'

His jaw twitched. 'Pills, not weed. I'd taken them from my mother's bathroom.'

'Why were you taking pills at fourteen?' Paige asked.

'Just because a kid's got stuff, doesn't mean the kid's got value. Nobody wanted me. Not my mother and certainly not my grand-parents.' His lips curled. 'Because, as you so astutely noted, I was the family fuck-up. Even before I did anything wrong.'

They watched him go back to his building, his step heavy.

'I should be more shocked, I guess,' Paige said. 'But honestly, my first thought wasn't "no way", it was "why didn't I see this before?" '

'Same here. Maybe because the senator is old, we just didn't see him as a pervert.'

'And Dianna is "his heart".' She rolled her eyes, furious. 'She had to have known.'

'I don't doubt it. But what I don't understand is why. Why the

MAC kids? And are there any other victims? It's going to be hard enough to prove he did it. That she knew will be even harder.'

'But you're going to try.' It wasn't a question.

'Absolutely,' he said grimly.

'We still don't know who killed Crystal.'

'Yeah, but now we know who had the most to lose.' Grayson tugged her to her feet. 'Let's go get some food and figure out what to do next.'

Twenty-four

Thursday, April 7, 11.10 P.M.

Paige looked up from her notebook when Grayson came through his mother's front door. He held Peabody's leash in one hand, a bag of Chinese takeout in the other. His cell trapped between his shoulder and ear, he closed the front door with his foot.

Paige let herself imagine what it might be like to see him do this domestic ballet every night. He caught her gaze and held it and she knew he was thinking the same.

Soon. Soon they'd be able to talk about whatever future they might have. But not yet. Violet didn't have much longer. If she was still alive. Adele was still missing.

And the senator was a child molester. He'd set all this trauma into play with his perversion. It made her furious every time she thought about it.

Grayson sat, still listening to whoever was on the other line. Too hungry to be polite, Paige started without him, watching his brow furrow, hoping it wasn't more bad news.

'Okay,' he finally said. 'You're sure? Thanks.'

He hung up and took the chopsticks she offered. 'Who was that?' she asked.

'Lucy. She checked the other names. More of the same. Only two died of natural causes. I reported it to Hyatt. We have an official serial murderer on our hands.'

'Any word on Violet?'

'No, not yet. They checked the names we gave them from Bond's law firm. None of them panned out. They have another lead from a maid in the hotel in Toronto, but her description is sketchy at best. Give me a minute.' He ate steadily, emptying his plate. 'I'm still hungry, but at least I can think now. Lucy found something else.'

He opened another carton, dumped noodles on his plate. 'She examined the photos of the ligature mark around Crystal's throat. She thinks the person who strangled her had one hand weaker than the other. The ligature is uneven in depth across the neck.'

Paige's smile was sharp. 'And our good buddy the slimy sex-pervert senator had a mild stroke in 2001. His left hand was affected. Sonofabitch. He *did* kill her.' Then she frowned. 'Wait. The strangulation didn't kill Crystal. The stab wounds did.'

'Which brings me to the other thing Lucy said. The autopsy photos show wounds that may not have been made by the same person. The angle of entry is too different.'

Paige bit at her lip. 'So *two* people killed Crystal?'

'Don't know. Lucy thought that maybe the first person strangled her, then may have stabbed her once. The second person stabbed her deeper. That was the fatal blow.'

'Shit. This changes a lot.'

'Not really. If McCloud's hands were too weak to kill Crystal, somebody helped him finish the job. Just like the driver helped him intimidate all those girls into silence.'

'The driver was dead years before Crystal's murder though,' Paige said, considering the logistics. 'He had to have had another helper, one strong enough to hang all the MAC victims after they were drugged.' She shook her head, rage bubbling anew. 'He raped them and then hunted them down years later and killed them. There is no hell hot enough.'

'Agreed,' Grayson said grimly. 'Although the best I can do is a needle in the arm.'

'We have to catch them first. At least we know where the senator is. We need IDs on his helper, and the broker. And we need to find Violet and Adele.'

'The broker has Violet and the senator knows who he is. But we can't pick up the senator until we have a complainant.'

'Adele,' Paige said. 'If the senator killed all the other MAC women, and if Adele didn't just run away from home, the senator either has her or knows where she is.'

'We still can't pick him up. We don't have a body, we don't have any proof other than Rex's story, which he's said he won't repeat in court. Other than that, we have nothing but very tenuous circum-stantial evidence. It'd get thrown out of a grand jury.'

'I want to scream,' Paige said, frustrated. 'This is like a giant circle with no end.'

'I know. I could use some good news about now.'

'I have news, kind of good. Do you remember Detective Perkins? He took my statement in the ER after the parking garage. He called while you were gone. He has an ID on the parking-garage guy. They got his DNA from your briefcase.'

'Well, who is he?' Grayson asked fiercely, his hand tightening to a fist.

'Name's Roscoe "Jesse" James. He's a professional fighter. Or was.'

'He's dead?'

'Perkins didn't know. James disappeared Tuesday night after his fight. He was last seen at his favorite bar. Security camera shows him sitting next to a guy who could have been Silas. The guy dumped something into Roscoe's drink and later said he'd give him a ride home. Roscoe's car is still in the lot – he never made it home.'

'Silas killed him?'

'Perkins said they're checking the vehicles found in Silas's garage. His van had a lot of blood in it. Same blood type as they found in the wood near the nursing home, which would be Kapansky's. They'll have to see if they can find James's blood, too.'

'If I hadn't seen him in action with my own eyes, I'd still have trouble believing Silas could have done all this,' Grayson said. His cell phone rang and he checked the ID. 'It's my mother.'

'Tell her thank you for letting us use her place,' Paige said.

'I will.' He hit the green button. 'Hey, Mom.' He frowned. 'Are you in a safe place? I just had that car tuned up. It shouldn't have just stopped on you like that . . . What are you doing *there*?' He let out a sigh. 'The GPS is only useful when you turn it on, Mom.'

Then the color drained from his face and Paige's heart started to pound. He surged to his feet, his face filled with fury. *'Who are you?* . . . Yeah,' he bit out. 'I understand.'

Blindly he set the phone on the table.

Panic grabbed her throat. 'What? What happened?'

'He has my mother,' he said tonelessly. 'And Holly. At first she said the car broke down. And then she said "I love you, Tony". When I was small and we were hiding . . .' His voice broke. 'If she ever called me Tony, I was to run as fast as I could.'

Paige kept her voice calm. He didn't need her getting hysterical. 'And then what?'

'Whoever has her knew she'd given me a message. He hit her. Hard. Then he came on the phone and said if I wanted her to live, I'd come with you. No cops.'

Paige made herself breathe. 'We need to call Joseph.'

Grayson stood. 'I'll call him on the way. You stay here.'

'No. Don't ask me to do that. I'll just follow you anyway.'

'He wants us both dead. I won't let him have you.'

Talking him out of leaving would be utterly futile but she wasn't letting him walk into an ambush alone. She swung her backpack to her shoulder. 'He can't have you either.'

He set his jaw. 'Then come. I don't have time to argue with you.'

She grabbed Peabody's leash and together they followed him out.

Thursday, April 7, 11.35 P.M.

Paige called both Joseph and Clay. The two men were talking to each other as they separately approached, planning their coordinated assault. Grayson drove with his foot to the floor, murmuring under his breath. Praying. Paige prayed too.

But she also had the laptop open, because doing something kept her sane. 'Your mother's smart. She'll do what she needs to do to keep Holly safe.'

'That's what I'm afraid of,' he said hoarsely.

She had no words to comfort him so she kept her hand on his

shoulder as city roads turned to country roads. They were somewhere near the airport. She could hear a plane coming in for a
landing. 'The broker wasn't on the list of ten we gave to Hyatt.'

'What does it matter anymore? He has my mother.'

His voice was anguished and it broke her heart. But she couldn't
let him falter now.

'It matters because who he *is* will determine how we take him
down. If he's a sharpshooter, we need to know. If he's a goddamn
cage fighter or an explosives guy, we need to know that too. Your
mother's life and Holly's life depend on it. So do Joseph's and Clay's,
not to mention ours. So get hold of yourself and think.'

'Okay. I'm thinking.' He drew a deep breath, and another.
'Maybe he wasn't the guy in the photo. Maybe the guy paying
Sandoval was a flunky and we've been chasing mist.'

'Maybe. But why would Sandoval have kept it? And why
would he have been killed for it? Maybe the broker just doesn't
work at the firm anymore.' She opened a new browser and typed in
the firm's name and *former*. It yielded pages of results that meant
nothing.

Paige tapped her keyboard nervously. Her thumb brushed the
touchpad and the screen jumped to the photographs she'd been
studying earlier – the ones of the MAC group photos that she'd
taken with Joseph's camera-pen. She started to move back to her
search screen, when her finger froze at a sparkle of light.

She was looking at the last photo she'd taken. A man's hand,
resting on another man's shoulder. The hand was manicured. The
right shape and size. 'Oh, my God.'

'What?' Grayson bit out. *'What?'*

'This afternoon when I went back to Reba's, Rex's stepfather
came in as we were leaving. A lawyer was there to see him, the
foundation's attorney. But he was there because Rex called him. I
snapped a picture of Rex's stepfather because he winked at me as he
was leaving. It was reflex. But I got the lawyer's hand.'

His chin came up. 'Manicured?'

'Yes. With a diamond pinky ring.'

'What was his name, Paige?' he demanded.

'I'm thinking, dammit,' she snapped. 'Stuart. Reba called him Stuart.'

Grayson stilled. 'Lippman? Stu Lippman?'

'Yes. Do you know him?'

'He was Bond's assistant on the Muñoz trial. Where is his office?'

Paige typed Lippman's name into her search screen. 'In the McCloud building. So is his condo. It's one of the penthouse suites. We were there, Grayson. Dammit.'

'The window. Do you remember the window? The one that was broken?'

'You said a foul ball. Or a big bird.'

'Or a bullet fired by Silas. Silas tried to kill him.'

'Then he hurt Silas's wife and abducted his child. But in Toronto? How?'

'It's less than an hour by private plane. We can check flight plans and manifests later. We're almost there.' His hands gripped the wheel. 'He's going to try to kill us.'

'I know. I have my Glock and the .357 in my boot. You have your piece?'

'Bashears took it, but Joseph gave me one of his. Beretta nine-mil.'

'Thirteen rounds. Between the two of us, we've got some firepower. If we can separate, come from front and back like we did Silas . . . It could work.'

'He's smaller than Silas. Don't know if he's combat trained.'

'With those hands? I doubt it. If you can get behind him, you can take him down. But don't kill him.' She put the laptop away, checked her guns. 'Once we have everyone safe, then you can kill him.'

'Call Joseph and Clay. Tell them.' He hesitated. 'And Hyatt.'

She stared at him in surprise. 'What?'

'We'll do what Lippman wants and buy the time Joseph and Clay need to set up,' he said grimly. 'But if the four of us fail, we still need to get the others out. Hyatt can send a team to Lippman's condo. Maybe he has my mother and Holly there. Violet, too.'

Thursday, April 7, 11.50 P.M.

Grayson slowed as he approached the place his mother had told him to come. The closest civilization was a mile back. There were lots of trees. Lots of places to hide.

'There's her car.' He stopped behind it, shone his headlights into the interior. It was empty. He pressed the trunk release on his mother's spare keyfob, his shoulders sagging. He'd been afraid and hopeful at once. Hopeful they'd be in the car. Afraid he'd find them dead there. He glanced down. 'Inside and trunk, both empty.'

Paige had slid to the floorboard of the Escalade by mutual agreement. They didn't want Lippman – if that's who was waiting for them – to know she'd come. They hoped it would increase their odds of taking him by surprise. They hoped.

'We didn't think they would be there.' Her voice was calm, steady, as were her dark eyes.

'We've just announced our presence,' he said bitterly. Now that he was here, he questioned the wisdom of the plan that really wasn't. He hadn't really thought it through. He'd simply reacted. *I'm going to get us all killed.* 'Might as well have ridden in with a stampede.'

'We knew we were walking into an ambush,' she said, still steadily. 'We're here to play along. To buy time for your mom and Holly. And Violet. We draw him out.'

He nodded. 'And take him down.'

'Right now there's one of him and two of us. In ten minutes Joseph and Clay will be here and we'll be four. I like those odds a little better. Especially since we don't know that your mother and Holly are even here. He could have them somewhere else.'

'I have a new appreciation for the lost-my-mind defense,' he murmured. They should wait for backup. But a lot could happen in ten minutes. *He could be hurting them.* And then Grayson's heart stopped, his decision made.

'It's Holly.' She'd appeared on the edge of the trees, stumbling into the light from his highbeams. Her hands were tied behind her, her eyes wide with terror. Tears streamed down her cheeks. 'A man's behind her. I can't see his face. Sonofabitch.'

'Turn off the headlights. You're probably blinding her,' Paige said.

He turned off the headlights and the maplight. 'I'll draw him, you bring him down?'

'He's seen you already, so that's how it's got to be. When you walk toward him, keep your body sideways. With your shoulders, you're like a broad side of a barn.'

'I've got the Kevlar,' he said, more to comfort himself.

'That'll only protect you so much. If he's too close, you could still be toast. Peabody and I will circle around. Take him from behind. Just like Silas. Okay?'

He'd nearly forgotten about the dog. 'Okay. Don't die.'

Her expression was grim. 'You too.'

He slid out of the Escalade, turning his body sideways. He heard Paige open the door on her side the exact moment he closed his. Good timing. *Let it continue. Please.*

'Let her go,' Grayson called into the darkness. He could no longer see Holly. She'd been pulled back into the trees. 'She's not who you want. I am.'

'So you'll trade?' a man called. It was the man on the phone. *Who hit my mother.*

Grayson couldn't remember how Stuart Lippman sounded. But right now, that didn't matter. 'Yes, I'll trade. My sister and my mother for me.'

'I want the woman, too. Holden.'

'She was hurt earlier,' Grayson improvised. 'I had to take her to the ER. Silas gave her a concussion before she shot him. They admitted her for the night.'

'You're lying.'

'You can call the ER, ask them. Right now, it's only me.' He walked toward the trees, keeping his body turned, angling his approach to force whoever held Holly to look at him and not where Paige and Peabody were running. With her black clothes and hair, she blended into the trees well. He couldn't see them anymore. 'Holly, it'll be okay.'

'Don't make promises you can't keep, Smith. I want Holden too.'

Grayson could hear Holly's keening cry of fear. *You'll die for that alone.*

'If you want Holden, then you'll have to go to the hospital and get her,' Grayson said harshly. 'She doesn't know anything anyway. She's a PI wannabe. Good fighter and great in the sack, but not a lot upstairs. If you know what I mean.'

'She's got enough upstairs to track down Adele Shaffer.'

'Who?'

'Don't play games with me, Counselor. You've got her picture all over the TV. She's a "person of interest".'

'I don't know anything about that. I've been busy trying to find Crystal Jones's killer so I can get Ramon Muñoz released from prison.'

Grayson listened for a response and when he heard nothing, started to move closer to the treeline. He reached under his jacket for Joseph's gun, shoved in his waistband.

He saw them then, Lippman and Holly. Lippman held her close, his gun at her head. Cold fury hit Grayson hard. Then he saw the glint of metal, too late. Heard the shot as all the air was shoved out of his lungs, the impact to his chest hurting far worse than the pieces of his car that had rained down on his back after Wednesday night's bomb.

He staggered backward, heard Holly's horrified scream.

'Grayson!' Holly yanked free, only to stumble when Lippman pulled her back.

Lippman's gun still pointed at Grayson, his expression racing from satisfaction to shock as Grayson picked himself up from the ground, then went down on one knee.

He expected me to be dead. Sorry, pal. Not today. He'd dropped Joseph's gun and now grabbed it, arcing it up, aiming at Lippman's head. But if he missed, he'd hit Holly. A split-second before he pulled the trigger, he heard a low growl.

Peabody. The dog appeared out of the trees from the right, lunging, and Lippman's scream tore through the air. Peabody dragged him backward, his teeth sunk into his arm. No longer able to hold his gun, Lippman dropped it, kicking at the dog, cursing.

Holly yanked free again and Grayson ran toward her, not seeing Lippman's left hand fumbling in his coat pocket until it was too late.

A backup. Lippman had a backup gun in his pocket. *Oh, God.*

'Holly,' Grayson cried. 'Get—'

In a blur of black, Paige leapt, throwing herself over Holly as Lippman fired again. Two shots. At Paige's back. Paige's body jerked and went completely still.

Grayson stared, horrified. *'No.'* He aimed at Lippman's chest, fired three times and Lippman went down like a rock. Grayson ran, dropping to his knees beside her, gently gathering her into his arms. *Don't be dead.* 'Paige.'

'I'm not dead.' Paige rolled to look behind her, the Glock in her hand, then came to her feet so fluidly that Grayson found himself breathless once again. Relief shuddered through him as Holly still sobbed. She was breathing. They all were.

'You're okay? You're both okay?' Grayson demanded.

'Knocked the breath out of me.' Paige ran to Lippman, who, although unconscious, also still breathed. She picked up both of his guns, put them in her pocket. 'Peabody, release.' The dog obeyed, sitting up, waiting for his next command. 'Good dog. Very good dog.'

Grayson lifted Holly into his arms. 'Are you hurt? Where are you hurt?'

'Judy,' she cried. 'The lady has Judy. She'll kill her. I tried to run. She'll kill her.'

Grayson and Paige's eyes met, stricken. 'Which lady?' Grayson demanded.

'She said she was a policeman. She had a badge. She said you were hurt and we should come. Then she tied us up. Made Judy get in the trunk. Then the man came. He said they would kill Judy if I tried to run. She's gonna kill her. It's all my fault.'

Grayson's heart stopped again. 'Morton.'

'Probably.' Paige knelt beside Holly, caressed her face gently. 'Honey, this is not your fault. It's not. But there's no one in the trunk of Judy's car. We looked.'

Holly shook her head. 'Not Judy's car. A blue car. The police lady's car. Over th—'

Another shot cracked the air, had them flattening to the ground once more. Grayson hovered, trying not to crush Holly. He turned his head, saw Paige's irate glare.

'Sonofabitch,' she hissed. 'What the hell?'

Grayson sat up, his fury intense. 'Fuck. Goddamn fuck. Morton did it again.'

Lippman no longer breathed, a new bullet in his head. Grayson could hear someone running through the woods and he and Paige surged to their feet, ready to start to chase.

But the roar of an engine had them stopping, looking at the road where they'd parked the Escalade behind Judy's abandoned car. A little black Mercedes appeared from the opposite direction. It paused by their parked vehicles and four more shots rang out before it took off in the direction they'd come.

Grayson looked over at Holly. 'Did you say the police lady's car was blue?'

She nodded unsteadily. 'Blue. W-with white stripes.'

The black Mercedes must have belonged to Lippman then.

Paige had run up to the Escalade. 'She shot out our tires,' she called. 'Two on our car and two on your mom's.'

'The Mercedes is Lippman's car,' he called back. 'Morton left her car here.' Hope sprang up in his chest. 'Holly says my mother is in the trunk of Morton's blue car.'

'I'll go look for it. You call for help.'

Grayson took out his cell, his hands shaking. He called 911, then Joseph. 'I have Holly. My mother's still missing. A black Mercedes coupé is headed your way. Stop the car. Detective Morton's driving.'

'The cop that shot Silas?' Joseph asked.

'Yeah. She was here, helping Stuart Lippman.'

'The broker. You got him.'

'Yeah, but Morton killed him, too. Do we have Violet?'

'No.'

'Dammit. Get here as soon as you can. I'm going to look for my mom.' He hung up, then looked at Holly who was very pale. He made himself smile, made his voice positive. For Holly. 'We'll find my mom. She's tougher than you think.'

Holly shuddered. 'The police lady said she wouldn't kill us. And then *he* came.'

'I know.' He carried her to where she couldn't see Lippman's body. 'I'm going to leave you for just a few minutes, to look for my mom. I don't have a knife to cut you free but Paige will.' He looked over his shoulder. Paige was nowhere to be seen.

'Grayson!' The shout came from over the hill. *Paige.*

He stood, his knees going weak when he saw her coming through the trees. On her right was Peabody, guarding her. Leaning against her left was a tall woman with red hair, walking stiffly, waving wearily.

Grayson had never seen a more beautiful sight than the two of them. He ran to his mother and she grabbed him in a hard embrace that had him grunting in pain. If Lippman's shot hadn't cracked his ribs, his mother just had.

She'd started to cry, her body shaking. 'You said it was over,' she accused.

'Actually I said there were loose ends,' he said. 'I'm sorry. I'm so sorry.'

'She was in Morton's trunk, just like you said, Holly,' Paige said, kneeling next to Holly, sawing at her ropes with a wicked-looking folding blade. 'I pried open the trunk with this knife.'

Holly nodded, still deathly pale. 'That's a really big knife, Paige.'

Paige folded it, handed it to her. 'It's yours. I'll teach you how to use it.'

Holly's nod was unsteady. 'Okay. But I never want to have to use it. Ever.'

Paige hugged her closely. 'That's the plan, Holly. That's always the plan.'

The cavalry had descended, Paige thought a few minutes later. Squad cars and ambulances. Cops in SWAT gear. And finally Hyatt himself. 'Everyone unharmed?'

Judy sat on the ground, Holly in her arms. 'Bumps and bruises,' Judy said.

Grayson slid his arm around Paige, wincing. 'Bruises all around.'

493

Hyatt looked down at Lippman. 'Who shot him?'

'The chest shots are mine,' Grayson said.

'Nice grouping,' Hyatt said.

'He shot me and Paige first.' Grayson fingered the hole in his shirt, giving his mother an encouraging smile when she made a distressed noise.

'He got me in the back,' Paige said. 'And it hurts like a damn bitch.'

Hyatt's lips curved. 'I know. But it hurts a whole lot more without the Kevlar.'

Paige rolled her shoulder. 'Yeah, I know that too. Head shot was Morton's.'

Hyatt's smile disappeared. 'I see. We have Detective Morton in custody. Mr Maynard and Mr Carter had apparently arrived at about the same time and parked their cars across the road. They held Detective Morton until we arrived. She had Dandridge's daughter in the trunk of her car. The child is alive. Doped up, but alive. She appears unharmed.'

Paige's shoulders slumped. 'Thank God.'

'The Mercedes was Lippman's car,' Grayson said. 'Morton may not have known Violet was even there.'

'But she's still a bitch,' Holly said stubbornly.

'Indeed,' Hyatt agreed. 'Come with me, please. All of you. I'll make sure you get medical attention for those bumps and bruises.'

He put them in the backseats of two cruisers, Paige, Peabody, and Grayson in one, Judy and Holly in the other. Peabody took up most of the seat so Paige found herself almost on Grayson's lap. She leaned her head on his shoulder, let herself relax.

'Nothing upstairs, huh?' she asked teasingly. 'I should be offended.'

He laughed softly. 'I panicked. Picked the most outrageous lie I could think of.'

She leaned up, whispered in his ear. 'So the great in the sack was a lie, too?'

'That was true.' He let out a pained breath. 'My heart stopped when he shot you.'

'Mine too,' she confessed. 'It happened too fast for me and Peabody to stop him from shooting you.'

'It's okay. You saved Holly's life. Thank you,' he said fiercely.

They came to a bend in the road where the little black Mercedes was parked along with Joseph's and Clay's vehicles, three ambulances, and a half dozen cruisers.

The morgue rig hadn't yet arrived. Paige was relieved that they needed only one.

'Check them out,' Hyatt told the medics when they'd piled out of the squad cars. 'Make sure they're okay.' He turned to Grayson and Paige. 'We found Mrs Shaffer.'

'Adele?' Grayson asked. 'Where is she?'

'In the hospital. A Dr Burke called the hotline after seeing her photo. She'd treated her for massive stab wounds as a Jane Doe this morning. The first responding officer reported the stabbing occurred just before nine. A witness saw a car driving away and discovered Mrs Shaffer in an alley near Patterson Park.'

'Senator McCloud,' Paige said grimly. 'He's hunted all the MAC women.'

'He'll be questioned,' Hyatt said, 'but he unfortunately has an airtight alibi. He gave the keynote address at a Rotary Club breakfast this morning.'

'Lippman might have done it,' Grayson mused, 'but it would be close. He'd have been hard pressed to make it from Patterson Park to the airport, then fly to Toronto to kidnap Violet, even if he had a private plane. Adele hasn't given a description?'

'She hasn't regained consciousness. We have an officer at her door, so that when whoever tried to kill her realizes they have failed, they will not be able to try again. Mr Smith, your home is no longer a crime scene. Your window is repaired. Once you have received medical attention, you may go home. We'll take your statements tomorrow.' Hyatt nodded formally, then strode to the squad car where Morton was being held.

Grayson skimmed his fingers over Paige's back lightly, frowning when she flinched. 'You need to be checked out by the medics.'

'I'm fine,' Paige insisted. 'What I need is a long soak in a hot tub.'

'Then that's what you'll have. Hopefully somebody can give us a ride.' They walked to where the others stood, Joseph and Clay having joined Judy and Holly. 'Joseph, Morton shot out your tires. We need a lift.'

'I'll drive you anywhere you want to go,' Joseph said. He looked at Paige, his expression profoundly intense as he held his sister tight. 'Holly told us what happened. That you threw yourself on top of her when Lippman fired. You saved her life. We won't ever forget that.'

Judy wrapped her arms around Paige. 'Thank you.'

Paige patted her back, embarrassed. 'Grayson saved me. I had to even the score.'

'So is it really over?' Judy asked. 'Please say yes.'

'Not quite,' Grayson said. 'We still have some bad guys to round up. And importantly, I need to get Ramon's conviction overturned. I'll file first thing in the morning.'

'After you sleep,' Joseph said. 'For now, let me take you two home.'

'And Peabody?' Paige asked.

'He saved Holly too. If he growls at me forever, I won't mind.'

Twenty-five

Friday, April 8, 8.15 A.M.

Grayson woke with a soft warm woman looking up at him and wondered if it got much better than this. He'd had her once during the night, hard and fast and desperate. He wanted her again, but slow this time. He wanted to linger. Savor. 'Good morning.'

She lay half on him, half off, her chin propped on his shoulder. 'How're you feeling?'

'Sore, but I'll live. How long have you been awake?'

'For about an hour. I've been thinking.'

'Oh, no,' he teased, then sobered when she didn't smile. 'About what?'

'It's going to be hard to prove the senator is guilty of sexual assault and murder, all these years later. He'll have an alibi and it'll be a good one. He can afford it.'

'Possibly. But I've worked cold cases with Hyatt's team before. Don't give up yet.'

'You'll need motive for a murder charge and you'll only have that if you can prove what he did to all those little girls. If Adele doesn't live, you won't even have a complainant. And even if she does file a complaint, it's her word against his.'

'The rape of a minor charges are going to be hard to prosecute,' he admitted. 'The evidence in the Crystal Jones murder is circumstantial at best. The murders of the other women even more so. But I won't stop trying.'

'I know.' She kissed his jaw, sighed. 'I started on something last night while you were picking up dinner. I've been working it in my mind this morning.'

He sat up and shoved a pillow behind his head. 'All right. Let's hear it.'

'The MAC program ran for sixteen years. That's a long time to get away with having a little girl go missing from the ice-cream party for long enough to be molested, every year.'

'You assume it happened every year.'

'They're all dead,' she said.

'True.'

'We know the McClouds' driver knew. He took the kids home. He probably took the victim home last. If the kids were being driven in groups, nobody would have known where all the others were at any given time. Plus, they were twelve. And Dianna McCloud simply had to have known. She chaperoned, every year.'

'I find it easier to believe that she did know than that she didn't.'

'I worked a timeline based on all I've read on the McClouds,' Paige said. 'Dianna married the senator when Claire, Rex's mother, was a little girl – nine or so. Claire moved out when she got married and had Rex. That was in 1984.'

'The first year of the MAC program.'

'It ended in '99, the year Reba went to the Peace Corps in Cameroon.'

She left the statement to hang and he frowned down at her. 'Surely you're not suggesting Dianna brought the girls there . . . on purpose?'

'Think about what Rex said his mother's response was when he told her what he'd seen. Claire said it never happened. That if he told she'd say he was delusional and send him away. That's an odd response, don't you think? Unless she'd learned to deny that it had happened to her.'

'I did wonder about that,' Grayson admitted, 'when Rex said his grandfather took the girls to his mother's old bedroom, which he'd kept exactly the same as when Claire slept there. Pink, like a little girl's dream.'

'Exactly. So if we assume the senator molested one daughter, what was to stop him from molesting the other, when she was old enough, especially once the oldest moved out?'

'That's the usual pattern . . . So you're saying to keep the senator from touching Reba, Dianna brings him other little girls? Like as a sacrifice?'

'It's possible,' Paige said defensively.

'It's a lot of conjecture,' he said gently. 'It might have happened that way, but the McClouds are just as likely to claim we're spinning tales from thin air.'

'If we knew what the senator did, we could work the family against each other.'

'It only works that way on TV,' he said. 'But there is one thing that bothers me.'

She lifted her head, brows arched. 'Just one?'

He smiled briefly. 'Brittany Jones. We never would have known about the MAC connection if she hadn't given us that medallion.'

'She wanted us to know. Maybe she wanted justice for Crystal?'

'Then why not just tell us? Why give us the bankbooks? She made it clear that Crystal was a thief, looking to score. Why did Brittany call Lippman, who I assume is the one who paid Kapansky to blow us up?'

'If we could find her, we could ask her.'

'If we could find her, I'd charge her ass for conspiracy to commit murder,' he said sourly. 'She gave me a key to a safe-deposit box. Why?'

'Why don't we get dressed, go to the bank, and find out?' She started to get up, but he held her a little closer.

'Because I'll have to get a court order first and I don't want to let you go just yet. Let's take another few minutes.'

She relaxed into him. 'I think we've earned that much.'

He thought he'd earned a lot more than that, images of lingering and savoring still playing in his mind. But first . . . 'I need to talk to you about something. This secret of mine that wasn't so secret. It will come out and it could be unpleasant.'

'Are you afraid of unpleasant?'

'No,' he said, and found it was true. 'But I don't know if you are.'

'After all this, you can really ask me that? You think I'm afraid of a little bad press?'

'Anderson said that when the courts find out about me, I won't be able to prosecute anymore – that there'll be too much conflict of interest.'

'Anderson was a crook.'

'But he could be right. I might have to give up my career.'

'That would suck. But you'd deal. You'd find another way to stand for the victims.'

'You sound so sure.'

'It's who you are. The job is just the means to the end. If you want to tell your story, tell it. I'll stand by you. But if you think it's nobody's business, then don't.'

'I don't want anyone to think they have a hold over me.'

'Grayson, you knocked on Rex's door, knowing Anderson would tell your secrets. You confronted Rex when you could have walked away.'

'No, I couldn't have walked away. It would have been wrong.'

'My point exactly,' she said. She leaned up over him, brushing his mouth with her lips. 'I think that you think too much.'

He ran his hand down her side. 'I was thinking this morning, too.'

'Oh, no,' she teased.

'Oh, yes. About how I'd rushed before.'

Her eyes darkened, impossibly. 'I liked it. But if you think you can do better . . .'

The feline challenge in her voice set his pulse pounding. He reached for her, took her mouth slowly, making her hum deep in her throat. When she reached for him he stopped her, linking their fingers together, rolling her on her back.

'Does that hurt?' he whispered. 'Your back?'

'Not enough for me to tell you to stop. Let me touch you.'

A shudder shook him. 'Not yet. Let me have you.'

'You do.' She lifted her hips against him. 'Grayson, please. Hurry.'

'No. Not this morning. Let me have you. All of you.' He dipped his head to her breast and her sigh turned into a moan. 'Every last inch of you.'

He lingered and he savored and he made her breath catch in her throat. When she urged him to hurry he slowed down even more until he had her begging. He kissed his way down her body and back up, wondering if he'd ever get his fill.

'Please.' Her whispers had become hoarse. 'Please. I need—'

He slid into her and her eyes closed. 'This?'

'You. I need you, whoever you want to be.'

'Look at me.' She opened her eyes and he knew exactly who he wanted to be. 'Yours.' Holding her gaze, he started to move. 'I want to be yours.'

He linked their hands again, watching every flicker of her eyes, every bite of her lip, increasing his thrusts until she writhed, until she arched like a bow, her body gripping his in one long slow beautiful spasm as she went over, dragging him with her.

It was quietly cataclysmic, different from anything he'd ever had before. Different from anything with her before. He hung over her, breathing hard, looking into her eyes as her body softened like warm wax. He didn't have words, so he kissed her, knowing that this moment he'd remember. When he lifted his head, tears ran down her cheeks. 'Did I hurt you?'

'No,' she whispered. 'It's just . . . so . . . big.'

He might have made a joke at another time. But not now. He understood exactly what she meant. This was sacred. 'I know.'

He rolled them to their sides, holding her as tightly as she held him. The minutes passed and he didn't want to let her go, but the ringing of the phone intruded.

Grayson reached out for it, not wanting to move. 'Hello?' It came out of him surly.

'Good morning, Mr Smith.'

Grayson rolled his eyes. 'Good morning, Lieutenant Hyatt.'

'Mrs Shaffer has regained consciousness. We get five minutes to talk to her. How fast can you be at the hospital?'

He was suddenly alert. 'Thirty minutes or less.'

'Then I'll wait for you to arrive.'

'What is it?' Paige asked.

'Adele's awake.' Grayson forced himself from the bed, looked out the window and blessed his brother. Sometime during the morning hours the Escalade had materialized on his curb. 'We've got thirty minutes to get dressed, walk the dog, and drive.'

Friday, April 8, 9.45 A.M.

Adele Shaffer was in ICU, Darren sitting at her side. Adele stared at the wall, her face as pale as the pillowcase. Darren rose when Paige, Grayson and Hyatt entered.

'Mrs Shaffer?' Hyatt said. 'I am Lieutenant Peter Hyatt, with the homicide division of the police department. This is State's Attorney Grayson Smith and his associate, Paige Holden. They've been investigating the MAC program. And the McClouds.'

Grayson gave the chair to Paige, crouching by the bed so that he was at eye-level with Adele. 'Hi,' he said with a smile. 'We need your help. Your husband said you thought someone was trying to kill you. You were right.'

Adele's eyes widened briefly, as if that was all the energy she had.

'The MAC program ran for sixteen years,' Paige said. 'Every year there was a twelve-year-old girl with curly blond hair, just like you had. Of those sixteen women, you are the only one left alive.' Behind her, Darren Shaffer gasped.

Adele closed her eyes. 'They said no one would believe me,' she breathed.

'We will,' Grayson said. 'We promise. Please tell us what happened.'

'They said they'd kill my family.' A tear ran down Adele's cheek and Paige dabbed it with a tissue. 'I didn't have a dad. My mother was always high. But I had three little brothers and I didn't want them hurt. They said they'd give us money for food. I didn't want my brothers to starve. So I never said anything.'

'It's time to tell,' Paige said. 'You were a MAC kid in 1994. You were twelve.'

'I thought it was the best day of my life,' she whispered. 'They got me a new dress. We had ice cream and so much food. Then the kids from the other schools started to go home, a few at a time. I was the only one left. She asked if I wanted to see upstairs.'

'Who's "she", Mrs Shaffer?' Hyatt asked quietly.

'Mrs McCloud. His *wife*.' She spat the word weakly, but her sentiment was clear. 'The room was pink. I hate pink now.' She swallowed. 'And then *he* came in. The senator.' Another tear slipped down her cheek and again, Paige wiped it dry.

'I'm sorry, Mrs Shaffer,' Hyatt said, 'but we have to ask you exactly what he did.'

'I never wanted to remember. But I never forgot. He pushed up my dress . . .' She began to cry softly. 'He raped me. I tried to fight, but he was too big. He held me down. Held his hand over my mouth. I thought I was going to die. I wanted to.'

Paige took her hand. 'I'm sorry, Adele. We're so sorry this happened to you. But please try to tell us what happened next?'

'He thanked me. I've always remembered that. He thanked me. Like I had a choice. Left me there, crying. A man came in. He was the one who'd picked me up from my house. He . . . washed me. I was too scared to move by then. He was the one who told me what would happen if I told. Then he put my medallion box in my hand and took me downstairs and put me in the car. *She* came, too.'

'You mean Mrs McCloud?' Paige asked gently.

'Yes. She made me eat chocolate. It made me sleepy.'

'She drugged you,' Grayson said.

'Oh,' Darren breathed, horrified. 'That's why you were so freaked by the chocolates that were left at the house on Tuesday.'

More tears ran down her cheeks. 'I thought I was losing my mind.'

Paige brushed Adele's hair from her wet cheeks, dried her tears. 'You weren't. So Mrs McCloud made you eat the chocolate. Then what?'

'When the car got close to my house they stopped. I was so groggy, I couldn't wake up. She pushed me out the door and I fell in the dirt. I woke up later and it was dark and I was cold. I went home.'

My mother didn't even know I was gone. My dress was ruined so I took it off and burned it.'

'Why didn't you tell me about this?' Darren asked.

Adele kept her gaze on the wall. 'I . . . it messed me up. I went to a mental hospital. I didn't want you to know. Didn't want you to know that I was crazy. Think that I'd hurt Allie. I went to see my psychiatrist on Tuesday. Then I went shopping. That's the truth.'

'I'm sorry, baby,' Darren said, anguished. 'I didn't understand.'

'I know. But I hoped you loved me enough so that it wouldn't matter.'

'Mrs Shaffer, who did this to you?' Grayson asked. 'Who stabbed you?'

'Mrs McCloud.'

Paige sucked in a startled breath. '*Mrs* McCloud?'

'The senator's *wife* stabbed you?' Grayson clarified.

'Yes,' Adele whispered. 'I asked her why . . . I told her I had a life. She said that was the problem.'

'Did you have an automobile?' Hyatt asked.

'I parked it in the alley. She took it. Left me in the dirt. Again.'

The nurse cleared her throat. 'Your five minutes are up. You have to go.'

'Thank you, Adele,' Paige said. 'I know this was hard.'

'They'll deny it,' she said wearily. 'I have no proof.'

'We're working on that,' Hyatt said. 'You concentrate on getting better.' He handed a card to Darren Shaffer. 'This is my direct number, with Assistant SA Smith's number on the back. Please contact us if you remember anything else. We'll keep you updated with our investigation.'

Paige followed Grayson and Hyatt into the hall, then leaned against the wall and made herself breathe. '*Mrs* McCloud stabbed her? I knew she must have known about the abuse, but . . . why? Why would Dianna McCloud try to kill Adele? And does that mean that she killed the others?'

'Good questions, Miss Holden,' Hyatt said.

'Very good questions,' Grayson agreed. 'We assumed that the same person who'd molested the girls had killed them as adults. For now, we need to separate the crimes. The senator did the sexual abuse – we know that. Adele's account matches Rex McCloud's, but I don't want to bring the senator in for questioning yet. We need hard evidence on the sexual assault. At this point, it's he-said, she-said.'

'It's unlikely you will find physical evidence of the rape,' Hyatt said. 'It's been eighteen years since Mrs Shaffer's assault.'

Grayson frowned. 'I know. I don't want to tip them off yet because we have to rethink the murders, too. We have circumstantial evidence that the senator killed Crystal. That hasn't changed.'

'You mean the uneven ligature marks around her throat,' Hyatt said. 'And the fact that Senator McCloud has a weaker hand.'

Grayson nodded. 'Yes. And that Crystal had two killers. The senator strangled her and a second person stabbed her. We assumed the senator would need help with the other victims, too. But now . . . Mrs McCloud changes things. She may have been the person to stab Crystal. She might have killed all the MAC victims or the senator might have.'

'Or they did it together,' Paige muttered. 'What a team.'

'But Dianna might still have needed help to get the victims hung after drugging them, and I don't know that the senator could have done it. We do know she tried to kill Adele, so we should start there. First step is to get physical evidence of the attempted murder. Then we can get a warrant to search the McClouds' home and see what we can find that connects to everything else. Until then, I don't want them to suspect we know or they could destroy any evidence that still exists.'

'Adele's car,' Paige said. 'If Mrs McCloud stabbed her and drove the car away, we might find fingerprints or blood. Or maybe she kept Adele's purse.'

'That would get us the warrant to search the McCloud condo. If we get the right judge, we might get into the estate too.' Grayson gave Paige a nod. 'You were right.'

'About what?' Hyatt asked.

'Paige thought Mrs McCloud was involved in the MAC assaults when the girls were twelve. I don't think either of us expected the senator's wife was a killer, though.'

'Attempted killer,' Hyatt said with a frown.

Grayson shrugged. 'She gave Adele a chocolate when she was twelve that made her groggy. That's how the Shaffers' dog was drugged and how Betsy Malone died.'

Hyatt looked impressed. 'Very good, Counselor. I'll get my people started on finding that car. Keep me posted.'

'I need a second before we leave,' Paige said to Grayson when Hyatt was gone. She stopped at the nurse's station. 'I'd like to check on a patient, please? Logan Booker.'

'Relationship to the patient?' the nurse asked.

'I'm his neighbor,' Paige said. She pointed to Grayson. 'He saved his life.'

The nurse smiled. 'I see. Logan's on this floor. He's stable.'

'I heard the doctors were able to save his leg,' Paige said, holding her breath.

'So far so good. His aunt came from Philly to care for him and to bury her sister.'

'Logan's mother,' Paige murmured. 'Poor Logan.'

'I know. When he's able to travel, the aunt said she'll take him with her to live. She seems like a nice woman. You can see him if you like.'

Paige looked up at Grayson. 'Do we have time?'

'Sure. Let's go.' But he didn't move, just stood there looking troubled. 'What is it?' she asked.

'I have to talk to Ramon Muñoz. I've been putting it off,' he admitted. 'I don't know what to say to make things right. But I need to talk to him. Today.'

She caressed his cheek to soften her words. 'You can't make things right, Grayson. He's lost his mother, his wife, six years of his life. You can't give any of that back. You can only give him justice by making sure that the McClouds and Morton serve the maximum sentence allowable by law. It's what you do best.'

He drew an unsteady breath, turned his face into her palm. 'You'll go with me.'

It wasn't a question. 'Try to keep me away. Come, let's visit Logan. Then Ramon.'

Friday, April 8, 10.35 A.M.

'Not your fault,' Grayson said quietly as they buckled up in the Escalade. They'd just come from Logan's room and it was Grayson's turn to give comfort.

'I know,' Paige whispered. 'He just looked . . . broken.'

'He's still foggy from the surgery. But he won't lose his leg.'

'Not what I meant. His eyes are dead.'

'He's in shock, honey. He's going to have a hard time. But his aunt seems strong.'

She nodded. 'Kind, too. And she's got resources. She'll know how to help him.'

Logan's aunt was a crime scene investigator with the Philly PD. She'd taken a leave of absence to care for him, she'd told them. She had already contacted a counselor who treated victims of violent crime in her area. Logan would get the help he needed. Then she'd taken them aside and asked for the true story. The cops had been cryptic about the gunman who'd killed her sister and injured her nephew.

Grayson was tired of secrets, so he'd told her what they knew.

'It's probably a good thing Silas is dead,' Paige murmured as he started the engine. 'Logan's aunt controlled her anger pretty well when you told her an ex-cop murdered her sister, but if looks really could kill . . . Well, lots of people would be lining up for their turn with Silas.'

'Silas wouldn't have lasted a day in prison. I only hope that none of his victims turn on Rose and Violet. You know, punish the family for the sins of the father.'

'I know,' she said, giving him a wan smile. 'So, where next?'

'North Branch.' The correctional institution where Ramon Muñoz was housed. 'It's a good two-and-a-half-hour drive.'

'You want me to put it into the GPS?'

'No, I've been there many times. I know the way.' He'd nearly made it to the highway when his cell phone began to ring. 'This is Smith.'

'It's Daphne.' She was back to the twang he hadn't realized how much he enjoyed. 'I got you a court order for the Jones sisters' safe-deposit box.'

He'd called her on the way to the hospital to ask her to prepare the warrant, only to find she'd started it the night before. 'Does Hyatt know?'

'Yep. I called him. He's meeting you there in thirty minutes with CSU. Oh, and Yates wants to see you asap. He left the message on my voicemail because he didn't have your new cell number.'

Executive Assistant State's Attorney Jeff Yates had been Charlie Anderson's boss. 'That was fast. I sent him an email when I finally got home last night, requesting a meeting to plan overturning Ramon Muñoz's conviction.'

'I figured as much. Just so you know, I heard that they're looking for you to come back to Homicide. The shit's already hitting the fan in terms of appeal requests on anything Anderson, Dandridge, or Morton touched.'

He'd figured as much, too. 'News travels fast among the defense.'

'That it does. The first stack of appeals were filed by Thomas Thorne.'

Grayson chuckled, surprising himself. 'It's not funny, but it is.'

'You won't think so once you come back. Have you started a brief for Muñoz?'

'No. I tried to get into the server this morning, but I'm still locked out.'

'I'll get it started so you'll have something to take to Yates.'

'You're the best.'

'Don't I know it. Oh, and before I forget, you asked me to get a court order for Brittany's bank account, the one on the register she gave you. I got it and called the bank for you. A thousand dollars was transferred every month from the account of Aristotle Finch of Hagerstown, Maryland. He died six months ago.'

'Which was why the money dried up,' Grayson said. 'Brittany was outa bucks.'

'Might explain why she sold you to Lippman outside the nursing home.'

'Oh, I hope we find her soon,' he said softly. 'Thanks, Daphne, for everything.' He hung up and turned to Paige. 'I'm not putting Ramon off,' he told her.

'I heard. Safe-deposit box, some meeting to discuss freeing Ramon, and Brittany is a greedy ho.'

He smiled. 'That last part you already knew. If this meeting goes as I hope, I'll have something firm to tell Ramon. I'd prefer that to going in with nothing but apologies.'

'I think Ramon would prefer that too. You want me to GPS Brittany's bank?'

'If you don't mind. Let's see what Brittany's been hiding.'

Friday, April 8, 10.35 A.M.

The lieutenant and his people were gone and Adele hadn't moved, her head still turned, still staring at the wall. She hurt, every nerve ending on fire. But she was alive.

And not crazy.

Darren sat in the chair behind her. Silent. The seconds ticked by, turning into minutes, and she wondered why he was even still here.

Then she heard a sound. A sniffle, then a sob. He was crying. Adele didn't think she'd ever seen him cry in all the years they'd been married. Slowly she turned her head, enough to see him from the corner of her eye.

She said nothing, just waited. He'd leaned forward in the chair, elbows on the bedrail, hands covering his face, his shoulders shaking. Adele drew a breath that burned. And let it out. Reached up and brushed his elbow with her fingertip.

'Sshh,' she said. 'It's all right.'

He looked up, anguished. 'Why didn't you tell me?'

'I was . . . ashamed. I thought . . . no one would want me. I was broken.'

'Adele.' His throat worked as he tried to control himself. 'You're not broken. You're perfect. You always have been.'

'You didn't know me then.'

'No, I didn't. You never spoke of your family. When we first met

509

I asked you about your family and you said you had none.'

'Because I don't.'

'But you told the lieutenant that you had three brothers. A mother.'

'Gone. All gone.'

He frowned. 'Dead?'

'Yes. Drugs and booze. Gunshot wounds. Drunk driving. By the time I was eighteen, they were all gone and I was all alone. My baby brother held on the longest. He promised me he'd stay out of trouble, stay away from drugs. I came home from work one day and found him dead. Shot to death, drug buy gone wrong. He'd been pushing, out of our apartment. I'd always seen shadows, looked over my shoulder, you know, since the senator, but when I found Andy dead like that, I just cracked.'

Compassion had filled his eyes, but at the mention of the senator the compassion became fury. 'And you went into the mental hospital.'

She winced. 'Yes. That was where I met Dr Theopolis. Who I went to see on Tuesday. I started to get better. I got a job, made friends. Went to college. Met you.'

The fury in his eyes banked, and he gently picked up her hand. 'If you'd told me about the senator, I would have believed you. And I'd never, ever think you were broken. I'm sorry, Adele. I'm sorry I didn't believe you when you said you went shopping. But you'd been acting so strangely and . . . well, I always worried that one day you'd wake up and realize you'd made a mistake. That you shouldn't have married me.'

'Why would I think that? Just because your first wife left?'

He attempted a crooked smile. 'I guess I was broken.'

'I was going to tell you,' she whispered. 'But I had to find out who was after me. I went to a private investigator.'

'I know. Your friend Krissy called the police when she saw your picture on the news. She told them that you went to see the PI to get material for the divorce.'

'No, not for a divorce. I just told Krissy that. I hired the PI to help me find out who was trying to kill me. I had to know I wasn't crazy and be able to prove it to you. Otherwise, I'd be handing you ammunition to use against me. To take Allie from me. You'd never believe I didn't have an affair.'

'What can I do?' he said. 'What can I do to make you love me again?'

'Nothing. I never stopped loving you.'

He swallowed hard. 'I love you, Adele. I can't promise to never be a jerk again because sometimes I'm stupid, but I do promise never to leave you.'

'What if they arrest McCloud?'

His jaw hardened. 'You'll testify. I'll be there with you every step. You'll make him pay. I just hope I can see his face without smashing it.'

'Everyone will know,' she whispered. 'Someday Allie will know.'

'You didn't do anything wrong, Adele,' he said fiercely. 'You were the victim. And you have nothing, *nothing* to be ashamed of. Allie will know her mother survived and got justice for herself and the fifteen others he molested.'

'All right,' she said. 'I'll do it. Are we okay?'

'More than okay. You're alive.'

'And not crazy,' she murmured.

He laughed, a watery sound. 'And Rusty's coming home tomorrow.'

She managed a chuckle that hurt her chest. 'No more chocolate for him.'

Friday, April 8, 11.10 A.M.

Hyatt and CSU's Drew Peterson were only a few minutes behind them, so they didn't have to wait in the bank's lobby long.

'You have the key?' Hyatt said.

Grayson held it up. 'Right here.'

The bank manager inspected the court order, then led them to the vault. He removed the box and put it on a table. Grayson inserted the key. It turned and slowly he lifted the hinged lid. Inside was a large manila envelope.

Drew opened it, his hands gloved. And he frowned.

'What is it?' Hyatt said and Drew looked up, puzzled.

'It's blue fabric,' he said.

Paige tilted the envelope to look inside and her mouth fell open. 'Oh, my God,' she breathed. She looked up at Grayson. 'It's Crystal's dress, the one she wore the day of the MAC ice-cream social. Remember the librarian said it was blue? That's the dress.'

'Will you excuse us?' Hyatt asked the bank manager. When the man was gone, he turned to Drew. 'Check it out.'

Drew took a UV lightstick from his toolkit, waved it over the mouth of the envelope. The fabric inside began to glow.

'I don't see any bloodstains,' Drew said. 'It's likely semen. We'll do a DNA on the semen and see if we can find hair, skin, anything on it that belonged to Crystal.'

'I can't believe she kept it,' Hyatt said. 'Why would she even think to?'

'At the time of her assault, who knows?' Paige shrugged. 'But later, six years ago, she was going to blackmail the McClouds. *This* is why she was killed.'

'She threatened to expose them,' Grayson murmured. 'This is why she went to that party. She must have told them she had proof. Has her sister been to this box?'

'Yes,' Hyatt said. 'The manager said she visited six years ago. She hasn't been back since.'

'She knew about the dress, so she knew about the assault,' Grayson said. 'Brittany wanted *us* to find out about MAC.'

'Why didn't she just report it to the police herself?' Drew asked.

'Because if *we* found out, it would bring the McClouds into the spotlight,' Grayson said. 'There'd be a scandal, which the senator and his wife would do anything to avoid.'

'*Then* she was going to blackmail them,' Paige said. 'Once they were implicated in the assault of sixteen girls, she'd be in a sweet spot. She'd get really big money.'

'Except she didn't know that, apart from Adele, they were all dead,' Grayson added.

'Why did she give you the key?' Drew asked.

'I think she got scared because we almost got blown up,' Grayson said. 'If we found the dress and nailed the McClouds instead of just implicating them . . .'

'It would take the heat off of her,' Hyatt said grimly. 'When we find her, she'll know what heat really is. For now, let's get this tested, Peterson. I want results as fast as humanly possible. When I bring in that ass McCloud, I want him to sweat.'

'Will do,' Drew said. 'I'll need something to compare it to.'

'I'll get you something,' Hyatt promised.

They'd left the bank when Hyatt held up his forefinger for them to wait. 'Excellent,' he said into his cell phone. 'Keep someone on them both.' He hung up and turned to Grayson and Paige.

'What did you find?' Grayson asked.

'Adele's car at the airport. Guess who the security video showed getting out of it?'

Grayson's pulse began to race. 'Dianna McCloud?'

Hyatt's bald head nodded once in satisfaction. 'One and the same. I had Detective Perkins draft a search warrant as soon as I left Adele's hospital room. Now it's signed and Perkins and his team are on their way to search the McCloud residences.'

'Both the condo *and* the estate?' Paige asked eagerly.

'Since the estate is where the original crime occurred, yes, the estate too. I'll keep you informed, Mr Smith.'

Grayson watched Hyatt stride away, then turned to Paige, a smile on his face.

'With Adele's eyewitness testimony and the DNA on the dress, we can put McCloud away for rape and his wife for facilitation. Then, if we're really lucky, we can maneuver them into turning on each other for all the murders.'

Paige smiled back. 'Just like TV. Except the prosecutor is better looking in real life.'

Twenty-six

Cumberland, Maryland
Friday, April 8, 4.00 P.M.

Grayson clipped the ID badge on his lapel. He'd been to North Branch Correctional Institution many times throughout his career as a prosecutor. Every time was important. Every time he'd be another step closer to getting justice for a victim.

But today . . . He'd never approached a meeting with so much dread.

'Relax,' Paige whispered. 'It'll be what it'll be.' She clipped her badge on her blouse. 'I feel twenty pounds lighter.'

'No shock there,' Grayson said. 'That's how much metal you left with the guard when you disarmed.' The guard's eyes had grown wider with each weapon she'd added to the pile.

'I feel very vulnerable at the moment,' she said.

I feel like I'm going to be sick, he thought.

They were escorted to a small conference room where a man in an orange jumpsuit waited. He sat quietly, looking down at the table, his manacled hands folded before him.

'Ramon,' Paige said softly. 'I'm Paige Holden. I was a friend of Elena's.'

Ramon looked up and Grayson had to fight the impulse to flinch. Ramon's face was battered, old bruises yellowed and fading. New bruises had nearly swollen one eye shut. Nearly. But not swollen enough to hide the man's blank expression.

Ramon's eyes were flat. Dead. Other than lifting his head, he didn't acknowledge that Paige had said a word. These were the eyes

514

of a man who'd given up. Who'd been beaten into submission. Who didn't care.

You put him here, Smith. You did this.

No. I did my duty. I did my job. He swallowed hard. *I did my job too well.*

Paige sat at the table, flicking a meaningful glance at the chair next to her. Grayson took the hint, sitting beside her. There was the tiniest light of hate in Ramon's eyes.

He remembers me. How could he forget?

Grayson couldn't find his voice. Silence filled the room and then Paige began to speak for him.

'Like I said, I'm Paige, this is Grayson Smith of the state's attorney's office. I'm so sorry for the loss of Elena and Maria. They were good women.'

'Guard,' Ramon said with no inflection whatsoever. 'Take me back to my cell.'

'*No,*' Paige cried when Ramon stood up. 'Wait. Please. I was with Elena when she died. I know what happened. Ramon, she died loving you.'

'No. She didn't love me.'

'She slept with Denny Sandoval. For you. To get evidence that you were innocent. She found it, Ramon. She found proof of your alibi. And it got her killed.'

Ramon's body went still. 'I don't believe it.'

'It's true,' Grayson said quietly. 'The evidence presented at your trial had been tampered with. Witnesses paid to lie. You were set up to take the blame for the murder of Crystal Jones. We know that now.'

'Elena was with Sandoval to get into his computer, Ramon,' Paige said urgently. 'She found photos that proved you were in that bar the night of the murder. And which proved that Sandoval had been paid off. He's dead now.'

'I know,' Ramon murmured. His eyes were still flat. He still stood, motionless. 'I saw it on TV. He committed suicide after he killed Elena.'

'No,' Paige said, 'that's not true. He was killed by the man who

515

paid for his silence. Who orchestrated the frame. His name was Stuart Lippman and he worked for your defense attorney. They were both dirty.'

'Bob Bond,' Ramon said.

'He's dead,' Paige said. 'So is Lippman. They'd framed other people for crimes they didn't do. Paid by the families of the true perpetrators. We know this.'

Ramon slowly sat. 'Elena did this?'

Paige nodded. 'She did. She started a huge chain reaction, exposing the dirty lawyers and a lot of other people. She and your mother hired me to help you. I'm a private investigator. They believed in your innocence. Elena never stopped believing. She never stopped loving you. I was with her when she died and those were her last words. She made me promise to tell you. So here I am. Your wife gave her life for you.'

Ramon's eyes closed, the hands he folded in front of him clenched into fists. 'Who killed her?'

'An ex-cop who was on Lippman's payroll.'

Ramon went still once again. 'Silas Dandridge,' he said.

Grayson blinked. 'How do you know Dandridge?' he asked.

'He came to the bar,' Ramon said woodenly. 'My brothers told me. For months after I was arrested he'd come to the bar and sit. Just sit. And watch.'

'Intimidating anyone who considered telling the truth,' Grayson said.

'Why didn't they tell someone?' Paige asked.

'Who were they going to tell?' Ramon asked. 'The cops? No. But it was no secret. Everyone knows Silas Dandridge.'

'He's dead,' Grayson said, and for the first time saw life in Ramon's eyes.

Briefly they flashed with fury and hate, then the emotion was gone. 'Good.'

'Jorge Delgado is also dead,' Paige said.

Ramon's nostrils flared. 'May he burn in hell.'

Paige nodded. 'I guess I can see how you'd feel that way.'

Ramon tilted his head in Grayson's direction. 'He can burn in hell, too.'

Paige drew a breath. 'He nearly died trying to prove your innocence. So did I.'

'Like it matters?'

'It does to me,' Paige said, clearly annoyed. 'I've been shot at, knifed, and nearly blown up. Since Tuesday.'

Ramon met her eyes, lifted his shackled hands. 'Pardon me if I don't clap.'

'I don't expect you to clap,' she said sharply, then she sighed. 'I don't expect anything from you, Ramon. That's not why I did any of this. I did it for your mother. For Elena. Because they loved you. Mr Smith did it because he recognized his case had been manipulated. That you'd been denied a fair trial.'

'And that you never should have been charged to begin with,' Grayson said.

Ramon closed his eyes. 'It doesn't matter.'

'What doesn't matter?' Grayson asked.

'None of it.'

'I met with Executive Assistant State's Attorney Yates before I came. In the light of everything we now know, we're applying for a reversal. To have your conviction overturned. Your record expunged. You'll be free.'

Ramon stood. 'Guard. Take me back to my cell.'

Paige stood as well. 'Did you hear that? You'll be free.'

'It doesn't matter. Elena is gone. My mother, gone. My life, gone. Even if I get out, I am not free.' He shuffled to the door, his ankles shackled as well. He turned sideways, waiting for the guard to open the door and Grayson saw the tears on his face.

It mattered too much.

'Mr Muñoz,' Grayson said, 'I did my job for Crystal Jones, the victim of a violent murder. I prosecuted you to the best of my ability to get justice for her.'

'And you want my forgiveness?' Ramon gritted out.

'No. I want you to know that I'll prosecute those who are in any way responsible for your wife's death as . . . zealously as I prosecuted you. Elena will have justice.'

517

Ramon nodded, just once. 'Thank you. For my Elena. But for me, you can still burn in hell.'

The guard opened the door and Ramon shuffled out, leaving Grayson and Paige staring after him. 'That's not how I pictured this meeting,' Paige said.

'Did you think he'd be grateful?' Grayson said. 'He's lost everything. You're the one who said I can't make this right and neither can you. We can only stand for the victims.'

She met his eyes. 'How did you get so wise?'

'I listened to you. Come on, let's go home.'

Baltimore
Friday, April 8, 7.45 P.M.

'Home' turned out to be the Carter estate. Paige tried not to gawk as she and Grayson approached the front door, Peabody in tow, but it was nearly impossible, so she gave up trying. The house looked like something from a movie.

They were greeted by Katherine, who instantly enveloped Paige in her arms. 'We are so happy you're here,' she said, squeezing until Paige had to gasp for air and Peabody uttered a very soft growl.

'You're choking her, Katherine,' Grayson said mildly, taking the leash from Paige's hand. 'And you're upsetting Peabody.'

With a breathless laugh, Katherine released her from her embrace. 'So this is the famous Peabody. I have something for him, if it's okay.' From her pocket she withdrew a dog biscuit as big as Grayson's palm. 'Brian baked it. A token of our appreciation.'

'If Brian baked it, it has to be good,' Paige said. 'I should probably wait until I get him home to give it to him. He'll get crumbs all over your house.'

'Crumbs can be cleaned,' Katherine said. 'Peabody is a hero. Holly and Joseph told us about last night. What you did for my daughter . . . Now I'm choking myself up. Thank you, Paige, for saving Holly's life.'

'It was . . . You're welcome.'

'I've heard nothing but talk of you from my children. Come, sit

518

with me while I finish dinner.' She firmly took Paige's arm and led her away.

Paige looked over her shoulder helplessly. Grayson just grinned and followed.

Brian and Lisa were already in the kitchen and one whiff had Paige's mouth watering. 'I think we forgot lunch,' Paige said.

'Sit,' Lisa said, pointing to a set of stools at the counter. 'Brian made snacks.'

Paige obeyed, snacking on something that she couldn't pronounce and that should have been served on a silver platter by a tuxedoed waiter. 'Where is Holly?'

Lisa and her mother shared an anxious glance. 'Holly didn't sleep well last night.'

'I suppose not,' Paige said. 'I worried about her. That was an intense experience. And she saw Lippman killed. She won't forget that anytime soon.'

'We know,' Katherine said soberly. 'We contacted a counselor early this morning. Holly sees him for the first time tomorrow. She wanted you to be there, Paige, if you don't mind. She said you'd know how she felt.'

Paige frowned. 'I do, and of course I'll go, but how does Holly know what I've seen?'

'I don't think she knows you saw your friend die,' Lisa said. 'I think she just knows you understand. You make her feel better.'

'Tell me where and when. I'll be there.'

Grayson leaned against the counter, his leg touching hers. 'So where is Holly now? And my mother? And Jack?'

Katherine sighed. 'At about five this morning, Holly decided she needed a dog like Peabody. Jack and Judy took her to the pet store.'

Paige made a face. 'She won't find a dog like Peabody at a pet store.'

'We don't think she means a protection dog,' Brian said. 'We think she means a Rottweiler in general.'

'We thought you could help her find one instead,' Katherine said. 'If you don't mind. A protection dog, we mean. It would make me feel safer, too – especially with those boys at the social center. I want Holly to have independence. A life. But I'm still her mom.'

'Peabody made all the difference for me when I was too afraid to be alone.' Paige scratched his ears. 'If you want, I can call my friend in Minnesota, the one who trained Peabody. I'm sure Brie would be happy to match Holly with a dog.'

'You set it up, I'll buy the plane tickets,' Katherine said. 'We could make it a weekend. Do girl stuff.' She lifted a brow. 'Meet your family. Since you're seeing our boy, you understand.'

Grayson winced. 'No family, Katherine.'

'None?' Katherine bit her lip. 'I'm sorry.'

'Not a problem,' Paige said easily. 'My grandparents are dead, but I have a lot of friends who would be delighted to meet you all.'

'Can I come?' Grayson said.

'Sure,' Paige said. 'Olivia can meet you and stop worrying about me.'

Grayson opened his mouth to say more, but stopped when his phone rang. 'Smith.' He listened, then said, 'That's quite a haul. I'm sorry I missed the search.' He grinned. 'Right now? Thanks.' He hung up. 'That was Hyatt. He said to turn on the news.'

Brian pointed a remote at a counter on the other side of the kitchen and a TV slid up from beneath. A second later, they were watching Phin Radcliffe standing in front of the police department. A cruiser drove up and a man was not so gently helped from the backseat. The camera zoomed to reveal a red-faced Jim McCloud. In handcuffs.

'Now *that*', Paige said, 'is an intensely satisfying sight.'

'Better if he were wearing an orange jumpsuit,' Grayson murmured.

'Soon,' she said. 'You'll make it happen.'

On the screen, Radcliffe was walking alongside the senator as close as the detectives escorting him would allow. 'Mr McCloud,' Radcliffe called. 'What are the charges against you?'

McCloud ignored him.

'We hear the charge against you is murder,' Radcliffe said, 'and two counts of rape. Mrs McCloud has already been charged with the attempted murder of Adele Shaffer, the murder of Betsy Malone, and for conspiracy to commit rape. Serious charges.'

McCloud stopped abruptly and looked into the camera. 'This is a total fabrication,' he said smoothly. 'The product of Adele Shaffer's tortured mind. We will prove these accusations false and help the poor young woman get the appropriate mental help.'

McCloud was then hustled away, up the stairs and into the precinct, leaving Radcliffe to expound on the life and career of Senator Jim McCloud.

'You can turn it off,' Grayson said. 'They're still searching the estate, but guess what they found hidden in the back of the senator's desk drawer? Crystal's purse.'

'*Yes*,' Paige said, the satisfaction she felt increasing tenfold. 'He's going down.'

'It held her cell phone – a disposable, which was why we didn't find phone records in her name. It also held credit cards, lipstick, and one canister of pepper spray.'

Paige nodded. 'Told ya.'

'Yes, you did,' Grayson said, then turned around when the front door opened and more voices filled the house. 'Come on. I want you to meet Jack. You'll love him.'

Twenty-seven

Saturday, April 9, 4.30 P.M.

Don't start without me. Please. Paige knocked softly on the door to interview room six. Grayson opened it and she was relieved to find they'd waited. Grayson had been at the precinct with Hyatt most of the day, going over the evidence recovered in the search of the McCloud residences. Paige felt a thrill of anticipation. They would fill in the gaps. Then McCloud would go away.

'I got here as fast as I could.' She and Holly had just emerged from the counselor's office when Grayson texted her to get down to the precinct asap. 'Your mother and Katherine dropped me off, then took Holly home.'

'How is she?'

'Still scared. She will be for a while. But I think the counselor helped. She goes back on Wednesday. I'll go with her.'

'Excuse me for interrupting your conversation with something as mundane as a questioning,' Hyatt said sarcastically. He stood on the observation side of the two-way mirror, along with Stevie who looked drawn, but alert.

This closure should be good for her, thought Paige. Daphne and Lucy Trask stood next to Stevie, flanking her on either side.

Detectives Bashears and Perkins waited to one side while Jeff Yates, the executive assistant state's attorney, leaned against the far wall.

On the other side of the mirror a man in a suit sat next to an irate former senator.

It made Paige smile. 'Sorry.'

'He's pickin' at you, Paige,' Daphne said. 'We all just got here. His royal pervertedness was just brought up from Holding. I say we let him stew a little longer.'

'We have someone else you'll want to see,' Bashears said.

'Brittany Jones?' Paige asked.

'None other,' Bashears said. 'We followed her boyfriend Mal to a hotel up on Lake Erie. She was there along with her son.'

'And a bag full of cash,' Perkins added. 'She'd closed out her checking account into which had been wired twenty-five grand right before your car blew.'

'She's in interview room two,' Grayson said. 'Lawyered up already, unfortunately. We'll question her after we're done with the McClouds.'

'And the DNA from the dress?' Paige asked.

Slow smiles spread across the faces of everyone in the room.

'It's a match, then,' Paige said.

'It is,' Hyatt said. 'It's showtime, people. Grayson?'

'I have to go,' Grayson said. 'Wish me luck.' He and Hyatt left the room, entering the interview room through a hall door.

'Senator,' Hyatt said.

'This is outrageous,' McCloud declared.

'Senator,' the suit cautioned. 'Say nothing.'

'I don't have to "say nothing". I'm innocent of all these charges.'

'Then this should be quick,' Grayson said. 'Tell me about MAC.'

'It was a charity run by my wife. One of her pet projects.' The senator waved his good hand dismissively. 'Low-income schools and poor kids got money. End of story.'

Grayson nodded. 'And they came to your estate for ice cream.'

'Once a year. Took forever to get all the ice-cream stains out of the upholstery.'

Hyatt shook his head. 'Kids are messy.'

'Adele Shaffer was one of those kids,' Grayson said.

'She's a deluded young woman. She needs help.'

Grayson's brows lifted. 'Your wife stabbed her.'

'No. The young woman is mistaken.'

'I'm afraid not,' Hyatt said. 'We have video of your wife driving

523

Mrs Shaffer's car. We found a pearl-handled knife in Mrs McCloud's trunk. The blood on it belongs to Adele.'

McCloud looked shocked. 'You're lying.'

'No.' Hyatt showed him a plastic evidence bag holding the knife. 'Dianna's fingerprints are on the knife, in the blood. She did it.'

'She . . .' McCloud shook his head again, bewildered. 'I don't know what to say. She needs help.'

'I'd say so,' Hyatt said. 'So back to Crystal Jones. How did you meet her?'

'I never met her.'

'Really?' Grayson asked. 'She was one of the charity kids who came to your estate.'

'My wife handled the children. I didn't get involved.'

'That's not what Adele Shaffer says,' Grayson said quietly.

'And I told you that she's delusional.'

'So you didn't rape Adele in your daughter Claire's old bedroom?' Hyatt asked.

'No!' The senator's face grew florid and his lawyer tried to calm him.

'What about Crystal Jones?' Hyatt asked.

'I didn't rape anybody! I'll have your job, Lieutenant.'

'Most days I'd tell you to take it,' Hyatt said. 'Today, I'm enjoying it. We recovered Crystal's phone from the purse she carried that night.' He tossed the purse, in a clear evidence bag, on the table. 'We found her purse in your desk, Senator.'

McCloud faltered. 'I didn't put it there.'

Hyatt shrugged. 'Your fingerprints are on it. And on the canister of pepper spray we found inside.'

'Senator,' his lawyer murmured, but the senator waved him away.

'No. I can explain. I did meet her that night. She'd come to my grandson's party and was found wandering through the house, very drunk. I had security escort her out. Later I found her purse and put it aside, intending to ask my grandson to give it back to her. My fingerprints are on the contents because I opened the purse, looking for her ID. I'm afraid the purse simply slipped my mind.'

'Really?' Grayson asked seriously. 'Interesting, because Crystal's blood alcohol was almost zero. She wasn't drunk.'

'She behaved like she was,' the senator insisted.

'We recovered the texts she sent right before she died,' Hyatt said, bluntly now. 'To your cell-phone number. It's been your number since before the murder. I checked. We didn't find Crystal's phone records because it was a disposable phone. And of course, we didn't check yours because we thought she'd come as Rex's date. We didn't know she'd really come to see *you*.'

McCloud blustered, 'Not true. I didn't know that woman. I'd never seen her before that night.'

Grayson picked up the paper in front of him. 'The day before the party she texts that she wants to meet you, that your power is an "*aphrodisiac*". You tell her, "*Not with my wife around.*" Then the night of the party she texts, "*Knock knock, I'm here. Rex thinks I came for him but you're the one I want.*" You text back, "*Meet me at the gardener's shed at midnight.*"'

McCloud's face had gone stony. 'I didn't send those texts.'

'So you didn't meet Crystal in the gardener's shed that night?' Hyatt asked.

'No!'

'And you didn't have sex with her that night?' Grayson pressed.

'No! I did not have sex with that woman,' he declared.

Famous last words, Paige thought and held her breath. *This is it. They have him.*

'Never?' Hyatt asked calmly.

'No, *never*.'

'I see,' Grayson said. 'So, what is this?' He unrolled the blue dress, protected in a large plastic bag.

'I have no idea. This is ludicrous. I'm leaving.' He got up and Hyatt was out of his chair in a split-second, pushing him back down.

'I don't think so, Senator,' Hyatt said.

'I actually think you'll be staying for a very long time,' Grayson added. 'This dress belonged to Crystal Jones. We found it in her safe-deposit box. It has skin cells that match her DNA on the underside of the fabric.'

'So?' McCloud asked belligerently. 'It's a dress.'

'It's a special dress,' Grayson said, then pointed. 'See this stain? That's semen.'

McCloud paled. 'That's disgusting.'

'Yes, it is.' Grayson put a picture of twelve-year-old Crystal on top of the dress. His expression darkened. 'It *is* disgusting. It's also yours. You *raped* this *child*.'

McCloud's mouth opened, but no words came out.

Hyatt leaned over McCloud's shoulder, murmuring in a menacing tone, 'And then you killed her when she threatened to blackmail you.'

'I didn't kill her.'

'You *strangled* her,' Hyatt said. 'Then you *stabbed* her.'

'No! I didn't stab her,' McCloud blurted. 'I strangled her. But I didn't stab her.'

His lawyer closed his eyes. 'Jim. Please. Shut up.'

'There were sixteen girls in the MAC program,' Hyatt pushed. 'You raped them all.'

'Then you killed them,' Grayson finished coldly. 'You killed them all except Adele Shaffer.'

McCloud's eyes widened. 'No. I did not kill any others. I didn't.'

Grayson leaned forward. 'Then why are they dead?'

Panic filled McCloud's eyes. 'I don't know. I don't know. Keith, get me out of here.'

'I can't,' his lawyer said. 'I told you to be quiet. You never listen.'

'Why?' Grayson asked. 'Why did you do it? Why did you rape all those girls?'

McCloud shook his head, finally mute.

Grayson stood up, gathered the evidence. 'That's okay. We got enough.'

Questioning Dianna McCloud was a great deal easier. Hyatt and Grayson teamed up again, but this time they took a different approach. They'd found photographs among Mrs McCloud's things that explained quite a lot. The first was a MAC group photo taken in 1984.

Stuart Lippman stood on the back row. There were other pictures – Stuart at his high-school graduation, college graduation, sitting at the defense table in a courtroom. He'd been her project.

And she'd taken his death very hard.

They'd found a lot of interesting things in Stuart's condo. One was a laptop, owned by Denny Sandoval. On it were the original files that Elena had stolen. It appeared that Stuart Lippman had killed Sandoval. Assuming he'd killed Bob Bond as well wasn't a big leap. Many of the dead MAC women had been hung in a similar fashion. That Lippman had also killed them made sense, especially given the close relationship he shared with Mrs McCloud.

Now they had to prove it.

When Grayson and Hyatt entered interview room four, she looked up, her eyes red and swollen. 'Go away,' she said hoarsely.

She'd waived her right to counsel, saying the only lawyer she trusted was dead. In her bloodshot eyes Grayson saw raw grief and the knowledge that Adele's survival and accusation spelled her own fate. He also saw that Dianna didn't care anymore.

'Sorry, ma'am,' Hyatt said. 'We need to talk.'

'I don't want to talk to you.'

'You loved Stuart,' Grayson said, ignoring her.

She began to cry anew.

Grayson ignored that too. 'He was the only person outside your family to have a condo in the penthouse suites.'

She looked up, surprised. 'He was part of the family. My part.'

'He was a MAC kid.'

She nodded unsteadily. 'He was such a little gentleman the day he came to the estate. So much better behaved than that brat of Claire's. Stuart loved me. I was a better mother than that whore he lived with.' She dabbed at her eyes. 'I took care of him. And he took care of me.'

'So tell me about the MAC kids,' Grayson said. 'Why did you start the charity?'

'I wanted to help children.'

'But your husband didn't.' Grayson dropped his voice confidentially. 'He liked little girls. You don't have to worry about sharing his secrets. He told us so. He told us he loved Reba.'

She looked uncomfortable. 'Of course he does. He's her father.'

'No. He didn't love her the way he was supposed to. He wanted Reba. Just like he'd wanted Claire.' It was a guess, but Grayson hoped to see how she'd react. He wasn't disappointed.

Her face twisted into a grimace. 'Yes, he did. I hated that about him.'

'You knew he molested Claire?' Grayson asked and Dianna nodded, reluctantly.

'Did you try to stop him?' Hyatt asked and she looked confused. 'She wasn't my daughter. It wasn't my place.'

Grayson wanted to grimace too, but kept his expression straight. 'But Reba *is* your daughter.'

'Yes. I had to protect her. That's what you do for your children.'

'Claire moved out,' Grayson said, remembering Paige's theory. 'And your husband started looking at Reba.'

'I had to protect her,' Dianna said defensively.

'So you gave him the other girls? The MAC girls.'

'Yes,' Dianna said, as if it made perfect sense. 'It wasn't as if they . . .'

'They what, Mrs McCloud?' Grayson asked. 'It wasn't as if they *what*?'

Dianna shrugged. 'Mattered. It was only a question of time before *somebody* did it to them, coming from those kinds of homes. I had to protect my daughter.'

Hyatt drew a breath and Grayson knew the lieutenant was fighting to keep his anger in control. 'Why did you kill Crystal Jones?' Hyatt asked.

'She tried to hurt us. Would have blackmailed us.'

'So your husband met her in the shed and strangled her,' Grayson said. 'But he didn't kill her.'

'It's okay,' Hyatt said. 'He already confessed. He said he only strangled her.'

Dianna rolled her eyes. 'He did a sloppy job. After he came out of the shed, I went in. The girl was still alive.'

'So you stabbed her?' Hyatt asked.

She said nothing, but her face spoke volumes. She'd done it, all right.

'How did you know she was Crystal?' Grayson asked. 'She told Rex she was Amber so she could sneak into the party.'

Dianna looked scornful. 'She also told my husband she was Amber, every time she tried to seduce him. My husband is an idiot who thinks with his . . . you know.'

'So your husband knew Crystal before the night of the party?' Hyatt asked.

'Yes. She attended a guest lecture he did for one of Rex's college classes. She somehow got Jim's cell-phone number, probably from Rex. She started texting him. Sending naked pictures of herself. Telling him how turned on she got by politicians. I saw the texts – I always check his phone. I wanted to know who this bimbo was. So I called the university, checked the class list. The students had to show ID to get into the guest lectures, heightened security and all. There was no Amber on the list. I got suspicious and talked to the professor. He remembered her getting cozy with Jim, but later sidling up to Rex. The professor told me her name was Crystal Jones.'

'You recognized the name?' Grayson asked.

'Of course. I have a photographic memory. I knew who she was and I warned Jim. The next thing I know, she's lied her way onto our property. I followed Jim that night when he went to the shed. He knew who she was and what she wanted. He killed her, or thought he did. I tried to stab her, but I didn't know where to put the knife.'

'So you called the one person you could trust,' Grayson said. 'Stuart.'

'He came right away. Knew we had to do damage control. He finished stabbing her, then came up with the plan to frame the gardener.'

'What about the other MAC women?' Hyatt asked.

'We had a vulnerability,' Dianna said. 'I had to fix it. It was just a matter of time before one of the others got the idea to do the same thing Crystal did.'

'So you hunted them down and killed them first,' Hyatt said.

'Yes, of course,' Dianna replied. 'I fixed it. I gave them chocolate. They fell asleep and died.'

'Why did you hang them?' Grayson asked.

She frowned. 'I didn't.'

'Somebody did,' Grayson said. 'Quite of few of them were found hanging.'

Dianna caught her breath. 'Oh. He did that. For me.'

'Who?' Hyatt asked.

'Stuart. He fixed them for me. That's what he was talking about. He told me a few days ago that I hadn't killed them all and that he'd had to fix them. That's what he meant.' Her expression became almost . . . reverent. 'He fixed them for me.'

Grayson and Hyatt left her at the table talking to herself.

Back in the observation room the others were still staring through the glass at Dianna McCloud.

'Oh, my God,' Paige said. 'She's . . . what is she? Crazy or evil?'

'Sane enough to stand trial,' Daphne said. 'That's all I care about.'

Grayson rubbed his forehead. 'Two down, one to go. I have quite a few questions for Brittany Jones.' He looked over at Executive ASA Yates. 'We've got her dead to rights. I don't plan to offer her any deals.'

'I wouldn't expect you to,' Yates said. 'Get in there and good luck.'

Brittany looked up when Grayson and Hyatt entered. Her eyes shuttered, her expression becoming sullen. Her lawyer introduced himself and stated that his client would be answering no questions.

'I'm Lieutenant Hyatt,' Hyatt said to Brittany, ignoring her attorney. He pointed to Grayson. 'Him, I think you know.'

Brittany turned her face away. 'I'm not talking to you.'

Grayson sat in the chair closest to Brittany. 'Then you can listen for a minute. You'll be charged with extortion and conspiracy to commit murder. That I was the intended victim makes me a little more than angry.'

'I didn't do it,' Brittany said.

'You stalled your friend at the nursing-home reception desk,'

Grayson stated. 'You knew we'd be there. You sold this information to Stuart Lippman who in turn hired Harlan Kapansky to place a bomb under my car.'

'You can't prove that,' Brittany said haughtily.

'Brittany, be quiet,' her lawyer admonished.

'We've examined all of Stuart Lippman's phone calls,' Hyatt said. 'Incoming and outgoing. On Wednesday night at 6.18 P.M., he received a call from a pay phone located in a gas station outside of Harrisburg, Pennsylvania. The security video at the gas station shows you, Brittany, making a call at exactly that time. A few hours later, Stuart transferred twenty-five thousand dollars to your bank account.' Hyatt's smile was cold. 'So you see, Ms Jones, we *can* prove it.'

It had taken a great deal of scrambling to get the gas station's security video. But, Grayson thought, the stunned look on Brittany's face was worth every second of effort.

She and her lawyer whispered to each other. Then her lawyer looked up. 'She gave you the dress. You never would have gotten the senator without the dress.'

That was probably true, Grayson thought. Still, he shrugged nonchalantly. 'The dress is nice to have, but I didn't need it. We have eyewitness testimony. The senator committed rape. Brittany committed attempted murder. They're both guilty.'

'The senator murdered, too,' Brittany said, her eyes flashing. 'He raped my sister, then he killed her.'

Her lawyer held up his hand. 'Can we make a deal?'

'Why?' Grayson asked. 'She has nothing to offer. I have everything and everyone I need. Either in custody or dead.'

Brittany's eyes narrowed. 'No, you don't, or you wouldn't be here. What do you want?'

Grayson nearly blinked. She'd read him well. He shouldn't have been surprised. She'd read him well when he and Paige had visited her house, catching his sympathy when she'd said about her son, *He's got only me*. She'd play havoc with a jury. All she needed to do was to convince one juror that she didn't know what Lippman had intended and he'd have a hung jury. Then she'd walk. He couldn't allow that to happen.

She'd tried to kill him. *She tried to kill Paige.* Fury bubbled up, and with it the resolution that this woman would go to prison for a very long time.

'I want a full confession,' he said flatly. 'Complete with details.'

Her lawyer's eyes widened. 'You want her to plead guilty?' He rose. 'No. Absolutely not. Let's go, Brittany.'

Brittany stood. Grayson didn't move, just watched her. 'You've got a son,' he said.

Brittany froze, fury of her own filling her eyes. 'Don't you lay a hand on my son.'

'Your son is in foster care,' Grayson said. 'He will be cared for. The question is, will you see him before he's out of college? Or ever again?'

She became pale. 'What do you mean?' Her lawyer tugged on her arm, telling her to leave, but she shook him off. 'What do you mean?' she demanded.

'Full confession and I'll recommend you serve your sentence in Baltimore. Anything less and I'll do everything in my power to see you locked up so far away that nobody will bring him to see you on visitation day. Ever.'

She lowered herself to her chair, trembling. 'You can't do that.'

Grayson's jaw clenched. 'Watch me.'

Her lawyer gripped her arm tight. 'We'll take our chances in court. Let's go.' He pulled her to her feet and she stumbled halfway to the door, still pale.

'The maximum sentence for attempted murder in the first degree is life, Brittany,' Grayson said. 'It might be better for little Caleb's foster mother to tell him you died. Better than him knowing his mother is rotting away in prison. *For life.*'

She turned, looking like she would faint. 'You bastard.'

Grayson shrugged. 'What'll it be, Brittany? This offer is rescinded as soon as you walk through that door. Think carefully.'

She closed her eyes. 'I gave you the dress.'

'And I thank you. But I suspect you did it more for your own health than mine.'

She opened her eyes and Grayson knew he'd won. 'Damn you,' she whispered.

He pushed a notepad across the table. 'Get busy. I don't have all day.'

She sat, slowly. 'What do you want to know?'

'Why did Crystal go to that party?' Grayson asked. 'Why didn't she just email the senator with her blackmail demands?'

'Because she wanted to see his face when she confronted him. *He'd raped her.* She wanted him to know she'd won. The shrinks call it closure,' she added bitterly.

That he could understand. 'Why did you put your son in St Leo's?'

'Crystal wanted it. The day of the party . . . She was psyched. She'd found out the senator was giving a guest lecture at a university. She had to pay to take the class, but she said it was worth it. It was an investment in our future. She went and met him, the senator. She said she was terrified and exhilarated all at once. She was going to make him pay for what he did to her. She hadn't expected Rex to be in the class too. That's why the senator did the guest lecture. Because his grandson was in the class.'

Brittany shook her head. 'She hated Rex. She remembered him, from that day. When she was twelve. She saw him with his fancy school uniform. St Leo's. She tried to talk to him that day. She had a new dress and she was so proud of it. But she overheard him laughing at them, at their bargain-basement clothes. She was so hurt. And then that old pervert raped her.' She stopped, her throat working as she tried to swallow.

'Crystal went right to bed when she came home. Curled up in the fetal position. I asked her what was wrong but she wouldn't say. She only cried. She didn't say until she found out I was pregnant with Caleb. Then she said she had a plan. That they'd finally pay. She told me everything. And she said that she'd take everything McCloud owned. That her niece or nephew would have the same private school uniform. St Leo's. That they'd have all the privileges McCloud gave his own kids. And Rex.'

She let out a breath. 'When she was killed, I knew who'd done it.

I knew it was the senator. But Lippman came along and offered me money. Fifty thousand dollars if I said nothing. I took it. But I couldn't make myself spend it. It was . . . dirty. It had her blood on it.'

Having our blood on the money didn't stop you from selling us *out to Lippman*, Grayson thought. 'So you put him in St Leo's.'

'Yes. Because it was what she wanted. And by then, I wanted the same thing. I wanted my son to have the best. The same as McCloud's family. It was Caleb's right.'

'How did she get the senator's phone number?' Hyatt asked.

'She slept with Rex. Waited till he was stoned and fell asleep and looked through his phone's contact list. Then she started her campaign, flirting, seducing. Somehow McCloud must have found out. So he killed her.'

'Why did she keep the dress?' Grayson asked.

'I asked her that when she told me her plan, six years ago. She told me the senator had raped her in 1998. That year the scandal with the president was all over the TV. That White House intern kept her dress. It was blue, too. Crystal figured one day she'd use it. After she died, I was afraid to. I knew Crystal was murdered by McCloud. I thought they'd kill me too, and I had Caleb to take care of. But then I needed the money because Crystal's old mark – the one in the bankbook I gave you – he died.'

'You never told him she was dead,' Hyatt said.

She shrugged. 'If he was stupid enough to not read the papers . . .'

'So he died and left you without income,' Grayson said.

'Yes. So I knew I needed to blackmail the McClouds. Then that Muñoz woman was murdered, then the bar owner, Sandoval. I knew it was about Crystal. I knew you'd come. I figured I'd give you enough to suspect the McClouds. Then I could get more. They wouldn't dare kill me now, not with Crystal's murder being reopened. They wouldn't want the cops to connect the dots. The rest you've figured out.'

'You'll allocute,' Grayson said.

'You'll get me a cell in Baltimore?'

'If it's humanly possible, I will. You have my word.' Grayson stood, incredibly weary. 'You'll be arrested now, taken to Booking. We'll talk again before your arraignment.'

He and Hyatt once again met the group in the observation room outside. 'I think we're done,' Grayson said.

Hyatt scowled. 'I have to give an update to the commander in half an hour. Do I need to know anything else? Any loose ends that could come back and bite us?'

Everyone in the room looked at one another, then shook their heads.

'I think we've accounted for all of the victims,' Grayson said.

'Looks like Dianna is at the top of our leaderboard,' Paige said. 'She killed Crystal, Betsy Malone, and tried to kill Adele Shaffer. She also killed ten of the other MAC women. Plus she facilitated sexual assault of a minor, sixteen times.'

'The senator committed sixteen counts of sexual assault of a minor, plus sexual assault against his own daughter,' Grayson said. 'And he tried to kill Crystal.'

'Silas killed Elena,' Paige said, 'Jorge Delgado, Harlan Kapansky, and Logan's mother. Lippman killed Sandoval and Bob Bond.' She rolled her eyes. 'And "fixed" all the MAC victims that Dianna didn't kill properly the first time.'

'Silas killed a lot of people before Elena,' Stevie said. 'We still have to sort through the weapons we found in his safe.'

'I may be able to help with that,' Jeff Yates said from the back of the group. 'The state's attorney himself got an email today, from Stuart Lippman's account. It's a detailed list of what he calls his "operatives". Some were cops, some were ex-cons. IA has the list. It will take some time to go through all the information and prepare charges. But Silas was on his list. As was Elizabeth Morton. He used intimidation and threats against their families to keep them in order. At one point Morton tried to quit and Lippman had her child hit by a car. Her son still walks with crutches, years later.'

'Oh, my God,' Daphne said, horrified. 'What a monster.'

'He was,' Yates said. 'But an organized one. He kept a roster of each "operative" and their jobs. I think you'll be closing a lot of cases, Hyatt.'

'I suppose that's a positive,' Hyatt murmured. 'Any more of my people on that list?'

'Not that I saw,' Yates said kindly.

Stevie was frowning. 'But Morton killed Silas. Why?'

'Self-protection,' Yates said. 'Lippman notes in the cover letter that came with the list that all of his operatives know the list exists, and if he's ever murdered or dies suspiciously, it will be sent to the state's attorney. I don't know who sent it, but Lippman trusted someone with the task. By making sure everyone knew they were on the list, he kept any one of them from going rogue and killing him.'

'But Silas tried to kill him on Thursday morning,' Grayson said. 'He shot the window out of Lippman's condo.'

'You'd seen him,' Paige said, 'when you rescued Logan. Maybe he guessed it was just a matter of time before you figured out who he was. He had nothing to lose.'

'With Lippman dead, his family would be safe,' Daphne said. 'Unlike Morton's son.'

'Morton killing Lippman makes a whole lot more sense,' Paige said. 'And that she deliberately left Grayson's mother for us to find. She didn't want to work for Stuart.'

'That will help her,' Yates said. 'She's going to do some serious time, though.'

'Wait,' Lucy Trask said. 'I may have one more body for you.'

'Who?' Grayson sighed.

'Tentative ID via his body art is Roscoe James,' Lucy said.

'The cage fighter.' Paige touched her neck, where the stitches had started to heal. 'He tried to slit my throat in the parking garage.'

'His own throat was slit,' Lucy said. 'He also had a high level of Rohypnol in his blood. He'd been dumped in the river and washed up this morning.'

'Silas killed him,' Detective Perkins said. 'I found them on the security video in the bar where Roscoe's car was parked.'

'Wonderful,' Hyatt grumbled. 'Somebody write this down and email it to me. I won't remember half the list.' He strode to the door, then turned. 'Good work. All of you.'

Stevie stared at the door he closed behind him. 'Wow. He's practically soft.'

Grayson studied her face. 'How are you, really?'

'Better,' Stevie said, but her eyes told the truth. 'Cordelia's still traumatized.'

'Then so are you,' Daphne said, giving her a hug. 'When our babies hurt, we hurt.' She looked at Paige. 'So when are we going to open that school of yours?'

Paige blinked. 'What? Really?'

'Yes,' Daphne said. 'Let's do lunch next week and we'll crunch the numbers.'

'Can Cordelia come to your school?' Stevie asked. 'I think she needs some confidence.'

'Cordelia needs a dog,' Paige said as the three women left together.

Stevie's voice came from down the hall. 'Dogs drool.'

Bashears and Perkins left to escort Mrs McCloud back to Holding, leaving Yates and Grayson alone.

'Is there anything else you need?' Grayson asked.

'Yes,' Yates said. 'I need someone to take Anderson's position. I've read your case summaries and I've seen you in court. You've been on the short list for a move up for quite some time. I saw you in there with Hyatt today. You two work well together.' He shrugged. 'Not many people work well with Peter Hyatt.'

Grayson's pulse picked up a little speed. 'He's not so bad. There's a heart under all that muscle and a brain under the bald.'

Yates smiled. 'If you want the job, it's yours. It's a promotion, you get a bigger office. Not a lot more money. You'll still try cases, but there will be more admin. That's the downside. More work for not a lot more cash.'

Grayson had yes on the tip of his tongue. But . . . 'I need you to know something first.' He told Yates the truth about his father. 'Anderson threatened to tell if I didn't back off the Muñoz case.'

Yates had listened carefully, showing no reaction, but now he cursed under his breath. 'First, who your father is doesn't matter. Second, if you'd come to me, I would have taken care of Anderson.

Under the circumstances I know why you didn't. But don't do it again. Third, this only makes me more sure that I've made a good choice. Another man might have backed off. You didn't. True integrity is priceless.'

'Paige said something like that,' he murmured.

'I'd listen to her then. Today is Saturday. When can you start?'

'I'll be there Monday morning.'

'Good.' Yates shook his hand. 'Congratulations on the promotion and, although I never thought I'd hear myself quoting Hyatt, "good job".'

'Jeff, wait,' Grayson said as Yates opened the door. 'Who will get my current job?'

'Who do you think should have it?'

'Daphne Montgomery. She's pretty amazing.'

Yates nodded. 'I'll take it under advisement. Enjoy the rest of your weekend.'

Grayson closed his eyes and took a moment to breathe, then looked up to see Paige leaning on the doorjamb. 'I thought you were with the girls,' he said.

'You're my ride home.'

From the look on her face he could see that she'd overheard. 'You think I made the right choice?'

'I think you recommending Daphne was pretty amazing. So what's your new title?'

'Senior Assistant State's Attorney.'

Paige laughed. 'As long as I don't have to call you that in bed, we're good.'

He put his arm around her shoulders. 'Actually, I was thinking more on the lines of "Baby, oh, baby, take me". You did promise to say that after all this was over.'

'And I keep my promises. I have integrity too. Can we go home now?'

It made his heart catch to hear her say *home*. 'Absolutely.'

Keep reading for exclusive bonus material from

no one left to tell

and an extract from the next in
the Baltimore series

did you miss me?

The story behind
no one left to tell

When I started writing *No One Left to Tell*, I knew my hero was a prosecutor with a past he wanted to keep secret at (nearly) all costs. The son of a serial killer, Grayson's life mission was making amends for the sins of his father. I had his story and his backstory completely clear in my mind.

It was Paige's backstory I struggled with initially. I knew she was based on my own karate black-belt friend and I knew Paige had recently relocated from Minneapolis to Baltimore to be a PI, but I didn't know what had prompted her to make such a drastic move. Before I started the book, I just figured she'd met Clay Maynard at a wedding (Evie's wedding in the *Silent Scream* epilogue), he'd offered her a job, and she'd decided to take it. But as I dug deeper, I knew that Paige had roots in Minneapolis. Her *dojo* was there – and a black belt's *dojo* is like family.

I turned for advice to Paige's inspiration, my friend Sonie. She thought long and hard then said, 'I would think it would take something big – and traumatic – to make her leave her *dojo*. One of the most terrible things that could happen would be if one of my students used a defense skill I'd taught them and was hurt in the process.'

So that's what happened to Paige – but not only was her student hurt, and killed, Paige was hurt in the process. The black belt who'd been so confident now knew fear.

Where are the no one left to tell characters now?

- Grayson Smith, having been promoted to the next level in the state's attorney's office, still prosecutes cases but spends half his time supervising the other prosecutors, including Daphne Montgomery (who still makes him muffins). Grayson and Paige recently married and are enjoying life as a couple. No plans for kids at this time, although Grayson's mother is constantly dropping hints.

- Paige Holden Smith manages the personal protection division of Clay Maynard's firm, having been made a full partner. She teaches both karate and general self-defense classes at the *dojo* and has been instrumental in adapting her training regimen to those with disabilities. Her classes are always full.

- Daphne Montgomery works as a prosecutor in Baltimore and goes on to become the heroine of *Did You Miss Me?*

- Joseph Carter continues to work in the police department and stars as the hero of *Did You Miss Me?*

- Stevie Mazzetti also continues to work in the police department; she goes on to be the heroine of *Watch Your Back*.

- Clay Maynard works as a private investigator in Baltimore – look out for him as the hero of *Watch Your Back*. Cordelia Mazzetti stars alongside her mom, Stevie, in *Watch Your Back*.

Fun Facts about
no one left to tell

- Paige's dog Peabody is named for Mr Peabody (from *Mr Peabody and Sherman*)
- I didn't know who Joseph Carter was until I started the scene in which he was introduced. That was the moment I knew he'd be Daphne's hero.
- I had no idea that Daphne was made up to look older! The scene where she shows up at Grayson's dressed as a sophisticated society woman was a hoot as it came as a complete surprise to me.
- I needed to place a bomb under Grayson's car but I wasn't sure how to write the scene, so I called my husband. 'Do you know how to make a bomb?' I asked. A long moment of silence. 'Why do you think I know these things?' he blurted out, annoyed. LOL. I ended up getting the info off of a website. Scary.
- The book video features a Rottweiler who was paid twice as much as the human actors were paid. Don't tell the humans.
- One of my favorite scenes is when Grayson comes clean with the Carters about his background but they already knew.

did you miss me?

Prologue

Marston, West Virginia
Tuesday, December 3, 3.14 A.M.

*C*old. *So cold.* Ford curled into himself, instinctively trying to find some warmth. But there was none.

Cold. The floor was cold. And hard. And dirty. *Hard to breathe.*

The wind was blowing outside, rattling windows, sending jets of frigid air around his body. Over his skin. *So cold.* A shudder wracked him and he struggled to open his eyes. It was dark. *Can't see. Head hurts. God.* He tried to get up, to push at whatever covered his eyes, but he couldn't. *Where am . . . what hap—*

Clarity returned in a rush and with it came blinding panic. He was blindfolded. Gagged. Tied, hands and feet. *No.* He fought wildly for a few seconds, hissing when the rope seared his skin. He slumped, his heart racing.

Kim. The image of her face broke through the pounding in his head. He'd been with Kim. Walking her to her car, so happy that she finally let him do so after three months of dating. Relieved that she finally admitted she needed him, because he'd quickly come to need her, to *crave* the way she could make him feel. He'd never known anyone to so perfectly match his interests. Wants. Needs.

Like she was made for me alone.

Fiercely independent, she always insisted that she didn't need a sitter, didn't need any guy to protect her. But not this time. *She asked me to walk her.* Because it was a bad part of town. *Because she needed me. She needed me and I fucked up.*

Where was she? *Don't let her be here.* Tied up. Gagged. *Please let her be all right.*

What the hell had happened? *There was an alley.* They'd gone through an alley because Kim parked behind the movie theater. *That damn foreign film.* She'd had to see some French film for class. Weird theater, sketchy part of town. He'd been angry with the prof for assigning the film to start with and was going to tell him so.

Kim didn't want him to confront the prof. They'd been arguing about it when he'd heard a noise. Felt . . . pain. *Oh, God.* The fear in Kim's dark eyes. Her scream. Every nerve in his body fired all at once and then there was the shattering pain in his head, right before everything went dark.

Kim. He threw his body forward and grunted, the exploding pain in his shoulder sending him back to the floor where he huddled, grimacing. *Where is she?*

He drew another breath, taking care not to inhale the dirt this time. Quieting himself, he listened for any sound – a whisper, a wheeze, a whimper. But there was none.

She's not here. He closed his eyes, fighting to control his pounding heart. *Please don't let her be here.* Because if she was here, she wasn't breathing. If she was here, she was hurt. Maybe dead. *No. No.* He shook his head hard, wincing when the pain spiked deep. *She got away. Please let her have gotten away.*

Away . . . from what? From whom? Where is here? The panic rose in his throat, choking him. *Calm down. Think. You know how to think.*

Thinking was what Ford Elkhart did best.

He closed his eyes, forced himself to calm. To think. To remember. *It's cold.* Which told him nothing. It was December, for God's sake. He could be anywhere north of Florida.

Why? Why me? He gave the ropes binding his wrists another hard yank, then swore when his frozen skin burned. *Why?*

He knew why.

Money. Ransom. It had to be. Kids of rich parents were prey. He wondered if they were contacting his mother or his father. He hoped his mother. *Dad won't pay a dime to get me back,* he thought bitterly, then pictured his mother and his heart clenched.

Mom. She'd be terrified. Out of her mind with worry. Because his mother had prosecuted enough of these cases to know what was happening to him, right now.

Enough of these cases . . . *Oh, no. Hell, no.* His stomach turned over as he considered the alternative. It was The Case. *Oh, God.* The case he couldn't wait to see over. The murder case that had consumed his mother for months. Those trashy Millhouses. Reggie was the killer, but the rest of the Millhouses were probably just as bad – they just hadn't been caught yet. *They hate Mom.* They'd harassed her. Threatened her. *Threatened me.* If the Millhouses were behind this . . . *I'm fucked.*

I'm sorry, Mom. She'd urged him to let her hire a bodyguard, just until the case died down. He hadn't wanted anyone following him around, snooping on him and Kim. He hadn't needed a bodyguard. He could take care of himself.

Hell. He'd taken care of himself so well that he was trussed up like a Christmas turkey. Probably waiting the same fate. He blinked hard, shook the tears off his face. *Stop it*, he barked at himself. *Crying won't help you get away.*

And he had to get away. *Kim needs me. So think. Breathe.* He forced himself to calm, willed his mind to hear the voice of his mother's friend, Paige, who taught self-defense. He'd taken Kim to Paige for instruction because he'd wanted to keep her safe, even when he wasn't there to protect her.

You were there, his mind mocked. *Standing right beside her. And it didn't make a bit of difference.*

He fought the terror that closed his throat. *Please let her be all right. I'll do anything. If something happened to her . . . because somebody was trying to get to me . . .* He'd never be able to forgive himself.

You might not get the chance to forgive yourself – or to save her – if you die here, so stop whining and think. He tried to remember what Paige had said, but he'd been watching Kim from the sidelines, admiring her body as she practiced the escape moves Paige had demonstrated. He'd been thinking about what they'd do when he got Kim back to his room.

He prayed that Kim had been paying attention, because he hadn't been.

So pay attention now. Eventually whoever brought him here would come back, if only to kill him. *You need to be ready to strike. To get away.*

Ford took an inventory of his injuries. His head . . . the back of his skull hurt like hell. *That's where the bastard hit me.* His right arm hurt too, but probably wasn't broken.

His legs . . . He tried to move them within the confines of the ropes. They seemed okay. Stiff from being tied, but not injured. *So you can run. When you get the chance, hit with your left and run like a bat out of hell.*

To where? He could hear nothing, no sounds of the city. Seemed like he was far enough out that getting back might be a challenge. It was cold and he had no coat. At least he had shoes. He might have to walk a long way. But he'd do it. He'd get back. He'd find Kim and they'd get back to their lives. He'd take her home, introduce her to his mother and Gran. He wished he'd done so already.

But first he had to get away from here. *Wherever the hell* here *is.*

Ford froze. Someone was coming. *Stay calm. Pay attention to details.*

A door creaked as it opened, an icy blast rushing into the room. His teeth would have chattered had it not been for the gag in his mouth.

He heard footsteps. Coming closer. Heavy footsteps. A man. Boots. He was wearing boots.

The footsteps stopped close to Ford's head and he could feel warmth from the man's body.

'You're awake.'

Gravelly. The voice was deep and harsh. Filled with . . . laughter? Yeah, laughter. *Asshole's laughing at me.* Ford bit back the fury that roared through him. *Pay attention.*

He heard the crack of knees and the warmth came closer. There was a scent. Aftershave. *Familiar.* He'd smelled it before, he was sure of it. *Where?* He tensed when fingers ran over his head, then hissed a curse when a fist grabbed his hair and yanked him up. *Fight.*

Dammit, fight. Ford thrashed, flinging his body to one side. A heavy knee planted itself on his chest, holding him down. His head was yanked to one side, exposing his neck.

'I'm back,' the man crooned. 'Did you miss me?'